WINDS OF DALMATIA

Tanja Tuma

June 11, 2013

Self-Published in June 2013
ISBN: 978-1483969220
LCCN: 2013906303
CreateSpace Independent Publishing Platform
North Charleston, SC

Contents

Author's Note

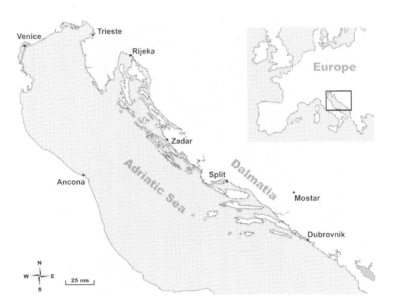

Modern Dalmatia is a province of Croatia. It includes the coast from Zadar to Dubrovnik with the many islands and isles.

Names of locations are written in modern Croatian, so that you can find out more about them on the internet. Striving for authenticity, the text contains some less known words from Greek, Latin, Croatian and other languages. They are all printed in italics and explained briefly in the Glossary at the end of the book. You will also find some non-English font characters, some consonants with a cap, which are pronounced in English as follows:

č, ć like ch in chair
š like sh in shut
ž like s in pleasure

I wish You a calm sea and pleasant reading!

Tanja Tuma

Part I

Past times

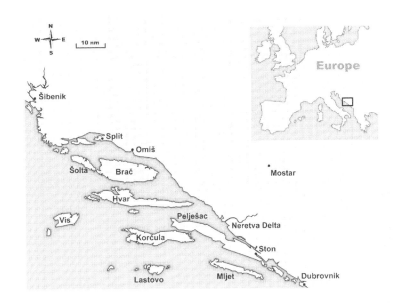

Southern Dalmatia.

Greeks, 6th century B.C.

Like every person, every war has a face. It leaves behind its horrible images grimaced with pain. It changes everything and everybody. History glorifies the heroes and condemns the villains, until one day, they all become names in textbooks or entries in encyclopedias. Victims, though, cannot forget, less forgive.

A photograph or short footage on the TV of the Croatian war for independence strikes my brain every time like a heat wave before the explosion. I tremble in fear and shame. During the day, I can control my thoughts and ban the painful memories quickly. I focus on my job and my research. Yet, during the nights, when my dreams escape my reason, the horrible images and cries come creeping in like evil spirits in the thick fog. My mind is an accurate surgeon of my memories. As a historian, I have a special gift for details. Thus, every night my nightmares visit me, ignoring my life, my success and my loved ones. The peaceful surface of the water stirs and cruelly brings up the atrocities in the same way as a torrent lifts the filth from the bottom of the pond.

Like thousands of Croatians, Bosnians and Serbians from former Yugoslavia, I am one of the victims of that bloody Balkan war ravaging the heart of Europe in the nineties. In my mind, the image of that war is the image of a man.

I was much younger then. My hair was not yet grey as it is today and my body was still firm and warm. I was a prisoner. Out of the locked room, where I spent most of the time during the months of my detention, I can still hear the noise of the war. It seemed distant, yet it was so close, inside me. Bang, bang, bang...Guns in the distance banged like blood in my temples. Today, I can still feel my heart pounding in my throat.

My face of the war is a man in his fifties, tall and dark. I cannot forget that we were in bed together. Not only once, we must have slept together many a time, yet, I cannot forget our first time. I was lying under him and could feel him entering my body. I was afraid of him, yet, I also welcomed him. Possessively, his hands were gliding over my hips. His lips slowly sucked at my breasts, moved up to my neck and ears to brush softly my heated cheeks. At first, our lips touched shyly like the lips of two teenagers, then, they joined in a passionate kiss. I moaned and gasped for air under his weight. His body felt strangely right. I must have enjoyed the sex with him. Suddenly, he stopped and sighed. He looked down at me. Our pupils bridged over years of solitude and longing. Hot tears welled slowly in the corners of his black eyes and ran down his stubbed cheeks onto mine. I think that was the moment of my fall. Each time, when the images of war visit my dreams, I can see his face, and I wake up in sweat and tears.

Outside, a pink dawn promises another glorious day on the

island of Pag, where I found refuge with my little Paula so many years ago. The thought of my baby saddens me and moves my sore limbs into action. I must get up and check on her. Only yesterday she received her last deadly cocktail of chemotherapy.

I take my soaked nightdress off. I slip into a thick gown. There will be time for a shower later. My back and my bones ache slightly, but I know it is only old age. Sixty-six; I never thought I would live that long. The corridor is dim, yet I find my step easily. I enter Paula's room, which has a wonderful view of the sea and the islands of Cres, Mali Lošinj and Veli Lošinj in the distance.

Thank God she's asleep. I can hear her breathing peacefully and for a moment, like a warm spring breeze, hope fills my day. Orange rays of morning sun overflow the room. Cruelly, they unveil the casualties of the night. I spot several loose strands of Paula's dark hair around her pillow. Like almost all of it, these have fallen from her skull during the night. They are curling lonesome and disconnected on the lavender blue of the bed linen. Paula's pretty face is pale, her cheeks sullen. She looks like an old woman in spite of her eighteen years. Her lips are gray and cut by deep dry cracks like wasteland in the middle of a desert. She was vomiting most of the day yesterday. What should I make her for breakfast? I pull up the blanket and leave the room silently, closing the door behind me.

In the kitchen, I start to brew some coffee and put the yeast on for fresh bread. I know Paula adores freshly made milk bread. I only hope her stomach will take it. While sipping my coffee, I try to think of a way to distract my baby from her pains and suffering. Her leukemia has turned nasty and no treatment seems to help. What good is there in all the wealth and money, if I cannot buy health for my baby? Will Paula live? I cannot think any further. Tears well up in my eyes and threaten to blur my sight. Then I hear noises upstairs; the flushing of the toilet, the creaking of the bed...

"Nona, are you still at home?"

At an early age, when she was barely speaking her first words, my Paula picked up this Italian word for grandmother and has been calling me by it ever since. It's music to my ears, so easy, so sweet: no-na, no-na, no-na... I cannot stop loving the sound of it.

"Yes, my love. I am downstairs. Will you have some tea?"

There is a moment of hesitation. Probably nausea and the duty to drink enough liquid are crossing Paula's thoughts. After some time, she utters a silent "Yes, please", and I put on the water for rose hip tea, which will soothe her stomach. While waiting for the water to boil, I start my computer and write a short email to my deputy director, Barbara Primic, that I won't be coming to work today. The ecological hotel Perovica will have to do without me until Paula gets better. I browse my last entries in the machine when I come across the folder of files about the history of Dalmatia I have been gathering since some ten years ago. Sometimes to remember the facts better, sometimes for fun, I tend to put down the events and characters as they might have been not as they are described in scientific papers. Maybe I could distract Paula with my tales. Maybe I should tell her about Korčula and its Greek settlers, or about the Emperor Diocletian, still the most important politician of all times coming from our shores. Maybe the story of Dubrovnik, the proud Republic of Ragusa and their struggle with Venetians and pirates would lift her spirits. Would she like that? I wonder.

The raised loaf must go into the oven. My tea tray is set to take it upstairs. I put it on her nightstand and kiss her on her cold grey cheeks. She looks at me unhappily, her big black eyes so familiar, so full of pain, and also of a strange light, which I know is the will to live. My baby will not give up easily and I am here to heal her with my love. For my Paula is everything I have, the only member of my family left after the ravaging years of the last Balkan war.

"Please, take one little spoon at the time. Your stomach is still upset and you need to be gentle with it."

My baby smiles naughtily.

"After the ordeal my stomach caused me yesterday, it would deserve to be removed from my body. The only argument against it is that wonderful smell from downstairs. Are you baking bread, nona?"

I caress her balding head very softly and nod.

"I am not going to work today. I'll stay here with you."

"But what will your staff at Perovica do without you? Can you do that?"

"Of course I can. I own it."

Paula gulps a spoon of tea and makes a grimace. Nothing tastes any good these days, but I know the only reason is her therapy. With the second spoon her face lights up.

"Acacia honey!"

I sit on her bedside and automatically my fingers start collecting the hair from her pillows. Paula looks at me:

"What are we going to do all day, nona?"

"After breakfast we can talk about history, if you like."

"You mean, you will open up your files for me? You will let me read you stories?"

I can sense a tinge of bitterness in her voice. Some time ago, when she was still healthy, she was curious about my research, but I didn't let her read my writings. I felt too ashamed. I make up all kinds of destinies for my characters and they often do terrible things; they hate, they are greedy for money, they cheat and lie, they kill and let others suffer, they make love and war. What would Paula think of me if she read all those things? It didn't seem appropriate at the time. Yet what is so different today? Is it Paula facing death which makes me go soft on the moral issues? Why have I been so tough with her in the past? My baby is expecting an answer. Her questioning eyes stare at me.

"Paula, I don't think you should strain your eyes reading my files. Not yet. I will rather be telling you my stories. The first is about a Greek woman who was Sappho's disciple. In the 6th century B.C., she came to Korčula from Corfu, called in Greek Kerkyra. Her name was Agape. She was a healer and a midwife."

"Nona, were there Greeks on Korčula? I don't remember that from school."

"Yes, there were many. Early Greek settlers were particularly fond of Dalmatian islands, I tell you. However, the major research and finds are fairly recent. Maybe all of them have not yet entered the schoolbooks. Anyhow, Korčula in those days was called Korkyra Melaina, the black island of a thousand springs. The settlers from Corfu added an adjective to their home island Corfu. Melaina means black. Melaina was a Corycian nymph, who was a lover of Apollo and in some legends a daughter of Melancholy. The pines on Korčula are really dark green. The most important though was water. The colony on Korčula was under Corfu's administration. It was led by a *tyrant*, whose name escaped the historical sources, so I made him up. He was a warrior, as he had to take the land by force from the local Illyrian tribes."

With a dramatic voice, I embark on Agape's story. I don't need to look in my files. I know all my stories by heart and remember every single detail I put down. My body may be weak, but my mind is as sharp as ever be it in business or elsewhere. I've always enjoyed suspense and drama. Now is my time to show it! I want my baby to listen and forget about her pain. I want my stories of lovers, conquerors, kings and queens, pirates and merchants to rouse her to life and prompt her to fight. Maybe the history of Dalmatia and my fantasies about my people in the old times are a good bag of tricks to deceive the creepy Death and make Him leave my baby's blood vessels forever.

* * *

A new spring day was breaking over the peninsula Pelješac, the last outpost of the mainland on the east, where vineyards and fields bloomed in striking green. The blue sea in between was peaceful. A strong man could swim over the narrow passage from Pelješac to the island of Korkyra Melaina – Korčula. Agape inhaled the healing scent of dark pines that gave the name to her new home, Melaina – black. She turned her cheeks to the soft

sea breeze embracing the morning flora in its warmth as though a
lover would kiss his girl after long passionate hours in the night.
The rough winds of winter seemed to have forever left the tiny
polis of Korkyra, perched on a narrow strip of land almost falling
into the sea. For the first time in a couple of years, the tall woman
with thick black curls tied in a bun felt peace in her heart and was
happy. The several soft goatskins hanging over her right shoulder
formed a bundle, which she was hoping to fill with various herbs
in the early morning hours while the medicinal plants were still
clad in the dew and had the most of their healing powers.

Agape, an unmarried professional in her late twenties, was a
very special citizen of Korkyra, the recent Greek colony grounded
by the sages of Corfu. The Greeks came to the island of Korčula
because they needed to trade with the ancient Hallstatt tribes
of the northern Balkans for their precious metals, amber and
wool. According to an ancient legend, Korkyra, or Korčula, as
the Illyrians pronounced the name of the island, was founded
long before the settlers built their stone houses around the harbor tower by the Trojan hero Antenor, returning from the most
ferocious battle of old times at Illium. Hearing the tale, Agape
would ask the most obvious question: where were the Greeks for
several centuries between Antenor and the present settlers? It remained unanswered, like so many other questions she had asked
in her life. Oh, cursed be all the Greek legends and tales! Forget
the good and ill-fated assumptions of gods' schemes and human
weaknesses! She abhorred the romanticized myths and legends
about the highly idolized god Zeus siring his numerous bastards
with mortal women around the Earth in spite of the watchful eye
of his wife Hera! Agape was weary of them as well as she was
annoyed by the superstitions which were still dominating every
treatment of the sick. Her citizenship at Korkyra Melaina was a
rare privilege for an unmarried woman, and it had been granted
to her not long ago for the good work she was doing as a midwife. She could not call herself a physician; the title was reserved
only for men who followed the line of formal education in *gymnasia*. She was a healer. It was a sorry fact that the Athenian
practices regarding the social position of women spread all over
Greece and even went with the settlers to the new colonies. Yet,
she was needed both by men and by women, treating all kinds of
diseases, performing surgeries and producing her own *pharmaca*,
drugs from potent wild herbs growing on the green slopes of the
island, which despite the sun's powerful baking of its rocks never
dried out or even lacked water. It was an island of a thousand
springs, which dwelt in its heart and sent their shots up to the
surface in the form of dark green pines, for everybody to see the
freshness and purity that was the essence of Korčula, Korkyra
Melaina.

Agape was proud of her achievements, though many times

she felt incompetent in her struggles for the health of her patients. She knew that her knowledge had limits, and those limits separated life from death. In secret, she doubted many of the contemporary beliefs, yet she could not oppose them with argumentation, with *logos*, that could clear all the questions. Not only was she busy from dawn to dusk with her work, she was also a woman and could not get a thorough philosophical and medical education. Her studies were scattered around lands and years in search for knowledge, so potent yet so dispersed in those ancient times. Nevertheless, on that lovely day, her heart was joyful and filled with the scented flavors of spring. She was cheerfully climbing up the hill, where there was a nice clearing with still tender stalks of pennyroyal growing in dark green patches. Pennyroyal was the herb which helped her patients with too many children. The strong mint-tasting infusion prevented an unwanted pregnancy and was soothing to the digestive organs of women whose men had insatiable sexual appetites. She would also prescribe pomegranate fruits to women, which grew wild all around the island and were ripe in late autumn, but her patients had consumed most of them by this time of year and it was still too early in the season for the unripe acacia fruit, another potent contraceptive. The acacia trees were in flower and they were emitting their white petals and sweet honey scent all around the island. The good mother Demeter was in pact with the healing deity Hygieia in establishing the balance between fecundity and the prevention of too many births. To Agape, all those remedies were not only the gift of gods and the blessing of nature. They were the everyday source of her income and wealth. Although she was living alone and did not have any rich protecting mentors, Agape was a wealthy woman.

She paused to look down into the valley, where she spotted a man on horseback, his bearded face turned to her screaming something incomprehensible into the white sun-beaten rocks. What was that? She recognized the horse and the attire of the *polis* official and focused her sight. The man saw her and started waving to her and beckoning her to descend, to come to him. Was it another emergency? There were a few wives approaching their term soon, but none of them was of a particularly high birth or a wife of an official. To Agape, it did not make any difference... a patient was a patient and he or she needed her help. She started the descent, not without regret, for she enjoyed her early morning walks and the regular picking of fresh herbs served her *apotheca* well. Anyway, the pennyroyal would still be growing tomorrow, while a life could be in danger and the patient might not see another day without her treatment. She had to hurry up.

"Agape, thank God I found you. Come quickly, up into the saddle, let's ride to my palace."

Agape recognized their ruler Arsenios. He was a strong warrior, so popular that the citizens of the colony elected him every year as a *tyrant* of Korkyra. Every time she saw his blue eyes, she had to think of Lesbos despite the coldness and reserve with which they conversed with each other. She thought little of him with his demagogic and stingy attitudes. For some time she had been asking him for a permission to expand her house with a shrine to Asklepios, the god of medicine, where she could more effectively treat her patients. He always found some vague excuses and referred to other projects in the new colony which were more urgent and more in need of his vast fortune and support than her sick. She would for sure not mount his horse unless she knew what was happening.

"What's the matter? Are you in a hurry to donate to Asklepios?"

"God, woman, mount the horse or I will draw my sword. I will tell you on the way."

"I will not, unless you tell me now! Who is sick?"

His voice hesitated, became softer.

"Please, Agape. It is my son, my little Timon. He had a cold, but this morning we found him nearly dead in his bed. He was breathing when I set out in search for you, but only barely."

A child is sick. Agape jumped up and almost fell to the other side of the horse, had not Arsenios caught her stout body and set her in front of him in the saddle. They galloped to the *polis* and Agape, not used to riding, was holding the horse mane for her life. She planned to ask several other questions to have some idea about the diagnosis, but could not. They arrived to the yard and slaves jumped to reach for her and took her immediately to Timon's bed. The child's cheeks were turning blue for the lack of oxygen. The one thing Agape could do without her medical bag was to open his mouth. She saw abscesses bursting with white and yellow pus, the whole mouth red with the ugliest inflammation of the throat she had ever seen. The boy's tonsils swelled so much that they inhibited breathing. It could be mortal. The boy was losing color. She had to act quickly.

"Bring me some boiling water, wine and a very sharp knife. Go!"

She turned the little boy of no more than five years, with a tiny, frail body, his white hair glued to his forehead by merciless sweat, on his side. She stuck her index finger in his mouth and felt the swollen tissue which was blocking the air. She pressed at it, and the tiny body jerked in the gasp for a breath. She repeatedly opened the respiratory channel until the servants brought what she had demanded.

"Light an oil lamp!"

Her voice was sharp and commanding. It left no room for disobedience. They did as she told them, and after she washed her hands and the sharp iron kitchen knife first in boiling water and then in wine, she put the knife tip to the flame. Without her index finger opening his throat, the boy was getting bluer by the seconds.

"Is he going to die?"

It was Arsenios in total panic. She looked him in the eyes and, despite the drama of the moment, could see Lesbos in his blue irises.

"Trust me, Arsenios, he is not. Come here and hold him tight. I have to make an incision to let the air through."

Arsenios came closer, unsure of what she wanted from him.

"Hold his head strongly, so that he doesn't jerk. I need another man for his shoulders. But the chest must be free."

A servant came forward with a shy look. There was no time.

"Come on, man. Hold the boy's shoulders!"

Agape shouted, but inside she was cold, calm and concentrated. She held the boy's chin high and looked attentively at his throat and the swellings obvious through the soft skin. Then she approached it with the tip of the knife.

"No, don't!"

Arsenios panicked. What was she doing? Precious seconds were lost again and the boy was almost still. No breath was coming in or out of his mouth. The room was silent. Fear suffocated everybody and set the moment in stone, as though they would be part of a marble relief on a temple.

"Arsenios, if you don't let me do the operation, the boy will die in the next minute. Control yourself and hold the head."

Agape's voice was sharper than the knife she was holding in her hand. The least she wanted was a dead child. She had to save him. She added in a softer voice.

"Please, you're a father and a warrior. We're fighting Pluto now. We must fight with weapons to get the boy back from the Hades."

His eyes were wide and dimmed with emotion and fear, but he was obeying her orders. At last, she was able to incise two cuts at the sides of the boy's throat. She did it almost slowly and with care. His head would jerk, but Arsenios held him in his wide palms like in Hephaistos' godly tongs. Immediately air passed through and despite all the red blood dripping from his white tender throat, the boy was coming to life. More air, more blood, more color to his cheeks. Arsenios met her eye. She returned his look and saw admiration, and again deep down she saw Lesbos in his blue irises. Then two tiny tears left his heavy eyelids. The great tyrant of Korkyra Melaina was crying the warm tears of relief. His child, his only boy would live. It was somehow embarrassing, all the emotions in the face of the man who would not have a second thought when delivering death sentences. Agape looked away, down at her little patient.

"I don't want to leave you alone with him. Can one of the slaves fetch my medicine bag from my house?"

"Yes, of course. Run, Theron, quickly."

A giant black slave moved forward like a panther. God knows where Arsenios had bought the man. He was no Greek for sure. Agape could not but smile triumphantly at her ruler. She beat Pluto and his deadly scheme one more time. She was a good physician, probably better than any man could ever be.

"Thank you, Agape! Thank you! I cannot repay you for what you did today."

"Oh, you will pay, my king. I have asked you so many times..."

"Oh, the shrine! Asklepios? It's yours. I will build you the biggest shrine you can imagine. Thank you, Agape."

Agape was still holding the boy's throat. The air made all the difference, but she had to stabilize the incisions and give the boy some sedative medicine to get him to sleep completely still. Only later in the day, would she infuse remedies to deal with the inflammation. There was one more worry, though. The boy was skinny and frail. Would he withstand a few days only on watered wine with honey? Her look travelled around the room and stopped at a woman whose face was ashen pale with terror. It was Timon's mother Chloe.

"Chloe, come closer and put your hands on the boy's forehead. He needs his mother's hand now."

They circled around Timon like gods around their throne throwing dice for the lives of men below. Timon's tiny body was gratefully soaking up the soft touches of his saviors. He was back to the babe sucking on a breast. He was reborn. Chloe opened her mouth to say thank you, but her words didn't leave her lips.

"We still need to take care. He's not completely out of danger."

The black slave came back with her medicine bag and she inserted two tiny catheter straws into the incisions. They were made from reeds and strong enough to withstand the pressure of the swollen tissue. Still, the boy would not be able to swallow anything, not even a drop of medicine without the risk that he would cough out the straws. She needed to sedate him somehow. Agape had a solution. She took out a bag with herbs and went to the kitchen where she prepared warm compresses soaked in herbs. She came back and they all put the compresses all over Timon's chest, on his forehead and over his eyes shut like in a deep sleep.

"He needs to rest now."

"Shall we leave him?" asked Arsenios in a small, uncertain voice.

"It would be best if Chloe could stay with him and make sure he doesn't move. I have to go to my *apotheca* and fetch more medicine. We need to bring down the infection."

"I'll stay here with Chloe."

The huge warrior knelt by the bed and put his big bearded head next to the boy's tiny chest. Agape was touched to see how he would do anything for his son. He would build temples and tame herds. He would love and he would kill for him, he would give his life in exchange for his, if only he could. He would breathe life into his weak heart. Another look at the sight of the family huddled around the bed and a sharp pain cut into her breast. She felt regret. What a sea of sorrows her life had been! Would she ever find love and happiness? Why was she saving the lives of the dying while she was living a life of the dead? The woman in her died a long time ago.

When Agape came back to Arsenios' home a few hours later, she was fully equipped. The family was still around Timon's bed and he was asleep and seemed peaceful enough. Agape's trained eye saw immediately that the inflammation was getting worse, and that the boy's defenses against the disease were down. The fever was rising and his cheeks were unhealthily flushed and hot. It was a serious case of *ankhon*, angina. Earlier she could have treated him with salty water to wash away the pus, now it was too late for that. She had a good supply of fenugreek seeds in her *apotheca* and she ground the powder and mixed it with sage honey. She had to risk and get him to swallow the slightly warmed mixture. As much of it should stay on the pus as possible. Then, reapply the small dosage every hour if possible.

She administered the medicine with the help of Arsenios and Chloe. Then, they washed his body with warm towels dipped in tepid chamomile tea and changed the linens. In the middle of their handling the boy, an old woman broke into the silent room. She had a big nose like an eagle's beak and a protruding chin, her coal black eyes were flashing in a trance like as intended madness, and a turf of ragged grey hair was hardly covering her skull. She was more crying than chanting the charms, pleading for help from Asklepios, the son of god Apollo and a mortal woman named Koronis. Her wails were shrill and loud, they were filling every corner of the sickroom with terror. Behind her stooped skinny figure, the big black slave was dragging a bleating little lamb obviously in mortal fear. Their clamant cries frightened the child and he began to stir nervously under the linen. Agape looked at the theater as though she would jump to strike down the old witch and the slave with one blow. She hissed in a low voice:

"Get the witch and the animal out of this room, Arsenios! Now!"

She was shaking with anger, and, halfheartedly, Arsenios

moved forward to the woman.

"Please, mama. I will come with you and we will chant and give our sacrifice in a minute. Just go out!"

But the little woman was not to be driven away. She looked into his face defiantly and screamed into the heaven.

"I implore you, my son! Call to the gods for the life of your son Timon! Ask forgiveness! I am begging for you the god of gods, the merciful Apollo! The son of Zeus and Leto, the most beautiful of all women on earth, take me instead of Timon, my only grandson! Here is the whitest of all lambs for you, my dear beautiful god Apollo!"

The blankets stirred again and Arsenios was getting impatient with his mother's wails and the animal's cries for help.

"Theron, take the lamb to the shrine and kill it ritually! Mama, go with Theron and sing chants to Apollo!"

"We must give the lamb here, at the bed of my grandson! Who is this woman? She should not touch Timon? Where is a physician?"

Arsenios looked at Agape. She was composed and concentrated on her job, but he could see the vein on her forehead pumping angry blood in the rhythm of her heartbeat. He had to gain control of the situation. Timon needed peace. Without a second thought, Arsenios took his mother in his arms and carried her outside despite her blows and furious cries of protest, Theron and the bleating baby lamb following in their wake. After they were gone, the servants closed the door and barred it. Chloe asked in a small voice:

"Agape, don't you believe in gods? Shouldn't we also chant charms to save the life. . . "

Ignorance was a mortal sin for Agape, but how could she blame a mother of a sick boy? Her anger evaporated and she became a comforting and healing authority again.

"Don't worry, Chloe. I do believe in gods and I offered to both, Asklepios and Apollo this morning. They told me I must do my job first or else they cannot help your little Timon."

"He's calm now. Can you stay here Agape? At least for a few hours. . . "

"Of course I can stay. We will look after him together, Chloe."

"Thank you. You're a good woman, Agape, and a good physician, too. Never mind my mother in law. She's a vicious witch. Whatever happens, she will say it is my fault Timon fell ill."

"Thank you, Chloe. Superstitions and charms! Timon needs you! But I can see another one will need you soon."

Chloe looked down at her round little belly. She smiled awkwardly.

"You know Arsenios. As soon as I stop breastfeeding, he's after me. I took precautions for some time, because I felt that

Timon needed me more than other children would. But Arsenios wants more sons and..."

"Well, you can have more babies, Chloe. And Timon will love a baby brother, I am sure. How old is he?"

"Well, this is his eighth spring."

Agape raised her eyebrows in surprise. Timon looked much younger than that, his constitution was frail and his humors obviously weak for an eight year old.

"Was he getting enough exercise? I mean before he fell ill."

"Timon hates it outside. Hunting or riding tires him out. He can read and write and he adores staying in. Arsenios took him to the woods a few times, but on each occasion, Timon was sick for days afterwards. He doesn't like meat and prefers honeyed almonds to any other food."

"Well, almonds are bad for angina, so they are banned from his diet for now. Honey is fine. Get him to suckle honeycomb. It's very good for children."

Timon was breathing peacefully under his linens, covered with a soft woolen blanket. Arsenios came back alone and smiled at the two women.

"I have my doubts when old cranks like my mother call for gods like Apollo! Were I in his shoes, I would run away and nothing could stop me until I dropped dead..."

They shared a hearty laugh and took the cups of spiced wine diluted with water from the servant's tablet. They could cheer for the moment. The boy's life seemed saved.

She was falling through the air, but slowly, slowly almost as though she would be a dove gliding over the sea. It was warm and sunny, and she was happy. She felt so free and she was enjoying the soft breeze warming her thighs and lifting her long, heavy hair in the air. She felt secure although her mind was trying to warn her that at one point she would hit the ground. She could not care less. She was enjoying her fall like there would be no tomorrow. Her heartbeat was slow and her breath peaceful. She remembered to open her eyes and look around. The sky was blue and the people beneath were like little ants hurrying around the narrow alleys of Korkyra Melaina. Good, she was home. She could see her house with the wide herb garden and the little *apotheca* at the end. She could see her slave Arida weeding the vegetable patches on the other side of the house. She loved the girl. She was always doing something, never slept in a lazy oblivion of her restricted existence. Maybe she should teach her to read and write, and help her to develop herself. On the beach, she could see children playing and running, and suddenly she got frightened that one of them might get imprudent and swim too far out into the waves. Then the thought came to her that the water of the lagoon was shallow and the bottom covered with soft white sand. She wished she could lie down into the warm sand

and sleep. She looked down onto the *polis*, and the thatched roofs opened to her sight showing slaves happily chatting in the kitchens around the herds. They were chopping vegetables and meats, cooking stews in the pots, baking breads in the oven and stealing cups of wine from their masters' *amphorae*. They looked relaxed. Was it festivity time? Why were there so many citizens dressed up out in the *forum*? She must come closer to see...What wonderfully colored gowns they were wearing! The colors were purple, blue, crimson, and gold contrasted with white. She must join them...She was gliding down closer to the crowds and the people below all of a sudden took notice of her. But, oh! What were they all laughing at? Was there a Dionysus procession going by? What was so funny? She could hear wild noise and she saw men exchanging obscene gestures in the air. Their middle fingers up like impertinent *phalli*. Why was that? Who was the target of their ridicule? Herself? It could not be. She was their physician, they should show some respect. Then she felt her skin. In agony, Agape realized that she was falling down through the air completely naked, as gods made her. Her pubic hair was curling in the sun. Her heavy breasts swayed around her figure with blows of the wind, and from below the people could see her vagina and the soft tissue of her labia like on a plate. She tried to press her thighs together and hide her sex. But the more she tried, the louder the excited cries from below and the more the crowds of citizens, men and women, were laughing their heads off. She could not hide. She was completely naked, exposed like a slave on the market. There was nothing she could do. She swallowed her tears of shame and looked closer at the people below. She could see one man who was not making fun of her. It was Arsenios. He stretched his arms towards her, begging her to come down to him. She had had this vision before. She was falling, falling...Until her body hit the tepid water of the lagoon. She was safe from the crowds there. Nobody could see her in the water...

"Agape, please weak up! Timon is burning..."

She felt two strong arms shaking her shoulders and immediately woke up to full attention. It was daylight. She remembered having fallen asleep reclining on a couch sometime towards the end of the long night, when the boy's breathing got more regular and peaceful. Arsenios was looking down at her, worry and panic in his blue eyes almost hidden behind bushy eyebrows and thick golden curls. Agape jumped from her couch and felt for Timon's forehead. The boy's fever had risen, it was the infection, which she couldn't bring down so quickly.

"We need warm chamomile tea and linen rags. It would be best to prepare a bath. We must bring the temperature down."

The servants needed no second command and in a moment brought a lovely wooden tub with golden and silver ornaments

around the edges into the room. They poured in some boiling water and Agape added sachets of dried chamomile to it, then after
a minute, they added cold water until the temperature was about
that of a human body. Carefully Arsenios and Agape lowered the
tiny burning body in. They washed and massaged Timon gently
all over. Then, under Agape's instructions, pitcher by pitcher,
they were slowly adding the cold water and the boy's cheeks were
losing the purple shade of mortal fever. The bath took nearly an
hour and after Timon was finally clad in fresh linens and resting
under the covers, Agape and Arsenios stepped outside in the garden, where slaves brought them fresh bread and olive oil for an
early breakfast. In the east behind Pelješac, the sun was rising
slowly, as though it would hesitate in fear of the day to come.

"Well, my son is not a strong boy, is he?"

Agape shrugged her shoulders, her eyebrows knitted in a worried expression.

"He will need more care. I need to bring down the inflammation or the fever will take him. Where is Chloe? I think she was
sleeping in Timon's bed."

Arsenios sighed, and his strong athletic body seemed to have
lost all posture; he was receding into himself. Agape still could
not comprehend this emotional side of their ruler so new to her.
Finally, he offered an explanation:

"I had a strange dream and woke up in the night. I sent Chloe
to our bedroom and watched over Timon myself. It's nothing.
I'm used to being on guard from my war years."

"How is she now?"

"Oh, Chloe? She's the image of health. She's expecting again.
I hope she gives me another son."

"Well, a son or a daughter, as long as the baby is strong and
healthy."

Arsenios shook his head. It was obvious he disagreed but
didn't want to comment on Agape's liberal thinking or upset her.
She was different from other women. She was so rational, so
composed when she had to take action. How she had made the
incisions to Timon's throat! He would never have thought that
he would ever find admiration for a woman! When he was pleading for a physician to the governor of Corfu, the administrative
superior of their colony, and when the old man finally wrote back
that he had found an appropriate person, he was at a loss when
Agape stepped from the ship and introduced herself. A woman!
How was he going to explain this to the elders in the *polis*, who
thought there was only one way of getting physical with a woman!
Her recommendations, though, were excellent; even the great Pittacus, one of the seven sages, praised her knowledge and healing
practices highly. According to her letter of presentation, she had
been studying at Lesbos, had spent some time with court physicians in Egypt and had been working many years as an assistant

to the military doctor in Sparta. She came to Korkyra Melaina when she found out on Corfu that they needed a physician in the new colony. She was the only one to have applied for the position, so the governor of Corfu sent her with the first ship to Arsenios.

She convinced them all. Arsenios had to change his opinion of her, too. She did a good job with Timon. There was a chance he would survive the stupid cold. Arsenios studied her stern, wide-boned face. With her severe expression and all the knowledgeable attention, she seemed like a man. He had been in battles and had seen men wounded, screaming in pains. He remembered how physicians lost faith and nerve in the turmoil of blood, cries of pain and shouts for attack. Seldom there was a physician so calm with a knife and with so much stamina as he had witnessed in Agape a day ago. No doubt, Agape was a brave woman. She seemed completely disoriented an hour ago when he came to wake her up. Quickly, like a soldier on the battlefield, she jumped into her role of an impermeable fortress, interested only in the work. There was not a trace of emotion or weakness in her expression. Who was she? What was she hiding behind this theatrical mask of indifference? Arsenios was convinced that everybody was of a certain humor and that we all could feel love, hate, compassion, aggression, we could display courage and cowardice, no matter how much we were trying to hide it. It was the balance between the heart and the head which made a great man. Like one of the Delphi sayings proclaimed: Know Thyself! He had a feeling that Agape, in spite of her selfless compassion and empathy with her patients, which made her a good healer, didn't know a thing about herself. Was it too curious to ask?

"What about you, Agape? When will we see you married? Aren't you lonely?"

"My king, I hold nothing of married life. My destiny is to heal people, neither hate nor love them. I have dedicated my life to the study of human body and soul. You cannot imagine how many doors stood closed to my ambitions, so I had to work very hard. I still cannot be a physician and it is only your grace and patronage that enable me to live and work as one in Korkyra Melaina."

"You know the council of elders demanded many times from me to find a male physician, but the Greek scholars have grown decadent and lazy. This is the new world. It's primitive in comparison to the old *poleis*, where there is a social life and parties, where there are *gymnasia* and theatres. For years, I couldn't get anybody to Korkyra, and people were dying unattended of simple, curable illnesses. Now we have you. I will pass a law by which you will be able to practice medicine officially. Also, you will get the *stipend* for it as a man would. I will insist on that. I cannot guarantee the job forever, though. Should a male physician with references come to Korkyra Melaina and ask for the job, I would have no choice."

"Thank you, Arsenios, then the job is mine for a long, long time. Besides, no physician will attend to women, so there will always be a way to earn my living here. And, you're right, it is very primitive here. We're but a bunch of peasants, and we'll soon be like our Illyrian neighbors – the *barbarophonos*. Although from what I hear, women have more rights and higher positions in that barbarian community than in a Greek one. Sad, isn't it?"

Arsenios was amused. He liked the conversation and he liked being both flattered and challenged. Nevertheless, he could feel an edge in her politeness. He smelled a rebel at one thousand *stadia*.

"Agape, you can't complain, can you? You're a citizen, you don't need a male patron and you can live your unmarried life as you please. What more do you want?"

Agape was on slippery ground. She could go on and quote from a long list of pangs and wrongs that women had to endure in this primitive society. Superb arguments were on the tip of her tongue, but she thought it better not to start a row with the king of the colony Korkyra Melaina, where after all, she led a happy life. She turned her critique into a joke.

"Well, I can write you a list of things and rights that I miss, my king. But let's not get cross with each other. For a start, some help with the building of the Asklepios shrine would be very welcome. I have the money myself, but I need your permission and support with the council. Were you serious about it yesterday?"

What a diplomat! She stopped on the point where his tolerance would tip over. Good, go back to your business, Agape! It is not the politics. It is healing. Back to where you belong.

"I never break my word. You will have your shrine. The council and I will supply the means as well."

Arsenios observed her blank expression. No matter how she was trying, her mouth became a thin, dissatisfied line. It revealed resent and disappointment. How did they start such a futile discussion? He wanted to be friends with this extraordinary woman, he wanted to get to her and warm her up. He was grateful for all she had done. They were a good team just an hour ago. He smiled apologetically and patted her hand warmly:

"Next, you will ask me to get you the right to vote, Agape. Be glad you're a free citizen."

"I think voting IS my right actually. If I am a citizen. Or am I not?"

Agape's voice became shrill and cried offense. The hypocrisy of the Greek society was sometimes too much for her to bear and her deep thoughts erupted from her in a volcano of brutality. What did that man think? She had just saved his son and his gratitude was to put her back in her place, below the men, many of them completely ignorant, even illiterate. Was he any better than his crazy mother? Was she, Agape, any worse as a woman? Her studies of medicine were extensive and they took her more than ten years. From the Lesbos *academia*, she travelled to Egypt and worked side by side with the best physicians in the world. She knew all about poisons, she learnt to perform surgeries and she acquired good reputation in treating women's diseases. She even helped cure the plague and studied writings about the human nature and the four humors. This villain, this *tyrant*, this complacent leader was nothing but a poor politician with no culture and little education. He could not judge her. Who was he? His kindness and emotions are nothing but pretense, a mask he had put on to awake her compassion, so that she would heal his son better. He didn't know her. She was so above such base thoughts. She would heal anybody, be it a dog or a man, so highly was she committed to the ethics of her profession. This Arsenios, who was he anyway? He came from Corfu with a troop of warriors and set the borders of the new colony. Then ships followed year after year, until one day she was aboard one. She found a lousy settlement, where drinking water was so unclean that a gulp from the *polis* fountain was the most dangerous of all poisons. Filthy animals drank from the same fountain from which women fetched water for the households. The sewage was still in the process of planning. People were dying by the numbers and it took her several months to beat it into Arsenios' thick head that he needed to develop the settlement in accordance with the basic rules of hygiene. He had lived in Corfu and should have known better. His greed for land and wealth was so huge that she almost despaired and left Korkyra Melaina for good. She had to write a complain to Arsenios' superior, the governor of Corfu, who backed her up. Finally, Arsenios had invested means and built the basic structures of the *polis*. However, there was no money for a *gymnasium* or shrines. How could she have forgotten for a moment who she was dealing with? Why did his blue eyes affect her? She should heed the Homeric verse: "Beware of Greeks bearing gifts!" Only she should say: "Beware of MEN bearing gifts!"

"I must go. Call me if Timon is worse."

"Agape, please."

He caught her open sleeve, and it almost tore from two forces driving it apart. She stopped and looked at her arm. Then she slowly lifted her eyes to meet his shining blue of a warm summer sky.

"I am sorry. I didn't mean to offend you, woman. It's the way of the world. What can I do?"

"Read and learn. And think, man!"

"What?"

"I'm going home. I'll come back in two hours to give Timon the medicine. Don't leave him alone."

She roughly drew the sleeve out of his grip and he let her go. She turned and started walking away. She could feel his look boring into her back, maybe appraising her figure. He was nothing but a brute! She turned towards the shore and decided to have a long swim in the sea. She needed to wash her body and clear her head. In spite of all her anger and hate, there was something in his eyes which deeply upset her. It connected her to her past in a strange way. It brought back the memories of the emotional turmoil, as beautiful as painful, she had once been dragged through. She would never let herself go like that again.

She was young and naive then. It was a long time ago at Lesbos. There was a sick young man and she was all alone with him. It was the year when she had attended Sappho's academy on Lesbos, where they were worshipping Aphrodite with wonderful hymns to life composed under the guidance of the greatest poet and woman artist of all times. There were no limits to their discussions; politics, business, morality and the world order. Debaters, either men or women, were equal! It was *logos*, which mattered, not their sex. Looking back, Agape realized, all that was in vain, futile. All those highly spirited women! As if slaves were debating about the morality and the social order of their proprietors; it could not make them free, they would still be slaves. Despite all their intellectual sophistication and enlightenment, Sappho's students were merely second rate people in the Greek society... they were women, and even Sappho's talent could not change that fact. Women could not vote. They could not take part in the government or be active in politics, and only exceptionally, if the male head of the family died and put it down in his volition, they could run a business. However, Lesbos was still better than other Greek *poleis*. Sappho's stepfather Pittacus despite being one of the seven sage men, also held women in their designated place. The privilege of education only meant that they got aware of their limited freedom even more drastically. It was a sorry fact that in such a cultured world, half of the population could not enjoy the fruits of civilization. The highly praised democracy was the sole privilege of men.

Agape came to the waterline. She looked around for a minute, then dropped her simple linen chiton and slipped into the tepid blue sea. She remembered her dream and flushed. What did it mean? Was Arsenios going to persecute her? Had she gone too far with her liberal statements? The water caressed and relaxed her tired body. The last two days were tough and the night was long. She had to watch over Timon. He would get well, but he would never be a warrior like his father. Her thoughts wandered back to Sappho. What a remarkable woman! She had a scroll of her poems somewhere, although she never read them. The melancholy would not do her well. Sweet poetry of love had done enough damage on Lesbos.

Back then, in the liberal climate of Lesbos, Agape still believed that knowledge meant power and could change the relations between the sexes. Wistfully, she remembered the speeches and debates which the greatest of all philosophers had given at Pittacus' court – Thales of Miletus. He was a guest on Lesbos, and nobody thought it strange that all of the students of Sappho's academy took part in his discussions. He presented his solutions to various geometric problems and spoke about all things divine and godly, but not in the sense of crazy superstitious oracles... his god was the supreme mind which shaped everything in the world, including men and women. When asked about the substance of matter, Thales talked about water, the element which Agape also beleived was the beginning and the end of life. Well, she knew about the beginning, for be it a foetus or a newborn, they would be each of them lost without their mother's waters and fluids. Thales' rationalistic approach to life was what she could believe in.

Before she came to the *academia*, she had been in training with an experienced midwife and learnt the secrets of women's health and childbirths. Her mother had sent her into apprenticeship at an early age, after her father had gone bankrupt because of false assumptions that Lesbos wheat can beat the Egyptian in price. She had to work hard. Her mentor, a midwife from Mytilene, Rhodopis, did not tolerate lazy girls or hours of idle pleasure in the sun. Work, work, work was all she knew. Agape worked a lot and learnt fast. When she joined Sappho's academy, she had her own license and had worked as an independent midwife in Eresus.

After her apprenticeship years, she felt she needed some time to think things over. She wanted to learn to read Egyptian, as rumors had it that Egyptian physicians accumulated precious medical knowledge in their books. She wanted to round off her knowledge and read them all. Her plan was to translate them and transcribe them in the Greek alphabet, which was more modern and understandable than the Egyptian hieroglyphs. Sappho's academy had an Egyptian teacher, a well known erudite, who could support Agape's ambitions. Against a symbolic fee, which she had negotiated with Sappho, she could enter the school for a couple of years, and continue her studies later in Egypt. Then, it all came differently.

The troubles started after one of the youngest of Sappho's students, Dorothea, committed a suicide and left a note saying that she could not continue to live without Sappho's love. It was preposterous. Sappho was approaching fifty then and she surely was too serious about her school as to start a love affair with a young girl. The *academia* closed down for some time and Sappho underwent an official investigation. Sappho's enemies and the rest of Lesbians were gossiping all the time, inventing erotic rites and

occult practices which could make even the king of Hades blush.
None of it was true. Agape knew that, for she was there. The
girl probably killed herself because her father wanted to summon
her home to Syracuse to marry his old friend. It was a political
marriage. He wanted to sell his daughter of sixteen to an old
fart of fifty, and Dorothea, who was a champion in philosophical
debates, sealed her own fate by taking poison. The trouble was
that the unhappy girl stole the hemlock seed powder from Agape's
apotheca, so Agape felt morally responsible. Dorothea had a lover
boy, who tried to save her by sucking the poison from her mouth.
She died, and he fell mortally sick. Overnight, the *academia*
became a morgue and a hospital, and Agape was watching over
the man who almost died for his love.

She was older and more serious than the rest of the students
and she had responsibilities. Her stay at the *academia* had a
purpose, and she dedicated all her time to learning. Most of the
time, she was alone and did not take part in the erotic games
and sentimental whirlwinds of her mates. They were there for
pleasure and education; they enrolled to spend their young years
in learning instead of just waiting for a husband, while Agape had
a life plan. But it had almost gone wrong. The young man was
lying in bed for days, sweating and gasping for breath, waking up
occasionally only to cry bitter tears over his dead beloved. With
patience and care, sliding spoonfuls of medical infusions down his
throat, changing his linens and washing his burning limbs, Agape
brought the man called Pamphilos, the first son of the richest wine
trader on Lesbos, back from the realm of Hades. When he opened
his eyes and apprehended her for the first time, her soul melted
like honey in the sun. For the first time in weeks, Agape could
see him as a man. So far, she had known most intimate parts of
his body, now she could see into his soul. She fell in love, but she
would not give away her feelings, and the matter would be closed
then and there, had there not been for Sappho, who brought the
two young people together.

Pamphilos was a few years older than Agape. He was aspiring
to a military career and his father was very proud of him. Like
many young educated men from Mytilene or Eresus, he was a
regular guest at Sappho's *symposia*, where he liked to listen to
the songs and to the sharp philosophical discussions. It was no
secret that some of the nocturnal discussions continued in obscure
corners of the garden in less sophisticated yet primordial body
language. Agape was aware of that as she often administered
herbal infusions or particular fruits to prevent the seed of such
extended debates from growing in a student's belly. But she never
took part in such debaucheries. Her friends were often teasing her
that she had no fun and lacked humor.

But Sappho liked Agape, and often took time to discuss a
moral or a health issue for hours with her. As a philosopher and

a poet, she was in favor of the idea that body and soul are an inseparable unit and that a physician should treat both equally. Medicine as a science was inferior and subordinated to philosophy. It was the prevailing idea of their time, with which the practical and rational Agape completely disagreed. Medicine was an exact science, one in which the right dosage decided between life and death. Many times, they would end up in a verbal repartee which Sappho as an experienced debater won over the young healer. When Agape lost her heart to Pamphilos, Sappho did everything to set fire to her feelings in good faith that it was precisely what Agape needed in order to grow into an understanding healer. Yet, she forgot how a broken heart could hurt.

In the honor of reopening the *academia* later in that year, Sappho invited famous thinkers and poets to a *symposium*. She encouraged Pamphilos, and helped him to write a long hymn to honor Agape and her healing powers. But Pamphilos also inserted several verses by the poet Anachreon on Agape's beauty. He and Sappho recited together:

> Spirit of Love, whose tresses shine
> Along the breeze in golden twine,
> Come, within a fragrant cloud
> Blushing with light, thy votary shroud,
> And on those wings that sparkling play
> Waft, oh waft me hence away!
> Love, my soul is full of thee,
> Alive to all thy luxury.

> – Supposedly Anachreon on Sappho, translated
> by T. Moore

Agape was speechless. Beauty won over her reason for once. After the evening closed, she took Pamphilos to her bedroom and explored the poetry of their bodies. Their love seemed so pure and infinite. It was only natural that words were consummated in long warm nights, kisses washed in tepid water of the bay and sweet promises exchanged over honeyed lips. Weeks went by, summer turned to autumn, and trees put on their golden attire. Both Sappho and Agape were assuming that Pamphilos, so much in love that his heart was aching and his soul was bursting, would propose marriage to his saviour. He did at last, but not to Agape. Hiding behind his father's decision to betroth a rich daughter of a *polis'* politician, he abandoned Agape as promptly as he had seduced her in spring. Agape was drowning in rivers of tears. She could not come to terms with the deception. She gave everything to Pamphilos, and she ended up alone and hurt. Who would ever love her? Her parents abandoned her, she had very few friends, then that love... Was there any chance for her to find happiness?

Or would she continue helping others while she could not heal the pain of her own heart? She thought of finishing her life. Sappho talked her out of the depression, and she seemed to gain the ground, when she discovered she was pregnant. Why hadn't she taken the precautions? Precisely she, a trained midwife, who knew the physical nature and consequences of love, she was to bear a child of the man who had turned his back on her. She knew there was only one thing she could do, and she knew how she would do it.

Agape stepped out of the water and, with the clothes in her lap, she sat on a stone in the hot midday sun to dry. Her skin was grateful for the bath. All over her tanned body, a sea of tiny salt crystals were starting to shine and to reflect from the grains of sand on the beach. Arsenios came to her mind again. He was a handsome looking man in his prime. He tried to make peace at the end of their conversation, but as always, she shoved the man off, proud, difficult, incomprehensible, her head high up as though she was a queen and he a slave. Why didn't she stay for a talk? Why didn't she give him a chance? Why was she being so arrogant and aggressive? Her pride made all human feelings difficult. Her sharp mind scared men away. Her bad memory of Lesbos shut her feelings in a wooden box, filled it with fear weighing more than hundreds of *talents*, and sent it to the bottom of the sea. There was no remedy for her soul, no medicine for her loneliness. "When anger spreads through the breast, guard thy tongue from barking idly." Maybe she should read Sappho's verses, and maybe she should think about them sometimes, too.

* * *

For the Asklepios shrine, the building adjoining Agape's home had to be knocked down. The new building, which rose in a few months, was beautiful. The tall, ornate columns carried the weight of the wooden roof with light indifference of the beautiful Helen lifting her golden hair. The rooms were spacious and full of light. The passages were built in such a way that fresh air circulated through, taking the unpleasant smells of the sick outside. There was an operating theatre, a prayer room with an altar to Asklepios for sacrifices, and two cubicles for patients. One was completely isolated from the other rooms – it was the quarantine. The white stone came from the island of Broc or Brač, from the quarries of the Illyrian tribes in the north of the island. Agape was beaming with happiness and good humor. The frustrated, angry citizen quarreling with her ruler was months away. With each stage of the building and with each stone set on the rising wall, Arsenios and Agape grew closer. On the day of the solemn rites to consecrate the shrine and offer sacrifices to Apollo, Arsenios invited Agape to a solemn dinner. She joined him on his couch,

feeling elated and proud. The higher the walls of her shrine, the
lower were her personal defenses. Her discussions with Arsenios
became more passionate and less articulate. It was a public secret they were having an affair, but they were very careful and
were never seen overstepping the limits of good behaviour. They
would meet in the mornings, Arsenios on a horseback with a look
of inspection on his face, Agape with skins and pots, looking for
healing plants. Agape still could not grasp how it happened, but
it felt right despite the fact that her lover was a married man and
his wife due soon.

After the day when their words crossed like swords, she kept
her tongue. Timon was getting better every day and soon he rose
from his bed. Arsenios and Chloe were out of their wits with
happiness and gratitude. So one evening, Arsenios came to pay
her in golden coins and tell her about the plans for the shrine.
They ate dried figs and drank sweet wine from Pelješac. Was it
the wine or the attraction of opposites? They clashed together
like two clouds in the stormy summer sky. Once the lightning
struck, they became inseparable like the forces in a storm.

Then the day came when her lover's wife, Chloe, was brought
to the shrine on a stretcher to be assisted better in her childbirth.
It started well at home, and it looked like the baby would not
take much time and effort to come to the world, but after a
few hours, the women got scared and preferred the professional
Agape to take over. For the labor got more and more difficult.
Chloe was bleeding and the baby didn't move for a finger in her
belly. Two servants supported her in the birth chair, and Agape
had already administered two small dosages of a dittany of Crete
potion. Chloe's body was losing strength. Agape was trying to
feel for the baby's position in order to help it get out with the
pressure of her own hands. In between the contractions, Chloe
whispered to her:

"Help me, Agape, please. I know you can. I don't blame you
for Arsenios. I really don't. He's always been too much for me."

"Dear Chloe, forgive me. I'll do everything I can, but for
now, focus on pressing and think of the son you're bearing. Now,
press..."

Witnessing the painful miracle of life like so many times before, Agape could not help but remember. Although she forbade
herself all thoughts and feelings while she was treating her patients, she couldn't help herself. Labor was always risky for a
woman. As it was the birth of a new life, the cord between
the two worlds was thinner than a spider's thread, both for the
mother and for the baby.

Still, labor was much less dangerous than what she had done
so many years ago on Lesbos. She could have gone to Mytilene,
to her teacher Rodopis, but she wanted to keep the pregnancy
a secret. Thus, she almost killed both... herself and the baby.

When her menses didn't come as due, she set about her bloody business. It was lucky that in autumn, the stems of Brassica oleracea, wild cabbage, were strong. She secretly pulled out the biggest plant from the garden of the *academia*. With a sharp knife, she carved the stem to the form of a smooth spike. She stole some lamb intestines and a ladle of goose fat from the kitchen. She washed the stem and the intestines first in water, then in wine. She boiled the fat and set it to cool. She prepared a large pessary, and filled the hollow part of it with crushed penny royal. If the foetus should persist to live, she would continue with the stem, now clean and dry, wrapped in a linen tissue by the bed. She asked Sappho for a few days of total peace in her cubicle and told her she would take some sedatives to sleep through her misery and gather her forces. Her teacher, fearing the worst, would not let Agape alone, and long days of waiting went by in frustration. In the end, Agape could convince her that all she needed was to be alone for a few days of complete peace. Sappho gave in and let her be, yet not without a good supply of dried fruits, wine, water, bread and cheese.

Agape prepared everything carefully. She inserted the pessary in the evening, before going to sleep. Her intention was to wait for the whole of the following day to see its effect. When the sun was up the next morning, there were no signs of menses-like cramps in her lower body or swelling of the breasts. She decided to wait and spent deciphering some Egyptian medical instructions regarding treatments of poisoning – the antidotes. In the afternoon, when the sun was already lower, a sure sign of the approaching dead season, Agape became restless. She took the pessary out of her vagina and inspected it. It looked soaked in mucus, so its juices had permeated the uterus. Obviously, to no avail. What was she to do? She was pacing up and down her little room like a lioness in a cage. She hesitated for a moment whether she had made the right decision. Maybe the baby was destined to live. Tears welled up in her eyes flickering with doubts as old as the human race. What if it would not die and she would have to bring it up on her own? It would not be impossible, she knew of a few women to have raised a child on their own. How would she stand the thought of having beside her living proof of her foolishness for the rest of her days? It would mean the end of her medical studies, and only Asklepios and Demetris knew if women would ever again trust her professional knowledge and practices of a midwife, unless she could treat herself successfully. The child would be a statement of the opposite. She could always say she had wanted the baby, but then the question of fatherhood would come up and hurt her every time like salt on a fresh wound. She had to go all the way.

Although she was strictly opposed to inducing abortion with mechanical means, for she thought it was not a safe medical procedure, she had to make up her mind. She had studied the writings of the ancients thoroughly, and from the objective point of view, it was the most efficient way to get rid of an unwanted pregnancy. Yet, it could not only mean death for the little creature, but also for her. A cold sweat ran down her spine. The evening breeze scented the eternally black airs of the Hades. She shuddered. If only she could consult somebody, maybe Rodopis. However, she knew what Rodopis would advise her to do – bear the child and get rid of it later, sell it into slavery or give it to a family without children. Labor is better for you than abortion. Yet how could Agape stand the humiliation? She would have to admit not only to Rodopis but to the whole world how weak she had been, how powerless her reason was against passions of the flesh, and how she had been duped by Pamphilos. Several women Rodopis had treated died of the consequences of an abortion induced by mechanical means. Well, Rodopis didn't have the knowledge Agape acquired, and, although her teacher was a wise herbalist, she knew little of hygiene. For one last moment, she gazed at the line where the sun was setting in purple splendor in the west. Her fate was in her skillful hands alone. Were gods against it? Hadn't the wise chorus of the divine orchestra punished her enough already? She believed only in herself, the rest was superstition. She had to act accordingly. Agape's blood froze in her veins like waters in the river of Styx. She washed her hands in wine. She took the cabbage stem and put a finger long piece of the lamb intestines on it. Then she smeared it with the grease. She crouched on her bed and took the stem in her right hand. It was firm and at least two fingers long. With her left palm, she leaned on the wall to support her balance, for she needed all her strength in her right. She slowly induced the stem into her vagina, up towards the birth channel and to the cervix. She flinched with pain when she felt the door to her uterus give way. Like a cut of a knife, sharp pain travelled through her nerves and hit the brain unprepared. She sank onto the bed, causing the stem only to penetrate further into her body. She felt a warm rush down her finger and knew she had done it. Her smile was bitter, for she was not out of danger. She could bleed out, which was a common death after a difficult labor, and an abortion was more dangerous than a labor. Powerful cramps were expelling the seed of love out of her body. She almost cried out in pain and only in the last moment stifled her mouth not to. She removed the bloody cabbage *phallus* from her body and arranged linen cloths to soak up the blood. She would not see it. She would throw the bundle away later. On her nightstand, there was a jug of wine strengthened with opium. She slept for days. There were complications, as apparently a tiny part of the lamb intestines tore away, stayed inside her body and caused infection. Using various baths and infusions, Agape gradually recovered, and it took her body at least a year to restore the monthly bleedings. After a thorough inspection of herself, Agape knew that in the future lovemaking she was free of worries and needed to take no precautions. She would never be pregnant again. At the time, she wasn't too upset, it seemed a practical solution. When she fell in love with Arsenios, though, she wished she could regain her fertility in some way. For once, her treatment of a patient was too perfect – it was forever irreversible.

A cry of a woman in labor brought her back to reality. Chloe was arching in pains, and the nurse kneeling between her legs at the opening of the birth chair, was waiting in vain for the new life to push through. Agape thought the baby got entangled in the umbilical cord somehow. She went to consult with Arsenios.

"Arsenios, I am not sure if I can save them both. Who do you want?"

"I want the boy. I can always take another wife."

Agape would have shuddered in disgust at his answer a few months ago. Now, she couldn't disguise a flicker of hope in her black eyes. They stared at each other for a long moment pregnant with options. Finally, Agape spoke:

"And if it is a girl, Arsenios?"

"It's a boy, I know. Now go and do your business."

Agape turned away from the rough man she loved so much and took the weight of decision on her shoulders. As it was, she was postponing her intervention for too long. It would be difficult, but she would try to save both, the mother and the child. Yet, like an unplowed field in the spring, there lay other possibilities ahead. If only for once, she could think only of herself...

She came back to Chloe, who was losing her consciousness for brief moments in between her wails. Her limpness became very dangerous to the lives of both, mother and the baby, struggling through the pains together. Agape stretched her hand and felt the pelvis opening. There was the baby's head, if she could move the tissues apart... She administered an opium potion, for she knew her next grip would be very painful. Chloe was hanging in arms of the slaves and with a small knife, the tip of which had passed through a flame, Agape carefully cut the perineal tissues between her legs. The baby's head, bluish, its tiny mouth almost inaudibly weeping, moved towards the floor. Without her knowing, Chloe's body jerked in the last of so many painful contractions, and the child was born. Almost immediately, Chloe's heart stopped, and she passed away without having heard the powerful cry of her little one, who was now selfishly demanding full attention. Agape saw the baby was safe in the hands of her attendants and stepped out into the yard.

"Arsenios, Chloe is no more... I could not..."

"And the boy?" he cut in.

"It's a girl. She's a big healthy baby. You can be proud..."

"Leave that, Agape! I needed a boy!"

The king turned around and left the Asklepios shrine without another word. Agape stared in shock at the wide shoulders leaving behind a dead wife, a newborn baby daughter and a desperate lover without another thought. What was going on in his thick head? Didn't he cherish the fruit of his love to Chloe? What base barbarian, what primitive animal would act like that? With bitterness she thought of her base hopes for their future together. She knew she had not done everything she should have to save Chloe. She was hesitating one moment too long between the mother and the baby. The moment which had drawn a line between life and death. The moment while Agape was dreaming of becoming the next queen. Oh, why had she abandoned only for a thousandth of a second her professional ethos of a healer? Was love to such a brute worth it? She could never be sure about herself again.

Arsenios went to his palace and in the weeks to come, he never asked about his daughter. He left her at the Asklepios shrine like an orphan, without a name or a person to care for her. At first, Agape was tolerant, finding all kinds of excuses for him: the shock of Chloe's death, mourning, new fights with Illyrians. Deep in her heart, she was still hoping he would come back one day and they would make love and raise all his three children, including the little survivor baby, together. Then it dawned on her: to Arsenios women meant nothing, nothing at all. For him, his female offspring and his dead wife were irrelevant, only Timon was of any importance as his heir and the future ruler of Korkyra Melaina.

The little daughter of the king did not seem to mind or notice her precarious position. In the arms of her wet nurse, she could never drink enough milk, she was always crying for more, more milk and more attention... That was all she wanted. That was the call with which she came to the world. She was thriving like a wild herb pushing and bursting in springtime. Agape loved her strong will and without noticing it, she got more and more attached to her. However, she went to Arsenios' palace to talk to him, but she was shooed away by the guards like a dirty beggar. She came back the next day. It was for the girl's sake, it was her heritage. Four months old, the infant hadn't been named yet. She wrote Arsenios a letter, begging him to see reason, to set a moral example as a ruler and acknowledge his blood. Yet, only a slave returned with a purse full of gold. Then she wrote a legal letter in which she beseeched him to take his daughter in his house and to raise her as it was proper or she would write to Corfu again. The black slave Theron returned with a chariot filled with furniture, linens and furs, and a brief note:

Dear Agape,

Please understand me and keep the girl as your own. I will support her and you with all the wealth I possess. I will come to see you soon and we will talk more.

Yours, Arsenios

A tricky flicker of hope shone back into her life with the little note. Maybe after the year of mourning... Agape brought the baby girl to a priestess and named her herself... Chloe, little Chloe, in the memory of her frail, soft-natured mother, the queen of Korkyra Melaina. Maybe by taking good care of little Chloe, Agape could repay for her past life, and maybe she would be able to forget the black secret which so many years ago under the warm Lesbos sun turned her heart to stone. She loved little Chloe as though she was her own. She was part of Arsenios, the rough warrior, the passionate king, who had softened her senses and quickened her juices after such a long time.

* * *

The air was heavy with the scent of sweet acacia blossoms when the following year, Persephone, the goddess of spring, once again showered the meadows of Korkyra Melaina with flowers. Agape was climbing the hill above the *polis* with a heavy, babbling burden on her shoulders. It was baby Chloe, who enjoyed early morning walks with her protector, safely tied to her back, with the most stunning view around. She was a little queen on her throne, and she gratefully returned the pleasure with cheers and smiles of a thousand innocent nymphs dancing in the soft green grass. Agape paused for a breath and looked down into the valley, where the shadows of the night were still cooling the dark green pines. She was happy, and her hopes for the future were high. Arsenios had written her a letter in which he was asking her to meet him later that evening. She would come, of course.

She had come a long way in her quest for happiness and balance. Layer by layer, joy lifted the dark secrets of her past and chased them away as sun dispelled the veils of the morning fog under its warm rays. She had a baby, though she hadn't brought her into the world, and she would have a man, though she had not wed him. Her basket quickly filled with bouquets of sorrel, lemon sage, penny royal and lime balm. Wild rosemary was in flower, and hungry bees were buzzing around the tiny purple flowers in swarms of noise which shut up the babbling baby for a moment. It would soon be time to fill the little stomach, so Agape turned down towards her house and her shrine, where god Asklepios took the life of a woman and gave another a future. She would return to the clearing among the pines in the twilight to meet the man to whom she wanted to give even more than she had already given.

Arsenios came to the meeting on time. He was as powerful as ever and solemnly presented Agape a gift, a wonderful purple scarf made of pure silk.

"Thank you, my king. I will wear it for the special occasions."

"Agape, you've done a lot for me. Thanks go to you."

"Well, how is Timon? He hasn't come to play with his sister for some time now."

Timon was the only member of the royal family who acknowledged his little sister Chloe and came regularly to Agape's to play with her. The older daughter went or rather was sent away after the death of her mother, to her aunt on Corfu.

"He's in training. I sent him to the camp on the north of the island. He must develop some muscles."

"Don't overstretch him. He's a sensitive chap. And very clever as well. The world changes, Arsenios. Today also knowledge counts, not only muscles."

"Agape, you still live in your ideals, don't you?"

"The day I will lose my ideals will be the day I die. So, tell me, what is the purpose of our meeting?"

Arsenios looked at her, but there was just cold in his eyes. No warm summer sky, no love lost. Agape was prepared for the worst.

"I'm getting married again."

That was not bad. She looked deeply into his blue eyes full of Lesbos, smiled tenderly, her spirits reaching the sky, and made a step forward. She knew that the precious purple scarf was her wedding gift.

"My bride arrives from Sparta in a few days. I thought you should know first."

Agape almost tripped in her step. She turned her eyes away to the black crown of the fresh dark pines. Tears welled up and she swallowed them together with a cold, painful lump in her throat. Shock paralyzed all her senses. She lost her tongue and was gasping for air. There was only one tiny straw left.

"Are you taking Chloe away from me?"

"That's precisely what I wanted to talk to you about, Agape. My future wife is very young, a thing of fourteen or fifteen years. She will not be too happy to look after another's woman baby. Hence, I wanted to suggest you keep the little toad, I mean Chloe, until she is of marriageable age. Of course, I will pay all the expenses for her, so in a way I will provide for both of you. You won't have to work so hard anymore."

"I don't mind working and I will not be maintained like a mistress, thank you."

"This time, Agape, I insist you listen to me."

She stood still in the face of that offense. There was nothing she could do, he was the king. He dismissed her like a servant. She was not on his life map any more. Still, she had to negotiate the position for Chloe. She had to compose herself and forget the failed hopes for love. She had been duped again. It was getting familiar. The whole year, while she was looking after his daughter, Arsenios was looking for a fresh young wife to sire more sons. She was tempted to curse his male descendants to be forever weak and sick. Instead, she said in a matter-of-fact voice:

"I demand one thing for Chloe. You must issue a sealed document that she is your daughter in the eye of the law and that she will be your heir, should the lots be cast in her way."

Did he hear her right? Arsenios blinked in disbelief mixed with fear. Was this woman a witch or a healer?

"Why do you think Chloe could rule Korkyra Melaina one day?"

"I will tell you why, my king," Agape continued in a hissing voice. "It is obvious that your semen for boys is weak and thin, and the one you managed to sire in all the years of your marriage to the queen will not live to rule, no matter how much you try to form him. The future boys will all be like Timon. Since you have sent your eldest daughter Arsenoe away to Corfu, I have my doubts she would ever return. Why would she? Why would she want to fight for her place with a queen of her age or an infant? She would find a husband in Greece and stay there. That makes my little Chloe the first in line. I just want justice for her, nothing but justice, my king."

Arsenios listened to her speech with his head down. Sorrow and confusion was written all over his face. He felt awkward. He had done nothing extraordinary, nothing the customs would not lay down, yet he felt unworthy. His cheeks sank and his look lost all sparkle. For a moment only, Agape almost felt sorry for him.

"Agape, do you demand justice for Chloe or do you demand justice for yourself?"

Agape lifted her head up, and her body grew even taller and stouter in the sublime posture of pride. She was hard again, the river Styx flowed in her veins, no emotion whatsoever, and she would not let him debase her.

"Justice for Chloe is justice for me. I love her more than I love myself."

The man shrugged his shoulders. He was defeated.

"Then, you shall have it. Chloe is my daughter. You took her out of my wife's womb to make a tool of control out of her. The gods will throw their lots if Chloe is to rule Korkyra Melaina after I pass away and explore the lands of Hades. But listen to me, woman. Don't you dare curse my new marriage and my new queen! I will find out about it and I swear, I will kill you both – you and the baby!"

"Bring me the document tomorrow!"

"Have you heard what I just said, Agape?"

"Oh, I have my king. Nobody can curse you more than you already have cursed you yourself! Farewell!"

She turned away and felt his eyes on her back, his anger hot with pride, his menacing thoughts hitting her like arrows in the battle. She didn't care. She would forget the man eventually. She could live with her defeat, with the loss of love, for she was used to winning and losing. Like the sun and the rain. Life was a mosaic of tiny stones of all colors. Some were bright and red. Some were dull and dark. It is the big picture which you could see from above that counted. A philosopher or a thinker had to abandon the everyday world of tiny stones to see the wholeness of the composition and to comprehend the essence of life. Her essence, her everything used to be medicine, which she almost lost to passion; now it was little Chloe. She would rule these lands one day. Agape would be the one who would raise the future queen of Korkyra Melaina into an educated and wise woman. Queen Chloe would get the best of them all...the kind nature of her mother, the heroic courage of her father and the knowledge of all the seven sage men of the world.

Romans, A.D. 311

I have been right to hope. Paula is feeling so much better today that I want to take her out for a walk by the sea. The hospital in Zadar has lent me a wheelchair. However, I still have to figure it out how to persuade Paula to sit in it. She would object, although she is still too frail to walk. However, if she gets sick or loses her consciousness on the way, I am surely not strong enough to bring her home.

The morning is fresh. The red earth smells damp of the rain that fell in the night. My heart is thumping in my chest as though it was about to blow up. Sweat is pouring down my back and I am suffocating. It is only a couple of yards uphill though. What is wrong with me? The strains of the last months have taken their toll on my body. The disillusion of watching Paula struggling with leukemia is poisoning me. I am tired and I've lost a lot of weight, which is anything but healthy at my age. I must rest for a minute. There is a nice big rock under a mulberry tree on the top of the hill, and I drag my legs to it. I sit down.

It is a majestic spot from which I can see the village, our house and the hotel Perovica, perched on the hill above a long white pebble beach. The building is not like a typical hotel at all, more like a huge village with more than a hundred tiny stone cottages from ancient times used by the fishermen to keep their nets in. In between, fabulous millennium-old olive trees cast their silver shadows over the tiled verandas of the hotel rooms. Well, only my silent business associate and I know the real figures of the enormous cost of the extravagant Dutch design. It is so pretty: worth every cent of it! I wipe my forehead and for a tiny second feel proud of myself. In the distance, I can hear and see Dario's boat returning to the port with his catch of fish. I get up again. I must go on. Will I be able to look after my baby and work at the hotel during the peak season?

A week after Paula's chemotherapy, I had to go back to work. The ecological hotel is anything but simple to run. It is a science of its own only to comply with all the regulations set by the European Union. Still, the eco brand brings in a higher rank of guests, who have well stocked wallets and do not nag at every expense. Over the years, not only the hotel set on the course of satisfying the eco tourists, but also the villages and people around it. There are sailing, surfing, hiking, fishing, and diving courses, as well as all kinds of other little businesses prospering around our little village of Mulobedanj. The islanders earn money, which is good for them and good for me. They needed to pocket quite some euros before they got used to us and accepted us. Paula and I come from mainland Croatia, so for many years the local people were suspicious of us. Sometimes I think I have more bought than merited my way into their hearts. Stained money for a good cause; so be it! I stopped feeling guilty about the money some years ago.

Paula has been more enthusiastic about Agape and the Greeks than I thought she would. All of a sudden, she wants to read everything there is on Dalmatia in the centuries before the Romans took its shores and conquered the old Illyrian tribes and the Greek citizens in their capable military coup. A year ago, my little girl enrolled into foreign languages, French and English, at the Zagreb University, but maybe she will change her mind after the treatments. She would make a good historian. In my point of view, knowing the history of your country, understanding and respecting the roots of your people, are basic to being a good hotel director and owner. You can easily get an accountant or a lawyer to run the affairs with tax authorities and handle the balance sheets, but for an ecological hotel like Perovica you need a visionary, a heart and a soul. If this malaise continues, Paula and I will be in trouble. Every bone of my body aches and when I set on my morning inspection of the new glasshouse, the steep, not more than a mile long path uphill feels like a mountain impossible to climb. I should probably go and see a doctor for my chest pain. Maybe I should simply give myself a rest.

I admire the glasshouse and the fresh vegetables and fruits ripening in the neat rows. Now the sewage water from the hotel gets recycled and my guests can enjoy organic food. The little van is loaded with crates and boxes. I join the ride downhill and stop at my house. Fresh strawberries, cheese and bread will delight Paula. I enter the house, and, surprisingly, I smell coffee.

"Hello, nona. I made some coffee."

I can see my baby is pale, her sullen cheeks glistering with sweat. She is wearing a white baseball cap turned backwards, for her head is by now bald. Her eyes are shining with slight fever, yet, she smiles warmly at me. She has gone through all this strain just to make me happy. I am a lucky woman, wrapped in the coat of her young love.

"Thank you, Paula. Do you want to eat something?"

"Not really, but I have to, don't I?"

I nod and start setting the table. She manages a few bites of cheese and bread. She will be fine. I just have to bring her out into the sun. She takes my hand and asks:

"Nona, I would love to know something more about the Romans in our lands."

It is my cue. While I start the story of Emperor Diocletian and his young friend on the isle of Šolta, I unfold the wheelchair from the corner. I manage to sit Paula in it, and while climbing the steep road uphill for the second time this morning, I feel no fatigue or strain. My baby is so light; she is like a feather. I try to convey the spirit of the splendid Roman age with saucy Latin oaths and blasphemies. Paula is amused and laughs brightly from the heart. Oh, I would be telling fibs until the end of days for this silver laugh of hers!

* * *

"By Jupiter, you have lived too long, Gaius Aureilus Valerius Diocletianus," murmured into his chin the old man sitting in his comfortable sedan chair. There was no roof above his head, so that the Great Roman Emperor could appraise the skies at all times. Despite his failing eyes and weaker hearing, his ability to forecast the winds and the weather had remained very accurate. No old age or grave illness seemed to have affected the sharpness of his thoughts. Yet, in his limbs and bones, Diocletian felt every one of his almost seventy years. His blue eyes lost the sparkles of command and anger, only the bushy white brows spoke of that once dangerously strong will which moved about armies and decided on a whim upon people's futures all over the territories of the biggest empire the world had ever seen.

It was a sunny summer day in Anno Domini 311, though the weather had been changing in the last two weeks of the hottest August month for decades. The old Emperor could feel the atmosphere turning to rain in his right ankle, swollen out of proportion, bluish and greenish, with red cracks in the skin, out of which yellow pus was seeping into the thick white bandages. The smell of it was repelling despite the constant changing of the dressings. It turned everybody's stomach, so people took flight as soon as they could. Shitty cowards, that was what they were, shitty cowards all of them. When all his physicians and courtiers were despairing and inventing new and new excuses to abandon him, he packed Filio, his Greek slave, and left his court in *Spalatum*. To hell with the most beautiful palace in the world, which he had been building for a decade, to hell with the wonderful herb gardens and lavender-perfumed baths that everybody else but him was enjoying. He found the air between the walls of his splendid palace polluted; there was a smell of decay and foul play in every corner. At the same time, he stopped trusting the cooks with the food, less so his entourage with their thoughts. He saw poison and daggers everywhere. So one day, without previous notice, Diocletian sailed to Šolta, the island across the *Spalatum* channel, to inspect how his fish were doing in the hatchery built at the end of a lovely bay called Nečujam, in his mother tongue, Illyrian.

"Oh, my Emperor, what were you saying?" asked the thin, delicately clothed young man at his side. Diocletian looked at his companion, whose pitch black curls encircled his softly tanned cheeks in an exquisite hair-do. Those Greeks were like women, spoilt, manicured and full of shit.

"Nothing, Filio, my boy, nothing... Let's go down to the pond, to speak to Antonius and see what we will have for lunch today,"

grunted back the old man, still feeling angry with his stupid slave
for the humiliation in the morning. The coward Filio with peach
like skin lifted him out of his bed and carried him in his lap
to the latrines as though he was an impotent sissy. Had the
sleazy Greek waited a moment longer, he, a long time warrior
and fighter, whom soldiers had hailed Imperator, Emperor, on
the battlefield of Nicomedia, would surely have managed on his
own. What a life, when a sleeky slave commanded his every day
needs and rituals! He should have him flogged! That was what
he should do! Thrash a whip down his pretty arse, and see him
sweat with blood and pain to show him who the *dominus* in the
house was. What would those waxed curls do in the jolts of the
whip, eh? Diocletian couldn't contain a little sadistic smile at
the thought of it.

"It is such a joy to my heart, when my Emperor smiles at me!
It is the Jupiter's flash to my faithful heart, Sir!"

"I don't think so, Filio, I don't think so. Now, do as I say!
Or does your back miss a thrashing?"

"Yes, my Emperor, right now, Sir, my light..." With the
sweetest epithets, the boy skillfully lifted the sedan chair and
wheeled it along the path. It was one of the latest inventions of
his master – a wheeled sedan chair with soft silk cushions and a
fur blanket to cover the legs and contain the pungent smell of an
old, decaying body.

"My Emperor, have I told you about Helena and me last
night? I haven't, how stupid of me!"

"Stupid is definitely your word, Filio."

"Now, you know she is alone for a week, for her husband
Antonius was sent on errands to Salona. Last night we were to
meet on the little beach around the corner. So, after you went
to bed, I took a blanket and a bottle of wine and went to my
meeting. She was already there, lying in the sand, waiting for
me. She was naked like a goddess, Venus from the waves. I
kissed her salty breasts and my *mentula* got stiff like a stick. Her
skin was wet and warm. Her vulva was burning with desire and I
sank between her legs and kissed the juices of her tights. Oysters
from Médoc couldn't taste any sweeter! Helena is as beautiful as
her name! Her want is like an eternal well, it is never exhausted.
I think she loves me. Well, I wanted to wash in the sea first,
for yesterday was hot and I was sticky with old sweat, but she
didn't let me. She had to have me right then. I plunged into her
softness with my hardness. I lost myself completely. When she
was bursting with joy, wetting my crotch with her essence and
crying out softly into my ear, I couldn't contain my semen any
longer. She didn't mind. She said she could have a baby, one to
grow smarter than her halfwit of a husband. And we didn't stop
there..."

"Filio, stop! Now! I don't believe a word you say! You're a

philetor like all Greeks. Your love and kisses are for men! You're a dirty lot, you Greeks, *paiderastia*, all of you! I should have killed every one of you when I brought my legions to your lands! What would a nice young woman like Helena do with a jerk like you? You're a slave and she's a citizen, stupid!"

Filio completely ignored the angry tone in his master's voice. He knew better – a barking dog never bites. He stopped the wheelchair and came around to face Diocletian. With shining eyes, he conjured him.

"But it is true, Sir! Why would I lie to you? She is as hot as a chestnut, I tell you. And we're meeting again tonight. Would you like to watch us, my Emperor?"

"What a pervert! I'll have you crucified, rascal! Just say another word about it! Bring me down to the pond, now!"

Filio quickened his pace and hid a little smile. Only when he was out of his master's view, his face dropped the smiling mask which had hidden his true thoughts. He hated Diocletian like nobody else in the entire world. On the other hand, he was in awe of him. There were so many sides to him. His sharpness of thought, his complexity filled Filio with the same wonder he had experienced when reading old Greek legends. Diocletian was like the skies in early spring – dark with cruelty and shiny with the warm rays of the high sun. It was such a curse that he had to work for him, precisely him. His life was in constant danger, fragile like a glass cup in the hands of the moody and malicious old man. Well, maybe not for long... The old fart should kick the bucket any day now, the way he smelt. Diocletian was looking at the distance, evidently lost in the images of something else. The story, which Filio had told about his evening on the beach was nevertheless exciting Diocletian's imagination. Somehow, he couldn't get it out of his mind. It was a fact that the Emperor never stopped wanting women, although the strength for sex had left his body years ago. What did Filio mean by watching them?

They came to the highest point of the winding path high above the blue bay. A ragged wild rosemary bush was perched on the cliff barely grabbing the white rocks with its roots. Or so it seemed. Like the old man sitting frail and pale in his chair, the bush reached deep into the ground, deeper than any lush flower of the season. There was a house of a farmer only a few minutes inland, where a meal was ready for his Excellency. Like every day, Filio stopped and clogged the chair, leaving the ruler alone with the magnificent view over Nečujam and the little village scattered around the fishponds. While his slave was away to fetch some figs and wine, Diocletian's mind turned to the fish. Last night he had a tasty meal. He started with oysters, fresh from his aquaculture, so he ate them raw sprinkled only with lemon juice and ground black pepper. For the main course, the cook boiled a big *Zeus faber*, one of his favorites. The spice sauce *Garum* and the green beans completed the fish nicely. The dessert was lavender honey cakes – an unusual combination, which he liked very much. On Šolta, Diocletian broke up with the long, copious meals he had to host in his gorgeous palace in *Spalatum*, counting ten or more courses, with a dozen boring guests eating to vomit and vomiting to eat. On the island, life was simple and the meals fresh, tasty, and light. He soon felt much better. If only his legs would serve him again. His villa on Šolta was not as huge as his palace in the city, but it was luxurious, with the dark green pines shadowing most of its yard during the day. Diocletian enjoyed sitting in the shadows reading or just napping away the hours until supper. Filio was usually somewhere near him, ready to jump at a hint, seemingly faithful and kind like a puppy, but underneath probably meaner than a junkyard dog.

Another day could bring another chance. . . He wished so much to walk again. He missed the love and affection of women. He missed his strength of a man, of the Emperor. He had lived too long. He should either get up and walk again or finish his imperial life. Brave men would fall on their swords. If only it were not so difficult to depart! If only not so many tasks were waiting for him! Despite his life struggle to bring back the power to the crumbling Roman Empire, he could witness it deteriorating like a dead fish in the sun. Not his fish. . . The old man was contemplating his *piscinae* below, nicely divided into tanks considering which kind of fish or shellfish was cultivated. In the peaceful left corner behind the pier, where the waters were relatively still even in rough winds on stormy days, there were oyster beds. They started the beds with oysters from Gaul, which had better flesh than the local species. Besides, they grew quicker. In the middle, where fresh water was constantly feeding the basins, they kept some wonderful specimen of *Mullus barbatus* or, in Illyrian, *trlja*. A few of them were big and old. They were swimming in circles in search of the keeper and the treats he might have in store for them, acting more like pets than fish for the table. Diocletian particularly liked grilled *Dicentrarchus labrax*, a kind of sea bass the tender white meat of which was a delicacy without comparison. Its breeding was far the simplest compared to the other species. Another wonderfully easy to breed species in the Emperor's tanks was *Sparus aurata* or *orada*, which was so plentiful that Antonius, the keeper, obtained a special permission from Diocletian to sell them to the fish market in *Spalatum* or in *Salona*. Finally, in the right corner, there were fresh lobsters tied to strings, strolling around the rocks, dark grey warriors with their huge claws from the bottom of the seas, now impotently waiting for the Emperor's desire to see them red and shiny on his supper table.

Despite the fresh breeze at the top, it was getting hot and the old man could not move from his chair. Where was that little scum, Filio? Was he going to pick the grapes for the wine? Oh, how could he be cursed with such Greek, a good-for-nothing servant? If only his wife Prisca was here with him! She knew how to pick and control the servants. Yet Prisca was no more and it was good so. She had betrayed him. She had betrayed his Empire.

"Oh, my dear father of the Empire, I am sorry. The peasants wanted me to try some wines, and I picked a fresh, cold white with a little honey and rosehip bouquet. Here, my lord, try some!"

"I swear you'll get to feel the whip by the end of this day, Filio! While you were getting drunk in the house, I was frying in the sun. Now get me in the shade. I will have a drink there."

Filio moved the heavy chair with the grunting old man away from the sun. He almost choked on the smell of the pus, which no perfumes or fresh air could hold back any longer. His master was really in a bad mood today. He should think of something to distract him. You never know when the Emperor could have a flashback of his persecution of Christians, and have him tortured as he had done with his own man Georgius in Nicomedia. Back then, the story of him and Diocletian's wife Prisca travelled through the antechambers of the Roman palaces with the speed of light. Filio poured his master some wine and placed a bowl of green olives stuffed with hard cheese and a piece of bread in his lap. How was he going to eat! His whole body stank like the plague. Filio stepped a yard back from his master.

"You know, my lord. I wasn't joking when I said you could watch me and Helena doing it. It would be fun and maybe we can look for a Helena for your Excellency, should you be feeling the wish."

Between munches and gulps of wine, Diocletian murmured.

"I cannot watch what is not there. Do you think I am so senile and blind?"

"No, of course not. Age does not hurt you, my lord. You're always fit and trim like a young man. Just look at your hair."

"What of my hair? It is whiter than snow..."

"Yes, but you still have the hair on your proud head, my lord. How many old men at your age are bald like ostrich eggs? I ask you... all of them are bald, and instead of a manly beard like yours, they have white and grey stubs protruding out of their chins."

With that said, Filio tickled the old man around his beard and laughed out aloud. There should be a way to put the old man in a better mood.

"Now, when I was working for my previous master in Nicomedia, I knew a very old rich merchant, who was suddenly widowed. Just like you, my lord..."

"Do not remind me of that, bloody fool!"

"Yes, of course... Well, that old man found a young and attractive peasant and asked her father for her hand. The father of the girl, actually much younger that the groom himself, couldn't hide his astonishment. 'What would you do with such a young girl? Silly, you should look for a companion of your age', he said to the suitor. The old man replied he wanted more children and that he would have them with the young girl. The father burst into laughter, saying it was impossible, for he was probably too old, and even called him an impotent sot. The suitor remained unimpressed and simply stated. 'Very well, whatever you think. But I can die soon and your daughter will be a rich widow, consider that.' The peasant saw reason and gave him girl's hand. The old man was a good husband to the girl, who was a beauty above all, and they got along well. After a year, the first son was born, then the second, and when their fifth, named Quintus, was walking, and a few years went by, the peasant was dying of curiosity and asked his daughter how that was possible. 'My dear father, why do you think my *dominus* has a handsome Greek slave?' You see, my lord, we could help each other. You get a girl, and if you don't feel like fucking her, I can do it for you. It'll be my pleasure!"

"Stop babbling, you idiot. If I need a woman, I can deal with her and I will. Stick to your boys, pervert!"

"You know, my lord, the other day I heard of a village in Pannonia, it's not on the coast actually, more in the centre of the province. Like you breed fish in your *piscinae*, they breed lovely girls for Roman veterans when they retire from the service and get their patch of land there. Like your fish and oysters, the girls are fresh and good quality, with no Christian nonsense in their heads. They cherish only Jupiter and Juno, Vesta, Flora, Minerva and such. Well, they obey, and perform rites only to the Roman deities. The veterans, instead of searching for a Roman matron who would terrorize them for the rest of their lives, they go to that Pannonian village and buy such a peasant girl from her parents. They acquire citizenship for her, teach her to read and write, some basic Roman habits, and make her pregnant every year. They say the sons of those girls are strong and clever boys, so maybe you should make it a law, *Lex Diocletiana Feminina*, or something, that your veterans should find healthy peasant wives to settle down with. It would be a win-win law for the Empire and for the soldiers."

"You can breed fish, but you can't breed people. At least, you cannot do it successfully."

"Well, my lord, may I disagree? You can breed yourself a nation of fine warriors if you choose. Maybe in the future you will be able to crossbreed humans. You can start experimenting with the slaves. I can sacrifice myself. I can be your first specimen. Just tell who I should..."

At last, Diocletian burst into wild laughter. The bowl with food fell to the floor and wine spilt all over his blanket. Filio breathed out. He finally managed to make the Emperor laugh.

"But, Sir. I am up to the job. I can copulate with any woman you might choose for me. I can say to my *mentula* UP! And it jumps like a soldier with a spear. I can ride any mule you ask me to, and you can see if it works before you make it a law."

"*Canus, canus!* Filio, you old dog, you can be funny. Oh, to breed fish. . ."

"I swear, my Emperor, you should think about it. What greatness those healthy sons could bring to our cohorts! They would be the future glory of the Roman world."

Diocletian's laughter died as abruptly as it had started. He looked sternly at Filio.

"No more about this! Our Empire is great as it is! We don't need your pervert Greek ideas to pollute our minds and disintegrate our families. All bad things come from the East. First Greeks and your disgusting *paiderastia*, then the Jews and this new religion, Christianity. It is the utmost religious fanaticism without any comparison. How can parents sacrifice the lives of their children to ascend to another world, Heaven, as they call it? How can wives follow their husbands into death? So those who are last now will be first then, and those who are first will be last. Who believes such nonsense? Slaves can never be masters!"

"You are right, my lord. I simply cannot understand why every day there are more and more Christians all around the world. There are even Christians at courts and in the higher ranks of the army now. It is a contagious disease, as you say rightly."

"You are a fool, Filio, but here you speak the truth. Christianity is the plague of the empire. We should kill them all. Once people are infected with their so called Scriptures, their brains melt to shit, and they stop thinking. All they bring about is loss. So many losses, so many lives spent for nothing."

Diocletian gazed into the distance. The dark green pines were softly rustling in the morning breeze, sounding like human prayers of thousands accepting death joyfully, willingly, blissfully like children receiving gifts, praying to die rather than pay their symbolic respects to the Roman rites. His mind travelled back to the times a decade earlier, when he had to put on trial one of his most dear commanders, Georgius. He was a fine young man, who fought bravely side by side with him, shoulder to shoulder with his Emperor. He was handsome, and women were all in love with him. Diocletian trusted him and showered him with gifts and attentions. Prisca loved the man, too. Diocletian didn't want to know how deep their relationship was and what it meant, but he knew his wife was very fond of Georgius. He forgave her. They had been together for ages. He wouldn't have minded if she just needed to have some fun. Nevertheless, Christianity was anything but funny. It undermined the essence of the Great Roman Empire; public order, tranquility, settled customs, habits and obedience. It was destroying his life's work and the traditions of generations. Octavius was right when he wrote: "And now, as wickeder things advance more fruitfully, and abandoned manners creep on day by day, those abominable shrines of an impious assembly are maturing themselves throughout the whole world. Assuredly this confederacy ought to be rooted out and execrated. They know one another by secret marks and insignia, and they love one another almost before they know one another; everywhere also there is mingled among them a certain religion of lust, and they call one another promiscuously brothers and sisters, that even a not unusual debauchery may by the intervention of that sacred name become incestuous: it is thus that their vain and senseless superstition glories in crimes."

Diocletian didn't have any choice. He had to join Galerius, that sadist and bloodsucker, though forever his ally, in the persecutions. He had to cut limbs, severe heads, crucify bodies, torture their sick minds, and crush their bloody faith in that tramp Jesus, who they had proclaimed their savior. It was no bravery to kill defenseless men, wailing women and clueless children. They killed them all; the ultimate goal was the total extinction of Christianity in the Roman world. Diocletian sighed in despair remembering. All the deaths brought nothing but loss. Loss of people, loss of workforce, loss, loss, loss... The persecutions, as he had feared in his enlightened moments of clarity, brought about just the opposite outcome. Those crazy zealots' faith was nourished by martyrdom. Crying in pain, dying on crosses, burning alive, they were baptizing their followers with blood instead of water. It was like a forest after a fire. Out of the ashes, from the roots of once powerful trunks, weeds would push up with new vigor, and soon hundreds of young green bushes would replace one tall tree. After the persecutions, the Christians with their fanaticism spread like a disease all over the Roman world. The stupid Filio was right. It was like an infection, like a huge pus lump threatening to burst and contaminate the Roman world.

Oh, Georgius! How he had loved to spend evenings with Georgius. They would exchange pleasantries, eat delicacies, talk about big battles and gorgeous women, listen to sweet music and have deep philosophical discussions on the new administrative order which had saved Rome. *Divide et impera!* Divide and rule, was the motto under which Diocletian in 293 delegated his Ceasar's power to two co-rulers, Galerius and Constantius, thus forming the Tetrarchy. It was not for charity that he distributed power, but for efficiency. His co-rulers had to work hard, employ bureaucrats, collect taxes, defend borders against the vandals, and bring prosperity to the Roman citizens, so tired of three hundred years in perpetual decrease in living standards. Georgius was a friend until that secret sect got to him and talked nonsense into his head. Or had he sucked it with his mother's milk in Lydia? Diocletianus did not know and could not care less. In the end, he had to kill him, too. Who would ever think that his wife Prisca would follow Georgius into death! Crazy fanatics! What a loss!

Diocletian thought Christian writings were full of ridiculous, fairy tale beliefs. The Holy mother Mary supposedly conceived her child Jesus with God without having slept with him, by the Holy Spirit. The Christians worshipped her as a Virgin until her death, despite the fact the woman had been married to Joseph. Well, Diocletian had deflowered quite a few virgins in his lifetime, and they surely weren't beyond fifteen years of age neither had they ever born a child. Then there was the crucifixion of Jesus, whom his own people, the Jews, turned in to their prefect Pontius Pilates in the end. It was beyond imagination what the author of their writings did with the short path to Golgotha, the hill where they had been crucifying thieves and criminals. He invented fifteen Stations of the Cross, followed with prayers and stops, at which Jesus supposedly met with half of Jerusalem. As far as Diocletian knew crucifixions, soldiers drove the condemned to the crosses like cattle, with whips and little time to chat and look around. There wasn't even one station, lest fifteen. And, the strangest of all was Jesus' ascension to Heaven in the arms of his father God. Diocletian's mentality of a soldier, of an Emperor and of a rationalist could never comprehend that tale for children which affected with madness such huge crowds all around his Empire. He couldn't believe a word of it, but he read the Scriptures thoroughly; to fight the enemy, you have to know him well. Christians were enemies like Sarmatians, Carpi, or Alamanni. They were dogs, undermining the foundations of the Roman Empire with their irrational religious zeal. He had to fight them and he did.

"Here we go, my Emperor. Where would you like to sit? In the shade? Shall I help you to the couch under that roof?"

"For a change, put me on the ground, Filio. I want to breathe in the fresh scent of the crushed pine needles today."

"My excellence must always crush something. In your younger years, I can imagine you crushing women..."

At the thought of moving his sore, swollen legs, Diocletian became impatient. In spite of the wonderful weather and lovely view of his lively fish ponds, everything got on his nerves.

"Now, I am crushing only the pine needles. And impertinent slaves like you, Filio, I can crush you. I can crush you like a flea in my linen, like a worm on the ground. I'll have no regrets, for you're a pervert and a thief, a scum, a son of a Christian whore, wasn't it?"

Filio let the abuses fly past his ears. His only hope was that old age and illness would eventually crush Diocletian, before he could do harm to him. For Filio knew there would be a time when all his jests and stories would lose Diocletian's attention and no humor could dam the old man's rage over life and destiny. Then, it would be him, Filio, to pay for it. He could see that Diocletian was grinding his teeth, withholding the pain as he was being lifted from the wheelchair. The Emperor's legs were like two tree trunks and the pus was leaking, stinking like a rotting rat in the field. Filio needed all his strength to disguise his repulsion, feeling his bile coming up in his throat.

"Would you like me to get some fresh mulberries from the hill for you, Sir?"

"Yes, go, I am sick of you. I don't want to look at your cheeky face any longer. Go, you stinking bastard!"

Filio didn't need another word. He knew that the Emperor would be in a better mood and more disposed after some time alone by the waterfront. Watching his fish swimming around, playing, growing, procreating. It was like contemplating Rome flourishing after his reforms. It made Diocletian proud and satisfied. With some arnica brandy to wash his open sores later, he would pass the time before lunch. Filio turned his head to see whether everything was all right and saw a skinny blond girl, maybe it was the eldest daughter of Helena, walking towards the ruler in the shadow.

Diocletian was watching the girl approaching, too. She was still a child, but her fine features were promising. Give her a few years, and she would grow into a beautiful woman. Her tunic was rough, though clean, and she belted it with a rope, behind which a bunch of tiny perfumed carnations were reflecting the rosiness of her cheeks.

"Come here, girl. Fetch your Ceasar a glass of water!"

The girl made a detour and brought him a pitcher of fresh cold water with a stalk of lemon balm in it. Diocletian drank gratefully. Water was sweet and he was feeling well. Funny, how all the wine he had drunk just made him thirstier. The girl stood beside him making faces. Diocletian noticed it.

"What is it? Why are you making such a face, girl?"

"Pardon me, Sir, but you stink."

"What? What did you just say?"

"I said that you stink. You smell like a corpse decomposing in the field, like a fish decaying in the sun. You stink!"

Diocletian roared in surprise:

"Who are you? Tell me you name!"

"I am Severa, Severina if you like, daughter of Helena and Antonius, the pond keeper. And you are Diocletian, our old Emperor, aren't you?"

"Yes, my rude little girl. And you're a spoilt brat, a girl without any manners at all."

"It's not bad manners to tell the truth. It's bad manners to lie. Don't your servants tell you to wash? Don't Emperors wash daily like all good Romans?"

"Aren't you afraid of me? Asking me such personal and impertinent questions?"

She looked at him with wide eyes. Maybe she should be more apprehensive.

"What can you do to me? You can't catch me, if I run, can you?"

"Not me, but my soldiers can. I just click my fingers and you're dust."

"And who would fetch you water and talk to you then? Besides, I can't see any of your soldiers around. They are probably avoiding you. Small wonder the way you stink."

Diocletian shut up. He was boiling inside. But there was something interesting in the way she spoke up, not to mention the bravery with which she presented her thoughts. The little girl was sharp. She had a strange kind of *auctoritas*, as though she had completed the military training on the ancient *Campus Martius*; she had the authority and courage of the bravest. What a shame she wasn't a boy! She could make a great soldier.

"You see, Severina, I am sick. Just for your information, I wash many times a day every day. But this stench is my curse. My legs are inflamed and they leak poisonous pus. This is why I stink."

As if the man in the shade, one of the most notorious persecutors and rulers, who didn't even flinch at severing limbs from the bodies of traitors or enemies, as if Diocletian was a little lost kitten, the girl replied in a sweet, clear voice:

"My poor Emperor! It must be horrible. Are you in pain? Let me see..."

"See what?"

"Your legs, the inflammations..."

"I can't. It is repulsive."

"At least put away the blanket. The heat is bad for every kind of inflammation. You should cool your legs."

"How can I cool them in this hot weather? Where should I stick them?"

She giggled as though it was a joke.

"In the sea, dummy. Ups..."

Diocletian's brows twitched at the language. Still, maybe she was right. Unlike the rest of the world around him, this girl seemed nice and sincere. She didn't mean harm, he could feel it.

"You have a way to speak to your Emperor, Severa. How do you know?"

"How do I know what?"

"That the sea and cold is good for inflammations."

"Oh, I know. My *avia* is training me to become a herbalist. She knows everything about the human body and I have to learn, too. I can read and write, you know."

"This is good. The first thing to know is to read and write, if you want to become something. What about my fish? Who will continue the aquamarine culture when your father gets old and sick like me?"

"I have three young brothers. But my *avia* says I should be able to earn my own living no matter what may come. She was born in Salona. When she was young, she settled on Šolta without anything. She had to start from scratch. She always says she survived only because she could heal people and help women in their births."

"Your *avia* is from Salona? What is her name?"

"She is Mira now, but she used to have a different name back then. Why do you ask?"

"Maybe we know each other. I was born in Salona. I lived there until I was fourteen, then I left with the army."

"Oh, I must ask her if she knows you. She never mentioned anything about it. But she doesn't want to talk about those ancient times. She says her life began on Šolta, where she got married and brought children in the world."

"Is your grandfather still alive?"

"No, he left us a few years ago. He was famous for his fish trade all around the *Spalatum* aquatorium. Quintus Portumnus of Šolta, maybe you've heard of him."

Diocletian shrugged his shoulders. How can he know everybody in his vast state? He lost interest in the girl's chatter as his legs began to ache. He knitted his brows above which tiny pearls of sweat were showing his suffering. The girl stepped forward and pulled the fur blanket away from his legs. He cried out in anger.

"What are you doing, spoilt brat?"

"Let me see."

Instantly, with soft breeze cooling his legs, the pain grew weaker. The girl approached him, undid the bandages and touched gently the purple skin next to the sores. She was concentrating on them and there was no sign of her being sick or disgusted. Diocletian was astonished.

"The smell, doesn't it bother you?"

"My *avia* always says *Nihi humanum mihi alienum est*, so nothing human is foreign to me, either. I don't think of the stench, I think of how to treat you."

"You're speaking wisely, my girl. I will reward you for that."

"First you will listen. Call your slave. We will bring you to the left corner of the bay, into the shallow water where underneath the seafloor, a cold freshwater spring cools the temperature all year around. It's good for the oysters and it will be good for your legs, too."

Diocletian whistled a few times, but Filio was nowhere in sight. Finally, he gestured to a few pond workers, who helped him into his chair and wheeled him to the desired spot under the sharp orders of Severa. Her voice was commanding the moves of the slaves as though she was moving troops in a battle. What a strange little girl! Diocletian could not stop wondering. At last, he was sitting on the white pebbles in the shallow, cold water and could feel relief. The strange blond child was right. He was feeling clean and fresh for the first time in months. She continued delivering commands.

"You, Anina, go and fetch clean, dry clothes for the Emperor. And find his slave to help him change. Quickly, move it!"

She clapped her hands impatiently. She was a born mistress, matrona! Then she turned to the old man, bathing helplessly in the sea with a nonplussed smile on his face.

"Don't worry, dear Diocletianus. I will fetch my avia and she will bring balms and tinctures to calm down your pain. She's knows a treatment for every ache."

Diocletian just gasped in surprise. The girl simply called him by his name as though they would have gone to school together. Before he could utter his protest, she turned around and ran along the beach like a wind. He sighed. Why should he protest if she called him by his name? That wasn't so bad. She made him feel younger. He sat happily, wondering how the world could spin in a young head like hers. She was a little witch! In the old times, when he was of her age, surely, he would have fallen in love with a girl like Severa.

The quality he admired most in all his life was brightness of the spirit. He didn't mind brusqueness and bad manners – he preferred those to stupidity. He had no patience with the slimy courtiers, who called him high epithets but disobeyed his reforms and were lying to his face. His Edict on Coinage suffered under the constant inflation of the prices. The Denarius was worth nothing, almost as little as a pebble on the beach. The Roman prices were going up daily. The greedy merchants and the careless debtors profited from the fact, grinning into the faces of the honestly working men earning their money with manufacture and agriculture. Diocletian wanted to restore the power of the Roman money and economy. His military rule, his administrative divisions and tax efficiency should find their counterpart in his economic measures. In winter 301, he issued Edictum De Pretiis Rerum Venalium, Edict on Maximum Prices. Many of his legal advisors were against the edict, and preached that the economy had a life of its own and that the edict could present new problems, more problems than solutions. Still, he made them work very hard to establish a list of thousands of goods, from jewelry

to meat and vegetables, which were all subject to the new law and
the prices of which were fixed to a maximum forever. Diocletian
cherished the vision that in a fair and completely regulated economy prosperity for the Roman citizens could be re-established.
Yet, those foolish and grabby merchants cheated him every step
of the way and more often than not ignored his provisions. There
was no punishment severe enough to stop the trade as it had gone
for centuries, in chaotic increase and fall of the prices and goods
depending on god knows what circumstances.

The sun was high in the sky. It was noon. Diocletian wanted to control the markets as he had always
controlled his army. Everything was perfectly clear in his mind;
a centurion was a centurion and wheat was wheat. What did it
matter if the grain was the product of Sicily and the opponents
claimed it should have been cheaper there than in the far away
Rome or Aquilea? Grain is grain and nobody should profit from
the people's need to bake bread. Diocletian plunged into the
painful memories of his failed monetary and economic reforms.
No matter how much he had tried to bring prosperity back, he
failed. With government control or without, most of the Roman
population grew poorer every day. It had saddened him when he
heard that so many wealthy businesses had gone bankrupt and
their owners, for the majority his close friends, had fallen on their
swords unable to face the losses. Where had he gone wrong? He
wanted to bring order and discipline, so efficient in all other fields
of state life, into the chaos of business and finance. Yet, there
were things he could not control. Like religious matters, where
new sects with various beliefs with origins in the Roman or any
other deities were breeding daily, business matters escaped his
firm hands and turned his improvements and edicts into worthless
papyrus. Trash, all trash... Why was he even bothering?

The sun was high in the sky. It was noon. Diocletian was
beginning to tremble in the cold water, yet there was no way he
could get out of it without help. Where was everybody? Was
that a ploy against him? Where was that lazy Greek of his?

Finally, the girl, Severina, was coming back, jumping over the
rocks like a little rabbit. Her hair was fluttering in the breeze. In
her right, she was holding a big basket. Behind her, Diocletian
could see Filio, running like crazy, throwing his arms in the air.
It had to be one hell of a surprise when the Greek saw the spot
under the pines empty and the Emperor gone. He overtook the
girl, pushing her clumsily.

"Oh, my dear Lord! Where have you gone? I was looking
everywhere to find you."

"You bastard, you were looking for me? Where were you, lazy
servant? I promise you the whip by the end of today. You'll see
how it feels..."

Severina watched the outburst of anger unimpressed. In her
point of view, they were losing time. She wanted to get her task

done and took over.

"Please, stop! Men, you're quarreling like two old wives at the fish market. Filio, please help Diocletian out of the water, dry his body and legs gently, and put a fresh tunic on him. Then I will treat his wounds with a special balm."

They both stared at Severina as though she was a ghost. Neither of them had ever been told what to do by a woman, even less so by a young girl. Severina remained calm. After a while, when she realized they weren't following her commands, she persisted.

"What are you waiting for, slave? We all want the Emperor to feel better, don't we? Move it, now, do as I say!"

Filio looked at his master, his face an outraged expression of bewilderment. Diocletian evaded his gaze and simply said:

"The girl wants to treat my wounds. Do as she says, maybe it will help."

"It will help. The goose fat and *arnica* balm will close your sores. And you won't stink like a pig anymore."

Filio, lifting the frail body of his master, almost dropped him back in the water, so shocked was he by the impertinence of the girl. Is she tired of her life?

"Careful, you fool! I almost slipped back into the waves! What shall I do with you, Filio?"

"I am sorry, my Lord. But, but this creature speaks to you in a way...I apologize for her and for me. She's young, she doesn't know you, master."

"Change my clothes and shut up! The girl has got more guts than all of your Greek tribes together."

Filio silently obeyed, and in a few minutes, Severina was greasing the sores with cold fat. It was greenish and it smelt fresh.

"What is this?"

"It is goose fat, *arnica*, sage, and royal jelly of the bees which were grazing on lavender. It heals open wounds and helps to restore the skin. I think you should take three baths a day in this cold strait, then dry thoroughly and treat the sores. And no blankets and no bandages. The air will help to dry the wounds and close them. Beside that, my *avia* prescribed a diet for you. She diagnosed you must have a heart failure and water is gathering in your legs because your heart is not pumping the blood well."

"My heart pumps well when I get angry. Why hasn't she come, if she's so clever, this *avia* of yours?"

"She said she didn't have time."

"She didn't have time for her Ceasar? What is she doing? Dying?"

"Mister, I don't think that is funny. My *avia* is a respectable healer and if she said she couldn't come, she couldn't. I'm here in her place and I'm treating you, aren't I?"

"Yeah, you're a great girl, Severina. Not like this scum, this fool of a slave I'm punished with. Come closer, baby, let me hold you. You said I don't stink anymore."

Severina sat against Diocletian's chest, and their eyes closed in mutual understanding. Although they had just met, it seemed they had known each other for ages. Diocletian was happy. His eyes watered with relief.

"My legs are truly better, the pain is almost gone. Thank you, Severina. I will reward you. Do you have a wish?"

"I do. I would like to study like boys do. I would like to be a lawyer or a doctor."

Diocletian smiled at her.

"The daughter of Helena, little Severina, I hope I will live long enough to see you doing just that. You're a clever child, you should study. It would be difficult for a girl, but I can help you. You see, people still fear me. I am still the first man in Rome."

"Thank you. You're not as mean as people say. I quite like you, actually."

"Who says I am mean? This *mentula* of a slave? Your father? Who?"

"It was my *avia* who said I should beware of you. And don't use vulgar language in the presence of a lady, it's rude!"

"I like your honesty, Severina, I like your courage! It's a pity you're not a boy, I could help you so much more!"

"I like being a girl. I don't need to show off and strain my muscles. I can simply use my reason."

Diocletian burst into a jolly laughter. The little witch had conquered his heart. She had an answer to every question. He fell in love, and Filio was in the way. He had to speak to Severina alone. He had to find out more about her.

"Filio, don't you have anything to do? Go to the villa! Bring this diet, this list of the dishes that I am allowed to eat, to our cook and order lunch in two hours. Meanwhile I will speak to this wonderful young thing who made my day today. Go, run!"

"And don't forget plenty of garlic, and instead of wine, hawthorn flower tea. Here, my *avia* prepared a sack for you. The cook should put some honey and lemon juice in it, so that the tea won't taste bitter. Or, he should add some sweet chamomile. Do you get it, Filio?"

Filio was grinding his teeth, but couldn't say anything. The old fart was obviously besotted with the little brat. Diocletian saw his face and teased him.

"Do you get it, Filio man? Or shall I ask the girl another question. Like, where was your mother Helena last night, Severina?"

Filio froze. What was the old prick getting at? What did he want from him? Probably his bowels spilled on the floor and his balls on a platter. Were they in his new diet, too? Oh, nothing could help his sick, rotten soul anymore. His body was decomposing, and in a few hours he would stink like a cadaver again. Filio knew that. Old sins were chipping Diocletian's life away like sea waves were gradually wearing away the rocks and pebbles of the shore. Severina replied in a clear voice:

"She was at home with us. We were reading Aesop's fables aloud. You know, my mother can read and write, too."

"Where was your daddy?"

"Why are you asking all these questions? He went to *Spalatum*, he had to sell some fish as *orada* were spawning for the second time this year and we had plenty. We dried and smoked some, but he had to sell the rest or the basins would be overpopulated and unclean. Oh, there are still plenty for you Diocletian, for fish you will eat every day now. You shan't have any pork or lamb, just poached fish with rosemary!"

"Did you hear, Filio, what my medical fairy just said? Go home and get the cook to start my new diet. And Helena, her mother, was at home last night. Did you hear that, you filthy lying *philetor*! I will see to it that you'll get your share, lying scoundrel!"

Filio didn't wait to hear the rest. The last words bounced off his back as he was ascending the path to the villa. Severina turned to the old man.

"What is a *philetor*?"

"Nothing, nothing, my child. You don't need to know all the vile words."

"Not all, but I would like to know this one. Is it Greek?"

"Yes. It's man's talk. It's rude. Forget it."

"I hate being treated like an imbecile. You should tell me."

Diocletian couldn't hide his surprise at her persistence. Severina had an independence of spirit which he had rarely found in men, lest in women. She reminded him of someone, yet he couldn't recall the person. She had an oval face with a tiny nose and thin pink lips. Her eyes were grey, intelligent, bright with natural inquisitiveness and wonder, but so cool and severe. She had a good name. It suited her perfectly – a severe, serious girl Severina. Her dark blond hair was thick and completed the image of a person who rarely squandered any time for trifles. She was busy, industrious, always learning. He wished he had time to give her opportunity to grow into a true Roman matron and marry her into one of the best regal families. It was a miracle that here, among fish basins and fig trees, a jewel of a woman was maturing, a woman fit to be the Empress of Rome.

"Severina, I like you. You're worthy of knowing. But I warn you, it's impure. *Philetor* is a man who has sexual intercourse with another man. In Greece, it has been very common, but we Romans find the custom disgusting."

"Oh, I know. Like Achilles and Patrocles, they were lovers, weren't they?"

"Probably, we don't know for sure. Homer doesn't really say it, does he? Anyway, it's obscene."

"Is Filio in love with a man?"

"No, I don't think so. He's in love with staying alive."

"Do you intend to kill him?"

"I could, you know. He's my slave."

"Will you kill him?"

"No, I won't. He's the only one that takes care of me. All the rest are gone..."

"Don't feel sorry for yourself, old man! You have plenty of people. You have an Empire full of citizens. What else do you want?"

Diocletian softly caressed her cheek. She was really a treasure and knew exactly what to say.

"Maybe I would like people like your *avia* not to think me evil. Maybe, I would like people to like me. Everything I did, I did for my people, for the Roman citizens. I wanted them to be rich and happy, not hungry and afraid. I even stepped back from power to prevent a civil war. Why is it, Severina, that people think I am evil?"

"Maybe because you have killed so many Christians."

"I had to kill them. They were disturbing the Republic. They were stirring our *pax romana*, the peace of Rome."

"Oh, they were nothing, just slaves and poor people. You could have let them live."

"You don't understand, Severina. Christians are religious fanatics. They are insane. They harm our rule from within. They disturb our peace and prosperity. Every other Emperor would do the same. Besides, I haven't stopped them, have I?"

"No, you haven't. My *avia* says they are just like your fish in the water tanks. You kill one, and thousands of eggs spawn at the bottom of the sea from which little fish grow and spread."

"It's a good comparison. They use fish as their symbol."

"Do they? I didn't know that. Why?"

"It's an acrostic. In Greek, *ICTYS* means fish, but the abbreviation stands for 'Iesos Christos Theou Yios Soter', i.e. Jesus Christ, Son of God, Savior."

"And why would they use the image of a fish?"

"They used to recognize each other in this way. In the early days, we didn't know what it means. Now we do."

"How come you know so much about Christianity? You hate them, don't you?"

"Yeah, I do hate them, more than anything in the world. But you know the saying: *Tuum nosce hostem*, know thy enemy!"

"My *avia* says, your wife was Christian. Is it true?"

"Prisca? She liked Christians, yes. But she is dead now."

"Did you kill her?"

"No, no, I couldn't. I loved her, you know."

His grey eyes filled with grief, and Severa got frightened he would cry. She simply took his hand in hers and squeezed his swollen fingers, laden with golden rings and precious jewels. Diocletian came back to life again, and started plotting and arranging.

"I will ask my niece Maxima, she's a Vestal Virgin, you know, to take you in and make you study medicine or law. You could become a Vestal Virgin in Rome. Would you like that?"

"Vestal Virgin? Me? A daughter of a peasant? I don't think that is possible..."

"Were not Marius, Pompeius and Cicero all of peasant origin, yet became rulers?"

"But they were as rich as Croesus, not like my father. He works with his hands..."

"Manual labour is honest work. Trading and intriguing are shameful. You should be proud of your father Antonius. He's a good man. What price is he selling the fish at?"

"The maximum, of course!"

Diocletian glanced at her from the side. He was sure the girl was lying. Everybody was ignoring his edict to gain more profit, why wouldn't Ante be selling higher, too?

"You said it is good manners to tell the truth. Now, do it! At which price is your daddy selling my fish?"

But Severa could not be brought out of her box. She simply nodded.

"The maximum it is, Sir."

"Maybe, maybe not. But let's talk about you. Would you like to go to Rome if I arranged it for you?"

"And leave my *avia* and my family behind?"

"Yes, yes, leave that old witch of your *avia* behind! You must think of yourself and your life. She's bound to die soon, like me. We don't count any more. Would you?"

Severa sighed. She could hardly believe her ears. For years she had been dreaming of leaving the island and going into the big wide world to study, but Diocletian's offer surpassed all her wildest dreams. Despite the fact that her parents were not too wealthy and she was only a girl, with the Emperor's support she could head for a proper education in Rome. It was a chance of a lifetime. Of course, she would leave her family. She knew what it would mean. She might never see her grand grandmother alive again once she left, but it was something the old woman would understand and approve of. She had to say something. She had to let him know she would go and she would not be afraid.

"I would love to go to Rome, if you helped me. Besides, I am sure my *avia* would approve of it. Look, there's your Filio coming down the hill. It must be lunch time for you."

"Indeed. Why don't you come along and dine with me?"

"Oh, I must tell my family or they will miss me. I'll be with you in a minute."

* * *

Filio was descending the hill at a slow pace. He wasn't sure what awaited him, but he soon could see that Diocletian was in a good mood, and smiling. What a relief! The way he had been grunting all morning, Filio was about to run for his life. It wouldn't be the first time. What his Emperor didn't know or might have forgotten a long time ago, was a rainy spring day which remained engraved in Filio's memory like a face on a coin, as though it would have happened yesterday. They were a group of Greek Christians, mostly runaway slaves, who, in a confusion, fell into Diocletian's patrol near Seres, their hometown. They were running east in order to find a better life and escape the oppression of Diocletian and Galerius, who were murdering Christians like sheep in a slaughterhouse. The Roman patrol immediately knew who and what they were, and in order to please their ruler, they took the ragged group of Christians to Seres, where Diocletian was staying for a week before moving his troops further on to the front. It was nearly some fifteen years ago, Filio was four or five years old. He was the tiny son of a Greek slave, Maria. He never had heard anything about his father, but his mother was a strikingly beautiful woman with wide black eyes, red lips like cherries and curly hair falling down her back like a wild mountain waterfall. Captured, she was trying to hide her face with a veil. Diocletian, inspecting the hopeless people, spotted her, singled her out from the others and with one blow of his sword cut the veil and the tunic from her body, leaving her split naked. She was in mortal fear, ashamed, her black hair hiding little of her olive skin and only barely wrapping her heavy breasts. He, Filio, was standing behind her, crying and screaming in terror. Impatiently, Diocletian gestured to the guard to shut the child up, to have him killed with a sword. His mother pushed him from her and the boy ran through the rows of legs to escape his fate. He never saw or heard of his mother again.

Little that Filio was, he wanted to avenge her, so after a few days of straying around like a dog, he slipped into the kitchen of the big Emperor. He hid in the onion basket, where the old cook found him asleep a few hours later. The cook, a soft man with a huge belly and little hair left on his skull, felt sorry for the little ragged boy. He gave him food and shelter, and took him into the household. Filio was washing the dishes, he was fetching water, feeding the fire and helping around the kitchen. Meanwhile he was growing stronger physically as well as learning more and more. Beside his mother tongue, Greek, he learnt Roman and Hebrew, and little by little mastered the basics of Illyrian. It

was unusual for a slave, yet supported by the cook, he learnt to
read and write, too. His handsome appearance, the inheritance of
his beautiful and unfortunate mother, charmed everybody. Filio
surely knew how to please the members of the imperial household,
be it men or women. Still, deep in his heart, he secretly nourished
the bile of revenge. He was too afraid to follow the religion of his
late mother, and he made offerings to the Roman Gods as though
he had never heard of Lord Jesus Christ. Anyway, he was too
young when he last had heard of Him, who had died on the cross
for all of them, embracing the pain with love for humanity. It
was a blurred memory, so distant, so vague, as though Filio had
never been part of the Christian sect. Yet all his life he worked
towards one single goal: to kill the man who disgraced and killed
his mother. Diocletian's cook, who loved the boy as his own,
looked after him and even sent him to school. Years went by
and no opportunity presented itself to Filio to fulfill his secret
goal. Diocletian's circle of friends, fellow combatants, his most
loyal men and women, was thicker than the walls of Illium. Filio
grew restless in his schemes to act. But how? Should he throw
poisonous herbs into a broth, others, maybe even his friends could
die. He had little or no military skills, so every sentinel would
kill him long before he would reach the old man's throat.

Things changed dramatically when they came to live in *Spalatum*, in the beautiful new palace on the Adriatic coast. There
the Emperor grew old and helpless. The more Diocletian's open
wounds began to stink, the higher up in the hierarchy Filio moved.
He could finally prove a real help to everybody who despaired over
the old man's constant grunting, bad temper and vicious smell.
He was one of the few servants who knew how to make Diocletian
laugh here and there. There was little or practically no gratitude
from Diocletian, but as his personal servant, Filio was earning
good money. He started hesitating over his initial intentions and
plans, forged in the distant childhood. Diocletian was an old
sorry sight of a man, and Filio could not bring himself to finish
him off. The Emperor, his mother's murderer and executioner
of thousands of innocent men and women, became old and frail,
and depended on him like a baby. Still, the odds, the old man's
moods, altering from thunder to sunshine like April weather, were
challenging Filio's existence by the hours. One moment Diocletian praised him and was nice to him, the next he shouted at him
and threatened him. Yet to tell the truth, Filio had never really
been beaten or punished no matter what.

It was high noon and the sun was burning the rocks and the
green bushes mercilessly. The old man was half lying, half sitting
in the shade, gazing into the distance. His eyes were flashing
energy and he was eagerly waving at the girl, jumping over the
rocks joyfully, shaking her head with fluffy blond hair as though
she had heard the joke of the day. What was this new interest in

a peasant girl? The daughter of the pond keeper and the woman, Filio was trying to engage into his ardent embrace as often as possible in order to drink in the sweetness of her mature love night after night. He would understand had Diocletian fallen for Helena's charms. But Severina, her daughter, why was Diocletian besotted with her? She was too young to get laid with and too old to be cute.

"Oh, here you are, my Filio! Have you seen Severina? What a treasure of a young girl! So clever! I feel so much better after the cold bath and the pomade she put on my sores. Can you smell?"

For a moment, Filio was stupefied.

"No, my lord, I can't. What should I smell?"

"Precisely! Nothing, nothing! The girl cleverly cleaned me and put this pomade on my sores, so I don't stink! Isn't this wonderful?"

"Indeed, my lord. You should not lose another moment. You should ask for a bride, maybe for one from Pannonia! Young and sweet like honey!"

"Are you making fun of me? Filio?"

Diocletian's mood was like a razor's edge – sharp and danger-ous on both sides. But Filio was genuinely surprised and happy for his master. He quickly added:

"My lord, why should I do that? You've been giving me food and shelter since I was born. I love you like a father. And you are a father, you know. You're the father of all of us, you're the *pater familias* of Rome. Let's put you in the chair. Our cook prepared everything as it was written on the papyrus – here, I brought you some cold lemon balm infusion; you should drink little by little, he says."

"I will stand up, Filio. I feel so much better now. I think I could do it. Just give me your hand and pull me up."

Filio was threading on thin ice. Should the old man collapse back, it would be his fault. But if he doesn't do as Diocletian demanded, he would face the morning scene again, when he barely kept the whip away from his back. He kneeled next to Diocletian saying:

"Let's get up together, Sir. Put your arm around my neck and I will hold you by the waist. On three, we jump up like one..."

He started to feel for the man's waist under the linen tunic with golden and purple embroidery.

"*Philetor*, would you like to rape me? You, you..."

Like a thunder from a clear sky, Diocletian shouted at his servant, who froze in mortal fear.

"Then, then you would put your finger in my arse and do your, your dirty... You're a rat, a scum, a pervert... Why don't you ever listen to me?"

Filio needed a moment. He stepped aside and threw a fright-ened look around the bay. The Emperor's shouts could attract sentinels and he would be doomed. Those men did not ask any questions or take any prisoners. His feelings died in him and gave way to fear. He would put Diocletian in the chair somehow, and this time, he would push him over a cliff at a solitary spot. He would shut up the old fart forever! Enough was enough! First, he had to think...

"The drink, Sir. Have a glass of lemon balm water, here!"

Filio poured the icy greenish water in the glass and passed it to Diocletian, whose crazy white brows were knit in discord.

"Drink your poison yourself, you sleazy Greek rat!"

Filio drank the glass and poured another. He repeated the gesture, and the old man finally took the glass from him with a shaking hand. He emptied it, spilling half of it on his tunic, and wanted more. Filio sat by him in the grass, searching for a joke or a topic to break the hostile mood and start a new conversation. In a minute, he knew, Diocletian would forget his outburst of anger and hatred.

"Sir, the girl, Severina... She'll grow into a beauty one day. I wish I could be free and rich to ask for her hand. I think she will make a perfect wife. What do you think?"

"Filio, you're born a slave and you will die a slave! Find yourself a kitchen girl. She could be good enough for you. Severina is a citizen and she's imperial material. I will send her to Rome to study medicine or maybe law."

"Oh, great! What a good idea! Then you will have your own physician! And a pretty one, not like that old Jewish fart at *Spalatum*. You'll be treated in style, by one of the most beautiful women in the Empire!"

"Yes, Filio, yes... sometimes you can get it! Halfwit as you are most of the time! Put me in my chair. Severina will join me for lunch later. We don't want to keep the wonderful fish waiting, do we?"

Filio didn't wait for another hint, he simply took the man in his arms and put him in the chair. Diocletian played along and held him around his neck. Filio was grateful that the pungent smell was more or less gone. He pushed the wheelchair uphill for some fifty feet when a clear voice reached him.

"Hi, Diocletian, I am back. My grandmother sends you this. Here!"

Severina gave him a silver ring with a bright ruby. Diocletian took it in his shaky palm, inspecting it, nonplussed. Nothing, no recollection came to his mind. Why was that woman giving him the ring? Shouldn't he be paying the money to the old bat for her medicine? Who was that *avia*, who communicated to him through signs and pomades? He nodded to the girl and thought of the purse filled with *aurei*, the most valuable of Roman coins, he would give her after lunch. And the letter he would send to Rome, to his prefect, regarding Severina. He silently composed the sentences for his envoy, enjoying the breeze at the top of the hill which was cooling his skin.

"I think we will have some northwest wind in the afternoon. It's dry and healthy, it will cool the air."

Filio and Severina looked at each other. Old people usually lived in their own worlds. What has a wind to do with the ring? Severina just shrugged her shoulders and smiled. She was indeed a nice change for the old man, but what if his temper turned against her, too?

"Would you like to know the menu, Sir?"

"Crap, Filio, crap! Do you think I am so old and senile that I can only think of shit and food?"

Severina broke in.

"Diocletian, don't use soldier's bad language with me, please. Don't you have any respect for me?"

For a moment, his blurred grey eyes locked with hers. Filio was shaking with fear. He tripped over a root and almost fell on his nose. Severina retained the presence of mind and held the wheelchair. She smiled sweetly at the old man.

"Didn't we agree, Sir, that honesty was the best policy?"

"Indeed. I like your spirit, but you should accept my bad language, too, Severina. It's part of me. You know, I've always been a soldier. I was hailed 'Imperator' at Nicomedia and given the grass crown by my troops!"

"My master is a brave man!"

"Unlike you, Filio! You're a coward. You shake at every sound! One day, you will be killed by your own fart..."

Filio didn't say anything. He and Severina exchanged looks behind Diocletian's back. They were approaching the frontal portico of the villa, where two tall statues were welcoming the wheelchair party. On the left, there was the god of war Mars in full Roman armor, his helmet bright with read feathers, holding a long spear, *pillum*, in his right hand, touching the *gladius*, the sword, with his left, his stony gaze set on the marble version of the master of the villa – a younger, bearded Diocletian, also in full battle gear. The sculptures were painted with rich colors, and they seemed almost alive with force, yet, they could not threaten the visitors, be it thieves or nobles, planted as they were in the ground forever. Upon passing under the portico, Diocletian lifted his right arm in imperial greeting. Sometimes, he felt closer to the cold marble statues than to the living people around him.

Their arrival stirred a commotion among the servants, and they were led into the shade, where two dining couches were prepared next to the rectangular piscine in the middle of the yard. Tables were set with pyramids of fruits; there were delicate tiny summer pears, sweet golden raisins and late figs, dried and fresh plums and almost black mulberries. On the other table, there were vegetables – some cooked, some stewed, some glazed with honey. The biggest table was reserved for fish and meat; clearly, the cook didn't obey the diet and in fear of displeasing Diocletian prepared a little of everything. Severina took charge and soon eliminated the dishes which were off limits. Diocletian listened to her benevolently and tamely as a lamb. They were chatting pleasantly, and Filio slipped away, only too grateful only to have survived another morning with his Emperor.

After lunch, Severina went to the kitchen to talk to the cook. Diocletian grew tired and heavy with sleep. His eyelids soon closed on the dark green shadows of the pines in the yard and he slipped into a pleasant, fresh dream. Before losing himself in oblivion, he thought of the blond, slender Severina. He couldn't remember, it might have been long, long ago that he knew a girl who was like her. Yet, there had been a lifetime of battles, governing and amorous pursuits between then and now, so his memories remained remote and blurred. It may have been before he joined the military, when he was still at home with his family in Salona. He would remember later, maybe tomorrow, should he live to see another day.

* * *

The sun had almost set and the shadows grew longer and darker, when he opened his eyes again. At first, he thought it was a vision. There was an old woman in front of him. She was tall and had thick grey hair. Her eyes were shining with blue arrows. She looked like a hundred year old version of his new friend Severina. Was the little girl real or just an apparition in his tired mind?

"Hello, Diocletian. Or shall I call you Gaius Aurelius, like I used to in Salona. It's been what... Fifty, sixty years..."

"Clara?"

"My name is Mira now, but yes, you're remembering. Did you get the ring?"

"Is Severina real? Or was it you who confused my mind?"

"She is real, don't worry, she is of flesh and blood. You're not that crazy yet. Severina is my great granddaughter, and she's the reason I am here."

The old woman't voice was harsh and her wrinkled face was clenched in a mask of hate.

"Why are you so angry? I only want to help the girl..."

"Oh, Gaius, your goodness sucks! Decades ago, you were meddling with me, now you're meddling with Severina. Leave us alone, we don't need you."

"What do you mean, meddling? We used to be friends, Clara."

"We were more than friends, you bastard!"

"What harm was there? We were fourteen."

"You gave me a ring and left me with a child. My father almost killed me."

"I had to go, Clara. I was in the army."

"You were shit and you will never change. Violent, proud, evil shit. Leave Severina alone!"

"Woman! Stop calling me names or I will call the sentinel. I may be dying, but I still have the authority of the Emperor of Rome!"

"I will call you what I want! You're no Emperor for me, scum!"

"Stop, Clara! What child? Did you bear my child?"

"As though you never have heard of it! Of course, we had a son! I sent you a letter from Šolta, where I had to escape from my family."

"Clara, I swear I didn't know. I have never received your letter. I think, I was at the Greek front then...I don't quite remember..."

The old woman collapsed on the couch opposite him. Tears streamed down her cheeks. With her palms, she was hiding her face, shaking all over her dried bony body, rocking back and forth in despair. What had she expected from him? For decades, she had seen her teenage love only on the coins and heard his words only when his edicts were proclaimed in the Roman towns. She was keeping her secret and would have kept it forever, if he hadn't raised her little Severina hope, filling her young head with impossible longing. Hope was poison! Mira knew what was left once the hope dissolved. She loved Severina so much. The girl was so much like her, so clever, so curious, and so brave. She could face anything. Mira knew she could. Yet to face the evilness of Diocletian? Those who had tried ended on the cross. It was better Severina didn't get her hopes up too high. After a few minutes, she resumed in a more reasonable tone.

"I sent you a letter a year after you'd left Salona. I asked you how I should name your son and whether you can provide for us. I had to get by on my own, which was hell. You can imagine my father, when he found out...Of course, I didn't tell him it was you, I was too proud. But, you, you, you should have come back and you should have looked after me, after us..."

While she was crying her reprimands at him, Diocletian seemed to be dwelling in a parallel universe. He was just staring at Clara Mira with eyes wide open, his eyebrows twitching uncontrollably, and for a moment, she thought he had lost his mind completely. Then, in a whisper, he was stuttering randomly, a question left his dry thin lips.

"Where is he now? The son, my son...What is his name?"

"He's dead. He died on the seas. His name was Gaius Marcus Pullus. Pullus was the name of the man who took me as his wife and adopted our boy."

Diocletian wasn't appeased.

"And his children? Where are they? They should be my heirs!"

"They live a comfortable life here on Šolta. Helena is the only daughter that Marcus could make to his young, frail wife. You probably have met her. She's married to Antonius, your fish pond keeper and Severina is their eldest child. Helena is a clever and beautiful woman. She's practically the manager of the aquaculture. She keeps the accounts for Ante, closes contracts with neighboring fish markets, runs the household. He does what she says, but all goes in his name. You know the Roman law."

"I must meet her! She should be the Empress of Rome, not a fish pond keeper's wife. I must..."

"Cut the crap, Gaius. She's happy as it is. If you made her Empress, your co-rulers would kill her first thing after you've kicked the bucket."

The old man started trembling. His eyeballs stepped out of their sockets, his face turned pale, and cold sweat ran down his spine. It was the end... Now, when he found out this wonderful news, he had a son, and a granddaughter, and a great grand-daughter, he would have to go.

"You've lived too long, Gaius Aureilus Valerius Diocletianus," he murmured in his chin.

"Indeed, you should have gone long ago."

The woman was sharper than a sword. His heart burnt with pain and his strengths were leaving him. He sank his head, closed his eyes, and lapsed into a stupor. It seemed as though he was gone.

"*Avia*, hello! Where were you? I was looking for you every-where."

"Oh, Severina, darling..."

A young voice, pure like the crystal waters of a spring, brought both of the old people back to life. The Emperor stirred and smiled at the girl.

"Here you are! I was waiting for you to come. I will have the letter for your departure to Rome ready tomorrow. Well, tonight! I will assign to you a couple of bodyguards and a servant. I think you should leave immediately."

"*Avia*, isn't it wonderful? The Emperor is sending me to Rome to study with the Vestal Virgins. I will have my profession, and a good one. You always told me I would get far one day."

"Severina, I am not sure. You're too young to travel so far all alone."

"She will have two of my best men. And there is an Egyptian slave at *Spalatum*; she would tend to Severina. She's a clever woman and can speak several languages. Young people must travel abroad, study and grow personally. What can Severa learn here among peasants and fish?"

"We must speak to her parents, Sir. We must talk to Helena and Ante."

Finally, the old people exchanged a knowledgeable look. Diocletian slowly nodded, saying:

"I hear the girl's father is away, and I am not going to live forever. I suggest her mother, Helena, comes to my villa tonight or first thing in the morning. I will have the letter ready, but she will make the final decision. Did you bring me the pomade, Mira?"

For a moment, Mira hesitated. Then, she searched in the pocket of her tunic and handed a little flask to the Emperor.

"Wait for the payment! Filio!"

The skinny Greek appeared right away. Diocletian knew he had been hiding in the shadow behind one of the pillars, probably eavesdropping. For how long had he been there? He would have to test how much the boy knew, and should it be too much, kill him. Until he arranges everything in Rome, the origins of the girl and her family should be top secret. The old woman was right; if his courtiers found only a tiny hint, they would all be dust in a matter of hours, even before he passed away.

"Bring me the purse from my desk!"

The few minutes of waiting were silent. Severina felt the laden atmosphere between the old people, but she didn't know what was wrong. She was glad that it was the Emperor who told her *avia* about her future in Rome, for her heart was breaking at the thought of the difficult conversation. She was excited. It was almost too much for one day.

"Here, is this the purse you wanted, Sir?"

"Yes, Filio. This is it. Take it, Mira! You and Severina have done really well, my legs are much better."

"Fine, I'm glad," said Mira, "but tonight before going to bed you should go into the water, cool the legs, then rinse them with rainwater, dry them, and apply the balm Severina gave you. Filio, will you do this?"

"Yes, madam, if the Emperor lets me."

"Thank you, and send Helena to me."

With those words, Diocletian motioned to Filio to bring him inside. He was feeling hungry, and from the arches of the kitchen, sweet smells of supper were filling the air. The women turned away and walked through the yard. As they passed below the portico, Mira put her arms around Severina's shoulder as if to protect her baby from the evil statues of the Roman warriors.

* * *

The sun had set behind the hills in the west leaving the skies burning orange and purple. The evening was like the ashes of a house after a fire; the hot day with its sophisticated plans and future changes for Severina seemed distant, chilled by the light breeze bringing a fresh pine smell from the hills. The surface of the sea was a peaceful mirror, like the silence between the old matron and the girl – it was nothing but a fake, false image behind which strong feelings and dangerous currents were boiling. There was tension in the air, challenged only by the noise of stones cracking under their feet on the path home.

Mira stopped, absent-mindedly picking some dark purple juniper berries from the bushes along the path. Her thoughts travelled in time, decades back, when she was a girl, not much older than Severina, and gave in to her passion with the young Gaius Aurelius. They had known and loved each other since they were children. First, they were mates in plays, later in work. There was little attention to the education and schooling of girls, but Clara could read and write. She was interested in botany. Her grandfather taught her a lot about plants, poisonous and healing. By the time she was fourteen, she knew how to control her body with plants, so she was rather sure her tea of dried rue would prevent her from getting pregnant.

They were both so curious, Gaius and Clara, curious and romantic at the age of fourteen. When she later followed the life of her once sweetheart who had become the Emperor of Rome, she had trouble matching the two – the boy who had left Salona so many years ago and the commander of the legions, the statesman, the strict ruler. It was particularly difficult for her to imagine him persecuting the women and children of the Christian sect. People would tremble in fear just hearing his name. He was the symbol of evil, death, and pain, compared only to a dragon in human skin. Clara pondered upon all this wondering whether it was all true or just propaganda to make the crowds obey him more. The Empire had organized a postal service, so even in the months when Antonius wasn't travelling to *Spalatum* with his fish, she heard news about Diocletian's retirement and life in his new marble palace in *Spalatum*. She didn't care any more, that part of life was over for her decades ago.

She put it behind her when she got married to Fidelius Pullus, who was more than true to his name. She always remembered him with gratitude and warmth, for after years of being alone with an illegitimate son, he took her for his wife and made her happy. They had two more daughters, who were both married to honorable merchants in Pannonia. Only once, after Fidelius' death, she made the travel and stayed with the two families for a year.

The salty air barely stirred. It was like the night so many decades ago when she was united with Gaius Aurelius. They were children. What did they know? Every evening, they went fishing for crabs between the rocks, but on that moonless night, instead of bringing home buckets filled with crawling crustaceans, they brought back their secret. It was Gaius who knew how to make love. He came from a rich family, and he had tasted kisses and embraces of the girls before. She was ignorant, but he knew how to seduce her and make her relax and enjoy. Afterwards, they met almost every night during that summer. Clara knew how to protect herself and drank rue tea many times a day. Yet, like the vigorous man, so was his semen – the conqueror. Shortly after he had left Salona to join the six times faithful Legio XI Claudia at Durostorum, Clara found she was pregnant. Her father threw her out of the house, for she refused to tell him the name of the lover who had planted the tree. Her grandfather, though, was much more tolerant, and helped her. He gave her money, and arranged for her to live with the local midwife, suggesting she should use the time to learn the trade herself. She did, but after the child was born, her life in Salona became harder every day. Her silence about the father of her little bastard son made her suspicious. Was it one of the married men from Salona? Or a foreign traveler? Who was it? Women didn't trust her, men made a detour around her. Clara took a new name, Mira, and went to the little village on the island of Šolta, where she could pass for a widow. Once Fidelius took her into his home, she was safe from all insinuations, which might have followed her from her old home. Married, under a new name and fairly independent as her knowledge of herbs and women's matters soon spread around the island, and as energetic as she was, Clara Mira built her home and family like Diocletian built his palace in *Spalatum*. Had he replied to her letter and taken her as his wife, she would have seen to it that they would start a strong dynasty, even stronger than the walls of the sumptuous palace. As life often turned out, she had her family, while he was alone in the cold rooms filled with precious objects: rugs, statues, and mosaics. They each became what they aspired to. Yet, as much as she was trying to bury her memories of him forever, she often speculated what destiny would have awaited their Gaius Marcus Pullus had Diocletian known about him and acknowledged him. Would her son have died so soon? Would he have lived to become the next Ceasar?

Anyway, the business with Severina scared Mira. She was an intelligent little girl, a treasure, the light of her old age, and Mira made a vow to prepare her better for life ahead than she had managed with her own children. Her granddaughter Helena was a tough case. She had been pig-headed and easy with her morals, even dissipated since her teenage years. When she got pregnant and Antonius proposed, Mira was more than happy to have given her away. He made a colorless, yet a good, hardworking husband. Mira knew that while Antonius was at sea, her granddaughter, the beautiful and passionate Helena, would take lovers and enjoy a night or two of wild sex with them. Helena picked only the most handsome ones, no matter if they were masters or slaves. That

Filio, the Diocletian's Greek servant, looked somehow familiar. He had to have been strolling around their house like a tomcat looking to mate with Helena before. Besides, he was as handsome as an *apoxyomenos* – athletic, nice skin and lovely dark eyes and hair. Had Helena been in bed with him? Well, blood wasn't water; one of the descendants had to inherit the wild sexual drive of Diocletianus. Apart from her infidelities, of which Antonius knew nothing at all, Helena was a good mother and certainly knew how to run the business. In a way, Helena was more a son than Gaius Marcus Pullus. With her character, she would make an Empress a thousand times worse than Agrippina!

Mira smiled into her chin. Severina relaxed and took her hand in hers.

"It's good to see you smile, *avia*. You looked so serious. Well, even angry just a minute ago at the villa."

"My darling girl! It's always tough and sometimes dangerous to mingle with power! You know what people say about our Emperor."

"Well, it's gossip, nothing but chit-chat of evil tongues. He's not a beast. He's kind and nice. He was so grateful for our treatment – he paid us twice, plus the troubles he will take to send me to Rome. Isn't that wonderful?"

"Severina, don't expect too much. Sometimes rulers may change their mind sooner than the weather turns. Anyway, we have to talk to your mother first."

"Oh, she will like the idea. Only, she would prefer the law for me. I could help with the business, after I come back, couldn't I?"

"You'd be away for thirty years! God knows if your mother will live that long."

"But my brothers will need me, too."

"In any case, you could help. We all need you, my darling. And we love you."

"I love you too, *avia*. I'm so much looking forward to the big world!"

"The world is big, but your wishes are bigger."

Hand in hand, they entered the house in the moment when Helena had lit the oil lamp, assembling her family for supper. As it was the custom, she let the *dominus*'s chair empty, waiting for Antonius to sell the fish and come back in a few days.

* * *

In the huge dining room at the *villa rustica* on the hill, the walls were clad in colorful mosaics showing various fish and other sea animals. Diocletianus was reclining on his luxurious couch, supported comfortably by silken pillows of vivid colors. He was alone and he was bored. The servants were bringing dishes, one after another, yet he couldn't eat much. He wanted to talk to somebody while he was dining, not just stare at the huge lobster mosaic on the opposite wall. The artist obviously found inspiration in the cooked animal, burning with pain in the boiling waters, for the reds were bright like fire in the light of the torches and the oil lamps.

"Filio! Filio, come here!"

It took a while before the black head showed at the threshold of the room.

"Come, my boy. Join me, I'm bored. Have you eaten?"

"Yes, they gave me something in the kitchen."

"Would you like some lobster? I should not eat it, but the cook is so scared of me that he cooks every desirable dish in the world. Come, have some!"

"With pleasure, Sir. Thank you."

Filio occupied the empty couch as though he would join an imperial dinner party every night. The lobster was delicious, its tender white meat peppered and scented gently with truffle oil. Such a delicacy, and the Emperor can eat only boiled fish and stewed vegetables. He could not devour any delicious sauces either, and above all, he should not touch the spicy fish sauce he loved so much, the *Garum*.

"Are we going to the shore after supper, Sir? The women said you should take another bath before bed."

"Yes, we will go, certainly. The cure is really helping. To think it was prescribed by a child!"

"Yeah, so much for the Roman physicians. . . "

"On the other hand, I can't expect anything better than I had at *Spalatum*. It's a province, it's backwards."

"Maybe your Excellency should travel to Rome before the seas close for winter."

"Maybe I will. What took you so long to join me? Were you headed anywhere tonight?"

"I wouldn't go unless you have given me the permission. I can't let you alone, I am your servant."

"It hasn't stopped you before, has it? So where did you want to go?"

"Your sentinel fetched me from the path to the village."

Filio sensed he was threading on thin ice. What was he going to say?

"Who is she?"

"Maybe it is he."

"Nice try. I know you're not fucking men, Filio. I have some knowledge of my stock, haven't I? So, tell me who."

Filio was sucking the tenderly cooked meat out of the joints of the fat orange red tail. He was gaining time. Maybe Diocletian would forget the question. Dementia had been entering his mind through a wide door ever since they came to the island.

"Come on, speak, slave! Do you think I will forget my question if you keep sucking on that lobster or what?"

Filio made a show of licking his fingers and placing the empty shell on the table.

"I am sorry, Sir. I just don't get such a feast every day! The lobster was delicious. Very spicy, it was good you avoided it. If it is true what the women said, the diet will help you, and once you're back on your legs, you will eat everything again. I like their approach. They look at your illness and the troubles of your body as a whole, not *per partes*. I wish your doctors in *Spalatum* have done that earlier and maybe you wouldn't have suffered so much pain. How are you feeling now? Shall I get you anything?"

"I am fine. I agree with you; the cure has done miracles in just one day."

"Miracles, indeed. . ."

"We will descend to the strait again. We will take a boy with a torch."

"We can do that, but there's moonlight tonight. It's almost as bright as daylight, for the moon is full. Will you have some fruit and cheese? Shall I fetch it?"

"No, no, sit and eat. They will bring it in. Now, where were we?"

"We were discussing your cure, my lord. Severina is clever. Who was the old bat that came to fetch her?"

"Oh, Clara, no, I mean, Mira. . . Don't call her old bat, she's my age!"

"Yes, the best of all ages. The mature age of wisdom and satisfaction, when you can look at your life and be happy with what you've achieved. The fulfillment, the completeness of it. . . Oh, I envy you!"

Tonight wasn't Filio's night. The Emperor's cheeks expanded in a cunning smile. He was pointing a finger at Filio's innocent looking face.

"Ah, you, sleeky cheeky Greeky! You don't want to tell the name of the woman you're going to bed with tonight, do you? You're trying to get me around my question with chit-chat, eh? Oh, no, look at me!"

Filio gazed at his master already stiff with fear. But Diocletian was amused and tapped a finger on his forehead.

"There's still some brain in here. It can be slower these days, but it is forever the brain of the Empire. Don't you fool me – who?"

Filio gulped down the lump in his throat and smiled the sweetest of all smiles.

"Oh, I've almost forgotten the woman. I only care about you, Sir. It is my imperative to serve you in the best way I can. You've been so good to me. Tonight, giving me such a wonderful dinner and allowing me to dine on the couch. I feel almost like a free man. Thank you, thank you so much."

"You will be a free man after I die."

The old man shuddered as though the chill of death breathed into his body.

"What a dangerous thing to say to a slave! Now, you will be trying to kill me, won't you?"

"Me, a free man! But, this is wonderful news! Have no fear, Sir. I could never kill you, Sir, even if I wanted. You're far too clever, and besides, you're a trained soldier and I'm a kitchen boy! Just by trying it, I'd risk my life. My future free life... Why would I want to do that to the man who promises freedom to the wretched me?"

"Precisely! You're not too clever, are you, Filio? Anyway, you're doing it again – beating around the bush! You, sleeky cheeky Greeky... Who?"

"Who what?"

"Don't overdo it! Who's the woman you'll be plowing tonight?"

"Your Excellency might be angry if I tell."

"Your Excellency will crucify you in person if you don't!"

"Helena."

"Helena?"

"Helena."

"She should come to see me regarding Severina."

"Indeed, she sent the news she would come. She wants me to escort her back. Not only escort..."

"So she is really whoring with you? I thought you were making it up..."

"She is... well, she's a woman in her best years... late thirties. Her husband, Ante, he looks all right to me, but she says he's dull... especially in bed. He finishes without her. You know what I mean. But she needs sex... Uf, she needs it badly."

"You're so much younger! How did she get you? Did she pay you?"

"Only once, then she didn't have to. I like her, well, I think I've fallen in love with her..."

In the midst of Filio's stuttering confession, Diocletian exploded into a wild, loud laughter as though the thunder struck into the room. He was wiping his tears, and a satyr-like look suffused his face.

"She paid you... only once, you say... she gave you a *denarius* and you were doing it under her instructions... you're a whore, a male whore, Filio!"

"It was ten, ten *denarii*, Sir."

Diocletianus was rolling with a hyaenae-like laugh. He started coughing, and Filio jumped to his feet to slap him on the back.

"Let me die like this, Jupiter, let me die of laughter. Oh, Filio, you can be so funny sometimes. Tell me one thing: would you do it with me if I preferred boys?"

Filio's face dropped. What a silly old man! And cruel...

"I would have to, my master, or what do you think?"

"You're lucky I don't like arses. But a woman paying a man for sex... I like her, what a matron!"

"Have you never heard of it before, Sir?"

"Of course I have, but those ladies were not fishmonger's wives!"

Filio took his chances.

"Well, Sir, when Helena pays ten *denarii*, I can tell you: she means business!"

Another roar of laughter almost made Diocletianus fall from his couch.

"You don't say, Filio... She means business... Ha, ha..."

"She said one *denarius* for each time... It took me the whole night to earn my wage!"

Now, the slave and his master burst in laughter together. When they calmed down, fruits and cakes were set on the tables. The servants who brought in the food hesitated at the door perplexed. The scene was indeed unusual; the ruler, who had been grunting impatiently for days at his slave as well as everybody around, was in high spirits and was having fun with the one who usually took the blame for everything bad in his life. What a nuthouse! Who was who in this household?

"Filio, you have my permission for tonight. But first my cure..."

They went to repeat the morning bath, and Diocletian returned in the best of spirits. The swelling of his legs was down, and he felt that he would stand up on his feet in the morning. When they returned to the villa, there was still no sign of Helena. They sat in the patio, the world upside down: while Diocletian was sipping mint tea, Filio gulped down wine. Where was she?

"I have been thinking earlier today: where did I get you, Filio? Who brought you into my household?"

"The cook – do you remember the fat Silvanus?"

"How could I forget Silvanus and his lamb stew? The meat was sweet and melting on the tongue. I'm really sorry he's not with us anymore. But where did he find you?"

"In Seres, Sir."

"Were you with the group of Christians which was seized by our patrol just outside the town walls?"

"I have never been a Christian, my lord. I share your views on the sect."

"Yes, I believe you. But, where do you come from?"

"I was but a child. I don't remember."

"Don't you remember your mother, Filio?"

Filio trembled in the breeze. What was Diocletian getting at? Just a minute ago, he promised him freedom and praised his sense of humor, and now Filio could feel the coldness in the air.

"I have a vague memory of her. She was tall, dark, and beautiful. I must have lost her very early, for I don't remember her ever caressing me or playing with me. I cannot recollect the town or the house where we lived. I don't remember any men, either. I guess, Sir, I am but a poor foundling. Silvanus was good enough to take me in and feed me. I think he surprised me asleep in the onion basket."

Diocletianus smiled in the dark. Yet, his smile froze suddenly. Like a thunderbolt, understanding struck him. Filio was the little boy who ran away from his sentinel when they gathered the Christian group in the market square of Seres. He was wailing like a puppy and they meant to kill him, but he got away. Well, his mother could not run, but before she died, Diocletian had some fun with her. She was really a stunning beauty. Filio inherited her looks. Now Diocletian understood everything. The boy had always reminded him of somebody, but he couldn't remember who. It wasn't so obvious when he was a child, but as a man, he was the spitting image of his beautiful mother. Diocletian was certain he was right about it. He had always had a good eye for remembering the features of a face. He would have to kill the servant now; there were two reasons for that. He could have overheard, who Severina was, and he used to be a Christian. Diocletian was convinced that all Christians should be executed: once a zealot, always a zealot... Yet, why hadn't Filio taken the chance to finish him off and avenge his mother when frequent opportunities presented themselves to him? Why? He could have done it many times, he could have pushed the chair from a cliff or drowned him in his bath, and maybe even gotten away with it. Well, it was obvious. Filio is nothing but a coward, and it was Diocletian who must take the final decision.

There was a commotion at the portico, and soon a stout legionary in full armor, drenched in sweat, with a pale, worried face was brought before him. He held a scroll in his hands: it was an urgent message from Rome. For an instant, Diocletian was confused, thinking of the letter in favor of Severina and her studies, which he had not yet written, so how could his niece already be sending an answer?

"Ave, Ceasar," whispered the soldier between short breaths, handing him the scroll.

The servants brought torches, and despite the soft orange light of the fire, when he finished reading, Diocletian's face was as pale as stone. Filio stood up with a questioning look. Diocletian coldly returned his gaze and, without any further comment, ordered:

"Pack my stuff. We return to *Spalatum* early in the morning. You go nowhere. You stay at the villa tonight."

His voice left no room for questions. Diocletian was the Emperor of Rome, and his break on Šolta was over. He had to return, to rule, to control and to murder if necessary. Filio turned away. Without another word, he left the dining room, his task set and clear. There was no time for trifle affairs.

* * *

The morning birds were chirping their merry song, inviting everybody to join in the festival of the sun rising in the east. Helena was smiling excitedly, ascending the steep path to the *villa rustica* at the top of the cliff, where she was to meet the Emperor. There was no hesitation on her part; if Diocletian were to provide for Severina to go to Rome, she would go. Helena was glad that her daughter would have the opportunity to succeed in the world and climb up the social ladder, which was very difficult, nearly impossible in the Roman society. Entering the order of the Vestal Virgins was a rare privilege, reserved for the girls born in the best Roman families, usually *patrician*. It was Pontifex Maximus who personally chose the girls. Still, the recommendation of the Emperor opened every door. Severina was not *patrician*. Ante and Helena were *plebs*, working with their hands, trading with fish and living in comfort. The Imperial Edict on Maximum Prices almost ruined them a few years ago, but inventive as merchants had always been, they soon found a way to avoid obeying the law without breaking it too obviously. Every law had its holes. They owned their business and expanded it all over the coast of Dalmatia. Šolta was a remote part of the Empire, but the building of the palace in *Spalatum* and the presence of the Emperor meant it became almost the centre of the state. Helena had heard of cases when the Vestals also took in plebeian daughters, for fewer and fewer parents conceded to the thirty year long term of service during which the girl became a woman, was studying, working, and teaching, strictly obeying the major Vestal rule of chastity. The vow of chastity could be difficult for someone like herself, but Severina was of a different temperament. While Helena loved the touch of human skin under her fingers, Severina had always preferred the cold feel of the papyrus. At nearly twelve, Helena had not even heard her speaking of a boy. Sometimes she wondered whether that was natural. In a few years, they would have to start looking for a husband for her. It would be tough, as the girl had some funny ideas and an unwomanly passion for freedom. Helena found it difficult to imagine how a man could control Severina. Well, there was always a way; she herself could always evade the authority of her *dominus* Antonius, couldn't she? Education with the Vestal Virgins would mean sure prosperity for Severina, and for her family, once she returned from Rome. Despite being in their forties when they finished their service, the Vestals easily got married and enjoyed the rest of their lives in the luxury of a state pension. On Šolta, Helena knew, men would wait in line to marry Severina after her Vestal term. She only wished she would live to see it.

Helena stopped for a breath, when she observed a large group descending the hill. Why were they up so early? Where were they going? Was the Emperor taking his morning bath in the sea as Mira had prescribed? By the way, what had happened to that Greek last night, who should have come to play with her? Helena came to the meeting place on the beach and felt very stupid; she was the matron, he merely a slave, still he let her wait like a trifling servant girl. Besides, she was paying him. She took a swim in the sea, waiting for him for another hour. Cross and discontented, she finally went home. Well, maybe, it was better so. All extramarital affairs, paid or unpaid, sucked when the secretive meetings became too frequent. Helena knew that as since the first month of her marriage to Antonius, she could not be faithful to him. There was something in her nature, something wild and unpredictable, which made her search on, want more, and try out other male embraces apart from her husband's. Ante was a good man, so calm, so reasonable, but boring, for the sake of all gods and deities, he was so boring that even the fish stopped swimming in the pond when he was around. Why had she chosen him? Was it precisely because she needed a steady rock, a shoulder to lean on? Or was it more the decision of her grandmother, who soon saw through Helena's excitable nature and wanted her to keep her feet on the ground? The group was coming closer and Helena could see that it was the Emperor's entourage indeed, with his personal guard and slaves burdened with trunks lumbering in tow. Were they all escorting the old man to his bath? There had been no rumor about his leaving or travelling somewhere. She stopped to wait for them on a wider section of the stony path. The fresh smell of wild rosemary was overwhelming, almost suffocating. Finally, they came closer.

"Good morning, Sir. I am Helena Antonius. You told my grandmother Mira to come and see you this morning. It's about my daughter, Severina."

Diocletianus had gotten up on the wrong side of the bed in the morning. His legs ached like hell and once again, Filio had to carry him to the latrines. This time, he gave in. The stench of the pus sores came back in the morning. Besides, urgent business was calling him to *Spalatum*. Galerius' letter was more than explicit: they needed him back to unite the struggling parties and prevent another civil war. Diocletian had, due to severe illness, abdicated the throne in the spring of A.D. 305. He knew very well that he was growing old and that he lacked the power to take the charge of the Empire for a second time. But now he needed to return to business and politics. He had to help his successors to bring the quarrelling parties to one table. The Tetrarchy had to persist. He saw the woman approaching and immediately knew who she was. It didn't lift his spirits, though.

"Where were you last night? You were expected and you didn't come. Disobedience... You should be punished."

Helena froze and looked up into the eyes of the Greek behind the Emperor. Their gazes locked, but they didn't connect. Filio's expression was impassionate. She couldn't fathom the reason for the Emperor's anger. The coarse, commanding voice told her she had made a fatal mistake.

"I am sorry, Sir. My husband is away and I had to look after the children and home."

"Another one who thinks anything goes before her Ceasar!"

"Please, forgive me, Sir. I am at your disposal now. Mira told me you would have a letter for me."

"I don't have it! Unlike you, who were wiping some shitty children's arses, I was busy with the matters of the state. Rome is in danger. I must prevent a war, woman!"

Helena blinked with disappointment. Why hadn't she come last night?

"I am sorry for that. It is about Severina, Sir. Do you want my husband to come for the letter of recommendation to your palace at *Spalatum*? You know that his ships make the passage nearly every day."

Diocletian's features softened. He should have seen the little Severina before having left Šolta. Or simply, he could have taken her with him.

"Where is your daughter? Why hasn't she come to see me off?"

"She was still asleep when I left the house, but I will fetch her, Sir. Let me fetch her, please. Just, can you slow down a bit? Maybe, I can get you some snack before you go on board?"

"Fetch her! Run!"

Filio didn't move from his spot. Every kind of delay was welcome. Helena nodded briefly, then lifted her tunic nearly to the waist, showing her long, muscular legs and ran downhill like mad. Those were the last minutes before Diocletian, so generous with his support to Severina, would go aboard. Would he ever remember his promises once he had come to his palace?

"I was just thinking, my Emperor. Why don't we take along some oysters and some fish? They will be fresher and tastier than anything you can get in *Spalatum*."

"Filio, maybe you should be the cook. Arrange that! Then go ahead, all of you. I want to be alone. You can come in a quarter of an hour to bring me to the ship. Understood?"

"Yes, my lord. Everything will be to your pleasing."

While the guards sat down on the rocks some fifty feet away from his wheelchair, and Filio went to get a drink for his master, the party of cooks, servants and workers continued the descent. The men were winking to each other at the sight of Helena's legs and buttocks, which here and then escaped the tunic. The Emperor looked at them from the top. He seemed almost like one of his portico statues. His hair was shining white against the blue of the sky, and his trimmed beard surrounded the tanned face of the man who would never stop fighting. Young or old, Diocletian would always take up his sword to fall upon his enemy.

Alas, his greatest enemy was inside his own body; pain, old age, dementia. But the worst of all ills was the doubt, the bewilderment, and the confusion of thoughts. Diocletian's physical strength was gone; he felt ashamed, the latrine business was too much for him. His mental powers weren't like they used to be. In fear, he had become suspicious of everything and everybody around him; food, servants, medicines. He couldn't trust his memory any more. His head was like an empty pot. So many times lately, he had forgotten simple matters of life, and felt powerless like a babe when Filio cautiously reminded him of them. He would forget little things like which day it was, which robe to put on, or which letters to reply to, or simply which book he was reading. Many times, he didn't even take notice of the moment when he would pass water, and Filio silently changed him like a shitty baby. Oh, he had noticed how the servant winced at the smell, and how he talked about him to other servants behind his back. Whispered words, uttered secretly, which condemned him to the life of a corpse. For some time, he had been neglecting even the smell of his sores, and would have continued to do so had not the girl blurted out the truth, the first to have been sincere with him in ages. But that porridge of his old brain – would it retain the image of Severina for a week? Who knew? Diocletian had asked Filio some time ago to carry a wax tablet with him at all times, so that when he thought of something important, he could put it down. Filio did his duty. He wasn't such a bad creature after all. Maybe in spite of everything, he could let him live. He couldn't kill everybody who crossed his path, could he? Warm tears welled up in his eyes and blurred his vision. They watered the deep wrinkles of his cheeks. Was he going to cry like a woman? The desperation of the old age... He should have fallen on his sword many years ago.

His thoughts were empty as though he was dwelling in some kind of a void, not in the décor of that grand landscape with lush green pines, clean white rocks and blue sea reflecting the sky. How could they be calling him to settle disputes among his successors, how could Galerius be counting on him, a wretched old man pitying each breath he took? He swallowed the tears and he straightened up in his chair. He had to go back to business. He had to do his duty. Or else, he would lose his *dignitas*, the only category which should outlive every Roman Emperor.

"By Jupiter, you have lived too long, Gaius Aureilus Valerius Diocletianus," he murmured into his chin with moist grey eyes. "There is nothing in this world for you, old man, go, go... put a coin under your tongue for Charon and close your eyes forever. Then let the fire take your painful limbs and purify your spirit, leaving behind only the ashes of your wrongs and lifting like a Phoenix into the sky your aspirations for the Empire to have a better life!" After his death, Diocletian wanted his body to be consumed by fire, cremated like the heroes who had been put on funeral pyres in the old times, when deeds were noble and women beautiful. He would give Filio his freedom. The memory of Diocletian should herald clemency and goodness into the times to come.

"Good morning, Diocletian," said Severina simply, and cut off his gloomy reverie.

"Hello, my little healer. Where have you been?"

"I slept longer today, sorry. How are you feeling?"

"Oh, pain, the legs again..."

"I suggest you take the bath before going on board. It will be hot today, and there's a light *bura* in the bay, so the journey will take a bit longer. But isn't the *bura* wonderful? *Bura* chased away the clouds and rains again."

"Yeah, wonderful... I am in a hurry, Severina. State matters, you know. But, yes, you're right. I must freshen up. Filio!"

Helena stood beside her daughter. They couldn't be more different from each other.

"Excuse me, Sir, the letter? Shall I send my husband?"

"Oh, I will send it in the following days. No, let Antonius tend to the fish! Filio, make a note!"

Everything seemed perfect. The sun was shining and the wind was steady, cooling the hot summer day. After the cold bath and treatment with the *arnica* balm, his legs didn't ache so much, and Diocletian set sail full of new vigor, as though he was heading for a new life.

* * *

Like every single gloomy morning in that long, grey autumn, Severina was waiting for a ship to drop anchor. She had almost banned the hopes of receiving the recommendation letter and travelling to Rome. She was simply using her time to study herbs, help her mother, and sometimes look after her younger brothers. She felt something would turn up sooner or later. Reasonably, since it was out of her hands, she didn't bother with it too much. Only sometimes, when she was all alone, she would shed a tear of frustration. How can fate play such silly games with her? She would do anything to study in Rome, anything... Yet, there was no word from either *Salona* or *Spalatum*. Without Diocletian, she would have to settle for less. She would be of marriageable age soon and her mother – for it was obvious not her father – would pick a groom for her. Severina was a free spirit and detested the thought of cooking, cleaning, and waiting on a man and on a family. Maybe, they would let her remain unwed. Since she had been healing the Emperor and his legs, everybody from near and far came to seek her help. Severina, at the age of twelve, was earning good money. Probably more money than any of the boys would make with the fish.

"Severina, Severina, I've got a present for you!" Marcus, the captain's son was shouting across the silent bay so loudly that the fish started to swirl and jump out of the water.

"Is it a letter?"

Severina shouted back with her palms around her mouth to carry her voice over the waves.

"No, it's a present, a real present from the Emperor! You will see!"

At last! Severina was excited like a bird in the tree full of ripe cherries. She couldn't stand still, and went to fetch her mother. Finally, the boat docked by the pier and the boy jumped off of it, holding a nice wooden box with golden carvings and Diocletian's insignia. The box was locked. There was also a sealed scroll, addressed to Severina. She took the box and the scroll. No way she would be breaking the seal and opening the box in front of so many curious eyes. In the home kitchen, she finally read the letter, full of kindness and warmth.

My dear friend Severina!

Thank you for your wonderful cure, which has done wonders: I can walk again, and all thanks go to you and your clever great grandmother. In the box you will find a small token of my gratitude, which is entirely at your disposal – it is a gift to you personally, and only if you deem it necessary you can share it with your family.
Do not think I have forgotten my promise to help you study in Rome. I have written to my niece twice, but unfortunately, I have not had her reply yet. She will write soon enough, don't worry. Should the seas close for winter before that, enjoy your life at home as much as you can. The regime of the Vestals is notorious for being very tough. The present Virgo Vestalis Maxima is a stern woman, who is probably one of the best legal specialists in the country. Do not worry. You are a serious girl. You will make it. I believe in you. Think thoroughly which way you will take – law or medicine. Either will be useful to our Dalmatia and to your Šolta. Well, I am certain I will have heard from my niece by the end of the year, and I will let you know accordingly.

Greetings to you and your family,

Yours, Diocletian,

Imperator Ceasar C. Aurelius Valerius Diocletianus Pius Felix Invictus Augustus, pontifex maximus, Germanicus maximus VI, Sarmaticus maximus III, Persicus maximus II, Brittanicus maximus, tribuncia potestate XVIII, consul VII, Imperator XVIIII, pater patriae proconsul

"Mama, mama, he wrote me a letter! I got a letter from our Emperor! Isn't that wonderful?"

Helena was at the box. She opened the heavy purse and her eyes lit up with greed. There were golden *aurei*, so many of them. It would buy their house and business many times over.

"Diocletian writes that I can dispose with the money."

"Very well, my girl, I shall just keep it safe for you. We will follow his will."

Severina nodded absentmindedly. She knew her dad would need a new, bigger ship. Still, she could use the money to avoid marriage, for which Severina was certain it would never agree with her.

"I need some time to think, mom. If I go to Rome, I will leave the sum at your disposal."

"It's all right, my dear. The money you earned with your treatments in the summer is enough for a new ship. Daddy has already ordered it. This should be for your needs only."

Severina embraced her mother tenderly. She loved her family. It would be tough to leave them and return an old woman. Still, there was a thirst for adventure and knowledge in her veins, and she could not neglect it. She wanted to see Rome and move around the powerful of the Empire. Oh, how she longed to be at Diocletian's side. She would be his doctor, his companion, his protégée. It would change the air she was breathing. Only one day, and she felt an affection for the man, who was commonly known as a monster. Severina knew that he was soft and human inside, and that it would be her task to reveal that humaneness of the Emperor. If only she could go to Rome before winter!

* * *

The festivities in honor of Pomona, the goddess of fertility, had gone by. The sacred letter to summon Severina to Rome still hadn't arrived. Mira was preparing her great granddaughter for other options in her life. Severina, having been the best in her elementary school *ludus litterarius*, would go to Salona and join the family of Turranii, who in a letter accepted that their boys would be learning with the *grammaticus* alongside with a girl. They accepted, of course, against a very fat payment. Mira had found out that the family had lost a lot of money and needed funds. Their loss had gone a decade back, but they couldn't recover from it. They had disobeyed the Edict on Maximum Prices, were heavily fined and nearly went bankrupt. Maybe, without Severina's tuition they would not be able to pay the *grammaticus* at all, which would leave their four boys without the basic education. Severina still had the big purse full of *aurei* intact. Thus, the question of Severina's education would be solved in an elegant way – she could more than afford the five hundred *denarii* per month. The girl was twelve, and in the next three years, she would master the Greek language, poetry, and oration to a certain point. It was more than what even very rich girls could expect, for women in Ancient Rome were only supposed to know how to manage a household and bring up their children.

Mira started her enquiries immediately after Diocletian had left in the summer. She never believed the old bastard would do anything right. Although Salona was a good alternative and kept the girl closer to her family, Mira could not ignore the sadness and the disappointment in the girl's eyes, always scanning the horizon for the ship which should bring her the sign that she had been longing for. What an old pig could kill the hope in the eyes of a young ambitious student! Mira was furious with the Emperor and wished him nothing but a slow and painful death.

When Diocletian's Greek slave jumped from Antonius' ship on the fifth day of December, she thought that the skies would clear and the questions would be answered at last. Filio looked even thinner than before, and headed immediately to Antonius house.

"Good day, mother Mira. Can I speak to Severina, please?"

"Severina has gone to the hills to pick some herbs. Tell me, have you news of Diocletian?"

"Yes, mother. . . "

"Stop calling me mother. I could not have born such a Greek creature, had I mated with an eel. Speak up!"

"Well, the news is young. Alas, my lady, our Emperor Gaius Aurelius Valerius Augustus Diocletianus died two days ago."

"Well, the old fart was bound to kick the bucket at last, wasn't he? Do you have the letter?"

Filio was shocked. Even in his most secret thoughts, he could not express his joy over the newly won freedom and the death of his master. For once, Diocletian had kept his word, and freed him on his deathbed. The woman was dangerous, speaking openly like that.

"What letter?"

"For Severina to go to Rome, to join the Vestals. Are you retarded?"

"Madam, I have the full mental capacities. There will be no letter, for it was the Emperor's niece who I personally suspect of treason."

"Why didn't you tell his household guards?"

"They were Maxima's accomplices. It would cost me my life."

"So, how did they kill him? Did they strangle him?"

"I think he was poisoned by the letter. The papyrus must have been impregnated with poison, but we will never know for sure. Maxima asked Diocletian to burn the letter after reading it."

"Maxima was his niece? The Virgo Vestalis? I come from Salona, and he had no niece with such a name. He had probably been screwing her, the old rascal!"

"I don't think so. But I am quite certain she had a hand in his death."

"It's your imagination. Why would she murder her most powerful protector?"

Filio looked at the old wrinkled face that despite everything still showed the pangs of a love which ended the fifty year old betrayal. Oh, yes, Diocletian was the master of hurting! He could mutilate bodies and break hearts easily. Nothing was sacred to the old man. When he had realized that he was about to die, he called Filio to his bed. Whispering, he asked him, if he knew who Mira, Helena, and Severina were, and Filio replied honestly that he had overheard their conversation at the villa. "Was it you, Filio?", the old man breathed into his ear. Filio didn't have to reply, for Diocletian realized what had happened. In his letter to Maxima, he made a hint about his long missed son and family. He also said he would change his will first thing when he would come to Rome in the spring. He was prudent enough not to mention any names, not that he would not trust his niece, but in case the letter should fall into the wrong hands. Well, Maxima's hands were the wrong hands. She sold the information to his rival Donstantius Chlorus, and even Galerius, his lifelong ally, could not prevent the poisoning. Still, the *medicus* proclaimed that the Emperor had taken his own life in full presence of mind and had drunk poison in his presence. Filio knew it was a lie, and ran for his life.

"She would, for she knew that Diocletian had discovered his long lost family recently."

"What do you know, slave?"

"Enough. And I am not a slave, I am a free man."

"Tell me what you know!"

"I know you had a son with our Emperor, and that the charming Helena is his granddaughter. Diocletian told me that in person."

Mira raised her thinning white eyebrows. Her voice lost the sharpness. Maybe the Greek wasn't such a traitor as the rest of them.

"Did he trust you so much?"

Filio's lips curved into a shy smile. He had to play his cards wisely.

"He did, yes. He lost his wife and his daughter years ago. He had nobody but me. When he was very sick there was nobody but me looking after him. He was grunting at me, he was scolding me, and he was bullying me. There wasn't a day that I wasn't afraid for my life. You know how he was. He had sunshine and thunder in the same sack. Still, he knew I loved him like a father."

"Did you really?"

Filio looked at her inquisitive face. He had to adapt the story well.

"I did. Diocletian asked me to come to warn you."

"Warn us against whom? You just said there was nobody but you who knew about our relations."

Filio was losing the thread. How would he bend the old bat to his will? He decided to strike *in medias res*.

"Am I nobody?"

"Are you threatening us?"

If looks were arrows, they would both be dead. They gazed at each other with hatred. Although the woman was old and frail, Filio was afraid of her. She was so stern. He dropped his eyes, pleading with her.

"I am not. But I don't know where to go. My life is in danger. Can I stay with you here on Šolta?"

"You're a weasel, Filio! Is that your name?"

"Yes, I am Filio Gaius, madam."

"There are conditions, though."

"I will do anything you ask. Just let me stay here, please."

Mira felt pity. What kind of life could the boy have had with a man like Diocletianus? Maybe, he could prove useful.

"Do you speak Greek?"

"Of course, madam. It's my mother tongue."

"Call me Mira. I am no madam. I work hard for my living. Do you read and write Greek and Roman?"

"Perfectly. I can also read and write Hebrew, Mira."

"You will work in the fish basins in the morning and teach Helena's kids to read and write Greek during the day. Can you do that?"

Now Filio was smiling, his white pearls of teeth shining in the sun.

"Yes, Mira. I will be the best tutor you can imagine. I promise."

"And keep your hands off Helena, or I'll cut your balls off!"

Filio froze. How could the old bat know about him and Helena? Well, in any case, Helena was too old for him. He didn't have to sell his sexual services any more. He was a free man. He had some money. He would buy a house and find himself a nice, juicy young girl. He can make the promise easily.

"I promise. You have my balls on a plate, Mira."

Thus, Filio Gaius, the former Greek slave of the Emperor Diocletianus and an eternal survivor, became part of Mira's Illyrian people. In the following years, he proved very useful to the community. Life on the island, far away from the intrigues of the court, was kind to him, too. The tiny, ragged Christian orphan became one of the pillars of the village scattered around the bay of Nečujam on Šolta. After a few years, he became a *Grammaticus*, and earned good wages, for the Edict on Maximum Prices, forbidding teachers to charge more than two hundred *denarii* per month per pupil, sank into oblivion. Helena got older and her juices calmed down, so at last, she could start to love and appreciate her husband Antonius. Severina went to Salona and was the best student in the Turranii learning group. The eldest son of the famous *patrician* family fell in love with her, and after having finished her education, she remained in Salona as Marcus Gaius Turranius's wife. She stepped up the social ladder and became a *patrician*. With the noble nature she had always had, she soon adapted to her new duties and became one of the most esteemed and enlightened matrons of the city. The old *avia* Mira lived to be a hundred years old, and even sailed to Salona to visit her first great great grandson, Gaius Marcus Pullus Turranius. She had always been very close to Severina. They wrote to each other almost every week. Mira was happy to see her girl settled and successful. She came back to Šolta, and died with a smile on her face, surrounded by her family and friends.

Nobody ever found out about Clara's secret, and in centuries weeds and bushes overgrew her grave in one of the most beautiful bays on Šolta, the bay of Nečujam, where under the surface of the blue sea, the walls of Diocletian's fish ponds have scared the sailors anchoring by the shore until the present times. Once again, the odds turned. While his flesh and blood had long died out, his walls and palaces won the race against time. So, maybe you did not live too long, Gaius Aureilus Valerius Diocletianus, maybe you lived just long enough to be remembered forever.

Ragusa – Dubrovnik, A.D. 1312

The thick walls of our house remain cool even in the hottest of
Dalmatian sun. I have heard on the news that today is to be
the warmest day of this summer. I am soaked with sweat and
exhausted, so after calling a hello to Paula over the bangs, cries
and loud music of a movie in the living room, I head for the
shower. I must cool down, my heart is pumping like crazy. What
happened to Dario's sister? How did she die? Did she commit a
suicide? Obviously, the police have started an investigation.

On my way home, I saw Dario Kadura all lost on his doorstep,
looking at two police cars moving quickly uphill. Dario, a retired
sea captain and fisherman, has been a friend since the first day I
came to this village nearly two decades ago. Some ten years ago,
his wife died in a car crash. For some time now he has tried to
show me more attention than is usual with friends. I have been
turning a blind eye to his courting. Today, though, I felt so sorry
for him. His proud figure of a man whose strong hands can easily
pull a net full of fish or hold a big tuna on a rod for hours was
limp, his shoulders stooped in humiliation. What did those men
want from him? When I came closer and asked him what was
wrong, he was hardly able to answer, his voice trembling and his
face shaking with sobs. I came closer and caressed his white hair,
and he fell into my arms. I comforted him as best I could, and
promised to help if he needed anything.

With trembling fingers, I open the shower and set the water temperature to tepid. I try to suppress the memories of rapes
and killings. The images my old sclerotic brain should have erased
long ago. Yet, like the flow of water, they keep surging up and filling my head with sorrow. Enough: I have to control my thoughts.
I have to make lunch for my baby. I put on a light summer dress
and go downstairs to meet her. Her face is alive. She looks happy.
She kisses me on my damp cheeks.

"*Nona*, I've laughed my head off watching The Pirates of the
Caribbean. Johnny Depp is so funny."

I put on a grin. There is no need to spoil her good humor.

"And sexy, isn't he?"

"Yes, he is. Sometimes, I wish I lived in the past times. People
were brave and took their lives in their own hands. There was
action and passion in the air. Not like today, when we can only
watch it on TV. What kind of life is it anyway? So boring..."

I will not argue, although I could. I have seen my share of
blood and action, not to speak of passion. I have had enough,
and boring is good for me. So I say:

"Do you know, Paula, that the pirates of the Adriatic were
terrorizing Venetian and *Ragusan* merchant ships for centuries?"

"Who were *Ragusans*? Italians?"

"*Ragusa* is the old name for Dubrovnik. Yeah, there is a town on the island of Sicily called Ragusa. I believe both names are of Greek origins. But the Republic of Ragusa was as famous and as rich as Venice in the Middle Ages. And the pirates lived half-way of each."

"Really? Where?"

"Oh, they were very active around Omiš and Makarska. They had a county of their own, and the ships feared them like the plague. Their famous leader was Knez Kačić of Omiš."

My heart misses a beat. Paula's huge dark eyes stare curiously at me. I love it when she looks at me like that. I shall never stop to amaze my baby. Oh, I love her so much. My poor girl is finally regaining her strengths. I cannot but take her in my arms. I press her to my bosom holding back tears of joy.

"*Nona*, you're choking me, stop!"

I let her go and turn to boil the water for spaghetti. Out of my bag, I take a lettuce, a few carrots, one large tomato, some garlic, an onion, parsley and a sack of mussels.

"Spaghetti with mussels today, Paula... What do you say?"

"I say I am hungry. I could do with some fries."

"Fries are no good. This will be better for you. Can you wash the lettuce, please?"

She makes a step to the sink and starts to clean the vegetables with a tiny knife. I take a bottle of white wine out of the fridge and pour a glass. Paula looks at it with a craving in her eyes.

"Do you want some?" I hasten to ask.

She shakes her head. Then she looks up at me.

"Can I have a beer, *nona*?"

I am not sure. With concern, I try to recall the instructions of her doctor. There were none regarding alcohol. Anyway, who would think about that after the devastating effects of each therapy? But it has been almost five weeks now. She can have a small one. I take a can of the Ožujsko light and hand it to my charming kitchen help.

"Here, the chefs must be hydrated."

"Yeah, with beer and wine... Cheers, *nona!*"

Our glasses clink. I get back to cooking. Soon, our simple meal is ready. We feast upon the spaghetti.

"*Nona*, do you have a book on the Dalmatian pirates?"

"Better, my love. I have done some research. I can print it out for you."

"I can read it on your lap top. No need to waste the paper."

I know where this is heading. Young people can be so nosy. I do not want Paula to read my files or meddle with my emails.

"It will take you some time to read about Dubrovnik and their negotiations with the plunderers. I need my computer for work, so print it will be."

Paula turns as pale as chalk. She cannot be so irritated about it. Suddenly, she jumps up and heads for the toilet. I can see she

is not going to make it, so I offer her the salad bowl. She empties
her stomach into it. Mussels and beer – I should have known
better! My stomach cramps with hers, and I have to gather all
my strength to keep my lunch down. When she locks herself
in the bathroom, I go to my office and print out the story of
the *Ragusan* heiress Miljutina and her two suitors in the Middle
Ages.

* * *

Miljutina screamed with fear seeing the thin stream of blood
dripping down her hose to the ankle, soaking her long white linen
chemise. She hid behind a wall under construction when she saw
the mess on her dress. She had to do something and quickly, as
she could not go about the city like that, not on a feast day.

On the third day of February every year big crowds gathered in the city of *Ragusa*, today Dubrovnik, for the festivities in
honor of Saint Blaise, who was not only the patron saint of wool
trade and throat aches, but also the sacred protector of the city
huddled between the rocks of Prevlaka and the river Dubrovačka.
Peasants were streaming from Pelješac, fishermen were coming
from the islands as far as Lastovo and Korčula, and shepherds
left their herds in the hinterland in order to witness the holy
procession and enjoy the many free banquets given in the honor
of the beloved saint. The *Ragusans* had many reasons to worship Saint Blaise and did that with obsessive passion, unusual for
rational statesmen, businesspeople and merchants, whose brains
were always calculating profits and percentages. Yet, Saint Blaise
miraculously touched their hearts and opened the doors of love
and devotion.

In his life, Blaise was a physician and the Bishop of Sebaste in
Armenia. *Agricola* came as a governor to Cappadocia and Lesser
Armenia with the clear orders of the *Imperium* to extinguish the
Christian faith in that province. He immediately arrested Blaise,
who, despite the brutality of the Roman persecution, refused to
renounce Jesus. Blaise's cures were famous all over the country
and people loved him for his charitable deeds. On his way to
prison, he miraculously saved the life of a child who was choking
on a fish bone in his throat. After the cruel torture procedures
of the Romans, in which his flesh was torn from his body with
wool combs, Blaise was beheaded in 316 A.D. His good nature
and pious devotion made the *Ragusans* worship their holy patron,
whom they called Vlaho or Blaž. It was namely his apparition to
Stojko in 971 which saved the city from the Venetian fleet. The
Venetians wanted to invade *Ragusa*. In all secrecy and in the
cover of the night, they dropped anchor as near as at Gruž to get
the last supplies aboard before the attack on the city. With the
help of Saint Blaise, Stojko, the canon of St. Stephen's Cathedral, warned the city council in time, the *Ragusans* formed their

defense lines and the surprise moment was lost for the aggressors, who sailed away without a fight. The city was spared, and Saint Blaise had been the symbol of protection, peace and prosperity for Dubrovnik ever since. In winters children would pray to him when a cold would be making their throats sore, not to mention the merchants, who prayed to him for the safety of their cargo in foreign ports. The gratitude of *Ragusans* to St. Blaise was displayed in many ways – his image, holding their destiny in his precious hands, decorated the city walls and was engraved on their coins.

February the 3rd in the year of the Lord 1312 was a warm sunny Thursday, a wonderful day off work and off school. The procession on *Stradun*, the biggest street of Dubrovnik, was to be held at noon, in two hours, and Miljuta was in big trouble with her fancy dress. Over her chemise now soiled with blood, the girl was wearing a deep green kirtle without a waste seam; at her thirteen years of age her figure was still forming the lines of a woman. The kirtle was woven from the softest of Spanish wool, which *Ragusan* merchants were shipping and selling all over the world. The textile trade and industry had been rapidly taking off in the last decades, so that *patrician* daughters were clothed in fine imported textiles from England, Flanders and Italy. No *raša* garments from the rough Bosnian wool for the soft skins, only the finest of the finest fabrics in rich, deep colors – red, blue, green and purple, but never orange or yellow. Those colors were suspicious since Venetians had passed a law requiring the prostitutes to wear yellow; vice was to be separated from virtue at a glance. *Raša* was a rough and scratchy textile; the garments were usually dyed in natural colors or shades of brown and worn by servants, peasants or lower artisans. While the rich garments were clean and fresh, scented with lavender, *raša* was normally heavy with dirt and the sweat of working hands.

Miljuta's blood was soaking the fine green kirtle, and for a moment she forgot to hide behind the low wall of the growing city walls in the northern part of town, at the Minčeta plain. She looked aghast at her ruined dress, not knowing where the blood was coming from. She felt no pain, she hadn't wounded herself. What had soiled her attire was a mystery to her. Miljutina was born Menze, or Menčetić, and their proud *patrician* house was in the centre of the city just above the port, so that her grandmother, the notable Marina Menčetić, could monitor the traffic of ships entering and leaving the port of *Ragusa* day and night. The old Marina was one of the highest ranking citizens in the *Ragusan* state notwithstanding the fact, that she was only a woman, a serious flaw in the world of business and trade in Dubrovnik. She was the fear of all the young and old in the city, an iron lady with a cunning mind and important trade relations all over Europe. She was also Miljutina's only family, as her parents had been permanently away from Dubrovnik for years in a row, hence the girl barely remembered her *mama* and *tata*. But *baba* Marina was always there to look after her and offer her a safe life and education. There was only one condition which went without saying – *baba* had to be obeyed. No monkey business – everything had to be perfect: the clothes, the grades in school, the chores at home and above all Miljutina's behavior. She had to be a lady at every step, for one of those days, as *baba* explained to Miljutina, she would become a *patrician* matron, a wife to a rich *Ragusan* citizen.

"Got you, got you! It's your turn to count, Miljuta, your turn!"

Mihajlo or Miho, the son of Džore Kaboga, in Slavic, Kabužić was two years older than Miljutina, that is fifteen, and already employed. He could play with his younger friends only on holidays. Since two years earlier, he had been helping his uncle, the engineer and shipbuilder Galvo Kabužić, in his shipyard, learning the secrets of the world famous *Ragusan* shipbuilding. They had orders from the Spanish Armada, the Portuguese kingdom, the Saracens, and famous senators and merchants from Pisa and Venice. Their ships were famous – the *karakas*. Those huge floating bastions, which could take aboard up to two hundred passengers and crew with hundreds of tons of cargo, dominated the Mediterranean and the Black sea, not to speak of the Adriatic. Today Miho was playing hide and seek with the lovely Miljuta Menčetić, as their friends dissipated to get some sweet snacks before the procession. Miho was more than happy that Miljuta stayed with him for a while longer. For some months now he had been feeling a curious longing for the girl, and he had felt more than friendship or playmate companionship towards her.

Miljuta started to run away and down the narrow alley towards the sea. She felt she should hide her trouble from the others. The children, like adults in Dubrovnik were full of superstitions and might have mocked or even harmed her. But Miho jumped after her and caught her from behind. He saw foreman at the docks catching a whore in a light yellow dress the other day. The carpenter caught the woman from behind, turned her around to face him, then slapped her face; she shrieked, slapped him back and gave him a passionate kiss. Excited and trembling with a strange aching in his loins, Miho could see, how the foreman's rough hands untied the woman's bodice, and two beautiful marble breasts escaped the roped tissue prison. That, in his opinion, was how men had to behave. He could gather that there wasn't much under Miljuta's kirtle, not yet, but a kiss would do for now. And he copied the rough ritual. Yet, the noble girl fought back with a sudden revolt. He twisted her arms behind her back, and she screamed in pain. She burst in tears, struggling to get free. The hands of her eager playmate were strong. She was caught. Whining, she tried to plead with him:

"Please Miho, let me go. I must be home for lunch or my *baba* will beat me."

"Menčetići don't beat their children. I've got you and I am not letting you go, before you... before you give me a kiss on the lips."

Miljuta stared at him nonplussed. What was this? Miho used to be her friend. Who's this scoundrel, who is twisting her arms?

"Miho, what's gotten into you? You're hurting me. Kiss? I am not your mother to kiss you, are you crazy?"

"Well, I won't let you go without a kiss. I'm holding you."

"Miho, let go now or I'll tell your mother. Instead of a kiss she will give you a thrashing you won't forget."

"She will not. I am earning my wages and I am a man now. My mother and my younger sister respect me."

The Kaboga family or Kabužići were very rich and prosperous. Since the *karakas* had come into fashion, the two brothers, Galvo and Džore, invested all their merchant profits and capital gained from the sales of lands into the ship building plant. The demand overrated the offer by many times. Their clients had to wait for one *karaka* up to two years before the ship was built and in sea-going condition. Yet, trade companies from all over Europe were willing to wait, as the ships usually came with a crew. They could sail, guide the ship, keep and protect the cargo during the trips. Each crew was trained in naval defense by the *Ragusan* knights, and came aboard with swords and pistols for the maiden voyage. The *karakas* were basically merchant vessels, with three or even four masts, from which the vast sails could catch the winds and the ship would build speed. Nevertheless, for fear of the pirates, they had at least six guns aboard, sometimes even eight – four at each side. The Kabužići ships were seaworthy upon delivery and the client's captain, navigator and officers could take their first cargo on a maiden voyage directly from Dubrovnik. At the peak of his engineering career, the younger brother, Džore, Miho's father, drowned on a Sunday fishing expedition to Lopud. So nearly ten years ago, Džore's widow Lucia and her two children, with all their godly possessions, were temporarily put under Galvo's patronage, until the elder son Miho would come of age. All this had been meticulously noted in Džore's last will and carried out by the notary after his death. It was customary in Dubrovnik for *patrician* men to leave their family and wealth in the trust of close male relatives. The sailors for the Kabužići ships were recruited from the poverty stricken hinterland and the peninsula Pelješac, which despite all its fecundity and vineyards couldn't prosper under the Serbian rule. The *Ragusan Rector*, who in the 14th century was always a Venetian, nominated by the Doge himself, couldn't speak the local Slavic dialects and couldn't acquire the hinterlands despite the fact that his diplomats were trying every ruse to get the lands from the Popovo polje to Ston and the whole of the peninsula under the *Ragusan* authority.

"Let me go or I'll scream, and people will come and..."

Miljuta shut her eyes and in a fit of black anger let out a cry so shrill that it scared the birds away from the trees and roofs nearby. In a moment, she staggered to the pavement and was surprised to be free. With her eyes wide open, she saw Nikola Bono, a seventeen year old merchant from Makarska, shaking Miho violently.

"How do you treat a lady, you little shit, eh? Didn't your rich *tata* teach you anything?"

A heavy punch at Miho's nose brought blood into the boy's mouth, so he couldn't answer the question. He was terrified at the sight of Nikola's giant body, trained and muscled like a Greek *Apoxyomenos*, athletic and strong, with the wild black eyes of a pirate. Although he was just a minor himself, his father from Makarska, named Bono, or Bunić, bought him merchantmen rights a year earlier and deposited 500 golden *dukats* as the guarantee for Bunići's business deals to the *Ragusan* administration. Should the young Bunić make a debt and be unable to repay his client, the State would do this instead of him up to the amount deposited. Thus, the administration protected the business from fraud. If the debt exceeded the amount deposited and the debtor was not able to repay it, he could even lose his citizenship and become the property of the state, which would, despite its obvious anti-slave policy, probably sell him at the slave market in Venice or make him work for the creditor until the debt was cleared. The laws were strict, written down not only on parchments, but carved in stone. The Bunići were risking their necks aspiring to the business elite of Dubrovnik.

Nikola was a very clever young man. He had travelled abroad, had spent time with scholars in monasteries and was fluent in Latin as well as several other foreign languages like Venetian, Flemish, French and Spanish. He was cultivated and loaded with his father's money. He paid the Kabužići in advance for three *karakas* half a year ago, and was constructing a huge warehouse at the western end of the city walls, where he also lived, in a small, luxurious *palazzo*. His father visited only occasionally, nobody knew him, really. The Bunići were not a noble family, they were not a part of the *Ragusan patrician* society, and in spite of all their wealth would probably never be. Hearsay was their wealth had suspicious origins. It was said to have been acquired from the former *Pagania*, where for centuries Slavic tribes opposed Christianity and lived according to their wild laws, mainly from piracy. The Bunići might have been pirates like most of the landlords or so called merchants between Omiš and Makarska. Omiš, where the river Cetinja flows into the sea like an emerald snake protected by high steep hills and rock precipices, was the headquarters of Adriatic piracy. The loaded merchant ships leaving the port of *Spalato*, Split, and sailing through the channel between the island of Brač and mainland Dalmatia frequently got trapped in the strong *bura* with no bay for shelter on either side. If something went wrong with the rudder or one of the masts, they were doomed, an easy prey for the local small and flexible boats *ladas*, which would quickly drag the shipwrecks into the delta of the Cetinja. There they plundered them. Speed was important. The shady business of distributing and selling the ship cargo was carried out practically on the spot. The pirates transported the stolen goods by land routes to Makarska, and also disassembled the ship and used the wood for their own construction, so that before the *bura* calmed down and the Venetian military ships started looking for the lost ships and cargoes, there wasn't a trace left of either. The crew would be let free, and the captain, the owner of the ship or any other wealthy or important passengers would be ransomed for high amounts through various intermediaries. So, *bura* was a highly profitable wind, bringing more wealth to the area than the calm sea, *bonaca*.

Now, the strong pirate fists were remodeling Miho's noble face without mercy.

"Stop, Nikola, now!" cried Miljutina and the fists stopped, letting the boy fall down like a bundle of hay.

"Miss Miljutina, sorry, I got carried away. Are you all right?"

"Surely I am better than Miho now."

From above she looked down at her friend, who was so violent to her just a minute ago.

"What now, Miho? Was this a strong enough kiss for you or not?"

Miho wiped his nose on a sleeve and blinked away tears. This was too much for him; at fifteen he was no match for the older brute. Instantly, he hated them both.

"I will report you to my uncle, he's a senator and he will expel you, Nikola. You're not a real merchant, you're a pirate. You have no right to hit me."

"And will you tell your uncle the senator, Miho, what you were doing to Miljutina Menčetić as well? Look, she is bleeding..."

Both boys stared at Miljutina's kirtle and the blood soaking it around her ankles. Miljutina, who in the heat of the fight almost forgot her initial trouble, was shocked and staggered, suddenly feeling weak in her knees, on the point of fainting. Nikola caught her and lifted her in his strong arms saying:

"Allow me, Miss Miljutina, to carry you home."

Miljutina lost her ever sparking energy. She leaned her head faintly on his shoulder and put her arms around his neck, defying all good manners and in particular defying Miho Kabužić.

"Her *baba* will kill you, Nikola. You, Miljutina, she will lock you up for a month. You're mad, both of you!"

Miho turned his back on them and ran into an ally toward the church, where the crowd was gathering for the midday holy procession. The young couple was calmly watching his huge, clumsy steps trying to avoid pottery, some stray cats and curious old people jamming his way. Miho's hat was tilted and his straight brown hair was disheveled. His chemise bloody, his grey eyes white with anger and his dark blue woolen jacket unbuttoned, the boy looked like a lunatic. He was hurt, the pirate and the girl had humiliated him. In the heat of the moment he forgot that it was actually himself who had started the fight and that his behavior was anything but noble. His wild gestures were uncontrolled, he wanted to get out of their sight as soon as possible. And he wanted revenge.

Nikola sighed and put the girl down. It was time to solve her problem.

"Miljutina, shall we go to the sea, so that you can wash before you go home?"

"Wash, eh, wash what?"

Nikola couldn't believe his ears – the girl must be close to the marriageable age and yet didn't have any idea what was going on, while even he could understand the nature of her bleeding. How can a young lady be clueless as to her body's development? He was embarrassed to break her ignorance, yet they should move on.

"You know that you're not really hurt. Have you heard of monthly bleeding? Women have it once in every lunar cycle. The doctors call it menstruating. Has your *mama* explained to you what this is and why it happens to women every month?"

"My *mama* is with *tata* in Venice, she couldn't. Only *baba* is here, and she will be so angry. My new dress is dirty. Do you think I can wash it out?"

"Yes, but first you have to put rags in your underpants, so that you don't soil it again. And no women would blame you, they all have it. Your grandmother also had it when she was younger."

Miljutina shivered at the thought of revealing this new secret to her severe *baba*. Marina de Menze, or Menčetić, was a true dragon lady. Some saw her as a legendary *Ragusan* woman and admired her brave posture of a widow. She was very capable and intelligent, so her husband explicitly made her the sole executrix in his will, prohibiting any of his male relatives to run the company or touch his estates after his death. She brought up five children. The elder two sons, Luca and Mate, were both spoilt good-for-nothings and lost for the family trading business. Her daughters, Ana and Andrea, were either too shallow or excessively religious. Ana, the elder, fleshy girl, was married to a violent Serbian knight. The younger, melancholic Andrea chose the convent of the order of Poor Clares, who established the first orphanage in the city. Instead of having her own, she looked after the abandoned children of rascals and slaves. Marina's youngest son, Miljutina's father Lovro, was despicably lazy, but at least clever. As a handsome young man, he did everything to avoid study and work. Not yet eighteen years old, he went to Venice and was squandering his *mama's* money with a women named Lucretia. Marina could bet Lucretia had been dressed in yellow when he first met her. Against all sanity, they got married and came to Dubrovnik to live off Marina's. She was boiling with rage at this Lucretia woman, a wench from Venice thinking she could pass for a duchess in the far away *Ragusa*. Not with Marina. When Lucretia gave birth to a daughter, little Miljutina, Marina decided that she had had enough. She had to live with the fact that her children were no good. She chased them all away from the new baby. The sweet blonde and green eyed Miljutina, a girl with quick intelligence and a happy smile on her face, became the sparkle of *baba's* eye and was supposed to take over and inherit the vast Menčetići business empire. Marina worshiped her, educated her and made her a better person than any of her own children could ever become. Yet, part of Marina's education was also total obedience of rules. The much less liked part for Miljutina.

Miljutina started sobbing, afraid of what could await her at home and not knowing what to do. Nikola took her hand softly and tried to calm her down.

"Look, here's what we'll do. We'll go to my house. Nobody will notice. Today everybody is going to the St. Blaise procession on *Stradun*. We can bypass them all. You know, I have an old nurse, Nana. She's Jewish, so she doesn't care much for our church festivities. She's also a herbalist and a healer. She's at home now. She will explain all this to you better. Like a woman to a woman. Come!"

Miljutina followed him with unsure and awkward steps. Her will was melting down, she didn't know any better, coming home like that on St. Blaise day was unthinkable. So she followed Nikola, with whom up to that moment she had rarely exchanged a word. They made a huge detour to avoid the crowds and arrived at his house, which turned out to be one of the prettiest *palazzos* at the western edge of the city. Yet, when Miljutina beheld the wet nurse, Nana, she almost took flight. Nana's huge nose was set in the middle of her face, dark with sun spots and wrinkles, and her black eyes were shining with interest, moving from the boy to the girl and back. She was bent double, skinny, her long black hair pinned high, in a huge knot at the back of her head.

"What is it, young people, why are you visiting an old woman instead of celebrating the saint today?"

"Nana, we need your help."

"Do you? Why we? Not at this age. Nikola, she's just a girl!"

Nikola blushed, deeply embarrassed. He knew what Nana's secret specialty was for some young women, who after love affairs got in trouble and sought her assistance. In his heart he despised this kind of devil's cure. It was against God and Humanity.

"Nana, it's not that, really. Let's get in and talk."

The sun was almost setting when, a few hours later, Nikola and Miljutina were standing on the hill above the city, which for some time had looked like a permanent building site. The *Ragusan Council* was investing decades of profits into building vast city walls, which were to enclose the town in order to protect its wealth from uninvited intruders.

"Thank you, Nikola. You and Nana helped me a lot today. I had no idea... And I was so scared. How come you know the women's staff so well?"

"It's Nana. She explained everything to me when I was ten. Also about the girls, how they can get... err, you know, with child. Also about the boys, how they feel their needs differently when they grow. I was also taken to... never mind, I just know now."

"Well, I'd know it, if I were seventeen, too. Wouldn't I?"

"By the time you're seventeen, you'll be more than knowing. Probably you will be a mother yourself, Miljutina."

He looked at her tenderly and stroked her dark blonde hair with his palm. She was a beautiful girl, very different from other *Ragusan* belles, who usually had dark hair and brown or black eyes. Miljutina looked as though she came from the north; her eyes were deep green, her skin white like marble and her blonde hair thick and straight, unwilling to curl for the weight of it. She was also tall and skinny, quick in her pace and gracious at dancing. He knew that as he had seen her dance at the New Year's Eve festival. But, coming from a well established *patrician* family, she was unreachable for him. Miho was right, if her *baba* found out about their afternoon, he could end in the city stocks. His father would be anything than grateful for such a stupid slip of reason. Softly, he said:

"You know, Miljutina, you shouldn't tell your *baba* about today, she could harm me."

"Of course, I know. It will be our secret."

"And if Miho opens his mouth, I will see to it that he shuts up."

"Don't beat him too hard, Nikola. He's just a spoilt boy. You know his father died some years ago, so his mother has been doting on him ever since. I don't know what got into him today."

"Never mind, he'll get over it. I'll speak to him tonight."

Miljutina nodded, still looking towards the west, past the scarlet bay to another big building site of *Lovrijenac*. The foundations were set, yet there was no more progress for a while. The senators were still working on the defense strategy for the city state and as always, they were summoning taxes to pay for it. They said the biggest fortress in the world would be built on the site, and the fort would protect Dubrovnik forever, until the end of its days. But the *dukats* were yet to be collected and the site was peaceful. They needed some more years to start the construction, all they could do was to decide on the saying which would ornate the entrance gate: *Non Bene Pro Toto Libertas Venditur Auro* – Freedom is not to be sold for all the treasures in the world. Ah, money and wealth, it was what this city was ever about. Miljutina looked at her companion and their eyes met. Nikola smiled politely.

"You're a woman now. Soon you will be betrothed."

Miljutina's eyes sparkled and she let out a cheeky, throaty laugh. She suddenly felt so free, freer than for some time, yet rooted in the soil like a tree, with a new and overwhelming feeling of a bond to the young man who helped her without prejudice or hesitation. She flushed with a daring thought.

"Yes. It could be to you, Nikola. Weren't you the first to have discovered that I am a woman?"

She broke the spell, and with a jolt, started running down the slope toward the Pile gate at the northern part of the nearly finished city walls, where St. Blaise would be holding her and the city's destiny in his pious hands. Nikola stood on the hill for a while, his face stricken with emotions and unmoving, except for the faint light of hope in his black eyes. Could it be? Could ever Miljutina, the noblest of *Ragusan* maidens, the future heiress of the vast Menčetići fortune, become his wife? He knew he had fallen in love, and he also knew he should need all the patience to free the girl from her *patrician* grandmother's claws. If it was possible at all. She'd be fabulously rich with him, but his family had no roots and no tradition in Dubrovnik. Maybe if they went to live in Makarska. What would his father say, then? The man was spending a fortune to infiltrate him in the *Ragusan* merchant elite. He would be disappointed. And Miljutina, would she give up the cultural life, the theatre, musical and dancing soirées, for a simple life among simple people, practically illiterate, not all of them even proper Christians? He knew Miljutina was being educated privately at very high standards for boys, not to speak for girls. He was looking at her green dress getting smaller and smaller until she entered the walls and he couldn't see her anymore. The day was dying in the west with purple bleeding of the clouds, reflecting their dark shadows in the calm water of the city harbor. It was time for a move. With a smile on his face and a cunning sparkle in his eyes, Nikola headed home. Youth could always find the way, just like water, just like the river Dubrovačka. Nikola's energy built up fast and ran through his veins in powerful streams, flushing away the obstacles; in his heart, with the imagination of his amazing intellect, Nikola was thinking of how to court to his sweetheart. Or better, how to charm her *baba*.

* * *

Miljutina came to her home *palazzo* above the port, not caring
for the procession or the mass. Her religion had been fading away
for some time. All the poverty of the peasants and beggars, all
the injustice done to the slaves, all the suffering of the orphans she
saw when visiting her aunt at Saint Clares' moved her and made
her belief in God shake in its roots. As a child, she absorbed
her sacraments fervently, and prayed to Jesus and St. Blaise
with love and worship. There wouldn't be a procession without
her braiding wreaths of wild flowers and shiny laurel leaves for
the holy saint. Yet now-a-days the priests with their inflated
metaphysical speeches couldn't penetrate her teenage reasoning.
She was a practical girl, and she preferred talking to people of
flesh and blood to praying to some relics, bones and scepters. In
her point of view, faith was a matter of the heart. She kept aloof
from the popular fears and superstitious notions concerning the
St. Blaise relics. She rather prayed to the goodness of her fellow
citizens.

She entered the dark vestibule of the house, and went directly
to the kitchen. There, on the big tables were mouth-watering
local delicacies wonderfully arranged on plates, prepared for a
dinner party her *baba* always gave on St. Blaise day for her
numerous clients and useful state officials. There was marinated
tuna fish with little white olive buns, peppered fresh oysters from
Mali Ston, garnished with lemon slices, Venetian beef stew with
baby carrots and young green peas served in little dough baskets,
dried ham and sausages with melon slices from Africa, fresh dates
and arancini, as well as caramelized almonds. There was a walnut
tart with apple slices, baskets full of tiny sweet tangerines, and
plates of grayish dried figs decorated with fresh, aromatic dark
green laurel leaves. The guests would come in crowds as always,
eat and drink the plates away, and smile courteously until each
wall in the house would go slimy and sweet from their talk: her
baba was an important woman. She was generating income one
way or the other. Picking at a sweat meat here and another
there, tasting this sauce and that, sipping sweet watered wine,
Miljutina wandered around the tables as happy as a bee. Her
feast day was saved. Old Nana cleaned her robe and gave her a
pair of Nikola's breeches, a pair that had been obviously too tight
for him for years. Nana also explained to her all about the blood,
and gave her linen rags for the four days while this menstruating
business would be taking place. And after that, she was told, it
would reoccur every month. She was a grown woman now, she
could bear babies.

She thought about Nikola dreamily and understood, not without a shiver, how much she liked him. He was so strong and tall,

like a prince. His hair was black and curly. It reached to his wide shoulders and was neatly tied with a leather string behind his neck. Oh, she wished so much to let the string loose and plunge her fingers into those shiny curls! His eyes were black, searching, sparkling with knowledge, deeply set under strong, bushy brows. She was flattered by his chivalrous tenderness towards her. Men at his age would drink wine, gamble and chase women around. But he was so different, so serious, running his family business like a seasoned grown up merchant. He enjoyed reading and studying. And in his library, she was deeply impressed with his books. He probably had the worth of one thousand *dukats* only on the bookshelves. This was really very peculiar for him; a pirate that she had always thought he was. The kitchen door opened and *baba* came in.

"Miljutina, here you are. Where the hell have you been all day? We were looking for you all around town. Miho came with his uncle and they wanted to talk to me and to you."

Baba Marina hugged her beloved granddaughter, who got stiffer than a pole. Marina drew away surprised and waited. Miljutina turned away and said coldly:

"Miho is a fool, *baba*. I don't want to talk to him or about him, ever."

"Why? This is new. You two have always been great friends. What's happened?"

"Miho hurt me. He doesn't know how to play anymore."

"What did he do to you, *zlato*?"

"He twisted my arms behind my back and wanted to kiss me on the mouth. Like a tart in the harbor. He's a fool, *basta*."

Baba laughed aloud, maybe just for a moment too long. Miljuta was staring at her astonished, without a word. The old woman composed herself and tried to make her see reason.

"The boy's a rogue. It is improper to be forcing a kiss from you. But he will grow wiser, don't worry. And, well, he will inherit Džore Kabužić' share of the shipbuilding company, you know. He might be one of the richest young men in Ragusa, when he's of age."

"I told you, *baba*, I don't care. A fool can be rich or poor, but he's still a fool."

"Well, little rows like this are nothing, believe me. And the Kabužići came to see us with a special purpose today."

Miljuta became suspicious. Did Miho tell her *baba* that she let Nikola carry her and even put her arms around his neck? Did he report Nikola and his punch on the nose? She must know. She continued provocatively.

"It wasn't just a row. He was violent to me. If it were different circumstances, I can imagine him raping a girl. I hate him. He's nothing but a little shit."

"No foul words, please. You're a lady. He's nothing of the sort, just a boy in puberty."

"If you saw how he was holding me, you would think differently. What was the Kabužići business here, anyway?"

"You will know soon enough, my girl."

Miljutina stood still. She was overcome with the feeling that something important was brewing and wanted to find out what.

"*Baba*, I must know now. Is it about me?"

"It's about you and about all of us, Miljuta, darling."

The darling bit should have been highly suspicious, but the girl still didn't get the hint. Somehow, like a mocking spell cast over her sharp intelligence her thoughts were lulled by the images of the afternoon. She was floating in another world, where there was a young man who she could love some day. It was the stuff of fairy tales or dreams. What a change! She had always looked at Nikola, like the rest of *Ragusans*, with nothing but contempt.

"You will marry him. We betrothed you, Galvo and me. That's why they came here."

Miljuta just stared and couldn't get the meaning of *baba*'s words. She would marry Nikola... No, it was the sly little shit her *baba* sold her to, it was Miho. He had come to their house in her absence with his uncle and asked for her hand. She didn't need to know more. Without any questions, *baba* consented. The two fortunes would complete each other nicely: the shipbuilding and the trade, the two most powerful families in Dubrovnik tied together by her own flesh. The equation was perfect, unless... Miljuta was terrified. It was a trap – how to get out of it?

"*Baba*, wait, I am too young to get married."

"Not now, it is to be in two years' time, my dear. You'll be fifteen by then, old enough for marriage."

"No, it can't be. *Baba*, I... Please, let us wait until I am twenty-one, full of age. I can help you in business. Please, *baba*, let me choose my spouse, you were allowed to do it, too, why would you force me..."

"Little Miljuta, in two years this row will be forgotten. Miho is a nice boy, you will get along, don't worry. As for me, my choice was not the best, you know. Your grandfather, Stevo, was a bit of an adventurer, look how early I was left a widow."

"But you loved him..."

Now *baba* lost her line of reasoning. Love hadn't been a part of her vocabulary for a long time. She liked her business and she knew how much she loved Miljutina, but a loving relationship with a man had been none of her business for many years. To be exact, she hadn't cared for any man since her Stevo had died in a futile maritime conflict with local fishermen in the channel of Pelješac and her life changed dramatically. She was carrying a child, the last fruit of their love, which came into the Annals of

the City. They were together since a very young age, Stevo and
Marina, they practically grew up together. Stevo de Menze was
from a very prosperous family. They had produced several doges
for the office in the old Ragusa, before the Venetian rule, and were
a very proud *patrician* house. Her family was not exactly poor,
but far below the Menčetići status, so a betrothal between the
two was next to impossible. Yet, they loved each other since they
could remember. When Stevo was fifteen, his father found him a
suitable bride, Milica Djakon, from the line of the twenty generations of the rulers on the island of Lastovo. Her father, Djakon,
possessed vast fertile plains producing wines and chickpeas on the
island, but he also owned several merchant companies operating
under the *Ragusan* flag. Milica was as tender as her name, *mila*,
so very frail and so very beautiful. However, her soft charms
were lost on Stevo, who since he could remember had loved his
friend and neighbor Marina. Hers was not a frail beauty – she
was a tough playmate, a rock Stevo could rely upon and a partner he could always trust. There was something exciting about
Marina. She liked adventures and boys' games. In those times,
parents were obeyed and acting against your families or their will
was severely punished, even by exile or death; the least was to
bury their bad offspring in a monastery for life. After Milica and
Stevo's betrothal party and the public acknowledgement of it by
the families, Marina wanted to drown herself and jumped from
a cliff into deep, stormy waters below. She was dragged ashore
half alive. It was a turning point. She made the decision to fight
against the rigid rules and prejudice of the *Ragusan* elite. First,
she'd get some education. So she joined the newly established
Poor Clares, where she learnt to read and write as well as manage a business by figures. There were years to go before the banns
were read in the Cathedral, as the couple was still too young to
get married. Stevo was travelling, completing his education on
the seas. He secretly remained linked with Marina through copious correspondence, which was forwarded to and fro by his older
sister. For all deprivation of contact, their words hadn't held back
any of their sentiments. A few years had gone by and the yeast
banns were read, so that Milica and Stevo were to be married in
Saint Stephen's cathedral in Dubrovnik in the summer of 1283.
Milica was aware of Stevo's feelings and reluctantly sailed a week
before the ceremony to Dubrovnik despite the black clouds which
were wickedly gathering above the hill of Hum, the highest point
of her home island Lastovo. The storm caught the ship and they
all drowned. The last line in her diary said: "Oh, Lord, with
sadness I undertake this voyage, which should bring me home,
but will only part me from my dear family and the beauties of
my paradise island Lastovo and drown me in sorrow. I didn't ask
Stevo to love me. He doesn't, I know that for sure. Our parents
demanded that we love each other. What a sorry command I

got from my father: love him! There is no imperative for the verb love, unfortunately." Marina remembered all this as it were yesterday. She felt sad for Milica, yet eagerly awaited the day when her Stevo would complete the mourning and come to fetch her from the cloister. And the day came at last. It brought joy and bitterness – for his inappropriate choice of the bride, Stevo had to renounce his inheritance as a first born. His father consented to a slight severance of the Menčetići estates and let him bear their family name. With a symbolic sum, Stevo and Marina could start their new life together. They built up a new Menčetići trading company. Stevo's good contacts and Marina's excellent money management were the best of the inheritance they could get. She bore him eight children in twelve years, only five lived. At the turn of the century, Stevo started acting odd. He had had an accident at sea on his travel from Venice, since which he had been hallucinating in his dreams. The accident cost many lives and Stevo couldn't take it. After having left the island Premuda, the weather turned windless and they were left floating in the middle of the Adriatic for days. They lost their course and without them noticing, their freshwater tank leaked, so that sea water got inside. They had a shipment of Italian wine aboard, so in order to survive the captain and the crew drank watered wine, only the water was the sea. When they finally reached Ragusa, many died of dehydration. Stevo lived, but was never the same again. He committed himself to St. Blaise, kneeling and praying fervently in front of his statue. He revised his last will, yet constantly neglected his duties with the City Council. Marina jumped in or the family would be heavily fined for not performing its duties. He didn't work, and all responsibility was on Marina's shoulders. One day he sailed to Lastovo to conclude the annual contract with the family fish suppliers and never came back. He was reported to have been wandering about the island for months and crying in pain. Marina held position and waited to get her love back. It didn't happen, and her sentiments died there and then with Stevo.

"Love doesn't pay the bills, my child."

"You can't, we have to wait for *tata*, for his word, he will decide. It's the law."

Marina inhaled sharply. She had been fighting her whole life against gender prejudice, which pervaded business and politics, and she was not having it in her own house. With a stiff, suppressed anger she said in a very low yet clear voice.

"God knows where your *tata* is sporting. I have been the head of the Menčetići family for some time now, remember?"

"My grandfather, *baba*, he loved and trusted you, look at your fortune. He put everything in your hands. I would be nothing but a pretty decoration for the house of Kabužić, they're such pricks."

"They are rather high, true. But Miljuta, you're intelligent, well educated and cleverer than all their clan together. You will deal with the Kabužići, no doubts. Now, will you change for the evening reception?"

"Is Miho coming as well?"

"I would assume, he would like to meet his bride to be, not only her grandmother."

Miljuta's hopes dwindled away, she saw there was nothing more to do at the moment. But in two years everything might change. Maybe the Kabužići will go bankrupt and the engagement will be off. Her mind was on Nikola. What would he think when he would find out? She went to her room silently and let her maid help her with her hair and dress for the evening reception. There was a new silken kirtle stretched out on her bed, the color was pale blue. She wouldn't wear it – the blue was the color of betrothal, but it could never suit her green eyes the same way as the betrothal to Miho could never agree with Miljutina's life. She would put on her dark blue kirtle with so much golden embroidery it looked more golden than blue. Her only thoughts circled around how to avoid the marriage and how to avoid *baba*'s intention to accumulate more wealth. There was no remedy – Galvo Kabužić couldn't have children of his own; no matter how many women he had bedded, he would put everything into his nephew's hands, and *baba* knew this. But she didn't know how Miljutina felt about it – or she did and she just didn't care? Miljutina sighed. How could she swim against the current? How could she find a way to get closer to Nikola?

* * *

Another and another whole year went by since the agreement between the two heads of the families Kabužić and Menčetić, Galvo and Marina. The wedding of their scions Miho and Miljuta was an important affair of the Republic, two powerful families joining forces. According to the custom, the banns would be read in the cathedral on the wedding yeast day, which meant only a week before the actual wedding. It was the spring of 1314 Anno Domini. Dubrovnik was prospering, acquiring more business and wealth every day. There was no war and few conflicts, once the *Ragusans* reluctantly accepted Venetians as their overlords. The Venetians sent their doge and expanded their and the *Ragusan* business with the Ottomans. In a way, the Venetians were more encouraging than suppressing the *Ragusan* aspirations to growth and wealth. But wars can have many faces and even the most peaceful a bay could hide wild currents under its innocent surface, where swimmers were drowned before they knew what had dragged them to the bottom of the sea.

Mihajlo Kabužić had taken his ugly revenge against Nikola Bunić on the day after St. Blaise feast. He had him put in the

stocks on Stradun in front of the Rector's Palace with a false indictment to the City Council. Miho had reported to the council
about the heavy punch on the nose and seasoned it with a murder
threat to his person. With a speedy procedure and relying upon
the word of a *patrician* son, Nikola was brought to Stradun. It
was only for a couple of hours, but Miho was thrilled with his
success and scoffed at Nikola, throwing fish scraps and debris in
his face. It took some hours before the family solicitor of the
Bunići intervened with the Council and immediately a fair trial
was called for. He freed the young man from all charges easily,
as there were some more witnesses to the violent scene at the
Minčeta plain than birds and Miljutina herself. Miho was left
with a black mark for the false indictment, yet his uncle's money
soon washed it away. After this rotten intrigue, Miljutina was
even bitterer about her fiancé and didn't want to see him or speak
to him. Her *baba* insisted that the customs be obeyed, so occasionally Miljuta, acting deaf and dumb, had to be in Miho's company. But the citizens noticed well how she had washed Nikola's
face with fresh water and fed him wine and bread during the few
hours, which he shamefully spent in the stocks. Shame or no
shame, receiving a drink from the hands of his love, the young
man smiled happily as though he was in Heaven.

On a rainy Wednesday morning, almost to the day two years
later, Miho was writing down the accounts in Galvo's office. He
had yet to copy a few letters from today's post from Venice and
go to the Rector's Palace to deposit the promissory notes for the
new order, which their shipyard had received from Genoa. After
the winter break, spring was a time of hectic business activities.
The debt which would arise from the order of the Genovese merchant had to be dealt with properly. The law obliged all traders
and businessmen in Ragusa to register their debts or payable
claims above 10 *hyperperi*, which corresponded to the value of
120 Venetian golden *dukats*, within eight days from the date of
issue in a document drawn up by a notary. The registration offices were in Dubrovnik and abroad, at all *Ragusan* outposts. In
this way the City Council of Ragusa and its merchant law guaranteed some security for the transactions within its rule, which
resulted in Dubrovnik being a highly popular place with traders
from all around the world. It was the number one address for
business either with the Catholic Spain or the Muslim Ottoman
Empire. Galvo came in and put his wide hat on the table next
to Miho.

"Are you done, Miho? The notary will go for lunch, and you
will be a day late with registration. Time is money, don't waste
a day. Leave the letters and first go to the Rector's."

"*Bene.* I've almost finished, just this one number."

"When you get back, we have to talk. I will need to send you
abroad with the next Menčetići ship, the Lasta. She's leaving on

the high tide tomorrow. Now, run!"

Miho did everything as he was told, wondering on his way back from the Rector's where he'd be sent. It was so exciting to think he would go and negotiate in the name of their company, or maybe he would have to secure a payment, or even cash in a promissory note. It would be for the first time he'd be in a business situation on his own, although he had been working for his uncle for many years now and understood very well the financial instruments they were using to make the most profit. He was a well formed young *Ragusan* businessman with the prospect of marrying one of the most eligible maidens of the city, who'd bring in several thousands of golden *dukats* and an important merchant network of clients in her dowry trunk. And merchants always needed more ships, which his family, the Kabužići could always build. He'd be richer and happier. There was a saying that the fathers of Dubrovnik taught their sons commerce as soon as they started growing their fingernails. The acquisition and accumulation of wealth was the highest of all *Ragusan* virtues.

"Here, in this letter you will read a secret, my boy, which you should by all means keep to yourself. Don't discuss this with anyone, it can be dangerous. You know that with a papal bull, the bank of the Knights Templars was suppressed along with their holy order last year. We, the Kabužići, have taken a very high promissory note deposited at their monastery at Vrana."

"Yes, I know. It is 538 *dukats* for the Pittis, a three masted *karaka* with four cannons. I have copied the note myself and it is registered. Do you think it could be a problem? The *karaka* for the Pittis is not yet ready, we need a few more months."

"You're right, but I don't want to wait that long. The persecutions of the Templars since the Black Friday are getting more dangerous, and there might come a moment when the laws and rules become irrelevant. It was horrible, you were still a child in 1307, but you have heard of Friday the 13th in France, haven't you?"

"Yeah, Phillip the Fair, just he wasn't so fair in the end. But as you always say, should the merchant rules fail to be respected the whole world would fall apart. The note will be valid no matter what. The Templars may be gone, but their money and valuables are deeply rooted in business."

"In theory this is so, I agree. But you can feel the tone of the letter. And our Holy Father joins in the prosecution by supporting the heresy charges. They're absurd, of course. But should the Templars be abolished, we could face problems. Who knows? Well, I have made a new deal with the Papal Bank in Venice, with Seniore Sorini. He will procure goods for the full value of the promissory note of Vrana, the former Templer monastery, and we will bring the goods to Dubrovnik for sale."

"But you will lose the 11% margin we would have at the ship

delivery date from the Pittis. The interest was against the security, they're a reliable client."

"They're a good client, I agree, but their guarantee is no good
any more. I reckon the Templars' promissory notes are like chestnuts in the fire, and I want to get rid of ours as soon as possible."

"I see. Are you prepared to lose the difference? It is nearly
60 *dukats* with the transaction costs."

"No, I am not, of course. The profit is essential, or why are
we doing it? I calculated we can get a substantial price difference
with the sales of goods here. You will issue another insurance
promissory note with Seniore Sorini, so that we're covered in case
of a shipwreck."

"Who will pay against the goods in advance?"

"I have arranged a common split of cargo. Only there are to
be fewer partners this time and will get higher percentages: 8
karats Menčetić, 6 *karats* Bundići, 6 Pucići and 4 will be ours –
so all together 24 *karats*."

"Only 4 *karats*? We will be selling only 4 *karats*? Will there
be any profit at all?"

"Don't forget our profit is in all of the 24 *karats*, Miho. It's
good business – we're rid of unsure payment and that is in advance of delivering the ship to the Pittis. In case something goes
wrong, we delay the delivery of the *karaka* until the payment is
clear, but if it goes according to plan, we will win again. It will
bring us new orders. Besides, you have to show your qualities as
a future son in law to Marina Menčetić."

"Fine, if it makes Miljuta kiss me in advance. . . "

"Well, you have the insurance, the betrothal. It is more than
a promissory note."

Galvo and Miho shared a hearty laugh, like any men at any
time when bringing up the subject of women and sex. Miho had
acquired some experience with women in the last year. He was
enjoying a young peasant mistress, who he was meeting many
nights per week and shared her bed and bodily pleasures against
his uncle's few *dinars* to her family. The girl was doing it because
her family was starving after the last bad harvest. Yet, they were
young and fervent, and with time deeper feelings for each other
secretly invaded their nights spent together. Miho could wait for
Miljutina's tender kisses as well as he could wait for her golden
dukats.

"You must be very careful about one thing: as soon as you
come to Venice, you must make a copy of Sorini's promissory note
and register it with our consul Pucić or Pozza, as he is known in
Venice, and send it to Dubrovnik by another ship. Find a reliable
person for the postal package and don't sail with the Lasta until
you do. This is very important, my boy, the copy is our insurance,
so to speak."

"Why would he give us a promissory note for the cargo if he pays for it?"

"Well, I saved his face not so long ago and helped him with the Head of the Papal Bank in Rome, so he owes me one. But the promissory note will not be only for the cargo, it will also function as an insurance policy for the ship. I'm sorry to say that international merchant rules don't know naval insurance like we do, and this is the way to still have it. Don't worry, Miho. Sorini gets percentages when the cargo is delivered, so he is keen to do it. But the bearer of the note can have it annulled with our consul anywhere, should he present the original."

Clearly, Miho's mind had been wandering and he could not say later whether he had heard his uncle's instructions properly or not.

"You're not afraid of pirates, Uncle Galvo, are you?"

"Of course I am. They are not to be joked about. They are getting more dangerous every day. We should all be afraid of them."

"I eliminated one two years ago, didn't I? He looked quite impotent in the stocks."

"Slowly, my boy, slowly! That coup of yours was not very clever. I had troubles with the court of justice. The judge suggested a compensation for the hasty verdict and punishment to Bunić, and wanted to fine us for the false indictment. Those are serious matters. Luckily, Bunić refused, saying no money could buy back his honor. But he warned the Council they should be more careful next time, before they'd put an honest citizen in the stocks. It was monkey business, don't brag with it. Nikola Bona is gaining power and importance, he's a clever young man and a good client of ours. Three ships, and his down payments are all solid gold. No promissory notes or traded goods or such pigeons on the roof like we get from Venetians and Pisans. He pays in plain solid gold. Never forget – our client is our king!"

"I know, sorry, Uncle Galvo. But I hate him nevertheless. I am sure he is after Miljutina. He took her away that afternoon. I will kill him, if he has deflowered her."

"You'll find out soon. It's a crime to sleep with a *patrician* maiden unless you're married to her, why would he do it? So, it is the 14th of February today, you will need approximately 28 to 35 days to Venice, depending on the winds. Take a two days' break at *Jadra Nova* to go to the hinterland, to the Vrana Monastery and find out if you can cash the Pitti promissory note. Just do it if the monks give you money. Well, I doubt they will. It's before the expiry date. In any case, take it further to Sorini, everything is confirmed and arranged, I'll give you the documents. Stay with Sorini for a while to learn the basics of the Papal Bank. You will return in the end of May. Maybe we can arrange the nuptials for the end of June. I will speak to Marina."

"Miljutina will not be fifteen by then, she has her birthday in November."

"Never mind, Marina Menčetić wants you two under one roof as much as I do, and she wants it soon. She wants Miljuta with a baby, an heir."

Cheekily, Miho said:

"It will be my pleasure to give babies to *baba*. I can't wait."

"Well, soon, you will have your chance, my boy."

"I will indeed. I wish only she'd like me more. Can I buy her a nice gift in Venice?"

"Yes, find something really nice. 50 *dukats* are at your disposal."

"Thank you, Uncle Galvo, how generous of you!"

"It's an investment with high returns. She's worth it, believe your old uncle's experienced eye."

Galvo watched the boy rush out of the office. He took a flask of *travarica*, a greenish liquor made of wine brandy and strong herbs, from the cupboard, poured a tiny glass and pensively sipped at it. Sitting in his big chair with his huge belly tearing apart the ivory buttons of the woolen jacket, Galvo was mulling over why destiny had cheated him of his own son, of his own heir. He unbuttoned his belt and took some dried figs from the bowl, then, with the force of a waterfall, his eyes filled with tears. He remembered Nevena, his wonderful first wife, the only woman he had ever loved and lost, the angel that he hadn't appreciated as he should have, and who in the end hurt him beyond possible. On her deathbed, she confessed to him that she had hated him all her life. They couldn't conceive a child. Why? Galvo didn't know. She avoided physical contact as though he had scabies. The times he somehow forced himself upon her, he felt her restrain and reserve. She didn't belong to him. Nevertheless, he kept trying and loving her, for Nevena in her heart was very tender despite her robust physique. She was a tall woman, more like a monument of a woman, and he liked that very much. Her body was full, the breasts and hips reminiscent of the shape of the antique *amphorae*, filled with a life force stronger than any wine. At first glance, she could not pass for a beauty – the contemporary ideal was more a pale child-woman than a strong, red cheeked, healthy girl. But he was much into her from their very first meeting. He had hoped that in all the years she would come to love him. There was one time when Nevena got pregnant, but only later he found out it was not by him. She had a lover. Their son was born dead, they were punished. Nevena caught a birth fever and agonized for weeks over the lost child. Every morning, when Galvo came to check upon her condition, there was less life. The terrible truth about her sin was not confessed to a priest, she confided only in him, Galvo. She asked him for forgiveness, she whispered that she should have given their love a chance, that she was sorry. Galvo cried at her bedside like a baby, and forgave everything, asking God to let Nevena live. It was not to be, she died the following day with a soft sigh, as though a dove fluttered up into the sky. To Galvo, despite all her sins, she was indeed Nevena the innocent. He found some stray sheets of her diary, after she died and could read about her passion for the man she named G. It could have been that Greek carpenter, a former slave, whom the Kabužići got from the city orphanage, a handsome and talented man. He had left Dubrovnik very shortly after Nevena's death. It was a pity, for he was an excellent master ship builder. Galvo never really got over the pain and the guilt he felt. All the women after Nevena were just passing images, like clouds taking rain and blizzards elsewhere, far away over the sea.

Sipping *travarica*, Galvo could not imagine that it was precisely that dragon lady Marina Menčetić who knew all about Nevena's story. She had been given the three volumes of Nevena's diary, with the instructions to deposit them at Saint Clares after Galvo's death. For Marina and Nevena were bound by a strong friendship. It started in 1295, when Galvo left Ragusa and spent several months in Venice. There was a mutiny at the Kabužić shipyard in Lopud, and Nevena was alone. She didn't know what to do and sought finances and advice from Marina, who she used to know at Saint Clares and knew had a tough business mind. Had Galvo been able to he would read in Nevena's diary as follows:

* * *

Friday, 13th February 1293

Yesterday was my sixteenth birthday. This precious notebook, sheets of paper bound in leather, was my father's present. For the good grades at Latin and honorable conduct I've shown in the five years of my stay with St. Clares. I was really happy. Besides, I received wonderful news from my aunt, who came to visit me at the cloisters. Soon, I will be able to leave the convent and return to my family, for in a short time I must get married. They're still negotiating a husband for me, I am so curious. It will be so exciting. I am told, the dances, musical performances and public theatres have much improved since the Venetians finally installed their doge at the Rector's Palace. I'm also looking forward to playing with my younger brother Petar. I can't wait and can't close my eyes.

Saturday, 7th March 1293

My father is coming for me in a carriage and with an entourage in an hour, but first I must confess my happiness to the precious friend – my diary. The family has found a groom for me: the

younger Kabužić, Galvo. He's many years older than me, at least
six or seven. I don't remember what he looks like. I met him a few
times before school many years ago. His family is not precisely
first rank of *patricians*. My mother is much nobler, a descendant
of the house of Cerva. Only three generations ago, the Kabužići
still worked the land with their own hands. In the last decades
they have acquired vast territories at Pelješac, so they grow wine
and olive oil, or better their serfs and slaves do it. But on the
other hand, there is not much competition among the young men
for my hand. I'm out of fashion with my heavy build, tall figure,
wide cheekbones, black curly hair and dark eyes. I don't look
frail enough and many a *patrician* boy is several inches shorter
than me. I hope Galvo has retained some of his peasant stoutness
to match me. Tomorrow there will be a feast in the honor of my
return, and I will meet him for the first time in many years. I am
told we played together quite a lot when I was very little.

Wednesday, 11th March 1293

I spoke to Galvo Kabužić at the Sunday feast at our palace.
Thank God he's taller than me. He's so handsome, and to my
surprise, only five years older than me. He's travelled the world
and has been to Venice, where he spent a year running a shipyard
for a wealthy family friend. We danced, and he let his hand slip
on my waist, and he even embraced me once. I think he likes me a
lot, and immediately I felt grateful and attracted to him. At the
dance, our fathers solemnly announced our betrothal and people
cheered. My little brother Petar shrieked with joy, as though the
marriage was the New Year's fireworks. Actually, he was very hot
and purple in his face most of the evening. I suspect his humors
are not precisely balanced.

Saturday, 11th April 1293

It's raining again and Galvo has left on a ship south, to Constantinople. When he came to say goodbye, they left us alone
and he kissed me awkwardly, partly on my cheek, partly on my
mouth. I smelled his breath, thick with wine, and felt his acid
saliva wet my lips. My *mama* says the whole bodily business gets
better and I shouldn't worry too much, men usually find other
ways for their amusement and let you be once the babies are
born. I can't wait to have a baby. At Saint Clares I took care
of Nazareth, a little boy, for a couple of years. One morning we
found him at our doorstep. I wonder how he's doing now without
me, he must miss me. Petar was vicious to me today and tore
my new veil on purpose. He's a spoilt little brat. I am happy to
be away soon. Well, not so soon. We have to wait another year
for the yeast banns.

Tuesday, 18ᵗʰ August 1293

The summer heat is killing me. It is thickening all the bodily fluids in all of us. The stone houses are heated like furnaces, be it simple cottages, inns or palaces. It was so much fresher at the convent, with the big herb garden and huge fig trees for the shade, where you inhaled lavender and orange blossoms. Orange and lemon trees were a recent acquisition – Arab merchants brought the first plants to Dubrovnik only a decade ago, and our prioress immediately planted them. She liked the fruits and adored the months of sweet perfumes the tiny white blossoms sent in the air. Here, in the city, the smells are sometimes heavy with stale fish and feces, although in the major parts of the city the sewage is set underground, under the big stones of the streets and alleys. Even the daily flushing of the streets with fresh water doesn't help much. I don't want to think of the heat and the vapors in some Italian cities, where people empty their chamber pots and garbage into the open canals in the middle of the streets. It must kill people to inhale the stench. I envy the boys, who can go swimming in the sea, it is unfortunately inappropriate for the girls to go bathing. I try to wash in my chamber, and here and then I slip away in the night to have a proper bath in the cool waters of the bay. Passing the night watchers invisibly is not always easy. Well, Petar came home from swimming with a fever last night, he's in bed. At least he doesn't run about doing mischief.

Thursday, 10ᵗʰ September 1293

It's been three weeks since Petar has been tied to his bed. I feel so guilty about this, as at first I was almost glad he was ill and still. We fetched all the doctors we could think of in Dubrovnik and in the nearby towns. The first, a Dominican monk, was purging the boy so that he lost all the vital juices from his body and was shivering with dehydration. Then I fetched my former prioress, sister Angelica from St. Claires. She ordered bleeding, and my brother was again nearly lost after several sessions and full cups of blood. At last, my father, despite all prejudice, went to the Jewess, a surgica named Fava, who came suddenly from Provence to Ragusa and who shortly became very famous for her cures. She made some rude jokes about the four humors' medicine of Avicenna, practiced among Christian doctors, and first bathed Petar in tepid water with lavender and chamomile oils. She calmed him down with herbal infusions, so that he was asleep for nearly two days. Then she ordered constant care, liquid foods and lots of hot drinks. He was to be fed every two hours with as much broth, ale, soup or similar as he could swallow. It was a good cure and he got better in a week. Nevertheless, it

is obvious that Petar's health will remain very frail and irritable
also in the future. He's of a weak constitution. I wonder how he
will complete his education and do some travels at sea so vital for
the family business later. Galvo has been very kind; he came to
see him and played board games with him, while he was getting
better. He's a good man, my Galvo.

Sunday, 20th December 1293

The yeast banns were read today at the Cathedral after the Sunday mass. This time next week, I'll be Galvo's wife. We had
lunch at his house, discussing the wedding arrangements. We
were all very merry, our fathers from the good red wine produced
by the Kabužići at Pelješac, the rest of us awaiting the big event,
which will take place at Saint Stephen's next Sunday. My wedding dress is superb – pale blue silk with white lace and pearls, a
veil and a little silver crown to fasten my hairline. I am worried
about how we will pin it to my always disobedient and thick hair.

Wednesday, 30th December 1293

I wish I were dead. *Jugo*, the south wind with rain and black
clouds above the harbor is nothing compared to my lost illusions
about marriage and about Galvo. All my studies and readings
couldn't prepare me for the wedding night. I'm still feeling the
pains today. Inside and outside; my soul is bruised and sad, my
stomach aches. Maybe I will die at childbirth, many do, and I will
be relieved of my husband. I try to keep peace with his family.
They're all very kind to me, particularly his mother. I try to
swallow the tears in public. They say it brings bad luck to all if
the young bride weeps in her new home. Oh, sweet death, bring
me to Heaven soon!

Monday, 14th March 1295

Nearly two years have gone by, and in spite of Galvo's too frequent attentions during our nights together, we remain childless.
No conception takes place, while his brother has had a son and a
daughter, so the popular reasoning has it that my blood is spoilt
and I am to blame. Well, today he embarks on the Delfina and
undertakes a long trip, with a three-month stay in Venice. After
the death of their father, the head of the Kabužići family, the
brothers Džore and Galvo decided to invest into the shipyard at
Lopud. They sold all land at Pelješac and with the capital, they
built their first *karakas*, which soon proved superior to the Italian
ships. The Kabužići implemented several technical innovations of
the Ottoman ship builders. Galvo will be selling and promoting
their *karakas* with the world trading elite in Venice. Through our

Rector, he even obtained an invitation to the Doge's palace and the possibility to present the shipyard to the Venetian court. Despite all success, however, there is a dark shadow on the Kabužići family. Namely, Džore is dead. He drowned a couple of months ago on a fun boat tour with the boys, so Galvo was left with a new business and guardianship of his brother's widow and her children. I still can't love him, but I try to support him and we've come to a sort of compromise. Still, I am glad to be alone for a while.

Monday, 28th March 1295

As Galvo instructed me, I went to check on the shipyard at Lopud today. It was horrible. The men were not working, just sitting around complaining they were so hungry. Indeed, they looked like skeletons, lifeless and drained of all juices. Some were sick, lying in their shacks, come down with dysentery. I was appalled at the living conditions of our workers. I knew they were more or less slaves, yet the filth and terrible smell of decay in the shacks, the foul food and the lack of the basic hygiene shocked me. The workers, who should be healthy and weathered, were dirty and pale, with bones protruding from every joint of their sorry bodies. They had no latrines and relieved themselves in the corners of the shacks where they lived, ate and slept. Small wonder they were still alive. I was angry with Galvo, who left me with no authority and a huge burden. Very casually, he asked me to go and check on the works here and then while he was away, yet left me no money or power of attorney to withdraw it, and I had only limited means of my own, basically only for the household and my personal needs. I expected the yard would be operating, that he had posted competent people in charge who know what to do, but I found human debris in chaos. I was informed by the head carpenter, a Greek named Kosta, that the builders have to finance their own living out of their pays. Only he was given a monthly amount to buy food for the slaves. However, Kabužić didn't leave him the last pay, so that he's now nearly two months behind. I didn't ask him how much he might be putting aside for himself, but he looked as starved as the rest, so I left my suspicions unsaid. He also told me that in the last month many good hands, carpenters and smiths, builders and rope makers, have left and work now for other shipbuilders at Šipun or Cavtat. The slaves, though, have no choice. Many contracts are delayed, also for the lack of building materials. The three-mast *karaka* for the Menčetić traders will not be ready in time. On the dry dock, a few ship carcasses were left lying on one side, with the empty hulks waiting for ballast to be put in and scaffolds to be raised around them. I promised help, but I did not know what to do there and then on the spot.

Tuesday, 29th March 1295

Just after eight this morning I went to see Marina Menčetić, with
whom I spent a lot of time back at St. Clares, and told her
openly about our troubles at Lopud. She didn't seem surprised,
saying that lately Galvo has been hesitating between trading and
shipbuilding, and couldn't focus on one or the other properly.
We discussed the situation, and I told her of my limited finances.
As all former Clares, we cherished order and discipline, and she
suggested I work step by step: first, bring the workers in the yard
food and clothes, second, order them to clean and whitewash the
shacks as well as organize a quarantine for those ill with dysentery,
at last, make them take an inventory of the building materials –
what they have and what they need. Then, I am to come back
to her and Stevo. They will try to find a solution with the City
Council for me to withdraw some money in Galvo's name. When
I asked her about the delayed pay to Kosta, she turned livid: "No
pay until they've fulfilled all your demands. You must also check
with your exchequer if the Greek is telling the truth. Who's in
charge anyway? Has Galvo appointed anybody to pay the bills
and purchase supplies?" I had to admit I didn't know. She just
shook her head in disbelief. What would I do without Marina?
I've never been in such a mess. The truth is, Galvo trusts nobody
and I suspect he hasn't left anybody in charge.

Wednesday, 30th March 1295

I have occupied a room in a nearby village inn (actually, the
owners will sleep with the sheep for the time), as I intend to stay
here at Lopud until the situation is solved. I brought a Serbian
mercenary with me for protection, and a cook, and my chamber
maid, who is a very authoritative and practical woman. I checked
Galvo's notes and realized that all the workers we have been left
with at present are slaves – including the Greek carpenter Kosta.
He was brought from St. Clares while still a boy and has been
a faithful hand to the Kabužići ever since, be it at Pelješac, in
agriculture, or at Lopud, as a trained carpenter. He was getting
some salary which he was probably saving to buy his freedom.
As he seemed more intelligent and the others listened to him, I
directed orders and demands to him. I also presumed that he was
literate, as our holy order would see to it that all children read
and write by the apprenticeship age. He was a dark, cynical man
around thirty, of a tall and wiry body, with weathered skin and
a huge Greek nose. He obeyed, yet with restraint. I sensed that
he couldn't take commands from a woman. In particular, my
hygienic measures seemed unnecessary to him. He was mumbling
excuses and objections, and I went red with anger: "Kosta, do as
I say and do it quickly. Or, you will be personally responsible for

the material loss of all slaves who will die as a result of this filth here. Clean the shit or I'll have you hung!" By the end of the day, the quarantine was set up and latrines were dug far away from the shacks. It was hard work. At dusk they all went to the shore and washed properly with soap, for which I sacrificed some of my own lavender bars. With clean clothes they returned to the building camp, to the huge table under the olive trees. To reward their efforts, my *Ragusan* cook made them a thick lamb stew. They also had some bread and watered wine. When they had eaten, I brought a plate of dried figs and made them a speech. "It is very important that you restore your life forces as soon as possible and start working on the ships. With every day that you go hungry, our business goes hungry and our clients more unhappy with delays. I will feed you. But you must obey me. I am your mistress. You must keep yourself clean – pissing and shitting only in the latrines, and taking daily baths in the sea before you come to the table. I expect you to meet all the deadlines." The full bellied men cheered me with loud cries and kissed my robe, promising their lives for another lamb stew. Kosta was quiet, just staring at me with an intriguing smile. I must find out what makes him tick, he's the clue to the shipyard business.

Friday 1st April, 1295

Yesterday, the men cleaned, whitewashed and repaired the shacks. I ordered them to cut sage and wild rosemary bushes from the nearby hills and put them on the floor, so that good air would fill their lungs at nights. With nutritious food also the sick from the quarantine got better, and it was decided that they can join the rest in a few days. At dinner, the men finally had some color in their cheeks, and the fish stew with chickpeas found praise as a top delicacy. They're good workers, when they are motivated. I suspect Kosta turned them in my favor. I was relieved that the Serbian knights who were training the new crew had gotten some advance payment from Galvo and took the whole lot of hungry Pelješac peasants to the hinterland, where in six months they were to master the basic fighting skills. It was one worry less on my agenda. Still, I need to talk to Kosta about the inventory and orders for the new material. They must get back to construction work as soon as possible. When I get back to town, I will have to sell some of my jewels. I was thinking of the necklace and hair crown from my wedding ensemble, or, I could sell the whole ensemble, it was just gathering dust in the trunk anyway.

Sunday, 3rd April, 1295

Today around noon, the Greek, Kosta, presented me two neatly composed lists. I knew he could write. I scanned them through and decided I must know more, so I asked him to lead me around the shipyard and explain the lists in more details. I also wanted to make sample checks, as I couldn't get into trouble with the City Council, withdrawing Galvo's money only to find out a slave carpenter had cheated on me. He smiled into his black beard and asked me to follow him. First we went to the hulls on the shore.

"We use the skeleton-first technique, and then caravel planking of the sides. First we have to find a thirty meter long oak trunk for the keel, which we fix into place with two larch trees – they are more flexible. The major components must be grown in one piece, so that the ship can withstand difficult weather conditions. Without the larch trunks, the tough and rigid oak could break apart in the critical tensions caused by the winds or the waves. Then the hulk on the sides is formed, and with it the height of the ship is defined. It is the best of Croatian oak. Huge oxen drag the heavily loaded carts all the way from Slavonija for days. We make our own planks, and only oak is good enough for the planks; up at the sawmill on the river Dubrovačka. We will miss the carpenters who left us."

"We will get them back. I'll get the money from Dubrovnik. By the way, who was paying the workers? Our exchequer?"

"No, it was Galvo himself."

"So I will do it when I get back from Dubrovnik with the money. Put down the sums and names of all we have to pay. "

"You? Sorry, Madam, but women... you know, women don't usually handle money."

"They don't? If you won't take the money from me, there are others who will. I bet they will."

Kosta threw me a side glance – there was respect, astonishment and something else in his black pupils. My lack of experience only made me as blind as a bat.

"It is unusual on the building sites and in the shipyard... "

"Kosta, stop fussing. Who is in charge of the technical side? Who tells workers what to do next?"

"Mainly I do since Master Džore has left us. I have completed two apprenticeships under the wing of the Kabužići – first with Mile, the carpenter in Dubrovnik, then Džore sent me to Constantinople, and I served under an Ottoman shipbuilder for a couple of years. With this knowledge... "

"You're still a slave. Why didn't you flee?"

"You don't escape an Ottoman business partner of the Kabužići. I'd be killed before I'd even think of it. I am saving up to buy my freedom."

"Are you cheating on the workers' food to get ahead?"

"Madame Nevena, why would I do that? They're the only family and friends I have. Besides, Galvo only gives me my own pay and some *dinars* for the food. I don't have access to any other money."

His voice was trembling with offence. I knew I had provoked the man, but I needed to test his limits and loyalties.

"Tell me more about the ships. Where do you get the sails from?"

"We get the linen from the mouth of the Neretva river – the peasants there wave the tissue particularly strong, and wax it on both sides, so it is water resistant and tougher. Then, there is a local artist here who paints the coats of arms and does the wood statues and the furnishing of the cabins."

"Why are these rocks scattered around the building site?"

"They are for the ballast. Once the hulk is built, the masts fastened in the main keel trunk, and the lower story above the keel carvel built, we lift the skeleton on pontoons and fill the lower platform with heavy rocks. We fill the empty spaces between the rocks with gravel, which, when it gets wet, stabilizes the ship even more. Without the ballast, the ship would drop to one side and go under."

I was explained so many technical things I can't recall all of them. Obviously, the Greek knows his business. I checked on his numbers here and there, they were all accurate, so I concluded the inspection. The sun was burning high in the sky, and I was getting tired and thirsty. One last question I couldn't resist.

"Will you still work for us when you're a free man?"

"Yes, madam, I will."

"Why?"

"As I said, this is the only family I've ever had. It's better to be a dog of the Kabužići than a jobless wanderer. There'd be only one option left, should I lose my post here."

"Which is?"

"To become a pirate and kidnap or murder lovely ladies like you, madam."

"Mind your tongue, slave Kosta, I'm warning you."

I went back to my chamber at the inn to digest all this information. I was angry, yet his boldness excited my fantasy. I said to myself that this Greek dog would eat out of my hand before the end of the week. I'll make a lapping puppy of him.

Monday, April 11th 1295

I came back to the shipyard at Lopud with my purse full and my self-confidence boosted. I had sold my bridal attire and got a good price for it. One of the Pozzo's daughters was getting married, and the ship which should bring her wedding dress to Ragusa was lost at sea on her way from Venice. In haste, they paid 120 *dukats* for the blue silk and the white pearls. The supply to the shipyard is flowing again. Marina and Stevo have convinced the City Council to issue a court exemption and restricted power of attorney for me, so I could pay Galvo's due bills for materials and place several new orders from the Greek's list. I sent a fast courier to buy the pitch from the Macedonian pines, which was very expensive, but needed urgently to make the wood waterproof. As expected, the site was busy, there were some new faces, and, as I had left my cook with provisions there for the whole week, their cheeks were rosy and healthy. Following my orders, workers took a water break every hour and had two good meals every day without counting the early morning bread and wine. I inspected the shacks and the latrines, all were clean. So I stayed at the quarantine house, which was next to the coast, empty now and refurnished more comfortably for this purpose. After the first evening meal I announced payday and summoned everyone to get their *dinars* from my purse. They cheered me, and some had tears in their eyes as they took their heavy steps to their beds, tired and satisfied.

It was late in the evening, one of those chilly spring nights, when the air is closer to the winter colds than summer heats. The moon was bright and large on the horizon, silvering the still, dark surface of the sea. I sat on a cliff alone, wrapped in a woolen blanket, deep in thought, wondering how I could persuade Galvo to let me be more involved in his business. Since I left the convent, where I had a number of sensible tasks, I've been bored most of the days. After the first excitement of marriage was over and I could sustain my marital duties with less strain, most of my days have all been the same. All I've been supposed to do is manage the household expenses, plan the meals, look pretty and get pregnant eventually. The latter was not to be – I've gained some weight and my appearance was further from the image of grace every day.

I heard a cracking sound in the bushes behind me and drew my short knife from my stocking, yet it was only the Greek. He had a tiny bottle of *travarica* with him and two little stone cups.

"Madam, can I offer you a sip?"

"I didn't know you're allowed to brew alcohol here."

"The ballast stone suppliers brought it, in gratitude as you paid the bill. May I?"

"Yes, go ahead. It's been a long day."

I accepted the brandy and it warmed me inside. I felt even better after the second cup, so I became bolder.

"Tell me your life story, Greek Kosta. Was your mother a slave?"

"Well, it is not a nice story, madam. No, my mother was a *Ragusan* matron like you."

"So your father was a Greek slave, or?"

"He was only half Greek, and he was a trader. He was made a slave before my birth."

"How could he have been made a slave?"

"He was made a slave by the *Ragusan* City Council for the bad debts he had accumulated with his trading company."

"Was he a merchant? What was his name?"

"Another condition in their verdict at the time was that any of the possible descendants of his are not allowed to use his name, not even mention it aloud."

"But you were raised by the Sisters Clares, weren't you?"

"Yes, my mother took refuge at the cloister when she was pregnant. She had me there."

"Now, tell me everything from the beginning. I want to know. Don't worry, I am a former Clare, so your story is a safe secret with me."

"Well, you have my sorrowful fate in your hands anyway, madam. So, hear my story. My father was born in Constantinople. He was the son of one of the first *Ragusan* consuls there. Soon, he demonstrated a talent for being very persuasive, so his father had him trained as a merchant. He started trading with spices. He was dealing with the Arabs a lot, took on their ways of trading, and the business was growing. It all went well, or so it seemed. Then he transferred his operation to Ragusa, where his father found him a wife, my mother, and soon they got married. But what she and her family couldn't have known was that all was on loan – by the age of thirty my father had copious loans with the Templars (and they used force to get to their money), with the Papal Bank and with practically all of his suppliers. Yet, he registered his company with the *Ragusan* City Council and deposited the obligatory sum with the notary. He was hoping to repay the debts with the help of his new, more profitable business here. But the company and its profits showed a snail-pace growth. Many established *Ragusan* traders didn't care to work with a newcomer. After a couple of years, the creditors tracked my father down and started to prosecute him. First they took in the deposit from the Council. Then every ship brought more creditors, and my father sold practically all his possessions. My mother's dowry was also eaten up by debts, so they lived in her family *palazzo* for some months. Then, the City Council struck again – there were more debts reclaimed, also some trading taxes to be paid and my father could not come up with the sums they demanded. He wanted to escape from Ragusa, but the night watch caught him and brought him to the Rector's dungeon, where he should await trial. The mildest possible sentence would be loss of citizenship and expulsion. My mother tried to save him, hired a lawyer, who would prove that my father was being mobbed by the *Ragusan* trading clique and similar, yet, he hung himself before the day of the trial. He was sentenced

posthumously – he, his wife and his child, should there be one,
are to be enslaved and sold at the slave market; the sum should
repay the taxes. My father's name was never to be mentioned
aloud in the history of the *Ragusan* Republic again."

"How do you know all this?"

"My mother left a letter with the prioress. She gave it to me
when I was full of age – ten years ago. When I concluded my
first apprenticeship, I asked the Council to state a sum for my
freedom – it is 300 *dukats*. They told me it should be more, but
that the good prioress asked them to show mercy. They're giving
me a chance; at the price of 300 *dukats*. Also, I'm forbidden to
register a company with the *Ragusan* authorities ever. If I pay
for my freedom, I can find a new family name, but am not to use
my father's. He'd be the shame of Ragusa forever."

"What a start in life! This is unfair. How are you to undo
your parents' faults?"

"I know, but what can I do? Escape? I would be running
for the rest of my life. I decided I would work and learn, buy
off my freedom, then find a wife and start a family. Džore had
been very good to me – he made both apprenticeships possible
and promised me the job of the master ship builder when I am a
free man."

"What about Galvo? Has he treated you well?"

"Yes, he needs me even more than Džore. He hasn't got the
faintest technical knowledge, so I think the job will be mine.
Galvo is very capable in the commercial arrangements and promotion – we have so many orders, we cannot follow with works."

"Could I have known your mother? There were only eighty
seven sisters when I left the convent."

"I don't think so. My mother died when I was seven years
old. She was a *patrician*, yet they were not very rich. But she
was proud, and when she got a hint of her fate – to be a slave
– she collected her personal valuables and with a trunk full of
jewelry, silver coins and silk attires came to ask for refuge at
the Convent of Saint Clares. You know that thirty years ago
the order was still very poor, the school was just beginning, and
only few *patricians* sent their daughters to the convent for the
basic education. So the prioress took my mother in and made
good value of her gift – she bought the lands around the cloisters
and started the herb gardens. The lavender field brought income
and the school picked up. My mother taught me Greek, and the
sisters taught me reading and calculation. They loved me like I
was theirs. From an early age, I was able to repair many things.
I've always had a gift for technical things. When I was twelve, I
started to work."

"And your mother's family?"

"They renounced both of us in order to protect their fortune.
They soon sold everything and went to *Jadra Nova*. I've never

seen any of them."

"Your mother, why did she die?"

"She got that illness, a light fever. It was winter, and *jugo* was bringing dark clouds and heavy rains for weeks in a row. After a while, she got out of her sickbed, but she never smiled again. A deep sadness overcame her and her moods got blacker every day. The prioress spoke to her, gave her new chores and tried to find a way not to let her wander the corridors alone. One night, she simply wandered off to the cliffs and threw herself into the waves."

"It had to be tough for you."

"Yes, I was crying for days, and the sisters nursed me like a baby. They brought me a little puppy, Resko, he watched the convent gate for years after I left."

"I remember Resko. He was half blind when I came to the school. The sisters had pity on him and fed him until his last breath. I used to stroke him..."

"His wet kisses certainly cheered up my nights after my mother was gone. For years he slept with me. I had a good life with the Sisters Clares. Instead of one mother I had many, they were so good to me."

"Couldn't you become a priest?"

"Slaves are not allowed to enter priesthood. Many don't believe in Jesus, you know."

"Do you believe in God Jesus?"

"I do, madam. The sisters taught me to love our Lord."

"Call me Nevena, Kosta."

I don't know why I stroked his hair and softly ran my palm down his cheek. My eyes itched with tears held back. I'd never heard a story like that. Poor little boy without a father! It is a sorry start in life without a name and a citizenship. And he lost his only family – his mother. He turned to me and hugged me tightly. He was clearly moved. Then he stood up:

"I don't speak of my past every day. Sorry to have bothered you, Nevena. Good night."

"It's all right. I asked you about your past. Good night, Kosta."

Kosta walked away towards the shacks, where the men were already snoring. He left the cups and the brandy behind. The moon was now high in the sky, dominating millions of stars twinkling from the firmament. I couldn't go to sleep and poured myself another drink. I was wondering what kind of society treated its citizens so badly for loss of money. My faith into the fairness of the republic was severely undermined.

Wednesday 20th April 1295

I am doomed. I have to leave Lopud soon. The works go on well, so that the shipyard managed to meet some deadlines and it seems that the Menčetići *karaka* will be finished with only two weeks' delay. We've had the sails delivered today. Before fastening, they must be painted with coats of arms. Kosta has been coming to speak to me every night since last week. At first, I pretended I wanted the reports on the works, how the building progresses, yet soon I realized my too tender feelings for him. Tonight, when I went into my cottage, he followed me.

"Nevena, this tension between us and all the unsaid words – we must find a way to be together. We can't leave it like this."

"There is no way, Kosta. I am the wife of your boss."

"I can find another boss and anyway, my owner is the Republic of Ragusa. I love you."

I stopped breathing. I didn't know what to say. Galvo sometimes says he loves me, but I'm too busy to listen to him. Now, this man came up, enslaved, yet more liberal and noble in his thinking than most of the merchants in Ragusa, who have lost their freedom to the rat race at a young age – who will have more, who will be richer and who more powerful sooner. He put his arms around my waist and drew me closer. I felt his lips on my lips and was surprised by his sweet breath. I let go, and for the first time in my life I knew why the beautiful Helen left everything to follow her Paris to Troy. I'd do the same. He softly undressed me and quickly removed his tunic and breeches. His chest was hairy and dark, for a moment I thought of the image of the devil. Then any thought left my head, and I was swallowed by the swirl of passion. His soft kisses were everywhere on my body – on my breasts, belly, lower. I followed his example, and with sighs and moans we came to live our love. He held me in his arms until dawn and promised to return tonight. I'm doomed, for I can't leave him. I'll stay here for a couple more days. Maybe, with time, the passion will dry up like a well in the sun.

Friday 13th May 1295

I am back in Ragusa among the cold walls of my personal prison – the Kabužići palace. I have saved our shipyard and ruined my life. I doomed my soul, which will burn in Hell forever. For, there's not a flower in the garden which would not bring to my mind the sweet reminiscences of my forbidden love. I float about on the soft clouds of daydreams. They're like feather cushions. Our kisses in May were even sweeter than those in April, our nights burning with more lust than the sun shining at noon. I can't look my sister-in-law in the eyes. I have the feeling that every servant can read my dirty thoughts. I confided to Marina, and this is the last time I am writing in my diary. Before Galvo has returned, I must get rid of my writing. This notebook could mean death by hanging for me and Kosta, for adultery is one of the most serious criminal acts. I should throw the diary away, but I can't do this – it would mean throwing away my love, the most precious moments of my life. Finally, I reached a decision. I will entrust the diary to Marina Menčetić. She's proven a true friend. After my death, she can bring it to the Saint Clares, for our children to know how we lived and loved in Ragusa in the year of the Lord 1295. Goodbye my diary. Goodbye my love.

* * *

Galvo woke up with a moan. The *travarica* stupefied his mind for an hour or two, and he slipped into irritable dreams, yet afterwards he knew that his dry mouth and heavy head would demand their toll. Maybe he would be a bit more at ease if he knew that Marina Menčetić, after having read Nevena's highly compromising diary, threw all three volumes into the deepest sea. Even the sisters, the Clares, could be corrupt and dishonest sometimes, and the young Kabužić didn't deserve a blemish on the honor of the Kabužići family. That was the friend Marina had been to Nevena. That was the kind of wife she had been to Stevo. Her decisions were hard, yet always right.

* * *

Miho was happy. Outside of the office the day was clear and the air smelled of rosemary and thyme. The country was drowsing in the sun after the winter chills and the big fig buds were humid, shining with the warm spring rains. He had little time to prepare for his first voyage, so he started right away. He put together the documents and made written notes of his assignment with great care. His small trunk was already taken to the ship, and he only had time to say goodbye to his family and Miljutina. He found his fiancée reading a huge Latin book. It looked like a healing handbook with many illustrations of the herbs. She barely looked at him, and he could perceive a secret joy in her eyes at their parting. She had turned against his unfortunate attempt to kiss her, he knew that. Maybe he should buy her a book instead of a nice kirtle. She's that kind of girl, always reading. When the Lasta set sail the next morning, he couldn't see her among the crowds waving goodbye at the harbor.

The journey along the coast toward Spalato was uneventful, with a steady southeast wind moving them along their course. The Lasta was one of the first *karakas* built in the Kabužići shipyard at Lopud. She was 75 feet long and could take nearly 200 passengers and crew aboard, as well as 200 tons of cargo. She was one of the first three-mast ships with a high square stern and the

rudder placed at the back. The stern was nearly ten feet above
the waterline, and the rudder had to be operated from the middle deck, so that the helmsmen shouted to the steering crew like
seagulls night and day. The crow's nest at the top of the middle
mast was the highest end of the ship. Should the watch boy fall
down, it would be to his sure death, as the waterline was 80 feet
below. The guns, which were more for fright than actual shot
precision, were three at each side of the ship's belly. There were
four proudly inflated sails with imposing coats of arms painted on
them, showing off like courting peacocks on the horizons of the
harbors where the ship was eagerly expected by the merchants.
The triangular front sail bore the Menčetići family coat of arms,
the big, lower, square one on the middle mast displayed the *Ragusan* Republic coat of arms, and the smaller middle one, just under
the crow's nest, had the proud Serenissima lion, the symbol for
Venetian suzerainty, painted in gold. The sailors, especially the
Slavic ones, joked that the watch boy in the crow's nest above it
was a lucky man, as he could piss and shit on Serenissima without
any consequences. In the Adriatic, the winds were unpredictable.
When the weather was really tough, and the watch boy, scared
and trembling, had to tie himself to the mast with ropes, so that
he wouldn't fall, not on few occasions he came down hours after the storm with wet breeches, the Serenissima sail soiled as
collateral damage. The sail on the back mast, at the stern, was
reserved for the saint of the city of Ragusa, to St. Blaise. He
would protect the *Ragusans* and the cargo in rough weather and
tough battles, were it at home or at sea.

On the steady winds, the *Lasta* was doing over eight knots easily, and Miho was admiring
her speed, knowing nevertheless how clumsy the Lasta was to
maneuver in spite of her name meaning swallow, the bird known
for its swiftness. She was a wonderful sea lady, a floating fortress,
like Marina Menčetić, her owner, a brilliant business woman with
a vast income and an incredible network, yet rigid in her old ways
beyond words. It was uncommon to own ships in the whole, as
this involved too much risk for a single merchant. For some time
now, the *Ragusan* merchants had shared not only the cargo risks,
but also the ownership of the vessels, in order to disperse the
losses and share the profits. Loss of ships and cargo was frequent
– either the pirates or the rough winds got them. But no, the
Lasta was fully owned by Marina as in the old times. She had to
have everything under control. What was his place in her family
hierarchy as her future son in law, he wondered.

On the steady winds, Makarska and Omiš passed by without
any pirates in sight. There were only fishermen with their *ladas*,
setting up and pulling nets. At Jadra Nova, he had taken the
land trip on horseback in vain, as the Knights Hospitallers, who
took over the Vrana Monastery and some of the finances from the
Templars, didn't want to cash the Pittis document in advance.

As instructed by Galvo, he continued to Venice, arriving in the middle of March and reporting to Seniore Sorini on time. The deal was arranged, and Miho spent many a merry night in the back alleys of the Serenissima drinking and whoring. He met a Spanish medical student, who upon the sudden death of his beloved, decided to join the Crusaders. Pablo sold him a huge and very precious book on medical science, The Qanun's materia medica by Ibn Sina, called Avicenna, an Arabic doctor whose major medical work was translated into Latin by Gerard of Cremona. The Spaniard needed the money quickly to buy a horse and armor and hire a page, so the price was heavily reduced. Miho wasn't sure if this vast manuscript was a good choice of a gift for a fifteen year old *Ragusan* belle, whom only per chance he had caught reading about herbs, yet, he understood it as a better investment of 45 golden *dukats* than dresses and precious textiles. Those were easily obtained in Ragusa as well. Just in case, he bought her a wonderful pearl necklace, earrings and a golden ring with a huge pearl in the middle.

On the 2nd of April, he stood at the docks under the watch tower of the Serenissima where the soldiers were supervising the traffic with austerity and strictness. A leaving ship was heaven for pickpockets and criminals. Also Venetian slaves would give anything to get aboard a *Ragusan* ship, as they were free personas as soon as they did so. So it was written in the seventh book of the new *Ragusan* Maritime Law. No wonder slaves all around the Mediterranean were crowding their vessels like bees honeysuckle. It was never a problem for *Ragusans* to get the ship hands for loading, even for free, at any port in the world, be it in Venice or in Constantinople. Miho watched as the Lasta was being loaded with cargo.

"Seniore Kabo, please, here is the bill of lading. You can supervise the loading from the shore. Your uncle, Seniore Kabo, is our dear friend and business partner. Please, take the bill."

The Venetian official was nice and slimy. It would be at least his several weeks' pay that would come just from the taxes of the riches being carried aboard the Lasta.

The facades of the beautiful *palazzos* were glimmering in a cold, sunny morning. The canals, on which one of the richest cities in the world was built, were packed with boats, and the streets and bridges as well were flaring up with activity and loaded with gay laughter. Venetians dressed in rich colors and they liked to show off their wealth, not hesitating to put on their best jewelry just to go to the fish market. Women were protected by half naked black bodyguards, either their eunuchs or slaves. The huge men looked like murder should anybody approach their *padrona*. Children were running between them all dirty and clothed in rugs of various races and births, so that you couldn't tell who was rich and who was poor – they just played and rallied the narrow streets together.

"Carico a bordo! Tempo, tempo!" Cargo aboard, quickly, quickly, Miho's foreman shouted with a list and a pen in his hand.

"Carry in the grain!" Miho counted one thousand and fourteen *staria* of first rate Sicilian grain, as the bearers dragged their feet into the middle section of the *karaka*.

"Next go the spices!" There were 12 pounds of cloves and 7 sacks of dried cinnamon sticks, to be followed by the most precious 4 sacks of dried pepper seeds. One brick of saffron, bought from the fabulously rich Polo family, was not taken to the ship storage room, but deposited ceremoniously in a small wooden chest next to Master Miho's feet. Saffron was very expensive, it would be taken to his cabin and locked up.

"Now the salt, go, go, men, move, quicker, quicker!" 17 sacks of flower of salt from the famous Saline di Sicciole were loaded aboard.

"Lead and metals!" 146 sticks of lead, 189 copper plates and 198 sheets of finest Spanish silver were put in the storage compartment below the cabin Miho shared at night with Captain Marjan.

The bearers were sweating, the more they carried, the more their backs were bending under the weight of the cargo, which would not end before some two hundred tons of various goods had been loaded. There were still 654 sacks of Spanish wool waiting in the nearby warehouse as well as several bundles of fox furs and 19 bales of soft, colorful oriental silk. The worth of several hundred *dukats*, more than a lifetime of earnings for many a merchant, was being carried into the vast belly of the ship.

In the stress of the moment, Miho didn't think of finding a captain of another ship sailing to Ragusa at some later time, to deposit the copy of the Sorini promissory note as insurance. It was getting late and he should go aboard soon, yet his uncle's instructions were clear. He lifted the saffron brick and shouted at the foreman.

"I'll be right back, I have to see Seniore Sorini and say good-bye."

He thought it was a good idea to leave the extra copy of the promissory note in the hands of their reliable business partner, who in the month to come could easily place the postal package in the hands of a trustworthy sea captain to bring it to Ragusa just in case. The letter was sealed with his stamp, and Sorini couldn't know what was in it. Anyway, the man had been more than helpful all those weeks, and the business relationship between the Kabo and Sorini houses went a long way back. This last matter well settled – Sorini took the letter package with a warm smile and put it in his locked drawer immediately with the promise to take care of it first thing the following day – Miho could step aboard his seaway home, to wealth and happiness.

* * *

Miljutina took the fact that the nuptials were planned for the end of June with silent indifference and a reproachful grudge against her family, who was more or less her *baba*. She had her own plans regarding her life, and, should Miho really come back by the set date, she knew for sure she would never end up in his marital bed. She was livid with her *baba*, who had seriously disappointed her. There was no possibility to talk to Nikola, as he was always busy, and when they occasionally bumped into each other in town, he just politely greeted her and passed by. It was painful – she was counting on him, and he nearly ignored her. She was prepared to elope with him, leaving her family, her *baba* and all the Menčetići gold behind. But he wouldn't speak to her, although there was a deep sparkle in his black pupils, and she could often notice a tender flush in his cheeks when their paths crossed. Her only consolation was Nana, who she visited every now and then and discussed medical matters with her. Nana was Jewish, the only daughter of a famous *medicus*, who, without a son, passed the knowledge on to her. She was a living encyclopedia, she knew everything about the human body, and Miljutina found out about many a useful cure for the pains her *baba* had been feeling in her bones for some years. She bravely read the books Nana lent her from Nikola's library, yet she never could meet him at his home. He was always at his offices above the port, working hard to build the new merchant name of Bunić. Sometimes, Nana was telling her anecdotes about him; how he had been as a baby, then as a boy, how he had several tutors at the same time, one of them speaking only Latin to him, another one Greek, so that Nikola was perfectly fluent in both languages at an early age. Nana always travelled with his entourage and was responsible for his physical wellbeing. His father understood that Nikola needed spiritual and physical support. Miljutina listened to Nana's tales and thought about how different her *baba* was with her – hard, cold and unforgiving. There was little tenderness in Miljuta's life.

It was the middle of June, but there was absolutely no sign of the Lasta, despite the fact that several ships, which had left the Venice port at a later date, arrived safely. Galvo Kabužić was half blind with rage. Not only Lasta and its cargo vanished into thin air, there was no sign of the copy of the Sorini's promissory note either. The nuptials were postponed until further notice. In the crisis over the Lasta, they were the last thing to be considered. *Baba* was worried about the ship and cargo, but being a clever business woman, she had taken several precautions and paid an extra insurance deposit with the Papal Bank as well as demanded a new building contract against her advance payment for the cargo from the Kabužići in case of shipwreck. Should Lasta fail to arrive, she would have another ship. Family or no family, business is business, no love lost there. Financially, she could cope with the loss of the Lasta and survive, but she would have to work at least a year to compensate it. For her relative to be, Galvo Kabužić, it was far worse – he could be losing the cargo, had frivolously put the insurance in the hands of the obviously not so clever boy, and besides, with Miho lost, he would lose his main heir, and last but not least, his only liaison to the Menčetići. In finances, Miho proved a fool, and Miljutina's harsh words – "Be it rich or poor, a fool is a fool," – resounded in Marina's ears. With the marriage, she was counting on Miljutina to control their finances. For some time now, the girl had been involved in Marina's every day trading, and showed a sharp intelligence and a quick, practical mind. It came as a surprise to the other merchants and cost them dearly when they underestimated Miljutina's business apprehension. Well, no Miho, no marriage and no control. It would be such a pity.

On a hot July Sunday afternoon, Galvo Kabužić came to see her. He seemed years older than when she had last seen him. His richly embroidered tunic of dark blue silk only partly covered the shirt crumpled with sweat beneath. The tunic was too short, so that it couldn't cover his thighs in hose, which only emphasized the bulk of his belly. Marina, still fit and elegant for her age, observed this with remorse, knowing well how badly the love for food and wine can soften and degenerate ageing men. His balding head glistened with sweat, and the scent coming from him spoke of neglect. He was blinking his sky blue eyes, set deeply into the folds of pale pink flesh, no manly suntan in his cheeks. He had to be spending all his days in his office, or in his dining room, eating and drinking. With a shaky voice, he asked her to support a search party for the Lasta. He knew that another of her ships, the *Tica* would take off for Venice soon, so he thought they could stop for a search on the way. She told him that it was an utterly stupid idea, as they would only bring the fully loaded Tica into the viper's nest – it was clear that the Lasta was either sunk by the weather or the pirates took it. She sent him away, airing and spraying the room with lavender tincture hours after he'd left. The old fool should wait for the ransom message and the copy of the promissory note, there was nothing else he could do at the moment. Besides, wasn't he also the sole beneficiary of the fortune of both the Kabužići brothers should Miho be lost forever?

The summer went by, and Miljutina was beginning to laugh again. The season was high, ships coming in and leaving the port almost every day. She was working with her *baba* at the office and learning the trade fast. She was not only literate in Latin and *Ragusan*, she was very talented in mathematics and accounts, putting down meticulously every amount, be it in *mincas* or in *dukats*. And above all, she loved it. It was the best pastime ever, like an exciting game. She was so proud to be responsible for the book keeping. Her *baba* registered with the authorities that Miljutina was performing trade operations in her father's absence instead of him, which was approved by the Council's notary as an exception with some somber sulkiness. Some *patricians* thought it was improper for women to trade and run a business, as it was a shame for a man to work with his hands. A high born lady should be protected from the dirty world of money and debts, profits, interests and losses. But the Menčetići women knew better and closed some very good deals.

That late August Sunday afternoon, Miljutina was upset and went to speak to Nikola. After the mass and the obligatory Sunday lunch, she walked over to the Bunići *palazzo* and pushed open the door to Nikola's library.

"Good day, my friend. Why don't you speak to me?"

Nikola lifted his eyes from the heavy volume, startled and completely unprepared for the girl's attack.

"Miljutina? But, but, I do...I mean, I do speak to you...It's just..."

Miljutina looked like her *baba* for a moment – cold and serious, although he could see a sparkle in her green eyes and a softness around her lips. In the last two years, she had become a woman, tall, and nicely formed, with high breasts and wider hips. Her rich blond curls were pinned high, and her long neck curve bathed in the soft thin hair which could not be tamed into the bun. Unruly, the hair stuck to her neck damp with sweat. There was a black velvet strip with a huge pearl around her neck. Her silken kirtle was dark green, like on Saint Blaise day two years earlier, when they first spent a few hours alone. Nikola often thought of that afternoon. He would do anything to be able to spend his life with this vivid and stunning *patrician* girl. It was not easy for him. He had to use cunning and the whole network of acquaintances which his family had built around Europe over more than two decades. Miljutina stood proudly before his desk with a veil over her head, so fashionable with *Ragusan* maidens in those days. It slipped slowly to her shoulders and cleared the view of her collar bones and the quick heartbeat in the cavities around them. She was waiting for an answer. She could command ships if she wanted to. He would be her obedient sailor, her helmsman. He smiled with tenderness, almost indulgently. He wasn't prepared for the storm that broke out of the girl's throat.

"Don't you laugh at me, Nikola Bunić, or I will give you a punch on your nose, like the one you once distributed..."

Flushed in her cheeks, she threw a postal package on his desk.
"What is this? You tell me!"

It was unsealed, the strange stamp in the form of the letter K in wax broken. It was what he thought it would be. He unfolded the letter which had only a few lines:

Dear Miljutina!

August 1314

I am sending this letter with the peasants bringing dried fish to Ragusa.
I hope it will find you in good health and at peace with God.
I promised you'd give the man 20 grossi for the delivery. Devil shall take him, if he doesn't deliver the note as he promised.
The Lasta was captured by the pirates at Omiš. I tried to escape, but the pirates fished me out of the waves. They found out who I am and want a ransom from my uncle, an amount so big I don't know what to do. They say several thousand golden dukats. Please help me, ask your baba to support him, should he be in trouble to pay. I will repay you all, I promise, when I am saved.
Please bring this message to my uncle as soon as you get it.
It is a tough life here. I have to work in the fields every day, but they feed me well. They say I must be fit for my fat ransom and that they will improve my soft muscles with outdoor work. They even have a Sarracen medicus, who checks my heartbeat and examines me daily. I feel like a horse. They think I am their golden boy with prospects of golden dukats, and they call me Zlatko – Goldie.
I don't know whether the other passengers made it, I am completely isolated. If they live, the relatives will get a notice like my uncle. I hope this will be soon.
I love you and we will be married as soon as this nightmare is over.

Yours, M.

Nikola put the paper on the table and looked her in the eyes.
"So, have you taken it to the old Kabužić, Miljutina?"
The girl shook her head and collapsed in the chair opposite.
"I don't trust him. Despite all logic, I think he'd do anything to have the boy killed. My *baba* says that he has changed after the loss of the Lasta and has tried to cheat on one of his clients. He's become an old, greedy bastard. Besides, he wouldn't be able to pay a huge ransom out of his own pocket, even if he wanted to. He would have to borrow and I know who from. I have been checking his credentials in this last year thoroughly. His business has never been very profitable, his accounts are insolvent most of the time. He has been covering the fact with vast expansions. This year, his shipbuilding plant in Lopud has doubled in size,

last year the big warehouse in Lokrum and the fishing company
on Lastovo. All the Kabužić money is in his production – stock
of wood, metals, half built ships. He has been taking orders, but
has been financing most of his production with loans. I think the
Lasta expedition was a desperate attempt to get to the cash from
the sales of goods. I don't know how he pulled it off, anyway."

"So what do you think we should do?"

"I don't want to marry Miho, but I don't want to have him
killed either."

"That's why you came to see me?"

"I came to ask your advice, but I can go..."

"No, no, stay. We'll think of something."

"Well, I know he's a little shit and he loves me as much as I
love him, which is not at all. I know he'd been holding a mistress
for a while. They say she's a nice girl, the youngest daughter
of our olive oil supplier from Pelješac. How stupid! This whole
charade is being staged for money, and there is none. But his life
has just begun, my God!"

"There is some money in the Menčetić trunks, believe me,
you're to be very rich."

"Yeah, hell will freeze over before *baba* parts with her gold."

"I see."

"Old Kabužić's intentions were probably to finance another
shipyard with my dowry, only to make more debts. Miho's but
his puppet."

"Would you like to get free from your betrothal vows?"

"By all means, if there's a way..."

"*Baba?*"

"I think I might be able to handle her."

"Good. Let me get some refreshments... Have you ever tried
coffee? It is a fashionable drink at the Ottoman Court. A trader
brought a sack of seeds."

"Anything. I could do with some wine."

She was shaking all over, her lashes holding back tears with
utter restraint, her cheeks hollow with worry and despair. The
letter put a new responsibility upon her. Miho was her childhood friend. They practically grew up together. And this pirate
business was clearly beyond her capacities to deal with, so by
intuition she sought the help of somebody, who could have some
knowledge about the ransom business. She would prefer it if
there was no word from Miho at all. But that could mean she
would have to wait for years to be free again. Her fiancé would
have to be officially declared dead or missing. How easily and
carelessly old greedy fools could spoil the lives of their offspring!
And without ever having asked her what she wanted, what she
expected from her life. All *baba* intended to do was to sell her
for prosperity, and for the first time in her life she would make
a very poor deal. Miljutina, shaking all over her body, choked

on revenge and resentment. Here was the man she loved, not the shitty shipbuilder's nephew with a big mouth and petty character.

"Let me get you both, coffee and wine. Calm down, Miljutina."

When he made a few steps closer to her chair, she stood up in a jerk and took him by the hand. He paused and looked her in the eyes. After nearly two years, they were almost the same height. Suddenly, she moved forward and embraced him, and without thinking, Nikola kissed her on the lips. Virgin or no virgin, Miljutina returned his kiss with an open mouth, their tongues searched deeper, their bodies pressed together in an invisible seal, in a cloud of young passion, subdued for so long because of compromise and prejudice dictated by the high society. They kissed and kissed, it was not to end and not to be. She was destined to become another man's wife, and he was to save that man. She knew he could and she wished he wouldn't. She was in love with Nikola, and hated the other and their marriage prospects. Nikola had been dreaming of her bosom since before it was showing under her tunic. They were drowning in tenderness, sliding to the silken Turkish rug on the floor, and he tore the strings of her kirtle and his velvet jacket from their bodies with haste. They would save Miho later, now it was the moment to break the iron ring of rules and belong to each other. Just this once and then... When Nikola stood up to lock the room, Miljutina threw her tunic to the floor. Her naked marble curves shone in the afternoon sun spying on the lovers viciously through the shutters. Nikola took off his shirt, but held on to the breeches. He couldn't go on, it was irresponsible, and he could go to jail for it. Besides, she was worth to be loved and cherished like a wife, not get laid in a study on a summer afternoon like a slut. But before he could compose his thoughts and get his heated head to switch on the self-control, Miljutina was standing close to him, so that her skin radiated her heat to his chest.

"Nikola, make love to me, now!"

With this whispered cry, she kissed him again with all the passion and skill, as though she had been doing it for ages and not for the first time. Her naked body with small orange shaped breasts was warming his chest, he was losing his mind. She pulled the strings. He trembled when the breeches fell to his knees. Her hand pushed his face down to her breasts, and he kissed and sucked the rose buds of her nipples. She tasted and smelled of lilacs in bloom; he was subdued and couldn't control his sex anymore. It had been in the stars, they had been the star-crossed lovers from the first moment he touched her. He knew it, she felt it. It didn't help to deny their love, avoiding being alone or trying to look the other way. Their hearts were pounding the rhythm, showing them the way to perdition with a drumming parade. Kissing the alabaster skin of her body all over, her hands touching him tenderly, aware of his spear, they sank to the floor together. She spread her legs and stared at his black pupils with wide open green waters of her eyes. With every quick movement, they came closer to ecstasy. How could they have been living without each other for so long? How could they have been treading on their tender love and walking by like strangers for months? Miljutina arched upwards and left out a soft cry. Nikola wanted to withdraw, but her strong legs held him inside her. He came and could feel how his semen was searching for life inside his girl lover. Miljutina was kissing his lips passionately. There was no return. Now it was time for loving. They continued in the fateful embrace and came together again and again, their juices pink with her virginity like the early buds of roses.

"I love you, Miljutina," he whispered at last, exhausted.

"I love you, too, Nikola," she said, and with a throaty laugh she added:

"It will be tough to ignore me after this."

He undid the bun of her light hair with tenderness and sunk his face into the golden locks. She smelled of lavender and her sweat propagated a tinge of dried figs and almonds.

"I've always thought of you. My heart was always with you, my love."

She kissed his hair and held him tightly, never to let him go. They rested in the embrace for a while. Miljutina came to life first.

"Where's Nana? Do you think she could hear us?"

"She's gone out. I don't think she heard us."

"Well, you're lucky to have her. She was my only link to you in the last year."

"Miljutina, it is wrong what we've done. You know that, don't you?"

"Is it? Why?"

"We're not married and you can get with..., you can get..."

"Pregnant. I wish I had, but it is not likely."

"Why?"

"Tomorrow is my monthly time. Today was probably the safest of all days to make love."

"You have developed some knowledge lately..."

"Yes, I have. I hated the surprise and fear when I was bleeding for the first time. So I have read a few medical books since. We could not have conceived a baby, not this time, not just yet."

"There mustn't be another time. Well, not until we get married."

Miljutina smiled to herself and thought there would be many more times in life, as long as they live. She would certainly not marry Miho after this afternoon. They spoke about Miho and came to a conclusion, so when the day was setting, Miljutina put her clothes on and went home. Thirsty like a desert without rain, she drank at each of the fountains in the city, the water only momentarily putting out the heat in her body. At home, her *baba* was waiting at the door for her. Deep creases on her chin displayed anger and were promising there would be the devil to pay. Her voice was low and clear, words sharp as razors.

"Where have you been all day?"

Miljutina looked around, there was nobody in sight. She decided to fight back for her rights. The selling of innocent flesh and souls for golden *dukats* had to be stopped there and then. She returned a defiant look and replied in a low voice:

"I went to Nikola Bunić and slept with him. I seduced him to deflower me and I hope I got pregnant."

Miljutina's face was pure teenage insolence and revolt. Marina Menčetić could not comprehend what her granddaughter was saying. She was just staring at her.

"Either you accept him as you future son in law, or Mihajlo Kabužić is nothing but dead meat."

Baba's face turned pale, almost ashen. She swayed like a cane in the wind and leaned on the doorjamb, shaking all over her body. The old woman with a tiny bun of grey hair, dressed in a black kirtle with shiny golden threads and pearls around the collar, lost her composure. She couldn't comprehend, what was coming. Why is the girl so hurt, so angry? Didn't she understand she would marry one of the young *patrician* heirs and continue the family line in business? What was Miljutina thinking? That she would marry for love? Surely the girl was just provoking her with this Nikola. Marina Menčetić, the scare of *Ragusan* officials and traders, looked like she was losing the ground under her feet. All she had worked for, all her ambitions were swept away by a girlish anger and defiance. Her black eyes shone with a vicious light, her face was like the sky before a summer tempest. After some minutes of complete silence, while even flies and insects stopped buzzing in the air, Marina composed her mind and lifted her chin.

"What do you mean? How can we save Mihajlo? Can Bunić save him?"

"Yes, he can. First, break the betrothal with the Kabužići. Then he is prepared to go to Omiš and bring your shitty would be bridegroom back. Then you can marry him yourself, if you wish."

Marina's understanding almost brought a smile into her stern features. Miljutina's brisk insolence didn't offend her much, she knew the girl's temper too well. It was becoming more interesting, however, how the young Bunić's mind worked. It was his father's contacts in Omiš and Makarska who probably held the Lasta and the boy Miho. With cunning, she could get both, the ship and the Kabužić boy back. And pirate or no pirate, if this was his scheme to gain Miljutina and if he had planned all this from the beginning, he surely was a match for her granddaughter, actually for both of them. Her intuition was telling her that either young Nikola Bunić or his pirate father might indeed have organized the raid well in advance. Did the young pirate really loved Miljutina so much? He was risking everything, though. But how could she blame him? She herself loved her more than she could ever imagine to love anything in life. The girl didn't have to know, but she was slowly changing sides. Her voice still sounded harsh and the reproaches severe.

"I hope this is true, Miljutina. Miho should be saved at all cost. The old Kabužić has become a pig to deal with. And of course, the Lasta, too, must be retrieved. But you shouldn't get in bed with Bunić before you're sure of him. You will end up with a pirate bastard in your womb. Your betrothal is over, anyway, you're no more a virgin, and I wouldn't want to be offering damaged goods. I am not a cheat."

Miljutina's face lit up like a candle in church. She thought it would take longer to persuade *baba* to break off the engagement. She would think her grandmother couldn't care less if she was still a virgin at the nuptial or not, that woman would have planted a pirate bastard to the Doge's bed, if *dukats* only kept rolling on. She sensed a subdued respect in the rough language, respect for whom... Nikola? She smiled broadly and jumped to embrace *baba*, kissing her warmly on both cheeks.

"I am so happy to be damaged. I've never been happier in my whole life and the pains of love are sweeter than honey, *baba*. So, Nikola's father can come and ask you for my hand?"

The proud old woman pushed the girl away.

"I will not be in liaison with pirates! We're a good *Ragusan* house, our roots go back to the first settlers, actually we are descendants of the Trojans, we are..."

"Not you *baba*, you're not getting married. I will be in liaison with Nikola and the pirates. And like it or not, I am already."

For the first time in her life, Marina was speechless. Her face was a mask, but under her coldness, she felt with Miljutina, it was what she could have done at her age. This girl had more guts than half of the men in the city. Her youth and love marched happily with the danger. She embraced the risks of life with enormous hugs. How the caution is thrown to the wind easily when you are fifteen and in love! She didn't know what to do, and just stared at her. Her granddaughter was stamped with the passion of love like a letter sealed with wax. But this one had been stamped with a pirate seal. What could she do now? Good night to all her aspirations... Good night to all her schemes... Was it still possible to protect the Menčetići wealth, name, and reputation? The pirate paid for everything in cash, he could be richer than Kabužić...

When the official ransom message came at last in the first week of September, Nikola was well prepared as to what he had to do. It was brought to the City Council by an itinerant monk, Brother Stevo. He carried a written scroll sealed by *Knez Kačić*, with the names of persons who were in the pirates' hands and would be killed by torture within six months following the date of the letter, should the ransom monies not be paid to his account in the bank in Kotor. The prisoners would be released twenty days after the payment at the Makarska monthly fleece fair. Miljutina copied the message and brought it to Nikola. Without a word to the Council Nikola saddled his mule, took his leave of Miljutina and headed north.

* * *

Miho waited and waited. Not a stalk of wheat moved in the warm breezes of the longer and longer spring days, and his situation remained unchanged during the exhausting field work in the summer months. Why didn't the pirates send their ransom request to Ragusa, what was keeping them? Didn't they want the money as soon as possible? All of a sudden, in September life got much easier for him. Obviously things started moving and Miho wandered what message *Knez* Kačić got from Ragusa to be so well disposed towards him. Less work in the fields, good food and plenty of wine, and the *Knez* even offered him the pleasure of some girls. Miho thanked him and tried to keep his posture with the family where he lived. It looked like his uncle was willing to pay at last. Still, time was dragging on slowly, at a snail's pace. Miho's impatience couldn't be calmed down, he was boiling.

The weather was getting more sinister and the days were shorter. Heavy clouds loaded with cold rains dragged along the coast, and the temperatures were lower as summer eclipsed into autumn. Miho stood on the cliff over the river Cetinja, not far away from the village which housed him. The other prisoners, if there were any, were probably hidden somewhere in the hinterland. He was looking out across the grey sea with foaming waves. He shivered in the wind and thought of these last months away from Ragusa. He hoped Sorini had sent the papers with another ship as they'd agreed. Only later, around the port of Pirano and approaching the soft hills of the Istria peninsula, Miho realized that Sorini, if he was a bastard, could open the sealed package and render the promissory note invalid just by presenting it to the *Ragusan* consul in Venice. It would be a disaster as his uncle needed the cash badly, every one of those *dukats*. The shipyard was a hungry beast – the stock of wood, the builders, the metals and stone weights, and of course, the pitch, which had to be imported, because the local product was not of good quality. Miho hoped dearly that Sorini didn't open the letter, so that his uncle got at least some value back, if the ship with the cargo and his nephew was taken by the pirates.

And taken certainly was the right word. After having left the port of Spalato, they encountered a wild, cold *bura*, not unusual in springtime in those waters. It had started so suddenly that the captain couldn't find a shelter in time. The high waves were banging at the ship from all directions, the horrible noise of thunderbolts made everybody's hair stand up in fear, and the trumpet-sounding wind sent the passengers to the cabins below deck. They felt as though they fell directly to Hell. The captain knew those waters well, and in his last attempt to save the Lasta, he steered the ship toward the mainland, where a narrow strip of sea, one mile from the coast, was calm. The *bura* usually blew over this strip and built up the high waves only on the open sea. For the well loaded *karaka* there was still hope that they would have a rough but safe passage to the south. There was no mooring between Omiš and Makarska. When they came closer to the land, in an instant, five *ladas* surrounded them. The fishermen were calling to the captain to throw down the ropes. They gave the impression as though they were willing to help them out in a difficult nautical situation. Captain Marjan knew better and ordered the middle big sail raised up. They had to escape the seemingly friendly hands as quickly as possible. There was confusion all around, and before the sail was hauled up, several heavy anchor ropes fell into the sea. The men from the *ladas* dived into the waves within seconds to catch them and pull them into the smaller, manageable boats. Miho came aboard and heard his captain shouting in distress:

"You, fools, you've thrown the ropes to the pirates! Up with the sail! Cut the ropes, now!"

Everybody was immobilized, and amidst a roaring tempest, the world stood still for a moment. The captain moved first and took an axe from the tool chest. He ran down the railing and with strong blows started cutting the ropes, which swayed to the waterline. In the chaos, a sailor's hand was in the way and two of his fingers went into the sea with the rope. Blood sprayed the captain and the passengers behind him. The sailor was screaming in agony and pain, the crew trying desperately to lift the ropes and the sail.

"Aim the guns! Fire!"

The first ball missed, they shot far over the *ladas*' positions into the black waves. Only the second shot was aimed better, and an approaching swimmer got spun in a whirl of foams first white, then pink and purple, until his body finally floated to the surface face down. Guns fired again, but missed as the targets evaded the line of danger. The imposing *karaka* could not move into the right position against the attackers quickly enough. The little boats rode the waves like good horsemen on fast Arabian

stallions – with the agility of skilled maneuvers. The pirates
knew their waters better and were allies to the *bura*. With every
minute they were closer to the *karaka*. Despite the captain's
cries more and more ropes were thrown to the sea below. With
a thrashing bang, the first hooks hit the deck and immediately,
there were men climbing aboard like an army of cockroaches in
the middle of apocalyptic confusion and shouts. The soldiers shot
their pistols, but before they could reload, many were stabbed to
death, had their throats cut or their guts spilled all over the deck.
The stench of blood, sweat and secretion was suffocating everyone
but the pirates. They cried support to each other, and laughed
at the scared defenders and passengers. The attacking brutes
obviously took their life as it came – winning or getting killed,
drunk on joy, blood and violence.

The captain lost control, the sailors lost hope and guidance.
Save yourselves who can! The soldiers still fought fiercely, their
destiny was sure death one way or the other. But the main sail
was down and it was men against men, the ship's course was
stopped. She bounced uncontrollably in the waves like a wooden
toy in a pond. As the fight was raging, Miho hid, ducked behind
the sacks and the chests, looking for the first opportunity to jump
into the sea and save his own life. Many attackers were thrown
down from the ropes and into the sea, where the waves trashed
them furiously against the ship sides full of sharp shellfish. The
grey sea was getting purple, foaming with blood. Yet the vicious
men kept climbing aboard, kept coming from all directions, as
though *ladas* procured an inexhaustible flow of fighters with greed
in their eyes and fire in their limbs in the pursuit of the *Ragusan*
riches and gold.

Miho threw up when next to him a pirate, with a sabre cut a
soldier in two and his guts spilled in a bloody and shitty heap at
his feet. He ducked just in time, as the next blow was aimed at his
head. In mortal fear, his stomach turned again and he retched,
leaning too far over the railing. Another wave, and Miho fell into
the cold water ten feet down, into his own vomit. He plunged
deeper below the surface. He was a poor hero, an untrained
fighter, but as a *Ragusan* he spent many days at sea and could
swim well and for a long time. So he dived under the keel, swam
to the other side of the ship, avoided the many pirates and shouts,
and with powerful strokes headed to the shore. He almost fainted
from exhaustion when he dropped onto the pebble beach. He
looked up, focusing slowly his sore eyes. He couldn't understand
at first what was in front of him, approaching. He grasped at
last that a huge *lada* was being hauled to the water and came
directly at him. With his last forces, he plunged back into the
deeper water, swimming with all his strength to escape the new
danger. Some fifty feet from the shore, he felt a thump on his
head and lost track. He was dragged aboard the *lada*.

"Kill him, what are you waiting for, Stipe?"

The commander cried out loudly, but his sailor decided otherwise. When Miho was swimming, he could spot the shine of gold on his hands and wanted to check.

"He's got a golden ring with a huge seal ruby. No, let's take the boy to our *Knez*, he must be fit for a fat ransom. A *Ragusan* sissy fished from the sea, great catch, eh?"

"Good work, my boy. If he moves, thrash him. We need to reach the *karaka* fast, there are more catches waiting."

This was the last time the pirates hurt Mihajlo's body. His hands and ankles were tied up until he was brought to the *Knez*. The leader inspected the ring and recognized that the boy belonged to the famous shipbuilders' family Kabužići. Miho was explained his position as a hostage and was assigned to a family in the village. The head of the family was a friendly peasant, and he was responsible for Miho's wellbeing with his own life.

Spring was warming the country, and work in the fields and with the live stock abounded. Every morning he worked and cultivated the land of the family. He came to know how to plough with a bull, how to tend to the cattle and look after the sheep. He was learning about agriculture from the farmers and enjoyed all this new information as well as closeness to the animals. So far, as a city child, he had stroked a cat here and there, or played with a puppy. They would leave every morning for the hinterland, sometimes even before dawn and they came home in the twilight. At first Miho looked for an opportunity to escape, but he had no money, and his seal ring was temporarily confiscated by the *Knez*, so he had little chance to last the long trip to Ragusa. He worked hard, hoping that he would be spared, if not by a ransom, maybe at least as a slave. He was young, only seventeen, someday an opportunity would smile at him and he would come home in some way or other.

The peasant family was quite prosperous and very friendly. He slept with two older sons in the same room, with one arm chained to the wall during the night. The Roko family had some interesting members. Father Roko was about sixty, yet fit and quick in his motions. He knew everything about wine growing and sheep, he tended to several olive orchards as well as fields of grain and chickpeas large enough to feed a Roman legion. Mother Bruna was the picture of kindness, a true mother with a huge bosom and wide hips, dressed in the obligatory black and always smiling. Her good nature and love, not to speak of splendid cooking, kept everybody happy even the forlorn *Ragusan* prisoner. The most curious of all was the wife of the oldest son, Marin. Her name, Lucia, evoked light and sunshine, yet her skin was blacker than anything Miho had ever seen. She was slender and moved with elegant grace, her *raša* tunic showing more than hiding her stunning figure with high, firm breasts and wiry, muscular thighs.

Miho was very much taken with her features, which despite the dark color of her skin showed the narrow Mediterranean lines with deep black eyes, thin lips and a lovely nose. She was like one of the dolls that he had seen at the Sunday market in Venice, only that she was blacker than night, a dark, mysterious picture of perfection, a black Venus. His resolve to temper his curiosity was mollified; whenever he saw Lucia, he just kept staring at her. When once his eyes wandered too low into the cleft of her tunic, she threw him an angry glance, saying: "Don't even think of it, prisoner boy!" Judging by the age of her children, she had to be past twenty. She had two sons, six and seven years old, both the spitting image of their father Marin, only a shade darker. Miho had to act carefully so as not to provoke Roko's or Marin's anger. He found out very soon that the pirates' society was a very patriarchal one, where women showed ultimate obedience to men. The only exception to the rule seemed to be Bruna, whose good humor brought smile to Roko's face at any time. Together they guided the family life in harmony and love. All the decisions were taken by Roko and all the tasks, which were assigned by him daily to the members of the clan, had to be fulfilled without objection.

Despite the modest house and conditions of the Roko family, Miho was given a proper straw mattress with linen, which was scented with lavender, and two sets of raša clothes, so that he could always be clean. His original clothes were taken away from him. Obviously, there was a pattern in maintaining the prisoners. The Rokos were not doing it for the first time. Although they watched him closely, they shared everything with him; their festivities and sorrows, their food and wine, work and troubles, in a word, they involved Miho in their life. Bruna in particular showed him devoted kindness, which brought tears into his eyes and made him think of his mother, how sick with worry she had to be waiting for the word of her son's life or death. Sometimes Bruna even gave him a treat, a sweet or a fruit and without letting anybody else notice, stroked his hair or blew him a kiss on the cheek. It was a rare occasion that they were alone. There was always a man present around him, for his flight would be blamed on Roko and severely punished by the Knez. After a while, Miho stopped looking for an opportunity to flee and immersed himself into their life with full verve. There were moments when he felt more like a guest or even part of the family than a prisoner. If it were not for the irritating checkups, which left no doubt as to why he was treated so kindly. At first he thought he was being observed by the medicus because of his head injury – his skull hurt for weeks after the blow in the sea and he still felt shaky after long hours in the sun – but the checkups just went on and on. One day it dawned upon him that he was being reared like a swine. He was a source of cash for the Knez, that's why all the attention.

Yet, for all his slavery and hard work, he had praised himself lucky so far. Many died a terrible death on the day of the raid. He could remember well how all the soldiers from Lasta were massacred and thrown into the sea for little Adriatic sharks to feast on the parts of the bodies. The ship was dragged into the mouth of Cetinja river, anchored and fastened with ropes. She was completely hidden from the view of the other ships passing by, her position secured and protected by the high green cliffs left and right of the river. For some weeks he was hoping for a Venetian military patrol to rescue Lasta, yet his hopes vanished quickly. The pirates of *Pagania* were a wild lot and there wasn't a ship that would venture near Omiš or into the mouth of the Cetinja river. The cargo, as far as he could observe, was loaded on mule trains and dispersed in all directions within hours of the capture. Although he heard many times that the pirates also disassembled ships and used the high quality oak planks for their own constructions, Lasta was left intact. Well, the guns and the powder were taken ashore and positioned along the impressive line of pirate guns at the river mouth. Miho was surprised to see how much mercy the violent *Knez* showed to the sailors and lower crew members – he simply let them go. Or, were these simple men bribed accomplices to the crime and were going aboard another ship at some other port, so that again they could throw ropes to the bandits below in a feigned panic? Well, the captain, the helmsman and the navigator were caught alive and brought before the elders of the village. The three of them were obstinate in their revolt. They demanded justice, so the *Knez* thought he would show them justice and had them hung, all the three of them, one from each mast of the proud ship they had been commanding. Their decaying bodies swayed in the wind, and the smell of flesh decomposing in the sun attracted the vultures. For more than a full month, the cries of happy, well fed birds echoed in the fjord, and the memory of the sound still made Miho's mind freeze with terror.

Roko was not only a farmer but also an excellent fisherman. However, Miho was not allowed to join on the sea-faring trips. Often they were after schools of sardines, which were usually chased into the channel by playful dolphins jumping out of the waters and showing the fishing positions to the fishermen. Then all the men from the village would quickly board their swift *ladas*, following the fish train for several days until the boats and nets were full. On those days, Miho was chained to the wall in the chamber of Roko's sons, and Lucia would bring him his meals. He liked to chat with her, though usually it was not really a conversation but a monologue as most of the time she kept silent, only nodding to his words here and there and smiling reluctantly at his jokes. After she was gone, there was a soapy smell of sweat and lavender in the air, which incensed the wildest day dreams, escaping the chains on the wall and exciting the boy beyond reason. He was trying to visualize her breasts, her pubic hair, the color of her belly and the sound of her and Marin's lovemaking. Soon, it was him instead of Marin, and many times he waited until the silence embraced the night, so that he could quietly relieve himself. He would have gone mad with sexual obsessions were it not for the boys, who came to the room at any time of day to play with him and chat about how children play in Ragusa. So Miho told them about his old school, about the street games, gang fights and religious festivals. He was more than happy to be talking to them, and they listened with their eyes wide open, drinking in every word from his lips. The seven year old Donato was very intelligent and technically gifted – he kept bringing to Miho his toys and the wooden gadgets he devised to make his life more interesting and easy. The younger, the six year old Marco was more introverted, and spoke about birds and nature as well as shared his observations about life in the village. Miho was getting useful information and insight into a society which was organized by laws so different from the rest of the civilized world.

One Saturday afternoon in June, when the men were at sea and Miho was alone and bored in the little room, Donato and Marco brought him water, soap and fresh linen. Hours were like days. Miho was tired of the world, chained to inaction. He had found out in the morning that the men went chasing a school of tuna fish, so there was little chance they'd get back sooner than in a week. It was Marco who first spoke:

"Zlatko, you know, Donato and me, we think that our mother likes you too much. She keeps asking questions about you, and Grandfather Roko burst out in anger the other day."

Miho shuddered at the name they used for him, Zlatko, Goldie, which was more or less a code name, so that people could not form any ties with him during his stay or later. He couldn't get used to it and was now mad with the boys. Before he could speak, Donato observed:

"This place stinks to high heaven. It is the chamber pot. You really should do something about it. Maybe we should devise a side opening in the wall, so that you can piss and shit directly outside."

Miho inhaled the thick air, humiliated, and yanked the chains.

"And how do you think, young man, I can do it with these chains on?"

"I know. I'll take it to the dung heap for you. It is not your fault, I was just thinking of how to do something about it. Here, soap and water. I'll leave the door open, so that some fresh air can get through."

"Then come back, Donato, I am too young to be alone with Zlatko."

"Yes, I eat little boys for dinner. Boooah!"

Miho swung the chained arm in Marco's direction, made a horrible face, and the boy shrieked with laughter. Donato took the chamber pot away and Miho started washing awkwardly, with the heavy metal on his right hand. Marco stepped closer, took the cloth, dipped it in water and soaped it. Then he scrubbed Miho's neck, ears, throat and armpits, like his mother cleaned him a few times a week.

"You see, my aunt, Pavlina from the village, she says that *Ragusans* eat babies as a delicacy. I mean the babies who don't have mother or father."

"Nonsense, Marco. Stupid woman! Your aunt doesn't know anything. Ragusa is one of the few cities in the world which has an orphanage, at the cloister of Saint Clares. They look after the children until they can go to a higher school if they're orphans of merchants, or until they can enter apprenticeship with a master carpenter, rope maker or smith or wherever there is a place for them. As the master is not given a fee to train the poor boys, the orphan apprentices have to work for him double time before they can leave and work elsewhere."

"What is an orphan?"

"An orphan is a child without a father or a mother, you ignorant little peasant."

"It is good to be a peasant, better than a soldier or a knight. What about girls?"

"You mean orphan girls?"

"Yes. Where do they put them?"

"Again, it depends on the status of their deceased parents. If a girl is of high birth, she will learn to read and write and be sent to a chaperone until she's betrothed and married. Her dowry is safely protected by one of the senators. In other cases, they put them into the rich households to work in the kitchen and be maids."

"Girls would read and write? Here even boys don't learn to read, only the *Knez* and some of his men can read, and the priest."

Miho was surprised. Indeed, in the two months he spent in this little village without a name, the children never went to school. This really was a backward area. He heard the bells for Sunday mass and he would love to go, but was forbidden. The Roko family never went to mass either, they were obviously still pagans. Donato came back and put the washed pot near his bed. He sat on the bed opposite and watched his young brother washing the prisoner. When Miho grimaced as the water was cold, he burst out laughing.

"Oh, Zlatko, you're indeed a sissy. That's what the men said when they brought you to our house. They said, 'This is a sissy we fished out of the sea'. I'll die laughing..."

"But the sissy can read and write Latin, Italian, Greek, and knows the world. You're but ignorant little sheep."

"You don't know a sheep from a ram, you're ignorant, Zlatko."

They all laughed. Miho didn't mind his young friends teasing him. Marco was tenderly wiping the soap from his chest and belly, while Donato inspected the wall near his bed.

"It is built with huge rocks, impossible to make an opening, or the wall would collapse."

"Wouldn't you like to learn? I mean to learn to read and write, boys?"

Now, they both stood still, staring at Miho. An awkward silence fell. When the boys stirred, the usual excuse came out.

"You know, we don't have the time. We have to help in the fields and in the vineyards."

"Yes, I know. But when the men go fishing, we're so bored, all three of us. We don't go to the fields for days. If you find me a book, some paper and two pens, we can give it a try."

"Books corrupt sane minds, says our grandfather. They are no good."

Donato was taking side with the old traditions of his family as though there would be a fight. But Miho saw the possibility of doing something useful and spoke softly.

"Yeah, some books are bad or tedious. But there are other books, big stories of adventures, and there are handbooks about building, shipyards, navigation, the stars. You can live here and enjoy finding out about other worlds just by reading. It's wonderful. You can read about pirates..."

Miho got carried away and stopped in the middle of the sentence. All three burst out laughing and couldn't stop until Lucia came into the room and cut the party with a harsh voice.

"What is this? Why is Marco washing you? You're not a baby, are you?"

Now the boys shrieked with joy looking at Miho alias Zlatko, whose terrible embarrassment was written all over his face as he was clumsily trying to wipe the soap from his back with one arm immobilized. Lucia watched his wet, naked torso dispassionately, and waited patiently until the boys finally calmed down. Donato took away the water basin, the soap and the linen, and they left the room while Lucia was hesitating.

"What was so funny? What were you laughing about?"

Miho looked her directly in the eyes and thought he would not be able to utter a word. He swallowed, she was waiting in timeless peace and finally he said:

"They were teasing me about the way I was caught by your men at sea, and I was telling them about books. Can I ask a question?"

"Yes, it wasn't a pretty sight, with a thump on your head and bleeding. Yeah, you can ask a question."

"Why doesn't anybody teach the boys to read and write?"

Lucia almost jumped with horror, then, carefully and slowly, she answered in a low voice.

"Very few people here can actually read and write."

Miho, all of a sudden, found a spark in her dark eyes.

"Can you read and write, Lucia?"

She looked back at him without the usual evasion, straight and proud.

"I can."

"Where are you from, Lucia?"

"That's enough for today. Bruna will bring you your dinner in a while. And my advice to you, *Ragusan* sissy boy: Be careful who you pose which question to."

Miho sat on the bed as the key turned in the door. No more Lucia, no more boys for company. He was alone with hours to kill while thinking of that look of hers. Who is this black beauty? Had she been captured? Had she been sold as a slave? How could he find out? He layed down and got drowned into his bodily delusions. He almost ached with curiosity and yearning to know more about her. He was still deep in his fantasies when the door opened, and Bruna came in with a plate of cheese, fresh bread, olives, dried figs and wine. Miho sat up, his mouth watered. Bruna sat to face him and smiled charmingly. When he finished, she asked mockingly.

"So you can read, Zlatko, and you're educated. We should have known this, you're an important heir in Ragusa. So the *Knez* says."

"You know that in Ragusa the majority of children go to school, where they also learn calculation. There are several schools in the city. I went to the Franciscan monastery. We need all the knowledge we can get. The Venetians are bastards and would cheat us at any deal."

"Ah, the Venetians. We've had many. They are harmless here, you know."

"I bet they are. As though my education can be of use to me now..."

"Well, actually, it can. I want my grandchildren to learn the basics; calculation, reading and writing, some Latin, while you're here."

"No problem, I would love to do it. They're lovely boys. But why doesn't Lucia teach them, she knows to read and write, I presume she also knows some calculation."

"Roko is so pig-headed sometimes, he wouldn't allow it."

"Why not? What harm can be done?"

"Well, he sees threats everywhere. Like, should the boys get educated, they would want to go into the world and who would tend the fields then? And they would rebel against the *Knez* and get killed. They would forget about fun, they wouldn't get married. It goes on and on, the nonsense."

"Donato is very gifted with tools and gadgets. Marco is very pensive and can observe nature and men with striking precision. My guess is Roko can't keep them here on a rope. They're no prisoners. If they want to leave one day, they will, with or without education."

Bruna sighed. She stared at the wall for a moment, then, not without hesitation, asked Miho:

"But you can teach them, can you?"

"Yes. I need some books, two pens and blank paper, or better, if you can get wax tablets, as paper will be too expensive."

"I'll go to the *Knez* tomorrow, to get the permission and the materials. Then I will speak to Roko and make him see reason. We should make use of you, my boy, for we'll be feeding you for some time, I guess."

"Oh, such hope you're giving me, Bruna!"

But he smiled and looked forward to playing at school with the boys. Bruna came back next morning with some paper and two books. That was what the *Knez* gave her, along with some wooden frames for the tablets, so that with applied wax they could start immediately. The books were two popular volumes which Miho knew. The first one, *Summa Theologica* by Thomas Aquinas was Miho's horror in his Franciscan school; he had to know each and every argument proving the existence of our Lord by heart and be able to provide his own discussion of each of them in Latin. The other was actually his gift for Miljutina, the *Qanun's materia medica* by Avicenna, translated into Latin by Gerard of Cremona. Both of the works were far too complicated for the boys with no knowledge of Latin to start with, so in his head, Miho devised a plan for teaching them the alphabet, and composed some simple written stories about business deals and the history of Venice, simple contracts and basic letters, which could motivate Donato and Marco to read. He instructed Bruna how to prepare the tablets with wax and the following morning, Lucia brought him breakfast and the eager boys.

"Lucia, how come that the *Knez* has permitted all this? And without Roko's knowledge?"

"Well, Bruna has a way with the *Knez*. Their understandings go a long way. Actually, he ordered her and you to achieve the maximum in the shortest of time whatever the work in the fields. You have to prove worthy of trust, the *Knez* is a dangerous man."

"Will this hurt my relations with Roko and Marin?"

"Well, there are other things which displease them. Just be careful."

"Now, Donato and Marco, *salve!*"

The boys gulped with wide eyes. They grasped it must mean hello and nodded at last. So in the following five days they were working eight to nine hours a day with pauses for the boys to get some air, eat and sleep. Miho realized that the teaching was very rewarding and the boys were progressing really fast, so that by the end of the week they could rudely spell out their names. With every meal she brought, Lucia was beaming more. She started to speak openly to Miho, and one evening she told him her life story, how she came to marry Marin. She was a hostage, just like him. The pirates caught her when they were on their way to Constantinople with her mother. Her mother drowned, and she, Lucia, was taken ashore and put in Roko's family to await the ransom. Her father was one of the most powerful spice merchants of Venice, the illustrious and fabulously rich Francisco Caravello. He was thirty years older than her mother, who came to Venice as a gift from his Abyssinian business associate Ibn al Tarik from the Tigray region. Al Tarik had come to Venice and got acquainted with the Caravello clan, which opened the way to his spice trade into Europe. So Al Tarik to show gratitude sent his youngest daughter, the beautiful Aamina Benevenuta. The Italian name was added later by Caravello. Francisco took the thirteen year old girl into his household, and she was taught Italian, some basic Latin and reading. Francisco was married to a pale Sonja of Slavic origin, from Aquileia, who spent months in her bed coughing with cold and fever. He was excited by the beautiful black Aamina and soon shared her bed. Aamina was in no position to reject Francisco. She embraced the thirty years older body of her white lord with slave-like devotion. So eventually, at fifteen, she got pregnant by him. Lucia was born on the Ascension Day amidst cries of joy. The enthusiastic crowds of the Venetians were celebrating the symbolic marriage of their city to the sea. In his golden barge, the Doge of Venice would sail out of the canals into the middle of lagoon and throw a golden ring into the waves of the Adriatic. Thus, year after year, Venice declared its love for the waters which brought them wealth and prosperity. Francisco thought this an omen and, despite the fact Aamina was not a Venetian citizen, he acquired the citizenship and recognition for her black baby Lucia. She was still his only child when she and her mother embarked fifteen years later on a voyage to Constantinople, presumingly on some secret trade mission with the Sultan in Francisco's name. By then, Lucia was a young beauty with knowledge of Latin and a good merchant education. Her main advantage was that Aamina taught her to read and write Arabic. The ship was taken, and for months Lucia waited for the ransom money from her father. Only years later, Lucia found out, that Francisco had died of a stroke the moment he was told about Aamina's death. His wife Sonja miraculously healed, got out of sickbed and refused to pay the ransom for Lucia. So, she was to become the *Knez*'s mistress. In the last moment, she was saved by the marriage proposal of young Marin

Roko.

Miho took all this in. So, they had both been prisoners, they had slept in the same bed in the same room, chained to the same wall.

"*Hal beemkanek mosa'adati?* Can you help me, Lucia?"

Miho's Arabic was heavily accented, but Lucia understood him and opened her eyes wide in shock.

"*Hal tatakallamu alloghah alarabiah?* Do you speak Arabic?"

"*Qaleelan!* Just a little. My uncle thought it was a good idea and hired a private tutor to teach me. He says we should establish good trade relations to the Ottoman Empire and their merchants. We import the pitch and the wax from Constantinople."

"You've scared me. Sorry, I must go now."

Miho was confused. He thought Lucia would be pleased, but she dashed out of the room with a confused expression as though the Devil was chasing her. Why? What was her pain? She couldn't miss Africa, for she had never been there at all. It must be her mother and the adaptation to this peasant life on the Cetinja river, which couldn't suit her.

The next day, the men came back, and he had to go to the fields, work hard and hold lessons in the late afternoon. Roko had to agree to his grandsons' forced education. The *Knez* didn't tolerate any disregard of his orders. Hence, he obliged gruntingly and made Miho pay dearly for it. By the time the men spotted a huge school of sardines and left to chase it on a late July moonless night, Miho was half dead with exhaustion. His muscles shivered with pain, and his head was banging with Latin conjugations drilled to oblivion. Bruna brought him his evening meal and a jar of lavender ointment he should apply to his limbs to relax. Between gulps of wine and bread soaked in olive oil, Miho stuttered.

"Thank you, Bruna. The cost of education... Will Roko ever be normal to me again?"

"This is normal. He was too curiously sweet before. But it will take some time before they come back. You're young, you'll recover soon."

"I wish to sleep, I'm so tired."

Bruna stroked his hair and left with the empty tray. Miho fell down on the mattress and soon in the black night he was dreaming of the sunny streets of Ragusa and fine citizens strolling from the Sunday mass on *Stradun*.

"*Salam!*"

"*Salam!*" Miho's voice surprised his dreams, the language drill getting through his sleep.

He felt hands stripping down his tunic and getting at the strings of his breeches. He was speechless and by the time he properly opened his eyes, a black woman's body was on top of him, tiny lips kissing his lips with passion.

"*Uhibboki!*"

Voices whispering "I love you", were contrasted by hasty, arrogant movements of the black woman, who had the situation under her control. His right hand was chained to the wall, he was immobilized. She, in contrast, was free, her snakelike body oily with a soapy sweat smelling of vanilla and roses. Miho remembered the smell from somewhere, but in the heat of the moment couldn't remember where. It was to do with home and kitchen, a feast in Ragusa. He was breathing heavily. She was finding spots on his body, touched them with her hands and tenderly sucked on his skin with her tongue. Miho was burning on a stake. With the fire in his loins, he thought that it was like Hell – a black Devil was having her ways with him at last. Yet, with every tender stroke, his lips were trembling for more. He was aching with love, feeling her wet sex on his thighs and trying to catch another kiss from her lips, trying to reach for her breasts, for her buttocks, his free hand clumsy with chained frustration. She was evading his intentions, mastering every move with skill and command. Her hands were moving too fast, he couldn't hold her in his arms, and she kept slipping up and down his chest. His member ached with excitement, sticking up in the dark night like a lonely pillar of a demolished temple in which dreams of goddesses were feeding the dreams of eternal love and passion to the boys. With awkward efforts he was moving his loins to get inside her, but it was only Lucia who dictated the pace, and all he could do was wait for it to happen. He couldn't make love to her, he was being made love to. Humiliated, subdued by passion, yet with boyish tears in his eyes, he kept repeating "*Uhibbok*"!. Lucia smiled, moved her hips, lifted and released her muscled belly and continued her dance of a black bird, devouring the whiteness of the boy's body with embraces of her black limbs. He was panting and almost came, felt his semen banging in his skull, when finally she sat on him, took him inside her wet rose and for a few long moments stopped all action. Their eyes met, and the current of heat travelled from one body to the other. Their lips came together in a kiss longer than eternity. When they breathed air again, Miho forgot the chained arm, banished the frustration and let her lead the way. She knew it so much better, he was only too happy to be in her warm hands. And Lucia's eyes burnt like candles in a dark church, she was coming with sighs and streams of joy, wetting his belly and making him scream with ecstasy. It seemed to him that hours went by, until he finally couldn't hold back and exploded like a volcano. She smiled and looked amused, but he couldn't care less. He wouldn't mind dying inside her if that was what she wanted.

They lay still for a while, before Lucia started getting dressed and helping him back into his breeches. When she leaned over him to get his tunic, he caught her face and planted an innocent peck on her cheek. She laughed, and he said reproachfully:

"You forced yourself on me tonight!"

"Yeah, you were dreaming of it from the day you came to our house, weren't you?"

"I liked you, ok. But rape is a serious offence in Ragusa!"

"I've never heard of a raped man. You were enjoying it. I almost lost you to pleasure."

"Ah, Lucia, the couple we are. A former black slave woman is forcing a white chained prisoner. The world is a crazy place, *habib*."

"Good night, my prisoner. Be careful tomorrow."

"Good night, my black angel."

Sooner than usually, the men came back. The catch was so huge that they had run out of nets. The family was busy salting and drying the sardines. Some were being pickled in salt and sealed by olive oil, the bigger ones were dried in the sun. The dried fish were collected after a few weeks by a vagrant merchant, who mentioned he was headed to Ragusa. Miho found the opportunity and entrusted him with the note to Miljutina, trying to warn his people in advance of what was coming. He had trouble writing the treacherous words of love, yet they had to be there, the note was to save his life. As a free man, maybe he could take Lucia with him. Or, she would never leave the boys and he was just another boy to her. He waited patiently for a feedback to his note, to be summoned by the *Knez*, or a change in the pirates' attitude, yet for several weeks the world stood still again and nothing happened. He assumed in the end that his note had not travelled to Ragusa, but was presented to the *Knez*, whose drunken cronies laughed heartily over his declaration of love to Miljuta. His nights were filled with black dreams. Lucia was engraved in his mind forever. But she was married, and technically, there was no way they could be together.

Then one day in late autumn he saw a young rider on a mule trotting toward the home of the *Knez*. Miho could swear it was Nikola Bunić. Hopes rose high in his heart; maybe, as a *Ragusan* merchant, Nikola could help to get him out of there. The rider was looking in his direction, but led the mule to the centre of the village, directly to the house of the pirate *Knez*. Miho despaired. He was mistaken, it wasn't Nikola. Several hours went by until the mule trotted into their yard, and Nikola descended, asking in a clear voice if he could speak to Mihajlo. Roko presented a respectful smile, and they sat together at the stone table under a huge mulberry tree. Immediately, refreshments were brought by a kitchen girl; salted fish, pickled olives, bread, brandy and wine. Nikola filled the cups and toasted Miho with a smile, saying:

"Here you are, Kabužić, let's drink to the deal of your life!"

"*Uzdravlje*, I never thought I'd be glad to see you, Bunić."

They drank another cup before Miho asked with caution:

"What do you mean by this deal? Did you bring my uncle's ransom?"

"I don't think he's paying, Miho."

"But... why not... They will slaughter me like a pig if they don't get the money. I am a Kabužić, my father's heir, he must pay!"

In a trembling voice, he searched for further arguments in favor of the ransom. He was in panic and shivered with cold in the evening wind. His eyes were wide open and white with horror. Nikola bent to his travel bag and took out a warm sheepskin cloak, padded with soft wool.

"Here, put this on. You will need it for the travel."

"Where are they taking me?"

Miho was so shaken he couldn't find the sleeve opening with his hands, and it took him a while before he was wrapped in the cloak.

"Well, I said we must make the deal of your life. It is for your life, actually."

"Do you have the money? Will you pay for me?"

"What makes you think so?"

Nikola knew he was abusing the situation, but he couldn't help it and postponed the facts, not without amusement. Miho was his rival. Not so long ago, he had abused his *Ragusan* oligarch position and humiliated him in front of the citizens, and, above all, he was technically still engaged to Miljutina, they were to be united by marriage. So, deep in his heart Nikola nurtured hatred for the young blue blood.

"Well, why are you here, then? What do you want from me?"

"Here you go. I can save you and take you home to Ragusa. There is one condition; forget about marrying Miljutina. Break the betrothal in writing. She will agree, don't worry. And you will live your life again."

"This is not what my uncle and Marina Menčetić are expecting from me. I can't..."

"Forget the old Kabužić, he doesn't want to pay for you. Don't you understand, my friend? Whom did you give the extra insurance, the promissory note for Lasta?"

"Hell, it was Sorini. This pig... has my uncle received it through another ship to Ragusa?"

"Of course not, think again! Kabužić is furious, he went to Venice and Sorini simply said you wanted the package brought to our consul in Venice. The consul played deaf and dumb, maintaining it was just another of his numerous everyday deals. He hadn't thought anything of it. And that he cannot undo a carried out deal. It is clear he had been bribed, but how will you prove it? A stupid thing to do. How can you trust such a villain as Sorini? Really! The ransom request has come in the meantime, and Galvo didn't react to it at all. I'm telling you, he doesn't want to pay for you. He would probably compensate the loss with your inheritance. Unless you spoil his plans and come back with me."

"You have a point, Bunić. Galvo could be after my father's wealth, and if I don't get free, he's got it all for himself. How do you know about Sorini anyway, who told you?"

"Never mind who told me. It was pretty obvious you had messed up. Ships were coming to our port for months and nobody knew anything about you. Your uncle put two and two together soon. He had huge financial difficulties and I had to extend my advance sums for the ships he's building for me to ensure I will get the ships at all. But what do you lose, Miho? You're young, you don't love Miljutina. She was your bride for money, and now you can choose another wife, a woman you will love."

"I can't, it's impossible."

"Why?"

"Never mind, I just can't."

"Suit yourself. My proposal is to forget Miljutina."

"But you, Nikola, you can't choose anybody else. You must have Miljutina."

"Yes, I do. I must have her. There is nobody else for me in Ragusa or anywhere in the world. I'm sorry."

"So, it's either me or her."

"No, it is you and her. I want you both to live happily ever after, just not in one bed under the same roof."

"Why would you want me to be happy? I'm worth more dead to you. When I'm declared missing, you can grab her, and Galvo can grab my share of the inheritance."

Nikola sunk into silence. He was slowly losing his patience. It took him a lot of strain to persuade father to intervene with the *Knez*. Since Nikola was building their name and fortune in Ragusa, any traces of contacts to the pirates could be fatal. He travelled for days thinking of how to persuade the pirates to abandon the ransom, and in the end, he had to make some fishy deals with them to legalize the stolen cargo. All to get this spoilt boy free! All to please his beloved Miljutina, the queen of his heart. Nikola could not speak up openly, not now, at least. He was trying to get the man out, yet this spoilt noble merchant was not playing his game. Miho was too curious, too inquisitive. The conversation was leading nowhere. He replied quietly at last.

"I have my reasons."

"You don't want bodies under your marriage bed, do you? But you have them already – the captain, the soldiers, all were killed. Did you set up this coup, Nikola?"

"You are a fool, Miho! The promissory note... I could not foresee, you'd be so stupid, could I? Besides, the pirates take any ship entangled in the *bura* at Omiš – how could I forecast the weather, am I God or what?"

"It's all so fishy. I just don't believe all these coincidences. And how do you know so many details about everything?"

"Listen, Kabužić! My father spent a fortune on my education. I work hard day and night to build the business. I am no murderer. My ships and their cargo are in danger just like yours in stormy weather...Only, I take precautions. I respect the rules and obtain insurance. Stupid boy!"

"Don't you think I do the same? Why are you here? Shouldn't the monk bring the ransom?"

"Did you forget? You uncle will not pay!"

Miho sank in dispair.

"How did you find me?"

"Stop asking questions and start worrying for your life."

Miho swallowed hard. Bunić had a point. He should stop poking into why and how, and get home quickly. Later, when the image of Lucia has faded in his mind, there were several maidens in Ragusa, and many would do anything to be his. Miljutina with her aloofness and her own ways in business would soon become unmanageable, and maybe the whole betrothal thing wasn't such a good idea. Let Bunić have her, the little witch. Still, he felt bitter about the matter and hated to be indebted to his opponent.

"How will you pay the ransom should I renounce the marriage to Miljutina?"

"None of your business, I will. If you give me your written word to break up with Miljutina, we will leave this place tomorrow. Your seal ring and your personal possessions will be returned to you, the weapons will travel with me. We will ask the *Knez* for a bodyguard through *Pagania*, so that we can pass his lands without further troubles. You must have had enough harassment by now. So what do you say? Is it the deal of your life or not?"

"It surely is a deal and I accept it. Where do I sign? You have the wording ready, I presume."

Nikola smiled. He could see the boy had a sharp mind and, to a certain point he admired his courage. He didn't break into sobs and plead for his life at any cost. In the end, he wasn't left with much choice – he had to play along or stay in chains. Nikola presented the scroll, and Miho read it quietly. It was in Latin, the official language of the Republic of Ragusa, and simply formulated their arrangement. Miho took the quill from Nikola's hand and signed. They sighed at the same time and laughed. Another fill of glasses, and Nikola turned to casual talk.

"I can see the Kačići have treated you well. You're tanned and muscular. Were you working in the fields? "

"Who, Ka..."

"The family of Roko, the family you were staying with. You do know that they are all related to the *Knez*."

"They never told me their family name, just first names. I thought it was Roko. Isn't Kačić the famous pirate leader? They always called him just the *Knez*."

"Well, who cares about the names – *nomina sunt odiosa*. Let it be. How early would you want to start tomorrow?"

* * *

Their mule train paused above Prijeko, the northern part of Dubrovnik, where the city walls were yet too low to obstruct the view of Stradun, the basilica and the port. The walls needed more construction to form a serious defense line. It was their last stop before entering the city, and they should not be late. It would be a pity to spend another night under the stars and not to enjoy a hot bath and a hot meal in their homes. While the cold November night veiled the alleys and the narrow town houses in a curtain of mysterious fogs, the harbor was clear and still glittering orange and purple skies as the sun was setting in the west. The bay was nearly empty. There were few ships anchored over winter in the *Ragusan* port. The owners preferred the peaceful bay of Lopud, which was even called *Mrtvo more*, the Dead Sea, for its perfect protection from the rough winter winds. The sea was tranquil and harmless like a vast, still pool. Its dark silver surface reflected the gold of the sun. It was indeed a bay of a million golden *dukats*, no wonder the whole world was in love with Ragusa.

Miho looked at Nikola. They had dismissed the Kačić body-guard some miles before the city, both avoiding the city guards and wanting to pass as uneventfully as possible.

"What guarantee did I have that you would not strangle me on the road, once you had my letter signed?"

"None, I guess."

"I had one. Miljutina wouldn't be happy, if you came without me. And she's not likely to believe you if you lie to her."

"Yes, that. And you had my word of honor."

"Well, it's just a word. Like my uncle's word. Like my word. Words are vessels of assumptions, postulates, nothing more. Empty vessels..."

"I agree. Deeds distinguish the man, not words. And here you are, home at last."

"I guess I didn't know you, Bunić."

"No, you got to know my fists first. It was a bad start, sorry."

"I thought then I was in love with her."

"Well, also love materializes with deeds, words are not enough."

They laughed heartily, each thinking of his love nights of the past summer. Miho grew serious. Like a worm, a question was boring in his brain. He couldn't help himself.

"Have you had her, Nikola?"

Nikola froze. This was not a subject to discuss. Should he lie to his new friend? For on the road they talked and talked and realized they were not so much different. With every little travel comfort Nikola arranged for Miho on the road, with every stew he cooked or wine he bought and they enjoyed together, more of Miho's initial bitterness dissipated in youngsters' jokes and new confidentialities. Miho was stunned by Nikola's intelligence and humor, good-hearted nature and courage. He began to look up to him as though Nikola was his older brother. After all, he was the one who saved his life and stood up for him when nobody else would. It was a revelation trip for both of them. On the other hand, Nikola realized he should make friends more often if he ever wanted to be part of the *Ragusan* elite. Nobility could not be bought with money, he needed to socialize. Miho was not a bad boy, just very arrogant and proud, qualities he lost forever working in the fields and tending to the cattle fearing for his life in Omiš. He changed so much in this last year. He had matured. Only how he trusted that his uncle would save him no matter what! Nikola knew only too well that nobody ever could be trusted completely, be it a man or woman. And he was so lonely with this wisdom, so very lonely. He needed a friend. His voice was colder than he intended.

"I haven't heard the question. Why do you think this is your business now, Miho?"

"But you surely had your fingers in the whole of Lasta business? Don't think I would report you to the Council, I would just like to know."

"Are we friends, Mihajlo Kabužić?"

"We're friends forever."

"In this case wait until our hair turns grey, our bellies round up and we're old goats peering under the kirtles of young girls passing. When we get into the City Council of Ragusa – then I promise, I will tell you everything you want to know, the whole story of this business."

"I hate you when you sound like a deal, Nikola Bunić! The devil should get your deals, not me!"

"Let me just give you a hint, Miho. Beware of unknown sailors on board of you ships! You should well know the man you sail with!"

"So, the sailors betrayed us... Who would think that, poor bastards!"

"Poor they seemed to you and to the captain, yet there is a dangerous network out there..."

"And how do you know it?"

"I don't. But I still have a father... Luckily, I do, my friend."

Nikola's mule trotted and neighed impatiently, it was time to move on. The baggage train with two noble riders entered the Pile city gate of the Republic Ragusa or Dubrovnik under the golden, protective hands of St. Blaise. They were loaded with riches beyond any price. Their baggage was youth, freedom and love.

Ottomans, A.D. 1501

My diesel car glides smoothly along the narrow country road, filled with tourists on their evening jogging, as if they must all at once make up for the fat they are going to eat later. The radio is playing Ravel's Bolero, a piece of music which expresses the eternal battle between the waves and the shore perfectly. I try to listen, to immerse myself in the wonderful tune, yet I cannot. Pain and sorrow cloud my thought. Mercilessly, they attack my mind like reappearing daggers until it is without any sensation and feeling. My tears have dried some miles ago. Mechanically, I turn the wheel while recalling my past sins. I let myself go and loved a man, now I have to pay the bill. Why does God hate me so much? Will I ever break free from the vicious circle of guilt?

A week ago, Paula's health got worse and I took her to the Zadar hospital, where they kept her in. The chemotherapy has not brought big improvements. The doctors claim there is only one more chance left – a bone marrow transplant. I will check that with the University Medical Center Ljubljana, though. They shall repeat the tests there and we will see if the transplant is indeed an option. In Zadar, they analyzed our DNAs and established Paula and I are not a perfect match. They asked me whether Paula has other close relatives.

Under no condition I shall think about Paula's family and relatives lost in the war.

The warm August evening sun casts its purple on the horizon, where dark blue clouds are gathering with their false promise of rain. The tourist season is at its peak and my days are stretched between hospital visits in Zadar and work at the hotel. Luckily, the hotel is full and our guests are as happy as bees in their quest for sunshine, sea, good food and sweet wine. It is so difficult to keep a smiling face around them. I know my bitterness and a sullen face would drive them away sooner than rain or bad weather. My employees are capable and professional, so I can delegate most of my tasks to them. From their sympathetic looks can I see their deep commitment not only to their jobs but strangely also to me, their boss. I am surprised. For years, I have kept my emotions and personal life very private. Many times, they have thought me cool and tough on their poor working morale – a hereditary weakness of easy life in socialism. They were used to the reverse slogan of Amex: Get paid now, work later! I had to put my foot down and teach them to work harder and take job responsibilities seriously. With many foreign business coaches, but more due to the tough economic situation in Croatia, we managed to get the wheel spinning. At the Perovica ecological hotel, we make a capable, kind and highly professional team, who do not rest on our laurels. Our yearly on-line survey every November confirms we are doing a god job. What's more, it gives us new ideas on how to improve our services.

The eight o'clock news on the radio bring me back to the road and reality. Another bomb attack in Turkey cost five lives. According to the report, the rebellious Kurds in the south of the country have been made responsible for the massacre. My thoughts glide to the last story I have brought to Paula to read. The Turks have always been a strong military nation. In the Ottoman times, they conquered half of the world, including the neighboring lands of Kosovo, Serbia and Bosnia. Our people have suffered under their rule, which on the other hand brought technical and cultural progress. When the Empire fell apart, the conflicts among the Catholic, Orthodox and Muslim populations have caused more evil than the Devil feared by all three religions. Atatürk reformed the crumbling empire and changed it into a democratic state, yet I sometimes have the feeling that even today their culture, based on Islam, does not agree with democracy and western values. I wonder what Paula will think about little Ayesha and her tricks around the Neretva delta some hundred years after the Battle of Kosovo. One thing, I am sure of: the suspense of the story will keep her thoughts away from her illness at least for a while. I have to ring up Ljubljana first thing in the morning. We have to have a second opinion. My baby, my Paula, she must live.

* * *

Marin was dizzy. He could not watch the belly dance much longer without having serious trouble mastering the pressure in his breeches. He was pressing his arms and hands in his crotch, sitting cross-legged on the fluffy, artfully ornamented Turkish carpet. His dark blond hair stuck to his neck; thick strands were falling on his forehead. He was excited, bathed in sweat all over, his body was burning in a fever of a troubled boy. Suffocating, he stared at the vision of colorful silk scarves waving in front of him. In the heavily perfumed room, his eyes remained fixed on the naked bellies and moving tops. His brain was empty of thought and reason as though all his senses had left him. The music was loud and powerful; *gusle*, a single-string Balkan *lyra*, was fighting for the solo with two flutes and four terrible drums beating wildly, their rhythm enhanced by the chimes at the ankles of the dancers pounding their bare feet at the soft rugs.

There were three women dancing. Or, they were three charming sorceresses. The tallest was dressed in emerald green silk and performed skillful twists and turns, catching the eye of many comfortably seated man. Marin felt her eye caught his more often than those of the other guests, and he flushed poppy red every single time. The eyes of the dancer were open wide, black, her thick, long eyelashes moist with excitement. She was smiling with the pleasure of catching the rhythm with her hips and shoulders, moving each part of her magnificent body as though it wasn't attached to the rest of her being. The loveliest part was her white, soft belly, where a big emerald stone in a silver ring hid the belly button, shaking wildly or turning in sophisticated circles as though around an invisible axis. Her companions were clad in crimson red silk and supported her performance in a terrific choreography of movements driving crazy every single man in the room. The pressure among the guests of the ostentatious dining party was building up like a river behind a dam after spring rains. Marin did not notice much around him, for he was lost in his blurred vision of the girls. He could not form any coherent thought and just stared, trying in vain to keep under control his heartbeat and lustful wishes.

He had never seen anything like this in his fifteen years of life. It was as though their bellies, shaking, circling, and tempting had a life of their own. Oh yes, he had seen a woman naked. In fact, not only one, there had been a few, but they stood still, they were not moving in such a seductive way, they weren't sending their hips to obscene heights and shameless lows like a crazy choir of witches. He turned his head away in hope that their images would somehow disappear in the stucco lace ornaments above the doors and windows of the palace of Abdullah al Bina, their illustrious host for the week. Abdullah ordered festivities in honor of his excellence Hadim Ali Pasha, the Grand Vizier of the Ottoman Empire. Hadim Ali Pasha was famous for his heroic conduct in the Mamluk War. Not only once, he had risked his life for the Sultan. Bayazid II showed gratitude and made Hadim the highest minister of the state, the Grand Vizier. Abdullah was a close friend of Hadim Ali Pasha, who was bound to arrive any day now on his first official visit to Bosnia.

Naturally, Marin did not know all this and could not care less. He was a young apprentice from the Adriatic coast, who came into his master's service at an early age, not even ten years old. He worked very hard; in the peak of summer, he harvested salt in the shallow waters of the Ston channel, and during the autumn fogs he would pick oysters until the skin of his hands, hurt by the sharp shells, looked like raw meat. All linen and leather bandages could not protect his fingers from the still and innocent looking sea creatures, which had been cultured in the clear waters of Ston since the Roman times. Once the delicacy for the Roman emperors, oysters, were now highly praised by the *Ragusan patricians*, who also liked to invest in the maricultural fields. Since Bosnia was occupied in 1463, and soon also populated by the Ottoman nobility, the trade between Ston and Mostar, along the beautiful Neretva delta and valley, opened widely and offered more income. Despite the fact that the Turks quickly mastered the local Slavic dialect of their serfs, the Turkish nobles, the *sipahi*, did not like to travel to foreign frontiers, so fishermen had to bring the oysters to the clients themselves. They did so during the winter months, when business was slower, and in the cold oysters stayed alive and fresh for many days. In summer, they had enough income supplying the coastal towns. The bad side of the winter travel was that the waters of the Neretva were high and torrential, rowing or steering against them practically impossible. Thus, they had to go over land. They packed the shells in oak barrels filled with cold seawater and took the difficult route to the north with mules and donkeys. The oysters were alive when they unloaded the wagons, which on their way back to the coast carried grain, rare spices, silk, and Bosnian wool for the *Ragusans*.

Abdullah adored seafood, so as soon as he had found out about the mariculture in Ston, he sent messengers to arrange regular purchases. It took at least four days of travel in each direction. When Abdullah's palace smiled at the tired men and mules dragging the oyster train uphill, the fishermen knew that they would be welcome, and that they would spend a few days bathing in his kind and almost proverbial Muslim hospitality. The palace was monumental and richly furnished. It was for the first time in his life that Marin entered an Ottoman palace, and this one in all its glory and luxury. He marveled at the comfortable rooms, he relaxed in the freshness of the Turkish bath, the *hamam*, and he ate foods and sweet delicacies with exotic spices and lots of honey and nuts. What a feast on his palate!

His master, Hrvoje Salić, was severe, and sometimes demanded almost too much work from Marin, but he was not a bad man. In the years of Ottoman raids and wars, in which the Turks strived at annexing Bosnia to the mightiest of empires the world had ever seen, business was slow. He had to fight hard in order to feed every mouth in his household. He would not even have taken an apprentice in the middle of the war crisis had he not felt sorry for Marin and his father when they came on his doorstep some five years ago. They were terrified peasants in ragged clothes, oblivious to everything but the safety of food and comfort. They had just miraculously escaped an Ottoman *deli*, a frightening cavalry unit formed more or less for raiding. Their home was a village near Metkovići which was a day's donkey ride from Ston. Ston was *Ragusan* territory and had been since one of the most important city centers of the Republic for decades. Had they gone back to their place across the border, the Turks would have come again, and Marin would be taken with them as a janissary as sure as there was God in Heaven. The Turkish military machine was insatiable – they abducted thousands of boys and brought them to Istanbul year after year to train the famous army of janissaries. It was a hard life, and their military service lifelong. So the boys and men would not often return to their families. Thus, Hrvoje Salić took the boy into his household and gave him a roof over his head along with his family name, Salić. It was only for protection at first. He acquired the *Ragusan* citizenship for the boy, who he reported as his remote nephew, although there was not a drop of blood they shared. The boy's father, who left a purse of coins with Hrvoje, left reassured, knowing that his son would earn every breadcrumb of his living. Marin was a good shepherd and knew a lot about farming; besides, he was growing like a weed and could soon manifest his strength. Indeed, the boy proved an extraordinarily useful and intelligent apprentice. Hrvoje, still hoping for a son of his own with his young second wife, Olga, loved him very much.

Since the first beat of music and the appearance of the half-naked beauties, Hrvoje sensed Marin's confusion at the sight of women in silk breeches. The faces of the dancers were partly veiled, yet their lustful dark eyes were shining. It was not the faces or the cleavages that aroused men. It was their white bellies, widely exposed to voracious looks bellow the breasts, where their ornamented tops were shaking with the wild rhythm of the music. Hrvoje knew it was necessary to hide the excitement. Men had to pretend that they were not looking at the dance at all. Their Turkish host Abdullah, in his early fifties, short and wrinkled, with a nice balloon of a belly protruding at his waist, was casting his glances at the guests suspiciously, as though he was only waiting for a pretext to strike at them. Hrvoje was scared when he saw Marin's reaction. It was terribly dangerous to show your attraction to Muslim women too obviously. The dancers looked like they were the daughters of Abdullah, yet based on the experience of his years trading with the Turks, Hrvoje was guessing they were his host's younger wives. Like their prophet Muhamed, all Turks could have several wives. The richer the man, the more beautiful the wives in his *harem*...

Hrvoje was sitting cross-legged behind the boy, agitated as if perched on a hot pan, trying to poke him in the back and warn him. At last, the boy turned around, with an annoyed, questioning look.

"Stop staring like that at the bodies of the girls! Look at their feet. Do you hear me?"

"Why? They're just dancers..."

"You don't know anything. Just stop if you'd like to keep your head on your shoulders."

"But..."

"No buts! Listen or you will get a thrashing..."

Marin could gather fear and urgency in the voice of his patron. He turned red as a crab in boiling water.

"Sorry, I didn't mean to..." he stammered.

"I know. You do not understand. This is particularly rude to Abdullah. They're his wives, you know."

Marin smiled. What incredible stories his master would think
of sometimes.

"You probably mean his daughters, Hrvoje."

"No! They are his wives. You heard me right. Do as I say."

"I will. Thank you. Sorry. . . "

Marin turned around again, focusing his eyes on the chimes
at the dancers' feet. But the lady in green didn't like her attention squandered on the floor. She bent forward, with her
breasts shaking wildly just above Marin's nose. With a wiz, her
scarves trimmed with tiny twinkling copper coins, caressed his
hair. Marin could smell the rose water in her thick black hair,
which was falling to her waist like a waterfall on the Neretva
river. He jolted back slightly, and the bulge in his breeches became visible to everybody, the shame of an uncontrolled young
man, offering itself and waiting for a girl to touch and enjoy it.
Abdullah noticed it and clasped his hands angrily. He called in
Arabic:

"Enough! Ladies, stop! Go to your rooms while the men dine
in peace!"

Before an older, veiled woman could gather the animated girls
and take them away, the tallest dancer, who had provoked Marin,
stepped forward, dancing wildly with her crazy hips above Abdullah's head. She looked him in the eye, rebelling, announcing
with her alluring and provocative moves that she was not done
with her audience yet. Enough was when she wanted to stop
and not a second earlier. The musicians paused half heartedly,
scanning the face of their lord, but Abdullah burst into laughter,
calling to her indulgently:

"Dance, Ayesha, dance, my little one, until you drop dead on
the floor. My pearl! My beautiful angel!"

Ayesha's eyes lit up with new ardor. She took Abdullah's
hands, pressed a quick kiss on his palms through her veil, and
lifted her arms, clapping her hands in unison with the chimes on
her feet. Abdullah smiled and joined her, gesturing to his guests,
including Hrvoje and Marin, that they should follow. Everybody clapped their hands. The musicians fired their instruments
anew, joining in with a song in which the word *habibi* was like
a wolf wailing lonely in his winter woods in the Jahorina mountains. The belly dancers encouraged the audience and surprised
the men with glaring eyes and new artful motions in harmony
with the drums and their young, perfectly curved bodies. Abdullah relaxed and shook with their dance as though he was a
little lamb jumping around a green pasture. The party was at
its peak, and the old veiled woman stepped into the background,
shaking her head in disbelief. Marin cast a side look at Abdullah
shyly. He wanted to apologize somehow for his rudeness, but the
old man smiled broadly as though they were brothers.

"Clap your hands, my boy! Up in the air with them! So that

we can all see them!"

Men roared with laughter at Abdullah's insinuations, and Marin, not quite understanding what he meant, obeyed his good-humoured host, who used the local Slavic dialect to communicate with his guests. Even Hrvoje put his worries aside and joined in the whirlwind of the music. The girls were dancing as though possessed by a strange dynamism, by a force springing up from long days of monotonous inactivity, when their shaded existence seemed like a vacuum in the rooms entirely isolated from the rest of the world, where the only man they ever saw was their eunuch guard. The *harem* was like a waiting room for life, but the party was life in its full essence – music, beaming faces and wide smiles on them. They were born to excite, not to feel bored.

Marin thought that the heat, the dance, and the excitement would last forever. He clapped and clapped, his sore hands feeling no pain through his bandages, while his head was burning with joy like a lantern in the night. His erection calmed down, and he cast his tensions aside. At last, he could look at the green dancer Ayesha properly. She was beautiful, and her temperament was one of a wild cat. Abdullah was not only the richest man he had ever encountered, he had to be the happiest man, too. Marin would die of trance if only he could touch a girl like Ayesha. She was shooting her black arrows in his direction. They held each other's glances while his hands were clapping and her hips were swirling upwards and downwards in harmony with the short convulsions of the drums. They touched across the air. Marin felt it, and Ayesha did, too, but nobody else noticed. The music was slowing down and with a graceful final turn, Ayesha lay down on the carpet before Abdullah, who stood up and raised her green veils. He tenderly kissed her on both cheeks and dismissed her like a child. A graceful, green swallow, she flew away with her silken wings. The music died out with the exit of the dancers. A man holding a *lyra* came forward.

"No recitation now! Let's have some more sweets and more music! And bring in the smoking pipes."

The servants, who were waiting discretely hidden behind the curtains, stirred into action. Abdullah's wish was their command. The men were chatting, eating, and smoking long into the night. The party, sheltered from the cold winds outside, shared the smoke with their generous host. The evening faded away, yet the images of the fantastic dancers did not lose a shade of their brightness and color. They gleamed in the men's dreams like stars shining in the black of the night.

* * *

Does any rose, in this rosegarden world, lack thorns?

– Hayatî Efendi

Ayesha slipped into the warm cloak held up by Fatima at
the gate. Their guard, the eunuch Ibrahim was waiting outside
to escort them across the yard into their part of the palace, the
harem. The girls in red followed, bending to the wind, shivering
in their scarce garments.

"How was our dance, Fatima?"

"You were great, but there are some things we have to discuss
later."

Fatima's voice was subdued, but Ayesha could hear she was
angry. She assumed why. Fatima would have never approved
of their vivid and dynamic choreography had she seen it before
hand. She was from another age. Actually, she was of another
age. She was as old as Abdullah, so nearly fifty, a grandmother to
her. Ayesha tore down the veil concealing her face and quickened
her pace. Fatima noticed it, but did not say anything. She was
confused and scared. The performance was too daring and she
suspected that Abdullah tolerated it for two reasons: first, he
didn't want to scare the infidel guests with the usual punishment
for rebellious women, and second, Ayesha could twist him around
her little finger for anything – he loved the girl much too much.

Fatima was Abdullah's first wife. She thought that she was
past jealousy. So many years had gone by since Abdullah took
her in his bed after their wedding ceremony and the celebration
which brought some of the finest Ottoman families around the
same table. They feasted and danced for a week, forgetting the
feuds and conflicts over lands and positions at the Sultan's court.
She was sixteen, and Abdullah was a year older. When after
the first evening they retired to their chambers, they discovered
physical touch and love for the first time. Both filled with knowledge and importance of sensual pleasures from the stories of "One
Thousand and One Nights", they learnt each other's wishes and
preferences gradually over the years. In the first decade of their
marriage, Fatima gave birth to two splendid sons, and Abdullah
avoided taking a second or a third wife, as it would have been
the custom. He chose going to the war with Persians rather than
hurting Fatima and their wonderful love. Yet, in the eleventh
year of their marriage, he had to abandon the battle line in a
hurry. Fatima fell ill with fever, and the doctors despaired over
her. His father arranged a hasty marriage to Selma, his second
wife. She was gorgeous. Her inquisitive grey eyes hidden behind
thick black lashes and her Greek nose behind the veil disguised
her voluptuous lips, always ready for a kiss. A tall, strong woman
with wonderful waist-long curly hair, she was a superb companion; she loved reading and discussing life and morals, or more

precisely, how to abandon or loosen the rigid Muslim customs. For Abdullah, who was lonely without Fatima or his warriors, she was a superb choice, not to speak of her prestigious family connections. Selma was the daughter of the Caliph of Cairo, Al Mustanjid. Such a good match should bring stability into Abdullah's family. So they thought! Yet Selma proved to be a vicious character, full of intrigues and schemes. Her only goal was to get rid of Fatima and to prevail in the *harem* hierarchy. She knew her aspirations could come into life only by using her seductive impact upon Abdullah, so she put into practice all the courtesan tricks of her powerful sexual appeal. For weeks while Fatima was recovering her strengths after the fever, she held Abdullah in her bedroom practically day and night. After his initial restraints were completely liberated from all prejudice and shame, Abdullah was drinking the poison of her erotic plays and pleasures. He ignored his work, switched off his reason, and he plunged himself into a physical slavery to Selma. Fatima ceased to exist for him.

According to the custom, Fatima was the head of the wives and their children. She also presided over the *harem*. Every morning she met her bed-ridden Abdullah to organize the family life and report to him about new developments in the household. She suppressed her hurt feelings, hid her sorrow over lost faith, and buried her love deep in her heart. So, when Selma finally got pregnant, and Abdullah's lust was appeased, Fatima fought back. She encouraged Abdullah to find more young wives and to fill his *harem* with exotic courtesans. Aroused by the idea of fresh nocturnal adventures, he took her advice and soon the *harem* became populated by exotic young faces. Selma could still hold her erotic spell over Abdullah for some years, but lacked the momentum to challenge Fatima's authority in the *harem*. Abdullah, while dispersing his sexual attentions around his several wives, always nurtured his respect for Fatima and considered her his life companion. He trusted her and confided in her in every aspect. On many occasions, Fatima solved conflicts behind the curtains and made his life at the court easier. Despite all new sexual liaisons of her husband and friend, she never grew bitter and wisely accepted her role of the mother in the family. In the most difficult moments of his life, she faithfully stood by him. Now, after more than three decades of their union, they both grew old and tired. Maybe it was time to step down from the stage and let the young have their way. She could calm down and relax. She could look at life perched on a soft cushion of a *divan*.

"I'd like to have a bath, Fatima. I'm soaked."

"Sorry, young lady, it is too late for the *hamam*. You must go to bed. Put the veil back. We're still in the courtyard, Ayesha."

"Oh, Fatima, I'm so annoyed by the veil. It's suffocating. In the room, it was hot and I couldn't breathe. And what's the point of hiding my face while my belly is exposed."

"Do as I say, Ayesha. I'll arrange for you to be sponged before sleep. Then I'll come and kiss you good night."

Obediently, the girl followed her servants Abida and Banan. They led her into a tiled room, warm and cosy all days and nights. The tiles were shining in the bright blue and red colors of the fine Arabic arts. Ayesha stepped into the tepid water of the ground pool. Her former dance companions, now dressed in plain sleeveless *raša*, came with soft linen towels and buckets, from which perfumed vapors were rising to their nostrils. It was hot water with rose oil, and the wonderful sweet smell was intoxicating. Ayesha sat on the tiled bench, and Abida and Banan undressed her and started to massage every inch of her body with towels soaked in the tepid, oily water. Ayesha enjoyed the feeling of cleanness.

She was used to delicate skincare since an early age. She had been raised in the Sultan's palace as the only daughter of Sultan's close friend Hassan, who died on the battlefield shielding his ruler. At the time of her father's death, her mother was charged with having committed adultery with one of the janissaries and was stoned to death, so Ayesha could not even recall her face. She had been an orphan for as long as she could remember. The wives in the *harem* knew how the Sultan felt about Hassan, and in order to get the Sultan's attention, they were spoiling the little girl without restraints, granting her every single wish. Yet, they had children of their own by the Sultan, so they felt no real affection for Ayesha, who grew into an aggressive, often rebellious and most of the time stubborn child, always looking for trouble. Ayesha could see through the false love the Sultan's wives enveloped her in, and she very soon started to terrorize half of the *harem* with her whims and outbursts. When something went against her will, her wails would wake the dead from their tombs, and no beating could shut her up. They were looking for the first opportunity to get rid of her. When Abdullah al Bina's family got decimated by the plague seven years ago, and Ayesha was eight years old, they sent her to him under the pretext that she should get used to the new family and the new country, Bosnia, before her marriage. It was a happy move for Ayesha. In the peaceful and wise Fatima, she found the mother she had never known. Fatima realized Ayesha's passionate character and discovered her artistic talent very soon. She hired musicians and dancers to teach the wild little girl to play the *lyra*, sing, and dance. Ayesha's rebellious energies focused on the song and dance practice. In the evenings, Fatima cuddled her in her bed and told her old stories from the Quran. She loved her like her own daughter, and her love was contagious. It was not long before Abdullah was calling for the two of them every evening. They were reciting old Arabic poetry or enjoying Ayesha's dance shows. He taught them to play at chess, the new board game that he had learnt and brought home from Persia. When she mastered the rules, Fatima was a serious opponent. Ayesha, though, lacked the patience and was quickly annoyed by the pawns claiming her queen. Even after the private wedding ceremony between Abdullah and Ayesha, their evenings continued in the same way. As his sons were away at war, they were the only family he had.

Abida slid the towel between Ayesha's legs, wiping her private parts thoroughly. Ayesha stirred impatiently.

"Stop that, you stupid girl. I don't like it."

"But, my mistress, you must be clean. Didn't you see the master's looks? You can be called upon later in the night."

"Nonsense! Uncle Abdullah will be too tired and stoned tonight. Haven't you seen the piles of food he devoured at dinner? And the pipes..."

Banan took Ayesha's left foot and started massaging it.

"You never know, mistress, maybe he would feel lonely after the party dies out."

"Well, in that case he'd call for Fatima first."

"What you did at the dance tonight, lady, was a very brave thing. The boy could be beheaded for such a gesture in a Muslim house."

"He's cute, don't you think?"

"You mustn't look at other men. You're married to Abdullah. You must always hold his eye or none at all."

"Technically speaking, I am. I do love him, but I can look around, can't I? Besides, if I only looked at Abdullah while dancing, I would fall over my feet many times. I need my eyes to see where I move."

"Yes, but it looked like you were flirting with the boy. You could get a beating for this."

Ayesha burst into a merry laugh.

"A beating? From Uncle Abdullah? Me? Never..."

"You know the rules, my lady."

"The rules are made for such as you and Fatima. There are no rules for artists like me."

"You should be more careful."

"No, you don't understand. I love life and I hate the *harem* with its high walls and tiny garden. I want to break free..."

"Maybe you can ask Fatima to take you on a trip together with Ibrahim."

"You still don't get it. I don't want to see the stinking sheep and the muddy fields and the ever dirty peasants. I want to see the world. I want to visit Ragusa and Venice and Istanbul. I want to sail the seas, not sit on a mule for a tour of our estates. I haven't been taken to Mostar since summer. I am a prisoner, not a wife!"

"You're exaggerating. It's the way of the world. Women shouldn't be exposed to dangers, they should be protected."

"Stop saying the word protect. It means life prison, nothing else. Anyway, what do you know? You're nothing but ignorant slaves."

The girls were visibly hurt. Abida and Banan spent all their days with Ayesha, serving her, cleaning up after her, washing her clothes, and no matter how tired they felt, in the evening still practicing belly dance with her. There were few young girls in the *harem*, so Ayesha lured them to dance with her with the promise that if a wealthy guest would particularly like one of them, she would insist he should take her into his *harem* as a lawful wife, not a concubine. In their position, it was a good offer, so they followed their mistress in her trail. Yet, their pride was hurt each time when their cheeky mistress rudely reminded them of their status in the household. Abida murmured:

"Calm down, Lady Ayesha. Let's dress for the night and go to your room. Fatima will soon come and kiss you good night."

An hour later, she was cuddling in her room, warmed by the embers in the brazier. The spacious bed in her sparsely candle-lit room was filled with cushions and blankets woven from delicate camel hair and wool. The walls were decorated with the bright ornamental red *kilim* design, which gave the room a mysterious glow. Ayesha and Fatima were lying on the bed next to each other. The girl's head was on Fatima's bosom, and the older woman gently stroked her long black hair.

"Fatima, do you think the boy is from Ragusa?"

"No, darling. He comes from Ston, the little town on the coast."

"Has he come to Adbina before?"

"No, Hrvoje used to come on his own with his barrels of oysters. The boy must be the apprentice."

"Do you know his name, Fatima?"

"No, and you shouldn't be asking questions about a boy. You're married, remember?"

"You are married, Fatima. I am just his wife legally, but in reality I truly am not."

"You mean because he hasn't slept with you yet?"

"Yes. And because he loves me like his daughter, not like his wife."

Fatima could not help herself asking.

"Has he ever tried?"

"Tried what?"

"To sleep with you, silly!"

Ayesha lifted her face and looked Fatima in the eyes. She knew how much the old woman loved Abdullah, and was reluctant to tell the truth. Even so, Fatima would know it. Ayesha was a poor liar and could not hide anything from her for long. Better to speak up.

"Do you remember the late August night when you felt tired and left us alone in the evening? Well, he tried then."

Fatima's heart missed a beat. How could she not have noticed it? Was the girl pregnant, and was that the reason Abdullah was so forgiving tonight?

"And... How did it go?"

"It didn't."

"What do you mean?"

"Fatima, your Abdullah is an old man. He could be my grandfather. He could not do it to me. He could not penetrate me, not even after I tried one of the courtesan tricks with him. Sorry, I just wanted to be a good wife. He burst into laughter and stroked my hair. Later he told me that I was too young and that we would try again in some years from then. I know I betrayed you in a way, but I love you both so much. And I was afraid you or Abdullah would send me away, should I not become his wife in the deed."

Fatima's face was pale and stern like stone. The girl's confession spilled disaster over the family like a sack full of foul beans. Abdullah couldn't prove a man with a beauty like Ayesha? That was dangerous for all of them. Virility was an integral part of the image of the *sipahi*, the nobles who held high posts in the Ottoman Empire. There were very few exceptions, like Hadim Ali Pasha, the Grand Vizier, who made his career as a eunuch, helped by numerous women's intrigues and the Sultana herself. In the end, it was the Sultana who asked Hadim to accompany her husband to the war in order to keep the Sultan away from foreign women and prevent him from bringing back exotic new wives. Hadim fought bravely, saved the Sultan's life and became his most trusted friend without having to prove his manhood as a procreator, which was exceptional. Everybody else had to sire as many children as possible. Abdullah was no Hadim, and he needed to demonstrate his virility.

Their two sons served the Sultan well on the battlefields of the Empire. Since some years ago, Fatima had hoped that Abdullah could stay at home and reign peacefully in Bosnia. He made huge improvements in the local farming and administration. Everybody adored him, either Muslims or Infidels. His policy was to let people free in their customs and beliefs as long as they worked hard and paid the taxes. So nobody was persecuted for the unusual mixture of Christian faith and pagan rites they were still practicing in the Bosnian hills. He left Christian churches intact and built mosques opposite them. At the dawn of each new day, the church bells and the cries of ayatollahs were competing for the people below. Whom should the subjects trust with their hopes in the life after death? Every religion was painting its own image of the way to the Paradise. The ways and paths might be different, and the gods called by different names, but the promise of the Paradise was only one. Peasants listened and strived. With their eyes directed into the Heaven above, they endured famines, illness, long cold winters, and hunger on earth. No matter how hard they worked, their struggle was tough, the path clad with sharp stones and suffering.

"Maybe he didn't want to sleep with you, Ayesha. You really are like his daughter."

"Fatima, forgive me. He would if he could. But don't worry, I didn't tell anybody."

"And you mustn't. For you know, Abdullah and I, we still sleep together sometimes... He's not impotent."

"That's what he told me, too. That you've been his true love since he was a child, and that he never felt much love for anybody else."

"Did he say that?"

Fatima lit up despite the seriousness of her worries.

"Yes, Fatima. I do understand him completely. You are so nice and kind. I love you, too."

Ayesha caught Fatima's hand and kissed it warmly.

"Thank you, darling."

Fatima sank deep in her thoughts. She returned the kiss on the mass of black curls, yet she could not drop the subject.

"Why did he try then?"

"He said he needed more children. He wanted to have a larger family or even another son. I'm sorry."

Fatima saw tears in the girl's eyes. She knew Ayesha was clever and emotional, but she would never have attributed her so much tact and sensibility. There was reason and love behind her image of a spoilt beauty. Fatima's anger and plan to scold her for the provocative dance evaporated.

"My little girl, don't be sorry. I wish he could have a child with you. It would indeed enhance his position, and ours accordingly."

"But it's impossible. We never tried again."

"Maybe he will tonight. He seemed thrilled by your performance. Although in my point of view, you deserved a thrashing. How dare you look at that Infidel boy like that? Are you out of your mind?"

"Oh, the boy... Isn't he cute with his blond curls? Do you think he liked me?"

"It was too obvious to everybody in the room how much he liked you! He made quite a scene with his penis up in his breeches. By the way, he risked his head."

"Not with Uncle Abdullah. He's too nice to punish anybody."

"Don't be so sure, baby. You don't know the anger of hurt pride in a man. Proud men are like elephants; they stroll around, peacefully sniffing for leaves and fruits on the ground until something stings them. It may be a just a bee sting in the trunk or an imprudent fly in his nostrils, but it can send the elephant flying into a rage, thrashing everything about him. So, show respect to your man and behave, my baby."

Fatima pressed a kiss on Ayesha's forehead and wrapped the blankets around her. She signaled it was time for rest. Ayesha held her possessively around the neck for some more minutes and would not let her go before giving her dozens of tiny kisses all over her dark, wrinkled face.

"I love you so much, *Anne* Fatima. You're so good."

Fatima put out the candles and silently left the room. A moment later, Ayesha was dreaming of freedom and foreign cities made of marble and gold. In her dream, she was flying across the sky free as a bird.

* * *

All that is in the world is love
And knowledge is nothing but gossip

– Füzuli, c. 1483 – 1556

Abdullah was lying on his vast bed supported by the colorful silk cushions and wrapped in soft lamb blankets. The textiles on the walls were crimson red, dark purple, blue, and yellow. Thick carpets covered the floor. The furniture was low and polished. In the soft light of the oil lamp, Abdullah slowly undressed and dismissed his servant. It was a nice party tonight. The guests from Ston are a funny lot. He did not blame the boy too much, Ayesha was clearly provoking him. She was extravagant and untamed. He sighed deeply. With both hands, he put his jeweled turban on the side table, revealing his too quickly balding head. His beard and moustache were still thick and bushy, with gray strands changing the color from black to silver. He moved his body around the world clumsily those days, for he had gained too much weight since he was not fighting battles for the Sultan anymore. His sons distinguished themselves at the side of Kemal Reis, who in the last few years had defeated the great Venetian fleet a couple of times and finally established the Ottoman control over Greece. Abdullah could stay out of it all and rejoice in the success of others. Comfortably seated, he took a book by his favorite Persian poet, Füzuli, and opened it at a random page. It was written on paper, the new invention which was pulled out of Chinese prisoners by hideous tortures and quickly prevailed in book manufacturing. It was so much lighter than parchment. You could take a paper book to your bed, while with the parchment books, reading was only possible standing behind the wooden chests to which the books were chained, so that an avid reader could not steal them. Abdullah loved books. They gave him intellectual challenge and a sense of luxury. His library was a mirror of his wealth. Füzuli's verses of love and philosophy travelled through his brain softly as though smoke was rising from incense, but his concentration wandered away, back to the party of that evening.

In his mind, he was seeing again Ayesha's belly moving in circles, her green, sleeved arms gliding through the air, now up, then down, like a swallow's chase for insects on a summer evening. She had grown into a beauty, and he could be proud. He should overcome his paternal feelings for the girl and take her properly, sleep with her and get her with child, or else she could become a threat to all of them. Like in an open book, he could read the audacity and the unruly thoughts in every move of hers. It should make him hot for her. Her penetrating black eyes should bring up the rough male want to subdue her, to fight with her the sweetest of all wars – the war of honey and pains of love under the blankets. Yet, he felt nothing of the sort. Ayesha had always been a child to him, and now she was a dangerous young woman. He had to think of something, he had to find a solution for her. Maybe he should divorce her and summon one of his sons to Bosnia and marry her to him. They both already had several wives, but they were both men in their prime – warriors and obedient servants of Allah. Either of them would surely know how to discipline the young woman who possessed the gut to flirt cheekily with other men in the room.

There was nothing to do about it tonight. He made sure Ayesha was locked up. The *Ragusans* were leaving tomorrow anyway, so no contacts could evolve between the Infidel boy and Ayesha. He spoke openly to Ibrahim – the eunuch is to guard her chastity upon his life. Still, Abdullah could find no peace in reading. His household, his *harem*, his family... decimated, taken to Heaven, a long, long time ago... All but his Fatima were gone. Ten years earlier, he had eight wives, five sons, and eleven daughters. He forgot the names of them all, so long ago it was. After Bosnia was finally part of the Ottoman Empire, he came there as the Sultan's special delegate to set up the administration, to build mosques and to enhance agriculture. Abdullah was given a *hass*, an estate so huge that it needed the full time management of several men. There were silver and copper mines in the north, in the mountains near Srebrenica, and vast fields of rice in the south, leaving acres of wheat fields and green pastures for stock in between. The rice fields were new in the area; the crops were more reliable than wheat, which in a rainy summer rotted away, leaving the whole population hungry and destitute. Rice loved rain, and when the weather was persistently dry, the new irrigation system helped feed the fields with waters from the Neretva. In 1490, the Sultan called Abdullah to the court in order to report on one hand about the situation in the new province, and on the other to advise the court the future steps to take in the occupation of the Balkan area. The conflict with Venetians was boiling even then, due to unsolved territory claims in Greece. The southern border, with *Ragusa*, was becoming dangerous. Abdullah prepared thoroughly for his trip; he collected the documents, he consulted with the Mufti and with local Imams. In the lovely March sun, he kissed every one of his vast family on both cheeks and left for Istanbul. He never thought that in five months' time there would be only Fatima left. By a fortunate coincidence, his two oldest sons had gone to the military school a year before. That had saved their lives.

They could never investigate properly how and why, after all the years of good health, after the Turks had implemented many new sanitary measures like clean water and a separate sewage system, in 1490 the black death struck again and devastated the populace of Bosnia with such force that more than half of it succumbed to the illness. For many decades, they had been remembering the big European plague only from the tales of the octogenarians. The horrible illness mostly spared the Bosnian peasants, whose tiny villages were scattered around the hills and isolated. Yet, the busy Ottoman settlements, trading with east and west hectically, were struck severely. Two thirds of the Turkish population got sick, and most of them died. The illness broke out just after Abdullah had left Abdina, and was ravaging for eight months. Fatima wrote to him about the disaster and its death toll. She urged him in her desperate letters not to come near Bosnia as long as possible. He was grateful to Allah for each of her notes – they were not only news, they were the news of life. By the time her first letters reached him, a few cases were diagnosed in Istanbul also. However, efficient Arabic physicians knew how to confine the sick and how to limit the sickness. In the new territories like Bosnia, few if any doctors were around. Abdullah was at the point of losing his mind not knowing what was happening to his wives and children at home in Abdina. Only Fatima and her two sons survived the plague. He thanked Allah for that. It seemed to him like a sign of God that he should not have taken any more wives, that forever, he should have stayed faithful to Fatima.

Oh, his Fatima! She was a true saint. He would never forget her aged face when he came back the following spring. He had left a strong woman, a pillar of his *harem* and family, who ruled not with a whip but with a kind word. Yet on his doorstep, he met a bent old woman whose eyes lost the sparkle. Her face was thin and wrinkled. She turned into a grey, sad woman who seemed like his mother. In long nights, between tears and sighs, she told him of each and everybody; how they caught the illness and died a painful death. It was a true wonder that she was still alive at all, despite the fact that she had been nursing all of them. She was alive, or rather, her body was alive, but her spirit was dead and broken. Abdullah tried to mend the evil and hired new workers to farm the lands and repopulate the community. Many poor people came from Pelješac and the coast, the Vlachs were lured from the north-east, and the shepherds descended the hills in the north of Abdina to start a more comfortable life around the fertile plains of the Neretva river. New animals, new crops, and a new life force invaded every corner of Bosnia. In the midst of all that excited noise, surrounded by rapid progress and development, only Abdullah's house remained forever silent. Fatima, thin as a shadow, less than half of her former weight, was moving around like a ghost, her eyes still reflecting the shock of pain and suffering she had sadly witnessed. No children were crying for attention, no running feet were disturbing the governor's afternoon nap. For months, he and Fatima were inseparable. They cuddled in their big bed, cried in each other's arms, made love every night with new hopes of a second coming, yet they couldn't conceive any more children. In the stress of the Black Death, while nursing the sick and administrating the healthy, Fatima had stopped her monthly bleedings, and she grew old and disillusioned.

Then, the Sultana sent them little Ayesha, a troubled child for a troubled couple. In her motherly way, Fatima soon established a connection with the little rebel and made her study art and poetry. Ayesha loved her singing and dancing lessons, and developed into a true artist. They acquired several slave girls to serve as Ayesha's companions. Finally, some life came back into the huge, luxurious *harem* halls. Fatima gained weight, got the color back in her cheeks, and happily dedicated all her time to Ayesha's education. Ayesha returned her affection warmly, and her character seemed to improve with every kiss from Fatima. The women in the *harem* were also providing for numerous orphans. The children loved Fatima and Ayesha. They were trailing behind them everywhere like a swarm of little bees. When the little ones were asleep, Ayesha and Fatima would join Abdullah in his chambers. Abdullah would wait impatiently to spend time with two most precious women in his life. A year ago, for the sake of appearances, they performed a marriage ceremony between him and Ayesha. Officially, he had two wives now, but in his heart, there was only one. No matter how many concubines Fatima brought to the palace in order to get him to enlarge the family, he would not touch any of them. He only had eyes for his mate, his companion and the love of his youth, Fatima.

On his pillow, he left the poetry book open and forgotten. He went outside. In a sharp, commanding voice, he asked the guard to bring Fatima to his bedroom. He wanted to see her tonight. They have to talk about little Ayesha. It was important they settle her down. Somehow, they would find the solution together.

* * *

Oh God, let me know the pain of love
Do not for even a moment separate me from it
Do not lessen your aid to the afflicted
But rather, make the lovesick me one among them...

– Füzuli, c. 1483 – 1556

It was one of those moonless and starless nights in which neither a cat could see its own paws nor a man could in any way perceive a figure walking in the yard. Was that shadow a pillar or a man? The pitch black veil covered the shapes of the world like a sea of dark troubles. Only around the pools and open streams of water, the pale stucco patterns were fused with the wreaths of white fog descending from the water into every corner of the palace. It was like a cold thick curtain, stifling all sounds and strangling all air. In the silence, Fatima woke up with a jolt, sensing a hand on her elbow.

"Please, wake up. Come to Master Abdullah with me, he wants to speak to you, madam."

"Now? It's the middle of the night."

"I know, I'm sorry."

Fatima threw a cloak around her shoulders and, passing Ayesha's room, silently opened the door and peeked in. The soft bundle of the girl's body was motionless, obviously the day had drained the energy out of her, and she was dreaming her sweet dreams. Fatima wondered what Abdullah wanted, but was pleased he summoned her. She wanted to talk to him. She was worried by the news of her husband's sexual disinterest in women. She didn't know how she would tackle that sensitive point in their conversation, but she knew she had to. On the other hand, she was flattered and pleased she was his only one at last. Entering his bedroom, she greeted politely:

"*As-Salāmu ʻalayka!*"

"*Wa ʻalayki s-salām!*"

Her husband was reading a book, comfortably wrapped in soft wollen blankets. Not without difficulty, Abdullah got up from the bed, his heavy body stumbling on ever shorter and thinner legs. Fatima quietly pretended she did not notice his unbalanced exercise. He finally came closer and took her in his arms. They held each other for a while.

"How is she? Is she asleep?"

"She's all quiet in her bed. She sleeps like an angel."

"It was a vicious thing, what she did today. What are you going to do with your spoilt daughter?"

"Abdullah, what are you going to do with your young rebellious wife?"

"You know she's not my wife, Fatima. Do you have any ideas?"

"I don't know. Just please do not send her away. It would break her heart. Mine also. And yours, too, my Abdullah."

"I know. Still, it is getting awkward. Ayesha doesn't know any limits in her boldness. She was provoking the Infidel in front of my eyes, Fatima. You know we can't allow that."

"I know. I am sorry. I did my best to put some sense in her stubborn head. Ayesha is wild and she has her opinions. It is difficult to undo the first seven years of wrong upbringing. You know how the Sultan's wives treated the child. She was their toy, their token to favors, rather than a person. What could I do? "

"I know, you did well all the same. I was thinking maybe if I divorce her and we marry her to our Yusuf."

"Yusuf has three wives, and his first, Layla, is a soft woman. She won't be up to Ayesha's character should the girl decide to play foul. I don't know. Will we destroy Yusuf's life in order to get rid of our problem?"

"I know what you mean. Ayesha is a defiant young woman."

"Can't you... I mean, you're her husband. She's emotional. If only she got pregnant... "

Abdullah looked at Fatima with sorrow, then sighed from his full body regretfully. He sat down on the edge of the bed, adjusting the gold-trimmed cushions trimmed behind his back before he spoke up.

"Stop, please. I am three times her age, and since 1490 I cannot sleep with another women. I just can't. I'm not less of a man for it. I know the Sultan and the court would think me incompetent should they find out. You know the reason. We lost so many children during the plague. I still think our great Allah sent me a message then."

Fatima remained still. What was she supposed to say? On the one hand, it was her life's dream coming true, on the other the position of the Bosnian *bey*, the governor Abdullah al Ibn, was threatened.

"Could we ask the Sultan to send one of our sons home and prepare him to take the *hass* over from you?"

"Not until the Venetians are expelled from Greece for good. Yusuf and Ali are good commanders, our army needs them."

"How long do you think it will be?"

"Maybe a year, maybe two. Who knows who the Venetians will buy next year to fight their wars? They have no honour and no courage. They would do anything just to have another year of trading and minting money. And some of our caliphs are even doing business with them. It's a mess."

"You say trading... That gives me an idea... "

"What kind of idea?"

"Can we buy a baby?"

"What do you mean?"

"Can't Ibrahim travel through Bosnia and find a pregnant girl and bring her to us? There must be thousands of them. He can bring her to the *harem*, and we pretend she's your concubine and the baby is yours."

"And you think the product of two stupid peasants can bear my name? Are you..."

"Stop the nonsense, Abdullah. Your blood is as red as the peasants'. Look at the janissaries, they're brave soldiers and great thinkers. They are one of the keys of our success."

"My son shall not be a janissary! Woman!"

"So how will you get another child... Shall we look for a new wife? Can you please pick one that will wake you up! For I am your age and too old to bear children."

Fatima's voice revealed panic. Abdullah was watching her in shock. He came to honor her sharp mind and intuition, and he knew she was right. He must have at least another child, or, after the next visit to the Sultan's court, he could be dismissed from governing Bosnia. He loved the country, he felt so much at home in Mostar and in Abdina. The green hills, the fruitful plains and the river Neretva with its thousand streams flowing into the delta and into the sea. He loved the woods where he could hunt down the wild anytime he pleased. And the oysters. And the carps from the lakes, fat and tasty. Not to speak of the various vegetables, which tasted sweeter than in Istanbul, for the slower growth nourished them with more minerals. Speaking of sweets, the honey from the woods, which smelled like pines and flowers, was simply the best he had ever had. Food and comfort! That was his Bosnia, the country won by his ancestors in ferocious fights, and the country which had taken so much from Abdullah, yet was giving so much back. He was tired and old. He didn't want to move again. Oh, the days since his thoughts started turning around good food, nice poetry, dance and musical diversions and comfort. Who cared about women? Lovemaking is for young people, whose juices boil in their veins, and delicious food is for the old, whose blood meanders slowly and surely towards the infinite eternal fields of love like the Neretva flows peacefully to the sea.

In fact there were two problems: one was Ayesha and her wild ways, one was himself. He had to separate the two and think thoroughly before his next move. Fatima was sharp at pointing out the problem, but she usually could not see far enough into the future. She was so upset, he had to calm her down.

"Fatima, please, don't panic. We will find a solution. This idea of yours, about a pregnant peasant, is a good one. We will talk to Ibrahim in the morning. Now, come here and stay with me tonight, will you?"

"Oh, Abdullah, I'd love to. But you must understand... I

want all the best for you."

"I know, my love, I know. Come here, sleep here tonight. I'll send Ibrahim back to the *harem*."

There was such longing in his voice she couldn't resist. She knew he needed her company, not so much for amorous exertion, but more to overcome the loneliness and the feeling of loss. Despite his governing position, Abdullah was a lonely old man.

"It's fine. I will tell him. I'll stay with you."

Ibrahim was dozing on the *divan* in the antechamber. His face was nicely shaped, fine and sensuous, almost like a woman's, and his black eyebrows and beard were fastidiously trimmed. Fatima knew his head was shaven under his *fez*, still, she found him very handsome. He had worked for Abdullah since Abdullah married his second wife Selma while Fatima was ill with fever so many years ago. In her distress over sharing her husband with another woman for the first time in her life, Fatima cried bitterly on Ibrahim's shoulder. He consoled her as best he could and helped her take over leadership in the household. She knew she could trust him with everything. They became very good friends; her wellbeing was his life's goal. Sometimes Fatima thought Ibrahim would be more than a friend, had he not been just half of a man. His fate was that of many eunuchs guarding the harems in the Ottoman Empire. Many years earlier, he confided in her. Ibrahim was a weak, sickly child, the fifth son of his father Mohammed, and wanted to become a scholar or an *imam*. His older brothers were all in military training; they were on their best way to become successful soldiers and commanders. When Ibrahim was eight, his father made the decision and had him castrated, so that he could enter a *harem* at an early age. For years Ibrahim was obliged to do the things he hated most – military training, studies of administration and defense, and some some study of medicine. At the age of twenty, he entered his first job as a eunuch in Abdullah's *harem* and settled down. He was with them through the plague and helped Fatima nurse the sick. His knowledge of medicine helped them out in many moments of crisis – he would even help with births. He grew old with Fatima and Abdullah. Though he was physically fit and kept his fighting skills, he got tired more quickly and needed more rest.

Fatima put her hand on his shoulder and whispered into his ear to go back to the *harem* and watch over Ayesha. He nodded, still drunk with sleep, and staggered away. Fatima turned back to the room and smiled tenderly to herself. She loved the night, it was her night at last.

* * *

How doest thou know what sort of king I have within
   me as companion?

                                      – Rumi, 1273

It was still dark when Marin and Hrvoje were harnessing their
mules to the overloaded wagons. At Marin's feet, their watchdog
Pero, a tall mountain shepherd, was yapping furiously at the
barrels, jumping wildly up and down around the last, the fourth
wagon of the train, bound south with goods to sell at home in
Ston.

   "What the hell has gotten into this dog? Marin, do something
or he will wake everybody up!"

   "Hush, Pero, hush!"

   The dog stopped and looked at Marin for a moment, then
continued his crazy act as though possessed by the invisible devil
challenging the obedience of his dog's brain. Hrvoje put the bridle of the first mule down and stepped over to the noisy beast.
His heavy boot kicked the dog with force, and its wild barking
changed to pitiful yelps of pain.

   "Why did you do that, Hrvoje? He's just a dog!"

   "Yes, and I am a man with a head on my shoulders. I want
to keep it that way. We must get out of here as soon as possible
and as quietly as possible. You don't know what Abdullah might
think of your last night's insolence this morning. He might show
us his true hospitality today."

   Marin bowed to the dog and cuddled his head softly.

   "It's fine, just stop barking, Pero! I'll give you a nice bone
this evening."

   The dog returned a subdued look full of misery, still yelping
softly in agony. Then he moved to the leading mule of the caravan, taking up his position as watchdog. His looked at the last
wagon knowingly, as though he was saying he knew better, but
is ready to obey his masters no matter what.

   Finally the bridles were fastened, and the train left Abdullah's
courtyard. At a slow pace, the mules took the road to the south.
The morning was cold and foggy, so Hrvoje and Marin lit a torch
on each wagon. It was not long before the sunrise. After they
walked for more than an hour, the first light from the east was
promising a new day, hopefully sunnier and warmer than that
previous week. It was the rainy and humid late November time.
The mules were puffing with effort dragging the heavy burden
uphill. The east with its shimmering was behind them. Marin
turned his head and admired the rich golden dawn which didn't
give them enough visibility to put out the torches yet. Pero was
running around the wagons, always on the lookout for danger
from which he should protect his masters. He was still upset with
the last wagon, led firmly by Marin, but now his loud barks didn't

disturb anybody but deer and stray predators of the forest. They heard foxes woofing just a while ago. Hrvoje wondered whether a fox would come closer to their train out of curiousity, as they many times did. At this time of year their fur was thick and soft, and it would make a nice present to his wife. Marin was still concerned with the dog.

"What's wrong with my barrels today, Pero? Why are you barking at me all the time?"

The dog just stared at his master with empty black eyes, barking and jumping around. Marin shook his head, not knowing what to do with his faithful, yet unruly companion. He loved that dog. He was intelligent and well trained. On many occasions, Pero warned them in time to avoid trouble. But all the same – he was just a dog.

The sun came up and lifted their spirits. They knew it would not warm them enough and that only a good fire would keep them through the night. Nevertheless, it was like a miracle when the dark hills changed to the rich colours of the day. Some slopes turned bright orange and red with the autumn leaves of huge birches, others were of dark green, overgrown with tall, ancient evergreen pines resisting all seasons. The narrow path was stony and unkept as the route was seldom used since Bosnia had become Turkish. The Turkish traders avoided the Venetian territory and Ragusa; they preferred to deal with the eastern lands and Serbia. They were all under their rule now.

Marin was hungry, and, while walking, he took a piece of bread and cheese out of his bundle. He started to chew voraciously. Here and then, he threw a scrap to Pero, who jumped at it happily. Hrvoje looked back and smiled at them.

"The hungry pair! Don't eat your profit on the way!"

"I am sorry, Uncle Hrvoje. An empty sack cannot stand upright."

"Yeah, just keep walking. Abdullah's horsemen can still go after us if he rises on the wrong side of bed this morning."

"Uncle Hrvoje, when will we make a stop for lunch?"

"Your mouth is full and you're asking about lunch! Keep walking, my boy! We'll stop for the night in the late afternoon just before twilight. You remember the wooden shack above the gorge of Buna?"

"It's under the sky, the shack is so tiny! We'll be freezing."

"You complain? You're young and your blood is high. You'll think of girls to keep you warm. What about my old bones?"

"You'll never grow old, Uncle Hrvoje!"

Marin walked happily, with a satisfied feeling of a job done. They still had a week of travelling ahead, but he couldn't wait to get to the Žitomislić Monastery, where the monks were rich and generous and would serve them a meal fit for a king in exchange for some spices and incense they had loaded in Abdina. Life was good when the sun was shining, and God was with them. In a week they would come home and Aunt Olga would bake some sorts of wonderful spicy cakes for Christmas, for which only she knew the recipes and the names.

At last, after hours on the road, they found the clearing with the provisional hut and unbridled the mules to graze on the beechnuts which were plentiful in this time of year. Mules moved around freely. Eventually, when their bellies were full, they would return to the caravan by themselves. They were easy to care for and could eat anything. Yet Hrvoje always had some special oats ready and made sure that they got enough fresh water, for the wellbeing of his beasts was his main insurance on the way. The wagons with their precious load stood still under the bare trees.

Marin went into the bushes to collect the wood for the fire, with Pero in tow. By the time they came back, it grew dark. Hrvoje lit the fire and put a pot on it; he would make them a lamb stew from the meat he bought at Abdina. The one thing the Mediteranean people never were short of was salt, and another was spices. Soon the smells made Marin's mouth water, and he patiently sat by his master, waiting for the delicious meal. Suddenly, Hrvoje jerked with apprehension.

"Shhht! Somebody's coming!"

At the same moment, Pero jumped at one of the wagons and got into his yapping fit again, his eyes firmly fixed on one of the barrels. They all heard tapping at the wood, and the barrel started to lean first to one side then to the other. It looked like an invisible force was moving it, and Marin's eyes opened white with terror. Was Abdullah getting his revenge by sending *jinns*, the evil spirits, after them? Before he could run away, the barrel lost its balance and, with a girl's cry, fell from the wagon. The lid opened, and a skinny young boy, wrapped thickly in a fur cloak, materialized. Hrvoje came to his senses first.

"Who are you? What are you doing here?"

The creature dropped the hood, and the lovely face of the green emerald dancer from the previous night smiled kindly at the flabberghasted men.

"Hello, I'm Ayesha, Abdullah's daughter. Sorry I have frightened you. But there was no other way I could escape Ibrahim, our eunuch."

Now Marin found his tongue.

"And you were hiding in the barrel all the way?"

"Yes. It wasn't very comfortable. What's for dinner?"

Hrvoje's face was pale with worry. Dark suspicions were overriding his thoughts.

"Are you indeed Abdullah's daughter?"

"Yes. Who do you think I am?"

Marin was still trying to put the facts together while Hrvoje continued with the interrogation.

"So, where did you put the wheat which was in the barrel?"

"I spilled it out."

"Are you crazy? There were five pecks of wheat in there!"

"Indeed, it was a narrow escape in the barrel. I couldn't stretch my legs, so I'm hurting all over."

Hrvoje lost his patience. He moved towards the wagons.

"We're going back. We'll pack the train now and bring you back. Abdullah will either pay for the grain or give us another lot. What a waste..."

Marin couldn't believe his eyes. Finally, he found his tongue.

"Are you real or are you a *jinn*? You're so beautiful..."

The girl burst into a jolly laugh. She was no ghost. She moved closer, but the shepherd dog Pero jumped at her and knocked her to the ground. He lay on her body with his full weight, yapping excitedly at his masters, trying to show to them how right he had been this morning. Hrvoje came closer, leaving the girl under the dog. She was pale with terror, turning her face away from the sharp teeth and the saliva dripping from his snout. Hrvoje needed more information before he was to take action.

"So, why have you run away from home? Have you done anything stupid?"

Ayesha was trembling with fear, she lost her self-confidence. Tears welled up in her dark eyes, she was trying to cover her face with her hands.

"Can you get the dog down, please?"

"In a minute, first answer my questions, young lady. Why have you run away?"

"I wanted to visit my aunt in Ragusa. Abdullah doesn't like travelling outside the Ottoman borders. He didn't let me go either with you or with our eunuch. So, I thought..."

"Stupid girl! You wasted the grain, and you put yourself and us in a great danger! And we have to bring you back to Abdullah, don't you realize?"

"Please, take me to Ston with you. I have money, I have jewels, I can pay you well! You will get many times the worth of the grain. Nobody will know, I promise!"

Marin motioned to the dog to let the girl free, and Pero moved to his side obediently. Ayesha stood up and brushed the leaves from her cloak, throwing side glances at Marin in hope he would be her ally. The boy looked at his uncle apologetically.

"Maybe we could..."

"Shut up, boy! You know nothing! If Abdullah's men find her with us, we're doomed!"

Now Ayesha turned resolutely to the old man. She pointed at Marin and said in a clear, malicious voice:

"If you bring me back to Abdina, I will say he has abducted and raped me."

Hrvoje jumped at her with his hand raised. Before he slapped her, Marin leaped in between.

"Don't Uncle, please. Let's see what we can do..."

Ayesha sighed with annoyance and despair.

"You don't know how it is to be locked in the *harem* night and day. I'm bored to death there. Please, help me! I can walk, I will obey your rules, I will be good on the way and I will pay you well, I promise!"

"Promise, promise... The only thing you can promise us is death, woman!"

Marin assumed the role of intermediator, and Hrvoje was losing the edge; there was indeed nothing to do at the moment. Travelling by night was far more dangerous than keeping the girl with them. The men and the beasts needed to rest and to eat; they had been walking for more than eleven hours without a rest.

"Let's have some dinner, then we'll talk. We can't send her to the woods in the middle of the night, can we?"

Hrvoje turned around and stepped to the fire. He fell silent, not knowing what to do. It had been a hard day without this complication. He had to think, and thinking is better done with a full stomach. They ate in silence. Marin brought water in two wooden mugs for the girl and for himself. He handed Hrvoje a smaller waterskin with a green and red painting of a herb on it. Hrvoje held it high above his mouth and drank from it. It was for the first time in her life that Ayesha could sense the sweet smell of alcohol, a drink which was never part of the various beverages at the palace. At least not while women were present. She knew that men would drink *rakija* with starters, particularly while there were Infidel visitors, but she had never tasted or smelled it. Then Hrvoje took out some tobacco and stuffed his pipe.

"Marin, go and wash the pots in the creek!"

Marin collected the pottery and looked up at Ayesha and Hrvoje. Ayesha's eyes were watery. Marin headed towards the dark of the tree trunks. Hrvoje was knitting his brows in confusion. When Marin was gone to the stream, he spoke up slowly:

"So, what shall we do to stay alive, Lady Ayesha? You tell me, please."

Ayesha felt bad. The melancholy and weariness of the old man touched her heart. But young and free at last, she could not share the weight of his fear.

"Master Hrvoje, let's talk about this in the morning. I promise I will protect you and your son from Abdullah's revenge or anger. Please, don't say it. I said promise again... But this is the best I can do. Here, please, take it..."

From the pocket of her cloak, she produced a heavy leather purse trimmed with gold. Hrvoje shook his hands.

"Wait, maybe you will need the purse to get back home. You can stay with us tonight. Tomorrow we will spend the night at the Žitomislić Monastery. The orthodox monks there are honest and generous, maybe we can find a solution with them."

Ayesha was not too sure of that. She did not trust any church authority. Still, Hrvoje's suggestion should do for now.

"Thank you, Master Hrvoje. You will not regret your kindness."

"I hope so. One more thing: don't seduce the boy. Marin was head over heels besotten with you last night. I saw how you danced around him. I understand you're bored and like to play around, but we would all like to survive this ordeal. Yesterday, Marin's stupid reaction could have cost us our lives. He's young and crazy, women are all he can think about at the moment. But he's a good boy. You know what it would mean if you had a liason with him."

"I know. I promise I will leave him alone. Tell me where I can sleep."

"You will go to the shed with me for tonight, and I will put Marin on the sentry with the wagons. As God is my witness, I will strike you down and vultures will eat your warm guts should you touch Marin or just look at him. So don't play with fire! Do you hear me?"

"Yes, but..."

"No buts, Lady Ayesha, you will do as you're told, or you won't see the day tomorrow. You're much less of a threat to us dead than alive. Do you understand this?"

"I do, Master Hrvoje. And I promise..."

Hrvoje wasn't hearing her out. He picked his blankets and the gear and went to the shed, explaining the sleeping arrangements to Marin on the way. Thus began the first night of their journey, a night pregnant with sounds of owl cries and fox howls, a night of the game between the predators and their innocent prey.

* * *

Sleep sits heavy on mine eyelids.
Sing to me, brother, and refresh me.

– Marko Kraljevič and the Vila, Serbian national
epic, 15th century

The morning was still dark, so dark it seemed more like the middle of the night, when Hrvoje whistled his beasts and men into action. Ayesha would not walk, for the fear her figure could give her away. Hrvoje was not risking anything. She was lying on the first wagon, clad in an old cloak, with a dirty cap covering her lush black hair. Her right leg was immobilized with a long wooden stick and bandages wrapped around it. Her identity was that of Marin's younger brother Antunić, who fell down a slope and sprained his knee. Should they meet anybody, she had to pretend to be asleep. Luckily, for miles and miles there was no one in sight.

It was a lousy morning to be on the road. The weather turned grey and cloudy, so instead of a wonderful sunrise like the day before, first light was sickly hesitating to show. Marin was tired. He had slept fitfully on the wagon, exposed to the cold during the night. The sounds of the woods woke him up every couple of minutes. The dog barked at the pitch dark night every now and then, responding to the woofing of wolves and the cries of the owls. Marin was walking beside the last wagon of the train, trying to guess what Uncle Hrvoje had in store for the girl. There was time enough to brood over it, as they could not reach the Orthodox Monastery of Žitomislić before late afternoon. He could not see what Ayesha was doing on the first wagon under the severe eye of his master, but he could hear the silence broken only now and then by a raven crying or the wind blowing through the leafless branches. He knew that it was a good sign that Hrvoje took the girl along. Hopefully, his master would find a good solution for all of them. He had contacts on the route from Ston to Mostar, and Marin presumed he could find somebody to take care of Ayesha. Secretly, he wished they could travel to Ston together and he would have another opportunity to speak to her. His heart beat faster only thinking of her falling out of the barrel like a ripe peach from a tree.

Caught up in his reverie, he almost missed hearing heavy hooves beating the road behind him. Pero, the dog, though, did not miss the thudding sounds, and he yapped alarm long before they beheld the rider wrapped in a long black robe. Hrvoje discreetly untied his dagger at the belt. Then he went on as though it was nothing, sticking stubbornly to his trodden way. It was Marin who saw the monk first. He immediately recognized his black hat *klobuk* and black cassock, tied at the belt with a heavy cord. The cord had a large wooden cross at the end. It was a sign of absolute devotion to God. He was an Orthodox travelling monk. The monk held his high brown horse back and approached Marin in an elegant trot. Marin commented admiringly:

"You have a wonderful beast, Father!"

The man was young, though the long beard made him look ancient. His vivid brown eyes glared from under the abundant hair like two brown embers. He descended from the saddle and replied joyfully:

"Thank you, young man. I shall give it a bit of rest. My *vranac* (my black horse), has been galloping all the way from Mostar, and it is time for me to use my feet for these last few miles to Žitomislić."

"Are you going to Žitomislić, Sir?"

"I am not only going there, I live there, my boy. That is, for

another two days, to be precise... Then, I am going home. May
I join you on your way?"

"Of course, you may."

Marin smiled politely at the monk. Then he called over to
Hrvoje:

"Master Hrvoje, can Father... what is your name, Sir?"

"Slobodan Milić."

"Can Father Slobodan join us on the track to Žitomislić?"

A nod of the hooded head at the head of the train meant
confirmation. Merrily, Marin went on:

"My uncle and me, we're going to stay the night at Žitomislić.
The monks there are always so kind and hospitable, but you
should know this..."

"Yes, we're trying to keep the spirits high for our Christian
brothers travelling through Turkish lands. Where are you from,
young man?"

"I am from Ston. And this is my father, Hrvoje Salić. My
name is Marin Salić. We do salt and oysters. And you, Father,
who are you if I may ask in the name of God?"

"Blessed be his name. I am Slobodan Milić from the island of
Vis. I have spent my twelve years of education at Žitomislić. My
father is Serbian. He insisted I had an Orthodox schooling and
sent me to the Žitomislić Monastery a long time ago."

"Are there Serbians on Vis? I didn't know that. But my
education, Sir, is very shaky. I can read and write, and do some
calculations. I have been working from a young age."

"Well, you seem an intelligent chap. Never mind the monasteries. It's not for everybody. As for Serbians and Vis, it is a long
story how my family came to Vis one hundred and more years
ago. It was my great grandfather Štefan who came from Serbia
just after the big Battle of Kosovo polje. Have you heard of the
battle?"

Marin had not. He had never been to a proper school. It was
Hrvoje himself who sat with the boy during long winter afternoons in order to bring him by some basic knowledge of the Latin
Bible, along with some principles of their business. The only volume they had in the house was a modestly embellished copy of
the Bible including the Old and the New Testament. Hrvoje got
the book as a present from his *Ragusan* business partner when he
saved him from bankruptcy with loads of oysters for Saint Blaise
Day a decade ago. The book was very precious. Hrvoje said it
was worth more than the house, so it was under lock and key in
the cabinet. Only Hrvoje had the key, and took it out every now
and then to read. Marin shook his head.

"You haven't heard of the Battle of Kosovo?"

"I'm afraid no, Father. I told you I am but an ignorant boy."

"We can change that. If you're staying at Žitomislić, we can
do something with you and your poor knowledge. We'll talk

after dinner. I will tell you this sad and brilliant saga of how the Serbians lost their kingdom and the Ottomans lost their Sultan on the same day. Would you like to hear it?"

"Yes, Father, it would be my honor to learn from you."

Marin looked admiringly at Slobodan. He was so tall and handsome, so worldly and educated. Judging by his splendid horse, he had to be rich, too. Marin was a modest boy and grateful to his fate which brought him to Hrvoje and to the sea. He loved Ston and he loved the peaceful daily rhythm of the tide and waves, which licked the shores and almost never disturbed the lagoon with wild stormy foams. However, like most of the boys of his age, he sometimes yearned for wild adventures, a life of freedom and independence. His nature was such of profound emotions. When he was a little boy, he had tears and laughter in the same sack most of the time. He could sing some Bosnian folk songs about beautiful maidens and courageous knights, and sometimes he imagined himself being one of the men fighting for their fatal ideals. He looked up at Slobodan, who despite his monkish habit, looked noble and adventurous. His deep voice brought Marin back to reality.

"Who is the child on the first wagon?"

"Oh, him... He's just nobody... I mean, he's my younger brother Antunić. The stupid boy fell and broke his knee. He can't walk now, so my father put him on the wagon."

"Is the man leading the train your father? You've just called him Master Hrvoje..."

"Yes, he likes to be called master."

"We can put your brother on my horse if you want. The mule is really straining."

Hrvoje turned back with a polite smile.

"Father Slobodan, this is very kind of you. The boy is asleep now, and I think it is best we keep it the way it is. It's not far anyway..."

Ayesha, dressed as Antunić, stayed quiet. She knew she should be careful. She remembered that some time ago the prior of Žitomislić came to Abdullah with a solemn plea to let them continue their monastic order and keep cultivating their lands. Abdullah signed their petition in Latin and granted them their rights within the borders of their estates, provided that they pay the due taxes to the Empire on a regular basis. The Ottoman rule was above all practical. They were not keen to terrorize the population of Bosnia and thus lose the precious lives of hard working serfs and their nobles. Since the conquest, one by one, the Bosnian nobles, who used to serve King Tvrdko, came to Abdullah and paid their respects. As the governor of Bosnia, Abdullah was busy concluding various peace treaties and friendship pacts with them. He was the image of patience and dealt with each one individually, which persuaded many (gently but firmly) to take up the Ottoman ways. Sometimes they became Abdullah's vassals before they took the vows to Allah. Nobody really bothered about the religion – they were part of the Ottoman Empire and the *bey*, their governor, knew very well that their children would reject the Christ eventually for the belief in the new and the only true God, Allah. It was the practical rule of gradual assimilation, and it was a profitable way of getting the taxes paid in the meantime.

They mounted and descended the slopes for hours until, through the mist of a light autumn rain, they caught sight of the monastery walls and the bell tower of the chapel beyond. Slobodan led the way, and the door opened immediately. At the courtyard, the monastery laymen took the visitors' mules to the stables. Hrvoje turned to the monks with the question of where they were to sleep. The chubby monk with a bunch of keys in his hands looked at Slobodan, who nodded apprehensively.

"You will have two cells for tonight, one for the boys and one for yourself, my master. They both have fireplaces, so you can dry your clothes. Here, come along!"

Hrvoje almost dropped his bags. He meant the girl and Marin would be sharing the cell! How could he prevent this?

"Thank you, Father. Maybe I'll take the little one with me. He's injured and might develop a fever during the night..."

"Oh, is it so? Then first bring him to our apothecary. For sure Father Luka will find a remedy for his pains."

Now Marin jumped in. The apothecary could not be such a fool not to distinguish between a boy or a woman's limb.

"Thank you, thank you. I think it's best if I take Antunić with me. If he feels worse, we will come to Father Luka. Thank you."

Swiftly, he lifted Ayesha from the wagon and she only nodded silently, keeping her head away from Marin's face. Hrvoje paled. That was a dead end. He almost whispered:

"I'll check on you boys in a minute. Just let me take care of the goods and the wagons first."

The monk shrugged his shoulders and turned towards the refectory.

"As you wish. The vespers are at seven, and the dinner is served in the refectory after the vespers. You're expected to follow our ways here, you know."

Marin followed the monk, his knees shaking with excitement and the fear that he would drop his precious burden onto the muddy courtyard. They came to the small cell, and the monk put on the torch attached to the wall.

"There are some candles on the shelf, but don't waste too much wax, boys. It is expensive."

"No, we won't, Father. Thank you."

"Are you coming to the vespers? You surely would do with a nice prayer, wouldn't you? Young lads like you are full of sins even when they're not aware of it."

The monk winked kindly, and Marin replied fervently.

"I will come, Sir. I love your brothers' singing. It's magic. For my brother...I think he would be better off to stay here and get some rest. The wagon wasn't very comfortable."

"But I would love to come, Marin," said Ayesha in a clear, deep voice. She almost looked and sounded like a boy, like a young boy before his voice broke.

Marin froze, yet the monk laughed heartily.

"That's the spirit, you see! Your little brother is a good Christian! You can carry him to the church yourself. You're lucky tonight. A deer crossed our cook's path too narrowly. Dinner is venison stew with chestnuts. Do you like chestnuts, my boy?"

"I do. Thank you."

The monk nodded and closed the door behind him. The young people were alone. They sank into an awkward silence. Marin was worried about Ayesha wanting to go to the mass. It did not seem right.

"Why do you want to go to the church? It's not your God. It's hardly ours – we're Catholic and the mass is Orthodox."

"So, why are you going then?"

"It's polite to the monks who take such good care of us. It goes without saying. They offer us their hospitality, and we should follow and respect their services. But you...This is different."

"I want to see how it looks when somebody speaks to me in the name of God. We pray to Allah individually and the *imam* only talks about everyday things, he's not the word of God in Islam."

"The mass is in Serbian...They sing it, you know."

"Fine, I adore music. But I thought the Christians pray in Latin..."

"We do in Ston, but not the Orthodox in Serbia. They say they're closer to God in their native language."

"Is then the Bible translated into Serbian?"

"Yes and no. The fathers use the old Slavic dialect of the brothers Cyril and Methodius. But I can understand much of it. Frankly speaking, I don't know much more about it..."

"Do you know the Quran?"

"No, what is it?"

"It is our Holy Book, like the Bible. It's the word of our god, Allah, and written in Arabic. I can recite it verse by verse."

"I can't know the Bible by heart. It is much too long..."

The vespers were ringing and it was time to go. Marin felt uncomfortable. He gathered that Ayesha had had a thorough education. Yet, she was just a girl. There were various rumors as to how the Muslims treat their women. First, they could be

married to more than one wife. Second, women had to wear the
veil, but Ayesha, even at the palace, was skipping hers. She was
obviously a libertine. There was a knock on the door.

"Marin, are you coming? The mass is ringing..."

Marin unbolted the door and let Hrvoje in.

"We are both expected to come to the mass, Master Hrvoje.
The monk didn't take no for an answer..."

Marin turned purple with his white lie. Why was he protecting
her? What was so special about the girl that made him lie to his
benefactor and friend? Ayesha threw him a grateful look behind
Hrvoje's back, then immediately tried to calm down his tension:

"Master Hrvoje, it is better we leave our emotions out of this
and act as naturally as possible. The monks are not likely to
look under my blouse or trousers, are they? I'll stick to Marin
and pretend to be Antunić."

"Christ! Allah's bride at a Christian mass... The ravings of
a madman are less... Never mind, let's just try to survive this
evening, and we'll see what to do tomorrow."

Marin carried Ayesha to the chapel on his back. Her eyes
shone with curiosity. The chapel was full of warm candlelight,
which embraced the monks and the visitors like a grace of God.
At the altar and on the walls around it there were beautiful golden
icons. They reflected the light and the sentiments which so long
ago had warmed the artists' hearts and endowed them with the
divine inspiration to create such wonderful works of art. In their
bright glow, they represented different saints performing good
deeds to the people. All their faces were looking up, to the invisible master of their fate embodied in a huge golden eye of God at
the top of the altar. Ayesha, raised in the faith of Islam, which
never and in no artistic form whatsoever portrayed the face of
Allah, was deeply confused. She bit her lip not to ask questions.
Were all those men in the icons Gods? Or, was it only the eye
above them?

The priest who would lead the mass came in and kneeled in
front of one icon, then got up and turned to the altar with his
arms raised towards the golden eye. He started his pious chant,
and the monks answered in wonderful voices of great choir singers.
Ayesha and the Catholic men from Ston were mesmerized. The
mass was a profound spiritual unison with God, and it tied them
to the Universe with millions of invisible strings as though the
notes and the tunes of the psalms would be golden threads to
Heaven. It was a wonderful performance of light and music. It
was Heaven descending upon them, touching their spirits on the
Earth only for a few brief moments. God was everywhere, they
could all feel his love, and they could follow his miracles.

Marin had tears in his eyes, Ayesha nothing but deep wonder.
Hrvoje still looked worried. No chants could stop his thoughts
about what to do with the graceful new child he found in the

barrel instead of the precious wheat he was supposed to deliver to his *Ragusan* trade partner in a week's time. In silence, they marched to the refectory, where it smelled of meat cooked in spices. There was the scent of juniper, fresh rosemary, and thyme in the vapours of the clay pots. The sweet, bitter aroma of sage was vaguely floating in the air. Slobodan came in after them and motioned Marin and Antunić to a wide bench. They ate voraciously without taking notice of their neighbors. In the dim light of the fire, they could not see their faces anyway. Their empty stomachs forgot the chant of the spiritual Heaven and demanded their toll. The stew and a piece of still warm hunk of bread were delicious. The pitchers were full of fresh apple cider, their surfaces shining with little drops of moisture. There was even an apple and a handful of nuts for dessert. Ayesha, her hair hidden and her face bent low over her meal, ate up as though it was her last supper.

After the meal, Slobodan summoned the visitors to his cell. It was a huge room with bookshelves and several wooden benches at the walls comfortably padded with sheepskins. The narrow windows high in the wall were covered by thinned, nearly translucent goatskins, which gave the room a mysterious glow enhanced by the reflection of the burning logs in the fireplace. The visitors were seated and ready for history. Slobodan's face changed to a solemn expression – he was eager to tell them about the Kosovo battle. Marin was tired. He yawned in despair. The only thing he wanted was to go to bed. Under pressure, he almost forgot the incredible sleeping arrangements for the night. Slobodan started his tale in a deep reciting voice.

"This, my friends, is the story of heroes who are long forgotten on both sides. It is mostly a story of hate and betrayal, of murder and abandon. In the last decades of the 14th century, our grandfathers feared and hated the Turks, for they were notorious for invading Serbian villages or towns, and plundering the livestock, the food, the corn, which was scarce in those days. They would kill all that opposed them. They would abduct the young boys for janissaries. They simply lifted them on their horses and took them away like sacks of wheat or piglets. Thus, whole generations would be lost to our mothers and lands forever. They raped women and terrorized the elders. The villages had developed a kind of warning system, by lighting fires on hilltops, so that people could escape to the woods or hide in the churches. However, even warnings did not help much. The Turks were cruel warriors, and the peasants delivered to their mighty riders like sheep to the wolves. Towns, villages, sacred places like churches and monasteries... nothing was safe before the Turks. Our people were left bereft, hungry, and cold.

King Dušan the Mighty of Serbia and the Bosnian King Tvrdko were resisting the Turkish invasions for decades, when the rule of Dušan's son Uroš, a childless and incompetent weakling put our defense lines into jeopardy. King Uroš the Weak was nothing of the man to protect his lands against the brave and very much popular Sultan Murad and his victorious sons Bayezid and Yakub. During the last years of Uroš' reign, Serbia was losing hold of its territories and people were starving. After king's death, Prince Lazar realized the precarious situation and gathered a huge and brave Serbian army to stand up against the Turks. Prince Lazar sought the assistance of the famous Kosovo knight Vuk Branković and his noblemen. The Bosnian king sent an army under the commander Vlatko Vuković. But many lords, some rulers from the Zeta and Dalmatian towns, were cautious and hesitated to join Lazar in his efforts. He cursed them and engraved the oath in stone,"

> Whoever is a Serb and of Serb birth,
> And of Serb blood and heritage,
> And comes not to the Battle of Kosovo,
> May he never have the progeny his heart desires,
> Neither son nor daughter!
> May nothing grow that his hand sows,
> Neither dark wine nor white wheat!
> And let him be cursed from all ages to all ages!

"Wow! You surely can recite a poem, Father Slobodan!" Marin was awestruck.

"But many did join him. Like your great grandfather. Tell us about him."

Slobodan's cheeks were glowing in his passionate account of the story. He smiled at Marin's impatience and continued.

"My great grandfather was Štefan Obilić, and he was with the troops of Prince Lazar like his younger brother, Miloš Obilić. You will hear more of Miloš later. He is one of the most famous Serbians, our hero."

At the name Obilić, Ayesha froze. She heard the Ottoman version of the events on the Kosovo field, and Obilić was the devil in person in the Turkish history. That was the one and only time that the Sultan was slain like a dog behind the battle lines. And for what? As her astrology and history teacher Yusuf Al Hakam described the events to her, Murad was showing mercy towards his enemy, who eventually turned out to be his assassin. She averted her eyes to the floor for fear her look would give her knowledgeable thoughts away. But Slobodan didn't notice anything. With elated enthusiasm and in a declamatory voice, his narration filled the room beyond the hides in the windows.

"Štefan and Miloš were brothers by birth, yet their characters couldn't be more different. While Štefan, five years older, was a practical man and ran their wheat estates, so that peasants and knights never lacked either bread or ale, Miloš was more spiritual and sensitive. He was always dreaming of heroes and big battles. While Štefan shunned the war with the Turks and kept suggesting to Prince Lazar to try peace negotiations and alternative arrangements in the region, Miloš was looking for an opportunity to distinguish himself. Anyway, life was kinder to my great grandfather Štefan. But history kept the memory of my great granduncle Miloš. He was a true hero."

"What was the year of the battle?"

Hrvoje asked in a low voice. He had heard the story of Obilić and the Kosovo maiden a few years earlier at a banquet in Ragusa. The tales were popular and sung by wandering minstrels all over the region, but very few descendants of the fugitives were willing to relate the facts, so to the coastal people the Battle of Kosovo seemed more of a myth than a true event of the past. *Ragusans* and their famous republic were a world of their own, more tied to Venice and Italy than to the hinterland.

"The battle was fought on Saint Vitus Day, June the 15th in 1389. Prince Lazar gathered his troops near Niš. His army was composed of all of the Turkish opponents of the time: Serbians, Bosnians, Wallachians, Bulgarians, and Albanians, who all joined forces to defend their sovereignty against the Turkish invasion. At the front line, Lazar put several thousand splendid archers, who could hit a target at 500 feet. In the middle was Prince Lazar with his heavy armored cavalry, which soon caused havoc in the Turkish lines. Around the centre were more than 10,000 infantry soldiers trained in modern fighting. The heart of the Christian coalition was the splendid cavalry; many thousands of brave and skilled horsemen with long spears. All together, Lazar's army counted some 20,000 men. From the south banks of the Morava river, where he was pillaging the plains of Bulgaria and Macedonia, Sultan Murad I approached with his devastating force and stopped in the middle of the Kosovo field, where he positioned his thousand and so many archers in the front line. Vanguard riders were mixed among the archers to hide the view of a camouflaged ditch behind the archers' line, where many a Serbian hero found his last breath on a sharp spike planted into the ground at the bottom of it. Murad was a clever strategic commander who knew well how to make war, how to invade and subdue people. He had vast field experience, deadly to many a nation. The line behind the ditch was composed of janissaries, many of them stolen in the Turkish raids from precisely those hilly lands, from families of Serbian or Bosnian blood. The janissaries were masters of contact fighting, so the Serbians, already devastated by the casualties on the spikes in the ditch, were soon losing their left flank. Anyway, Murad's army was mightier and counted 30,000 men."

"Where were the Obilić brothers?"

Marin got carried away by Slobodan's vivid account of the

armies. He felt almost as if he was sweating under the chainmail in the hot continental sun, where the fate of so many, including him, had been determined for centuries.

"Štefan and Miloš were just behind Lazar. They rode their huge brown horses, for which people said they were like Hanibal's elephants once they took to gallop. Now, Štefan was a careful chap. His major weapon was the axe, by the skillful swings of which he cut Turks into pieces when they came closer. Limbs were flying through the air and blood surged from the cuts in whirlwinds of pain and hate. Štefan fought bravely, yet his focus was always upon surviving the battle. The younger, Miloš, however, while artfully waving his lance, was fighting without any second thought of danger. He was as wild as a young lion. The Turks noticed it and encircled him. Two riders on swift small horses caught his lance with their maces. Miloš lost his weapon. Another blow by the enemy, and he had to jump down from his horse. He would have been captured or killed on the spot, had not Štefan grabbed him and took him away on his horse far behind the battle lines. As his elder, Štefan told Miloš to stay behind the front and save his strength for later. 'There would always be another chance for heroic deeds, my brother! Stay behind for now!' Miloš was shocked. He came to Kosovo to fight, not to wait behind the lines and watch impotently how Serbian blood fertilized their lands. However, he needed a weapon and a horse. From an elevated spot behind the front, he could see how the Serbians were losing the line, clumsy in their heavy armors and tired of decades of struggle. When he judged their cause was lost, he made up his mind and started walking into the enemy lines. In his desperate rage, he entered the Turkish supply camp with a message for Sultan Murad I. He asked the soldiers safeguarding the baggage train to take him to their leader, as he had to deliver the message in person. The Turks would surely have shortened him by a head, had they not been afraid of the Sultan's severe authority. From his rich cloak trimmed with fur and padded with silk they could see that Miloš was a knight, so maybe his message was important for the Sultan. Thus, Miloš was waiting for Murad in his tent while the battle raged with its last blows and cries like a wild summer storm with clouds of dust and splashes of blood on all sides. Body parts were scattered on the green grass, and men's heads were planted in the soil, with blank, terrified eyes looking at the void. It was a massacre beyond human recollection, and men were dying by the seconds. Although they were astonished by the wildness of their opponents, the Turks prevailed. Their losses were huge and with a heavy burden on his shoulders and a paralyzing black fog on his mind, stooped like an old man, Murad dragged his body to his tent. He was soaked in Serbian blood. To Miloš, he was the Devil in person, thirsty for more Serbian blood and more killing. 'Who is this man?' the Sultan asked his aides.

Before they could answer, Miloš spoke up: 'I am a servant of God, my lord, and I came to bend my head in the shadow of the mighty winner.' The Sultan looked at Miloš for a brief moment and suddenly felt sorry for the young lad, a proud knight, who was defending his home against the intruders. He poured water in his glass and offered Miloš a drink. Miloš stretched his hand, in which the shine of a steel knife blinded the Sultan's vision only for a second. With a blow so brisk that nobody could have prevented it, Miloš cut the throat of the mighty sovereign and fell on his back, spilling Murad's glass of water all over his body. 'I'd rather drink Serbian piss than Turkish water!' he screamed at the guards who fell upon him. The Turks took their revenge. Miloš died a martyr death. They tied his body extremities to the fastest of Bayazid's horses, and Miloš was quartered like a common criminal. The Sultan's watchdog ate the heart of the hero Miloš for supper. The Serbians could not find or bury his body in the sacred land, yet his spirit is forever present in our proud folk songs. Serbians will never forget his courage."

The three visitors were pale and crumpled in awkward silence. They were from a different age and of a different breed. Was it really so courageous to kill a man offering you a drink in his tent? A century later, when the Ottomans gained some sympathy by their competent and tolerant rule in Bosnia, and the majority of Serbian lords had taken vows as Turkish vassals, such extreme acts and idolizations were far away from their lives. Ayesha was trembling with sentiment. Marin looked at the window with his mouth gaping like an open wound, remembering how not so long ago, he and his father had fled from a Turkish raid for fear they would take Marin as a janissary. The growing Ottoman empire needed boys more than ever in order to feed their military machine. He never saw his mother and his little sisters again. He did not know where and how they lived. He forgot the face of his grandmother, who he had loved dearly. He knew there were very dark sides of the Turkish reign, and he could follow Miloš' rage. Hrvoje looked at his feet, visibly ill at ease. The triangle between the daughter of the Ottoman governor, the Bosnian *bey* Abdullah, the Orthodox noble and himself was very thin ice. Finally, it was Hrvoje who broke the silence.

"So how did your great grandfather Štefan come to the island of Vis?"

Slobodan took a white cotton handkerchief from his pocket and wiped the sweat from his forehead. He also ran the tissue across his eyes, for he obviously shed some tears of sorrow over the lost heroes and past freedom of the Serbians. Then, he went to the table and poured four glasses of watered wine into the wooden cups on the tablet. He turned to his audience and offered them a drink. Not without hesitation, with the image of Murad and Miloš in their minds, they took the cups from the tablet and drank in silence while the monk continued his tale.

"On the next day after the battle, Štefan was looking for his younger brother everywhere. He wandered the battlefield where the piles of scattered body parts, some of them crusted and brownish, some dark red, still dripping with blood, were attracting clouds of insects and flocks of vultures, not to speak of the shrilling cries of dark ravens in the air. The whole plain was alive with motion and sound, yet so many dead soldiers lay there forever still. It was the field where humanity was dead and buried under the terror of war. He could not but shed bitter tears. He wished that men were not such a greedy lot and could be satisfied with what nature offered. The Ottomans were masters of great agricultural plains golden with ripe wheat. They had mountains for pastures, where stock got fat and milk had the taste of wild herbs. They had the wonderful coast at the Bosphorus, where fish was abundant. Why did they want to subdue their scarce lands and occupy their territory? Why did they come and cause havoc plundering the villages and cities of their Christian neighbors? On the other hand, why did not Prince Lazar hear his advice and start peace negotiations instead of war, for which such a diverse coalition was obviously ill prepared? To hell with proud sovereigns, who only ever think of their own good and forget the people! The news reached the dispersed Serbian troops that Murad was dead. His son Bayezid, after having murdered his own brother Yakub sat on the throne as the new Sultan. It was unthinkable to Štefan that one would smear his soul with his own brother's blood just for the sake of ruling. He kept wandering the plains of massive destruction, where the only prevailing wind was the repugnant stench of death and decay for days in a row. He met other warriors looking for their friends and family, he met women wailing into the grey sky, crying at God, who mercilessly took their beloved away from them. There was a girl among them looking for her fiancé, Milan Toplica. She was tearing her hair in despair, and her sharp cries were piercing the air like the shrill sound of *gusle*, cursing her lover's fate that he had betrothed her, as though she was the one to inflict death upon him. She was weeping and sobbing, asking everyone about Milan and her brother. Our people immortalized her pain a the song with these verses,"

> Woe is me, what fate I bear within me,
> I but touch the young and tender sapling
> And the fair green pine must surely wither.

Now Ayesha had tears in her eyes, too. She wished she had never run away from her dear Fatima and her fatherly husband. Abdina was the only home she had ever known. Why had she been so restless and curious of the world, which bore such evils

and dangers? She tried to hide her distress and averted her look
to the bookshelf. When she focused her eyes on Slobodan, she
met his blank gaze. She quickly dropped her teary look to the
floor. The monk shook his head. He stood up from the bank and
started to pace the room.

"Marin, I can see you've learnt of the ways of the world. Teach
your brother Antunić about it! Tears are for women. He almost
looks like a girl. No whining, please. Marin, you know it is your
duty as the eldest, don't you?"

"I do, Father. Tell us about Štefan. Did you know him?"

"No, I didn't. He was long dead before I was born. It was my
grandfather who told me the story of the battle. On the eve of
Saint Vitus Day, my grandfather gathered the Serbian children
on the hill above our mansion and lit a big fire. We would roast
crabs or little sardines on sticks and listen to his tale. I can recall
it just as though it was today."

"And your grandfather, does he live?"

"I don't know. I've had little news from home for a while. I
am very much looking forward to finally going back to the island.
I have not told you though, how Štefan Obilić came to the island
of Vis. Well, after the battle was lost and Prince Lazar killed,
the other Serbian leaders fled from the Kosovo field in order to
save as many men as possible. They planned to regroup and
fight back, but in the end, they did not. There were rumors
of treachery among them. People said Vuk Branković turned his
troops around too soon and fled from the field, and that the battle
was lost because of him. In our folk songs, Vuk is a traitor, but
we do not know for sure why he fled. I would say that when
Vuk realized the battle was lost, he indeed tried to save his men.
Anyway, the Turks also had severe losses and needed some time
to reap the fruits of their victory. After a week of searching the
battlefield pestered by flies and insects, Štefan finally went home.
Then, he found out about Miloš and the assassination. On the
one hand, he was proud of his brother's ruse and courage, on the
other hand he felt it was not the way to either win or lose the war.
So, that was it. Štefan was done fighting. When he returned to
his estates in the North, he sold everything and took his family
first to Ragusa, then to the island of Vis. He got married to a
local peasant beauty and built a fortress, where our family has
lived ever since. He invested in several large fishing boats and
employed local fishermen to go fishing to Palagruža, where the
waters are rich with sardines. He started to develop agriculture,
and he planted olive trees and vine saplings from Pelješac. He
changed our family name and coat of arms. Our name is Milić
instead of Obilić. I am the third generation of the Milić sons.
We, the Milić boys, we all have to spend our young years in one
of the monasteries for our education, but it is our only connection
to our proud ancestors."

Slobodan finished his narration, and all four sat still and deep in thought for a while. Then the silver chiming of the chapel bells cut into the silence. They were tolling for the midnight service. Slobodan stood up and said with a kind smile:

"Hrvoje, will you come with me? I think we should let the young go to sleep, or you will be travelling at a snail's pace tomorrow."

Hrvoje nodded in agreement. Marin took Ayesha on his back, and they all said good night. They had enough heroes for one night!

* * *

Don't ask Fuzûlî for poems of praise or rebuke
I am a lover and speak only of love

– Füzuli, c. 1483 – 1556

Ibrahim's horse neighed into the mist. The black vranac did not like the trip into the white thick curtain, where danger could lurk behind every tree trunk or at every turn of the path. It was morning. In a few moments, the fog would rise and gave stage to the winter sun, which was already shining through the white lace. Ibrahim was tired. Not so much from the lack of sleep last night, for in his long years as a *harem* guardian he got used to finding his rest in short intervals. It was more the argument he witnessed between Fatima and Abdullah. They screamed at each other, both in despair over the sudden disappearance of the girl Ayesha. Did villains abduct her during the night? Would the people who held her want money or blackmail the *bey* for other favors? Had she simply run away in search of adventures? Was she unhappy? Had she flung herself over a cliff and drowned in the Neretva river? So many questions were floating in the air. Every possibility was equally horrible and humiliating for his master. Abdullah was a kind man, but he was a *sipahi*, a vassal of the Sultan, and as such, he had to exercise military control over his lands and people at all times. How could he proudly control his army and govern the lands if his own *harem*, his youngest wife, was the perpetual source of upheaval and revolt?

Fatima had gone to wake Ayesha in the morning, and all she discovered was an artfully arranged pile of cushions, which under the blankets looked like a human body. She immediately called him, Ibrahim, and asked millions of questions. He had been up for some time and had checked on the girl, but the shape of the pile of cushions in Ayesha's bedroom fooled him, too. He sincerely thought it was the girl asleep. Yet, he knew she could not have left with the Ston oyster merchants; he got up to check on them before they left, and besides, there were so many other people around, somebody would have noticed something. Apart from a dog run wild there was nothing suspicious. So where was she? The bigger question – was she alone?

Ibrahim shuddered at the memory of Abdullah's subdued, angry threats.

"Bring back the little slut, and I will personally admonish a thrashing she should have had years ago! How dare she run away? How dare she do this to me and to Fatima?"

"I feel guilty, Master Abdullah. You are the lord of my life. You can end it here and now."

With such a dramatic declaration, Ibrahim kneeled in front of the purple-faced Abdullah. He bent his head and lifted his hands, offering him his sabre to punish him. Yet Abdullah just wove his hand angrily.

"Get up, you fool! It is not your fault. She has duped us all. Shall I kill all of us then? Rather start thinking how to proceed! Look for solutions. . ."

Fatima's sensible remarks that some rogues could have abducted Ayesha in the small hours of the night, and that a ransom demand would reach them in the following days, only made the tension worse. Abdullah shouted from his belly:

"Abducted? My most loyal men guard us and the palace! They guard you, too! Tell her, Ibrahim, tell her! You cannot abduct a fly from the kitchen without being seen! Besides, Ibrahim checked on her hourly – she slipped away, the little snake. She is curious, she wants to get around, maybe even seduce an Infidel. I will show her. If only I feel a hint of suspicion there were some boys involved, I'll have her beheaded. Right here, in the palace."

"Please, calm down. Let's not jump to any conclusions before we know where Ayesha is. Ibrahim, where would you look for her?"

"I'd go north to Mostar. She had travelled there a few times in her sedan-chair. She may know the route. That is, should she be gone voluntarily."

Fatima put her hand on Abdullah's shoulder, trying to keep him as calm as possible. It was more than the etiquette conceded a woman to do in public, but Abdullah was in such distress he did not notice it. He did not want to show it, but he was afraid for his beloved girl, and at the same time he was furious with her. His intuition told him it was not kidnapping. Yet, the fear was there. He had been enraged by her dirty tricks before, her bad nature and the slack upbringing. They felt sorry for the girl, so they let her dance and socialize with artists. Who knows what else but music they had taught her, the perverts? He felt it was also his fault. He was weak, which made him even more furious.

In the end, reason prevailed. They decided they would not raise a general alarm. They sent him, Ibrahim, to look for Ayesha, to find her and bring her home. In the public eyes, he was taking the girl for a trip to visit the other, minor Ottoman courts in Bosnia.

Finally, the sun pierced the humid fog and from minute to minute dissolved more of it. Ibrahim and his splendid Arabic horse were travelling under the bluest of all skies. They paused at the top of a hill. On the opposite side of the valley, up on a hill and encircled by a high wall, a lovely Roman chapel bathed in the sun. The walls were as old and crumbled as their function – to protect the sacred place against the Turks. The Turks had settled down in Bosnia and they did not intend to leave it. Many of Abdullah's subjects were still very much Catholics, and he let them practice whatever religion they wanted as long as they did their work and paid the tithes. When the tower of the chapel burnt down a few years ago, he even donated monies to build a new one. By doing that, he gained a lot of respect with the peasants. They slowly started to appreciate the progress that the Ottoman rule had brought into their lives.

Ibrahim's look fondly embraced the cultivated plains around the river Bunica, where the vivid green fields of thick winter wheat interchanged with fields of white winter turnips and dark green cabbage. The varying cultures were like an ornamented carpet, the fertile *kilim* of the nature in winter. The soil rarely froze south of Mostar, so they could cultivate most of the Mediterranean crops and cultures like figs, olives, cherries, walnuts, apples, pears, plums and Armenian plums or, as the locals called them, apricots. The apricot trees were still small, as they had planted them in Bosnia not so long ago, but when they blossomed in early spring, it was like a pink heaven on earth. The grapes were also cultivated, and dried in the sun. They produced little wine on the estates. The wine was all for exports, as Abdullah was personally opposed to alcohol and thought that drunks did too much damage in the society. He had seen warriors, usually the enemies, dying in the fight intoxicated and overly courageous. Abdullah as a governor completely controlled the wine production of his Catholic subjects as he found out that many families suffered because their men were drunks. The misery of women and children in such families was appalling, the fields untended and taxes unpaid. The Ottomans also reintroduced some crops like lentils and chickpeas, which constituted the peasant diet throughout winter months. Millet was a sort of grain which local peasants knew, yet rarely cultivated, for they did not know how to prepare it. New oriental spices were now available at reasonable prices and, with new cooking techniques, millet became a favorite dish for children. Another big change in the agriculture of the lands around the Neretva delta was the water mills. They pumped the water, rich with sediments, from the river into the rice fields, while other strips of fertile land were dried and planted with citrus fruits, especially mandarins. The orchards extended as far as the eye could see, and scented the atmosphere with their fresh blooms in spring. The mandarins from the delta of the Neretva were sweet and delicious, simply the best citrus fruits Ibrahim had ever eaten. The Neretva mandarins were very popular in Istanbul, where the Sultan's cooks devised a special sweet delicacy from them – mandarin juice mixed with honey and crushed ice from the high mountains, all served as a cold cream which melted on one's tongue and sent a million joys to the heart of the eater.

Ibrahim took a couple of fruits out of his bag and peeled them in the saddle. The fresh aroma of the mandarin zest reminded him of Fatima. He felt so sorry for her. She was clueless as to what to do in the morning. He could see how she bluffed. He knew Ayesha had been the topic of the couple's conversations for some time. She was a difficult girl. Yet, she seemed so innocent in her struggle for life. He could understand her longing for freedom. Many decades ago, Ibrahim was a little boy with a head full of aspirations and a heart sweet and soft like honey in the sun. He was his mother's pet, born last, when she was nearly forty years old. She was spoiling him. Ibrahim smiled at the memory of her soft hands and lips on his cheeks every night when she was putting him to bed. Oh, his mother's kisses and the sweet jasmine scent which embraced him on her bosom... Tears came to the eyes of the old man, so vivid were these memories of love and joy. His father, though, could not let him become what he wanted – a scholar or an *imam*. He was ambitious, and Ibrahim was but his tool in achieving a higher position at the Sultan's court. He mutilated his body and hurt his soul. Ibrahim, like so many Turkish children, never really had a choice. He was a sellable object in his father's greedy hands. After a year, the pain in his groin stopped, and he continued his education knowing well that he would never feel anybody touching his cheeks again. For the life of a eunuch was a solitary path! Other men got married. They kissed and caressed their wives and children. The eunuchs did not. They simply never touched another person. The castration of the body was the castration of his life. It meant that even love to men, however sinful it was, was impossible. Nothing stirred in his pants. Nobody ever put a hand on a eunuch. All the same, he knew how it should have felt. For at the age of twenty, Ibrahim fell in love. He fell in love with his mistress Fatima.

A hind jumped out of the bush and, for a brief moment, focused its lovely big brown eyes upon Ibrahim. Then it leaped into the bush. What a graceful animal! The horse neighed, as though amused at the hind's fear, and Ibrahim picked up his line of memories. The lovely, warm Fatima and the first time she cried on his shoulder! She had been married to Abdullah for nearly a decade and they had two wonderful sons, when all of a sudden she fell ill. She would expect her husband to stand by her, not to quickly take a second wife as though she had not existed anymore. It was the custom, but still she could not cope with it. It was then that they became friends. He would do anything to be her friend for life, for to be her lover... was unthinkable. Fatima was a warm, motherly person, and she touched people a lot. She touched her servants when she was telling them what to do, she cuddled her boys until Abdullah sent them away to military training, she stroked the Persian tomcat who was proudly enjoying his prime male position in the *harem*, and last but not least, she touched him, Ibrahim, her eunuch and guardian. Many times, she even hugged him tightly. Those were the times when he could feel her warm perfumed skin on his skin and her full breasts flattened in his embrace. He would inhale her scent and kiss her hair lightly, so that she would not notice. Anyway, she would not care. He was just a friend to her. It was on those rare occasions that his eyes itched with hot tears of frustration. He repressed his agony in her presence and suffered during his long night watches, when he was alone with the stars and cold dampness arising from the Bunica river. He felt warm in his groin, his cheeks glowed with sentiment, yet, he could not make love to a woman. He was not a man. Years ago, his father had decided his fate. He was a cripple and he had no right to love her, Fatima.

Ibrahim often asked himself whether it would be any different had he not lost his manhood as a child. Would Fatima return his love? Would she leave her husband and her children and go with him? The answer was clear as the winter sky above him – she would not. Despite his nonchalance and a decade of treating her with little or no respect, Abdullah was Fatima's mate for life. She would never love another, whether he were a man or a god, lest a cripple. So maybe being her eunuch and friend was not so bad after all. They could be together all day long. They could discuss things, they could invent and reinvent life and love in the long sleepless nights when other women entertained Abdullah. They could read poets like Rumi, Hafez and Füzuli together. Without guilt or a second thought they could sink sentimentally into every verse, they could admire the poets' skillful turns in content and form, and they could share tears of joy at the lines of eternal beauty. So what more could love offer? Were they not lovers in spirit? Were they not soulmates? Was not their touching more intimate than any act of physical lovemaking could ever be? Was this subtle way of living together not a form of love more elevated than penetration and animal outbursts of body fluids? Their platonic relationship compared to Fatima's marriage coupling was like comparing Hafis' sophisticated *divan* to the rough peasants' speech.

Ibrahim smiled and rejoiced. He set his horse to gallop into the valley, where like a flock of sheep the houses of Mostar proudly glistered in the sun. Oh yes, he loved the woman, and he was sure she loved him, too. The tender autumn breeze was like Fatima's soft hand on his cheeks last night, when she woke him up to go back to the *harem*. Her lovely autumn hands with thin soft skin like silk... As Hafez would say: "I wish I were a morning-clear lake and you the sun, reflecting in it."

* * *

How
Did the rose
Ever open its heart
And give to this world
All its
Beauty?

– Hafiz, It felt love

They came into their cell exhausted and bolted the door behind them. The fire was nearly extinct, and Marin quickly brought it back to life, so that the flames stroked the logs like lovers' minds burning in the heat of passion. Still, their cheeks remained cold, and no fire could warm their hearts tonight. The tales of the battle burdened them, and the weight on their shoulders was too heavy. Ayesha tried to clean herself with wet handkerchiefs. She was tense, worn out and dirty. All she wished for was a long afternoon in the *hamam*.

When the cell warmed up, Marin arranged his travel blankets and his cloak for an improvised bed on the floor. He let Ayesha sleep on the main bed, which rustled with fresh straw. She looked gloomy, and Marin felt sorry for her. Slobodan's history lesson was a trial for her. For him too, they all had to control their feelings. God knows how the Ottoman version of the events sounded. She sighed deeply and knitted her brows with worry. Marin spoke up.

"What is it, Ayesha? Are you in pain?"

Marin's kind voice triggered it off. Ayesha burst in tears. Her loud sobbing filled the cell like a cry of a hurt animal. Marin panicked. The monk next door could hear her. He rose up and quickly held her trembling body in his arms. His embrace suppressed her sobs in his shoulder. He could feel her warm tears through his linen chemise and caressed her back in an awkward attempt to calm her down. After some long moments, for Marin longer than eternity, she stopped crying. However, she didn't move out of his embrace. She put her arms around his neck and looked seriously up in his face. Her eyes were red with tears and black with the knowledge that something was very wrong. Marin understood it was something she did not intend to share with him, and even if she did, he could probably not comprehend it. Although there was not an inch between them, so closely embraced they stood in the glow of the fire, there was a huge gap between his life and hers. The gap, slippery and dangerous for two young people, was loaded with tragic Serbian poetry and the saga of Kosovo. That space between them was cold and violent, and it breathed death and terror like the cold southeast wind košava gaining strength between the Carpathians and the Balkans in winter. It carried along millions of controversies between the two most powerful religions in the world – Islam and Christianity. Yet, their bodies were glowing in the nearness, and the young couple felt comfortable in each other's arms.

Marin's hands slowly searched the curves of her body, while Ayesha stroked his blonde hair absentmindedly. Their unison was so unreal that it seemed like a dream afterwards. At one point of their cuddling and tenderness, they pulled down their clothes and did the same as millions of young people since the dawn of mankind. It was a hasty, scared lovemaking of two deer in the woods hunted by cruel men and vicious beasts. Boiling with the passion of their age and curious in their discovering the other, there was not much time for joy or sophisticated amorous play. In their minds, they were both back in the palace when Ayesha was tormenting Marin with her dance and Marin almost burst with the desire to possess her. When he penetrated her, she felt a sharp pain in her groin and gasped for air. Tears came to her eyes and she sighed. Marin pulled back and tenderly kissed her on the lips.

"I'm sorry. I didn't want to hurt you, Ayesha."

She relaxed and they continued their love dance slowly and carefully, so that Ayesha's pain was soon replaced by pleasure. It did not last too long, for Marin arched on her, and she knew she could be in trouble. Later, his rough hands and warm lips stroked her worries away, and lightheartedly they giggled and tickled each other under the covers until morning. When the flames in the fireplace finally died, their bodies warmed them, and together they were not afraid of anything. The black gap between their lives disappeared. They blended into one human being in the way no history could ever join two nations or religions.

* * *

Back on the road, Marin was gloomy and angry. Hrvoje did not speak to the monks at Žitomislić about Ayesha, as he had promised he would before they ran into Slobodan. Instead, on the following morning, he woke them up early, and again they packed the train with, Ayesha alias Antunić lying on the first wagon as though nothing happened. Here and then, he looked suspiciously at Marin's guilty face, shook his head, but said nothing. What

was he going to do with the girl? Would he take her with them
to Ston? Was it safe? Marin felt in his heart that Hrvoje was
deeply concerned about their safety, yet he could not leave the
girl alone on the road.

They passed the little villages of Počitelj and Čapljina, and
they stayed the night in an abandoned barn at Gabela. Marin
could not close his eyes, for his hair stood on end when in
the misty afternoon they passed a field full of the long abandoned *stećci*, the Bosnian tombstones with mystical inscriptions
on them. They were eternally reminding travelers that death was
their closest companion on the road. The *stećci* looked majestic
in their gloomy silence. The ornaments on them were beautiful,
with words carved in stone in a foreign language incomprehensible to most of the known world save to the Bosnian lords. The
monuments stood amidst the yellowish grass, dead on the surface
yet with life waiting to resume its course the following spring,
life, which was never to return either to the people buried beneath them or to the Bosnian independence and freedom. The
lords, seeking adaptation and life, had been widely Islamized in
the last decades, and they abandoned their dead relatives, like
their ancient faith, seemingly without too much regret.

With dark thoughts, they meandered along the old Roman
route, still partially paved for horse transport, around fields and
orchards. Hrvoje was stopping often to ask people about the
latest news. Should there be a large Turkish search party set on
Ayesha, they would for sure have heard about it. At Metkovići, to
Marin's surprise, they headed for the most expensive inn, actually
a border post. On the way to Abdina some ten days earlier, they
had just stopped to say hello, for they could not afford the cost
of boarding. The owner was a retired janissary, Mehmet, who
was born near Mostar. After twenty-five loyal years of fighting
and wartime spent in the Sultan's army, Mehmet came back to
Bosnia, married a local peasant girl and opened the inn, which
was very popular with travelers and therefore very profitable.
Hrvoje and Mehmet were good friends. They had known each
other for years.

When their wagons entered the yard, Mehmet was waiting for
them. He took Hrvoje, who was trembling slightly with fatigue,
into his huge soldier's arms. For a minute or two, they held
each other tapping their backs. Then they disappeared inside,
leaving Marin to worry about Ayesha, the cargo and the mules.
First, Marin asked the servants for a room, and according to their
disguise, carried the girl inside. She was trembling with fear, for
she immediately recognized Mehmet as one of Abdullah's vassals.
She was glad that the old man did not look at her too closely, but
still, this inn was very thin ice. She did not say anything to Marin,
who was busy feeding and watering the mules, and arranging the
wagons, so that they would not fall victim to rain, theft, or other

damage. When he was done, he went inside looking for Hrvoje. He was sitting with Mehmet in the far corner of the dining room.

"Where is A... Antunić, master?"

"Ayesha, she's being washed and dressed by the servants, Marin."

"What? He... she... What do you mean?"

"Marin, sit down and listen. Mehmet and I have made a decision. We think it is the best for all of us that Mehmet takes care of our problem. He's Abdullah's loyal vassal and he knows who Ayesha is."

"Yes, the daughter of..."

"No, my dear Marin. The girl lied to us. She's Abdullah's youngest wife."

"But what will he do to her if..."

Mehmet smiled and looked into Marin's pale face with guilt spilled all over. The older men could read the boy's face like an open book. Marin's cheeks were changing from purple to white. Hrvoje had his opinion about the night spent innocently at the monastery, but neither on the road and even less at the inn, did he want to dig further into the secrecy of the dark. The less he knew, the better. Now Mehmet spoke up.

"We hope nothing much, since Abdullah is a soft hearted man, and Ayesha is his darling. Still, we must be careful not to provoke his rage. We do not know what actions Abdullah has taken. Let me deal with it in my way."

Marin's eyes filled with tears. He did not understand the world any more. He was staring at the huge, dark skinned Turk, for that was how Mehmet was dressed and looked after decades of his janissary service. Although ageing, he was a large, imposing man. A long scar divided his left cheek and spoke of his previous life of violence and war. Mehmet was not the person one would want to meet on a solitary road either by day or by night. Why would Hrvoje drop Ayesha like a hot chestnut and leave her to this brute? What would men do to her, if they find out about...

"What does Ayesha say about this?"

Now Hrvoje cut in.

"She understands that this is the best way to deal with the situation. She is tired. She just wants to go home."

"Can I talk to her?"

Like clouds would start gathering on horizon before the storm, Mehmet's forehead wrinkled in an angry grimace.

"What's enough is enough, my boy! You certainly will not see Ayesha again! I have to guard her chastity. It is the only way to return her safely to her family. So far, as I understand, she remains untouched. Is this so?"

Marin's eyes met Hrvoje's severe look. The fisherman's black pupils widened with fear. The boy looked aside and murmured.

"What do you think, *effendi*, that I would disobey my good master Hrvoje? As God is my witness, I have not harmed her in any way."

A servant in a black robe brought fresh bread, cheese and smoked fish. She put a cup of greenish, aromatic olive oil in the middle of the table. Marin took a piece of bread, but could not eat, although he was very hungry. Thoughts could not stop digging in his brains. What did Ayesha really think? Did she agree with Mehmet and Hrvoje? She told him she was missing her mother or anyway the woman named Fatima very much. He sighed with frustration. He should not press to see her, or he would put them both in danger. He could only hope that her husband would not punish her too severely, and that he would never find out the secrets of the monastic cell in Žitomislić.

After dinner, he went to the room that he shared with his master, while Hrvoje stayed up nearly all night talking to Mehmet. He could not find any sleep again. It was the third night in a row that he more or less spent thinking about the two of them. Was he in love? Ayesha was such a pearl, indeed, a beautiful white pearl born out of the shell's pain. The brightness and the beauty of her surface were shining in vain. Nothing could cover the shape of her despair and emotional trouble. She wanted freedom, yet she was firmly enclosed. Like a pearl in a shell, Ayesha was a prisoner in the *harem*, confined within its walls and the Ottoman traditions, so much different from his own.

The following day, they finally crossed the last hills on their way to the coast. From the elevation, Marin could see the still, grey sea. It was infinite and peaceful in its eternal strength. From the cliff, Mljet, the island of honey, or Mileta, as the Romans named the greenest of all Dalmatian islands, impeded the view to the open sea. The legend had it that on his way to Rome, Paul the Apostle was shipwrecked on Mljet, the island of a thousand snakes. Marin knew the green bushes and pine woods, for sometimes, he and Hrvoje risked the passage to its shores, abundant with all kinds of fish. It was quite away from Ston, and their ship was small, not strong enough to endure the rough winds in the channel. The pink clouds on the horizon behind the ridges of the island were promising a sunny day. Marin inhaled the salty, wet breeze, and was already feeling better. He could feel how his home would heal his wrecked mind. How he longed for the sweet smells of Olga's cooking! He looked at Hrvoje gratefully, and with a sting in his heart, thought of all the pretence of the last days. All for what – for the shadow of a spoilt rich girl who spilled lies like dry beans out of a sack. She was the wife of another, who was not just anybody. She was the wife of the *bey*, the governor of Bosnia. Would he have acted differently had he known? Abdullah would put him on a stake and kill Hrvoje's family if he found out. For a moment, Marin lost his breath in

terror. What had he done? No more secrets, no more lies! His
master deserved better than that.

* * *

Ayesha woke up in a linen bed, in the fresh scent of lavender
and rosemary. She was not at home. Nevertheless, again, she
was under lock and key. She remembered the inn and the food
they were bringing into her room at mealtimes. At least she was
clean and bathed after a week of filthy rags in which the oyster
merchant put her to hide her identity. For days, she was washing
away the smell, and no scented oils could cover it. How could
people live like that – without a *hamam*? She sat up, and pain
cut through her forehead as though a sabre was splitting it in
half. Why did she have such crushing headaches when she woke
up? Were they putting something in her food? And, for how
long would she have to wait here in this tiny room with one little
window, covered by a sheepskin for keeping it warm inside?

Despite the blood pulsating in her temples, she stood up and
went to the window. The fresh air smelled of pines, and she
thought of the sea she was so longing to see. Ah, gone was the
only week of freedom in her whole life. . . She briefly assessed the
situation; could she sneak out through the window and climb
down the wall? They changed her into a woman's dress, but that
part was easy. She measured the window with a scarf, but she
realized with regret that the opening was far too narrow for her
body to slip through. She sighed deeply. What a funny little
adventure the week had been! Although the days on the road
were interesting, she could have travelled in better conditions,
with Ibrahim and maybe Fatima, on a horse and with an escort.
If only Abdullah were not such a stubborn ass. Why was he
keeping her inside his walls? He should know she was young and
curious.

Well, she had paid him back for his conservative rules, had
she not? She smiled at the thought of the boy Marin and his
tender, sweet kisses. It was the sin of sins – adultery. Cruelty
to one's wife was also a sin. Thus, she got even with Abdullah.
Besides, nobody would ever know. She decided she would not
even tell Fatima, for fear she would feel responsible for her. She
had to change her life in the *harem*. She had gained independence,
she thought. She had showed courage and endurance. Finally,
Ayesha felt like the mistress of her fate. From that moment,
she would not stoop to anybody. She would tolerate no more
patronizing decisions and accept no stupid limitations. She had
to speak to Abdullah and let him know that there were not many
options for their future: either she would have some freedom, or
she would kill herself, or even escape from home again, which she
knew was much worse for him in the public eye.

Mehmet came to her room yesterday and told her that the oyster merchants had left without her, and that he had sent a discreet note to Fatima. What a cunning subject, this old janissary! Risking his head with his intrigues, everything only to prove his loyalty to Abdullah and extract more favors from him. What else did he want? He had a concession for an inn at one of the most important crossroads of the country, he had vast rice fields, large mandarin orchards, and he had a bunch of dirty kids playing in the courtyard. She hated them all; Mehmet, the servants, his slimy young wife, the ruffled black haired children, who licked her boots when kissing her good night. They were nothing but vermin, bad eggs, human excrements. They locked her in. She was sure they were putting opium or some other drug in her food, so that she was asleep most of the time. She had to regain control of the situation. She would stop eating. How long would it take for Ibrahim or Fatima to come to get her? Or, was it this Mehmet who would bring her to Abdina? Certainly not Abdullah, he was too old and too fat.

Ayesha's dark thoughts brought tears to her eyes. How could she be so vulnerable and helpless at the peak of her physical power? She was of high birth. She came from the Sultan's palace to this village at the end of the world, after all. She should have some rights. Then, she remembered the rumors about her mother which had filled the couloirs of the Sultana's court. After her father had gone into the war and her mother gave birth to her, Ayesha, her mother was reported to be with another man, a lover – a free spirited commander of the Greek janissary division. The rumor had it that they had caught them together in bed. The man was beheaded on the spot, while the woman was stoned to death. Thinking back, she wondered whether her mother was truly guilty. It could have been a way for the Sultana to kill two birds with one stone. God knows why she had the man decapitated. Maybe he had known one of her vicious secrets, and she had to get rid of him. Ayesha hated the hypocrisy and the intrigues of the Sultan's *harem*, and all the vividly painted wives and concubines, hiding daggers up their sleeves. Anyway, she was much cleverer than her *Anne*. She would not end up under the stones. She would sooner finish this prison they call a woman's life by her own hand.

She heard some commotion in the courtyard and looked down to the muddy gravel. A rider was galloping in through the door. She recognized Ibrahim's horse. Finally, she was going home! In a few nights, she would practice her dance again, spend afternoons in the sweet idleness of the *hamam* and eat the foods she liked. Maybe she should be kinder to Abdullah after all. He provided a home for her, and he was married to the best woman in the world. Ayesha's face softened at the thought of Fatima's fresh, fruity scent and the warm embrace of her bosom. Maybe she would tell

Fatima about Marin. While Mehmet was hugging Ibrahim in the courtyard, Ayesha was wondering what Fatima would think of her.

* * *

With every new morning since Ayesha was back in the *harem*, Fatima's worries were deeper. She thought the crisis was over, when one evening, Abdullah, after several days of raging and scolding the girl, finally took her into his arms. She promised she would never do such a thing again, and in return, he would arrange a visit to Ragusa in spring. They would go together, travel safely with an escort and stay at the Rector's palace. Abdullah would write to the Rector immediately. It would improve the business relationship and mutual understanding between the two states.

Fatima was glad that they could find a solution, though it was not without her or Ibrahim's help. Ibrahim had to swear by his life that he truly found Ayesha locked in a room of the Metković inn and that no men or women who could tell the story of her vile adventure were around. Mehmet reassured them that they were adding valerian drops to her food and drink, so that for days she was asleep. The corrupt janissary wanted a lot of money for his services and, above all, for his silence. All the time, he was emphasizing that silence is gold, and the bastard really meant it. He was clever and had sent the note first to her, Fatima, and not to Abdullah. He knew well that she needed to cushion her husband's rage with diplomacy before he could sell his assistance well. Anyway, Mehmet was a brute, and she did not like negotiating with him. There were huge gaps in his story, and the biggest lie, for Fatima was sure it was nothing but a lie, was that Ayesha came to the inn with a group of pilgrims. Why would Catholic pilgrims take the route through Muslim Bosnia and stop at an expensive inn run and owned by a former janissary, a vassal of the Turks? The tale was implausible, and on many occasions, Fatima fished for more information, either from Ayesha or from Ibrahim, to support her suspicion that Mehmet had his tentacles in Ayesha's adventure. Ayesha did not want to talk about the episode, and her health and her mood were getting worse every day. Since she had come back, she never laughed, and even the promise of a trip to Ragusa did not cheer her up as it should have.

Then Ayesha's illness got worse. Her face was ashen and she lost weight. She dragged her young body around the corridors of the palace as though she was made of thick mud instead of healthy hot blood. She stopped dancing and playing music. Every morning, she puked her breakfast the moment she had eaten it. She got thin as a stick. Weak, she spent many days in bed, and whenever Fatima checked on her, she would find her sullen, with red, swollen eyes, as though she had been crying in her pillow for hours. Fatima decided to have a serious talk with her. There had to be a reason behind this drama. From her experience, Fatima knew there always was.

She came to Ayesha's room and found her asleep. At least, Ayesha's head, with her eyes closed, was spilling the black curls around the cushions and her body lay still. It dawned on Fatima that the girl could be pretending in order to avoid conversation. Thus, she softly sat down by the bed, waiting. Eventually, Ayesha would open her eyes.

After a few minutes, the girl stirred and smiled hesitantly at her. With a sleepy voice, dragging her vowels for a moment or two too long, she asked Fatima:

"What is it? Is it evening?"

"No, my dear. It is morning. Actually, it is the morning when you will tell me what happened to you. Everything, you must tell me everything."

Ayesha's look met Fatima's decided face. What was she to do? She could not stay in bed forever or pretend much longer. Hence, she started her tale with her decision to elope and hide in the cargo barrels of the oyster merchants. She told her about the minutes when the shepherd dog nearly discovered her before they were gone. Fatima interrupted:

"Do I understand correctly that you spilled the wheat on the floor and hid in the barrel? How come nobody found the wheat?"

"The barrels were kept in the huge sheep pen, and I spilled it all around the floor, so that the sheep and the chickens flying from their night racks to get their share ate it all. It was amazing how quickly it was gone."

"Crazy girl! You're lucky that Hrvoje didn't kill you just for the worth of the wheat!"

"I paid him."

"So you were dressed as a boy. Where did you get the clothes and where did you keep them?"

"I bought the rags months ago from one of our servants from the kitchen. Her son is my height. All she had to do was to clean them, and she earned a fortune."

"So, you had been planning this for a while? The last night when I came to you and embraced you. . ."

Ayesha sat up and put her arms around Fatima's rigid body. She pressed her cheeks to her bosom, inhaling the scent of love and trust, she had so deeply disappointed.

"Oh, Fatima, I wasn't running away from you. I just wanted to get out of here. I was running for freedom. I can't be locked up forever, I need some space, I am sorry."

"So, how was your space when in the evening the men found you?"

In a fever, Ayesha spoke about Hrvoje and Marin. She told her how kind they were and that Hrvoje did not even want to take her money, but she hid the purse in one of the barrels, so he had to find it eventually. She felt she owed them a lot. She told Fatima about Slobodan and the extraordinary religious service she had attended at the monastery. Fatima felt drawn to her tale with interest and fascination. She had accompanied Abdullah to Žitomislić once, but they did not go to the church, they just spoke to the abbot in his office. Ayesha described the chapel and the golden icons, and the magical singing of the monks.

"Ayesha, you were bold to enter a foreign church just like that. It's as though an infidel would enter a mosque. How did you know how to behave in a Catholic church?"

"I didn't. I just followed the murmuring of the others. You know, the Catholics here and those at the coast have different ways of celebrating the mass. At the coast, it is in Latin and more or less spoken, while at Žitomislić, it was in a language similar to the local Bosnian speech and sung. So the merchants didn't quite get it either. Believe me Fatima: it was worth it. It was a spiritual experience. I was deeply moved."

"Great. You were not converted by any chance, were you?"

Then Ayesha giggled and hugged Fatima tighter. She should have spoken to her *Anne* weeks ago. All this time in agony and fear, and she was all alone with her misery.

"No, not at all. I'm as Muslim as I've ever been."

Fatima put her arms around Ayesha and smiled. Finally, the girl's defenses were down and they talked.

"What happened then?"

"You remember Slobodan, the rider who caught up with us on the second day. He was a monk from Žitomislič, or rather a Serbian noble who had spent some years there to get educated. He comes from an island called Vis. After supper he invited us all to his cell and told us the most distorted story about the Battle of Kosovo. It was a cruel tale, full of blood and treason. Have you heard about Miloš Obilić?"

"Who hasn't heard about the sneaky assassin?"

"Well, you won't believe it. The Serbians are cherishing him as a national hero. The man who murdered our beloved Sultan in his tent is their national hero!"

"I've heard something about this, actually, from a minstrel who came to sing for us a couple of years ago. And there was more: something about a wandering maiden looking for her lover among the corpses."

"The very same... Disgusting business, isn't it? I had to keep my face straight, and I could see that Marin and Hrvoje had their reservations, too."

"Well, the history has not been written yet, my baby. The Serbians have been losing ever after the battle, and today they are vassals of the Sultan like the rest of the Balkan peoples. Except for the *Ragusans*, who have always been in business with us and never minded our ways of life, so we never invaded them, although I am quite sure that we could have. Ours is a military force many times superior to the rest of them. Go on! Then you moved on..."

Ayesha paused for a moment, hesitating. She had to tell Fatima the whole truth. How was she to bring over her lips the immense act of treason, the crime against her good-natured husband and her family? Not for the first time, Ayesha repented her short-sighted, senseless sin. She had not even loved the boy. The whole business had been more about excitement and curiosity. She knew that after she had spoken, everything would change. Fatima would panic. Abdullah may have her killed. He would be merciful to end her life with a sabre, not with stones. Legally, he could do either. She would end up like her mother.

Fatima was watching the girl's face, flooded with guilt, attentively. What had she done? Patience, Fatima, patience... You should not push her too hard. She would tell you now, and you would try to help her. Ayesha focused her vision on Fatima's eyes and shrugged her shoulders.

"I can't help it. I must tell you. I am probably with child. I haven't had my days since three months, and I am sick in the morning. I will tell you in a minute how it happened..."

Fatima's pity and her deep sense of humanity feared the worst.

"Were you hurt? Did they force you, my baby? Tell me, who..."

Ayesha shook her head, and tears ran down her cheeks.

"*Anne*, I was just stupid. Nobody forced me. I was so moved and shaken by the story of Kosovo that making love to the infidel seemed like nothing. It was a whim of the moment, nothing else. I am sorry..."

"How did he come to your room?"

"*Anne*, we shared the cell. We pretended to be brothers, remember?"

"And Hrvoje did nothing to prevent it! This filthy fishmonger will never sell any oysters here again, or I'll get him shortened by the head, I swear!"

Ayesha stopped sobbing.

"I think, *Anne*, this is the least of a problem. What will we do with the baby? I can't have it here, under Abdullah's eyes. Well, sorry, I was a coward not to have told you earlier. Maybe we could have done something about it... There are ways..."

"No, actually in my experience there isn't any method which wouldn't endanger your health. You can't abort a child without serious consequences. If you live through your bodily ordeal well, there are still scars on your conscience. Let me think... When exactly did it happen?"

"Did what happen?"

"When did you sleep with the boy? How many weeks ago was it? Exactly!"

"Well, today it is full nine weeks."

"When should you have had your monthly bleeding after that?"

"Two weeks later."

"And? Where was your head? Didn't you know by then?"

"I was filled with drugs at Metkovići kissing those dirty janissary's kids good night. What did I know? I was just longing to come home..."

Fatima embraced her and held her still. Ayesha was weeping silently, sobbing in her shoulder. They were both desperate, although Fatima had a strange feeling that the terrible secret could turn into an advantage for all of them. She just had to figure out how. Besides, she had to do it quickly, for in a month, Ayesha's belly would fill up with new life. She had to talk to Ibrahim. They would concoct a plan to make happiness out of misery. After all, turning the spear of fortune was their art. They had done it before. If Scheherazade had survived by telling "One Thousand and One Nights" tales to the cruel Persian king, they would all survive on their plan if they tackled it wisely. In the end, they would all be happy – Abdullah, Ayesha, the baby and Ibrahim.

"Ayesha, please stop crying. I will think of something. Just don't tell anybody!"

"*Anne*, I won't. I promise."

Now Fatima smiled, and with gentle strokes of her soft palms, tenderly wiped the tears from the girl's swollen cheeks.

"Smile, Ayesha, smile! Be happy! You're having a baby! And I will be a grandmother."

Ayesha's black eyes widened with fear. Sobbingly, she whispered:

"And what will Abdullah be?"

* * *

Days went by before Fatima spent another night in her husband's bed. In the shadow of a new life secretly growing in Ayesha's belly, she, Fatima, was bursting with new energy. It felt like spring, a second youth, though the first flowers in the fields were still sleeping their winter dreams under the muddy, frozen ground. Despite their advanced age, she was eager to prove to Abdullah that she was a woman, and that they could still enjoy making love and giving each other moments of unforgettable pleasure. When they were lying in his huge bed satisfied and warmly cuddled under the woolen blankets afterwards, she felt it was time she spoke up. She paused for another minute, listening to the fire crackling in the brazier thinking how young passions are quickly lived and spent like dry wood turning into smoke. Theirs was a love engraved in their souls forever like an arabesque. It was Abdullah who cut the silence.

"What is it with Ayesha, Fatima? She doesn't spend the evenings with us anymore, and she rarely speaks to me. Not that she would be impolite, I just have the feeling she is avoiding me."

Fatima was grateful for his opening. It seemed as though he could read her mind.

"Well, she is in a situation. The more I think about it, the more I find it can actually help us all."

Abdullah looked down at her face leaned on his shoulder. Suspicion arose in his black eyes.

"What situation? Nobody has hurt her. She hasn't been punished for the troubles she caused. What..."

Fatima returned him a decided look of contradiction.

"Abdullah, you haven't punished her, but life has..."

"How?"

Yes, indeed, how could she present the irresponsible act of treason and the young sinner as a victim of life to the wronged father and husband? For, Abdullah was clearly both – he loved Ayesha as a father, but he was also her husband, her lord. Maybe she should mollify the news with some of their discussions from before.

"Abdullah, do you remember the night when we spoke about finding a pregnant peasant and proclaiming her child as yours in the eyes of the public?"

"Well, yes, but what does this have to do with Ayesha's indisposition?"

Ignoring the question, Fatima continued her train of thoughts in order to envelop him and his fury, which would eventually burst out, to encapsulate him within her thoughts of a practical solution for their problem.

"Can you imagine loving a child which is not yours by birth, my dear?"

"Well, I love Ayesha...But..."

Fatima stretched up to kiss his lips. With tears of joy not entirely honest, but still very powerful, she whispered.

"We have such a child here, my love."

Abdullah got confused, then looked at her with profound tenderness. He replied to her magical words with an exulted, long kiss. His palm stroked her belly.

"But this is my child, Fatima, this is a miracle! After all these years, oh, Allah, thank you..."

"Not me, Abdullah, Ayesha has the baby we want..."

He froze. It took moments for him to comprehend. He was staring at Fatima, perplexed, trying to order her statements into some kind of logical flow. She could see how the color was slowly

raising to his bolding forehead. His whole body started to tremble. He jumped out of the bed with the reflex of a long time
warrior.

"Are you crazy, woman? What are you saying?"

"Ayesha is with child. She's pregnant... The child will be
yours!"

"But it is not mine! I could not touch the little snake! You
know that!"

"Yes, I know that, and you know, and she knows it, too. Yet,
nobody else knows it! You see, this could answer the Sultan's
future questions about your family and your strength as a man!"

"What has she done? Fatima, tell me clearly! Cut the sweet
talk!"

Abdullah was screaming his lungs out. The sentinels knocked
on the door.

"Is everything all right, *effendi?*"

"No, nothing is all right. Go and fetch me Ibrahim!"

The sentinels, too happy to get away from their master, ran
like lunatics. They had never seen him in such a rage, and experience told them it was not good to be around him then. They
threw a distressed look at Fatima and were gone behind the closed
door. Fatima saw Abdullah's hate and anger, his trembling lips
and purple color, and for a brief moment staggered in the thought
that he would hit her. Then she could see his eyes filling with
tears of defeat, with pain of impotent old age, and knew that
she had to turn the failure into achievement quickly, before the
disaster would hit them all.

"Abdullah, I know. It is my fault, too. She's a spoilt girl, and
she puts her trust in the wrong people too quickly. I will tell you
all, just please calm down."

"How can I calm down? Nobody has done anything like this
to me in my whole life. All the wives, the concubines... And..."

Fatima was not so sure about that, but she kept quiet. His
voice was still angry, but he kept it lower. She stepped toward
him and took his right hand in hers. With the other hand, she
touched his cheeks and said softly.

"I know you are right to be angry. It's wrong. But you see,
this could all be to our advantage. You will have a son again. You
will be a true man in your house. I will have a kind of grandson,
and we will play with him. I will raise him. As for Ayesha, she
has punished herself. She cut her dreams of the world off. Just
like that! Now, she will have to stay inside and take care of her
little boy like all mothers do."

"If it's a girl?"

"It'll be a boy."

"How do you know?"

"I can tell."

Fatima breathed in. She succeeded. Abdullah was focusing on the baby instead of the wretched girl. Her plan would work, and their fortune would turn. Soon, there would be sounds of children's cries and feet running around the palace again. Abdullah sighed, and she came closer. They embraced, and for a moment, she had the feeling he was weeping. But no, it was not like him. He slowly disengaged and said in a sensible, clear voice:

"Now, woman, tell me everything! Only then I will decide what to do!"

Fatima retold Ayesha's story. She omitted the details and parts of it which could enrage her husband, like the Battle of Kosovo and the mass, but she told him who the father of the child was. In the middle of her report, Ibrahim entered their room. Abdullah regained control over the situation and the conversation. In a sharp voice, Ibrahim was filling in the missing information. The eunuch confirmed the details and extensively described the inn and the circumstances in which he found Ayesha. Abdullah asked curtly:

"Can we kill the bastard, Ibrahim?"

"Kill who? Who do you mean, *effendi*?"

"Who, who... The little jerk who planted his seed!"

"He's from Ston. It is the *Ragusan* territory."

"I didn't ask where he is from and whose territory it is. Can we kill him?"

"Yes, we can. We can send an assassin."

"Right, I'm sending you. You will go tomorrow, the sooner, the better."

"Yes, *effendi*."

Ibrahim threw a worried glance at his mistress. She was pale. They had forgotten the boy in their plan. Naturally, Abdullah would want to dispose of him, should he accept the child as his own. Not a soul should be able to doubt the child's father! Poor little devil, he seemed like such an innocent young man and was working so hard for his life, which was lost in a second. Fatima contradicted weakly:

"Maybe we can buy his silence, Abdullah?"

Abdullah shook his head in resolution. He knew how easily secrets came alive with people being part of them, and he did not want any more witnesses of his newly acquired fatherhood but those whose life was more in danger should they speak up. The boy should shut up forever, before he could open his mouth and brag to his pals about how he knocked up the Bosnian governor's wife. He would massacre the whole city of Ston should it be necessary. He would shut the whole world up!

Fatima's question was still hanging in the air. Abdullah turned first to her, then focused his attention on Ibrahim, who seemed to support his wife's hesitation.

"And he will keep the vow? Absolutely not... I don't believe in the vows of the infidels, they're all crooked. You will do it quickly, Ibrahim, and nobody should know who you are. Is this understood?"

"Yes, *effendi*. You can count on me."

"Now leave us alone. I want to talk to my wife in private!"

Ibrahim was swaying on his feet as he headed towards the door. He turned and caught Fatima's eye. Their expressions were serene, yet there was light in the black of their pupils. They made it again. They saved the girl and the baby. It was good, for good people always find opportunities to perform good deeds. Save for the boy. Ibrahim felt his blood on his hands burning like salt in an open wound before they had even touched him. He was sorry for the young oyster merchant and his bad luck. Oh, the terrible victims of love...

* * *

The world seemed at peace, and the pinewoods smelled sharply fresh in the late afternoon when Ibrahim broke his gallop to spare his horse. He loved the smell, mixed with the scented wind from the south which was blowing the sweet perfume of flowering mandarins into his nostrils. His head cleared up from the humid salty atmosphere at the sea, and he decided to take a cold bath in the Neretva river. He would change his clothes, put up a shelter to spend the night, and cook the rabbit he caught on the way in a spicy stew. He would find some peace and sleep at last.

His horse was grateful when Ibrahim unsaddled him. The black stud neighed with relief. Ibrahim, on the other hand, could not feel the heavy burden leaving his shoulders. Less so; the weight of dark thoughts invaded the lovely spot where river pebbles shone white in the evening sun and oppressed him more than ever. What had he done? Could he have avoided executing Abdullah's orders?

He folded the Christian peasant clothes into a bundle for the *harem* servants to wash for later use. Naked, he stepped to the water line. His crotch was empty as ever, letting the air flow around the calves freely, only the little penis in the middle, which after the castration operation decades ago, shrunk to a nut, not only because of the cold air. He sank in the water, yet jerked out of it quickly. Shivering, he applied layers of soap to his muscular body with broad shoulders and a smooth, hairless chest. His wiry biceps mocked the true nature of his manhood. Abdullah's shape was that of a fat old woman compared to his. The oyster boy was like a little worm when his hands clutched his throat. Yet they were both so much more men than Ibrahim could ever be! They could propagate, while he could only die lonely and unlamented.

He was a good-for-nothing. Or, good for one thing – carrying out the orders of the *bey*.

For his whole life, Ibrahim could not forget the year of pain after the glaring forceps had cut off his scrotum and left him with a burning feeling in his crotch. He was eight when his father devised the bargain with the court, despite the fact there was always a good flow of slaves from Africa, who, if they survived the castration, could become good eunuchs. There was no need to spill the Ottoman blood. But his father was a good merchant; he sold it well, his blood and his pain. Ibrahim remembered the day as it had been yesterday. It was sunny and warm, and his father smiled at him and kindly took him by the hand. He said that Ibrahim was a good boy and that he had a special future in mind for him. They had to go to the local *hamam* first. When they turned to the *bimaristan*, the hospital, Ibrahim wanted to run away. Why would he go to see a doctor if he was not ill? His father, however, insisted they should visit the illustrious doctor Ibn Al Raizi, who worked for the caliph of Cairo and was a reputed surgeon of the Empire. Ibrahim, hoping that maybe his father would listen to his pleas and let him become a student of the famous Arabic doctor, gave in. He followed obediently. The doctor was waiting for them in the operating theater. His face was grey and old, his eyes tired. There were a few younger men around, chatting to the great medical teacher in subdued, serious voices. Ibn Al Raizi greeted Ibrahim and his father kindly. He seated him on the operating table and gave him a silver goblet with a bitter drink in it. Ibrahim drank the cup down and almost immediately grew sleepy. His next memory was that he was lying on his stomach, with his legs stretched apart and fastened to the handles of the operating table. It was an excruciating pain which woke Ibrahim from his sedated sleep. "We will keep him here for another month, *effendi*. We must monitor the healing of the wound. It is a sensitive part. We must prevent inflammation." He heard his father say, "But you left his penis, he's still a man..." The doctor stroked Ibrahim's hair. "He will never be a man, *effendi*. It's safer this way. He will heal sooner and he will be able to ride and grow strong like a man. That's how our Sultan likes his eunuchs – strong and healthy, to protect his *harem*."

Ibrahim never saw his family again. After he stayed at the hospital for several weeks and his wound healed, they sent him to a *madrasah*, the Islamic school where the Sultan's future officials received a special education. Only years later he found out that the Sultan had paid his father a fortune for him. There were very few Turkish fathers who were greedy enough to exchange gold for the manhood of their boys. After nights of tears, after years of disillusions, young Ibrahim wanted to find his father and kill him, but robbers killed the greedy old man on one of his travels a year before Ibrahim completed his education. Ibrahim refused to mourn his father. His hate changed to apathy. When he entered the *harem* of Abdullah, one of the Sultan's most loyal vasals, he found Fatima. She was more than he could have hoped for – she was his true friend. She was a gift of Allah to the wronged little boy, whom one of the most famous doctors in the Ottoman Empire Ibn Al Raizi had cut off his manhood a decade ago. He was a faithful servant to Abdullah, the *bey* of the new land, Bosnia. He faithfully killed the father of his future offspring. What right did a *castrato* have to kill the young father?

Ibrahim plunged into the cold river covered with the foam of the lavender soap. The riverbed was getting dark grey, nearly black in the last rays of the winter sun. Nevertheless, Ibrahim kept washing as though he could purge the sin of murder from his soul.

It was only two days earlier. He had taken some laudanum with him to calm his nerves and sleep, for with age and lack of habit, all physical violence had become difficult for him. All the way down the river towards the coast, he had been trying to find another solution for the boy. Yet, the stakes were too high! Should Abdullah's spies find out that the boy lived, they would kill him all the same, and the whole plan he and Fatima devised would fail. It would mean living in fear for the rest of their lives. He just had to do it. From his secret stock, he took a flask of sweet wine, mixed with honey and laudanum, a drop of which in a glass of water sufficiently dulled the senses of a man, but a big gulp could put a horse to sleep. He reached the coast on the fourth day in the evening. The horse, unsaddled and free, was grazing at a clearing on the cliff. Ibrahim changed his clothes. A Turkish eunuch turned into a travelling merchant.

In the twilight, shielded by humid white fogs, he made an observation tour and assessed the situation. Hrvoje's oyster farm was closer to the southern cliffs, where he could see pontoons with strings of shells growing under the surface. There was a small boat with a lantern tied to one of them, and he could discern the shapes of two men lifting something from the sea and washing, scrubbing some kind of poles. He walked along the path silently, like a cat, all the way to the house, where in the candlelight he could see a dark, stout woman in a brown *raša* dress setting the table. There were merry cries of several girls of different ages running around and provoking her. Peeping through the open door, Ibrahim felt the wish to come in and join them. The merry sounds of family harmony and joy opened long closed wounds in his mind. Ibrahim ducked behind the pomegranate bush pregnant with ripe red fruits, waiting to see the men enter. They were nowhere in sight, so he decided to wait until morning and observe the situation then.

Abdullah's instructions were clear. He had to make it look

like an accident and he should not leave any traces behind. They did not want to cause any troubles between the Ottomans and *Ragusans*. The Turkish forces were in war with the Greeks, so the last thing they needed was new enemies in the Balkans. Ibrahim decided he would pretend to be a Christian traveler from Bosnia. With ruse and kindness, he wanted to make the boy drink laudanum wine and drug him. Then, he would drown him in the sea and let the corpse float among the strings of oysters. The water would wash away the traces of the drug, and nobody would suspect murder. However, it had all gone wrong. The fate turned the wheel another way, like so many times before.

He stepped on the shore and wrapped his wet body in the thick fur cloak. Once his skin dried, he slipped into his *harem* uniform, padded with fur and wool. He had crossed the border a few hours ago, so he was on the safe ground. He had gathered the firewood before, so now he lit a fire and put on a pot for the stew. He skinned the rabbit and put the liver on a stick into the fire. Sprinkled with salt, it was a rare delicacy. While the meat was cooking, his mind was wandering. Under his fingertips, he still felt the cracking of the young throat.

On the night before the deed, Ibrahim slept in a bush above the cliff. At dawn, his ears registered splashes of oars hitting the smooth, grey surface of the sea. The fog did not lift up, and Ibrahim could not see who it was and what he was doing. He saddled his horse, left his skin water balloon hanging on a tree nearby, and nonchalantly took the horse by the bridle, guiding it directly to the oyster farm.

"Good day, my boy!"

Ibrahim yelled through the curtain of fog. The oars stopped for a moment, then the bow of the boat pierced the fog, and, seconds later, Marin was standing in the middle of the boat, smiling at the stranger.

"Good morning, Sir! What brings you to us so early in the morning?"

"I'm willing make a trade with you, boy!"

"Trade, eh? You should see my master for that. He's in the house over there."

Marin pointed at the house on the shore, where Ibrahim, uninvited, had witnessed dinner preparations the evening before. Ibrahim checked if the people from the house noticed him and heard them talking. Fog or no fog, there was nobody outside in the yard. Marin thought he was trying to see where Hrvoje was and said apologetically,

"But they're all at mass in Ston this morning. I had to come and check on the oysters and pick the lobster nets. They'll be back soon, in an hour or so."

Ibrahim sighed with relief.

"Oh, I don't need to buy fish. I only need some water. Some

rascals stole my water skin at the inn this morning, and I don't have time to go back. Here, take this wine in exchange for your water skin there on the boat."

Marin looked at his feet and picked up the balloon, which had seen cleaner and better days. Ibrahim was waving the lovely glass flask with the Venetian coat of arms on it, and Marin's eyes lighted up at the promise of a transaction in his favor. Hrvoje would be glad. Maybe Olga would be able to store the sage honey wine against cough in it later.

"All right! Let me come to the jetty, so that we can do our business on land."

He skillfully steered the boat towards the land and tied it to the jetty. He jumped ashore with the water skin in his hand.

"Here you are, Sir!"

Ibrahim took the balloon, opened the cap, and smelled. It was water, what else? Then he gave the boy the wine flask, smiling politely.

"Thank you so much, my dear fellow. Here, try some of the wine to be sure you made a good deal. It'll warm you up."

Marin took the flask and opened it. He smelled at it and smiled broadly.

"Thank you, Sir. It is wine, all right. I don't drink wine, only at festivities. My master would beat me if he smelled wine on my breath."

Without another minute's pause, Marin bent to untie the boat. Ibrahim had to react quickly. When the boy was at sea, it would be more difficult. And later, after the mass, for sure, his master would join the boy at work. Still, Ibrahim was hesitating.

"What's the rush, my boy? Tell me your name and what you're doing with this little boat. It's like a toy!"

They both looked at the tiny wooden nutshell of the boat and laughed. The boat was indeed very small, but it was only to tend to the mariculture. They never went to sea in it. Should they both come aboard, it would sink like a stone.

"I am Marin Salić, Hrvoje's apprentice," he looked at the sea and proudly filled his chest with air, "This here, as far as your eyes can see, is the biggest oyster farm in Ragusa. Our oysters are famous from the Rector's palace to the Sultan's court – they all love to eat them. And, you, where do you come from, Mister?"

"Oh, I come from Mostar. I am a merchant and am going to the market in Ragusa to buy some cloth for our ladies."

Marin threw him a suspicious look.

"Now, in early spring? The seas aren't open yet. The ships don't sail in winter. You won't get anything..."

Ibrahim moved fast. He jumped at the boy's throat so fiercely that Marin could not catch a breath to scream. With all the strength, he was pushing his fingertips at the throat arteries, asking Allah that the boy would faint fast and he would not have to stare in his innocent lamb eyes. Finally, Marin's brown eyes closed, slowly and gracefully, as though the boy accepted the end of the line. Ibrahim pressed harder and felt the vertebrae cracking under his fingers, the sound making him burn with pain. To finish the business quickly, he grabbed the bushy hair with one hand and turned the neck to the side. In a moment, it was over. All life left the boy's body, which became limp and heavy. Ibrahim put the water balloon and the Venetian flask back in the boat and heaved the body over his right shoulder. The family would be waiting for the boy, thinking he would return eventually. That would buy Ibrahim some more time. He could not leave the body there, so he took it along, to the river Neretva, and disposed of it there. He tied Marin to his chest with a rope, so that his dead face was leaning on his shoulder in an embrace. Should they meet anybody, it would look like Marin is asleep on his father's shoulder after a long ride.

After the whole night of grazing in the clearing Ibrahim's horse was impatient for action, so they came to the delta within a few hours without meeting a soul. At least that went well. But Ibrahim was sad and distressed. He could not comprehend why this murder, after so many in his life, stabbed at his heart so deeply. Was it because he knew the boy was to be a father? Was it the memory of the boy as he watched Ayesha's dance steps, his face charmed, his passionate eyes dimmed with blissful innocence? Ibrahim knew very well who of the two could have seduced the other into sin, and he was sure as hell it had not been the boy. Ayesha was curious and full of tricks. Now, she would have his baby, Abdullah would take it as his son, Fatima would love him and bring him up, while he, the natural father, had to die. And he, Ibrahim, the eunuch, the lover without love, the cripple of all cripples, had to kill him. His hand touched the boy's soft neck only to stop his breath forever. For a brief moment, they were entangled in a mortal embrace, joined in a fatal grip, two victims of their time.

After he had reached the banks of Neretva with dead Marin in his arms, he sat on the bank, watching the young man's serene, still face. There were primroses and snowdrops flowering prematurely in the bushes. He pulled a yellow flower cluster out of the earth and cleaned the red soil away. He stuck the tender golden petals in the boy's chemise. Then he lifted him and put him in the water as though he was putting a baby to sleep its his cradle. Marin's pale angel face was shining in the sun. Slowly, his rigid body floated down the river towards the sea. Ibrahim stayed by the shore, deep in thought, long after the corpse had disappeared from his view. How beauty and youth passed away, either by the laws of nature or by those of men, or simply without any laws. His chest filled with melancholy and he thought of the Christian symbolism of colors, about which he had read somewhere long time ago. Yellow was the symbol of renewal, hope, it was the color of light and purity. It introduced the season of Easter, when their god Jesus was resurrected to eternal life. So, the yellow primroses, the tiny suns reflecting their creator in the sky in the dirty muddy soil below, were not there in vain. Ibrahim was a dreamer. His eyes filled with tears of regret and longing for the love and life in the family he had briefly spied upon at Hrvoje's house the night before. His mind wandered to Fatima and all the children they had buried together in the terrible weeks of the ravaging plague. Sadness overwhelmed his soul. Only the poet Hafiz could express it in the ode he had written upon the death of his little son:

> Little flower, the spring is here;
> What if my tears were not in vain!
> What if they drew you up again,
> Little flower!

Ibrahim had to go on. He left the banks where he gave the boy to the Neretva river and continued his voyage upstream. After hours of riding at full speed, while the physical activity diverted his wounded mind and his spirits improved, once again ready to face the world, Ibrahim let the bridle loose and his horse was trotting more and more slowly. He had passed the border and he decided he should have a break before finding the spot to spend the night. As he jumped down from his saddle, his eye caught a rabbit, frozen by fear and immobile, staring at him from the bush. He did not hesitate for a moment and threw a knife at the animal, which was too frightened to flee. Hit! It would make a nice supper in the evening.

Ibrahim reached the banks where he took his bath only much, much later. He was still gloomy, but the pines freshened his breathing and brought life into his system again. He regretted that he had left his laudanum in the little boat at Ston. There was nothing to dissolve his heart's pain. Maybe it would be for the boy's family, to soothe their pain of loss. The father would get drunk on wine. The stout mother and the lively sisters would go high on tears and mourning. Yet, what will become of him, Ibrahim? Would he ever find peace at heart for what he had done? Is there any laudanum for the assassins of young innocent fathers? Like so many times before in Ibrahim's life, he shut the pain out of his heart. Life grew over it with tiny layers of rare happy moments. He locked his emotions in stone like a shell locks its pure white pearl inside its being.

The Blaca Monastery, 1916

My office at the hotel is not a nice one. Its square window, shaded by translucent beige curtains, looks on the backyard, where we keep the waste bins. In summer, I am not too eager to open the window and let the foul smell in. No matter how many times I make our staff clean the yard and empty the bins, the compost will smell like the compost. When I feel depressed, I think my life is like that junkyard, in which not ten but sixty-six waste bins hide garbage below their lids, each labeled neatly: paper, compost, glass and plastic. Only my labels would rather be family, children, men, education, business, peace, war, money, wealth, friends, health...For all but two, dustmen are long overdue to collect and empty them into one huge pit called Life of Maria Perić.

With a sigh, I pick up the folder with signed invoices. Knocking briefly on the door of the office adjoining mine, I do not bother to wait for a reply and enter. My financial manager and accountant, Pero Vidic, works diligently on his computer spreadsheets. Like many of my better skilled staff, he does not come from the village Mulobedanj. It was impossible to fill the numerous job vacancies with some twenty of its active inhabitants at the time. To my satisfaction, though, many young locals found work with us later and stayed at home, which in the end created a small, yet optimistic island community. My bin labeled business must have been one of the most effectively recycled matters. Pero takes my folder with a wide grin on his face. With the hotel filled to the last bed, the cash flow is smooth and easy like a wide river meandering to its delta. He swims like a fish in it. I nod and smile back, declaring I am done for the day.

The path from the hotel to the village leads me along the seaside in the fresh shadow of the thick green crowns of crnika trees. Those dwarf Mediterranean oaks, typical of the Adriatic coast, cover the shores along the western side of the island from Novalja to Tavernele, hiding in its woods wildlife, birds, even runaway sheep and goats, not to speak of stealing weasels and fox. The tourists though never see them, for they rarely step off the beaten track. The community regulation which forbids all car traffic on the way from the village to hotel seemed very unpractical at the beginning, yet proved beneficial to the environment later. We managed to negotiate free access for the trucks during the construction years, but today, only delivery vans before nine in the morning and after six in the afternoon are free to pass. Many tourists who like shadow better than the burning sun bring their chairs and blankets along the path, so merry greetings and kind nods constantly interrupt me on my way home. Suddenly, I can hear the unmistakable sound of Dario's pumping diesel at sea. What is my dear old fool up to again? He cannot maneuver the

boat on his own. I focus my look and can see another figure on
the bow of the barge. I do not know the man, yet I am relieved
Dario has company.

The memory of my last boat ride brings into my mind the
taste of his kiss, the smell of his skin and the touch of his rough
hands on my breasts. Funny, how thick old trunks can burn
once they catch fire. Surely, we burn in our last flames, but high
flames they are. The nights in bed with Dario are hotter than
many a night I have spent in bed with my husband as a young
woman, not to even compare them to the nights with my lover.
When morning dew puts an end to our passions, we frequently go
directly to our work without having closed the eye. His love fuels
my body. I feel young and pretty. At last, I am strong enough
to face the terrible waste bins in the junkyard of my life. Maybe,
my man number three will be the best of all. I certainly do love
him more than I have the other two.

My deep feelings have blurred my reason and made me lose
my mind completely. These emotions are bordering on addiction.
I crave to meet Dario during the day, wait for his call or message
on the phone like a stoned teenager, and creep out of my house to
spend the night in his arms. Paula is livid. I cannot comprehend
why. Is my baby jealous? Probably, for this is the first time in her
life she has to share my love with somebody else. She demands
I talk to her in the evenings and is even willing to give up her
obligatory sitcoms to keep me at home. I know she is sick, but
sometimes I think she is simply selfish. For a while, I have been
walking the line, catching balance between my baby's sickbed
and Dario's passionate embraces. Then I made up my mind. In
my lifetime, I have been enough of a mother, a grandmother or
whatever. My name might be Maria, but I am no Madonna. I
am a woman who needs love and sex, not only children's devotion
and sacrifice for their wellbeing. Paula is eighteen. She is clever
and strong. She must stand on her own feet, not in spite of her
illness, but because of it. My role is to let her go, to let her free
to be herself.

The thumping motor gliding into the horizon brings back the
guilt. How have they done it? How have they made every woman
an eternal sinner? I quicken my pace to banish the destructive
thoughts. Do I want to have somebody who entirely and helplessly depends on me, somebody who is incapable of life without
me? I do not. I want my own place under the sun as much as I
respect the freedom of the others. Paula's world and mine cross
at one point, but we must live separate lives. I do not want to
suppress her. I have seen so many women ruin the lives of their
children and grandchildren by interfering, controlling and taking
charge of their fates. Like the mother of all mothers, Bruna, who
wanted to protect her son from the draft during the Great War.
I hasten to come home quickly. I want to print out the story

of Bruna, the mother at Blaca. It will give Paula some food for thought. She must grow up and stop being a jealous, demanding baby. I need air to breathe, time to live and a body to embrace.

* * *

His vision, from the constantly passing bars,
has grown so weary that it cannot hold
anything else. It seems to him there are
a thousand bars; and behind the bars, no world.

– Rainer Maria Rilke, The Panther, translated by
Stephen Mitchel

After the bread loaves were put in the hot oven and the fish soup ready to simmer for another couple of hours, Stijepan Lavrić sighed with relief. He needed a break. Awkwardly, he approached the narrow passage to the little kitchen window and opened it in order to let the heavy fish fumes escape into the sharp morning air outside. Through the grid, he could see bright sunshine, the sharp light of the first rays of the day, casting purple shadows of rocks and stooped trees in the water basin behind the monastery building.

Although it was early in the morning, Stijepan, a pleasantly round middle-aged man briefly called Stipe, had been busy for hours. On the fourth of October 1916, Saint Francis Day, the labor of the season was returned to the hardworking farmers and fishermen on the biggest Adriatic island, Brač. The stingy, rocky land had released its fruits; the vines were heavy with the last golden grapes, which were to be picked as late as possible to produce a sweet white wine, the fig trees were full as well as the lovely, seductive pomegranate bushes, arched with many fresh apples hiding millions of sweet seeds clad in juicy purple meat.

Brač was bathing in peace and sunlight, the last warmth before the harsh winter winds. More than four hundred years had gone by since the first Glagolitic monks fled their cells at Poljica, a community near Split on the mainland. In those times, Turks were killing and plundering Bosnian folks who in terror left their homes and inhabited the Dalmatian coast. The coastal people, on their turn, sought shelter on the many Dalmatian islands. In the solitary safety of the southern ridges of the island Brač, hidden below the cave Ljubitovica and the mighty cliffs of the mountain Malo čelo, Little Forehead, the destitute hermits started anew, working the meager commons, growing wheat and raising goats, leading a life of poor hermits in awe of their Lord Jesus Christ. Since then, the Monastery Blaca grew into a dominating stone fortress, the center of the cultural and spiritual life of the south of Brač.

Stijepan was in a frenzy. His huge body moved skillfully around the kitchen, lifting lids from the pots, shuffling pans and cups, adding spices and salt to his creations. He was a cook, but when the staff was short, he would also do other chores around the monastery, where he had been employed as a laic for the last twenty-five years. His mother brought him to Don Nikola after his father disappeared and left the family with five children destitute. There were too many mouths to feed, so she asked Don Nikola to employ little Stijepan when he was still a young boy. At first, the prior trusted him only with the garden and the goats, yet very soon Stijepan showed his talent for cooking. He spent all his free moments at the monastery kitchen, learning and absorbing the secrets of good dishes, as well trying everything that was cooking. His appetite was insatiable, as he had never eaten his belly full until he came to work at the monastery. Years later, when the senior cook got married and left Blaca, Stijepan took over his chores with devotion and care. He loved to think of new ways to surprise the old and the young of the household with new tastes from old dishes. He adored children, and they returned Stijepan's love eagerly. Namely, Don Nikola started an elementary school for the children from the surrounding villages in 1912, so Stijepan's great joy of each day in the week was to prepare a warm meal for a dozen of hungry mouths. It was more the need to eat than the zest to learn that brought them to the classroom, still, for many it was their first giant step into the world.

Despite restraints, the simplicity of the diet and numerous fasting days, he loved to cook for Don Nikola, who was, like all the priors of Blaca, born in the Miličević family from Poljica on the mainland. Stijepan paid particular attention to the menu when guests were invited, which was a rare occasion. Most of the time Don Nikola led a solitary life, absorbed in contemplation and prayers. They all respected him and his devotion to monastic rules, but only few really shared his passion for God. The world outside was out of joint, as the poet did write, and only few believed God could truly intervene with human malice. However, Don Nikola Miličević was a great man; he led Blaca in an impeccable way and even edited and printed The Rules of Life in Blaca, so that his descendants would know how to follow them. Well, without a doubt, his nephew, young Niko Miličević respected them, despite the fact that his eyes were turned to the sky burning with scientific interest, not only religious zeal.

A breath of rosemary came to his delicate nose, which brought him back to his pots and pans. Stijepan was planning a delicious menu for a celebration; fish soup, *scampi al bianco*, mutton goulash with corn bread, young cheese and fig cake. Although on the mainland people were starving and children dying of malnutrition due to meager harvests and the raging war, the monastery was well stocked. They had bought enough wheat to compensate for the July drought, the corn for the fuming *polenta* was plentiful, and the fruit trees gave enough to last through the winter. Their pigs were well fed and the goats gave milk for delicious cheese. The news from the mainland of the poverty and the misery in the trenches seemed far away. However, Don Nikola would always remember the soldiers and poor starving civilians in his prayers, and demanded of the congregation to do the same.

Stijepan obliged despite the fact that he did not understand much about that war apart from the fact that it was apocalyptic in its dimensions. The casualties were not counted in individual men but in thousands nearly every day. Like all Dalmatians, he hated Italians, who wanted to march into their lands and enslave them. It was no secret that Italians had attacked the Austro-Hungarian Empire on the Isonzo river in order to occupy the whole of Dalmatia, from Istria to Dubrovnik. The papers reported, that the Dalmatian battalion had been transferred from Galicia to Isonzo, and that more young men were needed to defend the fragile western border. Stijepan was glad that his Luka was still a minor, so that the draft could not take him. No matter the destitute situation and the horrible suffering around Europe, the aging cook managed to live in his cocoon; the newspapers on his night table remained unread, he cared little to listen to the news brought to the kitchen by the staff and the suppliers. The work in the house, in the kitchen and in the garden demanded all his energy and strengths. Well, he was not getting any younger, at forty and only with great difficulty his obese body moved through the chores of the day.

How could Stijepan get so fat on the basically simple monastery regime? Well, he had been starving as a kid in the village of Pražnica, so when he came to work for Don Nikola, it was like Paradise. Stijepan ate with gusto, and he could not leave food uneaten; after every meal, he took great care to eat all the scraps himself, enjoying the feeling of his belly filled. The more he heard about the famine, the more he enjoyed eating. With years, the food and the fat took their toll. He grew bigger and bigger. Bruna, his wife in the village Milna on the western side of the island, turned her face away in disgust when he came home for the Assumption of Mary in August.

Since they had been married on a bright winter day eighteen years ago, the arrangement with Don Nikola was that he could keep his job at the monastery on one condition; his wife and his child should never visit him at Blaca, but, he could go home for big holidays. Only reluctantly Bruna consented to the terms. She let Stijepan keep his job, which guaranteed her and the baby security in times when hundreds of their folks *Bračani* had to look for work not only across the channel in Split but also in the faraway America. With time, Stijepan managed to convince Don Nikola to let his son Luka come to Blaca for his school holidays, when the boy would help around the herds and bring some life into the silence of the thick grey walls. Luka adored his *tata* and made friends with Don Nikola's nephew, Nikola Miličević Junior, whom everybody called Niko. Niko never missed an opportunity to challenge Luka with new knowledge and interesting conversations. The boy was so bright. Oh, if only Stijepan had money! He would have sent Luka to school, so his son could have a better life. With the little land that Bruna worked at Milna and his pay from the monastery, they were not starving. However, it was not enough for the high school at Bol. After his primary education, Luka had to seek apprenticeship at the village Pučišča, where he was learning to cut the famous white stone of the island. Luka's secret passion was history. In the evenings, he was reading the books avidly, turning the pages with difficulty, for his hands were rough and the cuts in them deeper than the cuts he had made in the white stone during the day. Stijepan knew that Luka secretly nourished the ambition to continue his education and discover the world. Each time he accompanied him to the monastery, Luka spent hours with Niko, Don Nikola's nephew. What they were talking about was a mystery to Stijepan.

However, at noon a festive meal should be ready. Apart from Don Nikola's nephew and his Austrian friend, the elders of the villages, which were once part of the monastery land, were invited to join Don Nikola in the celebration. They would discuss politics and the Austrian intention to draft more Dalmatian men for their western front, where on the Isonzo, the Italian and the Austrian army were caught up in a never-ending attrition war, oblivious to thousands of human lives perished in vain.

"Don Nikola asked if you are ready to serve breakfast, Stipe," asked a voice coming through the tiny window from a man as thin as a stick. Lovro was from Istria and joined the monastery life as one of the laics, the staff who each had their responsibility in the economy and in the organization of the daily life at Blaca. Lovro was in charge of the agriculture of the monastery: he managed the vineyards, the olive groves, the crops in the garden and in the fields, the goats and the cow which gave milk and butter.

"Here I come. It's ready, Lovro."

Stijepan took the buckwheat hot cross buns out of the oven. He put some fig and lemon jam, a chunk of butter, a few poached eggs, some cold milk, and steaming coffee and tea on a large tray and carried it to the dining room. Focusing on the tablet, Stijepan lifted his eyes only when the food was safely put on the table.

"Hello, dad!"

His father's heart jumped with joy. It was Luka sitting at the table with Don Nikola and Niko. He rushed into his embrace. Embracing his son's tough and sun burnt body, he babbled with excitement:

"Hello, my dear boy...What a lovely surprise! Hello...Let me give you a kiss...Here..."

The joy of the old man brought a smile to Don Nikola's face. With a hearty laughter, the son, who was a head taller than his father, lifted the cook's round body from the ground and swept him around the room. Niko, the junior priest, looked the other way, paling, as though a faraway pain stabbed his heart. Once, almost so long ago that he could not remember, he had a family like the boy Luka...Then he came to Blaca, to step in the shoes of his uncle and head the monastery after his death. It was a sad and lonely time. He had no friends. There were no children miles around. Even the dog and the cat were old and lazy. A vision of Stijepan as a young man playing with him in the yard flashed into Niko's mind. It was the day almost twenty years ago when he first came to Blaca. He could have been no more than ten or eleven. He missed Poljica, he missed his mother and his father so much. He was crying in a bush, where the young cook found him. They played hide and seek, with one limitation...no sounds, no cries or laughter; the monastery was a place of prayer and silence. Among stifled sounds of amusement, tears of laughter were running down their cheeks. He survived...learning and praying with his uncle, and in secret, playing with Stijepan. Niko had his doubts about whether he could have become a reputed scholar only with books and prayers and without Stijepan's warm attention. He wished he could lift the old man in the air, hold him and dance with him like Luka. But his uncle, Don Nikola, would disapprove. Besides, the twenty years of studies left Niko frail and weak. His scholarly hands could lift nothing heavier than a book or sheets of paper. He could never compete with Luka's strong arms. Niko subdued his feelings once again, while his thoughts wandered to his only passion – the stars and astronomy. His recently published articles and public speeches had already made a name for Niko Miličević in Vienna as well as in all the lands of the vast Empire.

"Enough!"

Don Nikola's stern voice left no room for play. Luka put his father down and looked at Niko apologetically.

"Bring two more plates, Stipe, and have breakfast with us. I think Luka has something important to tell us."

Stijepan's eyes lit up. He rushed to the kitchen and brought two more plates as well as more food. He knew Luka's appetite. While he was putting everything on the table, Niko stood up and filled their cups with fresh rosehip tea. They ate in silence. After his first hunger was satisfied, Luka spoke up.

"Father, I have finished my school and apprenticeship. Since August, I've been employed as a stonecutter in the quarry."

"Really? Your mother hasn't told me. So, you get a better pay?"

"Yeah, I do. It is not a gold mine, though, and we're working very hard. Most days, we do some ten to twelve hours. Our boss was given a huge order from America. A government building. . . "

Niko woke up.

"This is great! In Europe nothing goes. . . Nobody's building. . . "

"Everybody is tearing apart, ravaging, demolishing. It is a barbaric and horrible war. All sides should stop and listen to our Holy Father."

After Don Nikola had spoken, the three men continued their meal in silence. Stijepan felt the tension in the room rising. The atmosphere was laden with different opinions, which remained unsaid. He knew that most men disagreed with Don Nikola's pacifistic views, which strictly followed the neutral position of Pope Benedict XV. Many Dalmatians felt betrayed when the Church had not condemned the Italian attack on the Austrian western border and the Italian *sacro egoismo* of Antonio Salandra, a nationalist beyond comparison. The position of the Holy Seat was not to take sides but to condemn violence at all fronts and help the victims no matter of which nation or religion. In his childlike mind, Stijepan, who could not understand the complex diplomacy of the Pope, thought it was nothing but hypocrisy. How could you not condemn the Italians, who wanted to occupy Dalmatia? They were the aggressors, not our Emperor, dear old Franz Joseph, who first lost his son, then witnessed his nephew being murdered in Sarajevo. What a disaster was this business of war! He switched the subject to lighter topics.

"Now, Luka, my boy, you came with a tiding! Is it a girl? Are the wedding bells tolling?"

Don Nikola and Niko looked at Stijepan nonplussed. Was the man really so simple? Could he only think of food and procreation, while the whole world was on fire? Luka smiled politely and shook his head in negation.

"No, daddy, no such things. . . The one who will catch me has not been born yet."

"Oh, my boy, that's what I thought twenty years ago, too! Look at me now! I have two bosses. . . one is the Reverend Don Nikola Miličević, the other is your mother. And when she got me, I was working here, in Blaca, not cutting stones half naked behind the beach, where the village girls could pass by and cheer me."

"Father, I. . . "

Luka was uneasy and felt guilty. How could he break the news to his father, who had always been so loving and honest with everybody? For months he had been acting in great secrecy, for he knew that his parents would bitterly disapprove of his intentions. However, he knew it would be his only chance in life. Luka did not know what to say. His cheeks were glowing with purple shame. Niko decided to follow the merry tone and break the tension, so he continued the story of Stijepan and Bruna.

"Well, Luka, I was about your age, when Stijepan told us about your mother. He wanted to leave us, that is, he wanted to leave the monastery, but we both pleaded with him to stay at Blaca. Uncle made the decision, which was good and clever for all of us. Oh, I remember how jealous I was of your mother, Bruna. I hated her for trying to take Stijepan away. You know how the world of a young teenager is either black or white, either good or bad. All of a sudden, Stijepan, who had been mine only...I mean my dear friend, disappeared over the weekends. I was left alone with goats and farmhands, who didn't play with me..."

Don Nikola lifted his eyebrows.

"Most of the time you were in *gymnasium*, anyway. For your holidays, I was there, too, Niko, remember?"

"Of course, you were. But I needed pals to talk to."

"A priest talks to God. He does so from an early age. There are no conversations with friends to outdo the sacred bond. You have never put enough faith into your life. I doubt that..."

"Oh, but little Don Niko was praying all the time, Don Nikola. He never missed a mass. I have never seen a child in such zeal for God and Heaven."

"Ah, Stijepan, for Niko Heaven has a scientific connotation rather than a religious one. He studies the stars instead of aspiring to them."

"My dear uncle, let me quote David: Jehovah counteth the number of the stars; He giveth names to all, Psalm 147:4."

"Niko, the stars are the symbols for the knowledge of all goodness and truth. They're not a physical entity, they hold spiritual meaning."

With a loud clink clank, Luka put down the cutlery. He folded his rough hands, one palm over the other, like in a prayer.

"Excuse me, Don Nikola, sorry, Niko. I have to speak up now."

The three men shut up. Stijepan scanned his son with an expectant look sending him sparkles of love.

"Dad, you know I love you and Mother very much. You have done everything you could for me. I am grateful to you both. My profession is respected, although not so well paid. Well, times are hard. I think it is time for me to move on. I must leave Brač and go into the world..."

"Will you be going to America?"

Niko's voice betrayed a tremble of worry. Stijepan was waiting for his son to reply.

"No, I am not going to America, Niko."

"So, where are you going, my son?"

Luka sighed. His blue eyes were set in the distance over the sea. His light, almost platinum hair curled on his forehead. Luka was a handsome young man, ready to get married and to give

Stijepan and Bruna grandchildren. But he was going away from Blaca, away from Milna and Pučišča, and away from Brač.

"I will be going to Celje, to the training camp of the Imperial Army. I want to get enlisted to serve. My friend Nenad is already there. He will have finished the training in a week and will be assigned to General Svetozar Borojević at Isonzo. I hope to be trained for the Austria-Hungarian Mounted Dalmatian Rifles and follow Nenad. I have already learnt how to shoot in my free time."

The three men were staring at the boy as though he had lost his mind. The first to speak was Don Nikola.

"But Luka, you're still a minor. I don't think even our Emperor is so mad as to be recruiting children for his suicidal mission at Isonzo."

Luka almost burst with anger. He stifled a juicy curse not to offend the priests.

"Don Nikola, with all due respect, when I finish the training, I will be eighteen. The limits regarding the age for volunteers can be bypassed. And I am in good physical condition. I can do my duty."

Then both Niko and Stijepan woke up from their shock.

"Luka, my boy, it is out of the question. Your mother did not bring you to this world to have you end up as cannon fodder on the Carso. I am a simple cook, but I know there's nothing to win there, just rocks. There are no sublime goals in the war, just suffering, killing. The only winner is death. No, I forbid you..."

"Dad, I have been living on my own since I was twelve. You cannot forbid me anything."

"Luka, my dear friend... Why will you volunteer to go to war? You must kill other men in the war. It is so non-christian, it is inhuman... They report from the Isonzo the most terrible things. Shelling, wounds, famine, thirst, even cannibalism... They call it frozen hell. And Stijepan is right... They fight over some rocky slopes. It is nothing for you..."

Luka's lips quivered. How could even Niko not understand him?

"Why? You're asking me why, Niko? I will tell you why. Because those rocky slopes are the border of our country; the border separates us from the Italians, who are after our land, after our lives. We don't need them here in Dalmatia. Do we? We have to fight for our land..."

Niko interrupted him.

"Yeah, but who cares in the end? Empires are not natural entities, they do not represent nations. They come and go. Italians will not come to Brač, will they? Besides, Luka, in such chaos you should look after your own interests. There are enough older men who get enlisted against their will and have to fight."

Now Don Nikola added.

"We are all Christians. This war is a disgrace in the eye of the Lord."

Yet, Luka, as though he hadn't heard him, continued his belligerent arguing.

"Niko, my interests are the interests of my country. The Emperor promised support and promotion to all soldiers after the war. When we win our Emperor will reward me; he will promote me, he will grant me a scholarship. I will be able to study in Vienna. I will be able to pass my Baccalaureate and continue to study history. This is my only chance."

"If you survive... Do you know the death toll at Isonzo? You're risking your life, Luka! There must be another way!"

"Niko, please, you cannot understand this. Your education was laid in your cradle with your name – Miličević. I have worked very hard at the quarry, thinking that I would be able to save money and go to the high school. But the pay I get is miserable. The army is my only solution. So stay out of it, please!"

"Luka, have you told your mother?"

Stijepan's voice was on the verge of panic. His only boy, their only child is going to waste his life for nothing. He was trembling all over his body. Silence fell on the room, again the silence shouting disagreement of all sides. At last, Don Nikola Miličević calmly stood up from the table. His voice revealed outrage.

"Young Mr. Lavrić, I think you should obey your father and listen to God. Now go! I will not dine with a future murderer. Our life here at Blaca is striving for peace. I beg you to leave the monastery right now!"

"Uncle, please!"

"Niko, shut up! I'm running this institution, not you! I will run it as I see fit! Thank you for your company, Luka. Stijepan, I think you have a lot of work today. My guests will be here in a few hours. Niko, stay here, we must speak."

Luka stood up, his cheeks purple with humiliation. He came to see his father and accepted the cordial invitation to breakfast from the two monks whom he had considered friends. Instead of understanding, instead of showing respect for his patriotic decision and the courage, which could also save Blaca from Italian occupation and plundering, Don Nikola coldly swept him aside like a street dog. Why was his father working for such a man? What was the prior hiding behind his image of humanity? He swallowed hard. He still needed to talk to his father.

"Excuse me, Sir, I didn't mean to offend the sacred place with my personal decisions. May I help my dad in the kitchen and talk to him privately? That is why I've come here."

Don Nikola looked at Stijepan, who was on the verge of tears. He was breathing heavily, his jaws shaking in distress. Maybe the son would take pity on his ageing father and come to his senses. In a more comforting tone, he said:

"You may, Luka. And you're always welcome to confession. Do not hesitate to talk to me. Your patriotism is positive, and I can sympathize with your feelings. But this war is not about defending your country. I hope we will have time to discuss it. The rumor has it that our Franz Joseph will draft all young men, such is the death toll on all the fronts and such is the need for soldiers. It is well possible you will not be left the choice at all, Luka."

Stijepan lifted his big body from the chair and started to pick up the plates and the leftovers.

"Come on, Luka. Let's do the dishes together."

Niko's sad look followed the father and the son leaving the room.

"Uncle, you were too harsh with Luka. He's still an ignorant boy. He cannot understand world politics while working in the quarry. We need to show him some affection, not scare him away. We can talk him out of it, you'll see."

Don Nikola sighed in distress.

"Niko, I am not used to such confrontations. And you know I am right."

"I know, uncle. Maybe Bruna can influence the boy."

"I doubt it. She doesn't even know about all this."

"Uncle, can I fetch you something from the kitchen?"

Don Nikola looked at his nephew sternly. He knew Niko was waiting for an excuse to follow Luka and Stijepan and talk to them behind his back. What business of his was this young stonecutter Luka? Why was Niko always so involved? Without waiting for an answer, Niko left the room, which fell silent.

* * *

He who has no soul
needs no gold,
He who has a soul
needs no dung.

– Srečko Kosovel, cons.5, Man in a magic square,
Ljubljana, 2004

Bruna could see the dog jumping up and running outside, barking ferociously. All of a sudden, the animal switched to friendly whining.

"Oh, it's him, at last."

She ran outside and took her son in her arms. His skin was warm and damp from the long walk from Blaca. She buried her head in his embrace, so familiar, yet so new. Luka had become a man. Soon, she would lose him, and he would embrace another woman. She wondered how his life at Pučišče was. Did he go out dancing? What was he doing during the weekends when he did not come home?

"Hello, mother. I thought you were the girl from next door. You look younger every time I come home."

Bruna smiled. She loved receiving the compliment, although she was aware that Luka had to be honestly shocked by her appearance. She had lost a few pounds again, despite taking great care to have regular meals. But she had been so sad and lonely. With longer evenings and works in the fields closing for the season, she had too much time to think about her solitary life. Her husband was working in the monastery, but she was the hermit. In her son's eyes, she saw the reflected image of a tired peasant, whose face was wrought by the work and the sun in the fields. Wrinkles around her wide blue eyes formed a spider net, not to speak of two deep creases alongside her Roman nose pulling her thin lips lower, in an almost perpetual expression of sadness. Her lines reflected the nights she had cried through in her tiny solitary house in Milna. Her fuzzy hair was bound in a light blond bun at the back of her head. She was wearing a neat white linen blouse and a dark brown skirt, which was fastened by a simple leather belt, obviously cut and shortened several times. Bruna was thin and pale despite her dark tan. Luka was worried, yet, he was careful not to show it.

"Mom, you've worked too hard again. You know you don't have to. Dad should support you and the house. And I can help, too."

"I know, dear, I know. Well, I had to strive through the season, although the drought took all the olives. We have very little oil this year."

"We can get some lard from our neighbors. I passed by their house and their pigs smell. . ."

"I know. Was Marija at home?"

"Yeah, she was. I stopped for a glass of water and offered to take her hogs for a swim before they are slaughtered."

"Oh!"

"She just laughed. She told me little Maja got married last Saturday, to an Austrian."

"Yeah, she met him while she was working as a maid in Split. It was a bit awkward, for she is only sixteen. I think she's expecting. Well, she might return to Brač sooner than Marija realizes. Her Austrian has gone to the front."

"Which front, *Mama*?"

"I am not sure. I think Galicia."

Luka was sunk in thought. How was he going to break the news to Nenad, who had a crush on his lovely neighbor and was probably dreaming about courting her in his lonely nights in the barracks? He himself had never really liked her. She seemed like a doll without any brain to him; red mouth, wide brown eyes and

long dark hair. With her curves and plump breasts, she looked
twenty at the age of fifteen. The voice of the woman Luka deeply
cared for woke him from his reverie:

"Come in, my son! I have cooked a nice venison stew with
fresh bread. I got some scraps of meat from our gamekeeper. For
once maybe I can win over your father's menu."

"Oh, they will be having scampi. It's for the gentlemen with
full bellies, not for eaters like you and me."

They smiled at each other cordially. The bond between them
was stronger than anything else in the world. For his whole life,
his mother was the only person Luka could always trust and rely
upon. She was a rock. She looked after him, she raised him,
sent him to school and finally, she arranged the apprenticeship
in Pučišče for him. Although it was not what Luka had been
hoping for, he knew that it was a good and solid profession. He
even felt proud of his work and could find satisfaction in carving
little objects from the soft white stone. Out of his pocket, he took
a sculpture of the Holy Mother which he had been working on for
weeks. It was the size of a palm, yet very precise and detailed.

"I have a present for you. Here, for your mantelpiece."

Bruna stared at a perfect replica of herself clad in the wide
robes of Mary. The hair was curly like hers, the eyes and the
brows. Her face was the same, and the hands hidden between the
folders of the stony tissue. Tears welled up in her eyes...

"Thank you, Luka. She is... She is wonderful!"

"Just like you, mom. You're wonderful."

They looked at each other for a couple of moments. Then
Luka turned around.

"It smells wonderful. Let's eat."

Bruna scrutinized his back as he stepped in the house. She had
a presentiment of something, but every tiding or problem would
be easier to deal with after their stomachs were filled. Mother
and son sat at the table, like they had done so many times before,
and enjoyed the savory stew cooked with rosemary, thyme, dried
and fresh tomatoes. The meat melted on their tongues, and for
a while only the tinkling of the cutlery interfered with silence.
Finally, Luka said:

"Mom, I have another surprise for you... coffee. Father gave
me a little sachet of ground Italian coffee, so we can have some.
Shall I put it on?"

"Oh, that's great. So, that was what you were hiding from
me! I knew there was something."

Luka turned to the stove with his face pale. By the late afternoon, in a few hours, he would have to talk to his mother about
his intentions. The memory of his father's tears and desperate at-
tempts to talk him out of it suddenly came to Luka's mind. They
could not come to any reasonable agreement, apart from Luka's
solemn promise to go and see Don Nikola for a private confession.

He had to give an oath to his father that he would come to the monastery next Saturday. What did the old man think? That the monk can change Luka's determination like *bura* changes to *maestral* in the afternoon? Now, with Mother, he had to use all his diplomacy. Filling a coffee pot with warm water from the stove, he said:

"Mother, what do you think about the Italians and their appetites for Dalmatia?"

Bruna's face turned purple. She had no political mind, yet her convictions were clear. She hated foreigners, particularly Italians and their Pope, who in her opinion had their tentacles in every church around the globe. Don Nikola, her husband's employer, was one of them... all the hypocrites hiding their fleshy passions under their long robes of monks. She hated them all. Still, she had to keep up appearances and went to the church every now and then. Luka's question brought a flow of foul words to her mouth:

"The shitty cowards will never occupy our lands! We're not like the ignorant Ethiopians, and even there, the Italians blew it. I am sure our Emperor will protect us. No matter how they are trying, they cannot break further east from the Isonzo. Every time I go to church, I cannot but pray that a flood should take them all, including their Holy Father. How can the priests preach pacifism and peace while those jackals are shelving our boys? That old fart, Don..."

"Mother, please!"

Luka knew his mother's hatred for the clergy, and to an extent, he could understand her bitterness regarding her marital situation, yet the words she was using were too much for him. She puffed through her thin lips sending a curl of grayish blond hair from her face. She looked at him defiantly.

"What? You said yourself they are nothing but a bunch of pansies! They tremble in their robes for their bodies which are of no use whatsoever! They could easily abandon the flesh and aspire to their souls, to higher spirituality... At least that is what they preach to the hungry folks, poor peasants, whom they exploit cunningly."

Luka smiled at his mother's revolutionary words. He knew their origin too well. His mother had always been missing his father, who could only rarely come home to be with her. Particularly when Luka was little and they were so much in love. She blamed Don Nikola for holding Stijepan away from her, believing the priest was only being jealous. His cook could love a woman of flesh and blood, while Don Nikola could only touch the stone Mother Mary in the altar. However, Luka liked the way their conversation went.

"Mother, are you a socialist?"

"No, I am not. I would not share the fruits of my labor with

lazy neighbors just for the sake of sharing. You father would
of course disagree... His respect for that monk is out of proportions... "

"Well, mom, we do all have a decent life with father's salary
and gifts from Don... "

"Oh, Luka, you will never understand! I would rather starve
than eat at the monastery table. It's like dining in the nest of
vipers! I would rather eat grass and snails than accept a dime
from that old fart! Look, what he has done to your father! He
has turned him into his hog, feeding him like Marija is feeding her
pigs! Do you remember the man your father used to be? He was
slim, handsome, loving... Now all he does is eat and grow... "

"I don't have the feeling Don Nikola is making father eat... "

"You're a fool sometimes, Luka. Food is Stijepan's tempta-
tion. It has always been... That's why he is a cook. But he
has grown fat since he has given up home and being with me at
least on Sundays... Don Nikola wants his scampi, or he wants his
roast, or pasta... What do I know? He just doesn't let Father
come home. While I am unhappy and cannot eat, your father is
sad and eating all the time!"

The words sounded too harsh in Luka's ears. However, his
heavy task was still ahead of him. Finishing brewing coffee, he
was pondering how to break the news to his mother. Her temper
scared him. Or, was he not to become a soldier? He had to gather
the courage. If he did not speak up now, when would he? Filling
two cups with the steaming black gold, he softly said.

"I agree with you regarding the Italians and the fishy policy
of the Holy Seat. I think the Church should condemn the Italian
aggression on the Austrian borders. And I also think we should
do something about it... "

"What can we do, my dear Luka? We're but poor souls,
peasants with no money... Who would listen to us, anyway?"

"Well, they listen to us when we get in the right circles. Believe me, they do."

"What do you mean?"

"Mother, I share your political views. I agree with you sincerely. And as a man, I feel that I must do my duty to protect
our lands. I got enlisted... "

"No! Luka!"

"Mother, do not worry! First the Imperial Army will train us
for a couple of months. I can shoot, I have a strong body! I will
cut those Italian melons in halves like I cut my stones! We will
win!"

"But, Luka, you're a minor... You cannot go... "

"I made my enquiries... There are ways I can join the army.
Anyway, I will be full of age by the time I am field trained. Please,
Mother, understand me... I need to give my life a meaning, a goal.
Cutting stones will bring me nowhere. I want to protect our lands

and be promoted. Our Emperor promised rewards to his soldiers after the war. I'll be able to get ahead, to finish the high school and to study. Wouldn't you like that?"

Bruna remained speechless. She had to think hard, not over-react and lose her son's trust. Her passionate hatred for Italians gave way to her fear for her only boy. She knew Luka too well. The least she should do was to treat him like a child and scorn his honorable intentions. She had to be wise now, or he would go. She saw the determination in his eyes. He would go to his war without turning back. She had to think of something. So, she slowly stood up from her chair and came to face him. She looked him deeply in his blue innocent eyes and embraced him tightly. Luka was surprised and interpreted her gesture as consent. His wonderful, proud mother! At least one of his parents was sound in his head in the midst of the havoc!

"Can I ask you something, my son?"

"Yeah, of course."

"Do you believe in God?"

Luka looked down into his mother's eyes, astonished. Why would she be asking him something like that? She did not mind if he believed, for he knew she did not. For her, God was an illusion which served leaders like the Holy Father and Don Nikola as an excuse for exploiting and enslaving the poor gullible peasants. Still, Luka had found faith and peace in the Christian view of the world.

"I do, mother. You know, I do."

"I mean, do you really believe in God, our blessed virgin Mary, her son Jesus and the Holy Trinity, Luka?"

Why was this so important all of sudden? She had almost never asked him about his beliefs or political views.

"Mother, I do believe in our Holy Bible. You should know..."

She cut him off.

"Good. Let's have our coffee. We can take a walk to the beach. You will tell me more about your patriotic decision, won't you?"

"Of course! Thank you, mother! Thank you so much! You're such a treasure. I love you!"

"I love you, too, Luka. You are my one and only..."

* * *

This morning I lay back
In an urn of water
And like a relic
Took my rest

– Giuseppe Ungaretti, translated by Mark
Thompson, The White War, Basic Books 2010

The huge bucket with pale orange shrimps was crawling with life. The males were waving their elegant pink scissors at the sky, and the females lay still, only here and there their long red antennae quivered in the air. Their moves were senseless, impotent, for there was no way even one of them could climb over the motionless hulls of those who had already drawn their last breath. They were all striving upwards, where the air and maybe a way to freedom in the clear sea waters lured them.

The heap of suffocating pinkish carcasses would normally whet Stijepan's appetite and his profound ambition to prepare the dish as best as he could. Any day but today... Today, the rosy crustaceans reminded him of the rare newspaper pictures of battles and the heaps of human bodies afterwards. The limbs of young boys and mature men were spread in every direction possible... an arm pointing in the air, fixed by the comrades' still bodies, a body missing one leg, both legs, or split open, with guts spilling over the others, a head looking up as if to blame the skies for the terrible stillness of eternity... And the eyes... the fear and pain reflected in those forever dead, wide open eyes. Timeless silence was their only connection; they were bound by its coldness and blackness, interrupted only by a few seconds of flash and fame in the lens of the war reporter. All those beautiful young men... when would this madness of the world stop?

Mechanically, Stijepan put some olive oil into a large saucepan, which was heating under the grill fire. The oil hissed on the heated metal like a wounded animal. The chopped onions followed into the greenish boil with a swish. They should fry to develop the right aroma before they serve as a bed for scampi. Some sliced garlic, and it was time for the real thing. Stijepan looked at the bucket again. The salty smell spoke of freshness. The scampi had been caught during the night and pulled out of the nets no later than in the morning. Many of them were still alive... A few onion chunks were already burning, their edges curling brown and burnt. He had to act swiftly, or the dish would be lost.

"At least you'll be swimming in wonderful white wine, my little fellows. I am sorry, but I have to cook you..."

"Stipe, are you talking to shrimps?"

Young Niko helped him lift the bucket, and with their palms they were spooning the crawling beasts on their last voyage into the saucepan. The heat of the steam which blasted from the saucepan was hurting their fingers and with effort they were taking the last of the beaten sea warriors out of the bucket.

"Ouch! Bloody stupid... Excuse me, Niko..."

"They don't give in easily, do they?"

One of the males was saving his final blow of his tiny yet sharp scissors to revenge the lot. He cut Stijepan deeply into the soft skin between the thumb and the palm. Blood was dripping from the wound onto the white tiled floor. Stijepan sucked on it while Niko wrapped a rag around his palm. The sizzling in the pan grew louder.

"Wine, we have to add white wine!"

Niko found a huge wicker bottle in the corner. Without hesitation, he uncorked it and spilled wine into the dish. The aromatic fumes woke Stijepan, who added some white bread crumbs and freshly chopped parsley. In a few minutes, the *scampi al bianco* were ready to be served. They could wait their turn in the corner of the grill for a while. After they saved the saucepan from the flame, Stijepan fell on the kitchen stool with all his weight. He did not count for how many times on that lovely Sunday he had burst in tears. Niko embraced the old cook, speaking softly to him:

"Please, Stipe, calm down. We will find a solution. He will not go, you will see. My uncle and I, we will do anything to hold him back. I have some money of my own and I am prepared to give it to him, so that he can continue his schooling... We should have thought of it years back..."

Stijepan was shaking with pain.

"I don't know... I don't know what to do, Niko. He's everything I have... My wife, Bruna... The life here..."

Niko's hands were stroking his back.

"I know, I understand. Please, calm down, my Stipe. We will find a solution, you'll see. I promise you, he won't go."

The old man wiped his eyes and blew his nose in the corner of his apron. Niko's heart bled with sympathy.

"Should my uncle see you..."

They looked at each other and burst into laughter. Simultaneously, they said:

"It's the final flavor that counts..."

When Stijepan served the dish on several wonderful porcelain plates, decorated with lemon slices and twigs of fresh parsley, not one of the guests could suspect the battle of emotions going on in the kitchen. They soaked their chunks of fresh milk bread in the savory white sauce, thinking how lucky they are to be at Don Nikola's table.

* * *

> With its golden rays the sun will shine
> on us, the European dead.
>
> – Srečko Kosovel, The Ecstasy of Death, Man in
> a magic square, Ljubljana, 2004

Luka's day at the quarry was over. He assembled his tools and put them in a leather sack. From tip to toe, his hair, face

and body were all coated with fine white powder, which filled
the air of the whole quarry. He looked more like a ghost than
human, but he was no scare to the people on the road, for they
were used to stone cutters and their appearance at the end of the
working day. He was headed to his rented room in the village,
where his landlady Milica had probably already prepared dinner.
He saw her sorting beans and chickpeas in the morning, so he was
expecting a hefty stew with lard and some smoked pork bones.
There was nothing like a good warm meal and a kind word after
a long working day. Milica was in her fifties, kind and motherly,
a good woman left a widow far too early. She rented her rooms
to a few young bachelor workers like Luka. The lodging came
with two warm meals and her friendly attention. Her tenants
were young boys away from their families, lonely and sad in the
pursuit of their daily bread. They were all saving their *krunas*
earned in the sweat of their chisels for their families.

Milica welcomed him with a smile.

"Luka, there's a letter for you."

"Good day, Mother Milica. Thank you. I will get washed and
be right back."

"The *minestrone* still needs another quarter of an hour. Take
your time."

She waved the blue envelope in front of his nose, teasing him:

"I bet it's from a girl, Luka. Will you be leaving me?"

"Mother Milica, how could I leave you? I am your man, forever..."

They laughed heartily. With a nod, Luka took the envelope
from her hand and saw in the left top corner it came from Vipava.
That had to be Nenad writing from the front. Impatiently, Luka
performed the evening ritual of scrubbing his sweated face and
body back to his human appearance. For a few extra *groši*, Milica
was doing his laundry, so he stuck his white shirt and pants in
the bucket in the lavatory. Fresh and with an air of lavender in
his nostrils, Luka went to his room. Twilight dimmed the room,
so he lit the oil lamp and leaned on the bed to read about how
his friend was doing.

Nenad Baričković, a sturdy and stout young man in his early
twenties, had been his friend for a while. He was a handsome
man with typically Roman features. His dark hair was thin and
straight, so for his Saturday dances he would use masses of lavender pomade to keep the strands in place. He was born in Supetar,
the most important port of Brač, which linked the island to Split
on the mainland. Nenad's family were quite wealthy fishermen
and farmers, but Nenad, the younger son, wanted to go his own
way. His inquisitive mind was never at peace. His light brown
eyes and pointed nose sometimes reminded Luka of a squirrel,
but while squirrels were shy and easily frightened animals, Nenad was brave and bold. His innocent appearance only inflamed

the girls more... they simply adored him. Nenad had been the hero of many feasts around the island, where tears were shed and hearts got broken after the music had gone silent. Luka could never understand what such a witty, bright man saw in his sixteen year old neighbor girl, Maja. She seemed so plain compared to Nenad's fire and ambition. After having completed his apprenticeship at the quarry, his friend soon went to Split, where had worked at the docks. They shared a passion for books, an uncommon interest among manual laborers, so they soon found a common ground for endless conversations. Whenever Nenad returned to Brač to see his family, they always spent time together, either going swimming and fishing or to go strolling at parties. Luka wished he had a brother like Nenad; kind, brave and manly. He tore open the envelope.

My dear friend Luka!

Vipava, 25ᵗʰ October 1916

After the last three days it feels almost like a miracle that I can write to you and report the conditions on the Isonzo front after the battle they already call the Eighth Battle of Isonzo. When I say report, I mean I will try to remain as objective as I can be. For if you think you have ever heard of Hell, you must know that here it is far worse. Believe me, my friend, you cannot even imagine it. One of the reasons why I am writing this letter to you is to be able to (hopefully) read it one day and know that it was happening not only in a nightmare, that it was not just a horrible dream or hallucination, but bitter reality.

But first let me tell you something about "naš Sveto", our Saint, as we soldiers call Field Marshal Svetozar Borojević. I know he is your hero, too, and you're keen to hear about him. On the eve of the battle, it must have been some ten days ago, he came to inspect our defense lines and spoke to us. It is a miracle how such a tiny may can be so strong and powerful. He is discipline in person. His orders hold this varied army of so many nations together. His command and authority are the glue of Hungarians, Czechs, Slovenians, Bosnians and us, Croatians. He is particularly fond of us, Croatians, but for tough alpine missions he likes to take Slovenians, who can climb the icy grey rocks like chamois. Although a tough commander, he is also a sympathetic man: when the first snows fell in September, he ordered warm uniforms and coats for the soldiers, and they whisper he paid for the shipment out of his own pocket. How different from his opponent, the ruthless and stupid Cadorna! We captured two Italian deserters who – also to please us, mind you – sang us a rhyme the soldiers sing behind his back:

"See Cadorna rampage, hear him roar! He's killed all the mice on the kitchen floor."

They say our Sveto laughed, but assigned them to digging
trenches all the same. For trenches are his most important strategic measure. Instead of one or two defense lines, we have dug four
in the Carso plain, where the soil is like on our Brač... hard and
rocky, the rocks being of soft limestone. Maybe soft for cutting,
but when you hit it hard with a pick or a spade, you feel the
resistance of the land in all your limbs.

I must try to describe the country for you. Once, I've been to
the Isonzo river, or Soča, as the locals call it, helping in a field
kitchen. Never in my life have I seen water so blue... like a sea
of emeralds. It is so clear you can see crustaceans moving from
rock to rock ten meters deep. And the mountains; they are the
highest I have ever been to. They say our Alpine soldiers are digging trenches and caverns directly in the rocky slopes. Amazing
country! The people are kind and loyal to our Emperor. They
don't have an easy life. In summer there is heat and droughts,
water is a permanent problem, in winter a harsh bura (yes, like
our bura) and deep snows, and spring and autumn are plagued
with torrential rains and floods, when the rivers Vipava and Soča
leave their beds to destroy the lives around them. Nowhere life
seems to spare the poor. What I hated most during August and
September, however, were not heat or days with bura blowing
around our ears, it was digging the trenches. It was worst in
September, when rains poured down from the sky, transforming
earth into sticky, heavy mud.

Had we complained about long hours with a spade and wanted our
elderly soldiers and Russian prisoners to do the job instead of us,
field trained soldiers, we were very grateful for every inch of depth
when the Italians started their seventh offensive. During the first
couple of days, a thick fog protected our positions, so the Italians, obviously too well supplied with ammunition, shot blindly
at Carso without bothering where their targets were. Apart from
terrifying noise, which filled mostly us, the fresh ones, with terror, few men were hurt. We even joked about their bad artillery
and out of date aiming techniques. We were soon to regret our
jokes.

Our positions were close to Nova Vas, where the civilians had long
ago been evacuated, and the houses completely deserted. Apart
from a few stray cats we could not find a living soul among the
houses with pink rosebushes and red gardenia withering on the
window sills. We only walked through the village to our fortified
ditches, which in the autumn rains were sticky with red mud.
The Italian bombardment practically erased the village from the
map after the days of annihilating fire. We held our defense line
in the trenches nearby, which were dug on the slope controlling
the field beyond us. As soon as the sun dispersed the clouds,
the Italians began shelling us, aiming poorly, yet striking at each
corner of the plain systematically. That time, they could see us

and hit us fully. I cannot tell you if I did my duty, whether I was a hero or a chicken, but I can and must tell how it was.

Our company, which has been reformed a few times in the last weeks, the last time when my comrade Bojan and I joined it only a few days ago, was at the front line, where Borojević placed few, yet, as he had told us, the bravest men. We were to hold the positions and shoot as many Italians as we could, until we were to regroup and abandon the front lines to let Italians fall directly into the crossfire of our machine guns of the second defense line. With a surprising tactical maneuver, positioning the second line as the strongest, our army reduced its losses and killed more Italians. You will see why the trick worked, although by the time we should abandon our front trenches and run back, not all of us could.

The Italian artillery focused all its bombs on the front line, expecting the majority of forces there. The ground was shaking with explosions, trees and bushes were on fire, and earth and mud from the puddles was raining on us. Luckily, we had good helmets, or the sharp stones would kill even more men. However, I completely lost touch with reality as men next to me were torn apart by the shrapnel shells or hit by hard rocks that were no less lethal than the steel projectiles fired from the enemy guns. Among the hisses of shots, the cries of the hit comrades and the stench of blood, sweat and mud, I lost my hearing. The action around me was like a silent movie without music, almost like a dream. I ducked in the trench, pressing my body to the wall, expecting the next bomb to explode right on me. It did not, and I could hold the position a bit longer, as long as necessary.

Finally, I sensed the rain of shells had come to a pause, so I tentatively looked over the edge towards the enemy lines. A stray bomb fell to the right of my position, and when I instinctively turned my head in the direction of the sound, some warm, sticky substance hit my face. I am not sure even today, but I think it was somebody's brain, an Austrian brain... I vomited into the trench, spitting bitter bile long after the Schnaps and Gulasch from the day before were out of my system. However, I had no time to lose. Either I should start shooting the bastards, or they would spear me with their bayonets like a Christmas pig. I was yearning for a gulp of water, yet I knew my canister had been empty for hours. I washed my face of the slimy human substance in a muddy puddle at the bottom of the trench, where I knew I and my comrades had been releasing our water and God knows what else in the last days of waiting for action. Again, I looked over the edge. This time, I saw them coming. I fired, and a man fell down. Euphorically, I reloaded. Bang! Another one hit the ground. I looked around me and could see I was not alone in our trench. Half of the company was aiming the rifles at our enemies, who were coming as though there was no end of them. They were coming in lines, like clay pigeons at a Sunday fair, again and again. They let us shoot them... I could see some faces... shocked and surprised as though they had thought they were going on a Sunday promenade, not to the enemy lines with loaded guns. I was reloading, shooting and reloading, until my bullets were spent. I agonized over my cartridge belt, searching for a few more. Empty... I prepared my two hand grenades. I pulled the pin off the first one and threw it into the enemy lines. Several Italians fell down. I bet a few of them shat in their pants. Bloody cowards! I flung the other one, quickly climbed over the edge of the trench and ran back towards our second line. When I fell in the arms of my comrades, the Bosnians, they cheered me. I could breathe at last, though I wished I couldn't. The stench was suffocating. I found some water and washed my face. A tall Bosnian with a red fez gave me his water canister, and when I took a gulp, I realized it was Schnaps. I didn't mind. I was happy I was alive and grinning like a fool in a circus. The incredible happened... I was still alive!

Luka, I saw so many men die on that day, I saw so much pain of the wounded and looked at body parts that should forever remain hidden from human eyes. Deaths were counted in thousands. It was like reaping a field of ripe wheat. The shells and the bullets took the youngest, the bravest and the best. After days of fighting, shelling, shooting and dying, the Italians suddenly stood still. We could not comprehend why. However, we rejoiced in preventing them from forming a corridor from Gorizia to Trieste, which their attack was all about. It had to be one of those cretinous decisions of their insane commander Cadorna.

My friend, my dear Luka! Think it over again about enlisting. You don't have to be fighting, not just yet. This war is exhausting for both sides and I am sure it will go on for a while. Maybe your turn will come then, but for now, stay on Brač, don't come near the army. You must believe me there is nothing noble about killing and trembling in horror of being killed in the war. Once you're here, there is no way out. The possibility of surviving is small, death is much more certain. I don't know if I can survive another such battle. They say the front will close down for the winter. I hope to be able to get some leave and visit you and my family.

In the meanwhile... stay put. Don't go to Celje. Even if you have enlisted, you can still back out, nobody will blame you... you're a minor, Luka.

Please write to me to the above address, and tell how my family and my sisters are. Or, go see them and ask them to send a word. Maybe you can help them with the writing, or they should ask Don Nikola. I need to hear from all of you. News from home keeps me more alive than anything else; the knowledge that there is a normal world beyond this stinky morgue, a world full of sun-

shine and love, which is waiting for me to return to.
With love,

Yours, Nenad

P.S. Have you had any news from your neighbor Maja since she's gone to Split?

Luka did not hear Milica calling him to the table. He did not even hear her knocking at the door. He lifted his eyes only when she opened the door:
"Luka, come, dinner is ready."
He just stared at her as though she was an apparition from another world. She realized something was wrong and cast her look to the letter.
"Luka, what was the letter about? Who wrote to you?"
Mechanically, he replied:
"It is from Nenad. He is at the front. . . "
"Oh, Nenad Baričković? I am glad he's still alive. . . Now, come eat your dinner, or you will perish of hunger!"
Milica turned around, but Luka did not follow her. Tears welled up in his blue eyes. He could not eat anything now even if it was the last bite of food in the world. He had planned to tell Nenad about Maja's marriage when they would meet in Celje, or later on the front. He unfolded the sheets and started to reread the message of horror, his friend's report from Hell.

* * *

What would you like to be, man, if it is hard
for you to be man? Become a street
lamp, silently spreading
its gleam on man.

– Srečko Kosovel, A Streetlamp, Man in a magic
square, Ljubljana, 2004

Autumn rains finally soaked the bushes and patches of land around the Blaca Monastery. Winter crops were gratefully showing its lush green, promising wonderful tastes to enhance the winter table. Yet, there was not much joy in the world, practically no hope for the future. The sky above the grey rocks around Blaca was black and closed with heavy clouds filled with foul prospects. The Great War went on no matter what weather. The last battles on the Isonzo took 33,000 lives on the Austrian and 6,000 more on the Italian side. The Austrian troops, composed mostly of Slovenians, Hungarians, Croatians and Bosnians, succeeded in holding their positions on Carso. Newspapers were full of horrible photographs of the casualties, and articles reporting the heroism and perseverance of the Emperor's soldiers.

Surrounded by bad news, Stijepan's worries about his unhappy family had no end. For days he was expecting Luka to come to see him and talk to Don Nikola. Suddenly, one morning, instead of Luka, his wife, Bruna, entered the monastery kitchen. She wanted to speak to Don Nikola. He quickly showed her off to the chapel, the only place where laymen and women were admitted. Then he knocked hesitantly on Don Nikola's door.

"Come in!"

The stern voice promised little understanding. However, Stijepan pushed the handle.

"Don Nikola, may I disturb you for a minute?"

"You already have. What is it, Stijepan?"

"It is my wife, Bruna. She has come all the way. Well, now she is here, at the monastery..."

"A woman? Here in Blaca? Haven't I told you years ago we're not a house open to public. This is a sacred place, a monastery."

"Sir, she's waiting in the chapel."

"The confession is on Saturday. Today is Tuesday... what does she want?"

"She wants to speak to you in private, Sir."

Stijepan stepped further into the room, leaving the door wide open. He awkwardly approached the writing desk covered with old volumes and papers. Suddenly, a strong current of air lifted a few sheets in the air and carried them off the table. Don Nikola jumped after them.

"Close the door, Stipe! Don't you see the draft will carry my work to the ground? Hasn't your wife told you what it is all about?"

Stijepan, picking up the papers, nodded in approval.

"She said it is about Luka. But she wants to talk to you privately."

"Without you, the father, present? Why?"

"I don't know, Sir. I don't mind. Please, will you see her?"

Don Nikola put a few large rough white stones on top of some of the papers which were about to float up and turned to Stijepan.

"All right, let's go, Stijepan."

They followed the long, dark corridor and stepped into the obscure chapel, where Bruna was sitting on the front bench with her rough peasant hands folded in her lap.

"A prayer to our Lord would not hurt you, Mrs. Lavrić, would it?"

Don Nikola was critical of anybody who would not kneel down in front of the altar of our Lord. The woman had always irritated him, he could not tell why. There was something so profane in her behavior. She rarely came to the confession, and even when she did she was always speaking of either Stijepan or Luka. A few times she had the audacity to bargain for Stijepan's salary with him. She would never admit any sins, although Don Nikola was sure she had committed not a few of them. The first was pride. She was treating his person as though he would be any other man in the world. Her respect for the Church was something to wish for, yet, he had to grant to her she did a good job raising her son and never really averted little Luka from the faith. She ignored his remark, and he could hear her say:

"Stijepan, I would like to speak to Don Nikola alone, please. It's... it's personal."

"Yes, of course, Bruna. Please, come to the kitchen window before you leave."

"I will, my dear."

Although the woman's mouth seemed full of honey, Don Nikola was apprehensive. He was sure the woman was up to something that he would not like. He fetched a chair from the corner and sat opposite her. With the soothing voice of a priest he asked:

"What is it, my daughter? What brought you to me in such haste?"

Bruna quivered with emotion. She hardly controlled her tears when she looked into Don Nikola's stern grey eyes. With a tremble in her voice, she said:

"Don Nikola, I need... Stijepan and me, we need your help. It's about Luka."

The priest moderated his tone.

"I know, Bruna. He wants to go to war. I am strictly against it and I hope he will soon come to talk to me. I will try to deter him from it."

"You must do more, father."

"I can assure you I will do anything in my power to make him change his mind. My nephew and I, we're even prepared to finance his education out of our own pockets."

"He would never take the money. He's too proud."

Don Nikola sighed with regret. It would be hard for him and Niko to finance Luka anyway, for the monastery had lost lots of income due to closed trade routes during the war. Many of their customers, who in the past had been purchasing wheat, olive oil and wine, were bankrupt and could not buy anything. The army could, yet the way was long, not only for the goods to travel, but also for the payment to arrive. Also, the last harvest was meager, so they had little surplus. He knew Niko had been saving all his income to purchase some powerful astronomy equipment.

"Bruna, it's an honest offer. We would do it."

She looked him in the eyes, noticing they mellowed. After all, Don Nikola was just a man.

"I know, Father. Thank you, I do appreciate your intention, but I know it would not work. I think Luka needs stronger ties to Brač. He should be prevented from going."

Don Nikola could feel Bruna had something specific in her mind.

"Speak up, Bruna. Tell me what you suggest."

"Father, do you know what a chaste and honorable young man my Luka has become?"

When Don Nikola raised his eyebrows in a silent question, she added:

"As far as I know, he hasn't had a woman yet. He rigorously follows the ten commandments."

"As we should all, should we not?"

The priest's sarcasm was lost on Bruna's insistence.

"Yes, of course. But I wanted to say that Luka's faith is above average for a boy his age. Maybe..."

"Maybe what, Bruna?"

"Maybe you could take him in. I mean you could admit him to Blaca as a novice."

She had Don Nikola's full attention now, yet it was not so easy.

"You know that the priests in Blaca have since the foundation of the monastery been the Miličevićs, don't you?"

Bruna was eager to explain more of her idea.

"I know. It would not be forever or even less to succeed you. Niko is your nephew and he will be the prior of Blaca one day. It would be just for some time in order to...well...in order to confine Luka and keep him away from his patriotic impulses."

"There's only one way he could live in Blaca...studying the Bible and preparing for his ordination."

"Yes, all that...I think you could persuade him. He can work hard, you know. You can give him chores. And he will have access to your library. He can read and study for his baccalaureate. What do I know? And when the war is over, he can resume his life...In the meanwhile, you can feign to prepare him for priesthood."

Don Nikola's face became purple with anger. Disrespect, profanity, audacity and pride...the woman was out of her mind to suggest to him such a deal. Bruna was trembling all over her body.

"Please, Don Nikola, please, receive my boy in Blaca. I don't want him to die on the front. Please!"

He looked down at the stones on the floor while Bruna continued with a tremble in her voice:

"If you're worried about finances, I can live without Stijepan's support and keep up the farm on my own. The difference can go to Luka. I am sure Stipe will agree with me..."

Obviously a mother's love was a powerful drive. Don Nikola suppressed his anger for the moment. Still, he had to explain to the woman how holy things work.

"Feign? Feigning to be a priest?"

"I mean, you don't have to consecrate him in the end... If you don't want to..."

"And if I do want Luka to receive his Holy Orders?"

"Yes, but... I am not sure whether he'd wish to..."

"Mrs. Lavrić, you should know that religion is a serious matter, especially if we're talking about a boy dedicating his whole life to priesthood. Once he takes his vows, he should not break them, or his punishment is beyond telling. We... You... you don't feign things here... Either you believe and focus all your efforts on becoming a holy man or you don't."

Bruna sighed with disappointment.

"So you're not taking him in... My poor boy... doomed... to die..."

She hid her eyes in her palms, shaking with sobs. Don Nikola took a handkerchief out of his robe and passed it to her. She seized it without looking up. The woman obviously did not understand. She was literate, but not much more than that. Despite her natural intelligence, she was not capable of grasping notions beyond her basic needs and emotions. Don Nikola resumed his preaching tone.

"Bruna, you're a mother. I can understand your concern. But you should understand the rules and the serenity of our institution. The first question is whether Luka wants to become a priest. If he does and as you say his faith is sincere, he will want to be ordained, he will aspire to it from the depth of his soul. I would have to talk to the Archbishop about it, anyway. But what I am trying to make clear to you is that Luka will put his heart into it eventually. If I persuade him to stay in Blaca and enter the seminary education, so that he doesn't enlist for the army, which I would prefer myself, it might be a decision forever. He might embrace the prospects of guiding mankind as one of us, the shepherds. It's a wonderful and noble vocation. Could you live with that?"

Bruna lifted her chin and solemnly looked Don Nikola in his stern grey eyes.

"Don Nikola, I would accept anything just to keep Luka alive. Anything! His life is my life..."

The priest nodded and made a cross on her forehead.

"I will do everything to bring your son to Blaca and keep him here. He will have a long and glorious life, I promise you. Now, kneel down, daughter, and pray to God! Pray for all the boys of this lost generation of the Great War."

Exalted, Bruna bent her knees. How wonderful! For once the priest showed humanity. Luka would spend the war behind the high, safe walls of Blaca, next to his father. She would cope alone like she always had to. After the war they would recuperate and

Luka would be able to choose his way of life. Mechanically, her lips formed the prayer for life:

"O God, our Creator, all life is in your hands from conception until death. Help us to cherish our children and to revere the awesome privilege of our share in creation. May all people live and die in dignity and love. Bless all those who defend the rights of the unborn, the handicapped and the aged. Enlighten and be merciful toward those who fail to love, and give them peace. Let freedom be tempered by responsibility, integrity and morality..."

* * *

See how in their veins all becomes spirit,
Into each other they mature and grow.

– The Lovers, Rainer Maria Rilke, translated by
John J. L. Mood

In the kitchen, Stijepan was sitting on his stool with a glass of water in his hand. The thick bean soup with fresh bread was waiting at the corner of the oven for lunch. He was wondering when either Don Nikola or Bruna would show up and tell him something. He felt neglected and pondered whether it was right to let Bruna always have her way. However, how could he blame her for her independence and self-will? What kind of life has he been providing for her and their son since the day they have fallen in love?

Solitary...lonely...sad...He knew the answers, yet in all the years he could not gather the courage to change it. He stuck to his job, his employer and the monastery routine as though it was the only thing in the world. The door opened.

"Stijepan, your wife asks you to see her off to the main road. You can take the rest of the day off."

"Don Nikola, Sir, can I really? The lunch is ready, so maybe I can serve it before I go."

"No, don't let Bruna wait. Lovro can deal with that. I'm not hungry yet, anyway. Go now!"

"Thank you, Sir. I'll be back..."

Impatiently, Don Nikola hissed:

"You have the afternoon off. You used not to ask me about it so many times..."

"I am sorry, Sir. I'll be back by dinner."

Stijepan bent his head, remembering the spring and summer evenings so many years ago when he sneaked out of the monastery to undertake the long walk to Bruna's house. They would spend a couple of hours together, talking, exchanging kisses and promises until it was time for him to go back and start baking bread for the following day. He was so much in love with her. Her wonderfully wild hair and clear blue eyes filled with energy and passion, her round hips and rich bosom, her bright laughter, so light and high, like the summer song of the cicadas. His emotions, after so many years, were now frozen, carved into stone by hours of Bruna's persistent nagging and complaining. Not that he would not care about her any longer; she was still the love of his life, the mother of his son. Yet, her critical comments had been poisoning his soul and stinging his heart for a while. Deep down he knew it was not her fault. He blamed it on himself; he felt unfit for love, fat and ugly, scared and unmanly. His pride and strength had long been drowned in the soups and sauces for his Monsignor.

When Don Nikola left the kitchen, Stijepan quickly assembled a picnic bag with some dried meat, cheese, fresh bread, dried figs and wine, delicacies which he knew Bruna could rarely taste. He also added a half empty jar of plum jam, a little jar of honey and a sachet of coffee. Maybe he would warm her up with a picnic under their mulberry tree in the mountain. They had the whole afternoon for themselves.

Outside the kitchen, he could see Bruna filling her goatskin with water from the well. She lifted her head and smiled kindly at him.

"Here you are, Stipe. I am glad you will walk with me. It's a long way to the main road. It would be so boring to walk alone."

"Well, you will have to slow your pace, Bruna. Your're swift as a young girl, but look at me: I might not be able to keep up with you. However, I have a nice surprise if we make a stop. Can you guess what?"

Stijepan gestured at the bag on his shoulder, and Bruna just nodded with appreciation. They left the courtyard and started slowly uphill. After heavy rains in the early morning, the sky split up and finally a shy winter sun rejoiced on the rocky slopes. When Blaca was out of sight, Stijepan stopped for a gulp of water. Trying to sound disinterested, he asked:

"What did you come to see Don Nikola about, Bruna?"

Bruna briefly resumed the conversation with the priest and their agreement on how they would persuade young Luka to stay at Blaca. Stijepan was thrilled with the idea:

"My Bruna, aren't you clever? That's really great! It will keep him away from the front. Don Nikola is a very kind man."

"Of course, I will have to give up your financial support to me and to the farm. I have figured it all out, and I can make it on my own. I can plant the crops, work in the fields on Sundays and close down the house during the week to go to Postira. In the absence of so many men, the sardine factory is looking for every hand they can get. Since the war, the demand for canned fish has doubled. I would be paid well. I think it would be only fair if we exchange your work for Luka's stay in Blaca. What do you think?"

Stijepan was apprehensive. He knew the severe ecclesiastical rules and the monastery regime only too well.

"What was the exact arrangement with Don Nikola? What would Luka be doing at Blaca?"

"He would take up the seminary education and study for his baccalaureate."

"Eventually, it means he would study to receive the Holy Orders, Bruna..."

She put her arms around his shoulders and looked at her husband wickedly.

"I hope not, Stijepan. The war will not go on forever. I hope to hide Luka here at Blaca until it's over. He's still a boy. He can make his decisions later, and I am sure he's not priest material. Luka's far too interested in girls and far too attracted to real life and real work."

Stijepan stiffened. Why was his wife taking the spiritual matters so light-heartedly? What if Luka decides to stay at Blaca forever? The monastery shelter could offer him support in his quest for knowledge, and the church hierarchy might offer possibilities for his ambitions.

"Bruna, I agree he should come to Blaca, and I will speak to Don Nikola tonight as to my pay, too. We will see, maybe the monastery can afford to form another priest. Young Niko is away a lot. I think it would do us good, and Luka could help Don Nikola with the school. Children are sometimes too much for the old man."

"I heard about the school. Some are very critical. Why would a peasant or a fisherman need to go to school? Stupid, narrow minded islanders... they cannot see beyond their boats and nets. I think it is great what Monsignor has undertaken, but I think the best thing of all is two hot meals the little rascals get every day. You know, many kids go hungry these days..."

In his wide embrace, Stijepan shook her tenderly with affection.

"My love, if you only knew what pleasure it gives me to serve the little rascals as you call them. I revive with every spoon they bring to their mouths. However, Bruna, we should think twice about Don Nikola's intentions. You see the priests consider it a very serious job to guide us in our faith. They study very hard. Would you like for our son to become a priest?"

In a jolt, she broke free from him.

"Never! I don't think it would come so far...!"

"Well, do not underestimate the power of faith. Our Luka is emotional. I am a simple cook, but I can recognize passion when I see it."

"I would know that, my dear, wouldn't I?"

Despite the laden atmosphere, they smiled at each other for the first time in a while. Their faces turned upwards, to the top of the mountain, they continued the ascent, biting their knees in the steep path, keeping balance on the wet slippery rock smoothened by centuries of use by men and beasts. Each was absorbed in their own thoughts, their minds occupied by long lost memories of their youth and love. It was a memory lane they were walking along, hiding little surprises at each turn. Not far away, only a few minutes off the main direction, there was the secret place of their first rendezvous under a huge mulberry tree, where they made love for the first time and where in late autumn Stijepan proposed to Bruna. It seemed not minutes but centuries ago.

"Are we going to stop for lunch at the mulberry tree, Stijepan?"

"We might, but the stones will probably still be wet. Well, we'll work out something there..."

Bruna nodded and sank in the memory of one unpleasant autumn afternoon eighteen years earlier when Stijepan was escorting her home. He had proposed a month ago, reaching the agreement with Don Nikola to continue in his job as a cook. Although the old man would never admit it, he needed Stijepan around his nephew Niko, a little boy with tears on his lashes and sadness in his heart, a ten year old from the mainland, torn away from his family in order to study and become the next prior. Little Niko was crying all the time, and only Stijepan had a way with him. Bruna knew why. Stijepan was the most wonderful man she had ever met. He was warm and kind, sincere and clever, yet not pushy or cocky. He was pure love. His dishes, of which Bruna could have a taste every now and then, on a few free Sundays, reflected his passion for nature and man. Herbs which lifted the spirits, oils which sublimated the tenderness and tastes of either sweets or meats that caressed the palate... her Stijepan was all that and more. He was handsome and tall, with thick chestnut hair and deep brown eyes. When she had first seen him in the church in Milna, and after having made some enquiries, she immediately found a pretext to go to the monastery for the big Easter service. He was there, and after the service, the prior shared his table with the visitors. They fell in love... She could not know then how much pain the marriage, in which her bed was empty and cold most of the time, would bring her.

Another of her bitter memories was a late October afternoon, a year before Luka was born, when they had made their confessions to Don Nikola. Bruna knew how the Church judged carnal relations before marriage, so she strictly denied that she and Stijepan had done anything inappropriate during their courtship. Don Nikola cited her The Corinthians:

"Each one should remain in the condition in which he was called. Are you, sister Bruna, in your primal condition?"

Bruna, who by that time knew she was in a condition, which was very natural to young women in love, yet changed from her birth, held his stern look and lied in reply:

"Monsignor, I am. I am in the condition most natural to a woman unwed."

She was so strong then. She could defy the devil himself to defend her man and his child who was growing under her heart. When later, she sat down with Stijepan to have a bite, he asked her:

"Did Father Nikola want to know if we... you know, if we have been impure... "

"You mean if we have slept together, Stijepan?"

"Yes."

"Of course, he did ask me. And you, did he ask you?"

"Sorry, what did you say?"

"I denied, of course. What business of his can it be what we do privately, Stijepan?"

It was their first serious row. Stijepan got furious and shouted from the depth of his lungs:

"You lied in confession? You haven't told the truth to your confessor? Are you out of your mind, woman?"

Bruna quivered with worry. She had obviously underestimated Stijepan's sincere religious feelings. Only too late she came to realize the effect her... in her view only reasonable... behavior had on Stijepan. However, she somehow kept cool about it.

"I was afraid he would refuse to marry us if I tell him the truth. Sorry, Stijepan! You know how much I love you! You know there's now two of us who need you."

"Did he give you absolution, Don Nikola?"

"Yes, he did. I suppose he did not expect me to picture him the details. I am sorry. I did not want to offend you."

She would never forget how Stijepan turned his back on her and, without another word, breathed heavily for a few moments. She could almost feel him weighing the arguments. She would never forget the sensation; she was suspended between his love for God and his love for her and the young family they were about to found. She was hanging on God's swing, pushed to and fro by Stijepan's faith. Only her husband's warm heart and good nature caught her and Luka in his embrace in the end. Otherwise, who knows how they would live...

They reached the crossroads where a narrow path led to the mulberry and its stone table and bench in the middle of the hill. The place was suspended in the heights, from where there was a fabulous view across the channel and over the low island of Hvar. Behind, one could see the dark back of the island of Korčula, and on the right the heights of the island of Vis, where many boats eager to catch the sardines around the archipelago sank in the mighty winds and sneaky currents. The sun had already dried the lovely stone cut bench which encircled a huge rock flattened and carved smoothly into a natural table surface. The traces of the overripe black mulberries had long been washed away, and the place shone pure and white like an altar. Indeed, it was an altar... a private altar of the couple who, after so many years, came to share the sacred prayer for the fruit of their love... their precious youngster Luka. Stijepan remembered another time when the place saw his worship... except that night he was worshipping love and flesh.

It was in the first months of his courtship to Bruna, when their summer evenings were filled with sensuality and joy. They seized every opportunity to meet and be together, not knowing that the tree of knowledge would grow not only flowers but also seeds and fruits of passion. Stijepan rarely regretted his love, although his life became very complicated after their wedding. In the moments of darkness, he would always remember their first time.

It was in the middle of the night, when the moon rose high above the western horizon. In its silvery light, hiding under the shadows, he swiftly sneaked out of the monastery and rushed to the meeting point on the mountain, under their mulberry tree, where he knew his love was waiting. It had been weeks since they declared their love for each other. Their meetings were rare and short. Under the stern eye of Don Nikola, who could not forbid, yet did not approve of any relations with the people outside his sacred institution and the hot tears of little Niko, who night after night leapt from his bed woken by nightmares, Stijepan had many obstacles to being with Bruna. She, on the other hand, had to walk for hours to see him, which meant she would be dead tired in the fields the following day. However, the stolen nights on their altar of love were magical, and on that July night his pace was quick to reach the rock. From some distance, he could see a motionless heap on the table, which he presumed to be his Bruna. He rushed closer to see if everything was all right, as he had often been afraid something bad could happen to her in the dead of the night.

Yet there, on the snow white stone, with moon illuminating her curly hair, transforming it to a silvery crown with tiny precious stones, lay his beautiful fairy, the only woman who cast a spell over him and captivated his thoughts night and day. She was fast asleep on her right side, with her hands folded under her chin, her clothes serving as a mattress, her body covered only with a thin blanket. Stijepan came closer and leaned over her. He touched the edge of the blanket, which slipped to the floor. The moon revealed her naked skin, her breasts with pinkish nipples and another crown of silver curls between her legs. Her buttocks and tights were muscular from the daily work in the fields. Stijepan knew how wrong it was, yet he kissed her awake, first softly on her cheeks, chin and forehead, then willfully on her mouth. Like in a trance, his hands reached for her full breasts. Without any warning, his actions became separated from his free

will, his brains completely divorced from his premarital vows. His
body took the lead. Bruna smiled and slowly rolled on her back.
She pulled his shirt over his head. Their skins touched as though
they belonged together since the dawn of times. They kissed and
explored each other until Stijepan, shaking with anticipation and
trembling in the agony of guilt and self-reproach, stripped naked,
too. In the heat of the night, he knew he was sacrificing everything he had believed in, yet his passion overran his mind. His
lips were sliding over the curves of her lustful body, and he took
great care to touch every inch of it. His senses, mesmerized by
the citrus smell of Bruna's skin, rebuked all the chaste promises
he had given to the cross in his earlier prayers. He should wait.
He should not make love to her, at least not yet. However, the
sensations swept him away. He was like a boat without a steer,
a vessel of emotions floating on a huge wave directly into a reef.
And he loved it; he loved her... his wonderful silvery reef... He
felt one with the moon, one with the universe, he felt like God
loving his Goddess... Soon the guilt was dulled and silenced by
sighs of lust and joy. He closed his eyes and merged with her in
the magic ritual on their mulberry altar. He gave himself completely. It did not feel wrong, not wrong at all. When he reached
the heights of passion, the intensity which exploded his brain, he
looked at Bruna. Her eyes were waiting for him, pale blue in the
white light, sincere and wide open, reflecting nothing but love
and submission.

They had made love several times that night, exhausting their
bodies until the first drops of the morning dew awoke Stijepan
to reality. He had to hurry down the hill to start the bread for
Don Nikola's breakfast. Bruna's merry, yet commanding voice
brought him back to the present:

"Show me the treasure you have in your bag, my husband!"

He did, and they ate in silence, savoring the perfect moment of
stillness. They knew something was bound to disturb the peace.
Indeed, a cry in the air announced a greedy seagull looking for
his share. They both looked up and laughed. Stijepan took out
of his breast pocket a small flask filled with sweet Porto.

"Try this, Bruna! It is similar to our *prošek*, although much
more aromatic."

Bruna took a gulp. The wine was sweet and strong. On cue
her cheeks flushed.

"My love, the color suits you! Have some more... Maybe I
can persuade you into some mischief..."

"And you are aware of the consequences?"

"I would take a risk with you."

They looked at each other tenderly, and then their eyes
stopped on the white stone surface of the table. Stijepan moved
closer and stretched his arm around her. With the other hand, he
held Bruna's face and slowly moved to kiss her on the mouth. She

was surprised, twitched, and returned the kiss dutifully, though somehow coldly. Stijepan understood. They had missed the ignition. There was a wall of silence between them. With an affectionate smile, he retreated in fear he would not be able to live up to his courage. He could not stand another humiliation. Bruna sighed and patted him on the shoulder. Friends they were, lovers not any more.

"Stijepan, whatever life has brought us, we should be grateful. We have Luka. And we must save him from this cruel war."

For the rest of the afternoon, they schemed and planned how they would control and influence their son's life. Stijepan blindly joined his wife's manipulation, forgetting that his son had a mind of his own.

* * *

It is also good to love: because love is difficult. For one human being to love another human being: that is perhaps the most difficult task that has been entrusted to us, the ultimate task, the final test and proof, the work for which all other work is merely preparation.

– Rainer Maria Rilke, Letters to a young poet

The shy December sun lifted the spirits of the stone cutters in Pučišća. In the sound of the chisels life felt right and simple; the atmosphere was filled with white dust and the sharp smell of young bodies hitting their daily production targets. The crisp winter air was vibrating with action and strength. Yet winter in Dalmatia was something else than winter in the Julian Alps along the river Isonzo. In his last letter, which was on Luka's bed table, waiting for a reply, Nenad wrote:

Dear Luka!

Vipava, 20th November 1916

Thanks for your letter and the news from home. It really lit up my day yesterday. As though the bright sun of Brač warmed my freezing body after I had spent another three days in the cold and muddy trenches on Carso. Thank you, Luka, also for helping my mother and my family with their writing. I understand you have little news about Maja... anyway, she needs to mature until I fetch her from her tedious job of a maid and make sure she has a couple of babies to look after.

I am glad and happy you followed my advice and told the draft committee the truth about your age. You cannot imagine how many difficulties we have here with young boys who in the heat of their patriotism got enlisted, lying about their age. Some are sixteen, seventeen, we even have a boy from Pula who had his fifteenth birthday a month ago. Borojević is very much embarrassed and angry when he is sent new "baby soldiers", as we call them. We could hear him scolding a bureaucrat on the phone the other day, and I was only glad I was not the man on the other side of the line. As much as we all respect their bravery, I must tell you there are problems with them all the time. They're not like you, though. You're a self-made man at your age. Still, you made a wise decision to postpone your military career. Or abandon it completely. I am looking forward to know more about your discussions with Don Nikola of Blaca. I didn't want to say as much to you before, but I've always thought you'd make a good man of the cloth. I don't know why. Maybe because you like to read and study so much, and you've never shown much interest in chasing girls. Anyway, I think you should consider Don Nikola's offer carefully. If it helps, write to me about it. I'm eager to know.

Here, the front on Carso has gone frightfully quiet. Apart from a few stray shells and bullets, Carso is peaceful and magical in its knee deep white snow, surrounded by high mountain tops and their dark green pines wrapped in thick white coats of snow and glittering in the sun like a million Christmas trees. When we're summoned to the front lines, it's like walking on clouds to Heaven, although, in truth, it is a path to Hell. It feels so good to return to the barracks. Borojević is sure there will be another Italian offensive before the end of the year, so we're all at full attention. Two nights ago, on our way back to the trenches, we came across an Italian platoon, no more than a dozen young men, without weapons, unshaven, in dishevelled uniforms with all their ranks torn from the coats and jackets. Luckily, I could understand their Italian cries that they surrender or else we would have shot them on the spot. Anyway, they were deserters, and we brought them to our headquarters, where they were shown into the commanders' house. I don't know what will happen to them, but the things they told us on the way were shocking. They said that behind their front lines, each time they were about to attack us, their commander Cadorna and his clique had posted machinegunners behind their line. The gunners were not there to shoot at us, but to shoot each soldier trying to retreat or hide from our shots during the charge. Many of their comrades lost their lives to an Italian bullet in the back. The casualties double... from the front they get it from us, from behind they are afraid of their own commanders. When their platoon was sent on a scouting mission, they made a unanimous decision to desert and try Commander Borojević' mercy rather than wait for an Italian bullet to finish them. They also told us that their commanders have received Cadorna's personal directive to decimate all the mutinous units. Can you imagine, Luka? Decimation, killing of every tenth sol-

dier of the unit randomly, in the 20th century! No court martial,
just a shot! The man must be completely crazy. He is severely
breaching the military penal code. He must think he is the new
Julius Caesar and the Isonzo is his Gaul! We love our Sveto only
better each time we hear such stories from the other side of the
line. We're blessed with his competence and mercy.
With your letter also the thaw has come to the Vipava valley and
transformed the roads in muddy traps for our boots and vehicles.
The last week was really tough. . . first, we had to tread in deep,
fresh snow, then, on the way back, when we were really tired,
we could barely lift our feet from the sticky, cold mud. However,
the rise in temperature also means we will be less cold during the
nights. You see, the mighty influence of the sun of Brač!
I have to go now. It's dinner time. I hope they will also give us
Schnaps, as the chill will kill me sooner than a bullet.
With my deepest respects to Don Nikola,

I remain with love,

Nenad

During work, Luka composed a reply in his head. He was
really embarrassed by Nenad's persistent interrogation about little Maja. How to tell his friend the truth, that a year after he
was gone, she went to bed with an Austrian officer, married him
happily and is probably already pregnant by him? Luka was wondering to which front the Austrian man was sent. It might well
have been Isonzo, and Nenad could even have met him. Luka's
other dilemma, as to his new situation and debates with Don
Nikola, was no lesser after Nenad's positive view. His thoughts
were wandering in the dark corridors of doubt. He felt torn apart
between his sense of patriotic duty and Don Nikola's offer to continue his education in Blaca and help the old man with the school.
It was a tempting offer.

Then another letter from Nenad came which was obviously
not written in his own hand. In only a few lines he reported
that he had been wounded in action and that he would come
home soon after his treatment, possibly by Christmas. Luka was
to inform his family. He was looking forward to seeing his friend
and hoped for him to stay at home until the end of the war. Luka
loved Nenad dearly. He was a good man and a true friend.

With bitter hesitation, Luka had followed Nenad's advice and
had gone to see the Imperial Army Draft Committee in Bol already in October. He was surprised how simple it was; he told the
committee that he had lied about his age, which was a common
case of patriotic zeal at the time. The recruitment officers were
very kind to him, explaining in detail why and until when he was
not to be enlisted. They let him go. Luka was only glad they
had not asked too many questions as to why he had changed his

mind. He felt terrible about it himself. Working double shifts at
the quarry, day dreaming of his future life of seclusion and study,
he could not ban from his head the thought that he was nothing
but a coward avoiding the action.

The only solace for his tormented soul was Blaca and the
long conversations with Don Nikola, which began on the weekend
following Saint Francis Day. Luka had fulfilled his promise to his
father and had gone to confession on that Sunday. Apologizing
about Saturday, when he had to work at the quarry, he expected
a reprimand and a lecture, yet, after the Sunday service, the prior
kindly invited him into his office. Luka knew the place from his
early age, when he came to visit his father and stared at the
infinite shelves of books from every century since the invention of
printing. Despite a huge fire in 1724, the monastery library was
rich with knowledge.

Don Nikola and Luka would sit opposite each other and talk
for hours. The earlier arrogant attitude of the church father was
completely gone. They met every Sunday afternoon since then.
Don Nikola wanted to know all about Luka's work and life as
though he was his own child. Luka, on the other hand, felt secure
and confident, disclosing to the old man his most secret thoughts.
He even showed him Nenad's letters and they analyzed the situation together. It came only naturally that Don Nikola inspired
Luka to further reading of the Scriptures and challenged him with
the notions of good and evil, the distinction between right and
wrong.

Luka was a thoughtful youth, yet his convictions about faith,
life and patriotism were still very rudimentary and vague. For
so many years he had been craving for intellectual guidance. At
last, Don Nikola quenched his thirst, explaining to him more
of the hierarchy of the Church, about Holy Orders and seminary
education. When the old man finally articulated the possibility of
Luka joining the Franciscan order, it was not a surprise. However,
Luka needed time to think it over. It was a decision which would
completely change his life. He knew he would have to commit
to celibacy and other strict rules, yet he found the prospects
somehow alluring.

There was one major question which plagued Luka's mind
since the last conversation with Don Nikola, a question which had
not been uttered aloud. Was Luka's faith strong enough? Surely
his name should give him power to believe in God's revelation
and embrace the kind of life through which he could help others
to find mercy in this crazy world. Was he committed strongly
enough to abandon secular life with all its joys and charms for
the austerity of discipline and study?

After long weeks of mulling over the pros and cons, Luka
decided to stop torturing himself. He was to see Don Nikola
the following Sunday. Surely the old man would be willing to

share his experience and help him find the right way out of the maze. His step was light and his spirits high when he entered the monastery kitchen warm with fumes from the stove in the middle of a sunny winter Sunday.

"Luka, my dear boy, how are you?"

"Hello, dad. I came to see Don Nikola."

"Yes, of course. Niko is here, too. But let me kiss you first. . . "

Vehemently, Stijepan, took his son in his arms and kissed him on both cheeks, sweet with the perspiration of a long walk. He had to let go of him to check the sizzling onions in a huge pan.

"Could you catch a ride?"

"Yes, actually, our young accountant is courting a girl in Milna, so he took me along in his car. I only walked down the road."

"Hungry?"

"Later. I. . . "

"So, have you decided to stay here with us, at Blaca, Luka?"

"I am not entirely sure, dad. We will talk about it today."

"You know what Mother and I think, don't you? We would like you to stay here very much. We both think it would be a great opportunity for you as well as a safe way not to be drafted after you're full of age."

"I don't know, dad. I still feel awkward about pulling back from the army. I. . . sometimes. . . think I am a coward!"

Stijepan took his son's hand and pressed it to his heart.

"My boy, I know who and what you are, believe me. When the time comes, you will serve humanity better than running from bullets and shells. You're not a coward. Since you were twelve, you've been earning your bread and butter. I don't know many boys who have done that. Please, Luka, not going to the front does not mean you are unworthy. It only means you may have a higher goal in your life."

Luka's eyes filled with tears.

"Maybe. . . If only Mother could understand my faith better."

Stijepan sighed. He knew that Luka was on the brink of joining the order, which could mean he would stay a holy man after the war also, the option, which in Bruna's secular views was absolutely out of the question. She wanted a life for her son, a wife, a family and children. But could parents really guide the stream of their children's lives as they saw fit? One moment hide them in a monastery, and the next moment bring them out and mate them with a local beauty. . .

"Luka, whichever decision you take now or later, it is your life. Not Mother's and not mine. . . Be true to yourself! Whatever you do, I will always love you. . . And Mother will love you, too."

Luka embraced his father. He had been such a support to him from his early age. So much like himself, his father honestly believed in God. Luka stepped into the dusky corridor with less

doubt in his heart. The door to Don Nikola's study opened. The
priest bid him welcome, and after some exchanged pleasantries
about the weather and the road, came to the point:

"I have spoken to the Archbishop. I went to see him during
the week, and he confirmed the possibility of your appointment."

Luka stared at the old man, suddenly uncertain as to what
to say. Don Nikola frowned, and his handsome face expressed
all his worry and care for the boy in front of him. Luka gazed
upon him as though he was seeing him for the first time. The old
man had a nice oval face with piercing grey eyes, a straight nose,
and wide cheekbones. He was a handsome and impressive man.
Luka could easily see him as a man of the world instead of a holy
man in a black robe of a monk. Yet, the soft lips were closed in
a strict line, expecting his reply. Deep wrinkles on his forehead
spoke of experience. He could have had a similar conversation
with another young men before. Luka said hesitantly:

"I am not sure of myself, Father."

"You have to make up your mind by Christmas. Luka, we all
have doubts sometimes. Only fools are always sure of everything.
Intelligent people are skeptical and wonder about the world. They
analyze, consider and reconsider things. However, do you know
what Jesus said to Thomas?"

"Blessed are they that have not seen, and yet have believed,"
murmured Luka diligently.

"Exactly! Faith in God does not involve certainty, nor does
it imply the absence of doubts. The question is whether you
believe..."

The young man was sitting very still. All of a sudden, he felt
free from all anxiety and saw where his path in the future should
lead him. It was a clean cut, like the cleft when a rock tumbles
down from a cliff with a roar, its edges sharper than a knife.

"I do believe, Father, and I have made up my mind now. I
will enter the Holy Order if you think me worthy of it."

Slowly, Don Nikola nodded in approval, and offered the young
man a kind smile.

"I think you will prove worthy, Luka. I have known you all
your life. Your father gave you a warm heart and your mother
fed you with determination. You know discipline, and you will be
able to follow the rules. I would not have talked to the Archbishop
unless I was sure of you."

Luka sighed deeply with gratitude. His tanned face and blue
eyes shone with enthusiasm.

"Thank you, Don Nikola."

"Though, there is something which I have to tell you first."

"Yes?"

"If you join us by Christmas, you will have to leave us and
complete your seminary education in Italy. Probably in Fossanova, which is south of Rome."

"That means I will have to leave Father...Mother...How would she cope with that?"

Don Nikola explained further.

"The seminary education at Fossanova will give you much better opportunities to widen your horizons. They need novices, and you need a place. Besides, here, the ties to your family might prove difficult, they might lead you astray..."

Luka looked at Don Nikola with a mixture of fear and enthusiasm.

"I've always longed to leave Brač...Will I be able to visit Rome?"

"You will. I will ask the Holy Seat for a special letter of recommendation, so that you're not bugged by some aggressive Italian policeman. Your passport is Austrian."

Luka's eyes were dreamy. He looked through the window into the winter sunshine behind Don Nikola. Was he ready to start a new life?

"When would I have to go?"

"We need to equip you with some knowledge. I reckon it will be late spring before we're through. Can I write to His Excellency the Archbishop?"

Luka was still hesitating. Going away suited him, but, he never thought it would happen so soon. He suddenly got cold feet.

"I can speak very little Italian, Don Nikola."

"Don't worry, you will learn quickly. As the Archbishop told me, they are planning to renovate a crumbled wing of the Monastery of Fossanova. Your stonecutting knowledge will be much appreciated."

Luka jolted in his chair. He searched in his leather bag and produced five little statues cut from the white stone. They represented five saints: Peter, Paul, Anthony, Francis and Luke. Each had a flat basement, so that they could be used as paper holders.

"I noticed you're trying to keep your papers in place with plain stones, so I made these for you, Father."

Don Nikola was visibly moved.

"This is very thoughtful of you, Luka. They're really beautiful. You have talent. Thank you."

"I should thank you, Don Nikola, for all your time and attention during the past months."

An awkward silence fell over them. They were both immersed in their thoughts. Luka was making an inventory in his head of what he would have to sort out by Christmas. Luckily, they had completed and dispatched the huge American order, so business was slow again in the quarry of Pučišča. The boss would not be too glad to let him go, as many stonecutters had been either enlisted or volunteered into the Imperial Army, and the production depended on young, less experienced apprentices or recently formed masters like himself.

"What about school here? Won't you need me to teach the children?"

"Niko's come home for a year. He was coughing so badly that his physician worried he might contract tuberculosis. He has to take a break from his research and rest for a couple of months at least. Niko will be tutoring you. Well, between the three of us, we'll cope. Until now I was alone, and I could do it."

Luka breathed in deeply. Indeed, Don Nikola was a great man, full of vigor and wisdom.

"I will resign from my job and cancel my room on the 22nd of December. I have some savings... I mean as my contribution for my entry into the monastery."

Don Nikola nodded with appreciation. The boy was not living in the clouds. He liked people who understood practicalities and thought ahead.

"Thank you, Luka, but keep the money. You will need it for the travel. There's a ship from Split to Ancona, where you take the train to Rome. The railway to Priverno, the little town close to the abbey, hasn't been completed yet, so you will have to find a bus or simply walk. It's about one hundred kilometers."

"It'll be a nice walk in spring weather, thank you, Father."

Don Nikola stood up from his desk and came around to the smiling Luka, who awkwardly offered him his right hand. Instead of shaking it, Don Nikola embraced the young man cordially and planted a kiss on his forehead. Mesmerized, Luka whispered:

"If only I could see into my future, Father! The thought that I am evading fighting for my country is such a pain. If I could only believe I can do something good without feeling like a coward."

Don Nikola patted him on the back.

"God will lead your way, son. All you have to do is to believe in Him. Then you will find peace in your heart and perform your duty. You will do the work He has foreseen for you. You will see that by choosing Him, by believing in His will, you will see your future. For only faith can see the unseen."

* * *

Bitterly true,
and with no consolation
is the thought of life.

– Srečko Kosovel

The *jugo* was roaring around the bay of Pučišča, where in the drizzle even the stones lost their natural whiteness and turned gray like the rest of the world. The sea was foaming, and the waves threatening to take away the piers and the boats tied to them. Few people were on the road, yet a wagon loaded with firewood overtook Luka.

"Whoa!" cried the driver and stopped the mule wagon.

"Are you Luka Lavrić, mister?"

"Yes, I am. Who are you?"

The driver took off his cap to introduce himself.

"I am Ivan, Nenad Baričković's neighbor. He's been back home since yesterday. Can you visit him? That is, when you can. I had a delivery in Pučišće, so he asked me to find you and tell you."

"When are you going back to Supetar, mister?"

"In the late afternoon, around four, I guess."

"Can I ride with you? It is my last day at the quarry, so I will be home early today."

"Are you leaving your good job at the quarry, boy? I heard it is getting many orders and there has never been a better pay."

Luka looked at the man more closely.

"Actually, the pay is as usual, neither better nor worse."

Luka lifted his hand to his cap and wanted to end the conversation, yet the man on the wagon poked into him further. With a serious voice, he asked:

"Are you going to war, then?"

"No."

Luka shuddered. Why was the man so curious? He started walking away slowly. The driver set his mules to follow Luka at a trot. He obviously wasn't finished with him.

"Well, you have your reasons, my boy. But I tell you something. . . stonecutters are the best people I've ever known. They're hard working, honest, good sports and faithful husbands. But what can you do. . . sometimes love drags us away from our work. What men wouldn't do for a girl lying on her back!"

The man burst out laughing at his own gag. Luka was sick of his intrusiveness, yet had to keep polite to get a ride later. He would have to tell him eventually, so what the hell?

"I'm going to Blaca for my seminary education."

The wagon stopped and the man cast him an incredulous look as though Luka was joking. Then he roared with laughter.

"That's a good one. . . ha, ha. . . Nenad's friend will become a priest? You're a bloke, boy! I like you. . . "

Luka smiled and let the man think what he wanted.

"So, see you on the road out of Pučišča at four, mister!"

"I can't wait, boy! You are a funny one!"

The sound of his belly laugh dissipated in the trot of the mules. Luka was finally alone with his plans. He was looking forward to visiting his friend in Supetar, although initially he had wanted to set out for Blaca that night. However, he would be behind

monastery walls soon enough. It would be a good thing to enjoy
a jolly reunion with his friend before that.

At the quarry, his boss told him he could come back any
time he wanted and added a tiny raise to his last pay. Luka was
grateful for the extra money as well as for his patron's sincere understanding and respect he had shown him as if Luka had already
received the Holy Orders. They parted in friendship. He paid his
landlady, who burst in tears as though he was going to the front
and not behind safe church walls. They arranged she would send
his furniture and things to his mother's house in Milna. At four,
he took the ride with Nenad's chatty neighbor.

While the mules were trotting in the heavy rain and the two
men were trying to cover their bodies with some dirty rugs, Luka
was thinking of the last time he saw Nenad. It was almost a year
ago at the Bol spring carnival, a rite which Venetians introduced
while they were lords of the island. Nenad was wearing a nice
dark brown suit, which was tight around his right arm. Like all
stonecutters, Nenad's right arm wielding a chisel grew twice the
size of his left. They were dancing along with the procession.
Nenad was putting his hands around girls' waists as though the
beauties all belonged to him. It was his last day on Brač before
leaving for Celje, before going to war. They got really drunk and
parted only when Nenad went aboard to sail to Split in the gray
morning mist.

"Whoa! Here we are, Luka! Please, pass my regards and love
to Nenad! If he needs anything, tell him I am always here. He's
a war hero!"

Luka was surprised. Why would Nenad need anything from a
brute spilling dirty jokes like nuts out of a sac? He nevertheless
politely thanked him for the ride. When he descended the wagon
and looked briefly up into the old man's eyes, he could see they
were full of tears. He stepped into the dark lobby of the house and
bumped into Nenad's mother. She held him tightly in her arms.
Was she sobbing slightly or was it only Luka's imagination? He
entered the kitchen, which was also a dining room with a huge
oak table in the middle. In the dim light of the oil lamp he could
see Nenad sitting at the table. He was still wearing his green
Loden uniform of the Imperial Army soldier, and his left breast
pocket proudly displayed a bronze medal for bravery with the
profile of Emperor Franz Joseph.

Nenad did not get up. He was staring at his hands folded
passively on the table. His handsome profile showed humiliation
and despair. Slowly, the soldier looked up and turned his left side
of the face to Luka, who in a split second saw why. He shivered
with shock. Half of Nenad's nose was missing, exposing the cavity
beyond the roughly healed wound. At first, it seemed to Luka his
friend was grinning stupidly, but then he realized there was no
upper lip on Nenad's face any more. The once sensual door to

Nenad's lustful mouth kissing girls and drinking wine was gone, and sheer teeth were obstructing the saliva from dripping to the chin. His left eye was sore and swollen as though some other piece of skin was implanted there instead of his eyelids with once long black lashes. Instead of hair on the left side of the head, there was a rough wound, glaring in all shades of pink and purple flesh, healed quickly and unevenly.

Luka pulled himself together and overcame his fear and cowardly aversion. He made a step closer. He stretched out his arms to embrace his friend, who just remained seated, with no energy for the move. Luka's eyes travelled down from Nenad's face to his body, and further to his legs. In the shadow of the table he could see the right leg of the *Loden* trousers neatly folded and pinned below the knee. Nenad's right foot was gone. Only then Luka noticed crutches leaned against the wall in the corner of the room. He made another step towards his friend, feeling the urgency of touching him, cradling him in his arms, comforting him with the strength of his love and emotion. He stumbled over his own foot as if two were one too many and fell on his knees in front of Nenad's clothes' stub of a leg. He would not show pity, it would be demeaning. He would treat his friend as the man he had always been. Luka took his friends' healthy stonecutter's hands in his and pressed them to his lips. He tried to sound cheering, yet plaintive sobs filled the room:

"Nenad, my friend, you're alive! You're alive! That's all that counts!"

A hissing, mumbling reply came back:

"I wish I weren't."

Nenad's mother, a strong and proud woman of fifty, pleaded with him:

"Nenad, life is the gift of God. You will be fine. The doctors in Vienna will put you in order. You will write books about what you have gone through. It is an important mission. You must live."

Nenad's disfigured face became a horror grimace of a monster. His body shook with silent sobs, and from his good eye a flood of tears poured onto Luka's hands. Luka was kissing those strong hands and drinking his tears as though Nenad were a bishop or a pope. Nenad broke the spell and softly caressed Luka's blond curls, which summoned Luka to his feet. Without letting go of his friend, he bent to kiss the good side of his face. Instinctively, Nenad offered his no lips back. The touch of cold bare teeth sent a creep through Luka's body, but he controlled the shiver not to offend Nenad, who hissed through his teeth, sending splashes of saliva on the table in front of him:

"*Mama*, please sum up for Luka. It is disgusting when I speak."

Mrs. Baričković put a bottle of brandy and a jug of cold water on the table. Then she sat next to her son.

"Sit down, Luka. It's a long story. I can tell you only what I know. Nenad's unit was sent to defend a village, Števerjani or something. They were trying to win back the position they had to abandon the day before. They came under a heavy Italian fire from their monster guns, and Nenad was thrown into a crater full of mud and water. It was so cold that he didn't even feel the wounds at the time. After another shot, a body joined him in the pit. He only saw the young boy had one of his arms cut off, so he could not hold himself afloat and would sink and drown surely. Nenad kept him afloat through the whole battle. They were rescued out of the pit hours later by the stretcher-bearers. Nenad's wounded foot got so infected they had to amputate it below the knee. However, the youth whom Nenad saved was General Borojević's young aide, a son of an Austrian count, so they are grateful and willing to help Nenad. After Christmas, Nenad will travel to Vienna, where the best surgeons will try to restore his face and lips as well as accommodate him with a solid artificial leg. They say Nenad should be able to walk again."

Luka nodded approval, yet he could see it didn't mean much to his friend. He was so deeply discouraged. His tears dried, but his face stayed impassive as if the conversation had nothing to do with him. Luka took his hands in his again and squeezed them gently.

"Nenad, we will all help you to get over this. You will heal. You will see what wonders doctors can do today. And you're a hero, our Emperor will reward you, I am sure he will."

Mother intervened with practicalities again.

"The first veteran pension has already been sent to us. If either the army or the Viennese family of the count pays for Nenad's treatment, he will be able to live comfortably with it."

From the back of the room came a deep man's voice. It was Nenad's older brother, who said:

"We will renovate a small fishing cottage we own at Zlatni rat, the Golden Cape beach. We will add a bathroom with a toilet and whitewash all the walls. The cottage has two rooms. It is warm in winter and fresh in summer. Nenad will be comfortable there. It's close to the city center, so he will be able to go to the library or to have coffee in the harbor."

A younger sister came forward with a plate of cheese and dried figs. She put it on the table, saying firmly:

"We will not leave Nenad to his sorrow. We will not abandon him."

Luka was moved. What a family! Nenad looked at his sister and his face grimaced into a kind of smile. He said silently:

"Please, Ema, sing to me!"

Ema took a tiny *lyra* from the corner and embarked on a long, melancholic Dalmatian folk ballad "Oh, my hand, the things you've touched". Her voice was sweet and clear, like a hymn of a thousand angels. With a nod of his head, Nenad summoned Luka to sit closer to him. He put his right arm over his shoulder and swayed in the rhythm of the song. Towards the end of the song, they were both humming along. The next song was merrier... "Jelica and Ive went for a walk". Nenad and Luka were swaying in unison, as if they were on the dance floor swinging girls in a lively *kolo*. When Ema put away her *lyra*, all were smiling and cheering. Before Luka took leave, Nenad whispered in his ear:

"Promise, Luka..."

"What?"

"Promise you will never go to war."

"I promise. Priests fight evil with faith, not with the gun. I will enter the Franciscan order tomorrow. I believe in God and in His Creation of the world."

"Good," was all Nenad said before he summoned for the crutches to limp to his room and go to bed. A long day ended with a merry song. Who could tell what the night would bring?

* * *

The candles were lit and a warm orange light embraced in love the three people having their meal on Saturday, 23rd of December 1916. They sat at the table in the modest dining room of the small Milna farmhouse: Bruna the mother, Stijepan the father and their seventeen year old son Luka. It was their last lunch together before the father and the son would join the Christmas festivities at Blaca, the fortified Franciscan Monastery, where after the midnight service in honor of the Nativity of the Lord, a modest banquet for some thirty most important landowners and industrials of the island would be held.

Stijepan saw to it that the meal was perfect; a fat freshly caught bass baked with onions, garlic, potatoes and rosemary twigs, served with a delicate lemon sauce whisked creamy from egg yolks. The side dishes were served with a deliciously steamed chard and fresh rocket salad. For dessert, Stijepan baked a cake the islanders called the Vatican bread, with raisins and nuts. Bruna made some fresh white bread to mop the sauce and dip into tasty olive oil. They rarely had such delicacies on their table, and they licked their fingers in the end. Smiles and cheeks hot with joy went pale, however, when Luka gave them an account of his visit in Supetar and of Nenad's wounds. In unison, Stijepan and Bruna looked at each other with relief. Their Luka would be spared the front in the Church hierarchy. However, although Stijepan also knew that Luka would remain in Blaca only for the spring months, neither of them had the nerve to reveal the fact to Bruna. She was having another piece of the sweet cake, chewing happily on the raisins. Between swallows, she said:

"Luka, what will be your first task at Blaca? What did Don Nikola say?"

"I will be studying for the seminary education and making up for the missing knowledge for my baccalaureate in Bol."

"What about the school? Aren't you going to help Don Nikola with the school?"

"Not for the moment. You see, little Niko is home, too."

Stijepan interfered knowingly.

"Well, I've always said that the Northern weather is no good. Vienna is drowned in fog and smog. He got some inflammation of his respiratory system, and his Austrian physician advised Niko to stay on Brač for at least half a year. So, he will be helping Don Nikola. He must do something besides staring at the stars."

Bruna did not know about Don Nikola Junior's scientific achievements, so she added:

"Contemplation of Heaven is every priest's sacred duty."

The men looked at her without commenting. It was clear they did not mind what she was saying regarding religious matters. In any case, they knew it would be insincere, for Bruna was more likely a pagan than a Catholic. However, they both loved her independent posture and temperamental nature. Away from Don Nikola's severe observation, Stijepan even found it amusing.

"My little pigeon, what would you know about priests' sacred tasks?"

Bruna made a grimace at him as if to say it was a low blow. She cleared the table and set a pot of coffee on the stove. When she finally collected herself, she briskly replied:

"And you, my Stijepan, you are a holy man, aren't you? Heart and soul of holiness you are! Particularly in the moonshine among the rocks. . . "

Stijepan blushed like a boy and started coughing. Luka turned away in disgust, realizing what Mother was alluding to. Trying to jest about it he said:

"Please, spare me the details, you two! I have no intention of imagining you two naked in sin!"

However, Bruna did not give up once she smelled weakness.

"My dear Luka, it's the rule of life and you will see one day that lovemaking is the ecstasy of love, the sublimation of all human emotions. You should always bear in mind that you are such a moon child, a fruit of love between your father and me."

Luka remained silent. There was no point in arguing with his mother that love was a spiritual rather than bodily energy, and that priests should remain chaste and pure for the reception of His mercy. She was so bright and practical, yet all divinity was strange to her thought. She would not accept a higher authority. Luka was glad that she had not argued with his decision to enter the Orders, and assumed she only accepted it because she was afraid he might get drafted. One way or the other, she supported him, and Luka had the feeling she even felt warmer towards Father. Maybe they would have a life after all. Mother was chatting on:

"By the way, Marija received a telegraph yesterday. Her Maja is coming home from Split to have her baby at home. As I presumed, Maja had to get married in haste as she was pregnant. She is due in the end of January."

"And what happened to the Austrian officer? Would he get a leave to follow her?"

"Oh, that's the sad part of the story. He was killed in action. Luckily our Emperor shows mercy to the families of his army men. She will be receiving a small pension."

Stijepan added emphatically:

"That is terrible. Maja is so young, a year younger than Luka, and she will be a single mother."

"I should say Marija didn't really sound sad. Maja has always been a vivacious girl. I think Marija has been afraid Maja could end up a single mother without a husband and his pension."

Luka felt bad discussing other people's personal affairs, and he said so:

"Mother, they are two strong women, and I am sure they will handle it without our help. Tell me more about your job at the tin factory. How do you plan to get there and back home every week?"

"Oh, we didn't show him, Stipe! Your father bought me a present."

Bruna went out, and the men sat in anticipation, grateful for a peaceful minute or two. Mother was too much for them both. They heard a bell in the lobby and got up to see what was going on. Mother was sitting on a black bicycle, hitting the bell handle again and again, enjoying the noise like a little girl; her cheeks were flushed with wine and happiness, her fair curls escaped the bun and flew around her eyes filled with blue flashes. In her heart, she had remained a wild child longing for action and fun.

"I will learn to ride the bicycle. They say it is not more than two hours and a half."

Luka and Stijepan laughed at her enthusiasm. It was so good to see her happy, the only woman of their lives.

"Listen, my boys! I will come to the monastery Sunday mass every week, and wait for you after lunch, when we can go for a walk and talk. Isn't that great?"

Father and son furtively exchanged a look of apprehension. A tiny moment of pregnant silence might give them away, might sow a seed of uncertainty which would set Mother on a trail. Luka did not know how long after Christmas he would stay on Brač, but for sure his mother would wreak havoc if she knew that shortly he was going to Italy, going away from her into the very nest of vipers. Her hatred for the enemies in black robes had not subsided with the prospects of saving her son from Isonzo.

"Mother, you cannot ride downhill from the road to Blaca! The path is too steep and rocky. You'll get yourself killed!"

"Watch me, boy! I can do everything if I set my will to it!"

Stijepan did not say a word. He knew Bruna was right. She was a hell of a woman, and he loved her. Maybe after Luka was gone to Fossanova, where he would be more than safe against the guns, Bruna would finally remember him, her husband. Perhaps she would spend more time with him. Her love for Luka was too strong; sometimes it seemed almost insane, like a kind of obsession. She acted and felt as though she was still carrying him as a baby under her heart, as if she would do anything not to cut the umbilical cord between them. Stijepan wondered how much that powerful love had affected, if not damaged their son. Could God love Luka any better than his passionately mad mother? Secretly, he rubbed a tear from the corner of his eyes.

* * *

The heart is not a penal code in which crimes and offenses are defined. Nor is it a catechism in which sins are classified. The human heart is a judge, just and exact.

– Ivan Cankar, A Cup of Coffee, translated by Loius
Adamič

In the beginning of May, no bird of the mountain in which the Blaca Monastery hid below the majestic rocks would keep silent in the small hours of the day. In the middle of darkness, males were puffing out their chests, starting their song to charm and attract their mates. In the bushes, in the trees, on the rocks and below the leaves, a majestic orchestra played the eternal tunes of love and sensuality. Before the lazy cicadas awoke with the first dew in the morning gray, thousands of olive tree warblers cried in the dark, longing for a friendly beak against theirs. The chirping of woodchat shrikes and invisible sparrows duly interrupted that message to the universe of females awaiting their partners, each singling out one special bird, the love of her life. However, they all went quiet when before the dawn larks began their song of a thousand violins, which mesmerized everybody. Without notes or a set score, they were sharing their pleas for love with human and animal couples shaking with passion in the cold spring nights. With morning light and the first sun rays, swallows shrieked their sound of warning, their goodbye to love and hello to the work of the day. Such was the concert of nature that many a young man, awoken by his hot blood and vivid dreams would not close his eye again until it was time to get up.

The shriek which woke Luka in that lovely May night, however, was not that of a swallow or of any other bird. It pierced the thick walls of the monastery, entering his mind like a shell on the front. It was the last night at Blaca for him. In the morning he would start his two-day voyage to Fossanova, where he would be acquiring his seminary education and helping with construction works. His tiny room was more of a storage room than a proper dwelling. It was in the southern part of the building, so sharp sea winds rattled the window glasses many a night. Still, his bed was regal compared to the pits and trenches where the Austrian soldiers were trying to close their eyes, if only for minutes.

The crying and weeping became louder. Suddenly, words were thrown in the air, harsh words which in a second shut down the birds' nocturnal concerto.

"Youuuu! Fucking liar! Youuu! All damm liars!"

Luka recognized the sharp woman's voice and knew whose squall got him to jump out of bed.

"Come down and look me in the eye! Liar!"

Luka looked through the window and in the moonlight he saw a thin stooped woman with a crown of silver curls coming down the path. She stopped to shout:

"Youuu! Fucking hypocrite! You took my soul away! Son of a bitch! Don of all dirt! Come here!"

Luka shivered with dread. The apparition hid her face in her hands and squatted lifelessly, shaking with violent sobs. When she recollected her forces, she went on at the top of her voice:

"Don Nikola! You are a liar! You are scum! You want to take my son away! What is so precious in my flesh and blood that you want it all for yourself! Will you fuck him?"

Had she been drinking? What got into her? But Luka knew the reason for his mother's hysteria. He did not only shiver with fear. He knew why she was furious. He knew that he and his father had deceived her. They avoided telling her the truth, cunningly concealed his departure to Italy for fear she would make trouble. Now she was here, at the door of the monastery, cursing like hell. How the hell could she have found out? Light shone in his terrified eyes... Ema and Maja were best friends. He had gone to say goodbye to the Baričkovićs the night before, for he did not want to leave Nenad without a farewell. Yet, he would leave his mother without a kiss... Before he could think further, another screeching indignant roar came from below:

"I have prayed every night since we spoke, Don Nikola. I have kept my promise, while you and your God have tricked me! My soul is mine! Do you hear me? I have my own will! I don't believe in your Jesus fucking Christ! And you don't either! You think I don't know, do you? But, I do. I know you're a fraud!"

Niko entered the storage room without knocking.

"I made sure that my uncle can't hear this...hear her. I've put another blanket over his door, and he's sound asleep in his room. I have also calmed Lovro down."

"What can we do, Niko?"

"I came to ask you, Luka. She's your mother."

A big shadow appeared in the doorway. It was Stijepan, alarm and terror written all over his squashy face.

"It's Bruna! She found out you're going!"

Luka shook his head. As always, Father was useless.

"Don't panic, dad! We'll talk to her."

Niko looked at the two men and straightened up.

"I will go down and talk to her. She has always liked me."

Tears fell down Stijepan's cheeks. He whined disagreement.

"She has only met you a couple of times."

"Still, father, Niko is right. She will sooner show reason with him than with either of us. Niko, please, hurry! Tell her I love her. Tell her I meant to come and say goodbye..."

Luka's voice quivered and broke in a sob.

"I will not lie to your mother, Luka. But I will talk reason into her."

Father and son approached the window. They could see the woman rise to her feet and proceed closer.

"And as to youuu, Stijepan! You're not a man, you're a lousy chicken! Whiiiiimp! How many times have you fucked me? Only that once to have me conceive that little liar!"

Again, she collapsed to the ground, her dress in disarray, howling and wailing like a wounded animal. Behind the window, in the safe darkness of the little room, Stijepan was shaking with sobs, too, his huge body convulsing in pain. Luka just stared through his tears, shocked by the force of his mother's emotions. It was pure hate, evil hate. How much had she held it back all those years for Blaca, Don Nikola and his gentle father? They could see Niko approaching with firm steps. He was obviously speaking to her in a low voice, but they could not hear him. Another shriek pierced the silence of the night:

"Curse on you, filthy little monk! Blaca should crumble to dust and you should fry in Hell together with that old fart of your uncle!"

They could see how Niko was taken aback by her foul words. He swung about and made a few hesitating steps back towards the building. Then, he took his cross in his left hand and kissed it, looked into the sky filled with the silver moon and shining stars, and turned to face Bruna again. He was a solid man of thirty, a scientist and a priest. He would not back off from a woman, no matter how ferocious and violent she was. They heard him say in a loud, firm voice.

"Come with me, woman, and talk to your husband and your son!"

Bruna was stunned, yet she would not let go easily. With a pointed finger, she threatened Niko and the building behind him.

"I tell you, little monk, this monastery has no future! There will be no priest to guide it after you die! I curse Blaca! I curse you and Don Nikola! I curse you to eternity!"

Niko assumed an authoritative position:

"Are you a witch or what? Stop! I don't care if thunder strikes me and Blaca here and now! But I refuse to listen to your obscenities! Come inside and behave like a human!"

Stijepan and Luka couldn't believe their eyes. Bruna stopped waiving her arms. Motionless, her face like a mortal mask in the white moonshine, she looked up to the southern windows of the monastery and said in a distinctive voice:

"I don't have anything to say to those two cowards! Let them live their grim lives! I don't want to set my eye on any of you monkish scum as long as I live!"

With that said, Bruna turned on her heels and started to walk up the slope, past the stone table under the mulberry tree, past her wretched life of waiting in vain, loving the absent husband and bringing up a treacherous son.

Back in the little storage room, Niko said goodnight to Luka. Stijepan could not move from the spot. He was still weeping silently, sobs shaking his whole body. The young priest took pity on him and put his arm around his shoulder. With a push, he gently led him to his room, murmuring soothing words and summoning the crushed old man to say a prayer with him. There were still several hours of the dark left, and after a while the birds returned to their hymns to love and life. Nothing interrupted their song again until the sun chased the shadows of the long night away.

The following afternoon, Luka boarded his ship with a big lump in his throat. Guilt was suffocating him. The thought of Mother and the childhood memories of her selfless love brought tears in his eyes again and again. He could not look ahead, and a couple of times he caught himself looking at the uniformed soldiers who were taking leave of their families to join the war on Isonzo. Maybe it would be better. Maybe, it was not too late to show courage. Maybe, he could still be a man.

When the sailors dropped the mooring ropes in the sea, and the ship was slowly turning to take the course for Split, he scanned the crowd on the shore. There, in front of them all, he could see his mother, waving her right hand in goodbye, trying to attract his attention. He lifted his hand in acknowledgement, and she sent him kisses through the air, hundreds of kisses from her warm, frantic hands to his young, handsome cheeks. He smiled. Oh, Mother! Your love is stronger than hate!

End of Yugoslavia, 1992

I lie here in the cold freshness of starch white linen sheets. All is quiet in the small hours of the night. Why do I feel like a corpse on the funeral pyre? As though I was waiting to be set free from the pains of this life and sent across the freezing Styx to another world, to the world of shadows, to the underworld in the eternal darkness. For Heaven will not wait for such a one as I...I am bad. I am not worthy, no matter how many pardons I was looking for with my work, my stories from the past, my history of Dalmatia...I am a bad woman. I have wronged so many people. I have murdered a murderer. The blood of suffering women who I listened to night after night instead of helping them is staining my fingers. Cries for help are echoing in my ears. My destination is Hell. My next husband will be the Devil himself. Another man will be another devil...Yet, there is Dario...my good old man...He is an angel. He loves me with the purity of a child. Alas, he came into my life too late. He could not absolve me from the evil. Sometimes, even angels fail...Sometimes even angels fall...

Why am I so certain that I will die on the day after tomorrow? I have never believed one can feel the moment with such accuracy. We cannot remember the moment of our birth, yet death is another matter. I know for certain that I will die tomorrow. What do I have to do? Shall I put down another list of matters to take care of before the operation? I have gone through several to do lists lately. I have been to the notary's to double check my will, and I have composed a memo that Barbara should lead the hotel Perovica in case I never come back from Ljubljana. I have put in order the files of my historical research and made two digital copies and a printed one for Paula to assemble one day. Maybe she will understand me better, maybe she will use the stories for promotion of this beautiful land, more sea than land, Dalmatia. There is not one thing I would not have dealt with. For since the first suggestion for this operation from the doctors, I have had the premonition that I would not live beyond it.

A sweet voice violates my peace, and intrudes on my tired brain: "But, you know, Marica, you know there is so much more to tell...so many secrets to disclose...first to Paula, then to the world...Don't you remember anymore? Are you so old?"

Oh, I am old, I nearly do not remember, and I surely want to forget. I have the right to forget after all this time. I do not want to dig all the garbage and all the vermin up again. It would do no good to anybody. It would only pollute my world with blackness and death like a black tide of spilled oil turns the most gorgeous beach into a cemetery for birds and fish. I have paid my debt, haven't I? Let him who is without sin throw the first stone! I have the right to die in peace...I want to sleep and think no more. . .

"Marica, if you die tomorrow and if your bone marrow does not save your daughter Paula, who will? You will be asleep forever. . . who will she have in this world to ask for help? You must face the truth. . . You must speak up. . . "

God, I am so ashamed. What have I done with my life? How can I tell Paula the truth? I will stain her mind with my sins. She is so innocent and pure. She knows only good things about her *nona*. If I tell her the truth, she will hate me!

"Marica, don't be so vain. You love the image of yourself you see in Paula's loving eyes. Don't use a terminally ill girl as your mirror! It is a fake image, and you are a fake! You are like the vicious stepmother in the Snow White story: Magic mirror on the wall, who is the fairest one of all?"

Oh, leave me. . . Haven't I had enough? Haven't I paid for all my errors with nights of anxiety and fear? Haven't I worked so hard that I lost track of day and night to build my business, to reinvent and rebuild my life? What else do you want, you selfish goddess of my conscience? My whole life was Purgatory and my death will be Hell. Please, let me be, let this child love me forever!

"But you had pleasure. It was wrong. You must pay. You must tell Paula. She has the right to know. It is her future."

It is her past and I don't want her to suffer for it. I have suffered for her, oh God, don't you see? I took all the pains of the bloody war on my shoulders. I have buried the horrible memories into my brain, so deep, that I cannot remember, I don't want to remember. I have left my three wonderful sons to keep my Paula away from the ugly world of judgements, the society of prejudice. I have created a spotless heaven for her on the island of Pag. I have spared her all the dirty details of the Balkan terror. It shall never be more than history to her, never! It shall never touch her life. It shall never dirty her soul, never! Don't you see how innocent she is? It is I who must suffer. Take me, God, tear me apart, kill me, rape me, torture me, but please, let my child live her pure life of an angel!

"Nay, nah, nah, nah. . . You're negotiating with God now, Marica! You have suffered for Paula. . . Who do you think you are? Jesus Christ? Do you think you can make a deal with God? Do you think you can swap your sinful life for Paula's? You would exchange your filthy joys for Paula's fresh breaths, wouldn't you? Aren't you something? You are a true counterpart of your devil lover. . . You are worthy of each other's crimes. . . "

I am bad. I have always known that. Jovan and I, we deserve to die in a thousand pains, and maybe our daughter must die with us, so that the evil leaves this Earth forever. How could I have loved a monster? How could a monster have felt love? It's God who loves, monsters hate. . . they kill. . . they copulate. . . they eat. . . they are beasts. . .

Truth hurts. It is cold and merciless. Why am I trembling? Am I afraid of death? I have defied death so many times...I will not be afraid now. I will not think of myself. There is no me any longer...I will prove I am worthy of the truth, that I am worthy of love. I will swallow the shame. I will write a note to Paula and I will confess. I will tell her everything. One day, she will know how much I have loved her and she will love me in return. She will know there is no such thing as war enemies in the face of God. She will comprehend that men can turn into beasts and that monsters can be human when they love. Who are we anyway? Sinful, lost, scared shadows, a weak race of people, who are desperately seeking God's protection, fighting fiercely against their evil instincts, hoping for Redemption in the far away Heaven above. I will write a letter to Paula. I will do it right now. She has been blind, but she will see. She will walk the path from Saul to Paul. She will still love me. I will prove my courage.

As for you, evil spirit, you, who think to be the mistress of my fate, you, voice of the voices, you shut up! I have faced life! I can face death!

* * *

"Are you awake, Paula, my dear?"

"Yes, nona. I cannot sleep. I am excited. It's the day after tomorrow..."

The rainy and grey day was giving in to the cold night, when the hospital lay in peace, hiding pains and fears of the patients in every corner of the white-washed rooms with grey vinyl floors. They were at the University Medical Centre in Ljubljana, waiting for the bone marrow transplant operation, scheduled in two days. They shared a private room. During the day, reading and watching TV between checks and various tests, and regular meals of tasteless food could subdue their anxiety. The nights, though, brought it up, like the river Ljubljanica sent its icy fogs upwards. The possibility that even nona's bone marrow would not help to cure Paula's leukemia was lurking from the shadows of the simple furnishings of the room... a table, two chairs, a wardrobe and two beds with two simple bedside tables, and a sink with a scare of the mirror above it. The white walls reflected the cold light of a street lamp. Paula was sad and afraid of the doctor's warnings that the operation is not entirely benign for nona either. During the tests, they discovered her heart was losing pace and force. Without really knowing or feeling it in any way, she had been suffering from cardiac arrhythmia. Operations and full narcosis with such a condition and at her age were dangerous procedures.

"Paula, do you want me to tell you the story of a woman from the last war?"

"You mean the Bosnian...Croatian...Serbian war in the nineties?"

"Yes, I just read about a woman from Split, Angela Bekić. There was a big article in Radar. I remembered I met her once, at the Medica Zenica in Bosnia during the war."

"Isn't Radar a Slovenian magazine? Can you read Slovenian, *nona*?"

"Well, it is very similar to Croatian. It's easier to read it than to speak it properly."

"Did you speak Slovenian when you were a child in Trieste?"

"Yes, I spoke Italian and Slovenian. And then you know, I studied more languages later... Latin, which I completely forgot and can only decipher reading, German, English, and French."

"Did you study history in Trieste?"

"No, no, my father was from Istria and mother Slovenian from the Brkini hills, so even before Trieste came under Italy after the WW2 in 1954, they went to Rijeka, which was an important port in Yugoslavia. The Italian population of Trieste became more and more indoctrinated by the revival of fascism and nationalism. It wasn't pleasant to live in a town where you were scolded and despised. I enrolled at the Rijeka Faculty of Arts and finished my studies there. Anyway, do you want to hear about Angela Bekić now or not?"

"I do, please, tell me."

Thus, *nona*'s story of Angela Bekić put yet another piece into the puzzle of women in Dalmatia. So many she had already stored on her laptop disk at home. It took her many years of thorough research. With her imagination, she was filling in the grey zones of life in the past. In her files, she represented a kaleidoscope of human destinies struggling on the shores of the Adriatic. *Nona* loved her work. Still, it surprised Paula that she would put together a life so recent. Usually, she would deal with the past centuries, searching for the threads to wave the cloth of Dalmatia in the old times. With interest, Paula listened to her tale.

"Angela was born in the year after the end of World War II in Split. Her mother Marina was a schoolteacher and her father, Ante, a municipality official. He obtained the job after putting down his weapons and uniform of a Tito's partisan. In the years from 1943 to 1945, Ante was fighting all along the Dalmatian coast, suffering fear, cold, and hunger. Tito's opponents were not only Fascists and Nazis, but also hordes of the terrible *Ustashas* from the Croatian puppet state *Nezavisna država Hrvatska* led by the collaborationist Pavelić, and in Serbia, the horrible *Chetniks* of Dragoljub Mihajlović. They butchered mainly civilians of the opposite nationality and religion. While *Ustashas* were sent into battles with the blessings of Catholic priests, the *Chetniks* sought the protection of their Orthodox Church fathers, but both were killing and raping in the name of the Lord. The *Domobranci*, the so called defenders of homes and Catholic faith in Slovenia, were formed later in the war, only in 1944, and they couldn't do so much damage, but they were nevertheless, exterminated as opponents of the communist regime in the woods of Kočevski Rog in 1945, days after the war.

Ante felt lucky in 1944 to have been transferred to the 8th Corps of the Yugoslav Partisan Army, famous for their liberation of Trieste on May 1st, 1945. His comrades who were fighting in the hinterland witnessed the evidence of the cruel and bloody raids between the *Chetniks* and the *Ustashas*, getting even with one another. Babies cut in two, mothers raped and killed in front of their children, old men disgraced and deprived of humanity. Only few survived the massacres, and they reported the sad events in the years to come.

Ante was a convinced pre-war communist. In his heart, he faithfully believed in the social revolution and in the brotherhood and unity of all Yugoslav nations. He believed in workers' rights, and he fought not only to liberate the land, which by then was to be a new Yugoslavia, but also for the revolution, which would bring peace and prosperity to everybody. Trieste was like Split, an international port with huge ship building docks, where work was heavy and pay scarce, where fishermen steered the boats into the gulf to follow the fish for the meager catch. In Trieste, he felt that people embraced socialism and communism with all their hearts. In the last months of the war, the citizens gathered some 3,500 volunteers to liberate the town from Germans. Tito's army with local communists established a new government in the time when the allies were negotiating the new border between Italy and Yugoslavia. Yet, Ante lost much of his faith and communist naivety during the forty days of the Triestine communist reign. To his dismay, the Yugoslav partisans took irrational revenge on the citizens, arresting and deporting randomly everybody who was Italian under the pretext that they collaborated with the Fascists and the Germans. People disappeared over night. It was like in the reign of terror in the revolutionary France, but this time it was not only aristocrats. They were taking in no matter whom as long as he was Italian. Years later, mutilated bodies were found in the karstic potholes called *Foibe*. In order to end the terror, the allies took over the city, and Tito's army withdrew. Trieste became Italian, as nobody wanted to live in the state of butchers and murderers. The old people would murmur things, but it was soon dangerous to speak up in the socialist Yugoslavia.

However, Angela's father Ante fell in love with Zorka, a striking blonde girl from the karstic hills above the city. They married in haste, and left for Split, where Ante laid down his weapons. In 1946, daughter Angela was born, and next year son Mario. Zorka was a quiet woman, she loved her school, where she taught Italian, and she spent days walking their dog to the Split's most famous nature resort, the peninsula Marijan. She never complained to

Ante that with the move she lost her background and her family. She loved him and cared for everything he cared for. In the late sixties, they bought a nice little stone cottage on the island of Brač, near Bol, where silence spoke the secrets of monastery ruins amidst the ripening pomegranate bushes in the tiny village of Murvica. They were a happy couple, and Ante was more than content to work for his community and to forget forever all the atrocities of the war.

You might think it strange that I know so many details of Angela Bekić's life, but days were long in the centre for women's rehabilitation center in Medica Zenica where I spent a year helping the sad occupants of that institution. Angela and I, we spent a lot of time together. You see, Paula, I never spoke much of the times during the war. It was horrible. You and I, we almost died back then. After our house was bombed and ruined, we had nowhere to go. We were in Zagreb for a while, at a refugee camp. The inertia was killing me. I knew there was nowhere to return to. Then I heard of Medica Zenica. They needed people to help set it up, so I went there, and you with me. It was late 1992. At least, I had a roof over my head and we were provided for. I worked voluntarily, caring for the women and children who were victims of the Serbian ethnic cleansing in Bosnia.

One of the major weapons for humiliating the Muslims were mass rapes of their women, leaving thousands of victims, the figures are between twenty and fifty thousand women, traumatized and ruined. After having completed a crash course in therapy and support, I talked to those women. By speaking to them, I kept their minds busy, working out the terror they had gone through. Their minds were so hurt: suicide, vengeance, shame, worthlessness, tears... I cannot describe the human misery. Some of them bore little *Chetniks*... children they got pregnant with during the rapes. Oh, you cannot imagine, Paula, the woes of the heart torn apart, beating for the innocent little baby and remembering its horrible conception... My main job was to document as much detail as possible, as Dr. Monika Hauser, who set up the Medica Zenica, was already at the time striving to proclaim rape as a war crime at The Hague Tribunal. Places, names, nicknames, dates... women then still remembered them. However, as years went by, their brains had to erase the atrocities, if they wanted to live on, to survive..."

Maria's voice trembled with emotion, and Paula noticed it. Darkness fell, so she could not see her *nona*'s face, but she was sure she was crying. She looked in her direction.

"Who was this doctor?"

"You mean Dr. Monika Hauser?"

"Yes."

"Monika is an angel. She is active in other parts of the world, where women are suffering like Liberia and Afganistan now, but

Zenica was her first women's station. If ever God sent an angel from heaven to comfort humans on earth, he surely sent her. She is the goodness in person. With huge efforts, collecting donations from Germany and worldwide, she set up Medica Zenica, a shelter for the victims of rape and sexual violence during the war. It was officially opened in spring 1993, still in the middle of the fights. The house provided medical treatment, psychological support, all possible social help to the victims... With support and help, she tried to make those suffering women whole again. But you never can, you see... "

"Was this Angela raped, *nona*?"

"No, it was worse than that. Listen to her story... "

"Angela was a bright little girl. She had a special gift for music, so she played the piano and sang melancholic Dalmatian ballads from her early age. Ante and Zorka had few relatives, but their friends' circle was big, as Ante brought home everybody whom he met at work. Zorka wined and dined them and they became friends eventually. One of such good friends was Vesna Parun, a famous Croatian poetess. They met at one of her poetry readings, Ante and Zorka invited her to their home, and she enjoyed many an evening chatting with them and resting from the important artistic world. Children would play with her, and Angela would sing a song or two. Vesna realized immediately that Angela needed to study music and encouraged her and the family to take individual lessons in piano and singing. Angela went to music school before she could read and write. She was singing at every occasion, and at every celebration her pure soprano, still unformed but promising impossible highs and lows, cut the air like a fresh breeze on a spring evening.

Angela's birthday was on Christmas day, which was more than welcome... they could celebrate without fear of neighbors reporting them for being Catholic and conservative. For in the new Yugoslavia, president Tito forbid all religions and all religious celebrations or festivities. There had been so many atrocities between the Catholics, the Orthodox and the Muslims in Bosnia during WW2 that the oppression of all other feelings but a celebration of brotherhood and unity under the dictatorship of the Communist Party was an offence and could get people in trouble. So even at Christmas, churches were echoing with silence, and priests seemed like the leftovers of other times and other cultures. Thus, no crèches and no Advent candles were reviving the story of the Holy family in the communist Decembers of the new Yugoslavia. It was a normal workday like any other day in the year. The pines were sold in the markets no sooner than on Saint Stephen's day, which was also a workday. On the other hand, the New Year's celebrations and strong alcohol flowing by the gallons in the workers' meeting at the factories were very much encouraged. The plum brandy was the spirit of bonding between three opposite religions and habits inherited from five different former states...the Habsburg Monarchy, the Ottoman Empire, and the kingdom of Yugoslavia with the Serbian king Karadjordjević on the throne, and the mess of the various puppet states during the WW2.

Angela grew into a lively girl, always on the move. When I saw her, years later in Zenica, she was still a stunning woman. She showed me photographs of herself when she was young. Her hair was straight, and she had vivid green eyes and a dainty smile, as tough she would challenge everyone to join her in her adventures. The world was her stage and her voice was there to fill it. Beside elementary school, she was also attending the music school, she sang in the radio children's choir and learnt to sail. Actually, she won a children's regatta a few times, beating the boys easily. 'It was all a matter of technique,' she would say with a light laugh. She adored life and action. Her ambitions were to study music and travel the world as an opera singer. However, in her teenage years, Angela lost her wonderful voice. She was fifteen, just having entered the Classical High School of Natko Nodila in Split. The cause of her loss was a commonplace medical mistake. Angela's physician suggested to have her tonsils removed, since Angela was suffering from frequent anginas and ate packages of antibiotics to keep the inflammations in check. It was a routine surgery, performed millions of times with no consequences. Yet, the day after the operation, her sensitive vocal cords were never the same. Her voice got lower and unclear. Her musical aspirations were over."

"How terrible... She was what... fifteen?"

"Yes, fifteen... "

"It is tough if you have to abandon your dreams so soon... "

"Angela decided to continue with her music, only she would play the violin instead of singing. She said it was nice, but her fingers would not listen to her brain, and her playing was good, yet far from perfect. It would not do for a professional career. So, she somehow accepted the situation. She turned her ambitions to literature and art history. That was also one of our favorite topics of conversation at Medica Zenica. We talked about Šibenik, the town, where she later lived and worked as a tourist guide and curator for several years. But, one thing at a time...

One spring morning, when the shells granted us a few days of silence and it felt almost like peace at last, Angela was telling me how she had met her husband Damir Bekić when she was in the last year of the high school. Her school organized an excursion to the Krka waterfalls above Šibenik. Angela told me it was the first time she was in the Krka National Park, as her parents took every minute off to go to Bol. She was overwhelmed with the majestic waterfall Skradinski Buk, named for its noisy presence in the canyon of the river, roaring down a magnificent travertine system.

The water was clear and revealed the bottoms of the whirlpools, water holes and streams. It was everywhere; it was falling from every rock in rapids, sending millions of crystals in the air, it was jumping over the cascades of moss and lovingly embracing the roots of the trees growing nonchalantly in the middle of the stream. There were laurel bushes thriving all around, fig trees, holm oaks, willows, sweet smelling elder bushes, pines, and wild asparagus bushes with soft, crunchy buds forbidden to be picked. Angela's senses were completely immersed in the greenery around her.

Soon she lost track of time and eventually, she lost her group and wandered alone along the wooden bridges, admiring the presumptuous fish swimming against the current in the open, not really seeking a place to hide from the visitors, for they knew well they were protected and could not be caught. It was getting late, and Angela got nervous she would miss the ship back, and the bus... How would she come home? The park was away from every traffic route.

'Can I help you, Miss?'

A young, dark ranger in a khaki uniform was looking at her with a warm smile. She appraised him from tip to toe. His head was crowned with chestnut curls, under which a pair of hazel brown eyes were inquisitively scanning the world around him. His uniform was simple, long trousers and a shirt with the logo of the Krka Waterfalls Natural Park. He was taller than Angela, yet not one of those heavy Dalmatian blokes, who would eclipse the sun if they stood in front of you. He was definitely older than her. He had a huge bag over his shoulder and a pair of heavy mountain boots dripping with water. It seemed he had not only been walking on the safe ground of wooden paths.

'I am here with school and I lost them. It is Natko Nodila High School from Split.'

'Yeah, I saw them earlier. They were going to enter the Electric Power Plant. But it is quite away from here.'

'Well, can you show me the way, please?'

'Yes. My name is Damir Bekić. I'm gathering samples of the water from various parts of the falls. You know, Krka brings along sediments and limestone particles. The limestone enters the structure of the mosses, and they form living barriers for the stream. It's all natural...'

'Interesting... I am Angela. So you're a biologist?'

'Yes, actually, I work for Zagreb University. We're controlling the water, the concentration of limestone in it, and above all, we keep an eye on pollution.'

'Is there any pollution here?'

'Not really. There's not much industry upstream. Let's go this way!'

Damir showed her the way uphill, which made her wonder whether it was the right way. Still, obediently, she followed the direction, the man walking behind her. It was awkward. The birds were singing loudly, and the water rivulets were speeding down to the valley and further to the sea. Only they should go upstream. The whirlpools, filled with bright green water, formed little streams flooding the wooden paths at lower places. At one such turn, Angela slipped and, with a splash, fell into a whirlpool. The water was freezing cold, and the strong current pulled her along with all its earth force of the seventeen slopes. It was taking her down, and for a moment, she almost lost her consciousness and gave in.

'Grab a tree, or grab the bridge! I'll get you!'

Angela was a sailor. She quickly regained her senses. She knew how to pull the ropes. With either hand, she grabbed a young fig tree. Then she looked around for a rescue from Damir. He threw her a long rope, and she wrapped it around her waist, forming a wide bowline knot. Slowly, he pulled her to the wooden path. It took all his strength, for the current was very strong. Finally, she climbed ashore, with her clothes, jeans and bright green cardigan, dripping wet. For a moment, he held her in his arms, as to warm her. Angela, who had little experience with boys, immediately felt drawn to him. Maybe it was the adrenalin, or maybe she was ready for a boy to rescue her from her ambitions. He used his walkie-talkie. They turned right, and soon there was a fellow ranger in a jeep, waiting for them on a wooden path. Standing by the car, he held a set of dry khaki clothes in his hands. Angela changed, and they drove to the main visitors' area at Skradinski buk. Her group was there, waiting by the boat, teachers looking at her angrily. However, Damir saved the day:

'Here is your lost sheep. You should be more careful with your kids. I had to fish her out of the rapids. She could have drowned. The water is wild here.'

Angela's teacher immediately subdued to the sight of the uniform.

'I am really sorry, Sir. Thank you.'

'Where should I send or bring back the clothes, Damir?'

Angela felt almost neglected. What a sorry ending of the trip. Damir scrambled something on a piece of paper, folded it, and put it in her hands. Only on the boat, thudding down the estuary, she read what he wrote: 'Angela, today I saved my angel. Can I see you again? Please, call me. If you don't want to, you can send the clothes to the Krka Waterfalls National Park.'

Angela made the call. They started dating. In her third year of university while studying art history and English, she bore him their first son, then two more in three years. They settled down in an old town house which Damir had inherited from his great aunt in Šibenik. Together, they made a heaven on earth at the address which was grand despite its name: Mali prolaz, Little Passage. The house didn't look much on the outside, one would say it was a bit run down, but they had a wonderful inner court filled with citrus and fig trees, where even on summer days the shadow was deep and fresh. The three-storey medieval building gave them opportunities to furnish each room in a different style. A kitchen and large dining room on the ground floor could sit ten guests, and they often had friends or family over for a Sunday meal. On the middle floor, they had three bedrooms, and in the attic, they furnished two study cabinets. It was a true Mediterranean home. After the maternity leaves, finishing her studies and supervising the renovation of the house, Angela got a job with the municipality as a tourist guide."

"So, a happy ending, is it? But, *nona*, how can you remember such details like a phone number? You amaze me. . . "

"Well, my girl, you know your *nona*. I crave details. Would you like to hear more? Are you tired?"

"No, I'm eager to hear the whole story. Go on, please!"

"Well, Angela said they were the happiest couple on the planet. Damir completed his PhD at the University of Split, and they lived comfortably for a decade, until the university in Thessalonica invited him to teach there for a whole semester and help them with their research. It was a well-paid job, for Greece was a European country with a much higher standard of living than Croatia. After six months, he came home a changed man. Angela said that she noticed immediately he had put on a lot of weight. Also, he became moody and didn't stop at one or two glasses of wine at lunchtime. The boys felt estranged to him, and since he frequently burst in anger and shouted at them, they avoided him as much as they could. A few years had gone by before Angela realized that Damir turned into a drunk, that he had become a serious alcohol addict. Her love died slowly with every glass Damir swallowed. He still worked at the university, but just barely. They threatened to fire him, for he neglected not only his research duties, but also skipped his teaching. The bottle was his best friend. Angela tried several times to persuade him to go into a rehab program. . . to no avail. He became an animal, unclean, fat, disgusting. Their love and marriage reduced to a few everyday phrases, Angela was working hard to avoid being at home. Somehow, the boys grew into young men, and their means still kept them all above water. They were good students and motivated to leave their home wrecked by alcohol and a violent father.

Such was their life until the spring of 1991, when the conflicts with the Serbian population living in the newly established sovereign state Croatia around Knin made their unstable life even more insecure. Angela and Damir were both middle-aged by then. Damir was over fifty, Angela in her mid forties. Somehow, they were victims of the events taking the wrong course. But the blame for the family misfortune was entirely Damir's. He failed as a husband and he failed as a man. I will tell you how.

His mother lived in the hinterland of Šibenik, near Drniš. She was a widow, a strict Catholic for her whole life, and an austere matron of the family. Unfortunately, she didn't see anything harmful in Damir's drinking a glass too many, as wine had forever lifted the spirits of men in Dalmatia. Angela stayed away from her as much as she could, but when the systematic shelling of the Catholic villages around Knin began, she wanted her to come to live with them, in Šibenik. However, the old woman would not leave her house for the fear that the police forces of *Republika Srpska* Krajina would plunder it. Then she got sick...breast cancer. Frequently, either Damir or Angela had to drive her to the Šibenik hospital for chemotherapy treatments. With sadness, Angela told me of the day which changed her life from worse to the worst.

Her mother-in-law called Damir early in the morning to ask him to pick her up. Her medical appointment was due at four in the afternoon at the clinic in Šibenik. He promised to get to her house in time, at two in the afternoon. As the main road was full of barricades, set up by various paramilitary Serbian units, becoming more and more dangerous, they would have to take detours along side roads. Angela left the house after breakfast, reassured that maybe in caring for his mother, Damir would drink less during the day. She had a group of Slovenian architecture students visiting the St. James Cathedral that day despite the war going on just fifty kilometers away. When she returned home at half past one, Damir was leaning on the table dead drunk. He couldn't even answer her questions, but she remembered his mother's appointment at the hospital and called her. The old woman was hysterical. She was crying into the phone that she had to come to Šibenik by four in the afternoon. Angela related to her what a glass too many meant for her son. He was snoring on the table, oblivious to anything around him. Her mother-in-law said she would ask a neighbor for a ride and call back. Within ten minutes, the old woman called to say that there was nobody who would risk the drive today as the shelling was coming closer. Angela decided on the spur of the moment...she would come and take her to Šibenik on one condition. Mother should lock her house at Drniš and stay with them until the conflict in the Krajina was resolved. The old woman agreed and thanked her with a trembling voice. In a whiny voice, she told her she was a good daughter-in-law and a good wife.

Angela wrote a short message to the kids: what they should take out of the refrigerator and what to do with dad when he wakes up from his alcoholic stupor. Then she walked to the parking lot above the market to get the car. In twenty minutes, she

was passing the first outpost, the Croatian one, and the policemen told her to drive back. They said fights were going on and
that the Serbians were gaining territories with the support of the
Yugoslav People's army. Angela hesitated. But then, somebody
would have to get her mother-in-law one of those days, so why not
she today? The policemen were tough to persuade. It was very
dangerous to drive further. They advised her to turn back and
prepare as the shells could even reach Šibenik later during the
day. Angela told them about the emergency. What would happen to her mother-in-law then? She had to go on. She insisted,
and finally they let her go through the post. Some ten miles later,
she bitterly regretted it. The fully armed *Chetnik* outpost told
her to take a detour. She fell into chaos in the village Ključica.
There were practically no men around save for the soldiers of the
Republika Srpska. They were taking the women without children
in one truck and the women clutching their offspring in another.
She heard the soldiers shouting at them, saying that they should
not be afraid, that they were taking them to a safe territory, out
of the range of the shells. Where was that, Angela thought, and
why would they do that? And where were all the men from the
village? She lowered the side window to see better. At that moment, a bearded soldier opened the door and dragged her out of
her car. In the heat of the crisis, she said 'Shit!', and he looked
at her nonplussed. Angela had an idea. She could speak English
perfectly, she was blond, she knew things... Maybe she could fake
to be somebody else. She started screaming in English that she
was a famous journalist, a reporter of the Guardian, and that
she wanted to be let free immediately. At first, they ignored her,
driving her car away. She got hysterical; she demanded her car
with everything in it back. She had taken her laptop with her,
for she had meant to wait with her mother-in-law at the hospital
and finish some work. The soldiers were just laughing at her, yet,
through their amusement, she heard some questions about what
they should do with her. At the top of her voice, she insisted
they should bring her laptop and she would prove to them who
she was. She could show them her articles. They made no movement to get her stuff back, but they became uneasy. Finally, they
made a call to their commander. Those were the early stages of
the war, when the Serbian forces still cared for their image of the
proud freedom fighters in the eyes of the international community.
Angela's hopes were up.

They waited in the sun for two long hours. At one point, the
soldiers distributed water in plastic bottles among the crowds.
However, the wailing of women and children was piercing their
ears. They were getting on their nerves, and the soldiers were
more and more impatient. They were pushing the people around
roughly, as though they were a herd of sheep. Angela remembered
the old partisan movies. The soldiers were like the Germans

on the screen. In the films like *Battle of Sutjeska* or *Battle of Neretva*, the Germans were beating the prisoners, snapping at them, like a pack of wolves hungry for blood and violence. Who and where were the good guys now? She had the feeling the whole situation was getting out of control. Any moment they could pull the triggers and just shoot everybody with their Kalashnikovs.

At last, a huge military jeep with the crest of the Yugoslav People's Army pulled up in the middle of the square. A tall, dark man of approximately her age stepped out. He seemed familiar to her, from the newspapers or from the news. Rešić, Reškić... Raškić, yes, Jovan Raškić... He was a Serbian leader from *Republika Srpska* Krajina. She remembered he was previously a doctor in Knin, but now occupied a high political and military post in the newly proclaimed Republic of Srpska Krajina. She hesitated; maybe he would see through her tale of a journalist. She had to give it a shot. Her English was her advantage.

'Hello, mister. I am Maria King, a journalist from the Guardian. You must let me free. You must return my car. You must order your soldiers to put back anything they might have taken from it. My notebook, my cell phone, my purse, valuables... You and your new republic do not want to make a bad impression on the international community, do you?'

Angela's voice sounded reasonable, yet trembled with fear. She realized that her life was in the hands of this authoritative man, who slowly put down his Ray Ban sunglasses and looked her deeply in the eye.

'Miss, I am sorry. You don't tell me what I must do. I am in command here. I give orders.'

'Yes, of course, but...'

'No but... Tell me!'

Angela's eyes opened with terror. She stuttered:

'Tell you what, Sir?'

'About you...'

His English was limited like she had hoped. Maybe, there was a chance... She repeated her story about writing a report on Drniš and about the Easter celebrations in the surrounding villages. She was breaking her tongue with Croatian topological names to make her tale more trustworthy. It was lame. Who would in the heat of war write about easter eggs? He seemed weary of listening to it, shouted a few orders to his subordinates in Serbian, and beckoned her to follow him into the jeep. He sat in the driver's seat with the words:

'We will check your documents, miss. Come with me.'

'They took everything from me, I have nothing. Everything is in the car. You cannot capture journalists. What kind of army are you?'

He started the engine on and drove through the crowds, sending up clouds of dust behind them.

'You have nothing to fear, Miss King. It is your name, isn't it? I am taking you to our headquarters, and we will only check.'

'And how will I get back?'

'We will see when we check.'

Angela looked at his profile as he was concentrating on the bumpy road ahead. She remembered from the news reports that Raškić, no matter what he stood for, was a handsome man. He was very tall, almost two meters, with a slender body, not spoilt by a beer belly like most in their fifties. His hair was nearly black, very thick, only here and there entwined with silver threads. His high forehead, tanned and wide, displayed deep lines of worries. Maybe everything wasn't so perfect in this new *Republika Srpska Krajina* after all. His eyebrows were black and the brown eyes under the thick eyelashes gave her a somehow warm impression, as though there could be human feelings and goodness in them. Maybe he was only doing his job and he would let her go in time. How would he check on her? She was lucky they had stolen her car and papers. It seemed even Raškić wasn't thinking of trying to get it back. Her laptop, mobile, money, purse became spoils of war. So he would have to look her up on the internet? Did they have internet in Krajina? Anyway, his knowledge of English... Angela knew that there was a reporter by the name of Maria King writing for The Guardian. Her only hope was that there wouldn't be any pictures of her beside her articles, a custom so popular lately to make the terrible news more personal, more authentic. She looked at the man again. Although he was a military man, he seemed to care about his looks and appearance. She could see his moustache was finely trimmed, and she could sense a fresh aftershave in the air. She was speaking incessantly, trying to persuade him not to drive further, to let her go now, to drop her off. He said it was safer for her to stay in his car and repeated that she had nothing to fear. The longer the drive, the bigger was her anxiety. It was more and more obvious that he would take her prisoner. She felt sorry for herself and started to cry. Through tears, she pleaded:

'Please, Sir, have pity. I have family in England. I would like to go.'

He shuddered, and looked her deep in the eyes.

'Miss King, nothing will happen to you. You are safe with me.'

How could she believe that? They stopped in the middle of the road. The man pulled out a black cloth.

'I have to bind your eyes. Safety precautions, you do understand, don't you?'

Gently, he blindfolded her. It felt almost as though he was stroking her hair. Still, she was terrified. How would she ever get away? So far, she was memorizing the few villages they were passing. They were taking narrow roads, nearly cattle trails. Maybe she could still find her way back, even if she walked. From now on, she was in the dark. She couldn't see the turns of the road ahead. It made her terrified and sick in her stomach. She wanted to see ahead, yet she didn't dare to remove the blindfold. Suddenly, her stomach turned. She said she would vomit, that he had to let her out of the car. He stopped at a corner of the road and let her expel her breakfast until bitter bile came up. He pushed a plastic bottle in her hand later.

'Here, you can wash your mouth. The blindfold stays. I cannot take any risks.'

They drove for a long time. Angela was exhausted by the time they arrived at a village school building. She didn't know where they were, but was grateful for the fresh air of pines and the fact that she could finally look around her. The school was silent and empty, as though the kids were on holidays. Raškić took her to a house across the street. There was a sign in Cyrillic next to the door: *Upravnik*, headmaster. He said to her in a low voice:

'These are our headquarters, the house of the headmaster. I will check your statements now.'

He turned to his guards and shouted in Serbian.

'Lock her in the headmaster's bedroom for now. I will give orders later.'

Two young men in uniforms of the Yugoslav People's Army with *šajkača*, a Serbian military cap, pushed her up the stairs, and the door key turned on her twice. She immediately approached the windows. They were wide and faced away from the school, to the hills across the valley. There were pinewoods all around with some newly leaved beeches shining in fluorescent green. Angela shivered with cold. They were away from the sea and its mild climate. Probably, it was somewhere higher in the mountains. Where? She couldn't see the village or town from her window, just hills, green and lush, in the prime of spring.

In an hour, a bearded man came in with a tray filled with fresh pastries and coffee. Raškić followed, took over the tray and sent him out. He closed the door behind him. They were alone. Angela was sure her story had caught ground, and he would let her go. Raškić actually smiled at her and poured them both coffee. He also filled two small glasses with *rakija*, plum brandy, offering her one. She took the glass gratefully. She wanted to clean her teeth and wash the vomit out of her mouth badly. Maybe, the brandy would do it. The glasses clinked. It was almost like two old friends drinking a toast together. They drank up. Then Raškić said curtly in Serbian.

'I checked you, *žena*. You are not who you say you are.'

Angela shuddered and protested weakly. It was over, but she was so shocked that she continued in English forgetting she should not understand him. She stuck to English, he answered in Serbian.

'But, I am Maria King. Haven't you found my articles in Guardian on-line?'

'I have. I have found some articles, and also a picture of Maria King. She's a young girl of maybe thirty, with a Hispanic face and black curly hair. No plastic surgeon in the world could change her into you.'

Angela remained silent. She held out her empty glass, and he poured her another brandy. The colorless liquid disappeared down her throat. As from a distance, his words reached her ears.

'What are we going to do with you?'

Tears welled up in her eyes. She thought that now they would accuse her of being a foreign spy and torture her to death to reveal the Croatian war secrets she knew absolutely nothing about. She switched to Croatian:

'I don't know anything. I was just driving to Drniš to fetch my mother-in-law. She is ill, you know. She has cancer. She needed to go to Šibenik to have her treatment.'

'Is it so? Where was your husband? Why didn't he go?'

Angela looked at the floor. An awkward silence filled the room.

'What kind of man would send his wife to the front line to fetch his mother?'

Angela burst in sobs. Raškić's question remained in the air together with the desperation of her last few years of life with Damir. What kind of man would do that, indeed? A drunk, a careless drunk, whose only thoughts revolve around the bottle... Raškić took a cup of coffee from the table and exchanged it for the brandy glass in her trembling hands. For a moment, he held her hand, trying to steady her trembling. She was too distracted to notice.

'Maybe we can work out something. Tell me your real name first.'

'Angela Bekić, Mali prolaz, Šibenik. I work as a tourist guide for the city of Šibenik. You can check this on the municipality page. My photo is there, too. I provide guidance in English, German, and French. I also take tourists to the Krka Waterfalls... I mean I took them before this...'

'Yes, before we founded *Republika Srpska* Krajina. You will take them again when the fights cease, don't worry. The justice will prevail.'

Angela looked up. Did she hear hope in his voice? Serbians were winning the territory, so the boys at the Croatian outpost said.

'I need a person with knowledge of English here at the headquarters. You know that UNPROFOR has positioned troops in the territory, and we communicate in English with them. Unfortunately, I speak little English.'

'Well, you worked as a doctor. You know medicine, and somebody else knows German and English.'

Raškić lifted his eyebrows in surprise.

'You know who I am, Angela?'

'Well, only from newspaper reports. I don't really...'

'Yeah, from the Croatian press, I can imagine. Anyway, here are your options. You're a prisoner of Republika Srpska Krajina. You can work for me and translate correspondence, documents, and reports, or join the other prisoners at the school. But in any case, you are here to stay and you'll be locked up.'

Angela froze. Those were the options. She sensed it was better to do the translations than to join the fate of the women imprisoned at the school. She had no idea at the time of the interrogation why they were capturing them. As I said, Paula, that was the beginning of the war, and little intelligence came through as to the nature of Serbian warfare. The only thing well known was that they were using the military resources of the Yugoslav People's Army from Belgrade, which was the pillar of Milošević in his expansion policy. Angela knew that Raškić was one of the intellectuals in the new Republika Srpska Krajina, the state of Serbians living in the territory of Croatia. She would try her luck and work for that enigmatic political figure. Sooner or later, the opportunity to escape would present itself. Maybe the NATO would back up the Croatian independence and help Tudjman to discipline the Serbians at last. They would liberate the territory, and she could maybe stay alive."

"It was clever of her. God knows what they would do to her at that school. Was it a logor, nona?"

"Yes, Paula. Though Angela had some doubts about it later. She confessed them to me. She felt like a collaborator, like a traitor. After all, she was helping the enemy with her skills, wasn't she? Still, when she realized what the soldiers were doing at the school, she stuck to her job. There were few logors, women camps in Croatia, but the one at Kijevo was terrible. Like the rest of them in Bosnia and later in Kosovo. Animals, men can be such animals!"

"And how did she escape from there?"

"The story is crazy. Angela told me she was beginning to like him. She said Raškić was kind to her, and she was grateful to him for... well, keeping her away from the logor. She soon realized he had fallen in love with her at first sight. She resisted her feelings. Yet, she was more and more looking forward to their long conversations about the history of Knin and Croatia, nationalities, conflicts and life in general. She said that he had explained to her the other side of the conflict, and that somehow, she came to comprehend the reasons for the Serbian revolt against

Tudjman. Still, she found their violence and mass rapes horrible, and on a few occasions spoke up to Raškić about it. She wanted him to break away from his troops..."

"And, what did he have to say in response?"

Maria fell silent for a while. The only sound in the room was her heavy breathing. Paula waited impatiently, fearing that her *nona* would stop her tale. Yet, in a trembling voice, Maria went on.

"Angela said he shut up and turned away. Sometimes, he would immediately send her to her room and be furious, but nothing else. Well, I am not sure about Angela's feelings, but it was obvious Raškić's love was genuine. He was courting her, and Angela, while accepting, she also feared his courtship. She was careful to avoid physical closeness, and he behaved like a gentleman; he never pushed anything, although she was literally at his mercy. She started to like him. She said during the nights she had dreams about him, about them running away together... she from alcohol, he from war. She felt terrible: a traitor, a cheap slut. She was a conformist, right? At home in Šibenik, she had adapted to a drunk, now she adapted to a mass murderer. However, she remained aloof and hid her feelings until one late summer afternoon when she almost got killed. The tension was increasing and she was trying to find out how the Serbian, UNPROFOR and Croatian forces were positioned. She wanted to escape. Raškić began to trust her more, yet used coded texts. Every message which she was translating only had numbers instead of names of the places. Random numbers, not even the coordinates. She would finish the text on the computer, and Raškić would insert the data afterwards. He was storing his correspondence in files protected by passwords. She said that she regretted bitterly that her computer skills were not good enough. Had her boys been there, they would have cracked the passwords easily. Thus, she never saw real names or places. In a case of a fax message, Raškić or his aides would blacken out everything which could give her a lead. On that afternoon, he went away and sloppily put the keys of the safe in his unlocked desk drawer. It was a one-time opportunity, and she grabbed it. Another man surprised her, yet Raškić returned in time to save her. Of course, when the lights went out, he came to her bedroom to claim the reward."

"So, he did rape her after all, didn't he?"

"Well, yes and no."

"To her horror, Angela received him with joy. She said she had fallen in love, too. There was no going back. She said she felt that he was the love of her life. It was like an Indian summer. She felt passion, tenderness, gratitude... and all the time horror. How could she love somebody who was responsible for war crimes? How could she? Nearly every day she heard what was going on next door, and she was making love to the monster in command? She put a warning into the text for UNPROFOR. SE-CUNDO MULIERIBUS IN CARCERE INFIRMORUM... help sick women in prison! She cleverly put it as a Latin citation in the text, as a saying written on a tomb in Knin, hoping that Raškić's medical Latin was not good enough to decipher it. Well, there came no reaction whatsoever.

Her Serbian lover came to her every night. She was trying to imagine that he was raping her, but she knew it was not true. She simply loved him. In his warm, passionate embrace, she managed to escape the nightmares, the terrible dreams she had every night after her lover left. In them, her friends and family were pulling her through the narrow streets of Šibenik with her head naked as a sheared sheep, the treatment of whores who slept with enemy forces during the WW2. She told me she didn't bother about protection, as she had long before lost her monthly bleedings. Her moods oscillated between despair and joy, between remorse and hope. Every day was like a walk on the razor's edge. It was a crazy, feverish autumn, in which for many days she stopped thinking of ever fleeing back to Šibenik. By the early December, Raškić trusted her fully. They even spoke of spending their life together, divorcing their spouses and getting married after the war, the outcome of which was becoming unsure. It was nothing but illusions, Paula. You see, even if they had managed to stay alive, there would have been no place on the territory of the former Yugoslavia where they could live peacefully. Once the nationalists incensed the pyres of hate, there was no amount of blood which could put out the flames."

"*Nona*, can I say something?"

"Yes, dear."

"I think this Angela made up her feelings for the man in order to survive the whole ordeal. There was no love, just fear and hate. She must have made it up, this love for the Serbian. Tell me what would happen to her if she turned him down? What choice did she have? Rape... well, mass rape!"

"I don't know, Paula. Maybe you're right. Love and hate have a million faces, and sometimes they dwell closely together. Who knows what face love has in a war like that? I am just recollecting Angela's life. I think you should know about her. Unfortunately, I have never written any notes on her."

"How did she come to Medica Zenica, then?"

"One day towards the end of the year, Angela got a funny gift from Raškić which opened the abyss of the dark depression like salt opens old wounds. He brought her an Advent calendar! She was crying in secret for days, for her sons and the joy with which she used to prepare an Advent Calendar for them each Christmas. Pain stung her heart like the bites of a thousand snakes. She should be in Šibenik with her family. She should be decorating the pine tree and baking cookies. Instead, she was whoring with the enemy. What kind of woman would do that?

Only then, she made up a plan. She would come back rich, so rich, that they would never have to be short of anything again. She would make Damir go into treatment. She would rebuild her life.

She knew of Raškić's money reserves in the safe. The huge amounts were for provisions like food and payments, but most important, he also kept some drugs and the money for them in the safe. Ever since an incident with Petar, Raškić's aide, which had almost cost her her life, she was kind to the brute, for she didn't want to risk another row. During daytime, Raškić was away a lot, so Petar was her supervisor very often. At first, they had short coffee breaks together, making small talk and chatting about trivial matters. Slowly, they became allies. Soon they exchanged secret signs behind Raškić's back, not always kind gestures, as two people working for the same demanding commander. She drank plum brandy during one whole night with Petar. Repulsive though he was, she needed to bond with him. It was part of her carefully devised plan to escape. Petar's trust was quickly gained over a bottle of brandy and with some flattering words. He even called her 'Angela, our *Chetnik* Dalmatian girl', and patted her cheek.

When Raškić was away for a couple of days before Christmas, Petar brought in a new supply of dollars and German marks. Now was the moment... she decided to act. On the following afternoon, Petar made a mistake which she had been waiting for: he was careless with the safe key. He put it on the desk, forgetting about it, and went about his business, whatever that was. She was working silently on a long text, a new plan of the international community for solving the Balkan problem. Petar didn't come back to fetch the key until the evening. She smiled at him and offered him brandy. They drank together, her glass filled with water, while she poured the man *rakija* enhanced by a strong dose of morphine. Raškić's secret drawer full of drugs was a blessing. Petar was soon staggering in his chair. Angela knew when the guards changed. It was a lucky night, for the last shift, both of the young soldiers at the front door, were to go to the front on the following day, thus presenting a one time opportunity to confuse the trails. She had checked the schedule in the office carefully. She waited until five minutes before the change. At the right moment, she put her dark green military coat and heavy boots on. She stuck her woolen scarf, a thick hood, and a pair of warm gloves down her trousers. She had taken the money out of the safe in the afternoon, while she was alone in the office. It waited under the desk in a simple plastic bag covering the crest engraved moneybag. Now she put it into Petar's bag. Should the guards search them, she could play innocent. She summoned him to his feet:

'Come on, Petar, let's find a peaceful spot and celebrate this!'
'What?'

The dose was too strong. He couldn't get to his feet. With difficulty, she pulled him up.

'Time for a pee, Petar!'

He smiled and obliged. They passed the guards in front of the headmaster's house.

'I'm taking him for a pee! I don't want him to pass water in Raškić's office, do I?'

Angela shrugged her shoulders innocently.

'He drank too much tonight!'

The guard laughed heartily.

'What else is new? Do you need help?'

'No, no, you can't leave your post. We'll be back in a minute.'

He gave her a dirty look.

'Well, hold him well, Angela!'

She smiled wryly.

'I've seen worse.'

'I bet you have,' was all she heard him saying in her back. She dragged the drunken man towards the little pinewood, where she leant his heavy body on a tree trunk. It was some hundred meters away, in the darkness. Surely, they would seek a hidden spot for his business, wouldn't they?

From the shadow, she had a good overview of the court, which was alight with streetlights. The guards were about to exchange their positions and give each other the latest report. She would wait until the situation was clear. Suddenly, a cry, like a wolf's or an owl's howl, pierced the dark night. The fresh guards and the ones she passed jumped in fear. For a moment, they ducked into the fighting position. She heard a click as they unfastened their rifles to shoot. They would fire away at any sound now. She held her breath. She had a feeling they were aiming at her directly. However, they must have realized the cry was coming from the school building. They stood up and relaxed. Angela knew it was her ticket to freedom. The pain of another woman would set her free. The guards would probably forget to report to each other about her and Petar, who slept like a log, oblivious to everything around him. She had to follow her plan now.

Sweating all over her body, she dragged the drugged man further into the wood, where there was a deep gully. He was as heavy as a sack of stones. At last, she shoved him into the gully and he fell down the slope like a corpse. She followed, and tried his veins to see whether he was still breathing, wishing with all her heart he would die of overdose. The pulse was there. There was no return. The risk was too much. She pulled Petar's military knife out of his boot, lifted his head, almost tenderly, and swiftly cut the man's throat. He stirred, and his eyes opened wide. She was afraid he could make a noise, but he didn't. The knife was sharp and the cut deep. He collapsed to the ground, this time for good. The blood drenched his fat belly, staining his bag. She carefully took out the plastic bag, leaving the money bag empty. Then she started to walk away following the gully downhill. When they would find him eventually, let them think he had taken the money and was trying to flee, but another villain robbed and murdered him in the attempt. There were so many around it wouldn't be anything new.

Her pace was giddy and she was trembling with fear and cold. She hoped Raškić would not search for her. Maybe they would meet sometime in the future, when everything was over, and she would explain... Not the murder, her longing for home... After walking for half an hour, she stopped and pulled all the warm garments on. She stuffed the money, packed in smaller, transparent plastic bags in her underpants, and filled her bra with handfuls of used, smelly banknotes. Didn't she have the most expensive tits in the world now? She smiled to herself with relief. So far, so good! There were some eighty kilometers of walking ahead! It was snowing heavily. Good, the snow will cover whatever traces she might have left at the bottom of the gully, where deer was seeking shelter from the bombs. She could see their tracks, and shuddered at the thought that there were bears and wolves treading those mountains, too.

The night was foggy and she couldn't see a thing in front of her. It was scary, yet perfect for the flight! She didn't want to steal any of the military maps for fear the Serbians would panic for their positions and send a massive search party after her. It would mean they would bring in the dogs which would find her tracks quickly enough. Yet, she studied the way home carefully. Her knowledge of navigation from the happy times when she was sailing the sea with her teenage friends helped. Some time ago, she had found out that the village, in which the street signs were all set up in Serbian Cyrillic, was no other than Kijevo, only an hour's drive from her home. She memorized some of the key points, and knew that she would have to walk southwest for days, or rather nights, before she would reach her people. First, she would try with her mother-in-law in Drniš."

"I told you *nona*, it was hate. She hated Petar. She hated Raškić, too. She would cut his throat just like that."

Paula snapped her fingers. There was silence on the other side of the room. Then Maria said in a low voice.

"She was forced to kill, but she was not proud of it."

"It was self-defense. If she hadn't done it, she might be dead now. Did she come home?"

"Well, she walked by night and rested during the days. The nights were long, so in two days, in the small hours of the day, she arrived to Drniš, which was curiously empty of either people or soldiers. She could see that her mother-in-law's house was empty, too. So the old woman must have come to her hospital somehow. Or was she taken prisoner like herself? The front door was locked, but she knew how to get inside through the cellar. She found some food and rested during the day, avoiding the windows and trembling that a pillage party might get hungry for the kitchen appliances and break in. She kept the cellar passage open, just in case. She tried the phone, but it was dead. She was wondering where her mother-in-law was. Had she made it to Šibenik? Who had driven her? Did her cancer advance? Was she in a hospital? Angela had been away for nearly nine months! She didn't know who was holding Drniš, and the electricity was switched off, so the radio and television were dead. She knew she had to get away as soon as possible. She found an old road map and took it. It was better than no map at all. She took some provisions and in the following night continued her solitary march to Šibenik. She was hoping that the lovely seaport was still in Croatian hands.

In the first light of a pale pink winter dawn, she entered the house at Mali prolaz four days later. The family, including her mother-in-law, sat at the table gathered for breakfast. They stared at her as though they would see a ghost.

'Mama!'

The youngest Tome, only seventeen, jumped in her arms. Then, Mario, nineteen, stood up from the table, and at last Bruno, twenty-four, held her in his arms for a long time. Tears poured down her cheeks. Her boys! So grown up, real men... She was beyond herself with happiness.

'Where have you been?'

A hoarse, hung over voice came from the back of the dining room. She looked into Damir's dimmed eyes and saw his reddened eyeballs, his irises shining with malice. Nothing had changed. She was back nine months ago in the same movie. Damir was drinking. She could have died on the front, she could have been raped, tortured, cut in pieces, he would hold to his bottle. She turned to her mother-in-law asking:

'How are you, Mother?'

The old woman stood up and embraced her.

'I'm better. They say they have cured me. When I die, it will be of old age. What more could I hope for?'

'How did you come to Šibenik on that day?'

'The Croatian Red Cross evacuated Drniš two days later, and they drove me directly to the hospital.'

Angela stroked the old woman's pale cheeks with her palms. Seeing her fingers crusted with mud and earth, she realized how dirty and smelly she was from her long march home and apologized. The old woman had tears in her eyes:

'Were you captured when you wanted to bring me to the hospital?'

'Yes. They wouldn't let me go. Last week, I could escape.'

'Didn't they release you, I mean, let you go?'

Damir was not even looking at her.

'No, they didn't. The commander was away and they weren't careful.'

'I see, the commander. . . Where is our car?'

'Damir, they took it away from me. I don't know.'

'How stupid of you! Why did you drive to the front?'

His mother took things in her hands.

'Damir, if for once you sobered up, you would remember, that it was you, you alone who should have taken me to the hospital that day. Angela, tell us everything! Where did they keep you?'

'I was quite close to Šibenik all this time, though I didn't know that for a while. I was in Kijevo. You see, the Serbians occupy a village or a town, and they change all the street signs. Also, I couldn't take a walk to find out, could I?'

'Mama, some women came home a few months ago. They captured them in spring, at the same time as they did you. They released them in autumn. They were saying that in Kijevo. . . that there is a women's prison and they. . . some were with child. . . '

'Bruno, don't worry. They used me as a translator, so I was working at the headquarters all these months. I was a prisoner, but nobody hurt me. . . they didn't release me, I escaped.'

Damir was watching her under his dark brows. He drank up his coffee and went to the door.

'I bought a new car. I used the savings. I can't commute to Split by bus.'

Angela just nodded and moved from the door to let him pass. He had neither a hug nor a word of welcome for her. He couldn't know anything. Even if he did, he should greet her. She had escaped death no matter how. Why was he so cold? Had they ever been in love? She smelled his breath, and it came back to her. It was not her Damir. It was the alcohol in his system. She was exhausted.

'I will take a bath and change. Then we can talk.'

'Mama, we have school. . . '

'I'll be here, Angela. We can talk.'

Her mother-in-law gently took her coat. Angela untied the muddy boots and headed for the bathroom. She needed a hot bath and a few days of rest. Then the whole nightmare will be over. Or, so she thought.

Her sons were happy that she was home. They celebrated Christmas together, and they even had gifts and a tree. It was a juniper bush, picked by the coastal road in a hurry, but it shined through the grey rainy days like a light at the end of the tunnel. Still, Angela was changed. She couldn't fit into her former life.

She took up her old job, only that there weren't any tourists to take around anymore. Šibenik was empty. . . a ghost town, a town of ghosts. People, the majority only women, were sitting around waiting for the shells sent from the hills above. Still, there were people who cared, and one such person was the director of the city museum. He employed her, asking her to work fast and long hours. She had to store valuables from various historical monuments around the city, take photographs of the items, and write protocols, then pack them up to be ready for transport should worse come to worst. It was fine. She got away from home, forgot the hostile drinking of her husband, and busied her mind with beautiful works of art.

However, she was restless and depressed. She felt as though she was on a run... either from the Serbians or from her husband or from herself. Her daily escape into the past lifted her spirits and filled her with hopes for the future. The war would have to end eventually. Then, she would go and dig out her secret dollars and marks. They would be able to buy a house or maybe two houses; there was so much money. She would buy a present to Damir... a motorboat, and she would heal him of his addiction, no matter what it takes. They would start anew. They would grow back together and embrace a new sunshine in their life. They would find joy and color, together again. In the colds and rains of January 1992, she could almost smell that new spring in her nostrils. Yet, judging by her husband, it was not to be. Damir was still cold and reserved towards her, but his mother made all the difference. She was looking after the house, cooking, supporting them. Like Angela, she had looked death in the face, and she appreciated life.

Did Angela think of Jovan? Did she miss him? Sometimes she dreamt of their hot nights together. Yet, she focused all her attention on Damir. With tenderness and activities, she managed to pull him away from his bottle for short intervals. When Šibenik was in a blackout for the fear of air raids, they would retire to their bedroom in the loft, draw the curtains, and put on a little candle. After long years of cold sheets between them, in the eyes of the danger, they would finally make love like two teenagers again. It was the beginning. Damir drank less, but there was still a strange uncertainty in his gestures, which Angela ascribed to her long absence. Many times his almond eyes were searching for an answer in hers, an answer to a question which remained unsaid.

Well, the new spring came with its full regalia: the merry birdsong, the warm sun, and the perfume of flowers, as though the shelling and shooting were from a different world. In April, Angela's body filled with new energy and new firmness. She was gaining weight. At first, she thought it funny, when she felt a small tickling inside her. It took her a while before enlightenment struck her: she was pregnant. Was it still possible at forty-six? She went to see her gynecologist, who confirmed her suspicions... well into her fifth month. The baby had to have been conceived sometime in late autumn. There was no way Angela could simply pass this child for her husband's. She would have to speak up. What would she say? Would she tell the truth: that she had loved the man? Would she say she had saved her life by sleeping with the commander? Would she tell his name? Angela wished she were dead. Why was she striving? Did she want to bear a little *Chetnik*, a souvenir of her detention at Kijevo? She found a moment when Damir was sober and they could talk.

'Damir, I must tell you something.'

She could see the coldness in his eyes. His cheeks dropped, and he bent his head.

'You mean the affair with Raškić?'

Angela lost her breath.

'What?'

'Well, people are talking in Šibenik. They say you were not in prison in Kijevo, but lived comfortably with Raškić.'

'And you? Do you believe I was in Kijevo for fun?'

'No, no... I know you would never be away from our sons. But what is it, Angela?'

'I am changed.'

'I can see you are changed. I may be a drunk, but I'm not a fool. Tell me, what did they do to you?'

'They... He... I had to do it or I would be killed.'

As soon as she had said it, she knew it had to be the truth. She would never have gotten away with the map incident had not Raškić been filling her with his semen every night. Had she invented that other Angela, enjoying the nights with the Serbian, in order to escape the reality? She was not sure. Was she that sick? Damir held his breath. After a minute of awkward silence, he said:

'Are you blaming me? Because I didn't go...'

'No, you couldn't...'

'For if you do blame me, Angela, think! If I had gone, I would have been killed!'

She looked into his eyes. They were full of spite and fire. How could he hate her so much? After all that she had done for him, for the boys and for his mother? She had to go on, though.

'It's not that... I...'

'What is it then? Have you done something against Croatia?'

'Damir, I'm expecting a child...'

'You aren't!'

'I am. I'm in the fifth month.'

'Can't you get rid of it?'

'Not any more. At least, the abortion brings risks... at my age. Besides, it's illegal.'

'But it's legal to rape a woman!'

Angela burst in tears. She remembered Jovan's kisses and tenderness. What would his reaction be if he knew? Would he protect her? Would he demand an abortion? Was it high treason for a Serbian leader to love a Catholic? Was it love or rape? Was it life or death? She wailed like an owl. All the bitterness of the past year came up like the bile after vomiting. She hid her face in her palms in shame. She should have pushed Raškić back. She should rather have died, cut his throat, jumped at the electric fence, drowned in the toilet, she should have done anything but let it happen. But she didn't. Oh, treacherous life... She had to stop it...

Then she felt Damir's arms around her shoulders. He was patting her on the back, whispering soothing words. Maybe there was hope after all.

'Damir, I could go away for a year and come back with the baby. We can say it's ours. Nobody will count months... It would bring new life to our family. The boys...'

'You're crazy! I could never bring up a little *Chetnik*! I'd rather strangle it like a cat!'

Angela saw coldness and hate in his eyes. She knew there was no place for her in his life. There was no future for them. Either raped or voluntarily, she was branded a *Chetnik* whore, and there was no amount of alcohol in the world that could make her husband forget that. He would always see the letter Č for *Chetnik* burning on her forehead, and he would surely hate the child. Even if she had given the child away somehow, for she knew it was possible, would he ever forget the fact that she was in bed with the enemy?

During the night, weighing all the arguments for and against, she made up her mind. After the family left the house in the morning, she sat down and wrote a letter to her husband. She would go away, suffer her detention to the end and bring the child to the world, and then make the decision on whether she could come back and continue living with him. If not, he would never hear of her again. She would disappear from the face of the earth, and he could tell their sons and the people in Šibenik anything he wanted. She packed some stuff in a suitcase and drove out of town. Her destination was north, she would try to get to Slovenia."

"And the money, *nona*? Did she pick up the money?"

"I don't know, dear. I met her later, when the baby was born, in Medica Zenica."

"Did she give the baby away?"

"I don't know that, either, Paula. I soon left Zenica, and I had to worry about you, about us, about other women. There were so many."

"I hope she's alive. Such a brave woman..."

"Yes, she had guts, didn't she?"

"Well, I hope she gave the child away and went back to her family. After all the atrocities, her husband should have seen reason!"

"Yeah, Paula. Maybe she did. Maybe he did. Good night, sleep tight!"

Part II

Life goes on

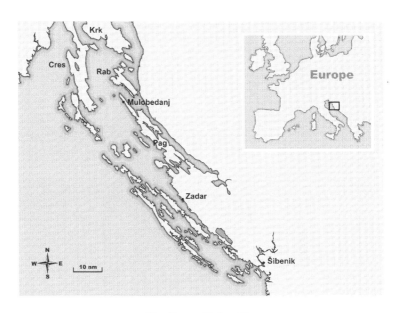

Northern Dalmatia.

Pag, 2009

The peaceful bay of Mulobedanj on the north Dalmatian island of Pag glistened with morning silver while the summer sun was sleepily rising on the horizon. Maria quickened her pace to come to the pier in time. Her greeting to the day, her short, solitary walk among the ancient olive groves, was finished. Her work began. She had to choose from the fish catch for tonight, before the fishermen sold it to the restaurants. She could hear Dario's diesel pumping along the calm surface of the sea. The noise was devastating. It was his boat, no doubt at all. He had to make some more miles, yet in the *bonaca*, the complete absence of all winds, it would not take him long.

Maria's white shirt and jeans were too hot for the day. She would change later. Her tan was deep. For a good part of winter and spring, she had been working outdoors, supervising the construction of the huge glasshouse where wastewater from the hotel could be recycled to irrigate fresh vegetables throughout the season. At her age, she was still a stunning woman. Her thick straight hair would have been silver for years hadn't she been dying it blond. She always wore a ponytail. The age agreed with her. The wrinkles and sun freckles on her face did not take away from the piercing look of her curious green eyes. Men still looked at her and admired her fine features and her fit, strong body on long, athletic legs always walking and moving. Maria, though, never took any notice of men anymore. She had had enough in her lifetime. "I don't need men in my life, I need life in my men," she would often joke, closing all further discussions. While Dario, the most successful of all fishermen in the north of the island, was constantly making advances at her, she pretended not to notice and remained friendly and businesslike. Buying good quality fresh fish was much more important to her than a love affair.

The path along the coast was wide and paved with polished stones, so that the tourists could walk barefoot and the bicycle rickshaws could transport goods and baggage over the five hundred yards from the village road to the hotel. With rocks at each side and evergreen shrubs, it meandered along the waterline. Here and there, there were tiny beaches with white pebbles shining like lampions. In between, flat rocks offered space for bathers to warm their bones and bodies from the first rays in the morning until late afternoon. The pines smelled harshly fresh and invited the loud choir of birds to chitchat their summer songs. The place was heaven, not meant for work, but nevertheless there were more people employed here in Mulobedanj and Dudiči than in the two towns of the island – Novalja and Pag. It was all because of the first Dalmatian ecological hotel, Perovica, named after the long bay with a pebble beach from where Maria was hurrying to the little harbour.

Hotel Perovica was perched on the slope like a crow's nest, two hundred yards above the beach Perovica, in the vast olive groves, which Romans planted two thousand years ago. For a while, the bumpy and rugged trunks had been objects of scientific research. The ancient trees became protected national monuments, and tended by a team of agricultural engineers from Zadar. They came once a month and checked on their condition. For centuries, peasants had well known how to grow olives. Now scientists with PhDs in agriculture were searching to discover the right treatments, the right fertilizers, and the watering regimes. Villagers had their fun with the Zadar people. They joked about them ignoring their instructions most of the time. Well, the islanders surely could understand their trees! They even named them – you could sit in the silvery shadow of Aurelia or under the vast branches of Poseidon, there were Old Martha and Jumpy Ram or Soft Baby, the folk imagery speaking to the guests from the tiny metal plates screwed to the uneven trunks was creative and vivid. Such a tree was so precious, that they even passed it on to the next generation separately – one heir would inherit the land and another the tree it grew upon – do not try to imagine the cadastral book of Pag! The olive trees were part of the hotel building; they were growing on terraces and through balcony floors. One of the most severe conditions set to the architects and builders fifteen years ago had been that no matter what, not a single ancient tree should fall during or after the construction of the hotel.

The building was a cascading mass of grey island stone huts, or so it seemed, for the facade imitated the fishermen's beach huts, which for centuries, people had been using to store the nets and fishing gear. The interior was simple, yet with all modern comfort: cable TV, shiny, tiled bathrooms, terraces with scented lavender and verbena bushes in clay pots, and free wireless internet access. The building fit perfectly into the landscape, except perhaps for the grey, metallic roofs, shining with hundreds of sun collectors. The electricity was from the sun, which was shining on the collectors for ten months of the year. The famous Dutch architect Gaastra Luivield, who got the commission to design and oversee the building of the hotel, won a prize for his design of the Ecohotel Perovica in 1997. Luivield was a great admirer of the Austrian Friedenreich Hundertwasser and his philosophy of environmentalism, so the hotel complex reflected the ideas of blending into the landscape and into the lives of the islanders. As the master Hundertwasser would say on planting and preserving trees in towns and city centres, "If man walks in nature's midst, then he is nature's guest and must learn to behave as a well-brought-up guest." Love for olive trees was the law in Perovica. Although Hundertwasser himself was invited to spend a week at the hotel when it was opened, he had not lived to see the place, really, only photographs, which he praised very highly. Gaastra Luivield, on the other hand, was an old friend of Maria's, and came every year with his blond second wife and four children aged from twenty-one to one. They would spend a week or a fortnight enjoying the fruit of his work and imagination.

The hotel had fifty-three very differently sized rooms, each with a view of the sea. The guests could admire the islands across the channel – Cres and Mali Lošinj. The town lights across the water were glimmering and luring dreams on the clear nights. The inside part of the structure, built directly into the rock and practically with no day light whatsoever, were household places like kitchens, laundry, elevators, spa area with small swimming pool and several whirlpool bathtubs as well as storages. The rooms had central heating, and many guests from Scandinavia enjoyed not only spring and summer but also winter months, Christmas and New Year in the rough fresh *bura* and in the sun.

The ecological hotel had been an enormous demand on the management, the investors, and the whole area, but in the last decade, it brought prosperity and life to the local people. Maria had had the idea years ago, and started the enterprise with huge investment capital and the support of the local municipality, which was desperate because the small villages were dying and the youth was devoured by the coastal towns Rijeka and Zadar. She knew from the start that in order to succeed, it had to be perfect. It was a fairy tale place, indeed, and the guests streamed in. Maria knew many of them by first names. They were coming in spring for the fresh wild asparagus, wild fennel stew, and carpets of wild purple cyclamens blooming. Summer attracted them with swimming and long evening picnics on the beach, where Maria's staff were serving prosciutto and the famous hard island cheese with olive oil and herbs. In autumn, vintage parties and olive picking tours were popular, and in winter, squid fishing and roast chestnuts. Each season was a feast. Maria made sure there was always music, fun and good food with strong wine. She would have artists come, musicians, folk dancers, even illusionists. The hotel had a small library, and the guests who fell in love with a book were able to buy their copy at the reception. Body and soul should feast equally and in perfect balance with nature in the lovely Perovica.

The sun was already high when she came to the pier and was waiting for Dario to throw the rope from the boat, which she would tie to the bollards. The boat landed, and in an instant, the hellish noise of the engine stopped. The bow was squirming with a heap of nets, entangling middle sized sardines and mackerels, just right for a wonderful Spanish dish – marinated sardines in olive oil and orange juice with slices of sweet red onions. It would make a wonderful starter for this evening, but she also needed something for lunch. She spotted some nice big dragon fish and a variety of smaller white fish. She could suggest to the cooks to prepare a fish stew with corn-broth – *polenta*. The local fish stew, or *brodet*, as islanders called it, was made with garlic, Mediterranean spices and ripe tomatoes, and cooked over a small heat for a couple of hours, then strained and served with filleted dragon fish meat. For vegan guests they would serve a wild asparagus risotto, and for those who did not like fish, chicken breasts in a white cream sauce with pasta. The salad bar was rich in the month of May owing to the new glasshouse. They could serve their own vegetables, fresh and crunchy. The several Novalja bakery shops delivered the desserts. The cooks would think of the details and extra dishes to vary the theme of the day, but Maria liked to set the basic tune to the hotel cuisine herself. She knew that on vacation, food was very important.

"Hello, Dario, what have you got today?"

Her polite smile could not entice the bearded character from the cabin. His mouth was spitting vile oaths and curses like hell spitting fire.

"Fucking dolphins, they tore my nets and feasted on my fish last night. I will get them one day, they're mocking me, cheeky bastards."

"Come on, Dario, dolphins are lovely fish, they bring joy, and when they're around, there's plenty of other fish, too. Aren't you a bit happy with your nets full today, Dario?"

"Shit, Maria, there could have been more!" And the flux of swearing never stopped, and not one curse was repeated by the other.

"When you clean the nets, bring the fish to the hotel. We'll take all of them. And separate different kinds, not all mixed up in all the crates, like two days ago."

"Yes, Madam, I will. Shall I also come and cook the fish instead of your chefs? They don't know how to cook the fish, your posh city idiots. What will you make of this?"

"My city idiots are chefs and have been trained in Paris and New York, by the way. They will make marinated sardines. I reckon there are at least three crates, and for lunch the rest, mixed kinds in a *brodet* with polenta and dragon filets. Maybe they will opt for bouillabaisse. You, of course, don't know what this is, so forget it. Keep a few sardines for your dirty grill, and come to collect the pay in my office afterwards."

"Yes, Sir, madam Sir. Which dirty grill do you have in mind? Damn the day when women got into command in Dalmatia. I must have missed the doomsday a while ago, Jesus!"

And his vile monologue went on and on. Maria shrugged and turned to the village to get home before Paula woke up. She was frail and sick these days. Only a week ago, she had her last chemotherapy treatment in Zadar. Maria's face darkened, her

lines cut deep pain. When they came to the village so many
years ago, Paula was only a baby, just over one year old. She
grew fast and was as fit as a fiddle. They bought a house at the
edge of the village, on higher ground, and Maria had it renovated
in the traditional style. In the shadow of the huge fig tree, they
welcomed their neighbors, talked to them, listened to their stories,
and played with their grandchildren, who came to visit. Back
then, there were only old people in the village, no work for the
younger generation.

In the first months of their stay at Mulobedanj, the villagers
were friendly towards them, feeling sorry for the grandmother and
her granddaughter who escaped the war. They could remember
them coming ragged and tired, with one sorry Samsonite suitcase
full of dirty clothes, and as it later turned out – money. They
were survivors. It was in the summer of 1993, after the hideous
massacre of Zenica, where civilians were brutally shelled at the
peak shopping hour. The world was shocked. First the Croatian
liberation army and their general Tihomir Blaškić were accused,
later the responsibility for the attack was attributed to the Serbian outposts at Vlašić. Nobody knew who was targeting whom.
It had been the craziest of all wars, and it was going on in the
heart of Europe. Maria and Paula made a narrow escape from
Zenica. All their family died, and all the belongings, including
the personal documents, had been burnt and lost forever.

The villagers were therefore surprised when they realized that
Maria was a very wealthy woman. When they asked cautiously
where she had acquired her wealth, she would reply with a joke,
saying that "shelled trees were growing banknotes instead of
leaves in the Bosnian war", and let their curiosity go by. She
stayed at the Slavko's inn at Mulobedanj through the summer
of 1992, walking baby Paula and chatting with everybody with
humor and kindness. In October, when her new personal documents were issued by the local authorities, she started to buy real
estate – first the house, then acres of the more or less wild land
above the Perovica pebble beach, accessible by a coastline path
only ten minutes from Mulobedanj. She had to put together two
brothers' denationalized estates in order to obtain four hectares
of land with half a hectare of an ancient terraced olive grove in
the middle. It was not cheap, yet Maria paid in cash, in American dollars or German marks, so they were all more eager to sell
to her. They needed the monies, for tourism was not bringing
anything during the war. When she told Dario who sold her the
olive grove in the middle of the lands, that she would like him
to continue to tend to the trees, and that she would buy all the
produced oil at a half of its market price, he was flabbergasted.
Would he still own the trees, as was the ancient islanders' custom? No, this could complicate the hotel business too much, but
he could exploit them and tend to them. The majority of the

price in olive oil was manual labor, so Maria was willing to pay for that. They closed a contract, and she started the virgin olive oil brand Perovička, for which she organized the bottling up and sold the whole first vintage somewhere to Slovenia.

She was a mystery to her surroundings – she spoke several foreign languages, could even read Latin, and knew absolutely everything about the Croatian history. With the land contracts corroborated by the municipality and taxes paid, she took baby Paula and spent the following winter in the Netherlands. She returned in spring with a dozen of surveyors, geologists, architects, and marketing experts in tourism and catering. They could all speak English, and a few of them some Italian, so she hired a girl from Novalja to act as a translator for the lively group of young professionals. They journeyed the island, the towns, visited the industries, and explored the countryside, talked to the peasants, inquired about fish catches, vintage wines, sheep, cheese, local agriculture, and life on Pag in general. It was obvious they were brewing something up, and in late spring, when they had tanned to their skins' limits, the feasibility study for an ecological hotel above the pebble beach Perovica was finished. Maria started her investment campaign with the banks, mainly German and Austrian, who were advancing their market shares in the Balkan region at full speed. The most powerful ones were the Hypo bank, the Reiffeisen, and the Erste Group. She would not deal with them at their headquarters in Zagreb or Rijeka. She rather invited their directors over for long weekends, paid their board, and wined and dined them sumptuously. Yet, eco-hotels were still a very new idea, and bank officials, all burnt red after an afternoon in the hot Dalmatian sun, could not see the profit in serving organic food and costly wines in the middle of Croatian nowhere land, where one of the most brutal European wars in decades was still going on.

Then, a pension guest who was staying every July for two weeks at Slavko's offered his support. He knew a friend of a friend, a wealthy man, who would be interested in finding the investors for her idea, yet they would all want to remain anonymous and communicate with her through a Cyprus foundation. Maria suspected this companion to be a foreigner, maybe a diplomat profiteering from the Balkan war or simply a tycoon. So this ghost partner became her business associate, if not even a digital friend (the only communication was limited to e-mails signed MM, which Maria immediately associated with Marilyn Monroe), and their cooperation laid the financial foundation for the first ecological hotel in Dalmatia. After a few messages, all in English, they conversed in a friendly way, chatted in a private tone, but without ever seeing each other. Maria could not discover his identity. She would sometimes set verbal traps for him, but he was a clever man (or was it a woman?). He never stepped into them.

Well, Maria was the manager and co-owner, the identity of her investors – she suspected behind her ghost partner not a single person but a few – was surely hidden under the shell companies, which were recorded in the Croatian business register as owned by other companies from Lichtenstein, San Marino and Cyprus. Later, also bank loans came into play, as her associate's companies issued guarantees many times over the amounts transferred. Money rolled and nobody was particularly bothered about where it came from.

Did she mind that probably huge money laundering was going through her hotel in Perovica? For a while, she had some reservations, but in view of the terrors she had seen during the war, Maria decided it was time to let bad money go into a good cause. The money would be spent anyway, and thus at least it created new jobs. The economy of Pag was growing in many places due to this new pearl of the Adriatic hotels, and life was generally better. After a few first years, when she had put all her efforts into the promotion at international tourism and catering fairs around Europe, the guests would not stop coming. They booked their holidays months in advance, paid in advance, and the cash flow was more than positive. The hotel was highly profitable, and the secretive ghost partner invisibly happy with his investment. Anyway, it was less stressful than dealings with war deaths. People talked, but nobody knew for sure what was going on behind the walls of the Perovica ecological hotel. Financial schemes of such proportions were science fiction compared to their time-honored village life. In the end, they were all happy to have jobs and a future to live for. With every improvement, the villagers asked Maria fewer questions, until they took real pride in their Perovica and their new, successful neighbor.

The house was still very quiet. Paula was obviously sound asleep. Maria went to the kitchen to put the coffee on. Then, she took some whole meal bread and fresh cherries from the cupboard, and set the table for breakfast. It had to be nutritious and healthy, for her granddaughter needed all the strength she could get. She put salami, sheep cheese, and cottage cheese on the plates, yoghurt, and juice out of the fridge, and took the steps to the first floor. She softly opened Paula's room and peered inside. Paula was lying motionless under the duvet. Maria strained her eyes, trying to focus, yet she could not see her breathing. She panicked and jumped to the bed. Paula slowly opened her eyes, smiled faintly, saying in a quiet, almost inaudible voice:

"Not yet, *nona*, though I feel terrible today. I was sick again just an hour ago. I'm fed up with it. Why don't I just die?"

"Paula, my love, please, don't talk like that, just rest."

Maria's eyes filled with tears. It was so horrible. After all the misfortunes, she was so much looking forward to see Paula growing, thriving, finishing her high school in Zadar, then going on to study French and German literatures in Zagreb. But it was not to be. The diagnose was terrible. Paula had been feeling tired and weak last November, so she went to see the doctor, assuming that she had a flu, or a viral infection of some kind. The doctor, alarmed by her blood values, immediately sent her to a hospital for more tests. In a week, the diagnose was set to their total nightmare – Chronic Myelogenous Leukemia. They went to the University Medical Centre in Ljubljana for a second opinion, but the Slovenians came to the same terrible conclusion and urgently advised chemotherapy treatments. In the last six months, Paula was receiving the second round of the chemotherapy cocktail, which made her lose much of her hair and left little hope of recovery. She fought, though. She was young and strong, and the survival rate was high – nearly ninety percent for five years. Many patients had overcome it, and lived for years. Maria hugged her sick girl tenderly, whispering softly into her thinning black hair:

"We'll find the cure, you'll be alright. You'll see, my baby, you'll see."

* * *

Dario put up a stool in the shade of a huge mulberry tree and sat on it, preparing his tools to sew the nets piled around on the stone floor: an old tennis racket to stretch the torn loops and mend them, a long sewing needle, a nylon thread, scissors, and a flagon of white wine mixed with water and ice. He pulled the end of the net, which the dolphins enjoyed tearing to get to the fish catch earlier in the night in his lap and looked for the first hole. He would be busy for a few hours now. Patiently, as the spider weaves his broken web, Dario's fingers surely looped the torn threads together. Going to the sea almost every evening and morning, living with the seasons, that was his life. He was looking forward to planning the next spot where he would set up his nets in the deep sea.

He was pleased with himself. They had given him a huge bonus at the hotel, nearly a reward for having decorated the crates with rosemary twigs and huge lemon slices. He thought of it in the last moment, more to impress Maria than her cooks. It looked prettier and gave some extra aroma to the fish. The cooks were happy and their chef generous, but Maria was nowhere in sight.

He reflected on his past with a sigh. He had been a sea captain on a dozen of smaller vessels in the Mediterranean area for years. In his late thirties, he fell in love, settled down, and got married. His Slovenian company Plovba, which at the time sailed under the Yugoslavian flag, paid him well, and he rebuilt the old family house in the village and modernized the olive groves with the

savings. He left his job relatively young, in his fifties, as was
the custom in his profession. The stress at sea took its toll on
the people. He had two daughters, university students, Olivia
and Mira, who rather travelled to Spain for their holidays than
come to see him in Mulobedanj. After his wife Ivana had died
in a car crash on the road from Novalja almost ten years ago,
the family fell apart and children escaped their home never to
return. First, they were gone to school in Zadar, coming home
each weekend with bags full of dirty clothes and empty stomachs.
Later they were off to the university, one in Split, the other in
Zagreb. Dario had been all by himself for a decade now. It
was the toll of lonely, depressive, and boring winters. Olivia and
Mira had had enough of its grey fogs as little girls. Out of the
tourist season, the coastal towns and villages were dead and still
like graveyards after the four months of non-stop joyful cries and
feasting. The inns and holiday homes in the village were empty.
There were only a few houses occupied around the year, owned
by older people, so the children had no company of their age and
were glued to the television set or to the computer. They had a
long slippery drive to the Novalja elementary school during the
week – either Ivana or Dario took them in their old Volkswagen.
Christmas mass in the little chapel of Lun was an event. New
Year's was dull, and January could not bring enough sun to warm
their homes and their lonely hearts. The winters were wet and
cold. Grey fogs were dragging around the walls and orchards,
rains fell from the heavy black clouds, which seemed like the
sea upside down. Downpours were broken only by days of the
freezing *bura*, when shutters sang their tunes all nights long, so
that nobody could close an eye for days. Yet the *bura* meant
cold and sunny weather with an azure blue sky, and the spirits
were up with this sharp northeast wind. The heaviest of all winds
was *jugo*, the wind of desperation. It brought heavy rains with
dark souls from the south, as the old people used to say. Many a
suicide happened while *jugo* ravaged with rain and darkness over
the coast.

Dario pricked his thumb with the needle and swore under
his breath. He sucked on his finger, salted with sea and sweet
with the taste of blood, and looked over the bay toward the inn.
Tourists were coming to the shadowy terrace for breakfast. It was
a small, family run business of his friend and neighbor Slavko,
who inherited the inn from his father. They were distant cousins
and spent many winter evenings chatting and drinking together.
The whole of Mulobedanj used to be one huge property owned by
one man, Angelo Kadura. A hundred years ago, the old Kadura
decided to divide his huge estate among his three sons and a
daughter. Dario's grandfather Izidore, his fourth child and third
son, got some olive trees and some barren land along the coast.
The village a good mile up the hill went to the first son Ante,

the bay area with a little tavern and the port to the second,
Milivoj, the daughter, Oriana, got some cash as a dowry, which
her wretched husband lost in gambling and drinking. The big
villa on the hill at Lun remained in old Angelo's hands until he
died. Afterwards, they used it as the local elementary school.
Angelo Kadura was a big man for the community of Lun. He
had modern views and started the catering and tourism business
while the ragged peasants were still tramping the rocky pastures
behind their sheep. He also obeyed the ancient tradition and
separated the inheritance of the olive trees from the inheritance
of the land they grew on.

In summers, Slavko's niece from Zagreb, Emilia, helped him
at his inn. Peeping from under the rims of his straw hat, Dario
could see how a group of young Slovenian boys teased the girl
and looked under her skirt as she was serving them breakfast.
The wooden tables were long and Emilia had to lean and stretch
to pour coffee to the guest in the corner. Dario frowned. He
disliked the northern arrogance, yet he could see Emilia smiling
charmingly at a blond boy at the top of the table. Emilia's skin
was the color of the sea-soaked olives in November, tanned and
soft. She was dark, with thick curly hair, now plaited in one loose
braid over her left shoulder. Big brown eyes and a typical Roman
nose rounded her tiny mouth which never stopped smiling at the
guests. She was not too tall, rather plump, with the full, firm
breasts of a seventeen year old girl. Full of sparkle in her black
and white uniform of a waitress, she moved around the tables,
telling jokes to the guests all the time and bringing them the first
joy of the day. With her around, Slavko's inn filled with guests,
and he could easily earn the money for the long winter months
of nothing. Maria would have Emilia at her hotel any time for a
double wage, but Emilia was too fond of Slavko to abandon him,
and after the supper was over at eight in the evening, she liked
to ride her motorbike *vespa* to a remote beach or to a *konoba*,
tavern in Novalja, to have fun with her friends. Zrče, the famous
discotheque in Pag's largest bay, was the place to go, and no
boy's heart was safe from Emilia's charms. Yet, no matter how
much fun she had and how early her *vespa* brought her home the
following morning, she was always there for the breakfast tables
at seven. She loved the months at sea, and she adored her uncle
Slavko, the tiny village of Mulobedanj, and his guests.

Dario was about to finish his sewing and his wine when he
saw two strangers stopping by the tables and asking Emilia about
something. She waved in his direction, and they approached the
top of the pier slowly. Dario looked up from the leather boot into
the man's face. He was somebody from Novalja, a younger chap,
whom he might have met before. He could be a police officer.
Dario was not sure.

"Mr. Dario Kadura?"

"Yes, indeed. What is it?"

"You're the brother of Marina Kadura?"

"I am. What about her?"

"I'm afraid there's bad news. Your sister was found dead in her apartment yesterday morning."

Dario blinked, and his blue eyes watered with confusion. He could not believe his ears. It was only last night he had spoken to Marina, more precisely quarrelled with her over the phone. She was angry and shouted at him at the top of her voice for not picking up his spoilt daughters from Ronchi, the Trieste airport. They had been returning from their holidays in France, where they had gone to polish their French in a course paid by their extravagant, artistic aunt, his famous sister. Dario was livid with the three of them for not coming to see him and spending some time at home, in Mulobedanj. Marina had raised her soprano, so that he thought the phone would break down and her anger echoed in his ears until morning. He hated rows and he hated the reality that his only sister, seven years younger than him, thought him a primitive rascal with no culture. Anyway, the man said she was dead, but it could not be, dead people could not shout.

"What do you mean, dead? I spoke to her on the phone last night, she was scolding me..."

The young man took off his blue cap, and only now Dario noticed a tiny logo of the Croatian police RH MUP – Ministry of Internal Affairs. The young man wiped the sweat from his shaved head with a handkerchief.

"Was it last night or the night before, Mr. Kadura?"

Dario was lost. He was still mad with Marina. The exchange of foul words was still vivid in his mind. She called him a smelly fish fuck and crazy captain Hook and the like. It could have been as well two days ago, not yesterday. Marina Kadura, the star of the world's biggest opera houses and a favourite of her vast audiences, was more pig-headed than anybody else he had ever known. She had been singing since the day she was born, even her baby cries were musical. Her famous mezzosoprano carried a sentiment almost beyond human perception – it was like the voice of Heaven. Nevertheless, most of her time off stage, Marina was quarrelsome and demanding. As a singer, she possessed the absolute pitch and was a perfectionist. Many a conductor despaired over her, for she would scold him for the tiniest dissonance in the orchestra. Naturally, since their early age, Marina had always found something wrong with him, her brother. Likewise, with every man she had met. Twice she was married and divorced. She had lived in several steady or less steady relationships, but abhorred the marital routine and despised men in general. Her attitude to being a wife was the one of total civic disobedience – she had never cooked, cleaned, or done any of such wifely chores for her men. As long as they could take it, she could love them.

Then it was over. Her only true love was music, and she enjoyed singing to the point of erotic satisfaction. The only people whom she absolutely adored and loved were Dario's two daughters, Marina's nieces. They were angels in the hell without fire, as she used to call the world.

"I don't really know, now," he mumbled slowly, unable to think.

"Can we go to your house, Sir, and have a talk?"

"Yes, yes, just a second, please. Let me get these nets sorted."

Absentminded, Dario meticulously folded the long net and collected the needles and the scissors in a tin box. Then he turned to the men in blue.

"Please, come this way, officers."

* * *

Emilia looked up from the coffee pot as the two policemen who spoke to her a minute ago escorted *barba* Dario up the pier. What was wrong? What happened? She wondered often in the past how people could live without crime in this tiny and restricted community. The tourists never got mugged, young boys never got beaten. Whores and cheats avoided the Perovica hotel, and so did the local gangsters, who let Maria Perić in peace and she often wondered why. Since the collapse of Yugoslavia, Slovenian and other Yugoslavian tycoons had bought up all the best spots along the Adriatic coast. Russian oligarch's luxury yachts were polluting the charming seas around the archipelagoes from the coasts of Istria to Boka Kotorska. Each year, Abramovich' prestigious yacht Luna harbored in the lagoon of the city of Šibenik. That was the implementation of the so called free economy in the former Eastern Bloc. However, Pag had not been witness to any of those vile aspects of tourism. Sometimes though, such a newly rich party came from such a yacht to eat and drink at Slavko's. They would anchor their boat in the middle of the bay and climb into lifeboats still larger than the local fishing boats. They would order food in advance on the phone, and eat and drink long into the night. Slavko was looking forward to those orders as he overcharged as much as he could. They could not back out of the payment once they had eaten the food and drunk the wine. Slavko cunningly would take only cash, no credit cards, feigning his establishment was too backward to handle the plastic money. They had deceived him with worthless plastic a few times in the past, and he knew better than to accept it again. At such occasions, he would cook the best of kid or lamb under the ambers, or an octopus stew with young vegetables, or *brodet* with *polenta*. His friend Dario came along and helped him in the kitchen. They would chat and drink half of the profit away during the evening. Emilia would rush between the tables, all

smiles, being jolly and flirtatious with the elderly, who drank in
her youth, while sharing private women's jokes with their wives
who soon could feel the weight of the sun and strong red wine
in their heads. The guests would return to their boats past midnight, all happy and full of Mediterranean tastes.

Now, Dario. What was going on with Dario? Emilia must
send her little friend on a spying mission. She scanned the bay
under the terrace, where children were playing and cheering in
the shallow waters.

"Andrea, can you come for a minute, please?" she called at
the top of her voice over the fence. The head of a little girl came
to the surface and cheered.

"I can dive like a dolphin! Have you seen me, Emilia?"

She was beaming happily.

"Come out of the sea, I need your help here, Andrea."

"Watch me now!"

With a scream, the girl plunged head first under the surface
again, and all Emilia could see was her round bottom in a red
bathing costume, which would not sink so easily. A few moments
later, she stood straight up and turned her cheerful face to the
fence.

"Have you seen what I can do? I am a diver now!"

"Yes, Andrea, now dry up and come here, please."

Emilia was worried, but could not help smiling at the water
scene. What a charming little girl! She wished so much she had a
little sister like Andrea. Emilia was an only child, burdened with
all the responsibilities and expectations of her big city intellectual parents. Her father, Ivica Karbić, was the general manager
of a publishing house owned by an international children's publisher, Terod, her mother, Branka, a librarian at the University
Library. Both were successful and bored. They lived in the centre of Zagreb in a huge old apartment, which they redecorated
according to the latest Italian interior design style. Emilia felt
like a stranger in her room. It looked like a first aid station or
a space ship chamber from the Star Trek, anything else but a
teenager's cozy den. It was all white, always clean to the point of
sterilization and void of all sentiment. The two prevailing colors
were white and petroleum green. On rainy days, it was like a grey
monastery cell, where she had to study, learn, read, and fulfill her
parents' ambitions. The following year, she would finish her high
school and continue her studies at the university. Her parents
were quarrelling over the subject she should take. Maybe, they
should ask her at some point what she wanted. She had enough
of school, and did not fancy the idea of going to the university at
all. She could run Slavko's inn here on Pag and earn her living
easily. She was certain she did not need any further education.
School sucked.

Andrea came to the terrace at last and smiled broadly.

"Will I get an ice cream after I help? Is it a mission? Where do I have to go? Do I go by sea or by road? Shall I get my bike? Is it dangerous?"

Emilia shook her head at so many questions in one breath. Andrea objected with a disappointed whine.

"What, no ice cream? And I left my dolphin diving for what?"

"No, no, you will get your ice cream, and it is not dangerous, and you don't need your bike. Will you go to Dario's house and listen at the window to what *barba* Dario and the men are talking about. Be careful, don't stay too long. When you find out, what it is about, come back here and tell me."

"And you will give me my ice cream then, right?"

Kids were tough negotiators, no half promises that you could forget later.

"I promise, I will."

Andrea put on a dry little beach dress and stepped into her trainers. She winked at Emilia with a conspiratorial look and started marching up the hill. She was back after a good quarter of an hour and reported with a sullen face.

"There are three men and Dario sitting at the kitchen table. They are not from our village, for I've never seen any of them before. I was listening for a while. They were speaking in complicated words and I didn't understand all of it. It was about *tetka* Marina. She's lying dead in her apartment in Rijeka, or so the men said. One man in a sports jacket seemed like a boss or something... He was asking Dario all kinds of questions about her. I couldn't hear well, you know, they spoke in a low voice, and *barba* Dario is very upset, he was... he was... Maybe I am not supposed to tell this... You can forget the ice cream, Emilia."

Emilia looked seriously into her eyes.

"My little Andrea, it's not about the ice cream, but you know how much my uncle Slavko and I love Dario. We want to help, so tell me everything you've seen and heard."

Andrea dropped her shoulders and let out a deep sigh.

"*Barba* Dario was crying, Emilia, with huge tears. I've never seen a *barba* crying before. I couldn't watch anymore and left."

Andrea suddenly had tears in her eyes, too.

"It is so sad, I hate Petar, but I would cry if he died, too."

Emilia hugged her.

"There, there, Petar is very bad with you sometimes. But you love him all the same, he's your brother. Come, vanilla or chocolate?"

Andrea smiled faintly through her tears.

"Both, please."

"Come on, some sweet vanilla to dry your elephant tears and the chocolate to bring out that lovely smile of yours."

Emilia was waiting to be able to talk to Slavko and tell him her worries about Dario. Yet, her uncle mysteriously disappeared into the cellar. She was not happy with the police in Dario's house. The time for lunch was approaching, so Emilia could not ponder on the story much longer. Guests were coming to the terrace. They sat at the tables ordering drinks and waiting for their starters. They chatted animatedly about their morning at the beach and the books they were reading, or how the water was, and of course, about the wonderful nature and the sea. Another major topic of their chats was what was for lunch. The menu was simple – pickled sardines with olives and oregano pasta as a starter, some mixed salad in between, and grilled veal cutlets or hake stakes baked in butter, mashed potatoes and steamed young peas as a side dish. The dessert was ice cream.

Emilia was running around the tables for nearly two full hours, the kitchen was at top speed. All the guests were hungry at the same time, all wanted a siesta at the same time, all wanted sun and sea at the same time. It was the rhythm of the mass tourism flooding the Dalmatian coast in July and August every year. Now, there was a table round of young Slovenian boys, "knights of the pot table", as Emilia often teased them. Emilia liked one of them. He was older than her. He had to be a university student. His name was Tomaž. Like many northerners, his skin was fair, and the sun bronzed only the freckles on his nose. He had long blond hair with some bleached strands. His eyes were bright grey and shone under his dark eyebrows like two alien suns. His strong, broad shoulders spoke of the fact that he was an excellent athlete. He liked to show off. In late afternoons, when the *bonaca* transformed the surface of the bay into a huge space mirror, the whole village would get to admire his water skiing stunts. He could leave one ski behind, or bend abruptly, or even jump over the tiny reef near the cost. It was neck breaking and daring, but he enjoyed the adrenaline and was aware of the girls' admiration from the shore. His stunts always coincided with the time when Emilia was laying the tables for dinner, so she would be watching his jumps sporadically. She pretended not to be too impressed, but the truth was that in spite of the boy's annoying peacock attitude, she was mysteriously attracted to him. He was vain and she knew it. He had a reputation for not being the most candid of characters, and she knew that, too. She followed him on Facebook and found a new photograph every day of his partying and the latest love affair. They were saying that chasing girls was his favourite sport. His Facebook status, though, remained single. Emilia did not want to be posted on his wall as the latest of his amorous conquests. Indeed, he was not exactly a knight in a shining armor, but he was throwing passionate glances at her, and she noticed it. She wondered about his intentions and at the same time, tried to ignore him. However, Emilia found herself thinking of Tomaž and his dark blond curls nearly all the time.

Tomaž was obviously besotted with Emilia more than he

wished to admit and spent every possible minute around her trying to impress her. He had never met somebody like Emilia. She was a classic Roman beauty and so unreachable, always aloof and distant. It made him crazy. He wanted her. There was a girl in the final year at his high school in Ljubljana, but she was dull compared to Emilia's bright laugh and shiny dark eyes. He was at his wits' end with his seducing strategies. It was clear that Emilia was ignoring him. Her face was always cold, her look empty, like a wall of an impermeable Middle Age fortress.

One morning he came to the terrace and wanted to help her with setting the tables. She served him a cappuccino and chased him away, declaring him spoilt and incapable of any real work. Nearly every evening, he was the last guest of the day and, after she was done with clearing the tables, he would buy two beers and invite her to drink with him on the pier under the stars. He even brought her flowers from his morning runs up the hill – sharp smelling carnations with delicate purple flower petals. He would entwine his bouquet with rosemary twigs. She said thank you and put them in the vase on the bar without any further comments. On every possible occasion he asked her out, yet Emilia declined with a secretive smile. Was she seeing somebody in Novalja? Did she have somebody in Zagreb? Was she just cautious? Did she think they could at best enjoy a summer romance and she was not that type of girl?

The lunch was over, and Emilia cleared the last of the tables. She had managed to tell Slavko about Dario's visitors. He immediately went uphill to Dario's house. He still had not come back. Emilia wanted to know what was going on. There was nothing she could do but wait. The old friends Dario and Slavko would probably talk and drink long into the afternoon. They needed time alone. Tomaž sat in the corner overlooking the sea and called her over. She breathed in deeply and came closer:

"What is the pot table ordering? We are not in Amsterdam, and we do not serve hashish weed to our guests, you know."

She was watching him from above through her thick black lashes, with her cheeks flushed.

"Emilia, why don't you have a cappuccino? It'll be my treat. Sit with me and talk to me. I can see you fed the crowds well, so you're off now, aren't you?"

"I could use a swim first, I'm soaked. Maybe later... Thank you."

Tomaž knew what was coming and prepared well for his invitation. It was either then or never. He had to get Emilia alone on his father's motorboat and away from the crowds. He was not a gigolo, but one thing he knew – if he ever wanted to seduce the girl, he needed to separate her from that restaurant, from her people and her daily chores. He wanted Emilia all for himself. Only for an hour, maybe two... He wanted to embrace her, feel her and kiss her on the lips. He wanted to make love to her.

"We could take the boat out. My father is having his siesta now. You filled him up with that wine of yours; he will be sound asleep at least for two hours."

"What do you mean filled him up? I think the man is of legal age to drink, don't you? He ordered the wine, am I not to serve him? He's our guest, Tomaž. What are two bottles of red? By the way, your mom drank along, so maybe they won't appreciate you disturbing their siesta just now."

Tomaž's cheeks flushed with purple shame. He was happy for his parents to have a fulfilling sexual life, but he was livid with everybody in the little holiday village to have noticed it. It was so humiliating. Mom and dad would go shopping by boat in the morning and come back hours later all sweaty and salty, their eyes sparkling with mischievous secrecy. How could old people even think about sex? It should be far beyond their age. He was deeply embarrassed and did not know what to say. Emilia saw his red face, understood immediately that she had gone too far, and added quickly.

"Don't worry, be happy. It's nice to see a loving couple of their age. My parents are so cold to each other. Instead of words, they exchange ice cubes like some huge American ice machines. They talk to each other only to quote prices of objects nobody ever wants to buy but them. Like, 'have you seen that rug, darling? It's pure Pakistani wool and all hand woven.' Who the hell cares about rugs these days? Besides, children wave those rugs with their thin fingers... Disgusting, parents are just disgusting! Come on, Tomaž, let's go to the beach and have a swim."

Tomaž lifted his head and looked Emilia directly in the eyes. She felt sorry for him. He could use her moment of sympathy and he would.

"Emilia, let's take the boat and go to an island nearby, for example Dolfin. It's just a quarter of an hour. I have my thermos full of instant coffee, and I will take some biscuits and mineral water. We can have a picnic on the boat. Have you eaten lunch at all?"

Emilia looked at the horizon. She was not hungry after having smelt fat, fish and potatoes for a couple of hours. Why would she not go, go away just for a couple of hours? Tomaž was nice and she liked him. Slavko was obviously still away, there was enough time before supper. If they were to take the food and coffee with them, it would not mean they should go too far. Besides she would love to try to ski on water. Tomaž could show her.

"Will you take the skis? I would love to try it once. I can ski, but I've always done it on snow so far."

Tomaž got up and started towards the inn.

"Yes, of course. The skis are in the boat. I will show you, it is so easy. Will you come, then?"

"I will. See you on the pier in fifteen minutes. I'll just change quickly and leave a message for my uncle."

"Super. I'll take the food and drinks. Thank you, Emilia, thank you so much. I will do anything you want."

"I hope you will. Can you steer the boat on your own, by the way?"

"Of course I can. I can anchor it much better than my father."

"I bet you don't have a license, do you?"

"Fuck the license, I can steer it with or without it."

Tomaž was getting impatient like all young men on the brink of an adventure. Yet, Emilia was not going to stop teasing him just yet.

"And the water police from Rab? Aren't you afraid of them?"

"Just come, don't worry. Nobody but seagulls comes to Dolfin. Not in this heat."

Emilia smiled and went to the house. She took her bathing bag, and changed into short pants and a T-shirt. She put on her smart Ray Ban sunglasses. Then Slavko returned with a sullen face, grey with worry.

"Where are you going, Emilia?"

"Slavko, I'm going for a swim. I'll be back in time for supper."

Emilia made a move to embrace him. Her eyes were questioning his.

"Don't, sorry, Emilia, later... We will talk later. Now, I need to be alone."

Slavko looked at the harbor, where a motor boat started with the tall blond Slovenian boy behind the steer. He did not like that boy at all; teenage arrogance bolstered by his father's money. Slavko knew the couple. Andrej Klun, the father was a director of a big national bank in Ljubljana. His wife, Anja, was a nurse. She was very attractive. Her dark tan and thick blond hair, her shining blue eyes, and above all her positive attitude were very appealing and made the woman in her late forties look years younger. Slavko liked her, but did not think much of Mr. Klun or even less of the young Klun.

"Not with that good for nothing boy from Slovenia, are you?"

Emilia inhaled deeply. She hated limits. She was seventeen. It was her right to see whom she wanted. In a polite but determined voice she said:

"Slavko, I'm just going for a swim. Tomaž will also show me water skiing. I've been looking for an opportunity to try for days. Besides, your niece is very much capable of looking after herself. She's seventeen, you know."

Slavko knew when he lost the battle – there was nothing he could do to prevent Emilia from taking an innocent afternoon bathing trip. She was nearly eighteen, taking her high school exam next year, and she was the dearest person in his life. He sighed with sorrow over his friend's situation – his sister dead, daughters away, love not returned. Who is he to stand in Emilia's way? In a deep voice, he slowly answered:

"Very well, see you later, honey. Have fun, but watch out for the sharks."

"There are no sharks in the Adriatic, you silly old man."

Emilia stood on her toes and kissed his stubby cheek. Then, like a whirlwind, she was gone through the door.

"No sharks, yeah, baby."

Slavko only knew better – aye, sharks there were, evil little sharks with small sharp teeth and many sets of teeth growing over and over again – at least one for each of the human sorrows.

* * *

With a sigh, Dario rose from his chair at the dining table. The room was dark, heavy shutters were blocking the midday sun out, but he knew every step in his house even in pitch dark. He headed for the huge cabinet, where glasses and liquors were stored for difficult moments. He looked at the detective, who nodded curtly. Four glasses and a dark green bottle came onto the table. Dario poured a big jug of water, and they all sat down.

"My name is Ivica Kostić and I am a detective at the Department for Violent Crime Prevention and Investigation in Rijeka. These are my colleagues Marjan Batič from the Rijeka police department and my Slovenian colleague Andrej Bak from Koper. Andrej joined us as your sister has had some strong Slovenian connections lately."

The detective paused for a moment and cast a sympathetic look at Dario and his trembling hand trying to pour *travarica*, into the glasses. He was spilling it all over the plastic tablecloth with a colorful flower pattern. Dario took notice of the silence and added hastily.

"I know she's had a lover or a partner. His name is Milan Nemec. They've been together for a year or so..."

Ivica picked the little glass from the table. With a resigned look, the other two followed his example and took the filled little glasses from their grim host. Kostić saluted, saying:

"Here's to your sister – let her rest in peace. *Živeli!*"

Dario sipped the shot in and poured another round. He was completely lost. The police had told him on the way to his house that they suspected the cause of death was a drug overdose or some kind of poisoning. They needed to wait for the official autopsy results. He knew drugs were out of question. Marina was a strict and disciplined artist, and she never drank alcohol, smoked or took any drugs, even medicines if she could avoid it. Since they were kids, she was very much against all intoxicating substances and despised people who depended on them. Including himself, when he had a glass too many. Her only drug was music and it was legal, although Dario was not always sure whether her obsession could not have harmed her life more than a shot or two at the pier.

"Do you know how they met? I mean Nemec and Marina."

Ivica Kostić needed to know more about the woman, although he had the feeling that Dario had not been very close to his sister for some time. By a speedy provisional court order, they had access to Marina's telephone conversations in the days before she died. As all talks on the cell phones also theirs was recorded. Thus Kostić was privy to the last conversation between brother and sister, which was anything but friendly.

"I think they met at the Rotarian dance in Opatija, where Marina sang as part of her charity program. She told me they fell in love at first sight, and they obviously ended the evening at her place in Rijeka. I know they were seeing each other quite often, usually in Rijeka or at some horribly expensive hotel around Istria, but if they were more serious... I wouldn't know."

"They were very serious, so serious that Marina changed her will two months ago and put down Nemec as her main beneficiary. Still, we have doubts about its validity. There is no notary seal on it, only a solicitor from Koper co-signed it, and the witnesses are untraceable Slovenians, or so it seems. It's kind of fishy. That is why we asked our Slovenian colleagues about Nemec, and they told us about their investigation. But we'll talk about Nemec later. So, did you know about the change of the will?"

Dario opened his eyes in surprise. He did not care much about money or wealth, but he was hoping his sister would put down the girls as beneficiaries. At least that was what Marina was always saying – the huge apartment in Rijeka would be for the girls to sell and have a better life, especially never to have to return to Pag, to his dirty hole.

"No, I barely heard her speaking of Nemec. I thought he was a flimsy affair, just someone to pass the time with, to dull her sorrow over the loss of her husband some years ago. This is new. Marina often said she would put my daughters in the will. You see, it was an awkward subject, I never really asked her about the money or her income. I inherited the family olive trees, the land and the house, while Marina went into the world with nothing but her voice. I should not complain."

Ivica held his breath. This man did not know anything about his sister, or he was a psychopath beyond telling.

"Are you aware, Mr. Kadura, what kind of inheritance we're talking about?"

"Well, she had this huge apartment in the old town in Rijeka and I presume some money in her accounts. Maybe a lot of money, as her late Venetian husband was loaded. The man had money to burn, but he was simple and kind as a bear. He enjoyed many a sunny day of fishing with me. It was the only time in my life I could get along with my sister, too." His lips turned into a generous smile. "Giacoppo was a nice man, I was really sorry, when he died so suddenly. Marina could not recover from the loss. She had never been the same since."

Ivica's voice was sharp as a knife.

"You're lying to us, Mr. Kadura. You must know about Marina's wealth. We found out what you signed at the Public Notary Govač in Rijeka. You should be the executor of her will on 21st of March 2005, so five years ago. The first will, I mean."

"Oh, yeah, I did sign the document, but I never read it properly, and Mr. Govač, the notary, was so busy that day – he didn't have the time to explain in details what there was in the paper. He tried, but it was very complicated. I didn't ask any questions. There were pages and pages of legal mumbo jumbo, who would understand it? I sailed the seas, I understand ships, winds, and fish. Besides, I completely trusted my sister Marina, shouldn't I have?"

"Are you saying you don't know today how huge the inheritance was even then? You don't know anything at all about the hotel chain at Opatijska Riviera? Hotels like Excelsior, Galeb, Rajski otok, Bellevue and a few other five star luxury villas? The Seashell chain – does it sound familiar to you?"

"What hotels? It cannot be... Where would she get those? Marina had no talent for business or finances."

Dario started to sweat. Obviously, he had signed something he should not have. What on earth is this man hinting at? That he could have something to do with his sister's death...

"No, Marina did not. But Giacoppo da Vesta – he bought the hotels after the last Balkan war from the German and Austrian banks and renovated them all, then chained them up with other groups in Italy and around Europe and created one of the most successful tourist operations in Croatia. He brought well trained catering managers from Switzerland, Italy and Austria. They built up his business to the sky. Meanwhile, he got married to your sister. And you obviously never heard of it, eh?"

Dario ran his fingers through his hair nervously. He was at his wits' end. Only this morning his life was so simple – sea, fish, sun, Maria, nets. Now, death, suicide, or even crime and business invaded his modest stone home and threaten to crumble his world to pieces.

"I live a simple life and I hate the media, I never watch the news. They're all full of crap. I don't..."

"Fuck the media! You spent summers with Giacoppo! You took him fishing! You drank wine with him. You did talk to him, didn't you? I don't believe he never told you about the hotels. What did you talk about, anyway?"

Dario saw the detective's point, but was getting impatient with his shouting. Nobody should shout at him in his house. He had to stop the man. He raised his head, looked Kostić directly in the eye, and in his croaky voice slowly replied:

"We talked about the weather. On the boat you don't talk, the engine is very loud. And while hoisting the nets, you talk fish. Then we cooked the catch together. He adored our old recipes and he loved to eat, so we talked herbs and spices. I never asked him about his business or money. How do you think he would take it? It's bad manners to ask a brother in law about his money."

Ivica stared at him. The old man was right. You cannot go around asking your brother in law how much he earned and what he did or would do with his money.

"Giacoppo da Vesta had no close relatives but his old mother, Carla. So your sister, Marina, his wife, was his only heiress after he died. That was when she made her previous will, which you signed to be the executor of five years ago. I don't believe you didn't look at the figures and the appendix of assets which were bound in leather. Stocks, shares, all sorts of securities, bonds of various European countries like Greece, Portugal and Spain, some also Slovenian, then contracts with Italian, Austrian and Slovenian companies – the man owned half of this area, for Christ's sake!"

Dario was puzzled. He tried to remember the meeting at the notary; it was in autumn, heavy rains were pouring down like a black curtain and he was nervous, not used to the big city traffic and crowds after so many years of peaceful retirement on his island. He was not concentrated, and he was not following all the formalities. In fact, he could not understand the real meaning of the documents he was signing. Marina said he should not mind too much, she wanted only the best for him and his daughters. She was still in mourning, very sad and moody. In the months after Giacoppo's funeral, Marina was like a nuclear bomb – a tiny wrong word could trigger an explosion of screams and foul words. He just signed, did not ask too many questions. Well, it was obviously the wrong thing to do.

"What do you mean by hotels? Please, tell me now. I swear to the lives of my daughters, I didn't know about Marina's wealth and Giacoppo's hotels."

Ivica Kostić looked at the old, wrinkled fisherman. His blue eyes were clear like the water in a still lagoon. He was flabbergasted. The old grey head, in a way so clear and quick, didn't seem capable of concocting such a lie. Still, Kostić had seen much in the years after the war. People got crazier and crimes more violent every day. Let's go along with his version and see where we get. He sat down, poured himself a glass of water, and drank it in one gulp. He decided to explain everything and watch Dario's body language carefully.

"OK. So about fifteen years ago, your sister got married to this Italian old bachelor, who had just sold his several print shops,

more like huge printing factories, which printed for illustrious
Italian publishers like De Agostini and Mondadori. Also, they
were exclusive partners of the German Bertelsmann Book Club
and printed their editions for the entire European market. Do you
know in how many languages? Eleven, and the print runs for each
title were like 50,000 copies for Spain, 100,000 copies for Germany,
70,000 for France and 60,000 for Italy. Do you know how much
turnover one book title printed for Bertelsmann brought into the
company? Millions, not millions of *kunas*, millions of euros they
made with only one title. His plants were situated around Milan
and in the industrial basin behind Venice – Mestre. One day, our
Giacoppo simply got fed up with his business. He was plagued by
impossible deadlines and penalty suits over printed and delivered
books. He wanted away. Besides, as I could read in the media
clippings on the internet, he believed that the Chinese would soon
take the printing business out of European hands, and with his
giant plants employing thousands of workers, he didn't want to
be around then. The Italian unions are particularly demanding,
the workers go on strike for nothing. Imagine he would have to
reduce the wages or even fire all those thousands. . . So he sold his
printing plants and paper mills. And do you know what? He was
right. Printing was the first major industrial sector which the
cheap Chinese labor took over. With the huge income from the
sales of his plants and industrial estates, he first bought himself
a Renaissance *palazzo* in Venice, and restored it, oblivious to
the costs. Giacoppo da Vesta was just over fifty, his mother
was trying very hard to match him with a bride from his social
stratum, one to bear his children and secure the future of the
family."

Until then Andrej Bak sat silently along and just gave a nod
with his oval head here and then. Now he interrupted Kostić:

"Is she still alive, this mother of Giacoppo's, la mamma?"

"You bet. I came across a photo from the Vienna Opera
Ball this year. This mother of Giacoppo, she is a true Italian
patron. Carla da Vesta, widowed at forty, richly provided for
by her husband, she doted on her only son; he was her most
precious possession. She was trying to mate him like a bull for
years – it was a shame. All the Italian yellow press was full of
articles and photos at the time; Giacoppo was a more famous
bachelor than Berlusconi is claimed to be a famous fornicator
today. Giaccoppo must have loathed the mamma circus around
him and all her sly, cosmetically enhanced candidates with false
blond hair and long legs, all in a rat race for his wealth. He took
a year off discovering the Adriatic and enjoying a simpler life.
He drove down the coast of Dalmatia in his yellow Ferrari and
slept in small places, talking to fishermen, sipping the strong red
wine and eating simple peasant foods. He came to Mulobedanj
in June 1994, where he met Marina and immediately fell in love

with her. There was a picture of them at a concert in the Pula Arena in *Večernji list*. Later he followed her to every opera house around Europe. They got married very soon afterwards. Their romance was all over the Croatian tabloids. Just reading about it was sweet to the point of getting diabetes."

"Don't insult my sister in my house, man. It was a true love. I was there and I witnessed it. She loved Giacoppo like she loved music. And the man was mad about her."

Dario's intermezzo silenced the Croatian detective for a moment. Then he went on:

"I am sorry. I didn't mean any offence. Anyway, this love, Giacoppo's mother didn't find it too sweet. She was furious and hated Marina, so Giacoppo very soon sold his Venetian *palazzo*, and the couple lived in Opatija in a rented villa, where your daughters, by the way, were regular visitors, and where you personally brought them in a car. Do you remember?"

Dario just nodded. How could he forget? The place was like a castle, with a huge green park, where exotic trees and bushes from all over the world grew in harmony like people could never live along each other. He caught Kostić' voice hesitating.

"Maybe after Giacoppo had learnt some Croatian, he realized how deeply the last Balkan war had destroyed our tourism and industry. He was restless, looking for an investment, to park his printing millions, so he started to buy one hotel after another; first in Italy, one in Slovenia and a few at the Kvarner Riviera. He chained them up and established a good quality four-star brand. In all of them, he had developed vast wellness areas, which hooked congress guests, so they were coming in masses. He also hired new staff. For the first time in Croatian tourism, managers from the Hotel Management School of Geneva were running the hotels and villas, and they improved the price-performance ratio many times. The business thrived, so to the chain of mass tourism hotels, da Vesta added five star luxury villas, very popular with bankers and the investment business community. Marina and Giacoppo seemed a happy couple. You said that and you know it, for every summer they came to spend some weeks here with you. They financed all of your daughters' travels to workshops on different catering subjects and various courses of foreign languages. It seems they were training your girls to take over the hotels some day. You must know this, don't you? Very soon, he saw to it that Marina was his sole heiress. And, she saw to it that you and your daughters were hers. As I already told you, Nemec came into play in a new will, which is not in order, or so it seems. We're on the dry land with that. We need an expert legal opinion on which of the two wills is legally valid. The difference is huge – several hundred million euros either for you and your daughters or for Mr. Nemec and his cronies. First, we need to find out what really happened to Marina. Suicide is a possibility.

One way or the other, our enquiries have to find the truth. And you didn't know all this, you say. . . "

Dario looked at Ivica, understanding only a half of what he was saying. He could not control his feelings any longer, and tears blurred his sight and found their path around the wrinkles down the cheeks. This was all fucking unbelievable, like a nightmare, though he could not wake up from it in the middle of the day. This was happening, the detectives were here questioning him, and Marina was dead. Why would Marina kill herself? Was she depressed? She was hysterical, true, but was she despaired to the point of finishing her life? Should he talk to her more often? The other option was even worse. If the autopsy should show drugs, Dario was sure she was murdered. The person who had murdered her could easily harm his girls. What would those people do for the money?

"No, I didn't know all this. But this Nemec, should he have his fingers in Marina's death, wouldn't he want to do away with me and my daughters as well?"

Ivica's face lost all color. He should have thought of it earlier.

"He might. Where are they?"

"They're flying home from their French holiday today."

"Where? Zadar airport?"

"No, Trieste, Ronchi, today. I think their plane from Munich is due to land at 15.45. They said they would take a cab to Rijeka and the ferry catamaran to Novalja. They would come in the evening. We can't. . . "

Andrej Bak, the silent and pensive Slovenian with a fashionable goatee and stark white linen shirt, was already dialing his colleagues in Koper to send them on an hour's trip from Koper to Ronchi.

"Excuse me, Mr. Kadura. I forgot – what are the names of your daughters? We'll try to intercept them at the arrivals."

"Olivia and Mira."

Bak stepped through the door. He was anxious to get the police moving fast as the traffic around Trieste was very dense at this time of day. The officers on duty in Koper decided to play it safe and alarmed their Italian colleagues as well. Since the Schengen border regime in Slovenia, they had been cooperating more and more closely. He also ordered a photograph of Nemec distributed among the airport security, so that they could seize him in case he was after the two young women himself.

He was not too happy to chase Nemec again. It was frustrating. Should they catch him without firm evidence, they might have to let him go within twenty-four hours like last time. A capital indictment against Nemec at the Ljubljana Regional Court had gone wrong some time ago. It was one of those cases of nepotism, so common in a young democratic society like Slovenia. The prosecutor to be, a young chap named something Birkengar, whose sole quality was that he was the Slovenian General Prose-cutor's son, messed up big time. The star business and penalty lawyers defending Nemec had an easy job getting the tycoon out and all the charges dropped. The police were furious with the young Birkengar. Such an extensive and expensive investigation, the enormous manpower needed to go through the business doc-uments, various financial and tax experts hired to find the proof of criminality in Nemec's management procedures – all wasted, all to no avail. Nemec got free of all charges, so that in the fol-lowing months he could transfer all his real estates and assets which he had criminally obtained in Slovenia either to his son or to his wife. The majority, though, sank God knows where. Off shore companies, dubious bank accounts in Cyprus, maybe some Swiss hedge funds. Foul money always found its way into obliv-ion. Just like rainwater and even whole rivers could sink all of a sudden into the karstic soil. His lawyers even had the audacity to file a suit against the police and the young prosecutor to be, Birkengar, for media harassment and personal damage to their client. In the end, Bak had to pay a lawyer out of his own pocket to justify his police work against Nemec. It was nothing short of absurd.

Now, they had a hot lead on him again. For a few weeks, sev-eral Slovenian supervisory institutions had been systematically checking all of Nemec's companies. Sometimes they used the tax examination to cover their intentions, sometimes the police searched the premises and confiscated the documents and the computers. What the young accountant gave them was precious, yet they needed more firm proof to lock the man up forever. His off shore businesses were off limits, but the Swiss government and various international banks notorious for their secrecy in the face of charges had proved very helpful with bits of information. Nobody wanted money with a dirty trail. So slowly but surely, in-vestigators were tightening the rope around Nemec's neck. One of these days, they would catch him and put him behind bars with other common criminals. There he could set up another of his usual insolvency scenarios, this time in jail with lover boys to back him up.

Ivica Kostić and Marjan Batič came out of the house. The hot midday sun hit their eyes. They were blinking at Andrej Bak expectantly.

"We are in contact with the Italians. They will intercept the girls and bring them to the border, where our boys are waiting. Should they bring them to Pag? Who will tell them about Ma-rina?"

Ivica shook his head, astonished. "You Europeans really work together? Schengen, well, I thought it was just bollocks, you know, political propaganda..."

Andrej smiled thinly.

"I bet Nemec, being old school, doesn't expect this. Maybe, we will make a major arrest today, boys."

They moved toward their white Škoda Octavia, comfortably parked in the shadow. Dario was watching them leave from the doorstep with mixed feelings. Above all, he was sad, for no matter how many conflicts they had had in the past, he loved Marina very much. She was years younger and since her birth, he had always been protecting her. He was also one of her truest admirers and was collecting her musical recordings meticulously. Yet, lately they often quarreled. He felt he had failed her as her older brother. He should have been there for her more often after Giacoppo's death, not fighting with her, but talking to her and comforting her. She got involved with that Slovenian scum, Nemec, only because she was lonely. Now it was too late. Their last conversation cut a deep scar in his soul. It was too late to apologize or talk it over; the wound could never close and his mind could not heal.

When the seagulls cry

Emilia took off her sneakers and jumped into the boat, taking the rope off the bollards. She neatly folded it on the bottom of the boat and took position next to Tomaž behind the steer. They were so different. He had long blond hair, much longer than it was the momentary fashion, shot wildly around his bronzed face like spaghetti with the only purpose to anger his father. Emilia was almost two heads shorter. Her forehead barely reached to his shoulders; she had a round, small stature, and her skin was dark and olive. He was a snowy Alpine peak, and she was a deep sea lagoon at night, warm and inviting one to plunge in and stay there forever. He was all action and impatience, and she knew how to control her impulses and kept her feet on the ground. Emilia knew Tomaž was an ambitious and talented student. A year ahead of her, he had passed his high school exam with highest grades and was waiting to enter the Ljubljana Faculty of Medicine, one of the most reputable medical schools in the region. He would be a doctor. Her grades at the Zagreb high school Prva gimnazija were not bad, but she was not interested in medicine. She wanted to work with people, to help them and look after them. Could she decide to be a teacher? She was still uncertain as to what she would pick as for her course of studies next spring.

"I will speed up now. The boat will be lifted above the surface in a minute. Where will you sit, Emilia?"

"I'll take the top of the bow. I want to feel the wind."

"Just stay behind the railings. It took me so long to talk you into the ride. I don't want to lose you on the first wave."

Emilia laughed coquettishly. She was ready to enjoy some free time and have fun at last. Besides, it was all spiced up with the attraction she felt for Tomaž.

"You, city boy, you know nothing about the sea. I've served as a sailor on my uncle's boat since I'd learnt how to walk."

Emilia sat on the top of the bow, so that her feet were touching the surface of the sea, and clutched the railings. It was a good position, and she nodded to say that she was ready. Tomaž accelerated until the boat was floating on the sea, only lightly touching the surface. They soon reached twenty knots, and Emilia felt happy and free like the seagulls circling and crying loudly above them. They had to be protesting against the insolence of humans invading their natural territory. Emilia and Tomaž, with eighty horsepower driving the engine, felt aloof and powerful; they were masters of the sea. For a moment, it felt like touching heaven. Tomaž was very careful intersecting the waves, so that Emilia was seated comfortably. At the open sea, she raised her arms like the young lovers in the Titanic movie and glided over the blue like a queen. Suddenly, the engine was slowing down, and nearly came to a standstill, leaving the boat senselessly floating up and down on tiny waves.

"Emilia, would you like to try the skis?"

"Now?"

"Yes, now. The sea is quite calm and you never know if on our way back the *bonaca* will hold. Come here, put the lifejacket on, and I will prepare the lines and the skis."

Emilia was ambushed by her own courage. She was excited about trying, but suddenly fears strangled her whether she could do it. Sports had not always been easy. Since she was a baby she always thought twice before jumping anywhere. Yet, hunger for fun overran the hesitation. She started to take off her T-shirt, but Tomaž stopped her.

"Leave the T-shirt on, Emilia. Some corners of the lifejacket aren't so smooth, besides, if you fall, you won't feel the blow so much. You know, our speed will be from ten to fifteen knots; the boat must pull all your weight out of the water. Then, you just stand on the skis like in snow, your knees straight, like in a curve. You'll see it's easy."

Emilia was looking confused by the sophisticated lines with a triangle on one end, the bar being of soft black contact plastic foam.

"Jump into the sea and stay behind the feed. I will throw the skis in the water, and you put one after another on your feet."

"Don't I need some kind of water shoes?"

"No, you don't. Here..."

The first ski fell in the water next to Emilia, who had difficulties moving about in the thick lifejacket. She put her right foot in the ski sock and made a sign for the other. With both feet booted, she floated on the surface clumsily, like a trunk. Tomaž was showing her the starting position of the body with her skis pointed out of the surface, when she'd be pulled out of the water.

"Hold the bar firmly at the level of your chest and pull your knees to your belly, so that the skis are below your body, the tops just out of the water. You bend forward slightly, and when the line is starting to stretch, concentrate firmly on it. With a blow, you'll be pulled out. Then you just lean backwards and keep the balance. Should you feel frightened or feel pain or something, just drop the line, and I'll collect you. It usually doesn't work the first time you try, so don't worry."

"Err, are you sure? I'm scared..."

"Don't be. It's very easy. Let's go."

Tomaž checked the line on both side bollards. They were fastened firmly. Then he focused on the steer. He turned back once more and gave the floating plastic package in the water a victory sign. The motor was gaining speed, and after a few hundred yards Emilia was pulled out of the water with a powerful tug. But she held on to the bar, she would not want to quit now. After a few moments, she relaxed a bit and found a position in which she was more comfortable. It wasn't hard, indeed, and it was a big time adrenaline sport. She was enjoying it with full breath. It was so hip, just the right kick, much more fun than riding the motorbike. Her hair was blowing behind her and her lifejacket was squeezing her breasts, for Tomaž had fastened it tightly. No matter what, she was holding on to the bar, following the boat in curves and turns at full speed. She felt so free... She looked upwards to watch the seagulls circling above the show. The birds were shocked, too, they stopped crying. Some ten minutes had gone by, but for Emilia they were like hours. Her hands and shoulders started to hurt and her leg muscles were shaking with strain. She let go of the line and plunged into the water gratefully, for she was sweating all over her body.

After some time, which felt like eternity, Tomaž came back to pick her up. First he warped the line, then he took up the skis and finally he put down a little plastic ladder, so that Emilia, still wrapped in the orange lifejacket could climb aboard. She took off everything, staying only in her bikini. She was shaking with cold and excitement. Tomaž wrapped her in a huge towel and slowly steered the boat towards the island. The motor was fighting the long waves. Emilia sat on the bench in silence; the powerful adrenaline experience sunk deeply in her soul. They didn't say a word for another quarter of an hour, with their eyes set on the strip of land in front of them becoming bigger and bigger. The seagulls resumed their war song against the human intruders into their nesting area, the island of Dolfin. It was one of the few wild spots in the sea where birds and fish could go undisturbed by the tourists.

The further the boy and the girl were away from the village, the closer they were feeling to each other. Tomaž drove the boat slowly towards a little pebble beach, killed the engine and lifted it up from the rocky bottom. Emilia jumped onto the high pillow of dried sea grass, sank knee deep into the warm softness and pulled the bow ashore. Tomaž passed her over a cotton blanket and the cooler. The green cooler was heavy and almost tipped her over. She grabbed it with both hands at last and firmly set the box on the shore.

The bay was still and windless. They spread the blanket on the soft sea grass, which was like a pillow, made from layers of weed washed on shore for centuries. It was ancient though renewed after every storm. Tomaž opened the cooler, and with hungry eyes Emilia realized he had a full picnic in it. There was bread, olives, cherry tomatoes, hard sheep cheese, dried ham and a bottle of sweet sparkling wine, *Fruškogorski biser*. Neatly wrapped in kitchen towels were two champagne flutes. There were also grapes and some mineral water.

"I see why the cooler almost squashed me when I took it on land. Is this coffee and biscuits?"

Emilia was smiling. Tomaž was spreading the food on the
blanket in the space between them. He seized the bottle.

"We must celebrate your skiing courage. You were great,
Emilia. Only few girls are so strong and can keep at the line
for so long the first time."

"Serving food and keeping several plates full of food in my
hands is a kind of a work-out, too. I wouldn't let the line go for
anything. It was so much fun, thanks."

"You did well. Here, your drink!"

The cork popped and caused frantic activity in the bushes.
A rabbit took flight, realizing finally he was not alone with the
seagulls. They were flying in circles above the young couple feasting on the delicacies, drinking from the elegant flutes and chatting about skiing. They found out they had both been skiing
at Kitzbühl the previous winter with their parents. They could
have met and spent time together. Soon the bottle was empty
and their stomachs full. Their hunger was satisfied. The sparkling
bubbles moved from the bottle to their heads.

Tomaž put the leftover food in the cooler and lied back on the
blanket. Emilia did the same. They had run out of words some
minutes ago. Each of them was alone with his desire. Emilia
closed her eyes. She was breaking under the strain of her turbulent emotions. She wanted so badly to look at Tomaž. But she
did not let herself go. As long as there was no physical contact
whatsoever, she felt safe. What from? What was she so afraid
of?

Suddenly she felt a shade over her face and body. She nearly
opened her eyes with surprise, for where would a cloud come from
on such a sunny day, when her logic was challenged tenderly. She
felt Tomaž's lips on hers and returned the kiss without thinking
and with her eyes tightly closed. Breathless, Tomaž said softly
in her ears:

"Emilia, look at me, please."

She opened her eyes, and two little suns were reflecting in her
pupils. She was the goddess of the sun. Her eyes shone warmth.
Tomaž was captivated. Emilia's feeble defense was down, too.
She didn't mind what would happen next.

"Will you believe me if I say I love you?"

She smiled softly and believed with all her heart the words
she was longing to hear for so many weeks. She closed her doubts
away and put her arms around his shoulders. They were kissing
again, and here and then Tomaž's hands searched for her breasts,
buttocks, stopping smoothly at the waistline. Not so much later,
he felt her trembling under her bikini. Emilia felt he was aroused,
but hesitated. The boat trip was getting out of her hand. Was
this what she had been wanting for all along?

Tomaž felt she was keeping back from him and didn't want
to be too pushy. So he slowly touched her body, her thighs, her

breasts, kissing tenderly her face, lips, cheeks, hair... His body
was all action, but he moved slowly like a panther; suddenly,
there was time. He felt her warmth embracing him like eternity.
She was unique and true, like the sun slowly setting down at the
horizon. He never thought it possible to lose his reason so easily,
to forget his ambitions and goals. With every kiss he was feeling
more in love with this wonderful mermaid. If only this magical
moment between the worlds could last forever. Suddenly, things
changed. The situation got out of his hands, too. With surprise
and anticipation, he realized Emilia had dropped her bikini and
was lying all naked under him.

"Is it the first time?"

"Yes. Will you take care?"

Tomaž kissed her lips fleetingly.

"If I only knew how... "

"You mean, it is the first time for you, too?"

"Well, yes. I had to study so much and I, I...I wasn't ever in
love before... "

"Me neither. But, is it safe? I mean, I can get... "

"Just in case, I have... "

He took a condom out of the cooler. The package was soaked
with condensation and cold. He opened it with his teeth, and the
plastic ring with a foggy membrane in the middle was out. They
continued to play and touch before the moment came when he
put the plastic on his penis, bursting with desire. Slowly, without
losing each other's eye, they were moving in rhythm. Their heavy
breathing and their cries of pleasure mixed with the seagulls' song
above them; their lust was blending with the afternoon heat. The
seaweed pillow was soft and warm, and the blanket was wet with
the sweat of their bodies exposed to the sun. They were diving
in a whirl of sensations they could never have foreseen, while
crossing from childhood into adulthood. It was Emilia who came
first, and the spasms almost made her lose her consciousness for
a moment. She woke from her petite mort when Tomaž exploded
in her with a cry of a stag. After the sweet battle, they stayed
together relaxed and happy.

"I love you. I will always look after you, Emilia, my darling."

"I know. I love you, too, Tomaž."

They held on to each other for some more minutes until Emilia
moved under his weight.

"Oh, sorry, I must be heavy."

"You're not made of feathers, no. Shall we go for a swim?"

Tomaž kissed her and slowly moved on his side. Emilia was
already on her feet and she ran into the water. Tomaž looked at
his soft member. The seed was all over it, and the condom was
torn apart. He knew what this could mean. A sea of trouble suddenly arose in front of his eyes from the splashing water of the bay
where Emilia was swimming without a worry in the world. The

temperature... from cold to hot in a matter of seconds... And he tore the package with his teeth... the rubber broke. What could be done? There was a pill Emilia could take within forty-eight hours from the intercourse. It would infuse a high dosage of male hormones into her body system in order to prevent the conception. He knew the pills were on sale in pharmacies over the counter. But they were very strong and had bad side effects. Recently, he had seen a documentary. It was impossible. He had to be overreacting. This only time...

He decided to think it over and talk to Emilia later. There was still time. And in any case, they would have to get the pills in Novalja in the morning. So there was nothing to be done there and then. He threw his worries into the wind and joined his beloved in the splashing waves. He dived and bit her ankles tenderly, pretending he was a shark. When he swam up, he sang the tune of the famous thriller nah, nah, nah, nah... Emilia shrieked with joy like a child. She escaped from his mock bites and came back for his wet kisses. They were salty and yet so sweet.

When they came back to the village an hour later, the evening glow was burning in the west. Emilia was in a hurry to start the evening job around the tables. Still, before she came ashore, she stood on her toes, with her shiny wet hair spread around her glowing cheeks and reaching to her waist like a mermaid's and kissed Tomaž passionately on his lips. Slavko was looking from the terrace of the restaurant, shaking his head in disbelief and anger:

"O, my god. There comes trouble."

* * *

The *carabinieri*, two dark, stocky fellows, gallantly opened the back doors of the black Alfa Romeo. Dario's daughters, the Kadura sisters, Olivia and Mira, stepped into the burning summer heat, dizzy after an hour spent in the comfortable, air-conditioned vehicle. Andrej Bak was leaning on the former post house of the border which since ancient times had separated two worlds; the wild Slavs from the cultivated Romans, the communist Yugoslavia from the capitalist Italy, the Eastern Bloc from the NATO. He was watching the women through his wide black sunglasses, which could well hide his surprise. The girls were sisters, but they could not be more different from one another. One was tall, fair skinned and very serious. Her brows knitted in a bad temper as though she already knew the welcome party at the Slovenian border had bitter drinks in store for them. Despite the heat, she wore a long sleeved suit, a beige linen jacket, and long brown trousers, colors which suited well her dark blond bob but not her young age. Her moves were clumsy and her whole appearance was unattractive. The other one was short, she moved graciously like an elegant cat and her body was well shaped like a coca-cola bottle. She was quite alluring in her pistachio green dress so tight that it wrapped her bosom like a second skin. Her hair was dark and in gentle curls, it fell loose around her deeply tanned cheeks divided by a kind smile of white pearls and red cherries. The couple of the Italian *carabinieri* who brought them to the border in their car were staring at the lower part of her body as she paced in her stilettos behind her tall sister. What a girl! In her sky blue eyes, you could read energy and thirst for fun, while the tall one was clearly sober and cold as a fish. How could one father produce such different daughters! Or, were there two fathers?

Knowledgeably, Bak smiled into his goatee and greeted them kindly:

"Hello, my ladies! I am Andrej Bak from the Slovenian Investigation Bureau. How was your travel?"

"Show us your identity card first!" the tall, blond girl barked in reply.

Bak dutifully showed his badge, and they both approached their faces to the picture.

"Put down your sun glasses!"

He did as he was told, looking for understanding in the sexy blue eyes. There was none. Despite their differences, they were a shrewd pair.

"I am sorry for the unpleasant welcome party, Misses Kadura. It was for your safety."

"You better show more respect than those crappy Italians, who dragged us into the car without any explanation. For one moment, we thought we were on our way into one of the brothels, kidnapped, you know. The whole time the bloody fellows were just smiling and repeating *no lo so, no lo so,* as though they were in a kind of mafia movie. And we both speak fluent Italian."

Now, the lovely one spoke up in a clear voice.

"It would be really nice, Mr. Buk, if finally somebody told us, what this is all about. Is it our father?"

"Again, I am sorry for all this. Your father is well. Believe me! The rest I will tell you in the car. By the way, Andrej Bak, not Buk, is my name."

Before they could utter another complaint, he turned on his heels and went to his car. They could get hysterical and loud, he would not discuss the matter in the parking lot on the border. They seemed to understand that and followed him, dragging their big and heavy suitcases on wheels behind them. Bak made no attempt whatsoever to help them. He packed the girls and the baggage in the car and sat at the wheel. The blond Miss Tall was sitting beside him.

"I am Olivia Kadura and this is my sister, Mira, Mr. Bak. Thank you for fetching us, but please tell us now what this is all about!"

Bak started the car, and before he put it into gear, he looked at her sideways:

"Your aunt, Mrs. Marina Kadura, was found dead in her apartment in Rijeka two days ago. We suspect she made a suicide. However, there is a slight suspicion that she could not have finished life by her own will. The benefactor of her last will might have his fingers in it. So we decided to offer you protection until we are sure."

Without another word, he starting driving. After a few miles, Mira asked.

"Please, Mr. Bak. Tell us everything you know. Have you spoken to Father?"

"Yes, we saw him earlier today. We went to Pag, that is, my colleagues from Rijeka and me. He is very sad. Anyway, he thought you might be in danger. You see, the last person Marina presumably had contact with, was Mr. Nemec. Do you know him?"

Now Olivia took over.

"We have met him on a few occasions. He seemed quite a fishy character to me. Do you think he had anything to do with her death?"

"How did she die?" a question, obviously between sobs, came from behind. Mira was crying.

She met Bak's gaze in the rear-view mirror. They stayed connected for a while, then Bak shook his head.

"One question at a time, please... No, personally, I don't think Nemec killed your aunt. I have been dealing with the man for years and I doubt that he is capable of physical violence. We're still waiting for the autopsy results, but it looks like she took poison or drugs. Your father said she had never touched drugs, but there are a few traces of injection on her arms. Was she ill? Was she taking anything? I mean as a therapy."

"No, she was very healthy and never touched either alcohol or drugs. She never smoked. Her voice was too precious for her."

"And Nemec... Well, he seemed rather nice. He was an elegant and cultured man. He took us out to dinner one evening. We went to a nice restaurant in Mošćenice. Do you remember Olivia?"

"Yeah, to me, the man seemed just a harmless fraud. He was boasting of his business all evening. Something about a printing or a publishing house which he had successfully revived or closed. Anyway, when it was time to pay, his credit card didn't work, was rejected or something. In the end Aunt Marina paid. She always carried cash. I couldn't understand what Aunt saw in him. Why did she need him?"

"Can't you understand human feelings for once, Olivia? She was lonely. We should have been home more often. We should have lived with her. Maybe all this wouldn't have happened..."

Olivia just shook her head in disbelief.

"You can't babysit a middle-aged, strong-headed artist, Mira. Besides, she wanted us to be independent. She was the one who rented the flat in Opatija for us. You remember, don't you? She needed her space. You know she was peculiar. We couldn't have lived with her. Don't blame us! Blame the... blame her!"

At this, Bak nodded in agreement while Mira burst into tears anew. Bak turned to Olivia and their eyes met in mutual understanding. Mira was an emotional child, drowning in sorrow. It was up to them to keep a clear head and work on the problem.

Olivia's sharp grey eyes reminded Bak of the eyes he had loved a long time ago. He turned his gaze back to the road, where instead of the lights of the vehicles in front, he imagined his wife's eyes. When the sparks burnt up in them, it was with pure force – of passion and reason, each fighting for their rights. Bak had loved her more than anything in his life. She was his soulmate. Her name was Mojca and she was a nurse at the emergency unit, where they had met one night over two stupid drunks, who stabbed each other nearly to death over a shot of brandy. After the wounds were patched up, interviews over and the drunks sedated to sleep, Mojca and Bak had a cup of coffee in the empty hospital cafeteria. He remembered the rising sun above the roofs of the sleepy city, the Ljubljana castle overlooking the medieval houses along the river below. They didn't say much, but immediately there was a sense of comradeship connecting them. Only a few months later, they got married, and a year later, they had a daughter. They got along well and understood each other's jobs, always focused on the lives and wellbeing of others, never on themselves. But their marriage lasted a decade, no more. Bak never knew why. Yet, without an obvious reason, his Mojca became distant and cold. He found out she had met someone else and had an affair with him. Despite therapists, despite their daughter's pleading with them to stay together, they could never get over the coldness. The third party was separating them like the icy mountain peaks separate two valleys. Bak could not put up with the shame of the affront, and Mojca could not warm to him again. Olivia was not the first woman who reminded Bak of his failed marriage. He had been there before. Yet, he never ever wanted to get into a serious relationship again. He buried himself in work.

"Can you please stop the car? I'm sick..."

Mira behind him was pale as death. She was gasping for air through the open window and it was clear she would burst with something else than tears that time. Bak put the siren on the roof of the car and pulled up by the road. Mira jumped out of the car and headed into an olive orchard. It had turned completely dark outside. The moonless night was casting its velvet over the land and the fields. Like ghosts of the underworld, the big, irregular olive trees were spreading their shadows over the field. Mira leaned on a tree and it seemed as though she was throwing up, but she could also be crying. Only violent jolts of her body were visible from the road.

"Mira is so tender hearted. She loved our aunt very much. She was little when we lost our mother, and Marina... Well, she gave us her love... in her own way. What was left of it after she had sung her arias."

"I'm sorry. I am the bearer of bad news... "

"It's not your fault, Mr. Bak. Just find out the cause of her death. I'll go to see how my sister is doing... "

"Yes, do. I have some water in the trunk. It was very cold when I bought it a few hours ago... "

"Get it, please. She could wash her face with it... We need some time now... Are you taking us to Opatija or to Pag?"

"Where would you prefer to go, Miss Kadura?"

"Bring us home. Take us to Pag, please. We need to see our father... "

"What about the ferry?"

"We can still catch the last one at half past eleven. But in the season they work the nights through. They go every hour."

Bak just nodded. Suddenly, he felt sorry for both of them. Olivia, so brave and reasonable, her eyes dimmed yet dry. She had to be hurting inside, too, but was too ashamed to show it. He imagined seeing her tears, although they were not bursting out of her eyes. He could feel her pain, the worry for her sister, the concern for her father and the anxiety in the face of events, which she could never have foreseen. Her stony facade, her controlled behavior would crumble, fall down like a house of cards in a moment. She could not fool him. He would take them to their father on Pag. It would not be for the first time he would be driving through the night. The girls should not be alone on an evening like this.

The coastal road, which in the times of the communist Yugoslavia the people built with voluntary work and proudly named *Jadranska magistrala*, was meandering around the bays above the cliffs of Velebit steeply falling into the peaceful stillness of the sea. The crumbled rocks below, polished by the sharp *bura* waves, stood sentinel like soldiers guarding royal palaces. It was a dark night. Silence was pressing the already gloomy atmosphere in the car. Without many headlights of the cars driving by, it was like driving through a huge grave. Bak would almost wish that the road was busy with cars dragging boats or every possible kind of trailers behind filled with the equipment to spend a year on an isolated island not two weeks at the sea. The end of July should be the peak of the holiday season. Yet, tonight, there was almost no one.

Passing Bakarac and Crikvenica, they were driving along the famous chestnut avenue in Novi Vinodolski. Like so many avenues sheltered by tall trees, it was planted by the Napoleonic troops two hundred years ago. Finally, around the tiny marina in the centre, they observed crowds in the streets, singing and partying noisily, obviously celebrating a local festivity, but more probably just rejoicing in the summer and good business. Olivia, who had been silent for nearly an hour, spoke up in a throaty voice.

"Mira fell asleep. We will be at Prizna in an hour or so."

"Yeah, I've been to Pag many times, either on holiday or on business. We used to spend holidays at the little village of Metajna. They were very friendly and the coast is wonderful there."

"I know Metajna. My father has a friend from WW2 there. They were fighting together against the fascists. The fascists were cruel rulers of our lands. I presume it was the same in Slovenia. What irony; nowadays, their descendants, I mean the Italians, have become most welcome tourists in Dalmatia. They like to eat and drink and go to restaurants. They spend money and we love them."

"I see what you mean. The world changes and the values follow the flow. The personal worth is nothing but expenditure. I can tell you stories of Slovenian tycoons, how they cheat and trick, lie and kiss asses. These days, people would do anything for a couple of euros."

"I still think Slovenia is much better off than Croatia. You have the European law, and once you sweep away the leftovers of the past, you'll be fine. Croatia, though, will need decades to get back on track after the last war with Serbia and the plundering of the wild privatization. Just think of all the hate and prejudice which are driving our society. We will never be part of Europe. We're so backwards."

"Actually, I don't see there is much difference between Slovenia and Croatia. Once you hand over the last of your war criminals to the Hague tribunal, you'll be in the EU in no time."

Olivia shook her bob in denial.

"I don't agree with you, Mr. Bak. You see, Croatians could have sent Gotovina to the Hague ages ago, but they don't perceive him as a war criminal. He's a national hero, who has fought in a just war. He's the liberator of Knin, the defender of the Bosnian Bihač. They will shelter him rather than turn him in for the sake of progress and better life. That's backwards, you see, Mr. Bak?"

"First, can we use our first names? I am Andrej. It will be easier. And as to General Gotovina, I know Croatians idolize him, but as far as I am acquainted with his case, he has committed crimes against the Geneva Convention. He should go to trial like the others. Do you know his military background was Foreign Legion?"

"Yes, I was reading about it. I don't really know the truth, but I'm telling you, for Croatians, he's a war hero. I saw posters of him on the walls around Zadar and other towns."

Bak nodded in understanding.

"War makes beasts even of decent men. In Slovenia, mass graves have been found just recently in an old mine near Laško. It is a sorry fact that they all carried the signatures of the WW2 heroes we used to learn about in our schoolbooks. Time always tells the truth, Oliver."

"Not always, not always. Usually the winners write history, Andrej."

Andrej Bak concentrated on the serpentine road approaching Senj, the city where the terrible, raging northeast wind, the *bura* sank many a ship in old and modern times. The blows could reach the speed of 200 kilometers per hour and could create high waves which mix and culminate into a deadly sea cocktail. They stopped talking, not finding another subject for a while. He was annoyed with himself, for with every minute he could feel the silence between them bursting with well-known feelings and a newborn tension. He had denied himself all gentle feelings. No more women, and especially not when they are involved in his job. As he was slowing down along the Senj *korso*, Olivia said in a low voice, obviously amused.

"You called me Oliver. This is a name for a boy. I am Olivia, you know."

"Of course you are Olivia. I am sorry. It's been a long day. I have travelled from Rijeka to Pag in the morning, back to Škofije and now back to Pag."

"Thank you for driving us to Pag. I called dad and told him we're coming."

"When was that?"

"When we stopped, you know, for Mira... He'll be waiting for us, he said."

"I could get some sleep in the car and drive back in the morning."

"This is out of the question! You will stay in our house, in my mother's study. Dad will have everything ready for you! Besides, we can talk some more about Marina and maybe come to some new clues together."

"I must be back tomorrow. I have a few meetings in Koper and Ljubljana. But thank you."

There was a line of cars at the ferry harbor, and they had to wait for an hour to get across. Mira woke up feeling a bit better. At last, they were turning left from the main road towards the little village along the bay of Mulobedanj shortly after eleven. Bak was visibly tired. His face looked pale and wasted. His eyes were red as though he was some kind of vampire. He was clutching the wheel for the fear of losing control of the vehicle. The last mile was the most difficult.

Dario was sitting on the bench in front of the house smoking. As soon as they drove into the yard, he turned on the light and yelled into the house. The girls hesitantly put their arms around him, and Dario sank in their embrace like shipwrecked. An older woman came out of Dario's house, and only Bak noticed her and greeted her.

"Hello, Madame. I'm Andrej Bak, Slovenian Investigation Bureau. I brought Olivia and Mira from the Italian border."

"Thank you and welcome. I am Maria, Dario's friend and neighbor. Come inside, we have some food ready. Would you like a drink? A little brandy?"

"No, thank you, no alcohol, please. I plan to leave early in the morning."

"I am sorry, young man, but I think you should stay one day and have some rest. If it's awkward for you to stay here with the family, I can place you in the hotel Perovica. I run the place. Would you like to go to Perovica?"

The father and the daughters came inside. They were looking at Bak waiting for his answer. He could feel it would be impolite not to take up their hospitality, so he gave in.

"Do you have the internet, Mr. Kadura?"

Maria offered a reply.

"No, he doesn't. But I have. My house is over there, on the hill above the pier, and after supper, we can go over, so that you can send your emails. Tomorrow is sleep time. You have to rest, the three of you."

"Thank you, Madam. Can I recall your offer for a brandy?"

"Maria, I am Maria. Here you are."

Maria poured the tiny glasses and they all drank up. Then they sat around the table, with a plate filled with cheese, olives and prosciutto garnished with pieces of melons and dried tomatoes in the middle. They ate in silence. It was after midnight when Maria took Bak to her house and when he came back, the house was dark and the girls obviously asleep. Andrej sat on the bench in front of the house and took a cigarette out of the box. Out of nowhere, Dario came with a carafe of wine and a bottle of mineral water.

"Thank you, Mr. Bak. Thank you so much for bringing my girls home. I was too confused in the morning. I should have followed you to Rijeka and to Koper, and take them over from the Italians myself."

"Well, I wouldn't have a day of holiday if you had, would I?"

Dario smiled. That was a nice attitude.

"Mr. Bak, would you like to go with me to lift my nets in the morning? My friend Slavko threw them for me, but we could pick them together, eh?"

OK346   PART II. LIFE GOES ON

"When in the morning are you going?"

Bak put out the cigarette and flung the stub away. When it flew over the yard, he realized how rude that was. But he was too tired. He could pick it in the morning. Dario could not care less.

"We can go a bit later, at half past six. It'll be a good catch, for the moon is in the first quarter."

"Right, I'll come, Mr. Kadura. I must be to bed now, or it'll be me falling in your nets tomorrow. Good night."

"Good night, Mr. Bak. You're a good man."

After a minute, Bak came out in a panic.

"Where do I have to go?"

"First door left in the basement. The light is on and I put some fresh clothes and the toiletry staff for you on the bed. The bathroom is next door."

Bak found it all; the simple room, the bed smelling of sharp lavender and all the tiny proofs of attentive hospitality like a carafe of icy water on the nightstand, and some dried fruits sprinkled with sweets in a bowl. After all, it was the hotelier's house, although Dario did not look like one. Bak took a long hot shower and crawled into bed like a sleepwalker. He sank into a sweet dream. He knew it was a dream, for it was about a girl. For ages, girls had not entered either his consciousness or his dreams.

* * *

Maria's desk in her home office was full of papers – mostly scanned and photocopied documents in Latin. Her laptop was on, glimmering in the dark, spacious room, the shutters blocking out the high afternoon sun. Only a little table lamp illuminated the scans of old Blaca Monastery chronicles, which Maria studied and embellished with her notes and commentaries in red. She was having an afternoon rest from the business and dedicated her time to her most passionate hobby – genealogy and history research.

The passion for historical research first started during her studies of art history in Rijeka, when by chance she found a book about her great granduncle, related to her through her Triestine mother. It was in Slovenian, but she could understand it and read it avidly. Then years of active life followed, when she completely abandoned the idea. After settling on Pag with Paula, she needed something to pass the time while giving meaning to her own life. She needed to find out about her roots. Moreover, she needed to leave traces leading into her future.

Although she kept her notes safely locked away, she wanted Paula to find and read them one day. It would define her life. A decade ago, when Paula was in boarding school in Zadar, she started the family history. Maybe it was her proof of existence. Soon the family history gave way to other events she discovered in the past. Dalmatia, the coastal area from the island of Rab to the Bay of Kotor, was historically one of the richest regions in Europe. How little people knew about it! The hordes of tourists visiting the beaches each summer had no idea that they were threading on the memories of Celtic, Illyrian, Greek, Roman, Ottoman and Venetian people, who long ceased to exist, yet left traces of their cultures in every stone. It became a true passion, a counterpart of her work at the hotel, where she liked to enhance her marketing and promotion leaflets with old legends and tales.

As opposed to the general habit of genealogists, she quit following strictly the male line, which was easier to trace in Dalmatia. She was after the women. What were their lives like? Women, either of high or low birth, changed their maiden names after marriage and assimilated into their husband's families. Maria wanted to find out about her forerunners, about the women in the past who shaped the society she was living in shoulder to shoulder with men, yet remained anonymous and forgotten. By digging into their past she wanted to know who she was, not in a transcendental or in strictly genealogical sense, but she wanted to study and understand women in the distant and recent Dalmatian past, in order to come to terms with the present.

Maria cherished life above all other notions. Life was not only a basic human right. It was a gift. She understood that every time the memories of the bloody toll of the last Balkan war creeped into her brain. She was grateful that she and Paula survived. The pessimism of the philosophers, who poetically despaired over not understanding how they came into this world with their profound fears and struggles with death, the blur of metaphysics, they were certainly not Maria's mantra. Her courage to fight for survival proved in action at the Bosnian front, when she was running from the shells with a baby in her arms. She didn't think there was anything heroic or mystical about death, just blood, violence and bad smells. Yes, Maria could still smell death when she paused for a moment and let the memories penetrate her thoughts. It was piss and human debris and sweat, with a sour tinge of horror adrenaline. There was nothing noble about it, no great ideas like freedom or justice, for which people perished – just the evil, plain death, the enemy of everything human.

Therefore, the subject of Maria's studies was life, not death. She wanted to set a course for her and Paula's ship to anchor in the safest of all harbors – happiness of the moment, the sureness of now. She took arms against Paula's illness and fought at her side against the vomit and pains of the chemotherapy. They would not give in easily.

For days and days, while the autumn rains or the rough winter *bura* were keeping her indoors, she was immersed in the passages of texts, mostly chronicles, business contracts, cadastral and parish books or some literary texts, mostly epics, which were describing the lives of women. It was pure detective work. From various clues, she somehow composed the life of such and such, not always sure or caring whether the woman was her blood ancestor or not. Then, she finally sat down at her computer and wrote the story, with vivid imagery, as though she was living her life in a distant past. It was not for her vanity she was researching her roots. She didn't care too much about the blood lines. They had been highly overrated throughout history, so many fools getting the fates of so many people in their hands only by blood inheritance. The old saying that blood was thicker than water meant nothing to Maria. She knew it was pure nonsense. You could relate to somebody who you'd just met more than you could relate to many a member of your own family. Her bitter experience was cemented in the foundations of her hotel, where her new life began so many years ago.

With a sigh, Maria took off her heavy frame glasses and closed her eyes for a moment. Her long eyelashes were damp with tears of strain as for some time she was trying to unravel a family story or more likely a family tragedy on Brač in the past century. She stood up and took another heavy book from the shelf. The rest of the huge oak bookcase trembled as she pulled the leather bound hardback out as though unwilling to let one of their friends go. She had enough of Blaca and the monks' metaphysics for the day. She would continue to write the story of the beautiful young daughter of the *Ragusan* merchant and nobleman Menze or Menčetić. Holding the huge historical volume in her hands, she let thoughts wander.

First to Paula, who was sound asleep in her room above and was at last getting better every day. Maria was so happy. She could burst with joy. Should there be God in Heaven, he looked down on her at last, absolved her of her sins, and inspired life in her girl. Obviously, the new medication, which Zagreb oncologists prescribed a month ago, worked, and after the painful days of Paula's body fighting the side effects of brutal chemotherapy, the girl was gaining her strength back. She needed a lot of sleep and she couldn't go outside, but for a few days now the vomiting stopped, and Paula could take her meals with her in the dining room.

The worries of Paula's condition stayed in the shadow of the sudden events, which stirred the peaceful life of the little village. Marina's death was in every mouth. How, why, who? There were a million questions, which the investigation would have to clear. Her poor friend Dario couldn't even bury his sister properly, for the body was still held in Rijeka for autopsy. Maria was glad that she could show her support to the family in such trying times. They were good people.

The heavy book recaptured her attention. Maria opened it at

the chapter about important *Ragusan* families, where she was trying to discern the story of Miljuta Menčetić, who was heroically
and for a reason refusing her family's marriage arrangements.
Dubrovnik in the 14th century was a dangerous place for a girl to
oppose the customs and the will of her elders. Well, any place in
any time can be dangerous for a young girl to throw caution to
the wind.

* * *

The terrace of Slavko's inn was nearly empty under the deep
shadow of the *crnika* trees, or *Quercus Ilex* as the botanists named
this dwarf Mediterranean oak tree with tiny dark green leaves. It
was so hot at three in the afternoon that even the ants were not
moving, saving their strength for the evening meal, when they
would pester the guests and collect food for their queen and the
colony deep below the ground. Maria sat at the outside table,
with a cigarette between her fingers, a steaming pot of coffee,
and the daily *Jutarnji list* in her lap. It was supposed to be
a serious newspaper, yet it was full of scandals and reports on
topless singers and financial thefts. She was wondering why all
the denounced and legally indicted criminals in Croatia were still
mostly enjoying their freedom with the monies they had stolen.
Or, politically correctly, they had privatized into their own pockets. Pocket privatization it should be called, not euphemistically
transition. The only transition Maria could see was the transition of goods from state ownership into the privileged households.
There was something deeply wrong with a democracy which could
not maintain a legal system to discipline criminals and protect the
citizens. When the first democratic laws had been forged by the
French Enlightenment philosophers three centuries ago and the
origins of today's democracy were idealized in the slogan "Liberty, equality, fraternity", only few had in mind liberty as chaos,
equality as abuse of the laws and fraternity as business network-
ing of morally base people.

In all now independent states of former Yugoslavia, legal systems and courts of law were deeply corrupt and malfunctioning.
Slovenia was no exception, although it had successfully joined the
European Union in 2004. Nothing but suspicious family connections dating from the communist revolution during WW2! Nothing but monkey business! She could read about prosecutors or
even court administrators, who were stealing documents, about
judges who left their lawsuits untouched until they fell under the
statute of limitations, and police forces more inclined to listen
to the politicians than to do their job. The villains were living
in peace enjoying their ill-gotten gains. In Slovenia the prosecution office was run by one family, in Croatia judges were friends
with solicitors; in the mess, corruption blossomed like weeds in

abandoned field. Wow, what is justice, asked the jesting Pilate, but never stayed for an answer. The criminal investigations all over the Balkan area were dealing with petty thefts while millions were sinking to the offshore paradises.

Maria despised the chaotic and corruptive governments which had changed the face of Croatia after the last Balkan war to the worst possible, yet she needed to be acquainted with its main players. Her business could not be an isolated island. No matter what, she strived for her personal ethics to remain pure and strict. But Maria of all people knew that only money and success could bring about a certain degree of ethics in average people, who at the edge would easily turn bad. The main rule at present in society was adaptation – karma chameleon, a man without conviction. Maria knew that a person without conviction is vulnerable, is trying to find a goal in life, and how terribly dangerous it could get when these goals are installed into their brains by mad politicians. The masses would take anything to be true; the emptiness of their brains allows the unthinkable to thrive there without any control at all. Just like an empty field invites lush weeds to spread and grow wildly. Given the circumstances, a docile schoolteacher could turn into a predator with a gun.

She looked up from the paper. A predator... Like that cat which Dario was stroking on the lower terrace. He was sitting on a stony wall, in the shadow, bent slightly forward, so that his unbuttoned shirt was showing his muscled stomach. His hands were huge and skin burnt by the sun into dark brown leather. He was a tall man, nearly two meters in height, and strongly built. He loved good food and wine. Contrasting his dark complexion, his full hair was white as snow and eyes deep blue and clear despite the age. His face with wide cheekbones could spite the rough winds at sea and the hundreds of wrinkles only played the expressions of his moods like a puppet theatre. Those days he was going around upset and unsure, carrying a mobile phone in his shirt pocket, which was so unlike him. His sister's death had pained the poor old man more than he wanted to admit. His face was at all times, difficult or happy, like an open book. No secrets and bluffing there, here was a man who was honest.

The cat was white and black, with thick, shiny fur. She was huge around her belly and her nipples were bursting with the approaching birth of a litter. Dario's hand was sliding softly under her chin, scratching the sides. She lifted her head and stretched with satisfaction. Then his huge hand moved slowly down the cat's spine over her black patch. He focused on giving her pleasure, his rough fisherman's fingers denying their strength and stroking the animal tenderly. She was purring so loudly that Maria could hear her at her table.

Suddenly, Dario raised his head and looked Maria directly in the eyes. "See, you could be in her place, I would make you purr with pleasure," his eyes were saying. He would hold her in his lap, tamed and passionate like his pussycat.

There was something crazily erotic about this old man playing with the cat. Maria blinked. Yes, Dario is a handsome man. She could imagine herself with him. She sobered in a flash of a moment. No love affairs!

"Are you expecting, Dario?" she yelled over the silence in a mockingly concerned tone.

Dario smiled apologetically. He knew better than to jump at Maria's defensive provocation about the pregnant cat in his lap.

"Yeah, indeed, I am expecting. I am expecting you, Maria, to come and turn a round in my boat with me." His blue eyes were shining with deep desire. She understood his gesture right. Maria lost her composture for a moment.

"Where would we go?" she asked cautiously. It nearly sounded like yes, with a hint of no.

"I thought about going to the isles of Laganj and looking for fresh asparagus. They must be sprouting after the last rains. Are you coming?"

He was still stroking the cat tenderly, and her purring sounds dominated the crickets' song. His look was serene, no hint of jeering in it. He had been in love with the woman for some time, and he could feel her interest and tender friendship for him. How she had come to his house a few days ago and helped him to clean up and welcome his daughters. She joked and scorned, but she liked him, he knew that. Something else, some past experience was holding her back, he could tell. When he approached her too much, she would back off in fear. Were they young, there would be plenty of time to pull down the defences. However, they were old, with the end of life approaching. They should live the moment and enjoy quickly the last beams of warmth and love. Yet, it was not to be. They had known each other for nearly two decades and were friends ever since Maria came to Mulobedanj. She had been very kind to him when his wife died. Some relatives reproached him he should have gone to Novalja on that day, but he could not – did not. He was sorry, but what could he do? It was his wife, not him, who had driven too fast at the slippery turns after all. And the older he got, the more complex the relationship with Maria was and more strained their communication, spinning around the daily fish catches and winter olive tending. Years went by, years they had missed... His blue eyes were expecting her answer silently.

"How long would it take to get back? I have to receive an important guest at six, and I would have to take my mobile with me."

Finally, Maria's defence walls seemed to crumble. She felt confused. Why was she so moved today? Was it the cat? Was it Paula's state of mind, which reminded her of the fragility of life?

Well, she didn't really care, she could control herself anyway, and she needed a break after the busy morning and monthly bank statements she was summing up for a report. Why not Laganj? Its Croatian name meant easy and light, just right for the tiny strip of pale green land in the middle of the blue sea.

"I'll bring you back in time, Maria. At half past five, is that soon enough?"

She heard his serene voice with no trembling, no passion. Maybe she was only imagining his sexual want a minute ago. It had to be her fantasy, for she had lived with so little emotions and physical touch all these past years, her only focus on Paula and work at the hotel. Yes, she had to be imagining things, why would Dario change his respectful attitude precisely today?

"Right, I'll be at the pier in a moment, let me take my bathing bag, I would love a swim as well."

Maria emptied the coffee cup, put the cigarette out and folded the paper on the table. No more tycoon stories, she would take some hours off. She loved to ride in a boat, the wind blowing her hair out of her ponytail.

There were still some waves from the morning *bura* when they steered out of the harbour. The boat was jumping up and down, and Maria was almost sorry that she had come along. She used to be sea sick at every occasion; just looking at a boat on the high waves made her stomach turn. Since the war, her stomach was like a rock, nothing ever bothered it.

The engine was screaming in agony, with pistons pumping in the chambers in hard rock rhythm. Or, it seemed to Maria, more like in the heavy metal music noise. They had to use hand signs to communicate. At last, they found the mooring block in a bay between the two little islands, the Small Laganj and the Big Laganj. Dario killed the engine, and dozens of white, screaming seagulls immediately took over the disturbance of peace. They were flying around the boat, doing acrobatic plummets and loops, thinking the fisherman would be pulling out a net full of fish in a moment and there would be scraps for their hungry bellies. After a while, the birds realized that was not the case, tired and left the boat and the two old people in peace. Dario brought out a flask of red wine, some cheese, olives and salted sardines. They ate in silence, enjoying every little note of the peaceful horizon and mopped the salty oil with soft white bread from Slavko's. It was made with milk instead of water, so it tasted sweet nearly like a festivity loaf at Easter. Maria thought of her mother's bread, baked in the karstic hills over Trieste, white as snow and tender as sweet cream. She had spent a happy childhood among the karstic vineyards.

Dario took out of the cabin a huge grey bucket, the kind to salt the small sardines in. He put into the bucket the flat basket for asparagus, strong shoes with worn out socks in them – Maria didn't want to guess for how long those had been worn – long trousers, a T-shirt and pants. He stripped naked and jumped in the water. Maria turned away in embarrassment – had he stripped in front of her before, or was today a different day? It took Dario several shouts to attract her attention again.

"Maria, get the bucket into the water slowly, please."

"Ok, sorry," she answered and smiled. "Is the water cold?"

"Well, it is. But I will dry in the sun on the beach. I'll be sweating by evening, though. . ."

She froze, again a sexual hint between the normal lines of conversation. Was he going to move on her or what? Maria lowered the bucket and watched Dario swim ashore. As far as she knew his passion for gathering either mushrooms in autumn or fresh herbs in spring, it would be hours before he would come back. She took off her clothes and lay on the bow with Ken Follet's Pillars of the Earth. She enjoyed the good story and the vivid characters. She had her doubts regarding the liberties of certain characters, especially the independent Aliena was suspicious to Maria, as women were deprived of many rights during medieval times. Yet, in principle, she loved strong female characters, and the book was a good read. She knew in her guts she was of the strong breed herself. After a while, she became immersed into the story and forgot about Dario. In between, she jumped in the water to cool off, without her bathing costume, for there wasn't a soul in sight. The sun was setting slowly and it was time to cover her skin and go, but Dario was nowhere in sight. They had to return, she had to welcome her VIP guest. She called Dario's name once, twice, louder and louder. She blew the ship's horn full volume. Only then she saw Dario dragging himself along the beach, shaky on his feet and limping on his right foot. His shirt was torn and he was bleeding. She jumped into the water and swam over.

"What happened, Dario? Are you hurting?"

With a worried gesture, she felt his chin and looked at the cuts, which didn't seem too deep.

"I am sorry, Maria. You're in a hurry, but would you believe it, I fell off the wall just like a ripe plum. It was at least three meters deep into the blackberry bush. I have thorns all over my body. I lost balance. It took me an hour to climb back. I didn't gather much asparagus by then."

"Leave the asparagus! What's with your foot? You can't stand on it, Dario!"

He took a sorry look at his right leg, where a heavily swollen ankle was purple like a freshly boiled crab.

"Oh, that's why it took me so long. It hurts like hell. I think it's twisted, if not broken. I don't know how I will swim to the boat, now."

Maria was a practical woman. In her life she always looked for solutions, and she immediately had one for the situation.

"I'll get the life jacket from the boat and drag you to it. Then I'll help you aboard with a rope."

"Yeah, do, please. And we'll use the pulley for the nets to help lift my weight, the leg hurts like hell. Would you be able to drive the boat?"

"Yes, but I will have trouble at the harbor. Anchoring is not my thing. Never mind, we'll call Slavko on the mobile and get him waiting for us on the pier, he will help."

Dario looked at Maria sadly. His plans for this trip were so different, how could he have been such a clumsy old chunk of wood? Old and out of order, that's what he was. Hell, he wanted to continue the afternoon courting Maria, for he had a vague feeling today that she felt more than friendship for him and was willing to admit it at last. But he fell from the wall, damned. No purring in his lap, he'd be happy if he could get home.

"Take off your clothes, Dario."

"Yes, mam. I wish it was under different circumstances you'd say this."

"Come on, dirty old man! Keep your pants on, just in case. I think I had enough sexy sights for one day."

"Indeed, I wanted to show you my treasures, but you turned away."

"I was afraid of your treasures, my friend! I am an old lady, Dario. I could get a stroke..."

"Not by looking at it, Maria."

They were laughing and joking, the best medicine for pain. The bucket was full, and Dario sat in the water trying to relax. Maria swam to the boat with the bucket and back with the life jacket. Luckily, Croatian maritime authorities were very strict about the basic boat equipment, and even old stubborn sea wolves like Dario were too afraid of the high fines to not have life jackets aboard. She dragged him to the boat, they joked along the way, and Dario had the audacity to fake clumsiness and pulled Maria's head under the water.

"I will leave you right here, old man. Stop being a child now!"

Maria yelled through coughs and laughs. In truth, she did not mind it. Suddenly, she felt tenderness towards this helpless fisherman, who loved her and messed up her afternoon appointment. With the help of the pulley, Dario got aboard, and Maria gave him a painkiller from his first aid kit. She made a phone call and asked her assistant to go and meet the president of the Croatian parliament who was coming to the Hotel Perovica in half an hour. They didn't have to hurry now.

Dario was leaning on the bench with his towel around his hips.

"Get us a drink, Maria, please."

She brought the wine glasses and filled them with red wine. They cheered and drank. The wine washed down the salty water and left a taste of strong, smoky bouquet. Maria sat down next to Dario on the bench. They faced westward, where the sun was sinking in a red and orange spectacle. She looked in Dario's eyes and saw the haze of the sun in his pupils. He stretched his neck and offered her his lips. Maria closed her eyes and pressed her lips to his. Their kiss tasted like sun and wine. It was warm, long and longing.

"Thank you, Maria," he said when they separated. She was reluctant to let go.

"It's only for medical purposes. You could say, another pain-killer, Dario."

He embraced her with his strong arms and pulled her close to his naked body. He kissed her again and again, until Maria was lying in his lap, tamed and happy like a purring cat.

"I love you, Maria. Will you make love to me, here on the boat?"

Maria thought of her men in the past. They were younger and tougher than Dario, but nobody worshipped her the way he did. She could sense all his respect and deep feelings in one wet kiss. And she loved it, she loved him. She felt drawn to his body with all the wrinkles and curves of age and experience. Yet, it was time to get Dario to the doctor's and get the boat home. Old bones were difficult to set and heal.

"Dario, we will continue where we stopped now. I promise you. But now, we have to get your twisted or broken ankle to Novalja and let the doctor examine it."

"Leave my ankle, search higher." He took her palm and pressed it against his breast.

"This is my pain, here. Feel it! In my heart, which wants to be loved again, my dear friend."

Maria's eyes got wet. She stroked his chest and kissed him on the cheek, holding him for a moment.

"Come on, my lovely man. Let's get you and your boat home first."

"Only if you promise me you will come to check on me tonight in my bedroom."

Maria smiled and said she would put him to bed like a baby. Then Dario limped to the steer and started the engine. The hor- rific noise silenced everything else. Maria freed the mooring and rolled the ropes. They sent a message to Slavko's mobile and set the course for Mulobedanj. An hour later, they should be back in the civilization. How would the villagers look at their relation- ship if things got serious? What would Paula think? Maria had only one thing on her mind; Dario's muscular chest and her cheek against it. She wanted him more than ever. The older you get, the more you burn with the passion of love and need for pleasure.

* * *

The evening was hot and the air thick with expectation. It should have rained days ago, the sky was charged with a gray mist, yet while the earth was crying for water, the clouds bypassed the island and moved further to Velebit, leaving Pag's crops thirsty and dry. They lay on the cotton blanket of the big double bed in Dario's house, enjoying the fan's breeze perfumed with the lavender burning stick Maria put in a vase on the night table. They were dressed, for they were too exhausted and too seriously involved in a conversation to think of making love. Their relationship was like a late summer sky those days – clouded and charged with electricity. Dario was sad about his daughters; the girls had left as quickly as Marina was put into the ground in the tiny cemetery at Lun. He missed them. He was hoping that they would stay for the summer, but they were both busy with their studies. He was happy that Maria was around and that they finally connected. Finally, they were together, a couple. Still, in all the wisdom and peace of their mature age, Maria and Dario could not find any good solutions to their problems.

Their first problem was Maria's granddaughter Paula. She hadn't taken it well that her *nona*, approaching seventy director of a famous ecological hotel that provided bread and butter for half of the island, was starting an amorous relationship with a local fisherman almost fifteen years younger than her. Besides, the man was a weirdo. Dario Kadura was seen as an eccentric with a moody temperament, who never spent too many words in conversation and had very few friends. Even his daughters left him, not to speak about his sister, who always nagged at him and complained about him to everybody in the village. Paula heard his sister, the opera singer Marina, died in dubious circumstances. She suspected that something was brewing between her *nona* and Dario since a few weeks earlier, when Maria steered his boat into the harbor one evening and Slavko helped him to the doctor in Novalja. She wondered even then how it could happen that the man broke his leg on the boat and where he had taken her *nona* on that wreck of a boat. He had only been her supplier up to then. He sold her the fish. Maria never really had a good word for him. She said he was unreliable and that she cannot plan the menu on his whims and moods. So, the hotel had many other suppliers as well.

All of a sudden, they became a couple. Everybody was laughing their heads off over the old fools. Paula felt ashamed and did not like the situation. She was sulking in the evenings when *nona* left her at home alone, doubly outraged by the lies that she was to go back to work at the hotel. Her health deteriorated again, and Paula got depressed with angst. She spent long hours in front of the television or on the internet, feeling afterwards all the lonelier. She wanted her grandmother to be with her and take care of her. When she discovered Dario in Maria's kitchen a few weeks ago, she was very upset. Her reaction coincided with her disease relapse. Her medical check a few days later showed that the chemotherapy did not stop the leukemia and there was little hope and time left.

Dario was trying hard to please Paula, and Maria was doing her very best to connect the two people she loved. They had supper together; lettuce, hardboiled eggs, and poached asparagus with a good white wine. It was a very silent supper, Dario sensing Paula's cold reserve towards him. There must have been thousands of volts in the air!

Maria, at the peak of the tourist season, felt too tired to act. They would have to get along eventually, her Paula and Dario. She felt too old to postpone her joy for later. Besides, her life was not a Christmas tree; it brought her many sorrows and few happy moments. Dario, with his wonderful sense of humor and love for nature, was one of them. If Dario and Paula didn't want to connect she would have to continue separating her time between them, and if they did, they could have some nice time together, the thrce of them. Maybe it was just her indifference which in the end made the girl and her aged lover start a heated discussion of the nature reserve around the island of Rab, where all fishing was forbidden within two nautical miles of the shore. Paula was defending their clever strategy with the argument that the Adriatic was overfished and several species were on the brink of extinction. Dario, on the other hand, was defending the fishermen's rights and their way of life. Of course, he practically lived in the waters around Mulobedanj and rarely came back with little catch. In harmony with the weather, the winds and the seasons, he always found the right spot for the following evening to set up his nets. In the end, after poking at each other for some time, they started joking and gossiping about the kids in the bay and the new love affairs mushrooming in the every day fuller hotel and apartments in the village. The hottest of them all was of course a new love between a Slovenian student and Paula's friend Emilia. The girlfriends spent much time analyzing Tomaž; every word he said was important, not to speak of deeds and attention he showed to Emilia. They both agreed it would be nothing but a summer romance, yet Paula was happy for her friend when she saw that the boy was a real gentleman. Emilia needed some emotions, a passion to sweep her off her feet after the coldness of her family from Zagreb. The ice between two rivals for Maria's heart and attention was broken. Paula even sipped a glass of wine and chatted as though there were no dark shadows under her eyes. Maria watched Dario and Paula, curiously wondering why they had never spoken before. After that she no longer lied to Paula about where she was going in the evenings. The magic of their mature love wrapped their nights in long conversations interrupted only by moments of passion. Also tonight was such a night. Dario took Maria's hand in his and leaned on the pillow against her.

"What are your plans then, Maria?"

She turned her face to look him in the eyes. Her expression was stern like carved in stone, it was neither happy nor sad. Behind the mask of impassiveness, Dario could feel her deep sorrow. He was looking desperately for some words of comfort and hope.

"We'll go to Ljubljana. I have arranged a medical for both of us in the end of September. I hope with this bone marrow transplant Paula can be cured. But it is not certain and we will see if our marrow systems are compatible."

"Can't they find out in advance?"

"Of course, they can. The last test showed a good positive probability. They said it could be enough."

"What about you? Is the operation risky for you?"

"I don't know. As much as I could find out it is not entirely without risks. But I'm fit, I'll be fine. Are you worried that nobody will bug you to change your underwear and clean your house?"

"Leave my pants, Maria. I prefer not to wear anything when you're around, you know that. As to this operation, I guess you have made up your mind."

"Paula is everything I have, Dario."

"The lady knows how to hurt my heart. Am I nothing to you, Maria?"

"Maybe something... my secret lover visiting my nights and entering my dreams... "

"We should surely drop the secrecy. Who cares what people say? We're two lonely old people. How could anybody blame us?"

She kindly stroked his white hair. He was still a handsome man, and she was glad she had him. She was so alone for such a long time. All her social contacts were superficial; they were suppliers, customers, builders, employees, performers, guests. There were almost no friends in her life. Hence, she forgot how it is to trust somebody and lean on him. Yet, she could not completely relax and let go. Or had she fallen out of the habit?

"You know how people are. They talk and talk... All of a sudden, they remembered their conversations with Marina. And she rarely spoke to anybody."

"Yeah, I know. She was very restrained. We only exchanged a few phrases in all the years I've been here."

"You wanted to say she was so aloof and proud. My sister was no easy character. She was particular and many times very unkind, especially to kids and women. You know, she had a theory about you. She told me once she was pretty sure your money was soiled with the war in Bosnia."

"Oh!? Money doesn't need any explanations. The hotel was built by the investors. I only used some cash to buy your land and to buy the house. It was not so much."

"I know. Back then nobody was interested in our land. You could have it for as good as nothing. Not that I am complaining about the sale. You left me the olive trees, and for the first time in my life I earned some honest money with my olive oil. Perovička – my first class oil! I was so proud. But Marina didn't see it. She never cared about anything but her music."

"I didn't know how to tend to trees. They are so old. I was glad when Luivield wanted to preserve them as part of the hotel complex. So your funny inheritance custom to separate the trees from the ground came in handy. I'm glad at least somebody is happy with me."

He lifted himself on his right elbow, and his left hand glided towards her breast. She stopped it on its way.

"Or, I will claim the difference in services. . . "

"You'd do a poor deal. I am too old for you or anybody else."

"Well, a good drink makes the old young. I'll have a glass of white wine. Will you join me?"

"Yes, please. And come back here. The fan is so nice."

"You can take off your clothes. You'll feel better and cooler."

"Men never change. . . "

Maria was smiling. They should banish their worries with a few glasses of wine for the moment. She remembered suddenly her first years in Mulobedanj, when Dario's wife was still alive and his daughters came around the building site of Perovica, chatting away curiously. Dario's wife didn't fit in. People from the village had been mean to her. Women were gossiping behind her back, and in long winter evenings, when they crossed her path, men looked away without a greeting. She was lonely and Dario was away at the sea. Those were difficult years for her and Paula, too, but the villagers soon bootlicked her every step, for they realized she had money. It was stressful all the same and no wonder one of the two of them got so sick. What mad scheme of fate to choose Paula instead of her!

The war was still all around them then. She could not banish the bad memories from her mind for years, and she kept seeing ghosts behind every tree trunk. She would not leave the house after dark for many years and shook many nights with fear while the *bura* was causing pandemonium with the wooden shutters. When Paula was away at school, she even spent some nights at the hotel. Then she found a way to control her anxiety: she started her historical research about the old times in Dalmatia. With her readings under the lamp, she could face the long nights of howling winds. Now, she had Dario and was grateful for it.

He came back to the bedroom with a bottle, two glasses, and a plate of small olives, soft cheese and crackers. She made space on the bed and took the glasses in her hands. He filled one after the other, the chilled golden wine causing the sides of the simple water glasses glisten with tiny condensation bubbles.

"Here, my lady. Any more wishes?"

"Thank you, very nice. Not precisely four stars, I mean the glasses, but will do for the moment."

"Sorry, I forgot the directors only drink wine from tall wine glasses. Shall I get another one or will you rather have water instead?"

"No, no. I was just joking. This is fine. By the way, you didn't tell me about your trip to Rijeka two days ago. Did you see detective Kostić?"

"Yes, I spent the whole morning with him and the boys at the police station. They also took me to the court, where I spoke with the judge regarding Marina's will."

"And what did they find out?"

"A lot, actually. I was surprised how efficient their investigation had been. This Slovenian boyfriend of my late sister, Milan Nemec, he's quite a character. They're still looking for him everywhere. There is an arrest warrant issued by the Slovenian authorities, which includes all the ex Yugoslavia territories except Serbia. He has obviously vanished into thin air. But it seems that he hasn't harmed Marina. That much they know. I guess he had other sins on his conscience. As to Marina, the Croatian police closed the case. They say it was a suicide and there is no point in further investigation."

"What do you think, Dario? Would Marina take drugs and kill herself?"

His face darkened with worry and guilt.

"What do I know, Maria? The ways of men are strange sometimes. After Giacoppo died, she had never been the same."

Maria saw he would need years to get over it. She wanted to bring him to other thoughts.

"What about Marina's will?"

"They are pretty sure that the Slovenian document is void. Still, we need to wait for the court council to issue a joint statement. They even tried to trap Nemec by sending to his address an invitation to the probate proceedings, but he didn't show up. So in a month or so this will be solved. But Maria, what am I or my girls going to do with this huge business empire? I don't know anything about it, and Mira and Olivia are so young. They've never had a job yet, and they still need to finish their studies."

"Don't worry. Marina also didn't manage the hotels on her own. And I am sure the dividends will buy you a new engine for the boat, or maybe even a new boat?"

"Maybe, maybe not. . . Anyway, my girls will know what to do. They should, really. We've spent a fortune on their education, time to show if it was worth a fig."

"I am sure it was. What does this Nemec do anyway? Does he own companies or is he a politician?"

"I understood he is one of the most notorious and successful Slovenian tycoons. He sent to hell several companies. He would simply empty their bank accounts. He was involved in selling arms and medical supplies to Bosnians during the war. I don't know where Marina found him. He is in every respect a true criminal. Bak told me there was an indictment against him a year or so ago. He got off the hook because of some kind of legal fault committed by the Slovenian prosecutors. Anyway, he neatly distributed his assets among his wife, who he never divorced, although I remember Marina thinking him a divorcee, and his son, who is some kind of left wing political activist. They also found out that he sliced a huge portion of his income into several Cyprus bank accounts, from which he invested back into real estates in Slovenia. They say they could track some of his investments to Croatia also. He always remained anonymous, pulling the strings of his straw men. Nemec is a clever man. I don't think they will ever catch him."

Maria's heart missed a beat. She remained apprehensively silent. She remembered the Cyprus straw man company which provided her with funds and bank guarantees nearly two decades ago and owned a big share of the Perovica hotel. Was it possible? Did he approach Marina because he knew the area? She would check her guest lists in the morning. Slovenians were quite rare, and despite the legal limitations regarding the period for which she could keep personal records on her guests, she never destroyed them. She simply took the lists out of the operating system, but kept them on for spring promotions or just in case.

"There's really nothing we can do. Just wait and see. I know it pains you that Marina's life ended by her own will, but it is better so. Your daughters are safe. You will get on with your life, Dario. Remember, it was her free will. She died when and the way she wanted to. She was a remarkable woman and a great artist. Stop feeling guilty. As to that Nemec, they will catch him eventually."

Maria's voice sounded strange to her, as though it hadn't come out of her own mouth. The hunch she experienced many times when she was researching remote historical events, the vague suspicion that names and places were connected and that she had only to put together the pieces of the mysterious puzzle, started to haunt her. She had the feeling that in some fishy way her hotel could provide a lead to Nemec. Was he her guest? Did he spend his holiday at Slavko's? He had to come to the village before and stay at Slavko's, or he would never put money into an entirely

unknown enterprise. Was it him who years later wanted to cheat
Dario's sister? Evil coupled with evil. She would conduct a thorough research tomorrow. If she was able to trace the stories of
people after centuries had gone by, she would track this Nemec
down for sure. Yet, what would she do then? She was not sure.
She was not sure at all what she would do with Hotel Perovica
then...

* * *

Paula was dreaming that she was still a little girl, maybe six
or seven years old. She was walking by the sea with her *nona*
Maria. The air was cold. A strong, freezing wind was blowing
from the sea, where high waves were roaring at the shore angrily.
They were foaming high up, menacing the rocks and the souls on
the shore. The atmosphere was gloomy, and in a kind of twilight,
trees, rocks, and bushes looked different, as though it was not the
same coast. They were dressed in light summer clothes. Paula
was cold, she was trembling and wailing to go inside, but her
nona remained determined to stay on her path and walk to her
goal, dragging little Paula behind her. Where were they going?
Paula's warm tears were cooling her cheeks. She wanted to break
away, but *nona*'s cold grip was firm as steel. She was telling Paula
something in order to comfort her. Paula couldn't understand a
word. The only sounds echoing in her ears were the howling of
the wind and the roaring of the sea. *Nona* was moving her lips
like in a silent movie. The only word she could read from *nona*'s
lips was the word must, yet she could not understand what she
was supposed to do. They came to the cliff, below which the cold
sea was hitting the rocks, sending freezing sprays to their feet.
Nona was smiling when she stepped over the cliff into the air,
holding Paula's hand firmly in hers. They mustn't jump, it was
too high. Paula cried out NO!
       She jerked from her bed in fear that her cry would wake up
nona. It was still dark outside. Through the darkness, slowly a
new dawn was creeping in, disclosing the world in its bare grey-
ness. Paula went to the bathroom and poured herself a glass
of water. She revived the scene on the cliff, still terrified of the
dream. She paused for a moment, trying to decipher the meaning, then, she dismissed even thinking about it. A dream was
just a dream and nothing else.
       However, Paula could remember a late autumn day when she
was six or seven years old, walking with her grandmother to the
opening of the hotel. It had taken a few years to build the strange
hut like construction, which to little Paula looked more like a
rock with bird nests than a hotel. The trees were growing out
of every corner. Lush green bushes and silvery leafed olive trees
were growing over the walls clad in simple, hand made stones.

Every corner of the construction looked different and as a whole, it made a playful impression. Even then Paula thought it was not serious enough, and wondered why anybody would come to spend time there and even pay money for it. On the day of the opening, they were late for the ceremony, so Maria was dragging her by the hand. Paula didn't want to go into the freezing cold and was nagging all the way. Suddenly, Maria stopped and bent down to her:

"Paula, I promise you will spend the first night together with your friends Mira and Olivia in your own hotel room. You will have a pyjama party. You must come along now and stop pestering me. We are late and we must run. Ok?"

"Where do we have to run?"

"We're going to the opening of our hotel, darling. There are people waiting."

"Will we have ice cream in the room?"

"You will."

"Coke, too?"

"All right, Coke, too. Now, come, quickly!"

When they finally arrived, a young receptionist looked after Paula. The only thing she could remember is her *nona*'s fear of cameras. Every time they tried to catch her face, she turned away and showed them her back. Another long forgotten detail came to her mind. *Nona* would never take off her huge sunglasses, even not when the sun had long set and it became dark. She was like one of those rap singers who thought they were cool with sunglasses indoors. However, in her eagerness to organize the girls' party, she soon forgot about it.

Now, years later, she remembered such little facts. Looking at the happening from a different perspective, she could see that *nona* must have been afraid of something or somebody. Why? She never harmed anybody and the islanders adored her. Paula couldn't think of a single person who would not like *nona* Maria. She was like a mother to all of them, and she was like a mother to her. Mother, mother... She didn't even have a photograph of either her mother or her father. *Nona* said they had both perished in the war. Their house, heavily shelled, burnt down, and in it all their existence. *Nona* said that at the time of the hit, Paula was outside with her. She was still a baby, and *nona* took her for a ride in her buggy. When bombs started raining on their town, she took little Paula in her arms and ran to the nearest shelter. *Nona* often said that she had been ever grateful to have made the right decision and immediately left the town. The Serbians occupied the territory within hours after the bombing. They took the women and children to concentration camps and shot most of the men. Nobody could return to the territory for years. Anyway, there was nothing to return to, according to *nona*'s testimony.

"What was my mother like, nona?" was a frequent question Paula asked when she was little.

As a child, she wanted to form an image of her parents, an image she would cling to and hold in her mind for the rest of her life.

"She was so beautiful," replied nona, "so beautiful that birds would pause to sing when they saw her."

Paula, aged seven, immediately imagined Disney's Cinderella, sweeping the loft, with tiny sparrows flying about singing a merry tune.

"What color was her hair?"

"It was blond, shining like wheat in the summer sun."

"Did she have a blue dress and a ribbon in her hair?"

"She had many dresses, yet she preferred to wear jeans."

"Could she sing?"

"Oh, yes. She sang and played at the piano."

"And my father... What was he like?"

There was the image of Prince Charming in his white royal robe, looking her mother tenderly in the eye.

"Oh, he was tall and handsome. He was also very kind."

"Did he love my mother?"

"Of course, he loved her. You're the living proof of it, my darling."

"Tell me nona, how they got married."

"Oh, but you've heard the story so many times, Paula. Don't you want to read a picture book instead?"

"No, no, tell me, how my daddy met my mommy."

Then Maria would look in the distance, her green eyes focusing on some far away time and place, and in a soft voice, she embarked on the story of the courtship during university studies, how she had met her future son-in-law. She went on, about how they got married, how their wedding feast was popular and which music they were playing, and finally, how they travelled to Venice for their honeymoon. It was a timeless tale of love, without any explicit dates or places. The only fact was Paula's birthday. The rest was a fog in the past.

Paula remembered her first serious row with nona, when she was turning thirteen and wanted to know all the details, names, places, dates. She needed to know the facts, not only vague stories. She wanted to visit her parents' grave. Nona lost her temper and slapped her on the cheek once. Finally, one windy winter day, when the ice on the new motorway between Rijeka and Zagreb was stopping the traffic and made blood freeze in your veines, she drove her granddaughter to Karlovac.

"There they are!"

Paula was looking at the strange grave with polished marble. There was a big grey tombstone with two names in golden letters: Pavle (1963 – 1993) and Ana (1967 – 1993). At the top of the monument was a huge inscription: *Obitelj* POLACI, family Polac. Immediately questions followed one another.

"So, is my family name Polac? But I've always thought my family name was Perić, like yours. Why is my surname Perić and not Polac?"

"Paula, you're Perić. It was complicated after the war. I had to get new papers for both of us. At the time your parents weren't dead but missing, missing persons. . . It complicated the matters. I had nothing – no birth certificates, no proofs of my former life left."

Nona's eyes were teary. Her face was pale, mouth strained with pain and sorrow. Paula was sorry to have put her guardian angel on trial. She realized how cruel and selfish her demands were. On the other hand, she was eager to find out more.

"Will we go to see our house one day, *nona*?"

"One day, maybe. . . But there's nothing to see. I think they even built a supermarket over the ground."

"Can they do that? It was our land, wasn't it?"

"Well, it's not so simple. We were renting the house."

"Can we buy flowers for mommy and daddy?"

"Of course, we cannot come every day, can we? It's too far away."

They bought a bouquet of white roses and put on two candles in the graveyard of Karlovac. *Nona* was looking around all the time as though she was doing something wrong. Well, that was the last time they visited the grave of her parents together. Next time, Paula went alone. It was in summer, during the heavy August heat, when she had just passed her driving test. There was the tension of the approaching heat storm in the air. Bees stopped buzzing, birds shut up in the thick crowns of cypress and oak trees, even the tireless mating song of cicadas was nowhere to be heard. She was searching for the grave for a couple of hours. The smell was overwhelming; the sweetness of thousands of flowers was stifling her. She had the feeling she smelt almost like a rose herself by the time she found the heavy grey gravestone. She gasped. To her surprise, she found another name below her mother's and her father's: Luka (1971 – 2009) Millions of questions in her head, she stumbled to her car, narrowly escaping the summer storm. The heavy raindrops were hitting her small new Renault like angry soldiers on her long drive home. Did she have an uncle? Was there more of her family and for some secret reasons *nona* didn't want her to know them? Who was Luka Polac?

She came home and told *nona* about Luka. *Nona* was outraged. No, there wasn't any other family member alive, she was perfectly sure of that. War took them all. It had to be a graveyard cheat. Either the city authority or somebody else obviously must have sold the grave for it was more or less deserted. She said she

would complain to the municipality of Karlovac. Somebody had
to use the Polac' grave and bury his relative Luka in the ground.
Was Paula sure there wasn't another family name after Luka?
Paula could not remember. It was a pity she hadn't taken a photograph of the stone. But she shouldn't worry – Maria would
arrange everything. It was sad but true that Croatian graveyards
filled up after the war, and a space with a real tombstone was a
privilege, said *nona*. Paula pursued the topic for a few weeks, yet
eventually, she forgot the matter.

When she thought about the incident later, so many things
had changed. Bitterly, she imagined herself soon to be put into
the ground next to her parents and next to the mysterious Luka.
She wouldn't live to his age should all treatments fail. Her life
seemed a huge hole without a beginning or end. Her parents, the
source of her life, were missing. . . Her future – studies, love, family, work, were escaping her. . . In between, rushing from dawn to
dusk, there was her good, hardworking *nona* and the terrible diagnosis of the clever doctors. . . Chronic myelogenous leukemia or
shortly CML. . . or simply a death sentence. . . The only question
left open was the time frame of her death. Would she die within
a year or would she, in spite of the terrible treatments, last for
a few years more? Sometimes, she felt depressed and didn't care
what life would bring. Other days were full of resolutions to fight
and kill the disease in her.

She thought of Neven, the only love relationship she had had
in her life. He was her schoolmate and they were together for a
year or so. Yet, he was so different from her. He loved sports,
while she loved books. He spoke of sport fishing, while she would
like to travel around Europe and see the wonderful monuments.
They connected, but only for a short time. She was ashamed
when she remembered their short holiday on the island of Vis,
when Neven made love to her. She was so disappointed. It was
so profane. There were no butterflies in her belly, and no stars
which shone on them from the sky. It was just coupling, like
two animals. She would never do it again, she promised herself.
Anyway, as it was, she would not live to do it again.

She wrapped her thin body in a thick bathrobe and stepped
in the yard. The dawn in the east started to lighten up the day,
displaying tiny drops of chrystal dew on tree leaves and flower
petals. Rosemary and blooming lavender hit her nostrils with
their obstinacy to attract the attention of every smelling organ
alive. They were fresh and strong, thriving in the corner of the
garden. Paula felt a rush of energy filling her body. Why would
she give in and die? Grow was the word of the hour, grow and
live. She faced the new day with new determination: she would
win this battle! She would undergo every possible therapy and
cure; no matter what it took, she would do it. She would suffer
the pain. She would overcome it. What could pain do to her!

She was young and strong! She would fight. If it took years, so be it! She wanted to live and greet every new day for the next sixty years. She wanted to love again and this time better. She wanted to learn and study. She wanted to raise a family and have three kids. She wanted to live to see her grandchildren. She could make it!

She smiled with the purple of lavender in her eyes. She was alive now, wasn't she? She would make coffee for her *nona*. What a wonderful morning it would be!

* * *

"Thank you for coming so fast."

"I started off nearly the moment I got your text message."

Emilia and Tomaž kissed and embraced. She hid her face in his shoulder. Tomaž felt her trembling and knew she was crying. How should she not? It was not only a summer storm, cloudy *jugo* weather with heavy rains and humid winds, which could go away in a few days. It was the dark sky falling on their heads. They would have to make some decisions and make them very soon. But first, they needed to be alone.

It was the last Saturday in August. Tomorrow Emilia would have to go back to Zagreb and start her last year of the high school. Her eighteenth birthday was in two weeks. When Tomaž came on the evening ferry to Novalja, Emilia was waiting, together with dozens of islanders welcoming their friends who came from the north, from Ljubljana, Rijeka and Zagreb, to spend the last August weekend in Zrče partying in the biggest beach discotheque on the Adriatic. Emilia and Tomaž reached the old cavern on Emilia's *vespa*, driving on the unpaved but well kept road through the ancient olive orchards for nearly an hour. Situated high above the northern cliffs of the island Pag, it was built in WW2 to observe the maritime activities in the opposite aquatorium, the harbor of Rab. The place stank like pest; it was obvious that sheep, wild and domestic, were using it as a rain shelter. Their hair and droppings were everywhere. In the twilight, the sea was dark grey, the waves trimmed with white foam as they rolled and rolled from the south.

"It was a rough passage. I was afraid the ferry would not go."

"Yeah, the weather is awful. We're nearly empty, only a Dutch family is still staying at Slavko's."

"When are you going back to Zagreb?"

"I wish never... How am I..."

Emilia broke into tears again. Tomaž held her in his arms and softly stroked her hair. This powerful girl, always teasing the boys and controlling the restaurant, keeping her proud head in the sky and her feet on the ground at every occasion, was now broken. And it was his fault. He had had more than twenty-four

hours to think the matter over, he had answers ready, yet he was
lost in the face of her tears.

Only a month back, when he approached the subject of the
torn condom after their love making on the Dolfin beach, Emilia
didn't look too worried. She said there was a very tiny probability
that this only time they could conceive, because her period was
due in two days, so she was supposed to be out of the danger
zone. The menstruation bleeding came in time, although it was
weaker. They both thought they were out of trouble and got away
with their calamity. They enjoyed their love affair without big
promises, yet knowing they wanted to be together as much as they
could. They planned to visit each other regularly, as Ljubljana
and Zagreb were well connected by motorway and train. While
the countryside would be passing by, he would dream of Emilia's
hugs and kisses. Now, a month later, there were tears and shame,
worries and pain. How would they cope with all this?

"Emilia, don't cry, baby. We will find a way. I love you and
you love me, this is all that counts."

"I'm sorry, let's go outside and sit under the roof. I can't bear
the stench here."

Tomaž took a bottle of apple juice and a can of beer out of
his Samsonite backpack, offering her a choice. It was his entire
luggage – the backpack which had up to then contained school
notes and books for study. Emilia grabbed the apple juice. The
drink was cold, and with some salty wind sweeping over her face,
she started to feel better. She didn't like the smell of sheep and
never ate lamb; she always visualized the little lamb babies hanging from the hooks, the butchers waiting for the blood to drain
out of their tiny, bony bodies, so that they could be skinned and
roasted on the grill. It was a powerful image, their bloodied white
wool, red and white, their ears flapping lifelessly around their pink
muzzles, death still reflecting in their black eyes, questioning the
world why.

"So, what do you think we should do, Tomaž?"

"It will be your decision and I will respect it either way. And
I'll stand by you, I promise. I will stick to you so much that you
will want me gone, you'll see."

Emilia looked up in Tomaž's eyes and leaned on him. He
put his arms around her again and just held her. Was it the
right moment to tell her about the options? He did some serious
thinking in the shortest and at the same time the longest day of
his life. He had devised a possible passage for them. Or, let her
talk it over and chose her own way. Would she include him in her
future?

"Did you tell anybody?"

"Yes, Emilia. I told my grandmother. She would support me,
I mean us. I'm sorry, but I needed an ally."

"You're so confidential with your grandmother?"

"I know it sounds crazy, but she's different. She lost her husband in the war, you know, my grandfather. Besides, I needed some answers and she's a doctor, or, she used to be. She's been retired for some time now."

"Is this the loud lady who took a room at the hotel Perovica in mid July, but spent all the time on our terrace?"

"I guess you can't miss my granny. She's the one."

"What did she say? Is the baby already...I mean, is it human?"

"At six weeks? Yes, but you know this yourself. You've had a biology class. It's all there – the gender, the color of the eyes, the brain...It's all defined. The two sets of our genes have united into this being. But from the medical or legal point of view, it's not yet a foetus even, so you have the option to...you know, the abortion."

Emilia thought of lambs again and her vision blurred. She always thought the moment when she would tell her boyfriend or her husband that she was expecting a baby would be joyful, with big hugs and *mama* jokes, with Christmas in her eyes and pride in his. Not like this, with tears and cries of need in which she became a huge trouble to herself and a burden to him, who was not more than a short summer romance.

As though he read her mind, Tomaž turned her to him and looked deeply in her eyes. He kissed her tenderly on her salty lips. Her first impulse was to keep away, but he wouldn't let her go and kissed her more. She melted finally in his arms and returned the passion with unwilling heat.

"There, you see. We love each other. We will find a way..."

"I don't know... One day I am a girl, enjoying my life, chatting with friends, guests...and the next I have to be a mother. How can one grow up over night? I can't do this. I want to go back in time..."

"Emilia, we can't undo what we did. We can't go back, we have to find a way forward..."

Tomaž looked at her swollen face smeared with tears and worries. She was still a child, so innocent and fragile. He tried to imagine her with a big belly or with a child at her breast. Impossible, she was too young.

"We never spoke about God, Emilia. Are you religious?"

"What has God to do with it? Are you?"

"No, but it is an issue, I think."

"Well, I have received all the Catholic sacraments, like every Croatian in the world, I suppose, but I haven't thought about it...I'm worried about my parents, school, friends...It's all over..."

"It's not over, Emilia. It's a new start. We're young and healthy, our families have means. We can have this baby...We were calling for it, the crazy seagulls were crying for it, remember? Now it is coming, the little one is coming his way."

His hand glided softly down her body as though he wanted to show the way, but stopped and tickled her at her waistline. Emilia jerked away for a moment, laughing through tears. She leaned back on him with a pensive smile on her face, thinking of their afternoon on Dolfin. So many days after Tomaž left for Ljubljana, she was remembering every detail, she was thinking of him and was holding silent conversations with him. He was with her all the time. She had been so wrong in judging him. She called him pothead, jerk, and other bad names, thought him stupid, pretentious and dumb. In principle, she didn't want to have anything to do with him. Until she found out one day that he was a tender man, maybe her soulmate. The short days they spent together after the Dolfin trip were the best days of her life. She could never have imagined there could be so much love under the sun.

"Maybe it is coming her way?"

Tomaž smiled.

"It's for us to find out, baby."

"But we live in different countries, and we don't have jobs, I haven't even finished the fucking high school. . . "

"Oh, sailor nature coming up now, is it? I haven't heard you say the f. . . word yet."

"I can do better. . . "

"Don't be angry. Let's discuss the options like two adults. . . "

"Which is exactly what we are not. . . "

"Again, it's up to us. As I said earlier, I talked to my grandmother. She finished her medical studies in Zagreb during or just after WW2. Can you imagine, in those days? Well, she has some influential friends in her profession at the Zagreb Medical Institute and at the faculty. She made some phone calls yesterday while I was there and arranged that I can enroll in medicine studies in Zagreb. It's a very good faculty, they say, even better than in Ljubljana. There were some issues with my knowledge of Croatian, but she offered to pay the fee and obviously, it worked. I will just have to attend a course in Croatian. Anyway, I will fax all my documents, certificates, and application on Monday, and will begin to look for a student flat in Zagreb as early as next week. . . "

"And who will pay for your flat?"

"She will, my granny."

"Has she won the lottery? Where does she get all the money?"

"It's a long story. She lost her husband in 1945, in May of 1945. And she never remarried. When the denationalization took place in Slovenia, she hired a good lawyer and got back much of her late husband's estate. He was a very wealthy man. He had a printing factory and owned a block of flats in the workers' suburbs of Ljubljana. She got only the flats back, but there are twenty units in the block, each over eighty square meters, so you can imagine the rents she's collecting every month."

"Good for her and good for you. Why do you want to study at all?"

"I want to make a difference, collecting rents is no profession. Anyway, she promised to support me financially if we decide to start a family. My only task is to study and I will have to renounce a part of my inheritance, the sum she'd be spending on me, in favor of my sister."

"How can you think of such obsolete things in this situation?"

"We were talking the night through, my granny and I. We discussed the issues from all possible angles. Our major problem, baby, is not money, but our youth and inexperience. We may be too permissive as parents, and later in our relationship have the feeling we have lost part of our youth. My granny says that it could lead to painful compensations..."

"So, you really think there is a slight chance we can have him, I mean her...You know?"

"It's not so slight, it's a fair option. And we should get married."

"Our priest at Kapitol would never marry me pregnant."

"We'll find another priest who will marry you pregnant and to me, an atheist."

Emilia burst in laughter. Now, they were talking. Maybe life is not so bad after all. She felt so confused thinking about the abortion. It was her constitutional right in Croatia to have one, the right many women had been fighting for since ages; the right to be the mistress of her own body. She read all about it on the internet. Yet, when she was there, when she found out how to apply for one and read about the procedure, it felt so wrong – to kill the fruit of love, in truth the first fruit of her first love. And all in the name of ambitions which could also be achieved later in her life. But she was alone and at first didn't even dare to tell him or her uncle or...A shadow came over her face like a cloud obscuring the sun.

"What about my parents? They haven't got a clue...In June, they let me go to Slavko's with a solemn promise I wouldn't get into trouble. How much more trouble could I get into than this?"

"Emilia, we love each other, this is no trouble. They will understand. They loved each other once. They conceived you. And we're very lucky that we have options. Many people don't, you know..."

"It was probably the only time they touched each other...I mean when they made me. I can't imagine..."

"Don't worry, you're not alone. I will be with you all the time, at every step. We will tell them together. But I don't want to push you into anything. You know that you still have the other option. Or a third one, my granny called her colleague, a pediatrician in Osijek, you can bear the child and you can give it away for adoption. It's healthier and more humane than abortion. All you lose is one year, and you started school a year ahead, at six, didn't you? So, it's no big deal."

"I'll come of age in two weeks. But why do you keep saying it is my option, my decision, my choice. What about you? It's your baby, too!"

"I want to leave all the gates open for you."

"But I want to know what you think. What do you want me to do?"

"Are you sure you want to hear this?"

"I do, more than anything in the world."

"Ok. I think you should... Anyway, it's going to be difficult. We will lose our social lives, I mean, our friends. Our parents will hate us. They will hate explaining to their friends and acquaintances what happened, and the society will shake their heads in disbelief – teenage pregnancy, in our times? And the boy wants to become a doctor? They will look at them as though they've done something wrong, and our parents will feel responsible for us, because they didn't prevent the misfortune. Although you probably know the statistics about adolescence sex – the kids are doing it in the primary school. So, we were old spinsters on Dolfin. Still, our friends will shun us, we're socially dead. We should change our Facebook profiles. We will only have each other, our baby and our studies."

"And the money your granny will provide."

"So you see, in my mind, my decision is for you and the baby. I'd rather be divorced in five years than going around with a stain on my consciousness or even worse, seeking for medical help or miracles if we stay together and you are not able to conceive at thirty. The abortion is not entirely safe. No operation ever is... "

"You're a clever boy, you, Einstein. I have known for more than a week that I'm pregnant and all I could think of was fear. Fear of Uncle Slavko, fear of my parents, fear of my school... Can I go to school pregnant? What when it shows? And you, you had it all planned in one day. You set up our life like the boat trip – the water skis, the wine, the food. And the girl fell like a ripe apple from the tree."

"Are you being sarcastic, Emilia?"

"Just a little... But how could you change so quickly? Yesterday, you were a gigolo showing off on your water skis, today, you're a family man. And how could you make up your mind for a married life practically overnight? The boys in my class can't decide on an aftershave or the music they want to listen to, and you... "

"Well, I had a mind trust, so to say a thinktank behind me. My granny is pure gold. Besides, she's eighty-nine and deter-

mined to examine our baby when it's born... She doesn't trust
other doctors. So basically, she will live longer because of us.
We're doing some good work here."

"Because of you, you dummy. I love you, Tomaž. Thank
you."

It was the first time she said it aloud, although she meant it
all the way. The serious, adult conversation came to an end and
their baby decision was taken. Her declaration of love sounded
almost like a joke. But it warmed Tomaž's heart and he kissed
her on her nose. Playfully, she shook her head with irritation.
The rain started again and there was no hope they would see the
stars tonight. But they had reached for them already, so to say,
in advance. Kissing and holding each other, they spent another
hour in the sheep shelter, chatting away about their plans and
keeping away all the bad thoughts and fears. It got dark, but
with the wind blowing strongly it was also getting very cold, so
they left the cavern and started the *vespa*. Emilia sat behind
Tomaž and asked:

"Who will be lucky first? Who are we breaking the news to?
Your place or mine?"

"Ladies first, baby. We're going to Zagreb tomorrow."

Emilia sang gaily:

"If tomorrow never comes..."

"It will come, but who knows what the future brings..."

"I do. It will eat and cry and produce mountains of shitty
diapers..."

Tomaž looked in her eyes with serious purpose:

"I forgot to ask you – have you ever played with Barbie dolls?"

"Yeah, but Ken doesn't have the thing, you know. Unlike
you..."

They drove away shaking with laughter at their teenage joke.
It started to rain. The sky was laden with thick clouds hiding the
moon and the stars. But the night was not over yet. Would the
rain stop and let the sky clear tonight? Would the moon and the
stars shine again tomorrow? Really, who knows what the future
brings.

Towards another life

The fog was thickening as they were descending the Vrhnika slope
in the central Slovenia, approaching the city of Ljubljana. It
was still dark when they left the island of Pag in Maria's car,
a comfortable and robust four wheel Opel Frontera, which was
so handy for the stony roads to where the suppliers or partners
of the Perovica hotel lived. The sun greeted them around Senj,
rising from behind the hill on which its century old fortress Nehaj
was looking after the port and the people below. It was the end
of September and quite cold for the season after the whole week
of rain and icy winds that closed the summer and made the last
tourists tremble with regrets until next spring. The sea was cold
and the weather harsh. All pensions and the restaurants closed
down for winter, only Maria's ecological hotel amidst rocks and
millennium old olive trees was still full of activity.

Maria was at the wheel, relaxed. She was used to driving
long distances from all her travels around Europe in the past.
Dario sat beside her, embarrassed in awkward silence afraid to
open his mouth and say something wrong. Paula was breathing
heavily asleep in the back, nicely wrapped in a blanket and her
nearly hairless head on a cushion. She was so thin and pale, her
shape was almost like a child's. Maria was explaining how the
Garmin road navigator worked, so that Dario could use it on his
way back to Pag. They reached the suburbs and it was not yet
eight o'clock. They were due in the Medical Centre in Ljubljana
at nine, so Maria turned to the petrol station and filled the Diesel
tank. They left Paula asleep in the back of the car and went for
a cup of coffee and an early bread roll.

"How are you feeling, Maria? Are you all right?"

"Dario, you must have asked me at least a hundred times,
and I tell you again: I am fine. I am not nervous, not afraid of
the little operation, and I know I will be in the hands of very
competent doctors. Please, stop worrying."

"I am sorry, but I have such a bad feeling. I wish I could be
around for the next week. I can find a hotel room and wait until
after the operation."

"And miss the big squid hunt? It'll be the dark moon next
week and the sea is colder. The conditions couldn't be better. Besides, you can't help us. You won't perform the surgery. Please,
take the car home, and I promise to call you every night and report on our progress. Then in a few weeks come back and take
me home."

"Home, you mean your place or mine? Will you be moving in
when Paula gets better?"

"When she's healed and she doesn't need me, I promise, I will.
Can you imagine the commotion among our village folks? They
will talk only about us."

"Oh, I don't mind, and you shouldn't, either. It will be fun. I am looking forward to it. And you must let me cook. I will show you at last what the Dalmatian cuisine is all about."

"I know. My fancy cooks at the hotel don't know a thing. No Michelin star can outsmart my Dario."

"I didn't say that. They can do the French stuff and the smart slow-no-food staff. For Dalmatian dishes, they should take a course, though. I can teach it."

"Actually, Dario, we can arrange that. Tell me now, what's the time?"

"It's ten past eight. Shall we take a sandwich and an apple juice for Paula? At the hospital you're probably booked for lunch, and there're hours by then."

"We will in a minute. Are you seeing anybody from the Slovenian police today?"

"Yes, from the Medical Centre I will go directly to the Slovenian NPU, the Investigation Bureau, where that tall detective Bak now works. He told me he has some interesting facts about Nemec."

"Good. I hope they find the man. I told you that I checked all my guest lists since many years ago, and Milan Nemec has never stayed with us. You can tell him that. What about Slavko?"

"What about Slavko?"

"Has Nemec ever stayed in his inn?"

"No, Slavko said never. I think he's got nothing to do with Mulobedanj. He met Marina at the charity ball in Opatija, and that was it. I wonder how he could have known all about Giacoppo's business and the hotels. Well, you know Olivia and Mira are starting to work at the hotels. The rascal is out of the game."

"Good for you and for them. They're competent girls and they will manage, I am sure. Where are they?"

"They're both staying in Rijeka. Olivia will be promoted in two weeks and she will start working in the management of the biggest of the Seashell chain. Not as an owner, more as an internship. Although the Slovenian fake will is declared void, we have to wait for the final court order regarding the inheritance. Mira still has some exams and the diploma thesis. She needs another few months to finish her studies. We talk a lot lately and they even listen to me sometimes."

"Who else would they listen to? They only have you, and you're a wise old man with grey hair and experience written all over your face, aren't you?"

"Don't joke around with me, my love. The hotel business the girls have to take over eventually is far above my head. As a matter of fact, it is far above yours, too. It's all finance and accounting, very impersonal. They will need years before they know something about it."

"It'll go quicker than you can think. Young people are so clever. With the knowledge of IT and foreign languages, the girls will be up to it in no time. Besides, they have the staff around them. They were running the business for all the years after your brother-in-law died. The young have the world at their fingertip or better at a click."

"I know. But their knowledge is sometimes very superficial. You know you still need experience. Would you have gotten the investors for Perovica at the age of twenty? Never! Would you have chosen such an extravagant design for the building? Would you have gone for the ecological mumbo jumbo? No, you wouldn't. But you did it in your mature age, and it's a big success. You see, you needed experience and wisdom to set the goal and reach it."

"And I had also a bit of luck. Don't forget my lucky charm."

Maria suffocated at the thought that detective Bak might reveal to Dario something to connect her straw man investor of Perovica to Nemec. Should she tell the Croatian authorities about her secret investor? Was it wrong to have taken the capital from an unknown source maybe smeared with blood of many years ago? Yet, what had she done wrong? Her hands were clean like her desk and the papers on it. She was not in the position to check the origins of the cash flow or trace it back beyond the Cyprus foundation which represented her shareholder. It was the duty of the Croatian tax and bank authorities, which obviously, like in all transitional countries, are blind or have turned a blind eye against a favor. She should not care. In the end, her hotel created many new jobs, saved the farms and agricultural land around it, and brought new life to the island. Dario's question put her out of her thoughts.

"What about Perovica? Have you put anybody in charge for the time you're in Ljubljana?"

"I told you already. I have. The staff manager, Barbara, will look after everything. She's young and competent. Since spring, I've been training her to be completely independent. I'm an old lady. I can die any moment of a stroke or something."

"You can't have a stroke. But I could. If you strike me with a...whip...or a surprise attack in the bedroom, wearing nothing but a black lace slip...or something."

"Or something? You're losing it, my friend."

"Ok, enough of this. Sorry. Shall I bring the fish to this Barbara then?"

"No, just go to the cooks, they will know what to do, and they will arrange the payment for you. But you could stop going out to the sea in rough weather. You're about to become a very rich man."

"I am rich when I am alone at sea fishing. I have the whole world to myself, and I can steer my boat anywhere I want to. "

She looked at him tenderly and stroked his cheek. His lips dropped on the inside of her palm and turned to kiss it. Without forewarning, tears welled up in his eyes. He was so worried. They had been together only those short summer months, and Maria was undertaking a risky surgery at her age. He knew Maria would not go back on it. Paula was her only family. Paula despite her bad moods and irritable behavior towards him, turned out to be a nice and emotional girl. You had to love her. Her vitality and strong will were unbeatable, and you could read fight in those large black eyes. When she regained her health, the girl would be a heartbreaker. Dario was sure about that.

"You're a dear man, Dario Kadura. Don't forget I love you."

"I love you too, Maria. Take care of you two in this foreign town."

"Ljubljana is a nice town and the people are friendly. I have always had a nice time here. By the way, can you tell me the latest news about Emilia's boyfriend Tomaž? Do you know what they will do?"

"Oh, it's quite a story. Who would think such a tough girl can get pregnant at her age? The boy should have taken precautions. Now, he enrolled at the Zagreb University, School of Medicine. I wonder how he got in. Every year they turn down many students with the best grades in their finals. He must have had some connections, or very good certificates from Ljubljana. He rented an apartment in Zagreb and lives two blocks away from Maksimir. They would like to get married and to move in together before the baby is born, but Emilia's parents are livid. They don't want to sign for her, you know the certificate. The girl is under age. She is about to turn eighteen. Well, they want to pull it through despite her parents. Actually, the marriage ceremony will take place in early November or late October, I am not sure, in the parish church at Lun and at the registrar's in Novalja. Our priest Ante was as happy as birds in spring when he was telling me about it. 'It's a miracle,' he said, 'to have a marriage at last after all those funerals in the last years.' I didn't think it was too tactful, mentioning the parish funerals. It was Marina's, and then also my wife's not so long ago. But I had my silent revenge... he'll wed a pregnant teenager with an atheist from Slovenia. There is God in Heaven, indeed."

Maria smiled at the words that reached her across the little table like a swarm of bees heading for sugar. Dario was so southern, so Mediterranean, so villager, when he let go. The teenage couple was as good a topic for gossip as their relationship had been ever since people had found out. What a village, this Mulobedanj.

"It sounds like a happy ending to me. At least, it is not often in these days that young people take responsibility for their actions. Don't you agree?"

"Yeah, he came across as such a snob, but I guess in the

situation, the boy was as good as he can get. They still have to finish school."

"Who cares about school, as long as they are healthy and the baby is fine."

Again, like a curtain of intangible presentiments, an awkward silence fell between them. Health was the only thing Maria could not conjure for Paula, she could only pray for it. It was so out of her power, probably one of the rare things she was unable to control, and Dario knew how this pained her. She had told him about the war, how they were fleeing from the bombing in Zenica, and how she lost everything. He imagined vaguely what that everything was, but Maria was so shaken when she was recounting the facts that he did not want to pose too many questions. Despite all the long intimate hours they had spent with each other, the woman was a mystery to him. Where was she born, where did she grow up as a child, who were her daughter and her husband, Paula's mother and father? How did they die? Dario sighed and looked at his companion tenderly... in time, all questions would find answers and they would live happily.

"Paula will get better, too. You'll see. After some years, she will be able to have babies. Everything is possible in our modern times, and you will be a grand grandmother. That means twice grand. Isn't that wonderful?"

"And you will be grandfather at least twice, my old man. You have two daughters."

"I hope more than twice, if they find the men to cope with them."

"We all find men who cope with us, even I did."

They looked at each other with the tenderness of all prejudice broken and all the knowledge in the world consumed. Then, they stood up. Maria put the euros on a plate in the middle of the table and headed for the counter for Paula's breakfast. It was time to go. It was time to get the treatment. It was time to act.

They came to the Institute for Oncology, which was not really an institute; the name was there to imply research and hope. It was a hospital for people with cancer, where hopes died last, while bodies were decaying in the fatal disease. The receptionist gave Maria and Paula the instructions. They were on their own from there on. So Dario kissed his sweetheart tenderly and hugged Paula, holding her to his chest for a few moments longer. "Get well, get well, and bring back your *nona*. I love you both," he whispered in her ear. Paula smiled faintly and nodded bravely, searching Maria's eyes for support. Dario left them. He would go to see the investigators, then he would slowly drive back to his island, where there were things to prepare. He would pick his olives soon and help Slavko with the wedding celebration. By then, his darling Maria should be home.

They admitted Paula in the hospital, where she would undergo additional tests. They didn't need Maria for a few days, though. She could have called Dario and driven back to Pag, but she wanted to be near Paula and visit her every day. More than anything else, sick people need moral support. Besides, the doctors might need her any time and she wanted to be ready. So, she checked into the Antiq, a small yet sophisticated hotel in the medieval town centre. Waiting at the reception, she leafed through tourist brochures. Her attention got caught up with the exposition The Ancient Greeks in Croatia at the Ljubljana City Museum. She had planned to visit the exhibition for a long time, she couldn't wait for it, as it would be the first time she would see one of the wonders only lately pulled out of the sea and restored to perfection... the beautiful *Apoxyomenos* from the island of Cres. It was a perfect occupation for the next two days. She would dive into the past. Once she completed the forms, she left the luggage at the hotel and set out for a walk. She was curious to see what was going on in the newest part of Europe.

Oh, she loved Ljubljana, even on a rainy September day. The streets were busy with people running about their errands. The sky was laden with dark grey clouds and the horizon almost black behind the white tower on the castle hill, where the flag with the Ljubljana coat of arms angrily fluttered in the wind. Maybe she would go there tomorrow. The little cafés and bistros along the river Ljubljanica were nearly empty. She could pick where to sit down and relax. She needed a bit of time for herself after the long summer with sun shining nearly every day and tourists pouring into her hotel, eating, feasting, chatting uncontrollably. Here it was an entirely different world. Slovenians all had a purpose, a goal, a deadline. So unlike the slow beat of Dalmatian towns, where people were sitting around tables endlessly discussing politics and drinking up their last coins, with lamentations about how they couldn't find work.

She bought a newspaper, a daily with the title Delo, Work in Slovenian. She would miss a word or two, but the languages were so similar she could easily understand it. She sat down under the roof of a lovely café and ordered a cappuccino. The headlines were trumpeting the local elections. The mayor candidates didn't spare one another, the political commentators even less so. She smiled at the photograph of the mayor of Ljubljana under the headline: Slovenian Berlousconi in the lead. One would think that after all the misery people would get tired of charismatic demagogues. Her interest was piqued by an article on Hit from Nova Gorica, a company which was scanning the possibilities to invest in casinos and hotels in Croatia.

Oh, her poor homeland, Croatia... How she pitied it! They missed the golden years of economic growth fighting a futile war and approached the European Union only in times of depression and crisis. Unlike Slovenians, who got away nicely back in

1991, the Croatian secession was horrible. Slovenians cleverly persuaded the Yugoslav People's Army and Milošević it was better for Yugoslavia to let them out of the federation. They seceded from the Federal People's Republic of Yugoslavia practically without a bullet shot. David who outsmarted Goliath... that was how the world press portrayed the tiny Alpine state.

Maria knew, though, that Slovenia was a young and corruptive democracy like all of them in the former so called Eastern Bloc. Men like Nemec were powerful and rich. Their capital was a network of connections with the dark forces from the past, operating through the current members of be it left, liberal, or right wing political parties. In their hearts, though, they belonged to another era... to the communism. They were blindly loyal to UDBA and OZNA, old Yugoslavian secret service organizations and their bosses, like Mafiosi to their godfathers. The invisible pillars of the society were the former regime connections. The politicians were but puppets, and the strings woven with the money stolen from the once nationally owned factories. The mayor candidates, who were fighting for the term, maybe knew maybe not, whose tune they would have to dance to for the next four years. In the meantime, the damage, distrust in democracy, was growing like a smelly hill of garbage. People stopped going to elections, and sadly lost their belief in the sacred rule of the majority. The mass media were sporadically following corrupt politicians as though they were little monkeys performing in a circus. Until a charismatic leader would show them the right way; his destination could easily be war. Tudjman and Milošević had taken their roads to hell, and the people with them, had they not? *Panem et circenses*... elections were like bread and games in the Ancient Rome. The scarcer the means, the fiercer the fight. Like rats, eventually, the humans would kill each other for food.

The morning was opening the curtain of rain and sunshine, bright yet hesitant and tender, pierced the heavy clouds. Maria paid for her lunch and coffee and went to the museum. She would have five hours of Greece, and their colonization of Dalmatia. At the museum entrance, there was a lively group of high school students waiting for the guide to take them around the exhibition.

"Madame, would you like to join the group for the guidance?" the lady at the ticket office asked her politely. Maria replied in an accented Slovenian, rusty for the years without practice.

"Do you think they will listen?"

Amused, she gestured at two boys who were fighting for a mobile phone, maybe to read the latest messages, and a girl in the middle who was pleading with them in vain to return her the device. Others in the group were laughing and teasing each other to show they were so cool and that they belonged together... to the same herd of sexually ripe, yet socially inadequate monkeys.

The woman at the ticket box smiled and nodded: "You'll see,

once they are inside, they will be mesmerized. Our curator is very interesting and he can certainly tell stories, so that even the coolest of the gang shut their mouths and listen."

"If you say so, I will join them. It will be a new experience."

She collected the exhibition guide, when a gong in the corner of the hall banged three times. The sounds echoed in their ears. Before anybody could react, a huge man stepped in the middle. In a powerful declamatory voice, he started his tour.

"My name is Simon and I will lead you through the exhibition. Let's see first if you know anything at all. Where did young Greek boys some twenty centuries ago go to for their initiation into manhood?"

The crowd fell silent. Maria was scanning the faces of the boys, who felt awkward not knowing such an obviously important fact. She was certain, though, that the guide meant Palagruža, the isolated island in the Adriatic half way between the Dalmatian islands and Italy. She had read an article about the findings there only recently. Finally, a tall blond girl almost whispered.

"Dalmatia?"

"What a guess! It was somewhere in the Adriatic, but where? And what were they doing there?"

Now eyeballs were turning around and some obscene gestures were floating in the air. At last, a boy's voice from the back said theatrically:

"Drinking!"

"Bravo! You see, nothing changes under the sun! The boys about fifteen came to this place to drink and to prove they would be worthy as men. Where? Nobody knows but me. Now, I will tell you and show you the place, in a picture, of course, if we make a bargain. You listen to what I have to tell you about the brave old Greeks, and I will tell you where this place was."

Shouts came from the back of the group.

"Yeah, man! Good trick, man! He's cool, yeah!"

Oh, he had them. Maria was feeling almost as one of the teenagers. She followed the funny custodian in sneakers and clothes of an American street gang member, his curly black hair long and tied into a ponytail, his body huge and muscular. He was watching his audience from under his thick eyebrows sharply. She remembered Agamemnon, the evil king of Mycenae, who couldn't rest until he gathered the Greeks to go to Troy and reclaim his sister-in-law, the beautiful queen Helen of Sparta. Such violence for one woman... or was it for the golden riches of Troy? Maria and the kids were wandering from room to room, admiring the exhibits and listening to the stunning facts. The culmination of the exhibition was a room, filled with light and sunshine and only one huge statue in the middle. It was the famous Croatian *Apoxyomenos*, found near Vele Orjule, a tiny archipelago off the island of Lošinj, some ten years ago. Maria had read about it.

They said it was one of the most important recent finds from the Antiquity. The beautiful athlete belonged to the Classical or early Hellenistic period, and they placed his origin in the 4th century B.C. He was part of the cargo on a Roman ship a few centuries later. The vessel sank, the *Apoxyomenos* never reached his new home of a wealthy Roman villa, but he reached us two millennia later. Now, she could finally admire it live.

She waited until the group had left the room and the girls had had their share of staring at the perfect male body, mostly the lower part of it. Then the sounds died out, and Maria was alone with the boy in bronze. She stared at him with her shiny eyes as though she could breathe life into him. She had done so with many of the characters in her genealogical research. She couldn't rest before she had the story of the person put down on paper. She knew hers was not an objective description of the past. Her personal understanding of history, all the assumptions, how once upon a time people could have lived, posed filters to the truth. Were historians, who were involved in the scientific research of the past and even traced migrations based on our genes, always completely objective?

She sat on the bench and leaned her head on the wall, gazing at the sculpture of the youth. He was twice the size of a man, and his shiny, polished body suggested a winner, his shoulders stooped and his muscles tired from the strain of the race, his body posture modest yet glorious. His head bent down, he looked satisfied, almost happy. In his right hand he was holding the *strigil* with which he was about to scrape from his body oil and sand before washing. The competition was over. It was the moment of silence and peace. "Beauty is eternity gazing at itself in a mirror", said Ruskin a long time ago. Maria's eyes filled with tears. The powerful emotion of witnessing perfection almost suffocated her.

What could have been this boy's thoughts so many centuries ago? Was he a racer? Was his discipline the javelin or the bow? His sensitive lips formed a tiny smile, which illuminated the symmetry of his face. Still, his joy was subdued and measured, as though aware of his mortality, of this magic moment. Maybe Apollo let him win this time, but would turn against him in the future races. In all his beauty and perfection, the *Apoxyomenos* was nothing but a toy, a darling of gods today, a castaway tomorrow. Unless the artist had immortalized his muscles in bronze, he would have been forgotten in a matter of a moment. How *Apoxyomenos* and his artist had tricked the time! The athlete's victory lasted forever, and nobody could ever take his content smile from his face.

Maria closed her eyes and thought of Paula. She was of the same age as this youth, yet her body protruded with bones and seemed week as a straw compared to the strong thighs and powerful biceps. Were there gods who played games with her, too?

Wasn't her love strong enough to cure the girl? Did the vicious gods need her blood and flesh as well?

The tears, which beauty inspired a moment ago turned bitter and slid down her cheeks rolling over the creases of her face. She blinked and finally closed her eyes again. Better not to think about the present. She would glide into the story of the past, of the famous Greek settlers in Dalmatia twenty-five, twenty-six centuries ago.

Long time ago Oscar Wilde wrote, "In such ugly times, the only true protest is beauty." It would be so Ancient Greek to fall into a dream now...

* * *

When it came to it, Milan Nemec surely knew how to run. He smiled as he sank into the softly padded leather seat of the business class flight to Cape Town. The plane was about to take off. He could relax at last. With no trouble at all, he passed all the security checks at the Leonardo da Vinci Airport in Rome. The Slovenian and Italian authorities could mean trouble, so he bought his plane ticket for Cape Town out of Rome over the internet. He borrowed the credit card of one of his employees and paid him double in cash. But he used the credit card only until Paris, for South Africa he reserved the first class ticket per telephone. It was easy...first class opened the doors to everything. He'd pay in cash and leave no traces behind. People would do anything for money, just anything. He chose the night flight to South Africa via Paris. Charles de Gaulle airport was chaotic, and during the small hours, he spent the time between flights at the men's restroom, just in case.

Anyway, he prepared his escape route carefully, so there was no way he would attract unnecessary attention. He even took care during the summer not to spend too much time in the sun, as he had read in an article that tanned people were more likely to stick out of the crowd. It was tiresome and he was not a young man any more. But he had to persevere until tomorrow afternoon, when he'd be spending a week in his friend's villa by the sea. Years back he saved his neck by producing a legal document which helped him to a few millions that his friend had been carelessly enjoying in his sunny exile ever since. Nevertheless, Nemec didn't trust him completely. He didn't tell him why he was coming, what his new identity was or the next destination he was headed to. Some secrets should remain secrets.

"Would you like a drink, Sir?"

The sweet voice brought him back. The stewardess was young and lovely as though from a picture book. Big brown eyes and a soft red mouth were inviting and Nemec smiled broadly.

"Yes, a good idea. I'll have a whisky, a single-malt, please."

Her petite body bent over the cart to fetch the tiny bottle from the bottom.

"Would you like some ice with it?"

"No, miss, no ice, please, but water. You know, you should drink a good whisky only with a few drops of water."

She smiled obediently and served him a chilled glass with a napkin under it, a tiny green bottle of Glenfiddich and a bottle of still water.

"Would you like anything else, Sir?"

Nemec leaned his head to the left. This was getting amusing.

"May I wish for a quiet sea, miss?"

A string of tiny pearl white teeth showed behind the redness of her lips. Mockingly, she put her right hand to a salute, saying.

"Aye, aye, Sir! We're having good weather on the flight. There is nothing to worry about."

Nemec smiled and nodded in thanks, then stretched his long legs in comfortable jeans. He was dressed neatly, but modestly, in clothes of mass production, no fancy brands. This was his second identity, which he slipped into while driving from Trieste. His name was Mario Čengić, a retired sea captain. When buying the passport, he realized Čengić had really existed and lost his life while protecting the bridge to the island Pag during the last Balkan war. It was scary to wear the identity of a man who died in combat. It was like being on the threshold of life. Like Čengić, Nemec knew the sea well. In his jet set life, he had sailed a lot, mainly in the Mediterranean. Not for work, it was pure pleasure. Every year he chartered a yacht, usually the longest and most luxurious they had in the marina at Sukošan, including a skipper and staff. Why should he worry about how to maneuver the ship, how to get provisions in small groceries on the islands, how to find anchorage in the evenings and clean the deck, if he could easily afford to pay the skipper and the crew? He adored holidays on the ship. He sailed for a few weeks in spring and some more in the end of each summer. Years he had taken his family aboard... his wife, Olga, and his son, Matej. Later, when Matej didn't want to come with him and Olga was long separated from him, he would either invite male friends to drink the nights through or young women who were expected to take care of his needs. Many were of Matej's age or younger. They were all beauties with gorgeous bodies. Usually they had excellent education and manners. The Maribor agency, which provided those women, was indeed well organized. Milan never pressed them for sex or gave them the impression they had to yield to his whims. He forgot about the paying arrangement, he wanted more. He charmed them with expensive dinners, which he personally enjoyed the most. The jealous glances of younger and more attractive men towards his table were like a balm to his self-esteem. Women all liked to drink champagne, so he ordered bottle after bottle. Not before long the girl, who feared the worst and had been prepared to face an obnoxious old crony, would relax and surrender to him. Then he would make love to their firm bodies, pretending he was young and in love again.

However, dozens of fresh young faces and bodies of Venuses vanished in a second when he met Marina Kadura. She was a different story. She was of his generation. She understood the same jokes, the same music, they admired the same antiquities. She came from the same world, Tito's Yugoslavia, where they were young and nurtured hopes at the same time. He fell in love with her, and it seemed to him that it was the first time in his life that he really loved a woman. He would have given anything for her... his wealth, his family, his life, had she only asked for it. He hoped for a long time she would. But she didn't want anything from him; that was his grief. She never really wanted anything from him...

With regrets, his thoughts turned to Matej. How quickly his sensitive son had grown. He finished his PhD in philosophy of law and passed thirty years of age. How time flies? He had the feeling he had missed out on his son's childhood. Later, chasing money and power, he had failed to take part in his teenage years and more or less ignored his transition into manhood, too. Did he know the name of Matej's first girlfriend? She had come with them on the yacht one year. She was a moody, dark rebel with piercings and short black hair like a boy. But Matej was smitten with her. How could he? He shared so few of his son's preferences. Matej loved to read books since an early age and soon took the path of a social activist, so he'd worked for Human Rights Watch and spent some time in America and in Africa. Nemec respected his son's way and could understand the youth's contempt for the transitional tycoon rat race which he was driven to undertake every day in order to have more; more money, more houses, more wealth and power, more of more... Nemec understood; he donated a substantial sum to the Slovenian branch of Human Rights Watch, which helped them at the start up. The NGO soon focused on campaigning for "the erased". The erased were people of various non Slovenian nationalities from former Yugoslav republics living in Slovenia, who after the independence for obscure reasons lost their identities and all social and economic rights to go with them. They had simply vanished from the official register of the citizens of Slovenia. Matej was eager in his pursuit of justice, the same way as his father was eager to accumulate wealth. However, Nemec would have to face the fact that he would never see Matej again. He had to think of a way to support him, though. You cannot live on ideas, can you?

His wife Olga was another matter. His teenage love, they got married after they had finished their studies of business in Ljubljana and Vienna, more out of a habit than true passion. For many

years, Olga, working for the local tax office branch, supported his
career and stuck her neck out for him to prevent too frequent tax
inspections in his companies. Then, in her mid forties, Olga found
out about his occasional escapades with young women and got
very bitter. They were constantly fighting while Matej was still
in college. One day Olga had enough and left them both...her
husband and her son. She packed her clothes and occupied their
weekend house in Strunjan, declaring she wasn't coming back.
She left her job and dedicated all her time to esoteric therapies
and wellness sessions. They didn't get a divorce, so Nemec was
paying for her life style. The male household with his son in
Ljubljana seemed to become more stable for a while. However,
they were too different from each other and with time, their dis-
agreements deepened and it was time Matej left home. He bought
him a nice flat in the old town center of Ljubljana and granted
him with a lifelong rent of 1,500 euros per month. With that,
he washed his hands of him as he had done some time ago with
Olga. They were all happy seeing the least of each other.

The day before, he had chartered a yacht in the Portorož
marina on the Slovenian side of the border and sailed out to
the sea despite the threatening weather report...storms and west
winds, sea very rough, wave height from six to seven meters.
There was nobody who took his boat out that evening. All ferry
journeys to Venezia and to Istria were cancelled. Yet, the brave
captain Nemec didn't have time to wait for nicer weather.

One way or the other, it was all over. They belonged to another era, to another man. Nemec knew he would never see his
family again. He had taken care of every detail. With bitterness,
he wondered how long they would think of him after he was gone.
For Nemec burnt his bridges and staged his own death. Thus the
prosecutors would have to leave his family in peace and let them
enjoy the inheritance. After his death, the assets had become
unattainable by any court verdict. What he needed for his personal needs had been transferred years ago into various South
American bank accounts. They were easy on the money's origin.
They accepted fugitives of all kinds, provided they were rich. Besides, Bak would now go after the other guy. Milan smiled in his
chin. Now the angry, sticky inspector would be somebody else's
companion. He was free. For the night before, Mr. Milan Nemec
had drowned in the Gulf of Trieste. They would never find the
body. How could they?

He sailed out at six and set course to Trieste. The twelve
meter yacht was jumping like a toy in the waves. The mariners
were shouting at him to come back, but he texted the marina
watch that he was only going to the next marina at Isola and
that there was nothing to worry about. They stopped the panic.
Why should they care, the boat was fully insured and in case of
wreck they would get a new one. The yacht engine wasn't the

strongest, but the wind was far too rough to lift the sails, so his progress was slow, not more than five knots per hour. It took him ages to pass the distant lights of the Koper and Trieste harbors. Finally he beheld the dark curves of the cliffs near Miramare Castle. He wasn't in a hurry, in summer darkness fell late. At a quarter to ten he came to the chosen spot in the bay. He had to put on the position lights some time ago, the green and the red. He killed the engine, and the yacht was bending dangerously with the unpredictable waves, so he dropped two long anchors. . . one from the bow and the other on the feed, both going some hundred meters deep. The boat was more stable. He was hoping that the coast guard would not be coming to his rescue. Was it nerves or the very rough sea? He was sea sick for the first time in his life and despite the fact he hadn't eaten in hours, his stomach juices kept bursting into his mouth. The trouble was that he needed to wait a few more hours for the next step, and he needed the energy to endure his death. So, with utmost disgust, he ate a few whole meal energy bars and, surprisingly, his stomach took the sugars in. He drank some water, too. Then he lay down on a bench outside, next to the rudder, tightly wrapped in thick blankets. In spite of the season, the air was cold and he was freezing. Slowly and not without sadness, he took off his wedding ring and threw his and Olga's life into the black waves.

It stopped raining, but the wind was still roaring. Black clouds were travelling to the east with a frightening speed. He closed his eyes and slept lightly for a few hours. When it was time to get up, he almost wasn't able to gather the energy. But it was the only way. He hooked his fluorescent green jacket sleeve and tore it at the railing, so that scraps stuck to it and the rest of the jacket fell in the sea. A boot and the cap followed. He left his wallet and all his documents on the boat, including his personal computer, camera and mobile phone. Then he took out his diving gear, put on his new, warm Henderson 7mm Aqua Lock Hyperstretch wetsuit with extra padded 7mm gloves. The underwater swim took an hour, thanks to the sophisticated underwater direction finder, the transmitter of which was positioned in a car, rented under a false name and parked on the beach parking lot. Without the clever electronics, he'd be lost in the black depth of the bay forever, and his death would be a little bit less staged. Janis Joplin was wrong when she was singing that freedom's just another word for nothing left to lose. Nemec knew freedom was a state for which you were prepared to risk your life and lose everything.

The jet plane was taking off with less sound that a 4W vehicle. It was another wonder of modern times. Nemec smiled in his moustache and took another gulp. The alcohol warmed him inside and brought color to his cheeks. In his mind he was still in the freezing waters of the Gulf of Trieste. By the time he reached

the Miramare beach, there wasn't a soul in sight. It was two
o'clock in the morning, and with difficulty, he dragged his diving
equipment to the trunk of an old white Seat, a car he would never
touch in his real life. He only hoped it wouldn't break down until
his next stop, the Autogrill rest area on the way to Venezia. He
changed into a dry, warm track suit and started the trip along the
coastal road to Monfalcone and further to San Canzian d'Isonzo.
There was no time to rest, not just yet. He knew the boat in the
middle of the bay would sooner or later attract attention. When
dawn started to color the horizon, he arrived on the banks of the
river Isonzo.

He put the heavy aqua-lung, the band weights, the mask and
the fins, the gloves and the jumpsuit in one huge, strong plastic
sack and tightened it with a strong rope at the end of which was
a small spare anchor. He waited for a good moment and climbed
onto the bridge, from the railings of which he pushed the heavy
package into the deep waters of the river. It was almost daylight
when Nemec turned to the motorway at last and parked the Seat
at the Autogrill Venezia Este. He took everything out of the car,
wiped all possible fingerprints away, locked it and left it for good.
He knew there was no way to escape the latest forensic methods;
a fallen out hair or a fiber of a tissue was enough to establish the
identity of the driver. But he also knew those methods take time.

With another remote control key, he unlocked a shiny black
BMW X3 and threw his bag into the trunk. Then he took out another bag and started for the toilet area, knowing well there would
be a crowd of truck drivers who'd try to shave and shower before
starting another workday on the road. He could easily blend in,
nobody would notice the change. He paid for the full service and
took a cabin, where he first put hair dye on his neck-long grayish blond hair, leaving some areas around the ears untouched. He
was very proud of his bushy hair, so rare for his age. Yet, it would
have to go. The hair dying took twenty minutes at least. In the
meantime he shaved, and with the precision of a surgeon, glued
a mustache under his nose. He had paid a lot to the hairdresser
in Croatia for it, and it was worth every euro. It was said to be
water resistant and had some silver strands in it to suit his age.
Finally, he changed his contact lenses and transformed his bluish
eyes into deep brown. Later, he also added a pair of heavy frame
glasses to his new image. He showered and washed out the hair
dye. Then, he cut his hair short. He wasn't quite happy with
the result, yet it would have to do. His final look in the mirror
showed a younger, although a pale and tired man. After more
than an hour, he came out in new clothes. His jeans and sweater
were smart, but not conspicuous. He headed for the restaurant
area, packing all the garments in a bag, which he threw on a construction lorry full of rubble. A worker will be happy with a new
tracksuit and a pair of good sneakers. He had a hearty breakfast

with ham, eggs, fresh bread, and lots of orange juice and coffee. Then, he started his long drive to Rome.

The lovely stewardess came back. Instead of a jacket, she was wearing an apron. It was dinner time. He heard the cutlery and the buzzing of microwave ovens from the service area.

"How would you like your steak? Well done?"

"Yes, please. Is there any salad?"

"Yes, Sir, it is a full menu from the appetizers to the apple tart. Wine? We have a red from the Venezia region and a nice Pinot Griggo."

"Bring me a bottle of the Venezia red and some sparkling water. Thank you."

"It'll take some time, we're full, sorry. I'll be back in fifteen minutes."

"Of course, thank you."

He sank in his seat and took the headphones out of the sterilized plastic sack. He didn't want to think about the last few weeks. He had to cut them off. Didn't he burn all the bridges behind him to be on his own and at peace? Didn't he leave his son and all his lovely estates in Slovenia and possible assets in Croatia to start anew? What would he do later in his life? He was looking for freedom. Would he really breed stock and live as a gaucho in the Patagonian plains free of thought? He was hoping for love and emotion. Would he remarry and have more kids? He could find a Brazilian beauty with a body of a goddess and live the day from beach to beach, from casino to casino. Well, one thing he knew well; he would never return to Europe. It would be too risky, despite his new name and existence.

He managed to set the radio to a station with classical music. The first few notes of the famous aria Habanera from Bizet's opera Carmen evoked memories. Opatija... Hotel Kvarner by the sea... The Crystal Hall and the Rotarian charity event in late spring, when lemon and palm trees were luring hidden sentiments out of locked hearts with their sweet perfumes. The bright, solemnly decorated hall, where half of the Slovenian and Istrian philanthropic societies were trying to bond business ties for the following year... Suddenly, the soft mezzo soprano raised a song of love and forced the powerful cry of an eternal rebel against all social rules upon the ignorant audience... On the one hand the freedom of feelings, the power and dangers of love, on the other, the audience less free than any street vendor on the korso... in between a deep abyss.

That voice, so colorful and tender... He knew that voice, he knew the singer. It struck him like lightning. Milan Nemec was falling down. He was diminishing. He was shrinking in his skin and turning into a grain of sand. In the face of the purity of the music he was nothing... Nothing but...

"But you're crying, Sir! Please, calm down. Everything will be fine."

Milan Nemec raised his fake brown look up towards the sweet young voice, his headphones still holding him prisoner of eternal beauty. He stuttered:

"My god, it is her, listen..."

He took off the headphones and approached them to the stewardess' ears. She was holding a tray full of food and wine and mineral water. She was clueless as to what to do next. Only music could break the silence between them. The sentimental mezzo soprano was like an invisible bridge between two foreign souls. Love was not always kind, it was sometimes more cruel than hate.

> Rien n'y fait, menace ou prière,
> l'un parle bien, l'autre se tait:
>
> (Nothing helps, neither threat nor prayer.
> One man talks well, the other, silent;)

* * *

Days dragged along like the huge grey clouds bearing autumn rain. September turned into October, and doctors were waiting for more test results and needed more scanning. Maria visited Paula every day, but apart from the time spent at her sickbed, she got bored in her hotel. She could not rest, she was used to action. She could have gone home, to the island of Pag. Yet, in her emails Barbara was reporting to her how efficiently she coped with the work, and the management and all seemed more than well. It would spoil the balance in the hotel Perovica, should she come back for a couple of days and then leave again... it would be no good meddling with Barbara's management style, for which Maria knew that it was very sharp. She understood that, as Barbara was young and had difficulty in winning respect and authority in her position. Thus, Maria simply stayed in Ljubljana, taking time off. She went to all the galleries, had been to all the exhibitions, and had seen theatre performances as well as had gone to a few classical concerts. Culture was nice. It was a rewarding way of spending her free time, but she was lonely everywhere she went. Only now she realized how much Dario meant to her and how much she missed their daily chats.

They spoke on the phone every evening, but days without uttering more than a few sentences were long and boring. Besides, the weather turned from bad to worse and while, on her island, sunny days were filling the olives with juicy oils, in Slovenia people had to put coats on, and evenings were cold and grey. When the theatres closed and she returned to her hotel room, there was a cold, empty bed waiting for her, and hours to kill in reading before finally dozing off to sleep. Maria needed Dario to hold him, to touch him and to keep her warm. All those years, living with Paula, yet so alone, without a man wrapped around her body...now, she did not know how she could have coped without it. One morning she had enough and called Dario to come to Ljubljana in order to spend some days wandering around Slovenia by car. In the afternoon the same day, he came to Ljubljana, and they went for dinner to a nice homely restaurant by the river near the black cat sign on the wall, chatting happily like two teenagers after school. Love knew no age limits.

"You should see Slavko, Maria. He's completely crazy. He got it into his thick old head that he would throw the biggest wedding party Lun has ever had for his niece. He wrote to all his guests. Well, he did not. Actually...you know, him and the computers...Well, he went to the young receptionist at your hotel, the blond one, what is her name...Neva or Neda, whatever, he asked her to print for him more than one hundred letters, which he sent to his guests and family members. His sister, you know Branka, Emilia's mother, well, she is livid with him. The pregnancy, the shame, the school...all in wrong order, she says. And now, to make it worse, Slavko wants a big fat wedding to underline the facts."

"Well, why make such a drama out of their age and order of events? They have the means to live and study. Why should they marry in top secret and not share their joy with friends and family? Emilia would be no less pregnant for it, would she?"

"Those are his words exactly. It's amazing. All the guests want to come, he's fully booked, and many checked in at Perovica or at the Tovarnele inns. They're paying their stay and bringing gifts for the couple. Crazy, isn't it?"

"So, the old fox will fill his purse before winter at his niece's expense? Cunning...I have arranged something for them, as well, you know. I've always liked Emilia. It's an outrage for her intelligence to work at that den."

"Don't be a snob, Maria. Slavko's restaurant has been in the village since ever. It's a place to go and sit by the sea with a beer or a glass of wine in the evening. You can't do that at Perovica."

"You peasants cannot, indeed. Our guests are enjoying it. Enough, you haven't come to Ljubljana to quarrel, have you?"

The waiter came with a bottle of white wine and filled their glasses. Starters came to the table and they ate the plate with smoked meats and cheeses in silence.

"The olives are poor this year. I don't know if there will be anything to pick at all."

"Well, I thought the sun was good for the fruits."

"Yes, the sun is good, but the draft in August obviously stressed the trees, so that they dropped most of the fruit. The rain came too late. You will have to buy your oil elsewhere this year, I will have very little to sell."

"Don't worry, we'll manage. Our guests come from the north, and olive oil is something exotic for them in any case. I'll buy it from Korčula. I know a good producer there."

"They're all thieves and liars, the *Korčulani*, don't you know that, Maria?"

"Aren't you a difficult man today, Dario? Shall I rather buy from Slovenians, maybe from Italians or Spaniards? And the lying *Korčulani*, your fellow citizens, should spill their oil into the sea?"

"I'm sorry. I missed you so much, and now I'm nagging at you. I promise to improve after tonight."

"What happens tonight?"

As soon as Maria asked the question, she blushed deeply, guessing the answer. She would never get used to men's sexual innuendo. They seemed to be able to switch to it in the middle of the courtroom, dinner, funeral... you name it. Were they always thinking only of coupling? Was she thinking of it?

"You're blushing, my dear. I think you've had the same thoughts in that huge bed of yours at the Antiq hotel. How can you stay at a hotel for old people anyway? Antiq! It makes me think of fossils."

"Nonsense, it's just a name. Besides, it is very pleasant, you will see."

"I won't see much of it. I like to close my eyes and pretend that I am a young stud."

"Oh, stop it, Dario. I can't eat and discuss those matters."

Dario laughed heartily shaking his head in disbelief.

"You talk like a nun. And we know you're anything but... "

"Don't you nun me!"

Maria stood up and beat the old man with her napkin. She was laughing as well now, enjoying his teasing. She knew exactly where it was leading.

"I love the foreplay... A napkin is a good idea, Maria."

Dario could not stop shaking with laughter. Bemused by his Croatian guests acting like youngsters, the waiter stood aside, hesitating to put the plates on the table. Finally, they took notice of him and sat down in awkward silence.

"Here you are; trout a la Triestine, baked potatoes and rocket salad. Enjoy your meal!"

They nodded thanks and started eating. The food was fresh and tasty, not even Dario could find anything wrong with the fish. They toasted with a glass of zelen, a white wine from the West of Slovenia.

"Dario, you were late today. Did you go and see your Slovenian detective first?"

"Indeed, I was with Bak for a couple of hours. You should see their offices, Maria! Our anti-corruption authorities 'USKOK' will never be able to afford something like that. Not to speak of the security checks. . . I think the Pentagon could learn something from those pedantic Slovenians."

"Were you given a body check, Dario? If they had emptied your pockets, you'd have been lucky not to land in a colder place than the Antiq hotel."

"Well, I was trying to persuade an attractive young police woman to give me a body check, but she only passed an electronic device all over my body. Soon, we will do everything only with electronic devices, nothing with bare hands. Anyway, I had a long conversation with Bak."

"And, what's new?"

"Bak lost all track of Nemec. The rascal simply disappeared. It looks like he has drowned in a naval accident, but they're still searching for the body. Anyway, Andrej spoke of fish and sea for most of the time. He invited me to go to the mountains with him. He says you can see wild goats grazing on the rocks."

"And Marina's case? Is it closed in Slovenia, too?"

"More or less. The Croatian police are sure it was a suicide. Well, the Slovenians, I mean Bak is not completely convinced, yet he has other cases and won't pursue the investigation. If I understood correctly it is also a question of finances."

"Maybe it is better so. Let her rest in peace."

Dario put down the knife and fork. His chin was shaking.

"Maria, I will never forgive myself. I wasn't there when she needed me. And to have taken drugs. . . she must have been really desperate."

Slowly, Maria took his hands in hers and held them firmly. Dario calmed down and stopped shaking. Maria spoke:

"Don't reproach yourself! People take strange decisions every day. At least, she was the mistress of her fate. When she had enough of it, she found the courage to finish her life. I am not sure if I am so strong."

"I know I would never do it. Think of Olivia and Mira! They are devastated. Mira hasn't done anything but cry in months."

Maria felt she should defend Marina's decision.

"Dario, it was her life. She had to have reasons."

"I don't know how to get the feeling of guilt our of my mind. It makes me crazy."

"You will, with time. It's only been a couple of months. Dario, you never told me who found her and how."

Dario breathed in deeply. It was crazy. He could not forget the day when he went into Marina's apartment after she had been found dead. The police, forensics dressed in white, with all kind of electronic devices, everything beeping and buzzing like in a beehive. They had taken her away by then, probably to the morgue. They told him her housekeeper, a young girl from Lika, Višnja, who was cleaning the apartment twice a week, found

her in bed, tucked in as though asleep, but dead. She came in
with her own key. Before starting her duty, she peeped into the
bedroom and closed the door to let her sleep. After several hours,
it seemed strange to Višnja that Marina had not come out. She
checked again, approached the bed, and saw her open dead eyes
staring into the void. In a shock, the girl called the police and an
ambulance.

Two days later, Dario walked about the big, lavishly furnished
rooms with polished antique furniture, speaking class and wealth
from every corner. Despite several richly decorated potpourri
plates emitting lavender and rose oils, there was a certain stench
in the living room... the smell of death. It was acid and bitter,
like the opened bottle of Cynar and two half-empty glasses on the
club table. Why had not Višnja put those away? She had been
cleaning, had she not? The police asked her the same question.
She told them that she was about to start dusting and vacuuming
the living room, but she came into the bedroom to see whether
Marina was awake first. Before that, she was doing the bathroom
and the kitchen. It was a plausible explanation. Marina trusted
Višnja, and the young girl adored her employer, the famous opera
singer. Thus, the Cynar was still open on the table. Dario felt
sick. He could sense the liquor's bitterness on his tongue... it
was like bile coming up and poisoning his mouth. Two forensic
technicians took the glasses and carefully emptied the content of
each in separate ampoules, then packed each glass in a separate
plastic bag and scribbled notes on every unit. They packed the
bottle, too.

All around Dario, police officers were shuffling through the
bookshelves, laden with heavy old volumes, and Dario could see
that they were clueless as to the fragility of the books they were
handling carelessly. He got upset and told them to be more careful. At one point, he even shouted at one police officer, she looked
very young, that in her whole life she could not earn the money
to pay one volume she was holding in her right hand. It was the
fragmental volume of Marin Držić's writings, the most important
Ragusan Renaissance playwright and poet, Poems from the 16th
century. The woman froze and put the relic carefully on the club
table. Then the two police clowns, as Dario called them in his
mind, Batić and Kostić, started picking at him, scanning his reactions for indices. He was hurt, sad and felt guilty even without
their insinuations. They kept asking him if anything was missing.
How could he know? There was too much of everything in this
fancy den! There were bronze statues, impressionist paintings,
tiny polished tables inlaid with ivory, huge china vases in the corners. The fucking place was a museum! Dario stopped at the
old Roman corner, where Marina kept three oil lamps over two
thousands year old and some coins from the era of the great Emperor Diocletian. In the hall, a wonderful late baroque timepiece

stood on two marble columns, decorated with climbing cherubs measuring seconds and minutes. Oh, he was lost in this world, and without Marina's voice, although she had scolded him many times, it was a desert... emptiness filled with vanity...

When he finally more fell than sat on her bed, and with his rough fingers, tried to feel the crumpled linen for his sister's shape, the police let him alone and stopped asking irrelevant questions. He remembered he just wandered away, got in his car and drove away, blinking at the road through a veil of tears. He felt so miserable and useless.

"I didn't see her body until the funeral. It was her housekeeper Višnja who had found her."

Maria stroked his cheek and looked at him warmly.

"Dario, she was a middle aged woman. She led her life as she pleased. She picked her friends, her housekeeper, and her tours. There was nothing you could do to protect her."

"I'll never stop thinking I could have done more. To remember that the last time we spoke we shouted at each other!"

"She was not an easy person. You never picked the moment and the tone of your conversations. It was always her. She called you and let you know this and that... But in your heart you must know she loved you. You were the only constant in her life. Men had come and gone. You and your family were the only family she had."

Dario's eyes watered. He took out a cigarette package and lit one. Out of nowhere, the waiter came running.

"Excuse me, Sir. You're not allowed to smoke here, I mean, inside. You can only smoke outside. Would you move to the terrace and have your dessert there?"

"What do you mean, I can't smoke! Am I a guest or a hound?"

"I am very sorry, Sir. But we have this new law. All public rooms are non-smoking. Please, I can lose my job if I let you. The fines for the pubs are crazy. Please, Sir, go outside."

"Come on, Dario. We'll get some air outside. Will you have coffee?"

Muttering foul words into his chin, Dario stood up reluctantly and moved towards the terrace. There were gas heaters with lamps in the middle of every table. The guests around them were smoking as though it was the last puffs in their lives.

"I see! That's why the restaurant is almost empty inside! What will you do in winter, my boy? Will you serve them dinner on sleds? Oh, you Slovenians, oh, those Europeans... what's the next thing they will think of?"

With an apologetic smile, the waiter saw them to a corner table, where a tall rose bush was filling the air with the perfume of its last flowers in the season. The buds were white with fringes of red. Dario waited until the boy hurried inside, then moved closer to the bush, and smelled the delicate flowers. On an impulse, he plucked a tiny bud and gave it to Maria.

"Thank you, Dario. I'll hide it in my purse, for the man is coming back with our coffees. Let's have a piece of estragon cake. It's delicious and not too heavy."

"Life can be sweet. . . "

"We've deserved it."

Dario threw a curious look at his companion.

"Do you have brothers or sisters, Maria?"

Maria knitted her brows in displeasure. She hated questions about her relatives. Her father and her mother had long been dead, and the rest. . . They belonged to another life, far away in the past. She rarely ever thought of them herself. Dario was waiting for her answer. The silence dragged about the table like evening fog. After a few minutes, Dario spoke up.

"I see. You don't want to talk about it. Why?"

Maria turned her eyes, shining with tears, to the rose bush.

"Dario, I wish I could tell you. I wish I could open up to you, and to Paula, and confess like in a church. My life, you see, is a building of cold stones. The past is frozen. Sometimes, I feel like the Iron Henry, with my heart banded in metal circles. I need you and your tenderness to break each of the iron bands, Dario. Please, wait until after the operation. We will take some time off and I will talk. . . You will listen. . . Maybe, you will not judge me too severely. . . "

Dario raised his hand and put it on the back of Maria's neck. He turned her head tenderly away from the bush, towards him, stroking her wrinkled cheek with his other palm. He looked Maria in the eyes.

"Take your time, my love. We have years to go. . . "

* * *

On a sunny late October Friday, Tomaž was driving his mother's car, a red Renault Scenic, down the scarlet slopes of Velebit, where oaks were burning in the last hot autumn sun of the year. Thin dark green pines were slightly moving in the wind, like lovers dancing a slow waltz, with their heads up, ready to resist the much harder winter fare of the *bura* blows. They were approaching the Prizna-Žigljen ferry line to the island of Pag. Emilia in the seat next to him was drowsy, with her head leaned on the warm window, her thick black curls spilled all over her pale face. Her full lips had lost the crimson red of their first kisses. She had had a rough morning. The sickness and the stress were wearing her out. Tomaž had to stop several times on their way from Zagreb. Once she needed to catch some air, then she struggled with her stomach not to bring up the little juice and tea she drank on the way.

He looked at her and still he found it difficult to believe all this was happening. Their lovely afternoon on the Dolfin beach, the unexpected pregnancy, his granny helping him out more than any person in his life – and above all, he couldn't believe he was going to have a wife and a baby in a few months' time. It was surreal. Like in an old black and white movie. Yet, Emilia was here, next to him, she was breathing heavily in the dense midday air, laden with the scents of the Mediterranean flora. He slowed down on the windy road leading to the ferry harbor. He opened the window now and breathed in some fresh air; he felt as though he was driving on a gigantic pizza. He smiled at his thoughts.

Was he sorry for the lost youth? Was he hesitating asking Emilia to marry him? It was funny, but once the practicalities as to where they would live and who would pay for the young family with no income and several years of schooling ahead, he was sure as hell. Marriage was the right thing to do. They were lightheaded in the summer, and they had to pay the price now. It was lucky they could. Besides, he loved Emilia more than he could imagine he would ever love anybody in the world. He knew that. She was not so sure about her feelings for him. In distress, she thought about an abortion, but it would send them into the world of adults with bitter memories which they could never get rid of for the rest of their lives. They had to step over the threshold of life at one point. Was there anything like the precisely right moment?

They moved in together into a tiny, one bedroom loft on the Bukovačka road, very close to the huge green park of Maksimir and just around the corner of the Medical Library. He had hired the tiny apartment for six years, and his granny paid the rent for a year in advance. She gave him the power of attorney for the grant which he would be receiving for the following seven years. He knew what it meant – top grades; his granny was not one to trifle with. He was sad when she insisted on arranging it through a notary service in case she wouldn't live to see his graduation. The weeks in September were all devoted to redecorating and furnishing. Luckily, he had some savings, so instead of new high-end skiing gear, he bought pots and cutlery, a microwave oven and some other low priced household commodities.

Emilia joined him in Bukovačka only last week, since her parents were trying every trick to get their girl back into the state before the summer. Her mother was suggesting Emilia should get rid of the baby. They met Tomaž with coldness and reproach, as though it was entirely his fault. However, he patiently waited for Emilia to come to him, and she did. Their first days together were like a honeymoon, and quickly, he arranged for the wedding before the families would interfere again. He smiled at the image of the two of them walking the baby to the park together in the afternoons. It was due in spring, in April. Apart from the problems the baby caused Emilia in the mornings, it wasn't showing yet. She was nicely curved, which was good for the labor. He studied it in a huge gynecological textbook, which he had bought in advance, for the subject would occur only in the third semester. Her flat, firm belly of a seventeen year old would soon reveal that there was a new life inside her body, which was part of him, part of that sunny summer afternoon on the island.

Tomaž had no second thoughts – he left his friends, his family everything and everybody behind to be with this Dalmatian girl and the little blind passenger on its way to existence. Soon, they would hear it, for it would disturb their nights crying for food and care. Well, his mother said so, once she got over the shock and started enjoying the fact that she would become a grandmother. His parents' only concern was that he was moving to Zagreb, away to another state and another life. His granny knew better – Emilia needed to finish the high school. She needed the trusted environment of her friends and family, for she would be in a more difficult position. Tomaž would adapt. The Croatian language wasn't so much different from Slovenian. His mother gave him her car, so that they would be able to visit. He was so grateful to them all and couldn't think of another ending.

When the car stopped, Emilia woke up. With dreams in her eyes, she gazed at the bare white rocks across the narrow channel, nothing but a hard mass of stones, between which only dwarf bushes of sage and thorns had enough persistence to grow. This side of Pag, the *bura*'s side of the island appeared from the sea like a desert. Yet, it was green in the middle and even had some fertile agricultural plains in the southeast.

"Hello, there. How do you feel?"

She nodded reluctantly. She was fine now. The voice reminded Emilia of the purpose of the drive. She was getting married and in the back of the car, there was her wedding gown, a simple champagne colored dress, which her friend Ana designed and sewed. Well, Ana wanted Emilia to shine on that special day, so with great care she showered the bodice with hundreds of little fake pearls. Although the dress was not too long, just above the knees, it came with a luxurious veil embroidered with silk and decorated with pearls as well. The little tiara would underline Emilia's rich hair and black eyes. Ana also thought of the neck tie for Tomaž to match his bride's attire. Tomorrow they would first go to Novalja with their witnesses for the civil ceremony, then to the chapel of Lun. Emilia thought it would be more difficult to get the permission for Tomaž, who had received no sacraments in a Catholic church, but the priest showed tolerance. She had never seen a wedding at the tiny chapel, but she thought it lucky, for the guests would be very few. Their invitations went to her parents, his parents, Slavko and a few villagers.

They drove for another half an hour before they gaped at

the big wooden road sign, embellished with olive branches and laurel leaves, with one big word written on it: VJENČANJE, WEDDING. Tomaž voiced their shared thoughts:

"Slavko! He was the wedding planner. We're in for a surprise!"

"I hope he didn't spend too much money on it. The sign is wonderful. Let's go back and take a photo for our Facebook. Can we do this?"

"Yes, great idea!"

They drove back and posed hand in hand around the sign for their wedding. The worries fell off their shoulders. It was such a nice day. Later, when they would unpack and talk the ceremony over with the few guests, they would have a swim in the sea. It was still nicely warm from summer sun.

When they parked next to the restaurant, Slavko came out of the kitchen, where things were hectic. Through the back window, Emilia could see many people baking, cutting vegetables, frying meats and shouting orders.

"Uncle Slavko, what is going on? What are all these people doing?"

"They are preparing your wedding, my dear! Hello, Tomaž. How was your drive?"

"Fine. Thank you, Mr. Karbič."

"Slavko, call me Slavko. You're family now."

Slavko embraced them both, holding and kissing them like little children. They could not resist his warmth and smiled, surprised, with thousands of questions in their eyes. The old man shrugged.

"Well, what do you expect? I had to do something. My competition, that woman from the hotel, Maria, left her wedding present before she left for Ljubljana. Here."

They opened the smart envelope with golden and green initials, entwined like two olive branches – Ecological Hotel Perovica, Island Pag. It was a letter with which they were to spend a week at Perovica in the wedding suite. They had never been there, but it had to be magic – the view from the top rooms of the hotel was praised in all tourist brochures.

"You see, to compete with this Maria, I decided to give you the wedding feast and organize it for you. This is my present. I hired help and invited people you know well, Emilia. Everybody came and brought presents for you."

"But how will you pay for the food and the drinks? Have you robbed a bank?"

"Don't worry about the money now! People are coming today and tomorrow. You see, Emilia, I have written to all our guests who have ever spent their holiday here and politely invited them to come and celebrate with you. You won't believe it – all called or wrote back, and they're coming. They will be staying at the inn and many are helping with the feast. Their presents are wines and delicacies. You will have the sparkling wine Srebrna penina from Radgona, our guests from Maribor are bringing the whites for the fish dish, and the family from Kras will bring the black Teran for the venison main course. I never knew Samo was working for the beer brewery Union, and he's bringing a huge barrel for the draught. It will be the best feast ever!"

"Slavko, are you mad? It was like begging. . . What have you written them?"

"Oh, the music, I forgot to tell you about the music. You will have a soprano singer during the ceremony in the church. This is Dario's connection, a student of his late Marina. When you come out and you are wed, Mrs. . . Mrs. . . What was the name? Oh, Mrs. Klun. . . Then one of our Slovenian guests is rehearsing some Dalmatian ballads on accordion. Here, the Heart Asses, a group from Rijeka, will be playing dance music from six in the evening until the morning."

"Please, stop, Slavko, stop! This is not true!" But the teen-agers were already giggling at the prospects of a nice, lively feast. They were already sorry that they couldn't have invited some friends.

"Well, I expanded the guest list, I hope you don't mind. All our living relatives are coming, Emilia. Tomaž, I asked your parents to bring along a few from your side. We also thought of your friends, the knights of the hot or pot or what-do-you-call-it table, Tomaž, as well many of your school friends from Zagreb, Emilia. Your lady mother, my snobbish intellectual sister, was of great help, actually."

Emilia laughed heartily. "Does my mom know who my friends are? She must have put it in the classified ads."

"No, she put it on Facebook, or one of the youngsters did. Don't you underestimate us! We usually know what you're doing, children. Well," his look travelled to Emilia's body, "we try to know, most of the time."

She slapped him gently on the chest. Tomaž stretched his hand to shake Slavko's.

"Respect, man. . . Thank you so much. We will work here during next summer to repay you."

"Yes, with that baby of yours, I will need all three of you here from June to September!"

The young weds to be were still shaking their heads in disbe-lief, when the lift-boy from Hotel Perovica came with a trolley to fetch their luggage and bring them along the windy path to the hotel.

"Now, go, children. Go with Mario and settle down in your fancy suite. Tomaž, please come back to go through the ceremony plan for tomorrow."

"We'll both be back in a minute, Uncle Slavko."

"No, you won't. Emilia, you take a rest. You look like you've eaten a snail. Have a nap. We'll arrange everything, Tomaž and I."

"But..."

"No buts. Start to trust your future husband, now!"

The old man's voice was quivering with emotions. His rough attitude and wild jokes couldn't hide his true feelings. Everybody will come tomorrow. There would be his family, friends, guests, singers, musicians... So much activity and happening in the last week! He was enjoying it with all his heart. It was life, full of colors and action, in the time when he was getting old and winter was coming to embrace the tourist village in a silence broken only by the solitary cries of the seagulls and howls of the gales.

Emilia couldn't control her excitement and broke into tears. She was embracing her dear uncle, sobbing into his ear:

"Thank you, thank you. How did I earn all this? All this love..."

"You don't earn love, Emilia. You either have it or you don't!"

They all arrived in time, so the following morning, all the parents met at the huge breakfast table, where there was coffee, fresh bread, cheese, prosciutto, pickled olives and *travarica*, the herb brandy, to lift the spirits. Tomaž's parents, Andrej and Anja Klun, took a sip from the tiny glasses filled with the greenish liquor. Despite the serenity of the moment, their eyes shone with mischievous thoughts. Opposite them, the bride's parents, the couple from Zagreb, Ivica and Branka Karbić, were sitting in silence, looking for words to start the conversation with their future in-laws. At last, Slavko came to the table in a white designer suit, his thin golden-rimmed glasses, and a big cigar in the corner of his mouth. He was proud and looked just like the late President of Yugoslavia, Tito. They all burst into a laugh and forgot the embarrassment. The words spilled out.

"My big brother, you look smart today. Are you getting married?"

"Where is the bride?"

Andrej Klun joined in the joke and was mockingly turning around asking, glancing with emphasized gestures around the terrace.

Slavko didn't seem either to hear or to notice their jokes.

"They're coming. Come on, you're going to Novalja for the civil ceremony. I'll stay behind and get everything ready at the chapel."

The party grew serious. They stood up and collected their accessories such as cameras, purses, car keys. Anja brought the wedding bouquet for Emilia from Ljubljana. It was wonderful – white daisies and tiny pink roses. She fetched it from the inside of the restaurant and they waited by the path for Emilia and Tomaž. How young they were! They were still children. Children would be raising children. Branka Karbić stooped to the idea; she seemed troubled and sad.

The couple came out of the shadows of the pines, which were propagating their fresh scent of resin into the morning air. They were both nervous and awkward in their gowns. Tomaž hurried up to his parents, kissed them on both cheeks, and gratefully took the lovely bouquet in his hands. He turned around and for a tiny moment, he was in the middle, in the crossfire of two loves – behind him was his mother with teary eyes, in front of him Emilia, smiling widely, showing two sets of pearls. With a wide smile, he gave the flowers to Emilia and kissed her gently. They would drive off in separate cars, each with his family, and come back from Novalja in one car, together, as a married couple.

After they had left, Slavko and Dario first sat down and poured themselves a shot. They knocked back their drinks in one gulp.

"Do you remember my marriage, Slavko? You were my best man."

"Well, you and Ivana were serious people, twice their age together."

"You know, I don't think that there is any recipe for happiness. Ivana was not very happy here, and she didn't get along either with the villagers or with my sister."

"Is there anything new regarding the inheritance?"

"Indeed. Last week we, I mean Olivia and Mira and me, were at the court. The will I signed as executor is valid. My daughters went to see the board of directors of the hotel chain yesterday. They have been holding meetings with various people. They are slowly penetrating the business. It is enormous. By the way, they should be here any minute."

"And you, you were her brother, so next of kin? Did she leave you something?"

"I should inherit all the cash from Marina's bank accounts. Her savings must be quite substantial. I don't know what I will do with the money."

"You can always give it to charity. The point is you have it."

"Yeah, I know. Maybe I should buy a new boat. I'll see. Shouldn't we go to the chapel? Our priest will get nervous."

"Let me just check the kitchen and take the sparkling and the glasses. It's all packed."

Dario helped his friend with the boxes, and they drove a couple of miles up the tiny road to where the little chapel overlooked the east and the west shore of the island. They heard singing from the cold, thick walls inside, where a singer from Rijeka, a beautiful young student of Marina's was rehearsing her arias. It sounded like the voices of angels from Heaven. They chose the repertoire together – *Caro nome che il mio cor*, Gilda's song from

Verdi's Rigoletto, then Rosina's *Una voce poco fa* from the Barber of Seville and for the end, a Slovenian pop song, "One Day of Love". With the playback it sounded like a whole orchestra. Dario and Slavko put the glasses and the wine in the deep shadow of a fig tree, under the polished marble table. The rehearsal was over, and they stepped inside to check on everything.

A long line of cars decorated with flowers built up along the road. The guests were gathering. The car plates were from all over Europe – Croatian from Zagreb, Osijek and many from Rijeka, Slovenians from Ljubljana, Maribor and Koper; then, there were Dutch, French, Germans and Italians. All came out of the cars directly into the sun and into Slavko's embrace. They were all dear guests, who knew the house and were willing to spend the last weekend before winter on the warm, sunny Pag. After the greetings, Dario took them over and poured them a little shot of *travarica*, to go with dried fruits, sweet almonds and tiny cubes of hard sheep milk cheese, aged two years and heavy in taste. They all knew Emilia and they all cheered the brave young couple who cherished life above everything. At last, Tomaž and Emilia came hand in hand, Emilia's veil tied at the back with a strand of her thick hair. They stopped at the threshold of the church and Emilia, among smiles and cheers, kissed her groom, then she disappeared behind her veil for the last time.

The service was noisy, a cacophony of prayers and good wishes in various languages. The chapel, packed with people, was like the tower of Babylon. The only time the wedding guests shut their soft murmurs was when the crystal soprano was filling the chapel with a song, and the seconds when Emilia and Tomaž were saying "I will". The last surprise was a lovely Slovenian pop song, One day of love, which numerous guests knew and sang along enthusiastically. In the heat of the moment, the priest forgave Tomaž his clumsiness during the mass. He sat when he should have stood up and murmured the prayers in the rhythm of a rap song. After the ceremony and the compulsory sparkling wine, they all moved towards the bay and Slavko's restaurant.

The crystal bay greeted the wedding party with the sun setting in all its glory. The tables, filled with delicate starters and wine bottles, were set around the terrace. The band was to come soon to play the dance music. Inside, there was a special table for the gifts, which was spilling over with good wishes and small kitchen appliances, blankets, carpets, gift vouchers, books, porcelain – you name it, there was everything. Tomaž took the microphone and in a short speech thanked them all in three languages – Slovenian, English and Croatian, Emilia added her thanks in Italian and German, and finally, in the familiar Dalmatian dialect, at which a huge applause and a stamping of feet exploded. The brandy and the sparkling were doing a good job. People ate and laughed. Speeches followed one another, all in the name of beauty and love. Tomaž and Emilia were ecstatic, in their element, surrounded by the people they loved. Dario stood up, and with tears in his eyes, he delivered his good wishes, too:

"Happy is the bride that the sun shines on. Dear Emilia, I wish you all the best and thank you so much for your help at the inn and hard work while your old uncle... Stop interrupting, Slavko... I said old. Should I say muttonhead? Where was I... while we, your old uncle, and my person – I am his friend of a similar age – were drinking away the profits you've made. Thank you for your loud criticism and thank you, Tomaž, for taking her away, so we can drink more at ease the future. Now, this taking her away cannot go without an obligation. You should look after her and the little one as we would. We will give you the set of rules later in the night. And..." A message beeped on his mobile phone, and he lost composure for a moment. He ignored it and continued: "I wanted to say that our secret information service has found out what happened back in the summer, thus you have consummated your marriage in advance. It is a good thing. Never wait until you're allowed to do something, for before everybody here present would grant it, you would get old and grey like Slavko. Shhhhhh, Slavko. Why are you interrupting me all the time? Where was I? Oh, so congratulations on your courage, which you will need in order to face the years to come. I am sure you will do fine and be good parents to your baby. Emilia, I wish you health and Tomaž, I wish you a son!"

Sounds of protests rose from women, what a chauvinist wish! Olivia and Mira were shrugging their shoulders in despair over their father. Slavko cried in:

"I wish you some sun, too, my old friend! Or the moon... To whiten your hair and illuminate your head!"

A trumpet started to play and drowned out the laughs. The first dance was reserved for Tomaž and Emilia, who set out on the dance floor awkwardly, swinging their bodies in a slow waltz. Soon, other couples joined them, and before anybody could think, the band struck a lively polka, and people were jumping up and down like lunatics.

Catching their breath, Slavko and Dario returned to their seats.

"Didn't you receive a message, Dario?"

"Oh, yes. I'll go to the pier to catch some air and read it. Can you lend me your specs?"

"Here you go. And come back – I have something special in my kitchen. It is twenty-five years old, pure, golden in color and brewed in Ireland. The young are pregnant, they shouldn't drink. But we can..."

"Don't open it without me, you bandit."

Dario sat down on a bollard at the end of the pier. The soft velvet night enveloped him like a warm cloak. The still surface of the sea was reflecting the orange lights from the restaurant. He was just sitting there. It seemed he didn't move an inch for ages. His head bent down, his body was shivering. It was some time before Slavko noticed it. He grabbed the precious bottle and two glasses, and approached his friend with a smile and outstretched arms.

"Here, let's have a drink to our health now, my friend. You're shaking! It'll warm you up, Dario."

Dario looked up with the watery blue in his eyes. He was crying. He gestured to the phone.

"She is no more. Paula just sent me the message. My Maria, my love... She died this morning, they couldn't save her. She is no more... She is no more... What am I to do, Slavko?"

"I, I... Dario!"

Slavko kneeled by his friend and hugged him. They were both crying in despair and frustration, shaking like old oaks in the *bura*, jolting and jerking with pain, ready to give up and fall down. How much pain can one person sustain? How many women would Dario have to lose? His wife, his sister, now his love...

"I wish I had stayed with her in Ljubljana. I wish I had been there, Slavko."

"You couldn't have changed anything. For a month now, you'd been travelling here and forth. At least you've spent some nice time together.... "

"Why? Why now? Why her?"

"Do we ever know why, Dario? Maybe she found her peace, maybe this is all for the best. They had been postponing the surgery for some time... "

"I knew that something was wrong, but she wouldn't tell me. She was such a pighead."

"She wanted to pull it through. Believe me, even if you had been guarding her night and day, it wouldn't have changed anything."

Dario was still, trembling with pain. As though all life warmth had left his body and only cold winds were shaking his limbs. Slavko forced a glass in his hand and poured the golden liquor into it.

"Let's drink to our friend Maria. She was a good woman. She was good to all of us. She was a saint. Her love was stronger than life... "

Dario looked into the sky filled with millions of stars, which reflected his tears still streaming down his wrinkled cheeks.

"I hope you're at peace now, my love. I will follow you soon, very soon... "

Slavko drank up, and decidedly poured himself another drink. With a blank gaze towards the black shapes of the coastline, he murmured, more to himself that aloud:

"Let's just hope her granddaughter lives and all this was not in vain..."

Dario burst out:

"Damn you! Damn you, God, and all the forces above! What kind of Bible is this? A life for a life..."

His furious cry of revolt against creation didn't stop the drums a few hundred yards away from beating their loud rock'n'roll song. The dance floor was crowded, and the guests were jumping up and down, their hips were shaking left and right, be it boogie-woogie or rock'n'roll, the perfumed, made up faces were smiling and crying with joy, eyes were shining...the wedding party was exploding with life! Nothing could stop the flow. Events were taking place as though a magic pen would have written them a long, long time ago...

Letters from beyond

Although spring was hesitatingly coming to Holland, the first hours of a new day were always dark and still. His room felt like the inside of a coffin. No birds were singing at dawn like in his homeland Croatia, where tits and sparrows were twittering their hymns even in the harshest of winters. Here, even the noise of the perpetual traffic, the warnings of horns and the screeching of tires, remained outside, muffled by the thick walls of the prison cell. In spite of that deaf silence, every day since he came to the International Criminal Tribunal for the former Yugoslavia Detention Unit, Jovan Raškić opened his eyes at 5 a.m., and was relieved to have done so. For during the day, he was able to control his nightmares with his reason. He could steer the stream of thoughts into the peaceful stages of his life, so that the horrible images could not ravage his brain in any way they chose to, as they did in the dark. It was his lifelong habit to get up early, either in his job or at the front during the last Balkan war.

At seventy, Raškić' body had lost the vigor of a warrior. Slowly, he dragged his bare feet to the floor in search of his warm slippers. He wrapped his shoulders in an old woolen sweater and headed for the toilet corner of his domicile. He passed the water and immediately flushed the toilet. He put on the light. The sharp, sweet smell of his urine and old age polluted the air, and he took great care to clean every drop from the seat and closed the lid. Back at home, he had never done it, and he could remember his women, his wife and daughters, always complaining about it. Meticulously, he washed his face, brushed his teeth and shaved with his wireless electric shaver. He hated it for its annoying buzzing sound of a wasp, but such were the regulations; all razors, cables or sharp objects were off limits. He put some aftershave on his cheeks and looked at himself in the mirror.

Almost twenty years had gone by. He was trying to imagine his face at the time he was at the front at Kijevo, making love to his translator Marica almost every night. She was the sweetest of all his prisoners. Raškić' black eyes flashed with the reminiscence of lust. Those were the times when he was strong and powerful, when his word meant life or death. At the bottom of his soul, he still secretly felt proud of it, no matter how much he had regretted his deeds later. Not in the courtroom; there, he was trying to explain to the prosecutors, to the judges and the lawyers, what made the Serbians of Krajina rebel and fight against the Croatians in the early nineties. They listened to him carefully, asked additional questions and put each of his thoughts down into the protocol. He liked their work and was glad he could at last tell the world the Serbian side of the story. He cleaned his silver rimmed glasses and put them on.

Until yesterday, when in the afternoon, a letter came from his homeland, from Croatia. Its words undermined all his reasonable posture. At first, it seemed impossible to him. He remembered quite clearly that Marica was not menstruating in the months they had spent every night in bed together. Yet, the picture of their supposed daughter left no doubt. Paula was the spitting image of him when he was her age, although her features were finer and her face leaner. She was lovely, a real beauty, and the thought filled him with pride. He had a daughter who wrote him a letter. Maybe he was not the last of the junkyard dogs under the sun. He should write back.

It was the first sign of any communication from his old life, which he had had in twenty years. Since the day when he decided to leave the war, to put down the arms in the fight which was not his fight any more, to run away and hide like a coward, nobody, neither his family nor his friends knew and cared where or what he was. The shame of that day when he became a traitor burned in his brain like the eternal fires of Hell almost for two decades.

It was in the small hours of the day like today, a morning like any other. In the distance, a hesitant grey light was slowly coming up from behind the dark mountain slopes. It was announcing another day in a row of too many, actually more than one thousand, in the loathsome Balkan war. The air was laden with tension. Birds and deer were hiding in their holes. The green wood was silent as though expecting a kind of a storm. Well, it was the Storm – *Oluja*. Intelligence reached Raškić in the middle of the night that the enemy had launched a major offensive along the front lines and with the help of the air force bombing the Serbian positions they were making very fast headway. The Serbian Army of Krajina should get enforcements from the Bosnian front or even from Belgrade quickly, before it was too late. However, everything was silent on the eastern front and their big leader Slobo was unreachable. Somewhere deep in the valley below the woods, dark fear of death dwelt in the meandering stream of the river Krka. It was on the fifth of August 1995. For a few weeks, he was back in his hometown Knin, ordering papers in the knowledge that the days of *Republika Srpska* and its SVK – Srpska vojska Krajine, the Serbian Army of the Republic of Krajina, were more or less over. He had never been in action before. He recalled asking himself what he was doing in that muddy trench below the old fortress. It was high summer, and he was dizzy from the humid heat radiating from the warm earth. In an hour or so, the August sun would heat the rocks and wake the dry blossoms in the fields below. They would come then, the Croatians. They would stream down the green slopes into the fields like grasshoppers, cleansing anything in front of them and leaving nothing but a desert behind. He would shoot. Could he shoot at all? Cold sweat shivered down his spine, and his black hair, interwoven with silver, stuck to his helmet. He had commanded troops, yet in truth, he was no soldier. It had come to that. They had all left their offices and rooms before dawn to defend Knin until their last drop of blood. He would have to kill somebody. Was he capable of actually firing his Kalashnikov at an enemy? Milošević would say again what a coward he was, how impotent in fighting for the Serbian cause, what a worthless shit of a doctor, that he should tend to chickens instead of soldiers at the front. The last encounter with his superiors still echoed in his head – chick, chick, chick, Jovan, chick, chick, chick...

He hated that war, he hated the *Ustashas*, and he hated the Bosnians. He hated them all for making him fight. He hated them to have taken away his life, his family, his profession, only to transform him into an obedient war machine. There were times in those years when he hated his Serbian brothers, too. Years before, he had still believed in their rights. He believed in the Serbian heroism, in their noble culture, and he believed in their loving God, shining from the icons and resounding in the hymns of the prayers. He believed they had true and honorable reasons to claim their rights, but nothing like what happened later. Vukovar, Srebrenica, Omarska, Keraterm, Trnopolje and Manjača – names of terror printed on the world map forever. They should not have harmed so many women and children. They should not have ruined so many lives. His combatants and himself, their commander – who have they become? Have they all forgotten the Ballad of Marko Kraljević? Have they all forgotten what made them fight the Turks for hundreds of years? Serbians used to be a proud people of brave warriors, but now they became nothing but a horde of butchers, trying to protect their last bastion, Knin. Jovan Raškić was ashamed. Two days ago, he had ordered his soldiers to burn their archives in Knin. He did not want the *Ustasha*'s police to feed on their bloody tracks and cause more death and more pain later.

Something was moving in the darkness of the woods on the other side. They were still far away, too far to fire, but they were coming closer... He had heard it was to be the biggest Croatian offensive since WW2. They would have to fight. What were his choices? "Go, Marko, [...] drink thy fill of wine!" Stop feeling sorry for yourself, Jovan, or they will hit you and you will die. Maybe even worse, you will be their prisoner. What would they have done to you, if they had captured you, the *Ustashas*?

Jovan banished the unpleasant thoughts away like a swarm of flies. Outside, he could see the first white fogs of the Dutch morning. With so much water in the plains of Holland and due to the proximity of the sea, there was always some mist in the air. Raškić threw a longing look at the light outside. He felt silly, almost like a schoolboy grounded for not having done his homework. He would so much like to breathe in the morning air, just once, just today... He would not mind the cold, even not

the rain. He knew he would have a chance to stretch his legs in
the courtyard after lunch, yet the freshness of the day would be
gone by then. What was the time? It was not yet six o'clock.
He should sit down to his computer and write the letter to his
daughter. Well, was not a computer print out too impersonal?
He looked at the envelope and took out the folded sheet with
two photographs: one of Marica and the other one of Paula. Her
message was brief, to the point, and she wrote it by hand. He
would do the same. Out of his drawer, he took a pen and a few
sheets of paper. He dutifully wrote the date in the right corner of
a blank page. Then, his thoughts wandered back to the summer
morning in Knin so many years ago.

The Croatians, the *Ustashas*, had always been a curse to his
family. He could not remember the face of his grandfather, who
had been tortured for days by those bastards. They finally hung
him on the walnut tree outside their house in the last days of
WW2. For decades under Tito, thanks also to the fact that his
wife Jovanka was a Serbian from Lika and in the spirit of *bratstvo i jedinstvo*, the brotherhood and unity among the so diverse
Yugoslav nationalities, the Serbians in Croatia were left in peace.
Then, Tudjman came to the power and helped the *Ustashas* back
in the saddle. He got himself some nice helpers. That Gotovina,
a war machine, the nightmare of Serbian boys, was he leading
the army in *Oluja*? Were the Bosnians coming from the east to
support the *Ustashas*? Serbian soldiers had raped so many of
their women that they must have sired a new nation, a new army
of orphans...Little *Chetniks*, children born out of violence and
hate, children who no woman took to her breast to feed...sordid
creatures of war that nobody wanted.

Did his daughter grow up convinced she was one of them? Did
she think she was a little *Chetnik*? Had Marica told her that?
Or, had she told her that they had loved each other, although
in a strange way, at the wrong time, in the wrong place? How
should he begin his letter? Could he write Dear Paula? No, it
is too intrusive. The tone of her letter was more matter of fact.
Maybe he should use her surname and put Dear Miss...What
was that family name that Marica adopted after the war again?
Perić. How did she find such a name? Did she use a passport of a
woman who died in a *logor*? What was her real name again? He
could recall every detail of her face, every contour of her body,
the smell of her skin, the taste of her kiss, but her family name
escaped his memory. He had to remember it. He would. It was
important. Since yesterday, he was confused and disoriented.
The image of his daughter and the knowledge of her grave illness
upset him. His head was a whirlwind of emotions. His thoughts
were circling around that fateful day when he thought that he
had broken up with the war for good.

Back then, on the slope below the old city of Knin, his body shook so hard that he heard his teeth rattle. He knew it was not the morning cold, for summer mornings in Knin are mild. It was pure fear. The stench of his perspiration hurt his nostrils. The noises of engines and hushed voices of people moving through the bushes were coming closer. He turned his eyes up to God and to Heaven. Heaven, what Heaven, he would be going directly to Hell. Media all over the world reported that the Serbians were the aggressors, and that they were losing the war. He was on the wrong side. Should they have caught him, they would have finished him on the spot without any court martial or lawyers to write down his arguments of defense. What about the liberators, who also tortured and massacred civilians? Would the society acquit them from all guilt because they won the war? Was not their fight just another side of the same bloody coin? Was it not the spinning wheel of basic human instincts, the call of hungry, dominating genes, which tell men to kill and to breed like animals? Where were human souls in that crazy Balkan massacre?

A few signal rockets exploded in the sky. The Croatians were already in the valley. Now they would have to march uphill. That would be tough. Who was afraid of them, anyway? Maybe my enemy would be a young boy, with a girlfriend waiting for him on one of the beautiful Dalmatian islands. He could be a Bosnian peasant, with a whole clan to provide for, including our bastards. Or, a history teacher with glasses and a poetry notebook in his breast pocket of the uniform? Who would come first? What had they done to him? Was he to take their lives just because they were not Serbians?

It was there and then that Raškić took his traitorous, cowardly, yet somehow human decision. He was an old man. He would rather die himself than kill another. He had had enough. He would step out of the vicious circle and seek the first opportunity to run. He had to be careful and wait until the fight was in full vigor, or his boys would shoot him in the back for deserting the battlefield. They had his orders to do so. He waited patiently for the right moment. Then, he ran as fast as he could. He jumped into the jeep, where his new identity was waiting, hidden in the trunk. After an hour's drive, he became somebody else. He was a sales representative working for Pliva Pharmaceuticals. With the money and a new passport, he started a new life. Unless he had come forward voluntarily, they would have never tracked him down. They caught the others. They put them in those comfortably furnished cages, grey and blue, upset and frightened like little rabbits, shaking for their sorry lives. Yet, they would have never got him. He was too clever for all of them.

Jovan Raškić, once a pediatrician, then a Serbian freedom fighter, a war commander and fugitive of a decade was sitting in front of a blank piece of paper, not knowing how to address the young woman of his own flesh and blood, who needed his help.

Not a muscle of his body moved while the ICTY detention unit was waking into a new day. The corridors were filling with muffled sounds of conversation in Dutch and soft tinkling of cutlery. The merciful Lady Justice was serving breakfast.

* * *

"Good morning. There was a letter for you yesterday, from abroad. I think Belgium or the Netherlands. They forgot to give it to you, sorry."

It was the nurse Ivana, blond and thin, quick paced and friendly, the early bird, as she was called. She pulled up the shutters and opened the window widely.

"Thank you, Ivana. Good morning."

"I'll be back later with the usual routine, you know."

Ivana made an obscene gesture with her hand and smiled broadly.

"Ass or mouth today?"

Paula was smiling too, now. It was their private joke, and parts of the body were actually code names for two doctors at the Zadar hospital oncology department, which they both very much disliked. One was a notorious ass-kisser. He was nodding at the head of the department no matter what the old man was saying. The other was boasting about his nocturnal sexual exploits while examining the patients.

"Ass, I am sorry. Do you feel worse today?"

"Well, I'll survive, won't I?" replied Paula with arched eyebrows and a questioning look.

The young women giggled. It was the blackest of all humor, a macabre death dance with slight hopes, but it was humor all the same. A soft breeze scented with crazy yellow broom in flower blew into the room. Every spring, the broom shrubs invaded the hills of the Dalmatian coast. Paula was grateful to be at the Zadar hospital and not in Zagreb or Ljubljana. Her medical state was very fragile. She was under strong drugs and constant surveillance of the medical team. After the failed bone marrow transplantation in Ljubljana, they were treating her with Glivec, to be followed by Cytarabine Interferon, which they said would bring better results. But in due time, so they had told her, another attempt at bone marrow transplantation was not out of the question, should Paula find a suitable donor within the circle of her relations. She had not known of any until a few months ago. She grew up with the certainty that the two of them, *nona* and herself, were the only family members who survived the last Balkan war, and that there wasn't any other person with her genes in the world. At the Karlovac cemetery, there was that strange grey tombstone for the *Obitelj* Polac, her unfortunate family fallen in the war, which was according to *nona*, solid proof

of that. Just a few days before her death, *nona* Maria told her
the curious story of Angela, a woman who was captured at the
front and fell in love with her jailor. Paula thought nothing of
it, as she knew *nona*'s passion for stories – she knew quite a few
of her fabrications from several historical eras – surely, it was
another one. If it were not for the letter. . . the last breath of life
from her. . . her last good night kiss. . . It revealed to Paula, who
her next of kin was. He was alive, though he should be dead long
ago.

Paula was shocked and terrified when she found out that she
was the daughter of the one of the most notorious war criminals,
doing his time at the Detention Unit of The International Criminal Tribunal for the former Yugoslavia in the Hague. Through
the story of Angela her mother had told her, it might not have
been in a rape she had been conceived, but in an act of love. Love
between two enemies, between a prisoner and a jailor – was that
possible? Why did they not hate each other? Were they not too
old for love? Was it the reason, why for years, *nona* was telling
her the tales of Dalmatian superwomen of the past, the brave
and splendid protagonists, who loved and received love against
all odds? Was it a kind of preparation for the big truth about
her, Paula?

Paula had cried through many nights pitying her fate; her
deadly illness, her loneliness, her sad mother, hiding such big
truths as an abandoned family and sons in her disappointed heart,
and she had cried over the fear of pain and death lurking in the
shadow of her shrinking future. How could she face death without having lived first? How will she go through all the physical
pains of another treatment? When the only person she had ever
loved, her mother, died and left her alone. Paula felt she had lost
everything in the world. She had no hope. Depressed and with
only one wish, to leave this world as soon as possible, she was
brought back to Croatia shortly after Maria's death in Ljubljana,
back to the Zadar hospital.

Here the nurses knew her much better. They remembered the
young woman, almost a girl, as a fighter. Paula might have been
seriously ill, but she never lost faith and humor. They knew she
embraced a good joke, she loved laughter and life. She had been
joking about her hair or the absence of it all the time. When
after many chemotherapies a year ago, she became as thin as
a straw, and she had to come to the hospital again, she would
say, that she came for a special rehab cure – diet and chemical
substances withdrawal cure, like a movie star. After she lost her
grandmother, Paula suffered in her black moods. The hospital
staff felt it and were afraid of leaving Paula alone in the room.
They spoke to the doctors and after a week, a famous Croatian
psychotherapist Dr. Irena Jungić, visited the hopeless patient for
the first time. Dr. Jungić was seeing Paula every other day, and

soon progress followed. Paula was getting better, her mood got brighter as the weather was more and more sunny outside with the coming spring.

At the beginning, Paula was just being polite and did not take the therapy sessions too seriously. She did not need a shrink. She needed the medicine to heal her leukemia. Patiently, Irena asked questions about trivial things in her life like her youth, friends, life, the hotel Perovica, her schools, studies, books they were both reading, avoiding all delicate topics. Paula did not tell her doctor anything about her mother or as it should have been – her grandmother.

One grey day, though, when the southern humid wind *jugo* was blowing and whipping the windows with heavy rains, bringing suicide into people's minds, Paula crashed. She cried in Irena's lap, babbling how she wanted to find out about her father, Jovan Raškić, the Serbian commander. Why did he persecute the Muslims and the Croatians? Why did he put up the women camps? How could he have "ethnically cleansed" villages of his former friends and neighbors? How could Mara, Maria, her mother, have fallen in love with him, who was the devil, the brain of the *Republika Srpska* Krajina? Why did she give birth to her? Why had she not aborted her while she could? Why had she let her live? She had been ill conceived. It was all wrong. Her leukemia is God's punishment, she had never believed in the stories of Heaven and Hell, but now she knew – God and Devil are there, fighting for her. Paula was losing her mind.

Irena held her in her arms, suddenly stiff as wood and cold as ice. Her uncle and his family had all vanished in one of Raškić's raids outside Šibenik. They never found their bodies. Four people simply disappeared, maybe in one of the karstic caves, nobody knew. Ten years later, the family set up a symbolic ceremony and a tomb stone with their names: Ivan, Borka, Angelka, Stevo... Stop the memories, now, you should be a doctor. This girl had nothing to do with the man. Irena was trying to concentrate on her job. Irena tightened her embrace to let Paula feel she was there to support her, but her mind was still a foggy mess. After a while, she blocked all her emotion out and became the doctor, the professional she was. Let's bring the girl to the facts again and calm her down. It was time to be very practical about the whole situation. First, she asked Paula:

"Does anybody else in the world know that Commander Jovan Raškić might be your father?"

Paula stopped sobbing, seeing Irena's point at once.

"No, nobody..."

"Did she tell him about you?"

"No, not as far as I know. My mother took great care to ensure that nobody could have found out about it during her lifetime. She suggested to me in her letter, which I received the day after she died, that I should continue to be very careful. She would have burnt all bridges and not even have told me till the end of her days, was it not for the slight possibility that my father's bone marrow might save me should hers not. She could not have known how right she was..."

"Yes, I've heard of your mother Maria Perić, she's a legend of the Croatian tourism. Didn't she set up the first ecological hotel on Pag? I thought she was your grandmother, though, so it said in your medical file. Strange, for all the publicity about the hotel, I don't think I've ever seen her photograph in the press. I wonder what she looked like."

"She was fit and stunning for her age. Since I remember, men liked her. However, you wouldn't find photos. She had never let any media take any photograph of her, she never stood up in public, no press conferences, nothing. I thought she was too modest. Well, I know now why. It was not only modesty. It was the fear that the past could catch up with her. Here, this is her."

Paula fished out a photograph of a tall, aged woman, deeply tanned, in jeans and white sleeveless shirt, smiling into the camera and coquettishly throwing her blond ponytail to the right. Her teeth were perfect, her eyes sparkling green. She was obviously more than fond of the photographer, as there was a joy of sexual arousal in her broad wholehearted chin. Paula saw Irena flinch and tried to explain that it was their neighbor Dario, *nona*'s partner, who took the photograph, and that she stole it from his house one day. Irena just nodded, thinking that Raškić could have had a hard time resisting such a lovely woman so many years ago. Maybe he had raped her like so many others, and the woman was only hiding the humiliation behind the tale of their love.

"Have you spoken to a friend about that man and your mother?"

"No, no... I am too afraid. You know how people still feel about the war. They loathe men like my..., like him. They're worse than animals for them. People lost families... My mother said in the letter, that he was not violent, that he..."

Paula stopped in the middle of the sentence, noticing Irena's face paling. She sat up in her bed.

"I am sorry, doctor Irena. I have made a mistake. I shouldn't be telling you this. Will you keep my secret?"

Irena banned the images of her cousins, blond teenage twins, from her mind and nodded quickly.

"Yes, Paula. There are rules I have to keep. I lose my license and my job should I tell anything that I get to know during my patients' sessions. Also, much of it is not true. Many patients are imagining things. Not you, though... I cannot and will not tell anything, you have my word, Paula."

Irena looked at Paula's desperate face, staring at the void

ahead. She was so young and so ill. Life tested her human capacities to the limits. Few people would be able to fight such blows.
Yet, there was a strange strength in this ash grey girl with thin
black curls more revealing than covering the head. Paula's lips
were pressed tightly together, her look, blurred with uncontrol-
lable tears, was focused on an invisible point ahead; she seemed to
possess a core of steel persistence. The vital force and optimism
of her mother combined with the soldier energies of her father.
Forget the man...

"One question, Paula. Do you have any physical proof that
your grandmother's story is true? Did she give you any documents?"

Paula caught her eyes – she nodded slowly, trying to wipe
away the tears that flew down her cheeks like two streams of
pain.

"Unfortunately, yes. She gave me a sealed manila envelope
on the evening before the operation in Ljubljana and asked me
to keep the envelope closed for her until she woke up from the
narcosis. Alas, she never did. Later, I studied the file thoroughly.
She wrote me a letter... enclosed was her old photograph. On the
other side, it said Marica, 1991, yet no other proofs of her previous
identity. There were some papers that she must have stolen from
the command post during the war, but there was also a huge load
of newspapers articles about the Raškić' process. When you see
the pictures of my..., of him, he even looks like me. Same eyes,
strong black brows and hair. Well, most of mine is gone now,
with treatments, his as well, I suppose with age..."

"Can I have a look at the file, Paula?"

Irena did not know why she wanted to see those papers, there
was no chance of finding anything for her use in them. Yet,
a strange curiosity, which made her one of the best Croatian
psychiatrists, surged in her brain. She wanted to find some trace
of his deeds, she wanted to study the violent man herself. To
create his psychological profile for further generations to beware
of such characters – all charming and nice on the outside, all evil
in their hearts. Had Raškič never thought about the Hyppocrates
oath he once had taken as a doctor, while his soldiers were raping
and killing? Where was his conscience? Paula looked into Irena's
stony face and slowly shook her head.

"I'm sorry, but no. I have to think twice even about my
confession today. I must live with it, doctor Irena, not you."

Irena saw the mistrust in her eyes. Nevertheless, she realized
that the girl had to have a reason for telling her about all this.
Paula was a strong and clever girl. Her confession was not just a
crying fit of a black moment. Maybe the reason was too obvious –
hope to find the better donor, hope for life. The girl needed moral
support, a hint of guidance as to whether she should be trying
to save her life by getting in contact with the criminal. Should

she catch the straw of hope or just let it go and die? Irena felt that was the basic question which Paula had asked her between the tears and between the lines. She had to stick with the girl. She was a doctor after all. Irena looked Paula directly in the eyes and said clearly.

"Paula, you want me to help you find him, don't you?"

"Well, I know where he is. We all do, don't we? He's being tried in The Hague, at the International Criminal Tribunal for the former Yugoslavia. He is in the famous Detention Unit. He will probably stay in prison until the end of his days, won't he?"

"He has spoken against Milošević, he explained many things about Krajina. He could get a lesser punishment. Not a life sentence."

"I don't think he could stay alive another day should he ever leave the prison."

"Yes, the charges, and the legal procedure are one side of the coin. The people who want revenge for their families are the other. You're probably right. He's dead one way or the other."

"He had been missing for so many years. Now, I can even write him a letter."

"Why don't you, Paula?"

"You mean before it's too late for both of us?"

"Yes, you should grab your chance to get well. Write him now. Maybe... you never know... He must have been a man once..."

Irena's voice cracked. This was too heavy. She knew her duty was to encourage the contact, in order to explore Paula's slightest chance of healing. Her mother had told Paula about Raškić for that reason in the first place. On the other hand, she felt nauseated by the thought that Paula would find him and he would respond. How would he react? Regret, remorse, desperation so many years later – they could not bring any of the dead and persecuted back. Irena sighed. Her eyes wandered into the distance behind the trails of the thick raindrops sliding down the dusty windows. What now?

"Yeah, you mean before he became the beast..."

"Paula, don't think of him like that. He's your father, maybe, your only living relative. Maybe his bone marrow can heal you. You should only bear this in mind. Leave the rest aside for now."

"Anyway, you know that my mother's name wasn't Maria but Marica, they called her Mara."

"And the family name?"

"She didn't tell me. She just said I should show him her old passport photograph and tell him I am his and Mara's daughter from Kijevo."

Irena's eyes blinked with swallowed tears. She was used to eliciting out secrets from her patients. Paula's, though, was a heavy one. How can a woman pretend so well for so many years? Why? How could she have deprived her daughter of a life filled

with laughter, brothers, sisters, uncles and aunts? Was there
a way to track down Maria Perić before she had met Raškić?
Maybe if she knew Mara's old family name, Raškić would not be
the only possible donor for Paula. Maybe they could leave him
out. There was a slight chance.

"What was the name of the woman your mother was telling
about days before the operation in Ljubljana?"

"Angela something... I thought at the time, what a strange
woman'a name for Dalmatia. But so is Paula, I have always been
the only one in my class, the only one at the whole school."

"Try to remember that something, Paula. There could be a
clue. After all, Maria was in her late forties when you were born.
She could have had a grown family by then, couldn't she?"

"I don't know. I wasn't paying so much attention to the
names. Anyway, if my mother had a family and children who
survived the war, they are surely Catholic and Croatian. How
would they react to a Serbian war bastard showing up at their
doorstep? What would they do with a little *Chetnik*?"

Paula shook with sobs – why was she so alone in the world?
Why had not her mother remarried or left her with some knowledge of her former family? Why only this filth of a man, who
allegedly had conceived her in the middle of planning raids or
another war camp or God knows which atrocity springing to his
sick mind?

"Paula, don't underestimate the power of wealth your mother
acquired with the hotel Perovica. I think even the Bishop of
Zadar would claim your kinship, be you Serbian, Albanian or
Gypsy, just for the sake of money. Also, the passions have cooled
down after so many years."

Paula shrugged hopelessly and turned her gaze to the window.
The rain stopped and the clouds were nearly gone. The sky left
some light through, maybe the sun would come up later. The
story of Angela sank in the back of her mind on the morning
when they told her about her *nona*'s death. It was such a sad
story, and she remembered having wondered that night what this
pregnant woman Angela had done with her baby in the end. She
could never have imagined the outcome. It was herself, Paula.
She was the unlucky little bastard. Would she try to find her
blood relatives, if she knew her mother's real name? How would
they look at her? Could she buy their love with her money and
business? Yeah, probably she could. They would put up with
her just for the sake of silver euros in their pockets. She had seen
what money could do to people in Mulobedanj. The country fell
into deep debts and wild privatization campaigns. Euros bought
everything – love, friendship, land, sheep, olives... Why would it
not buy some bone marrow from a next of kin? Yet, in their
hearts, those not to be found relatives would despise her deeply,
she knew that for sure. Like they must have despised her mother,

for she turned away from them at the time. Paula did not know that for sure, but concluding from Angela's story, her mother had to go away for many reasons. One was herself. If that family had existed, they had not been there for Maria when she needed them most. Paula shuddered – which was the lesser of two evils? To contact her criminal father at The Hague, or to follow the traces this Angela left at Medica Zenica in 1992 and to find the real Marica?

She could not think of why suddenly the story of Saint Paul's conversion came to her mind. As Saint Paul was still Saul, a zealot Pharisee on his journey to Damascus, a light from heaven flashed around him. He fell to the ground and heard a voice say to him, "Saul, Saul, why do you persecute me?" The lord Jesus blinded Saul, and freed his sight only after he realized the truth about God and his son Jesus. Was her name Paula because like Saint Paul, Maria was blinded by her previous life and saw truth only after she'd loved that man and gave birth to her, the fragile child of war? Do all those images from our childhood Sunday school influence our actions? Maybe there is something like Providence. Were we born to interfere with God's plan and execute our free will? Or, are we just particles of dust lost in the rough winds? Questions without answers for thousands of years. . . If only she could see in her mother's soul now, if only she could hold her one more time and feel her warm embrace. Her lips trembled, and her eyes began to fill with fresh tears like pearls of pain wanting to part from the shell. Irena softly touched her elbow and looked Paula straight into her eyes. Her decisive voice was low and harsh.

"Paula, you must find out the truth for yourself, remember your name. I think you must find your father first and tell him you exist."

Paula paled for a moment, thinking to herself, "Yes, Irena would want me to act, but could she take the consequences upon herself should everything go wrong?" She said aloud, reluctantly:

"What if Raškić abuses the fact that he had a love affair with a Croatian woman during the war and that he was sheltering her, thus saving her life? He might hope for a milder treatment by the judges."

"I don't think a love affair can change the verdict much. Anyway, the judges would probably think it was a rape after all. Their first concern is for the victims, who had suffered or died. Raškić, like the Nürnberg Nazis after WW2, will be tried not only for his infamous deeds, not only for the just treatment of the living witnesses, but for the future generations to know that even in wars certain acts are intolerable by the society. So that such war crimes could be prevented in future wars."

"It is so said and terrible, Irena. He was not just anybody. He was not a poor, illiterate peasant, who would blindly believe in the justice of the Serbian cause. Raškić was a doctor before the war. He took the Hyppocrates' oath. He should have known of the Geneva Convention. He should have remembered his oaths, bastard!"

"Calm down, Paula. It is not about him, it is about you. Focus on the purpose of your contact. Do you have his address in jail?"

"Yes, I do. He's being kept in the ICTY Detention Unit. I sent an e-mail to the administration a few days ago, saying I was his very distant niece. They sent back his address. It is only land mail, of course."

Irena's expression hardened.

"I heard of this luxurious prison where the former mortal foes, the Muslims, the Croatians and the Serbians, are playing chess, cards and cooking meals together, waiting for their verdicts while peacefully doing their time. It is safer and more convenient than freedom for them. Out there, they would be wild game, moving targets for revenge. Now the same laws which they had been trampling down keep them safe. They should all hang, if you ask me."

Paula heard a crack in Irena's voice, and again she became suspicious about their conversation. Irena is her psychiatrist, but she has also had a life. She might have lost somebody in the war, for she was very knowledgeable about The International Criminal Tribunal for the former Yugoslavia. Paula felt sorry that she had lost control and opened up to Irena. The weight of the truth on her shoulder was too much for her. She needed to speak to someone about her secret.

One way or the other, Irena had to respect client confidentiality and keep the story to herself. Paula looked at Irena's Mediterranean profile with dark olive skin. Irena was a thin woman, and the wrinkles around her mouth and eyes were deep. Who was this woman? All of a sudden, she had a funny feeling about her. During their sessions, Irena was professional. There were very short moments when she got personal, commenting on this or that. Today, she was involved in Paula's story more than ever before. It had completely absorbed her. The doctor that she was, she slipped and lost control, too. Paula wondered why.

"There's no death penalty at The Hague, you know. Raškić' process is still going on. I can follow the proceedings of the tribunal on-line. He keeps denying all responsibility and blames it on the others. He says he was only obeying the orders issued by Karadjić and Milošević. The verdict will be reached shortly, though, I think. It seems the judges are losing patience with him."

Irena nodded slowly, and said in a very low voice, though there was nobody else in the room.

"Yeah, you must move quickly, Paula. You should follow your

mother's will and use this information to your benefit. Send Raškić a letter informing him about your mother's death. Tell him about yourself, about who you are. Then we will see."

Paula nodded pensively and thanked her doctor for her support. Irena looked at the clock on the wall and stood up, letting her eyes wander to the horizon, where the distant shapes of the islands Molat and Ugljan were glistering in the sun. The time was up. Paula did not even notice when she left the room, closing the door behind her.

She thought about her mama and old age. Maria would not tolerate getting old – she was timeless. She kept fit with work and long walks which she had claimed she needed for work. When Paula was a child, she did not understand. It was only in the last year that Paula could comprehend the complexity and the genius of her mother's enterprise. The ecological hotel offered a unique and incredibly modern case study of how nature could be preserved and exploited at the same time. It was not easy to maintain balance. One had to understand the needs of the guests and the life of the villagers. Maria thought of various practical solutions and engaged a few whole villages in becoming suppliers for the Perovica hotel without losing empathy for the authenticity of their lifestyles. She would buy as much as she could from the locals. She would employ them in her kitchen, as service staff, or suggested other, preferably outsourced activities, which they would offer to her guests. Thus, fishing trips, tracking parties, surfing, scuba diving, and wind-sailing enhanced the tourist offer at this remote corner of the island, practically at the end of the world. Her guests were rich and they paid gladly for more fun.

Paula was trying to remember if she could ever detect that Maria might have secrets. She once had asked her how she could finance the building of the hotel.

"Oh, I got investors from abroad. I don't even know all the companies. I got their offers through some foundations which provided support for post-war business developments in Croatia. My plan to start in such a remote place was welcome, so I got the funds."

Paula wanted to know more about it.

"So you don't really own the hotel, *nona*, you just run it."

She got a quick reply.

"No, no, I do own it. At least I own the majority share."

"How much do you have exactly?"

"Fifty-one percent."

"And the rest? Who owns the other forty-nine percents?"

"As I said: various angel investment companies."

"Don't they share the profit with you?"

"Paula, aren't you curious? Of course, they do. But they also let me have lots of liberties with the surplus. You know, I am

happy to discuss it with you. The hotel is a very long-term investment, so I decided to use the profit to develop new services and
new supporting activities. I wanted to achieve certain stability
in the area, in which the stay at Perovica would offer a delightful
experience. Therefore, we built the glass house to produce our
own vegetables and reuse the water. We created a few jobs. You
also know that we have invested in many islander companies offering sports and leisure commodities for our guests. So, Perovica
is not just a hotel, it is a part of the island, a recreation area,
where tradition meets the modern times and heals people from
stress."

Paula was listening to her *nona*'s explanations with attention.

"I read in an article about how a group of angel investors
buried a company because they wanted a very high return on
their money in a very short time. Don't your investors want the
same? Can they just come and claim their investment back one
day?"

"It's not that simple. There are rules, and at the beginning,
we set them in such a way that the expected returns are very
slow and very low. It was still war when I started, and there
were many favorable options for me. Besides, since I have the
majority, I can always make the decision to reinvest the profit.
This year, we have built the glasshouse to reuse our sewage water
and grow fruits and vegetables. It was an international project
financed by the Croatian government and the European Union.
Our supply of fresh produce is much more reliable now. And
all the villagers can buy their vegetables from our garden if they
want to."

"Yeah, the strawberries are terrific."

"Silke Wahring is a treasure. She's worked as an agricultural
engineer in Holland and in Spain. The technology of painting
the glass with this special white coating to prevent the strong
summer sun from burning the plants inside is revolutionary. It
makes the cultivation here possible. People all over the island
want to follow the example, so that they would not depend on
the supply from the mainland so much."

"So the water with which sunburnt bodies are washed in the
evening can be consumed in the lettuce a few days later."

"Precisely. It was just an idea at the beginning, but I was
exploring it for a long time before we started the project. Ideas
are important, you see."

"I know, *nona*. But ideas cannot buy land and pay the
builders. Where did you get the initial capital?"

"Oh, it wasn't so much. I borrowed some from the banks, I
found a few sponsors. You don't need so much, you see. People
always think it is millions which earn millions. Not always, you
see. Sometimes ideas are worth more than millions."

In her bed, looking through the window into a wonderful

spring day, Paula could almost smell the sweetness of thousands of flowers, bushes, and palms in bloom. Only last year, the air was full of hope and beauty. She remembered how they were climbing the steep coastal path curving among the olive groves uphill. *Nona* was pushing her wheelchair. Paula refused at first to sit in it. She protested that she was sick, but not a cripple. She could not walk on her own, though, so she finally gave in to *nona*'s persuasion. She needed fresh air after a month of the acid smells of her sickbed. They made long walks together and chatted about this and that, mostly about the past. Paula smiled at the memory of the story which *nona* had concocted about one of the most popular political personalities in the Dalmatian history – the Roman Emperor Diocletian. It was just so like her strong emancipated mother to put the bravest of soldiers, the notorious Imperator, the persecutor of Christians and the hero of women, in short, one of the most efficient and ruthless rulers of his times, in a wheelchair, and let him be wheeled about by a Greek slave... Paula closed her eyes and thought of the girl who lived by the fishpond on the island of Šolta in 311 A.D. There was time to open that god forsaken letter later.

* * *

With a weary look, Paula came back to her sick bed. She was contemplating the letter in her lap, turning it over again and again as though she would be able to perceive its content without reading it. It was yet another envelope with another message from somewhere beyond reality. The envelope was thick. There had to be dozens of pages, folded neatly, almost like a literary manuscript. Her life seemed like an equation with two unknowns – x for her mother and y for her father. Could she open the letter and read it now? The address was written in ink, in capitals. Before her name, there the neat address quoted "Miss", and the postal code of Zadar was put left of the invisible margin of the rest of the address. The postal stamps were portraits of the Dutch queen, still young and smiling tolerantly at the world, the date and place defined by the seal; it was dispatched a week ago from The Hague. There were no signs whatsoever that the letter came from one of the most notorious detention units in the world. Paula did not know what was in it for her, but she knew what had happened to Raškić lately.

It was all over the media; after long months of his firm denial of any war crimes, defending the military actions as protection of the Serbian population, his wall of silence, which sheltered so many murderers and rapists, all of a sudden broke down; Raškić lost his appearance of a Serbian warrior and started to talk like a father, a husband and a doctor. He could not stop his flow of words, so while he was not confessing his crimes to the jury, he was writing them down in his cell. He was photographed in his cell with tears in his eyes kissing the Catholic cross on a rosary and asking the victims for forgiveness. It was pathetic, and too late for so many lost lives. It was too late for him, too. In another, less democratic world, he would long have hanged like a thief. In the middle ages, his body parts would have been scattered around the towns and villages which he had been terrorizing, without mercy. However, this was Europe, where human lives had a high price as long as they were in full view of the public. Who had been worrying about the lives lost during the Balkan massacre in some remote hills and dark woods, who could hear the cries of women and children behind the thick walls of former factories and schools?

Paula had watched his confession on YouTube with mixed feelings. He spoke about his profession and job as a pediatrician before the conflict with the Croatian politics escalated in Krajina. He worked in the hospital in Knin, which later in the war became one of the most notorious war prisons for Croatians and Muslims. He had a family, three daughters, at the time. The oldest, twenty-two, was studying medicine in Belgrade, the younger ones were still going to the high school in Knin. As soon as the first shots fell, he sent all his family to Belgrade. He said he had an apartment he inherited from his uncle there. His house in Knin, on the hill below the famous fortress of the Croatian king Dmitar Zvonimir, became the centre of the new Serbian movement. Jovan Raškić dedicated all his strengths to defending the autonomy of the Krajina Serbians, which had been pushed around by Tudjman's pro-Croatian regime. According to Raškić, it was an honest revolt of people afraid of the fifty year old memories of WW2, when the *Ustashas* had been killing and raping wildly everybody who was not Croatian and whose belief in Jesus was Orthodox. Raškić claimed that Franjo Tudjman was a reactionary and a nationalist politician. Shamelessly, Tudjman's right-wing political party Hrvatska demokratska zajednica – The Croatian Democratic Union – brought all the *Ustasha* ideology back to life; the glorification of the Catholic Church against the Serbian Orthodox religion, and the importance of the Croatian nationality. With the new Croatian constitution in 1990, the Serbians became just one of the ethnic minorities in the new independent state of Croatia. Revived were the old, feared fascist symbols like the red and white chessboard coat of arms in the middle of the new Croatian flag. The Krajina Serbians, populating one of the least friendly regions of Croatia, the Dinaric Alps, felt stung in their pride. They deeply resented the new HDZ nationalism and needed little encouragement by the Serbian president Slobodan Milošević to revolt against the new Croatian government. They founded *Republika Srpska* Krajina, the Republic of Serbian Krajina, where their goal was primarily to protect the Serbians

– their culture, Orthodox religion and values against Tudjman. Only later, this idea led to the plan of uniting all the ethnic Serbians and forging all their territories into one political unit – the Great Serbia, by removing all the non-Serbian populations, which were in the way.

Raškić explained all this logically and eloquently. If the audience had not known the outcome, it would have almost looked like a just cause. Yet, it was not for nothing that so many of his comrades were now in prison. He confessed that he had been very naive. He had thought the founding of *Republika Srpska* Krajina would not evolve into a war.

According to his words, Raškić's main job was to organize logistics for the soldiers, mainly volunteers, who came daily from Serbia and Monte Negro. He had settled them down in houses, abandoned by the local Croatians in fear of the RSK militia. Vojislav Šešelj's efficient military training made soldiers out of young, inexperienced rookies. To the prosecutor's questions about why they would train an army unless to fight and kill, he just remained silent. Raškić replied that in time he had understood, that the young Serbian men came to Krajina for drinking and mischief, looting and raping local girls no matter of which ethnicity. Then, the conflict front spread widely over the Krajina's long borders, and the commanders needed to keep the militant mob under control, so drugs came into play. It was easy to obtain them, either via Adriatic from Italy or via land routes through Romania and Serbia. Many of the young men perished in combat because their reactions were numbed, but so many new came every day.

He took care of all the details – organized the letters sent to the families of the fallen soldiers, even the coffins with the golden crest of *Republika Srpska* Krajina. Everybody admired and loved him for his comforting nature. In his defense, he said he had never been in action himself. He reported that in 1991, the front was behind the Dalmatian coast. There was a sudden cholera outburst in the nearby prison camp, so he and his medical team came to administer the cure and ban the deadly disease. It was the first time in his life that he saw a concentration camp, skinny living carcasses walking and pleading in pains. The commander was Krečić something, a huge man from Novi Sad, and Raškić ordered him to disband the camp and set up a quarantine, so that prisoners, particularly those who had caught the cholera, could be given the medicine and medical care. Some of the Serbian soldiers had caught the disease, too. He had ordered the whole village to be put under a quarantine, to be cut off for some time from the rest of the army. Those were his orders, and only in the ICTY hearing he discovered the true nature of problem solving. The camp leaders listened to him with pensive nods and took him back to Knin in a huge military jeep the following day. He believed he had been obeyed and men were cured, yet during the process he found out just how the camp had been disbanded after he was gone; in the simplest of all ways – all the prisoners and the sick Serbian soldiers were shot, poured over with gasoline, and burnt instead of buried. The medicine was for the healthy murderers.

The concentration camp and the spreading fights with casualties and deaths lead him to the conclusion that the mission of the Krajina army was war. But by then he was too involved to get out. He mechanically performed what was expected of him. Like medieval kings took daily doses of various poisons in order to avoid death in case of one of their courtiers wanted to kill them in that way, his brain was accepting new violence and crimes against civilians and enemy soldiers day by day. He could not die of poison now, but he would rather die of clear water – the truth. Yeah, he had administered drugs. Later, he started to take some himself; it was the only way to survive. He knew of the rapes, and he profoundly regretted his inertia.

The prosecutors wanted to know more about the rapes, for only recently the Hague court started to treat them as one of the war crimes against civilians. Raškić admitted that it was the policy of the Serbian army to rape Muslim women and keep them in detention for many months, so that they would bear Serbian children, little *Chetniks*. In this way, the memory of the winners would live on for generations. To the question of how men who a few weeks before had lived in families, who had wives and daughters at home, were able to do that, Raškić replied that interminable hours of mass rapes were only made possible by administering drugs to the soldiers. They were given several pills to sustain the acts, not only Viagra, also pills to lift their spirits and make them feel better. He had never taken part in the orgies himself, which did not make him less guilty.

The hidden centuries old propaganda was part of the big genocide plan to "cleanse" the territory between Krajina, Serbia and the banks of the river Drina of Muslims and Croatians. The river Drina should not be a Bosnian river anymore. It should become the border between Croatia and Serbia. The population in between should disappear. Such was the monstrous plan of two nationalistic leaders: the Croatian president Franjo Tudjman and the Serbian president Slobodan Milošević. All they achieved was heaps of corpses and rivers running red with blood...

In one video, Paula saw Jovan Raškić losing his composure. Tears were falling down his stubbled, grey cheeks and he was trembling like a leaf in the wind in front of the camera. He was a doctor, he should have protected and cured people, not let them be tortured and murdered. He realized that there was no excuse for his deeds and kept asking, in a shrill voice, the Bosnian and the Croatian people for forgiveness. He had spoken up, had he not? It was his personal way of the cross. He felt it was his duty to report to the coming generations of Serbians, Croatians and Muslims the truth, the truth as it was, without political color or distortion by any of the three sides.

Paula thought it was a special kind of irony, listening to what he was saying. Raškić advocated that there should not have been any war actions or killings. Diplomats should have discussed the conflicts for as long as they needed to find a solution, as they finally have done at Dayton. He claimed that the nationalistic passions were deep down only basic animal lust for sex and murder. He could not see it then, yet it was part of the Devil's game. He decided on self-incrimination, he would defy the Devil. It was a process, through which all soldiers should go. Nobody should ever give up their personal conscience, their fundamental responsibility to be human, be it war or peace. Jovan wanted to answer for his crimes. He wanted to receive a just punishment. He cooperated with the tribunal, which was the source of justice. What were his expectations? What kind of life awaited him? It would be worse for him to live with his memories every day than to end his days and escape the guilt.

Utter cynicism, Paula thought. He was talking in public about his nightmares, how he could not close his eyes without seeing the disfigured faces and the broken bones. For him it was bad dreams. For his victims, it was sharp reality and a struggle for life often ended by death.

The media commentaries about Jovan Raškić were divided. Some found his penance moving and said Raškić' medical personality surged up, that he was basically a good man and that it was only the system of the brutal war, which transformed him into a criminal. Many articles mentioned the importance of confession and penitence. Was that not the main point of the International Criminal Tribunal for Former Yugoslavia? To condemn the crimes and make the criminals repent. Was not its purpose to establish a new peace, with respect for the victims? Paula read in one of the papers a famous quote by the former ICTY president, Antonio Cassese, "Justice is an indispensable ingredient of the process of national reconciliation. It is essential to the restoration of peaceful and normal relations between people who have lived under a reign of terror. It breaks the cycle of violence, hatred and extra-judicial retributions. Thus peace and justice go hand in hand." She was not sure she completely understood all the implications of the text, but one thing she knew: her father had turned off humanity, he had closed his brain to reason and to justice at one point. She had little sympathy for his tears and shared the view of many journalists, who were reporting from the Balkan fronts during the war and had witnessed the atrocities. They were coldly hostile towards Raškič's pleas for pardon and stated openly that he deserved no milder treatment than the rest of the butchers in the notorious Yugoslav detention unit. The face of Lady Justice knew only one truth, engraved in stone, and stones do not cry, do they?

Paula thought of the timing of her father's public repentance. A month earlier, she had sent her first letter to him, with mama's passport photograph and one of herself. She briefly stated that she needed genetic proof that she is his daughter, who had been conceived with her mother at Kijevo. Did he break down before or after her letter? It must have been after. Something about her mama made him human. Enough hesitation, she tore open the envelope and started to read:

Dear Paula,

The Hague, March 2nd, 2010

Thank you very much for your letter, which filled me with joy over finding out about you and at the same time with profound sorrow over the death of your mother. Those were difficult times and your mother, Marica, was indeed very dear to me. I loved her and I love you, my daughter, for being a part of her. I am so happy, that you come to exist, thank you. Had your mother stayed with me a little bit longer, she might have made me a better man. But I understood she had to leave me to find a way back to her family. Desperate times cry for desperate measures. You will think, we, war criminals and prisoners at The Hague are not allowed to write about tender feelings, as we trampled so many down, but to some extent, we too are part of the same species as you are: the human race. They say the lowest part, the brutes, the criminals, but still, we should have more feelings than a worm or a dog, shouldn't we?

You are asking me for my hair and body specimen, by which the doctors could carry out the analysis and compare our DNA codes. Are we truly father and daughter, or is it only your mother's fantasy that she had been in love with me? One part of you hopes I could be your father and donor, the other fears of it. You would prefer not to be related to me. I understand. You're torn between the hope for life and the agony of the shameful facts of your origin and birth. You shouldn't worry. Should the DNAs match, they can perform the operation and carry out the transplant in full discretion without any trace of connection between the two of us here, in the Netherlands. It can remain our secret for the rest of our days, and I will understand if you don't want anybody to know about me and not to ever meet me in person. You must know one thing, my child – that I am not only the persona described in the media and known from the indictment documents, which I am told are put on the internet for the wide world to read. I am not a fake. Everything I have done in my life, I have done out of my sincere convictions, be it for better or worse. Some of them were very wrong, but some were good. Lately, I have reread the Bible and I found God. I pray to him for others, for you and your health and happiness as well, yet I know that there is no redemption for myself. I can only go to Hell. But I lost all fear of Hell and its eternal fires. I know I must suffer for all the bad things I have done or ordered them done. It is just. It is a necessary consequence. However, words cannot describe how happy I am to have found the tidings I had planted a seed. At least I keep hoping that Marica and I had conceived you all those years ago. I will die a happier man. You must be seventeen or eighteen now?

You probably know that I have children with my first wife, three daughters, who used to live in Belgrade. I sent them away to safety at the beginning of the war. After the war, or at least, after I quit the front and lived abroad, it took me years to try to find them again. I realized only recently that my first wife, Mirjana sold everything we owned in Serbia and took our girls to America. The lands our family had owned in Knin and the house are left empty. They all renounced me and changed their names. I haven't heard from them, and the letters I have been sending to the Belgrade address keep coming back unopened. Return to sender, that is all my life has become. Even our relatives don't know where they are and how they're doing. It was a shock at the beginning. I was angry and felt betrayed, as I've ever been a good father to them. I ensured their welfare and education, and spent much time with them, revising their homework, playing with them, spending holidays together. Not like with you, of whom I was not even aware until a week ago. I couldn't help Marica financially, I couldn't teach you to read and write, I couldn't do anything for you two. Yet, you sent me a letter, only you, nobody else. Never mind my old man's babbling. In reply to your question, I would like to tell you more about your mother and me.

She was the bravest of all women I've ever known. I will never forget the moment I first saw her. Her green eyes wide with fear, long blond hair scattered in sweaty strands around her face. She refused to board the truck with other prisoners, and a soldier came to me, saying, "This one is for you, doctor, she speaks only English. And she keeps repeating something like 'porter, urnalist', ere..." A young soldier boy pushed her disrespectfully towards my jeep. She was a tall woman in her forties, with a strong body in tight jeans and a black linen jacket. She looked directly into my eyes and said. "Hello, my name is Maria King and I am a reporter with the Guardian. You must let me go immediately, or this will be an international incident without precedence. You must give me back my car and everything in it. My computer, my purse, my stuff... Now, let me go, now." I would have let her go, would it not have meant sure death for her in that particular

situation. The next troubled youngster in a SVK uniform she
might have chosen to shout at would have shot a bullet through
her head. So I turned to my jeep and indicated to her she should
follow me and get inside the car. "We will check your documents,
miss. Come with me." My English was nothing like her perfect
Oxford pronunciation, but I soon had my doubts regarding her
journalistic identity. She had no camera, no documents, no purse
even or a notebook. She claimed she was abruptly dragged out
of her car and the soldiers took her stuff. She screamed that she
would report the theft to my superiors. Whom to, I thought to
myself, who do you think would listen to you for one minute in the
middle of this chaos? Nobody answered questions in the newly
established Serbian Republic of Krajina. Usually the quickest
answers came from the nearest machine gun. Then, her clothes
were all domestic brands, and when I mentioned this, she said
everything was so much cheaper here than in Britain, and that
she had been in Croatia for a couple of years as a reporter. It
took us nearly two hours up the winding mountain roads, and
she stopped talking after I blindfolded her. I was grateful, for the
suspicious avalanche of English words confused me. Her voice was
low and hoarse from fear. She spoke quickly and gestured like an
Italian all the time. She was explaining the British media market, telling me all sorts of things... Anyway, I didn't catch much
meaning. I felt attracted to her from the first moment. When we
arrived at Kijevo, I locked her up in the headmaster's house while
the rest of the women were taken to the school building. We had
a computer and a slow internet access via mobile phone, but no
matter how much I tried, I couldn't confirm her identity. I knew
she was a fraud, that she was nothing but a bluffing Croatian with
good English knowledge and education, trying to get away with
her lies. She would stick to her story, hadn't I offered her a staff
job, helping me with all foreign correspondence and guaranteeing
her personal safety, yet locked in a room, a prisoner. Stubborn
or not, Marica, as was her real name, realized she wouldn't last
a second out there. My offer was her best option. The communication with UNPROFOR, who were posting their troops in the
area, was getting more and more complex every day, so I needed
help. Nobody knew of her cover lie, and I presented her as my
personal prisoner secretary, so she was safe as long as she obeyed.
Despite the fact that there was certain intimacy growing between
us, I couldn't take any risks. I was careful with specific military
information, and also, I knew how close to Šibenik she was, and
I did not want to lose her. She worked hard and minded her own
business. She was skilled with words, well read, and she could
write in several foreign languages, not only English. All of a sudden, I was highly praised by our leaders like Karadjić and Mladić
for my excellent correspondence with the foreign troops. Marica
could transform an ugly attack into a self defense operation by

her skilful use of English, French or German phrases. She was
brilliant. In all our letters, she would always quote some historical event or a Latin saying from the past monuments from the
area, as though to teach the UNPROFOR soldiers about our culture in the past.

She was a prisoner with a special status, locked in one of the
rooms on the second floor, looking away from the school building
facing the hills. I ordered her door to be double fastened and
locked at all times, and window frames strengthened so as to be
sound proof. We met only while she was working at the office.
Alas, you can guess the nature of the school building now! It was
a women's prison. Marica, though, made no notice of the screams
and cries for the other side of the road. After a few weeks, she
asked me about it carefully. I evaded the answer. Even then, in
the midst of rightfulness of the Serbian cause, I felt ashamed in
front of her for what this civil war had become.

For Paula – permit me to use your precious name again – I have
come to believe that there are never, ever any just reasons for
war. Politicians who failed in their jobs, since the times of Cicero
and through the Middle Ages and modern era, misinterpreted
the greatest thinkers to justify their base instincts for killing.
Inspecting the Serbian cause from their perspective, you might
find Republika Srpska Krajina and its defense struggle for bellum iustum. All the elements are there; the Serbians in Knin
under Tudjman were deprived of their human rights and their
cultural tradition, their religion, and life; they were wronged. So
when I read the US Catholic Conference's statement from 1993,
saying, "Force may be used only to correct a grave, public evil,
i.e., aggression or massive violation of the basic human rights of
whole populations.", I can see the Serbians had reasons to rebel
and use weapons against the Croatian state. However, my dear,
when guns rattle and cannonballs fly, minds are blocked out and
men become beasts, they get to be their prehistoric selves again.
Everything civilized dies. There, you see, are the true reasons for
any war, be it just or unjust – men are blinded by the lust to
kill. Rape is just another way of expressing their base instincts.
Compassion, love, feelings are for women. Men are predators,
deep inside our system there must exist a war gene. The pacifists
are right – we should never take arms, never go to war. For one
step leads to another, and before you know it, there are thousands massacred at Srebrenica. The true cause for wars is men's
nature. The reasons are not outside us, they are inside us. Ergo,
wars are subjective, not objective. Subjective wars cannot be ever
justified by any objective arguments. Each morning, every one
of seven billion humans must wake up, must open their eyes, and
start fighting the bellicose impulses to which our nature drives
us. Each day, we must look for and give love. We must break the
chains of prejudice, stereotypes, aspirations to dominate, greed

for money and striving for wealth. We must free our spirits and open our souls to the others. For our own life and love can only exist in the eyes of another human being. Alone, I was nothing, with Marica, I was a man...

I think I fell in love with your mother at first sight. I could see she was so different from the women of Knin. She was so independent, intelligent, and industrious. She translated loads of papers every day and could even translate from Serbian Cyrillic. She was the best of all assistants. Once, when my military aide, Petar, was rioting and screaming and even shooting around the office wildly, she, pardon me, my child, made in her pants and asked me to let her change after I had disciplined the wild guy. Since then, we had a sentinel at my office door and nobody could burst in while we were working.

Sometimes, when the evenings became longer in September 1991, we stayed in my office and talked, about just anything. Later, deep snow fell on the hills around Kijevo and grey days of autumn rains left for crisp winter sun. It was a very cold winter, and heating was a rare commodity. We spent a lot of time together, just talking, discussing various topics, and carefully getting to know each other in the many of our diverse opinions. Having realized how educated she was, I tried with all possible means to detach her from the wrongdoings at the school. We would talk about subjects which weren't connected to the present war, but sooner or later we always found ourselves analyzing the three ethnic groups of the area from every angle, their history and frictions in the past, particularly in the World War Two. Ustashas and Chetniks were the terror of all in 1941, and we would compare their doings with the revolutionaries elsewhere in the world. Marica was persistently and subtly trying to influence me to abandon the Krajina cause and join my family in Belgrade. But I believed in the Great Serbia and couldn't think of abandoning my comrades, including Karadjić. I felt it was a thing of honor to defend my Krajina. When she compared our rule to the Reign of Terror in the French Revolution under Roberspierre, I sent her to her locked room. She didn't understand the Krajina cause.

Although a prisoner, Marica was treated with respect. My soldiers didn't dare to touch her; they thought from the beginning she was my lover. I even hinted in the direction here and then and said I would make her Serbian, it was my Pygmalion project, so that they would leave her alone. They laughed and poked fun at me, saying there were so many young, beautiful women to take.

Anyway, you probably want to know how your mother came to love me, the enemy. Thinking back, it was very natural. In the middle of fear and madness, I became her only protector. Another thing – her marriage was dead long before she met me. There had to be something terribly wrong with her husband. I think he must have been a drunkard and a brute. I can hear your question: how can anybody be more of a brute than a mass murderer, a war criminal? That man was a bad husband for Marica, believe me. Even today I don't know how it was possible that she had come behind the Croatian front lines and why. I presumed he had sent her on some errand and she was captured by chance. I still thought I loved my wife, but my feelings for Marica were so much deeper. I think there was something primordial in it. I felt like the first man in the world, protecting my mate from violence. Maybe I was dreaming, but I felt more like a man with her than with my soldiers. Anyway, I was in love like a boy, I couldn't keep my head straight. I was courting her in all possible ways. Sometimes I brought her a box of chocolates, another time a book or even flowers. I was so much in love. Once, I made my aide stop at a sunflower field to cut a bouquet for my Marica. She mocked me, saying I forgot she was my prisoner, not the other way around, but she put the sunflowers in a huge water pot and took them to her room in the evening.

One day, when I was starting to trust her fully and went to a meeting, leaving her alone in the office, she disobeyed my orders. She stole my key to the safe and took out the military maps of our positions. She was studying them when my aide caught her. Had I not come in at that moment, all would have turned out differently. You would not be, my child and she would probably have been killed. When I dismissed Petar, she stuttered she was sorry, that she felt nostalgia for home. She couldn't live under this pressure anymore. I stepped towards her and took her in my arms without a word. She embraced me and hid her face in my chest, sobbing softly, and I felt she was not only crying, but also trembling with anticipation. Then I kissed her. Her lips were moist and hot, salty with a stray tear and burning with fever and fear. She was afraid of her love, as I was afraid of what would become of us.

We were in our late forties, my child, and we both knew this was the first real kiss of our lives. You don't make mistakes about your feelings at that age anymore – we wanted each other more than anything in the world. Later that night, I made love to her for the first time. We had closed ourselves in the tiny headmaster's bedroom on the upper floor, and we both gave way to our feelings. It was the 30th of August 1991, my dear. I will never forget that night. I will not give you any more details of our lovemaking, although young people are more knowledgeable about sex these days. I don't know if you have ever made love to a man, so this might be embarassing. Just remember, we loved each other, I never forced your mother. I admit it was the privileged position of the commander that might have made her look at me with different eyes, but no force, neither physical nor mental. So, when you were conceived, if you are mine, it was in an act of pure love between two disillusioned middle aged people

who found a ray of sunshine in each other. Since that first night,
we spent almost every night together. Our love affair was going
on until Christmas when, without any notice, Marica was gone.
I knew she was alive, but I didn't have the time to search for her.
How she disappeared from my life and why we didn't stay together? Those, Paula, were difficult times, the front got worse
and worse. I had even been speaking to her about transferring her
or simply sending her home, but she didn't seem to want either.
Then, in late November, I brought her an Advent calendar with
little chocolates for every day until Christmas. I knew Catholic
children loved it. She burst in tears and didn't even thank me.
Later I realized she must have been struck by remorse. Somewhere at the coast, not too far away, she had a family, and she
had been lately more pretending to be my prisoner than she was
staying for the warmth of the bed we had shared. I had to go to
join a military operation at the front above Dubrovnik, so a week
before Christmas, I was away. I gave explicit orders regarding
her. She was to work for at least eight hours every day, translating a huge text of an international agreement concerning the
future state in the territory of Bosnia and Herzegovina. For the
rest of the time, the guards should lock her in the headmaster's
room. The boys reported every day about her and fetched her on
the phone almost every night – I missed her terribly.

When I came back on Friday, a week before Christmas, Marica
was gone. I drove all night to be there at dawn, and when I
entered her room, the bed was empty, I checked the bathroom,
nothing. I raised hell, but nobody knew anything about her.
They showed me her translated texts from the day before, and we
were all clueless. Nothing seemed to be missing at my office. We
searched the surroundings. There was deep snow, so there should
be footprints. Yet, we couldn't find anything. Marica vanished
without a trace. Surprisingly, Petar vanished, too. Some soldiers
were grimacing, but I was sure he had done something to her and
ran. I feared that he had killed her. He hated her from the very
beginning. Then, I was dragged into another investigation and
couldn't deal with Marica's disappearance anymore. A day after
Christmas, I mean the Orthodox, not the Catholic Christmas,
I ordered more cash for a celebration, when my bosses told me
that just two weeks earlier, so while I was away, my military aide
had collected a bag of money, which was to pay for at least half
a year of provisions. They meant Petar, and he was gone, and
obviously, it was he who stole the money. It was a huge amount
and I felt responsible. So, we searched and searched, and only
after the snows melted, we found Petar with the empty money
bag and his throat cut in the woods nearby.

That was the end of that. After Marica was gone, something
changed in me. I became like the rest of Serbian soldiers in this
despicable war. My remorse and my guilt will never leave me. No

matter what the verdict of the ICTY will be, I know in my heart that I deserve a life sentence and eternal fires. I have caused suffering and death to people. You know, Paula, corpses and bones in mass graves cannot forgive, they only condemn.

Maybe I can save one life, so precious to me – yours. Please let me know the result of the DNA analysis and discuss further steps with your doctors. I think it would be best for you to come to The Hague, and get the operation and treatment here. Will the Croatian Health Insurance cover it? Do you have money in case they don't?

Hope to receive your answer soon,

Love,

Jovan R.

Paula neatly folded the sheets back into the envelope. All power and life energy deserted her. She was lying still and silent under the comforter, shivering despite the hot sun outside. Her mind was empty of all thoughts. She was confused by the writing and could not focus. Her thoughts turned in circles, wandering in a sort of Purgatory, where her parents were tearing her soul apart. Her poor dead mother, so vulnerable, so loving, and tender, had sacrificed her life for her. On the other side, there was a father with his either false or genuine, in any case, belated regrets...In between, they occupied her thoughts with rivers of words. Their confessions came from another world, the dwelling of surreal ghosts. She let out a sigh and wiped the tears away. She must call for the nurse and organize the DNA test. How would she tell the staff at the hospital whose sample hair she's testing? Maybe she did not have to. Maybe she could keep it a secret for the time being and just try to save herself. She would think of her origins later, when she has some sure prospects of life ahead.

Funny, you would think it is a father's duty to acknowledge his children. Here it was in her hands to claim or disclaim her father. "The world is out of joint", lamented Hamlet. Oh, but to be, Paula wanted so much just to be...

Dario and the sea

The pitch dark, moonless night faded in the early morning twilight with the promise of a cold, peaceful day. The sea was like a silver mirror, which reflected Dario's figure, bending over the pier, meddling with the mooring ropes at the bow of his motor boat. There was *bonaca*, the absolute stillness of the winds and the sea. His spirits were high. In a low voice, he was softly humming a Dalmatian folk tune into his chin. In the early hours before dawn the villagers of Mulobedanj were still soundly asleep, and he would not be the one to disturb their dreams. At last, the long planned trip began to the east of the island Unije, into the narrow, mile long bay of Vogniśća, which at this time of year would be squirming with squid. He could almost smell a good catch, and his tired body lit up with the tinge of adventure. He was not the only one to hunt the squid on Unije. There would be other fishermen, and he was looking forward to chatting and drinking around other boats in the evening. The weather report and the wind charts for the following days were favorable, his jigs and rods all ready.

It would be a break from his life, which during the long winter months overcast him like a train of thick black rain, which *jugo*, the south wind pregnant with rains and sorrow, was bringing with its dark clouds. His house became a cold monument of fear and loneliness. The memories seemed to seep from every crack of the old walls, entering his brains like alcoholic vapors of the innumerable bottles of brandy he had been emptying to forget the images of the two women he had loved and lost in no more than a year. There were not enough bottles to drown the eyes and the smiles of his lover and his sister's wonderful voice, resounding and flashing through his mind in an endless ping-pong game. Maria and Marina, Marina and Maria... Why did he have to lose them both?

The only solace to the grieving man were his two daughters, Olivia and Mira, who after years of separation which they had spent at school and university, remembered their old father and came to visit almost regularly. He was glad when he noticed that the contacts between Olivia and the Slovenian inspector Andrej Bak had gone beyond the purpose of the long abandoned investigation. Dario suspected they were starting something, but nobody told him more, and he was too sensitive to ask. Anyway, he liked the man, and every time Bak came along to Pag, he took him fishing. The mountaineering northerner seemed to learn about the fish fast and above all, knew one thing, so essential to good fishing – keeping silent. Dario was much more concerned about his younger daughter Mira, who since Marina was dead, wandered about the world like a ghost. Her eyes were red, always filled with new tears. He tried to talk to her, but she closed up like a shell, hiding her pain deep in her heart. Apart from mourning, Mira seemed to be doing nothing at all; she stopped going to the university altogether, she would not start a job, she would never go out with friends. While Olivia finished her degree with excellence and started to work at the Bella Vista hotel in Opatija, the star of the Seashell hotel chain, founded by Giacoppo da Vesta, Mira just sat about and watched television at any hour of the day. In fact, she did not need to ever work in her life again, for Marina's wealth was enormous, and Mira inherited a good share of it.

About a month ago, they gathered in a courtroom in Rijeka, where the judge, in the presence of the notary Govač and a foreigner in a dark suit, read them Marina's will. There was money, there were shares and bonds, there were real estates, and businesses. The hotel chain Seashell included six four star hotels and three five star villas. There was also a yacht charter company in Zadar, Sails of Love, which had over thirty yachts in its fleet; mainly sailing boats, but also motor boats. The judge quoted that none of the companies were involved in any kind of legal procedures like insolvency, tax debt collection or other kind of publicly known legal actions. The total estimate of the inheritance was far over one hundred million euros, so the three heirs sat at the court hearing nonplussed, trying to comprehend their new situation. Considering those sums and values, their aunt had led a very modest life. The major assets were the hotels, which were going very well despite the economic crisis. Along with shares and bonds, they were bequeathed to the girls. Marina's apartment, her antiques, the cash, and the chartering business were left to Dario. They each had to sign a statement with which they accepted the inheritance. During their signing of the documents, the man in the dark suit left the otherwise empty courtroom. They were all three too absorbed in their new responsibilities, not least for thousands of jobs provided by their newly acquired businesses, to notice anything or anybody around them. After the court procedure, the notary Govač took them to his office to explain in detail how the property had been managed so far, including his suggestions for the future.

The days went by and Dario still did not know what to do with all the money. Like Mira, he cared little about the money. They both let their shares be managed by Govač' financial consultants. Only Olivia took the responsibility in her own hands, and patiently took the path of learning to understand and lead the Seashell chain one day. She bloomed in her new role. The hotel staff was capable and well schooled, and while they acquainted her with their operation, they treated her with respect and kindness. Yet, Mira was another story. She was a girl in the depth of despair; she was plunging into a sea of sadness and tears. No money could pay for her smile. Life had lost all color in her empty eyes. Dario tried to persuade her to come home and stay with him on Pag, but she would not. She had preferred to be alone in her grey rented flat in Zagreb. She would not live in Marina's flat either, which, empty, really looked like a museum. Olivia suggested to Mira that she should see a psychologist to deal with her depression, but the girl denied that her behavior was anything more than normal sadness over the loss of the woman who had been like a mother to her for so many years. Dario was left confused and did not know what to do. He needed Maria's advice so much. Where was she now?

In his lonely moments, either at sea or between his four walls, Dario was rereading the messages they had exchanged over the phones while Maria and Paula were in Ljubljana. He could not delete them. He drank in the sweetness of the tone and smiled at the naughty thoughts and wonderful companionship he had shared with his lover and friend for those short happy months. To his horror, there was also the last text message from Paula, which destroyed all his hopes. What would he do with the heap of money from Marina if he could not spend a moment of his life with his love any longer? What would he do with the heavy burden of guilt about not taking better care of his little sister? How would he live on? There were things he had to think about... His little one, Mira, so fragile, depressed, and sick with pain... What would he do with the inherited money? How would he find meaning in his future life? How would he go on?

He turned the ignition key on, and the hellish whistle of the starter turned into the loud pumping of his boat engine. The villagers were so used to the sound that they probably only turned around in their warm beds. Well, the first investment should be a new engine or a new boat for his tours around the northern islands of the Adriatic. He could buy a nice comfortable fishing boat, so that he could spend several nights a week at sea. It could be a small yacht, with plenty of room to sleep and cook. His boat was old and used, it barely had a toilet, a small fridge, and a gas stove to warm up an instant soup or cook some pasta. He thought of the fleet of yachts tied in the Zadar marina – surely, one of them could be suitable. In a moment, he changed his mind – what would a fisherman do with those fancy floating miracles? Sails of love... Goodness, the name was so kitschy, he would never steer a boat under such a name. Anyway, family yachts were no good for fishing.

He steered the boat out of the little harbor and set the course on his GPS. He would spend the first night in Osor, a little town on the island of Cres. He would fill his tanks with water and fuel, he would buy food and drink for the trip, and he would visit the old fishermen's pub *konoba*. Maybe he would get a little drunk, but far less than at home, for there would be people around him, perhaps some sailors or fishermen he knew. They would talk to each other, joke about women, and sing rough songs from the past. He would take a room in the little inn above the pub. He was old, and the morning humidity on the boat did not agree with his limbs any more.

The darkness was thinning and a shy morning sun was lifting a grey mist above the surface. Dario's boat cut the water, leaving a foamy trail of waves at the hem. Suddenly, he perceived a school of dolphins a mile ahead in the channel between the islands Pag and Cres. They were playfully jumping in the air, as though putting on a show especially for him.

Dario smiled, thinking of his childhood memory, when, sixty years ago, he accompanied his father, going fishing for the first time in his life. In those days, fish was abundant in the Adriatic. All the fishermen had to do was to close the bay in the evening with a net reaching from one cape to another and for the whole night slowly pull in the ends towards the beach. For the purpose, the whole village would sew their nets together and they would all close the giant loop, first with the boats, then they pulled the ropes reaching to the two ends of the bay together with their hands. They were pulling it slowly for the whole night, until in the morning grey they finally hauled the squirming bundle ashore. They shared the catch, and they put the fish on ice while sorting them into crates. Each fisherman got the fish proportionally to the length of his nets.

On that particular night, an extraordinarily big fish got caught in the mile wide loop of the net. They more heard than saw the whoosh movements on the inner side of the net. Full of optimism, they were hoping for a stray tuna male. No, no such luck. . . It was a huge dolphin, feasting on their catch. The men continued to pull and haul the ropes. They would trap the bastard eventually. With the approaching dawn glinting lightly in the east, the loop was getting closer to the beach, when the dolphin jumped over the net and swam a few yards into the black sea. Then, the strong water acrobat turned around and jumped back into the loop. At first, the fishermen thought there might have been a whole school of dolphins about and that the one got confused over something. The big black shadow jumped out again. Yet, in a moment, it leaped back into the net loop. And out, and back in. . . What was wrong with the dolphin? Why was it jumping in and out of the trap? Did it lose its mind? It should swim away to safety. All of a sudden, the men felt a jolt of the nets, and the thick ropes almost slid out of their hands. The huge black body of the dolphin virtually lay on the top of the net and created a window for two light gray youngsters to swim into freedom. The mother dolphin followed them, leaving the fishermen admiring her cleverness and patience. She was trying to teach her babies how to save themselves, but they did not follow, and in the end, she had to save them herself. Well, the fishermen's benevolent smiles died out later when they found a bite in every second fish. The dolphin family had a great meal and once again, men were doing the hunting for them. However, little Dario could never forget how he had felt about it; he was fascinated by the dolphin family. Despite the damaged catch, he rejoiced at their escape.

The boat held the course and Dario stepped out on the bow, where the fresh air smelt of salt and infinity. Suddenly, at a right angle, next to the tip of the bow a dolphin jumped out of water, throwing a curious look at him. Dario smiled and shouted at him merrily:

"Ey, little fellow! What do you want? Are you spying on my fishing positions? So that you and your clan can come to empty my net tomorrow, eh?"

The dolphin swam along the bow half bent so that its curious eye never left the fisherman's face. He seemed to be asking him a question... How could Dario hear or understand his sophisticated underwater speak?

"Well, no breakfast at Dario's either today or tomorrow, my boy! I'm not going to pull in the nets today. I'm going to Cres, and you will have to catch your meal yourself! Good luck, buddy!"

A swoosh of dolphin's powerful body muscle was all the reply Dario got. He knelt down and stretched his palm over the water surface. At first, the dolphin plunged into the dark and Dario was starting to lift his tired body up. Another swoosh, and the animal jumped higher, so that, for a fraction of a moment, Dario touched the silken skin of his swimming friend. His eyes filled with tears of joy... What a superb sea creature! How cute and clever! What would its future be in the face of of pollution of the Adriatic? No sooner than in a few years, he would go hungry... it would starve to death in its own home waters for the lack of fish. For the greed of men was mightier than the beauty of the sea.

With anger, Dario thought of the new developments in the aquaculture and fishing industry in the last couple of years. The domestic bottom trawls were fishing the Adriatic empty in order to procure food for the numerous blue fin tuna, which new maritime entrepreneurs were growing in huge net pens. The forced schools held in a tiny space littered the sea with their excrements a thousand times the usual. The tuna were actually shitting death into the deep blue waters. The farming of tuna was highly subsidized by the European Union, and with Japanese manic demand for its tender dark pink meat, it was quick and rather easy money. The Japanese came into the Adriatic with their factory ships, and bought the fattened tuna alive, directly from the huge cages. They prepared them on board, designing their sushi while steering back to Japan or to the next big airport. The Japanese claimed that the Adriatic tuna was superb, the best of all.

In a way, the farmed tuna were not eating only the future of the dolphins and other, blue fish species away, but above all their own. The fish farmers would catch the fish when young and put them into the huge cages alive with thousands of their kind. They fed them copiously. Yet, in the pens, the superb predator, used to swimming miles at high speed every day, could not propagate, and the species was dying out. Another question was with which chemicals the farmers could keep the aggressive predators from cannibalizing each other. Also, the fish population of mackerel, sardine and various squid and crustaceans, from the smallest to the biggest, disappeared into the tuna feeding supply. The sea was becoming empty blue water, devoid of life and necessary diversity. The greedy man did not even spare one of the most beautiful corners of the Adriatic coast, the fjord of Zavratnica at Jablanac; a huge tuna pen seemingly peacefully floated at its entrance. The almighty god Poseidon was slowly losing his battle against the almighty technological men.

With one last jolt, the merry dolphin swam away and left Dario pondering the future of his country. Soon, they would both be seeking their fish: the men and the dolphin. Was there a way to prevent progress? Was there a way to perserve the sea?

Dario went back to the cabin and adjusted the steer to the exact course of 280 degrees southwest. He was doing solid seven knots. On the horizon, he could see the island of Trstenik with its tall lighthouse on the hill. How many times he anchored at the little pier and took a break, having some bread and drinking some watered wine in the shade of the mighty fig trees? For a moment, he thought of doing it today, but then he decided to proceed and rather follow his plans for the trip. He made some coffee in his thermos and poured himself a cup. With a cigarette in the corner of his mouth, he could not lose the image of the lively dolphin greeting him in the morning. The longer his look was immersed in the calm blue surface ahead, the less he actually could see it. His focused pupils seemed to see deeper, they were scanning the water, X-raying its creatures and the black abysses and the mysterious depths. However, his look was turned inside. An idea flashed in Dario's brain; a possibility of spending his fortune on a good cause. Maybe, he could kill two birds with one stone and engage Mira in his enterprise, so that she would finally come out of her depression and start to live.

Every stroke of the motor was hitting his ears: yes, yes, yes... He would do it! It was the right thing, and even his late brother in law, Giacoppo, who with his business capacities had accumulated the huge fortune, would love it and approve of it. Dario knew he would. Yet, what should he do first? How would he realize his intentions?

Dario almost turned the boat around and went back. Then, he continued his stream of thoughts, for a good captain should not just steer and sail, he should know where and keep the right course. His trip to Unije would provide time to make a thorough plan. Dario made a mental list of meetings: first, he had to see the notary, Mr. Govač. They must estimate the total value of his share of Marina's inheritance and look at the options for the sales value of it all. He had to know how much money he can count with. Then, he would speak to Olivia and Mira and present them his new idea. In a way, his decision would very much influence their future also. He had a friend in Rovinj, a retired sea captain nicknamed Sale. He had to find his address and visit him. He should find out more about Sale's last working years, when he worked for the Center for Marine Research in Rovinj. He would talk to him. He would go to the Aquarium in Rovinj, and he would visit the institute in person. He would learn to use the internet in order to browse for information and options. That should be Mira's job. She has to teach and help him. They have to break the vicious circle of pain and sorrow together. It would be their project, while Olivia would look after the hotels. After all they were the weaker links, the sentimental losers, he and his little Mira, were they not?

Passing by the island of Trstenik, Dario became restless. He should immediately write his goals down, before his old rusty brain sends them to oblivion. He opened a tiny cupboard beneath the steer and took out a dark green logbook bound in solid leather. There was a symbolic sail engraved in gold on the front cover. Next to the logbook lay a wooden box with a selection of special pencils. They were able to sustain humidity and salt. He opened it. On the first page, there was a hand written dedication in black ink:

For the captain of my soul

I wish you would stay at home with me.

Ivana, 1998

His wife, who at the time had still been hoping that he would take an early retirement and stay at home with her. She had been so lonely during long winters in the little village, and she complained she needed him to help bring up the girls. However, the sea, a far more powerful mistress, dragged him away from his home and from her warm bed until he had lost her forever. Dario sighed. His eyes wet with tears of sorrow. So much love he had missed all his life long! Now, he was determined not to let that final opportunity go. Empty sheets greeted him. They were ready for his hand to write upon them.

Paula in The Hague

The plane was slowly descending, with a monotonous buzzing of the jet engines, gliding through the veils of the thick white clouds, which gave the impression of a beautiful lace woven by industrious and imaginative angels in heaven. All of a sudden, the elegant cockpit nose of the Canadair Regional Jet with the blue logo of the Slovenian national air carrier Adria Airways pierced the velvet fogs. Paula beheld an open plain, a vast flat land with hundreds of silvery canals and lakes, thousands of cultivated fields interwoven like a labyrinth of thousands of possibilities, like a limitless maze of forbidden joys, between which green pastures were hosting lazy fat cattle squinting in the midday sunshine. Nearer to the coast, vast glasshouses were sheltering summer vegetables and flowers against the delayed spring frosts of April. Yet, the most striking of all were the bulb fields. Billions of tulips, hyacinths and daffodils were showing off their beauty with vivid red, orange, blue, scarlet and yellow, making up with their colors for the shy light of the northern sun. It was so unlike Dalmatia, so different from the Balkans. It was Holland, the land of the canals, where happy people lived in peace and tolerance, assuming their smiles and postures as though their royals moulded them from clay and put them in their gardens like shiny garden gnomes. So unlike Croatia, where people were ugly with hate and grey with worries, and where despite the bluest of the sea and brightest of the sun, people were sad, deprived, and hurt.

In spite of despair gnawing in her brain, Paula was determined to do anything to stay alive. Her father's and her own HLA genes were a perfect match, approaching the number of loci of twin siblings. The oncologists who were treating Paula in Zadar and in Ljubljana, as well as the new specialist group in The Hague, unanimously agreed that the second transplant would almost certainly bring about better results, maybe also complete the healing of the young woman. Paula still demanded total secrecy regarding the identity of her donor, which the European privacy law was granting her anyway. After much thought, she made up her mind that ahead of all medical procedures, she wanted to meet her father and speak to him. She would go and see him the following day, a week before the operation, which was to take place in the Medisch Centrum Haaglanden.

There was much fuss about her visit and his personal security at the detention unit of the ICTY. The goal of the judges was to finish as many trials as possible and to read the verdicts openly to every suspect indicted with war crimes. In Raškić's case, they feared three possible scenarios: vengeance of the victims, escape options and suicide. Since the beginning, they refused to let Raškić out of the detention unit and wanted the operating team to derive the bone-marrow cells from Raškić within the facilities

of their medical unit. Not too enthusiastically, the doctors gave
in and planned the procedure in such a way that the chain from
the donor to the patient would still be short and efficient. They
would admit Paula to the hospital a week prior to the operation,
as they wanted to repeat the tests. Her health was precarious
indeed, since it had changed a few times from last autumn.

A week after she had received bone marrow from her mother,
it looked as though her situation would improve. The winter
months went by in high hopes, despite her sadness and loneliness
at the huge loss. There was little relief in finding out who her
father was. She was bitter about it, and she had made a decision
that she would destroy all evidence referring to the events during the war. She would continue to live alone. As soon as her
health permitted, she would continue her studies. She decided to
transfer from foreign languages and literatures to economics and
tourism, for she wanted to take over the Perovica ecological hotel
one day.

But then, all her plans evaporated like steam from a boiling
pot after another check at the Zadar hospital in February. Her
white blood cell count was once again alarming. The relapse was
tough. Paula thought she would never be able to climb out of the
abyss. Immediately, the father option came back into her mind.
She hesitated for a few weeks, until another possible transplantation remained her only hope. Her father replied to her letter with
a plea to meet her. There she was, gliding toward that colorful
land in the spring of her life, with fears of the man and hopes for
the father who was awaiting her.

In spite of the sunshine and clear skies, it was a bumpy land-
ing. The side winds were particularly tricky for planes at the
Shiphol airport. Paula took her bag and her trench coat and
headed for the exit. When she stepped into the airport lounge,
before heading for her luggage, she saw a man with the logo
of Medisch Centrum Haaglanden on his breastplate, holding the
handles of the wheelchair. Paula had time to observe him. He
was very tall and bulky, with reddish hair. She thought of a huge
oak leafing in spring, the buds erupting in pale brown and orange.
His blue eyes were scanning the passengers, and having noticed
her, they lit up in the welcome smile of a man who is always
ready to help. She came closer, and she read from the badge on
the left side of his chest: Helmer Lieuven, staff nurse.

"Hello, I am Paula Perić. I come from Zadar. Are you here
for me?"

"Well, hello there! Yes, sit in the chair, and I will take you to
the car."

"I hate to sit in the wheelchair. It makes me feel sick. Can I
walk?"

"Well, you can walk, of course. Just let's pick up your luggage
together. The chair will be for the suitcase then. It is for the

suitcase I brought it, anyway."

"You're funny, Helmer. Thanks."

They walked to the luggage band and he lifted her suitcase from it with the strength of a hulk. What was he before he worked in the hospital? Was he a dockworker? Rotterdam, one of the biggest seaports in Europe was not too far away.

"How was your flight, Paula?"

"Wonderful, thank you. The bulb fields are really something. I have heard of your tulips, but to see them..."

"Yeah, it is the best time of year to come to Holland. When you're out of the hospital, you must stay for another week and go to Keukenhof."

Paula blinked. If she should leave the hospital... She would go anywhere.

"How come you're here, Helmer? I informed your administration of the flight and the hotel where I'm staying, yes, but I thought I was supposed to check in at the hospital tomorrow afternoon."

Helmer opened his eyes widely and shrugged apologetically.

"It is not my fault. My boss, Doctor Siuwel, wants to see you today. He sent me to fetch you. Mind you, this is a royal treatment. My car is just over there."

Paula paced after him, not wanting to admit that she was losing her breath. Weeks in sickbed enfeebled her. Helmer handled her luggage and helped her in the hospital van. They left the airport area. Looking back at the departures area, Paula noticed an amusing sign: KISS AND RIDE.

"There is no KISS AND WELCOME sign at the arrivals, though!"

Helmer threw her a side look. He assumed he would pick up a dragging leukemia patient, barely able to sit in the wheelchair. Next to him, there sat a beautiful young woman with wonderful black eyes shooting fireballs. It was the hot summer sun of Dalmatia rising in those cheeky pupils, contrasting the paleness of her cheeks. He could see her thinning hair, cut very short and curling naughtily at the scalp, and he imagined a crown of black curls in its place. Her face was sullen, yet her complexion olive and her lips bright red. Her smile was warm and open, showing a set of tiny white pearls. Her whole body seemed fragile and fine, so unlike Dutch girls. She was stunning. Maybe he could forget the professional distance for a moment...

"I can kiss and welcome you, if you like. You look gorgeous, Paula."

Amused, Paula offered him her mouth, and he smacked a noisy kiss on it. They burst into laughter together. A friendship was born.

"Thank you, Helmer. I can really feel the Dutch tolerance now."

"Well, maybe you should visit the Red District of Amsterdam, not Keukenhof."

"Whichever sightseeing you recommend – I will do it all when I get out of the hospital."

"I bet you will."

They turned to the main road, and after driving for an hour, they left the motorway and took a narrow country road. It was new and shone black with fresh asphalt. Helmer had to avoid cyclists of every age, dressed either leisurely or in business suits; all people, young and old, were cycling somewhere, smiling yet permanently busy, with purpose in their eyes. Admiring the poplars along the canals, growing in a straight line as though an architect long ago had drawn it with a ruler, Paula's eyes caught the vista of a row of windmills with brightly painted white and red wings. Some of the wings were moving in the fresh wind from the sea.

"This is Kinderdijk, Paula. I took a detour, as the road to Leiden has been blocked for hours today. I heard earlier on the radio that there are traffic jams. Besides, this is a nice way to get acquainted with Holland."

"It's like a fairy tale. Can we stop and take a walk around the windmills?"

"Well, I still have the chair. Would you let me push you?"

"No, I'm sorry. Let's just drive around it then."

"And I can tell you the story of how Kinderdijk got its name. They say that on Saint Elizabeth's feast day in 1421, a huge flood washed up on the dyke a child in a crib. It was a miracle that the child was alive and safe, although hundreds died in the wild waters during the stormy day. Dutch have always been practical people with little imagination, so they simply named the dam Kinderdijk – Children's dyke. Cute, eh?"

"Just the story I wanted to hear. I wonder if there are more miraculous cribs in Holland for the likes of me..."

"I haven't been told why you are here. My boss just sent me to the airport. Do you care to talk about it?"

"Yeah, of course. I have leukemia and they found a donor in the Netherlands with a perfect match for the bone-marrow transplantation. The last time I received it, it didn't work."

"Oh, whose was it? I mean, who was your previous donor?"

"My mother... Unfortunately, she died during the procedure."

"Oh, I am sorry... I didn't think it was so risky for the donors."

"It isn't in principle. Yet, my mom was older. She was nearly seventy years old, and her heart was weak. She wouldn't tell me that. She wanted to help..."

Paula's face darkened. The pain stung in her heart every time she thought of her mother. At first, she was so angry with her. Why had she been keeping those terrible secrets from her? Why had she not told her the truth? Nobody at the hotel and nobody in the village could understand Paula's bad mood, when they spoke about Maria. Dario organized the funeral, and Paula followed the burial procession without shedding a tear. She was shocked by her mother's revelation. Like through a thick fog, she could hear voices of the large crowd of islanders paying their last respects to the woman who changed their lives with her hope. But where was hope for her, Paula, her daughter? The anger threw a huge black shadow over anything else. People ascribed her behavior to her illness and shook heads in pity. In February, after the feast of Candlemass, it was clear. The transplantation had not brought about healing. It had failed, and her mother died in vain. And now, she was to find another donor or die. Paula cast away her prejudice. She wanted to live.

In a way, she was glad to go directly to the hospital and not have to worry about anything. She must gather her strength for tomorrow, when she was to talk to her father for the one and only time. She had read so many reports about Jovan Raškić, the Serbian freedom activist, the Srpska Krajina military commander, the war criminal, the famous sinner, the crushed repenter. Now, she would meet the man...

They put Paula in a private room. It was peaceful, overlooking a lovely little garden with trimmed shrubs and colorful spring bulbs. They would not let her in peace; they pushed her around the hospital from the laboratory to the scanning rooms, from one sophisticated medical gadget to another. In the evening, when she finally had some quiet moments to read, Helmer's face poked into the room.

"How are you? Do you need anything?"

Paula's smile was tired and slow.

"I do. Can you give me something to sleep tonight? The whole day was like a madhouse. I am afraid I won't be able to fall asleep."

"I'll check your chart and come back. Anything else?"

"Yes. Could you hire a taxi for tomorrow morning at nine? I have an appointment. Doctor Siuwel knows about that. I forgot to call the taxi company. Also, they might speak only Dutch."

Helmer looked her in the eye. The fires of her sunny coast were gone, extinguished. She looked what she was – a patient with a terminal diagnosis.

"I am off duty tomorrow. I can bring you anywhere you want in my car. It's a new Ford Focus, you will enjoy the ride."

Paula smiled at his kindness. It was so sudden and so sincere. Was it a friend she found in Helmer, or did he expect more from their relationship? In any case, she had to go alone.

"I'm sorry. It's very private, Helmer. I'd prefer a taxi."

"I see."

"Thank you anyway. It's a very kind offer. Can I store it for later?"

"I understand. I would go there alone, too. . . "

Helmer's naughty smile spoke of dirty thoughts. Paula's senses woke up with apprehension.

"What do you mean, Helmer?"

With a serious face, he said.

"The gigolos in the Red Light District. . . "

He could not finish the sentence, for they both burst into laughter. The absurdity of his suggestion brought light into the grey room. Sex was life. Even talking about sex was life. With a serious conspiratorial nod, Helmer closed the door, leaving Paula's eyes wet with tears of laughter. Not much later, he reentered the room. He gave Paula a package of powder.

"Now, here's the stuff to make her erotic dreams come true. The taxi will be here at nine."

"Thank you, Helmer. You're so nice. When this is over, you must come and visit me on my island of Pag. Here. . . "

She handed him a business card of the hotel Perovica, and he put it in his pocket.

"At you service, Paula. In Holland, men serve women. It begins with a queen, you know. . . "

With a deep, theatrical bow, Helmer left the room. Soon, she fell asleep to the pitter patter of the raindrops falling from the sky as dark as the bottom of the ocean.

The following morning, Paula woke up into a different world. The sun was bright and the sky blue, and for a brief moment, she thought she was back in Zadar. The voices of Dutch nurses soon brought her to the day's schedule: her visit to the ICTY detention unit.

The taxi was a comfortable black Mercedes, next to which a driver in a dark suit was smoking peacefully as though he was on holiday. She came over and told him the address at Scheveningen. His eyes blinked, his brain flashed: The Hague Hilton! Popular opinion was not always kind to the legal tolerance. While the purpose of the comfort of the notorious detention facilities was to treat the prisoners fairly until they were proven guilty, people had passed their verdict long ago. The driver hastily opened the back door, and Paula sank into the soft beige leather. They drove in silence, which Paula appreciated. In her mind, she went through the list of questions she would ask Jovan Raškić.

She paid the driver, and faced the huge metal door. She rang the bell, and explained in English the nature and the goal of her visit. The guards showed her to the visitor's parlor. It was furnished with two blue leather armchairs, a pale green sofa, and a birch club table. All around the room, there were shelves with books in almost every language of the world, many of them in the languages spoken by the peoples of the former Yugoslavia. Next to the large windows, there were tall plants with thick green leaves cascading over the supporting railing like a waterfall. They created a relaxed atmosphere, conveying more the feeling of a park rather than a prison. It was the library. The man, who left her alone in the room after serving refreshments, explained shortly:

"Miss Perić, we cannot leave you and the prisoner alone. Despite the fact that he is your father. It is too risky. There will be a guard present behind the librarian's desk. All conversations will be recorded. It's for your safety. You should know that. We have security cameras in every room. Please, sign this statement first!"

Paula ran over the five pages of a printed document. There was a statement for every possible consequence or denouement of her visit. She looked at the man, wondering:

"Is Raškić so dangerous?"

"No, Miss. He's actually a calm man. Still, you never know. We cannot guarantee you absolute security. We cannot be legally responsible for you. His indictment is severe."

Without another thought, Paula signed the paper and passed it to the man. She could sign her death warrant one way or the other. That man's blood was hers. It was there to save her. She sat in the big leather chair and waited. There were no newspapers or leaflets on the club table or anywhere else which she could read to kill the time. She could get up and pick up a book. However, they should bring him in any minute. The time was dragging along, minutes longer than hours.

At last, Jovan Raškić entered the room, thanking politely the guard who saw him in. He straightened up, smoothed his thin grey hair, and adjusted the silver wire glasses. Although visibly aged and ravaged by his turbulent life, he made a presence with his tall and handsome figure in the room. She could imagine him commanding men and leading armies. However, she could not see him loving her mother. That was unthinkable. His dark, dimmed eyes glided over the room until they apprehended Paula. She was staring at him with her mouth open. His body flinched, he wanted to make a pace, but hesitated. His daughter Paula was so beautiful, but so pale and so frail. Her thick cream sweater with huge tresses along the front reminded him of home, of his grandmother always knitting a huge pullover from the homespun wool of the mountain sheep. She wanted to stand up. She made a movement, but then leaned back in the chair. Raškić nodded to her and approached the sofa opposite.

"Hello, Paula. Thank you for coming."

"Well, since you're donating your bone marrow, the least I could do is to meet you."

"Yes."

He stretched his right hand to shake hers, but she pretended not to notice and looked away, towards the bookshelves. She did not come to touch the man. She said:

"You have a wonderful library here. It takes a lifetime to read one wall of the books, at least."

His eyes followed her look. He sensed she was avoiding looking at him. They needed more time.

"We're lucky, indeed. And it is so international, so mixed in genres. . . "

"As international as the guests of this institution. . . "

Raškić looked at her. Her soft face with regular features, so feminine and lovely, was the opposite of the harsh tone and sarcasm of her words. Just like her mother, Marica. She could hit the nail on the head with the precision and sharpness which would hurt his feelings for weeks. However, hurting used to be his domain. He had to soften the tone of their conversation. He had to show Paula he was nothing but a man. In an apologetic tone, he added:

"There are even some books in *Serbo-Croatian*. . . Andrić, Krleža. . . "

She cut into his sentence. Her voice separated the notions, the invisible fences sharply, like a razor.

"Mr. Raškić, there is no such language as *Serbo-Croatian* any more. There is Croatian and there is Serbian. You, Serbians, you have killed the *Serbo-Croatian* language and the *Serbo-Croatian* people in your crazy war. I suggest we use Croatian, for we have both been born on the Croatian territory. Knin and Karlovac are in Croatia today, despite your big Serbian ambitions."

Raškić's shoulders sank. His expression hardened, and his face was like a mortal plaster mask. He shrank in the sofa and just shook his head in disbelief. After some long minutes of silence, he asked:

"Do you have questions to ask, Paula?"

"Will you speak the truth?"

"I will tell you everything. About my family, actually your next of kin, too. . . About your mother. . . About my reasons for joining the *Republika Srpska* Krajina. . . About. . . "

"Tell me why you killed? You were a doctor, a pediatrician. You were healing people, and then, click. . . You start an ethnic cleansing. . . You hurt people!"

"I didn't hurt your mother, though. You must believe me."

"Yeah, I suppose you didn't. What choice did she have anyway? What would you have done if she had rejected you? I wonder. . . "

A curtain of pregnant silence fell over them. In the view of Raškić's indictment, her mother's options were terrible. What would he have done with her mother should she have said no to his amorous advances? Finally, he almost whispered:

"War changes everybody. . . "

"Does it really? You think that people are all victims and offenders at the same time. They kill and get killed. They rape and get raped. They torture. . . don't give me that crap, old man! If you want to speak to me, speak the truth!"

He murmured.

"It is true. The line is thin. . . the oaths broken easily. War is crime. It turned us all into criminals. . ."

"Not my mother. She was an honest woman, not a criminal. . ."

"That's what you think. . . She. . ."

"I've heard the story, but I think it was her imagination. Her way to find an excuse. . ."

"She told you about us? I thought you didn't know."

Paula's voice became calmer, her tone more polite. Their heated exchange slowed down, like the flow of the river Rhine that in the Netherlands lazily approaches its delta. They could not afford to waste time in quarrels. They needed to talk.

"She didn't tell me directly. She told me through a story about a woman from Šibenik who went to fetch her mother-in-law and was taken prisoner by the Serbian troops. This woman's name was Angela, not Marica, and my mother's Maria. She mentioned a relationship with the commander in charge. Actually, she used your name and person, but it seemed very improbable to me even then. Why would that Angela feel love for the brute who had dozens of women captured in the nearby school and ordered his soldiers to rape and torture them? What does it mean for me? I will have to live with the fact that I am a byproduct of war, collateral damage, or a little *Chetnik*, as you called such bastards. . ."

Paula sank her head to her bosom, hot tears falling to the sky blue linoleum floor. They were treading a slippery ground, both of them. Her plan to ask questions was falling apart like a house of cards. She could not hold back the anger and the pain any more. Maybe, all this was in vain and she should simply accept her illness and let it slowly kill her. While she was sobbing, covering her face with her hands, Raškić started his narrative in a soothing voice, as though it was a bedtime story.

"I was born in the middle of 1944 in Knin into an old, respectable medical family. My father was a doctor, like his father before. We had a house in the old town. We also owned vast lands in the hills around the town. I had been living there for my whole life, also after I got married, with my wife and my three daughters. The ground floor of our house was my father's office, where patients came in and out at any time of day. They told me that my father joined Tito's partisans before I was born, that he had to flee from the *Ustashas*. They were looking for him. There was a rumor spreading in Knin that he was helping wounded partisans, which was against the Croatian NDH's law. Well, you have probably heard of *Nezavisna država Hrvatska*, the Independent State of Croatia in WW2 during your history lessons, so I

will not go into detail. In Yugoslavia, more people were killed in
the civil war than in the fights with Italians or Germans. Let me
rather tell you the figures. In 1941 the Nazi regime counted the
population of the NDH to 6,2 million. 3,3 million were Croatian, 1,9 million were Serbian, 700,000 Muslims and 150,000 Germans. The estimates are that during WW2 over 500,000 Serbians
were murdered, 250,000 forced to leave their homes and 200,000
forcibly converted to Catholicism. Some 50,000 perished in the
Jasenovac concentration camp. The total toll of the victims in the
territories of the former Yugoslavia for all the nationalities during
WW2 was one million. You can see that half of them were Serbian. We were like wild game – the Italians, the Germans, and
above all, the *Ustashas*, the army of the NDH state – all were
killing and persecuting the Serbians. You learnt about the poem
Bloody Fairy Tale, by Desanka Maksimović, where the poet described the killing of a whole generation of students in one day
in Kragujevac, which belonged to the Nazi occupied Serbia. The
Germans considered us *Untermenschen*, non-humans, animals, so
when they needed to take and kill hostages, we were in the same
row as the Jews. I am telling you this because it is important
to understand why, in the late eighties, we were terrified of the
new developments in Croatia, particularly of the independence.
Democracy was fine. Nobody wanted a one party system forever,
especially not the intellectuals. After Tito died, the economy
declined, so we needed a change. Yet, with democracy, all the
symbols of the *Ustasha* killing raids came back to Croatia: the
flag with its red and white chessboard pattern – it was the flag of
the NDH. The new currency *kuna* – it was the former currency
of the NDH. Presidents Mesić and Tudjman held nationalistic
pro-Croatian public speeches. The re-established position of the
Catholic Church in the society – the church had supported the
killings and the raids of the Serbians by the *Ustashas* in WW2.
One of their monks was even the commander of the Jasenovac
concentration camp. We were terrified. The rise of Tudjman,
who openly declared that the modern Croatian state was a rebirth of the Great Croatia and NDH. Have you ever seen the
borders of NDH?"

Meanwhile, Paula wiped the tears from her cheeks. She was
looking at the floor and listening passively. She could not see
where Raškić was going. She knew all those facts. They were
part of general education, well, not all of them. In the last twenty
years, Croatian children did not learn much about WW2 and
Tito's partisans. It was not the heroic past anymore. It was the
totalitarian communist regime. It was crap, one way or the other.
She wanted to know more about him and his family, not about
the politics and war. She said:

"I know. The border should be the river Drina. Later Tudjman and Milošević made the same pact, forgetting the Bosnians,

well, even worse – not only forgetting, they were trying to eliminate them. As you well know, don't you?"

"Look, Paula, I don't want to play the sacrifice lamb. I am what I am. I cannot change that. We started the conversation with the thought that war changes people. My explanations aimed to show, the independent state of Croatia was threatening if not even harassing the Serbians in Croatia. We reacted to their aggression with our aggression, which was originally defense. Do you know what they did to me in 1989? I was the head of the pediatric department at the Knin hospital. One day, I could not open my office door. I thought something was wrong with the key and looked for the janitor. Speaking to him, I realized I was disgraced and I didn't have an office or my job any more. A young doctor, who had come from Zagreb two years earlier, simply took over the department, showing me the writing with which my career was sealed. Just like that, overnight, I was back at the starting point. He told me to my face that the professors at the Medical Institute in Zagreb suggested to him to go to Knin, where promotion would be quick to reach, as there was only a Serbian head of department. His professors told him that Serbians were getting unpopular in any higher public position, so in no time he would take my place. I was shocked. He simply threw me out."

"Why didn't you go to Belgrade or somewhere abroad? You could find another job..."

"I loved to live in Knin. It was my home. I had a very tough time while I was studying medicine in Zagreb. It was so impersonal. I had very few friends until I met Marjana, who later became my wife. Were you studying before you fell ill, Paula?"

"Yes, I was in Zagreb, too. The doctors discovered the leukemia there. I enrolled in foreign languages and literatures, French and English. It was November when I saw the doctor. A nasty cold was dragging for a month, and I couldn't get better. I thought it was the climate at first, then this diagnosis. I quit the university and literatures, for I had been spending more time in hospital than anywhere else. I don't think I am interested in continuing..."

"Would you rather study medicine?"

"No, never. I am so fed up with doctors and hospitals I hope I will never see them again in my life. One way or the other..."

"One way or the other... What do you mean? You will not die, Paula, it will work. You will get well, you'll see. The colleagues from Medisch Centrum Haagenland lent me some books on the matter. When we spoke later about your case, they were very positive about you. They say that it's a very good match, that you're lucky. However, the doctors would prefer to have both of us in the same hospital. You know, the ICTY won't let me out, and they will have to do the operation here?"

"Yes, they told me. I think they're also concerned about your safety. . . "

"And that I might plan to escape. Honestly, I decided I am
not going to run any more. I decided to tell the truth, to shed
light on the events as I see them. I want to show the world that
our civilization and legal system hang on a thin thread and that
it is our duty to make it a strong rope. I want them to see what
extreme politics can do to a man, to every man. Do you want me
to continue?"

"As long as you're not putting my mother in the same category. . . "

"Paula, I loved your mother. Whatever she had done, I helped
to cover her escape and made my superiors ignore the chain of
events. I know it had been in self-defense, and I don't blame
her. Well, first things first. . . You were asking why I hadn't left
Croatia, when I saw it was no place for Serbians. I was too
involved in the cultural and political life in Knin. I was active in
various associations, musical, literary and others. I was a deputy
in the municipality council. I became one of the first Rotary
Club members in Split and organized charity events in Knin.
I was also one of the high officials in the newly formed Serbian
Democratic Party. I believed in our cause. Besides, I trusted that
we could solve the conflicts, organize our government according
to ethnicities in the territories, and live peacefully next to each
other. I could not accept the new Croatian constitution, which
defined Serbians as an ethnic minority. We used to make up one
third of population, even the old Croatian Parliement, 'Sabor', in
1867 recognized us as a nation living in Croatia. Under Tudjman,
we became a national minority. Although many lives were lost
and many Serbians left Krajina during the NDH reign of terror,
percentage-wise, we were still one quarter of the population. I
was naive. I thought we could work this out politically. After
all, be it Christmas on the 24th December or two weeks later, we
believe in the same God Jesus Christ."

Paula started to take interest in the matter. Maybe the Croatian war of independence was not such a black and white tale
as she had heard it presented at school and in the media during
her whole life. Tudjman was portrayed as a war hero, as the
father of the nation. Yet, when little by little, after his death,
the wealth of his family members became a matter of USKOK,
the anti-corruption authorities in Croatia and its closer investigation, many started to doubt him. Paula read somewhere on
the internet that if he had not been not dead by then, he could
be answering questions of the ICTY alongside with Milošević.

"When did you realize it was war then?"

"Not soon enough. In the late eighties, I embraced the idea
of democracy and sovereignty. I was the initiator of the 1990
referendum in Krajina. For the first time, we could express our
political opinion freely; we voted like the Slovenians, French, and

so many other nations. It was a new land, Paula. We had been living in the communist regime for decades. Nobody asked our opinion. We were told by the party what to think."

"Were you a communist?"

"No, I wasn't, although my father wanted me very much to join. He was so afraid. He was a member of the party. You know, I told you that he had fled and came home only after the war was over. Well, he joined the partisans in late 1943, but during one of the fights around Kozara, the *Ustashas* caught him. He would have been executed on the spot if they hadn't found out he was a doctor. They interned him into Jasenovac, the notorious concentration camp, where over 700,000 people suffered the fascist *Ustasha* torture. They estimate between 80,000 and 100,000 victims were Serbians. Well, you can imagine that my childhood was filled with stories of the *Ustasha* terror. My father never recovered and led a quiet life as the city's general practitioner. His patients adored him, but he was always afraid, always on the run from the flashbacks of the camps. He told me, the *Ustasha* held the concentration camp for children near Sisak. Can you imagine? They put children between the age of three and sixteen into a concentration camp, where they sadistically molested them. Some 20,000 of those poor innocent children perished. My father became the eye and the ear of the suffering. My gentle, suffering father... When he finally came home, he was only half of the man he used to be. He would burst in tears while watching old partisan movies. He was afraid of Croatians, terrified of their police. I think the only Croatian my father ever liked was Marshal Tito. I am glad dad died before all this mess started."

Raškić stood up and started pacing the room in front of the bookshelves. The guard stood up as well, but Raškić signalled with his hand that everything was all right and he would not try anything suspicious.

"They say little about Jasenovac in the history lessons these days. You, Serbians, you set up concentration camps for your enemies in the last war, too. Isn't that so? It's just a matter of force..."

"There were a few *logors*, camps, in *Republika Srpska* Krajina, and I am not proud of it. But the main atrocities, the shelling of Sarajevo and the Srebrenica massacre were in the domain of the Bosnian Serbians: Karadjič and Mladić. They are a different species; wild and bloodthirsty. Anyway, I fell to the propaganda of Slobodan Milošević that Serbians would live to see another Jasenovac in the new, independent Croatia."

"So when did you realize it was a war?"

Paula wanted to know what made this man tick. She wanted to explore the borderline of his humanity. Why had he crossed it and when? Would it be possible that she might cross it, too, in an extreme situation? Was it true that war changes everybody?

"In spring 1991, I realized that I have to take action in order
to press our cause. By that time, we had had another referendum, in which we, the Serbians of Croatia, declared we want to
live in Yugoslavia, or what was left of it. In the last hundred
years, Yugoslavia was the only state which sheltered the Serbians
from the fascist forces and from their persecution. Too late, I
realized what was going on; a genocide, which today my prosecutors describe as a 'joint criminal enterprise.' We were to ban
from their homes as many Croatians as possible and ethnically
cleanse the territory to join the Great Serbia. It was then, in
those raids, when we captured Marica, your mother."

"You realize that our conversation is recorded, don't you?
Just in case you don't know..."

Although Paula's historical knowledge was not like her
mother's, she knew he was lying. Yugoslavia was a kind of big
Serbia, and between the two world wars, Belgrade was feeding on
the prosperity of the other nations, showing its dominance everywhere it could. The NDH years might have been a trauma, but it
was not the whole picture. Yugoslavia was as complicated as the
pieces of its puzzle... Through her thoughts, she heard her father
speak.

"Everything here is recorded. Privacy is the luxury of the
free. I knew that before I came. However, Paula, I am a new
man. I want to confess, and may they use my confessions against
me and punish me. I used to be a doctor. Then, I was a beast, a
murderer, now I am just an ordinary man, a sinner. I don't care
about the sentence. Any sentence the tribunal can impose on me
will be easier than the one I carry in my heart. Like Milan Babić,
I have my conscience, too. Like Babić, I say, 'The regret that I
feel is the pain that I have to live for the rest of my life.' I had
suppressed my conscience, I turned it off during the war, and I
did things or let things be done to other human beings which can
never be justified. When I regained my senses and realized what
was right and what was wrong, I gave myself over voluntarily. It
was three years ago. I could have gone on hiding for ages, but
I decided to confess and to repent. I wanted to be part of the
society again, which I had not been under a false name and with
somebody else's money."

Paula did not know that. She was surprised. She always
imagined the police caught criminals by surprise, and had to tie
them up and bring them in. That man came up, though he knew
what humiliation and hate awaited him. She looked Raškić into
his eyes for the first time:

"Where had you been all those years? You vanished around
1995... three years ago, that is twelve years!"

"I fled to the Greek Cyprus and lived there a very simple
life of a peasant for two years, until I learnt to speak Greek and
could pass for a foreign doctor, yet not Serbian. Then I bought

another identity, the third one. I was Polish. I worked as a village doctor near Paphos. I could have gone on like that for another lifetime... The Interpol and the prosecutors would never find me."

"Why then?"

"I felt I had to pay my debt. I was following the arrests of so many of my comrades, even my former enemies. I was following their trials on the internet. They were not honest. Some were even arrogant and defended their abominable policy. It was not fair towards the people who had suffered. I remembered my father and his nightmares of Jasenovac. It was as though I betrayed not only the Serbian cause, but everything else, too; myself, my origins, my father. I had to act. My family, I mean my wife and daughters, they renounced me. I never hoped to find your mother again. I knew she was gone from me forever. I had doubts whether she lived. So, one day, I put a note on my doctor's office at Paphos saying that I would be away for a long holiday. I flew to Ljubljana and gave myself over to the Slovenian police."

They remained silent. Despite herself, Paula felt sorry for the man she could never call father. Somehow, he was honest in his suffering. He seemed sincere with his wish for atonement. He was a broken human being. A child could see that.

"I am sorry. It will probably help at the court that you came forward voluntarily. You might get a milder sentence."

Paula's voice did not show her emotion whatsoever. She made a clear and a matter-of-fact statement. Raškić made a few steps and stood behind her, so that she could not see his face. The guard jumped up in alarm, reaching for his pistol. He could not understand what they were saying in Croatian, it would be a matter for the translators later, but he was assigned to protect the girl. Then, he saw that tears were streaming down the old man's face. Nobody said a word for several minutes, Raškić was fighting to stiffen the sobs, so that Paula would not see or hear him crying. The Dutch prison guard was looking at him with wonder and at full attention, ready to draw his gun and shoot at him, should he lift a finger to hurt the girl in the leather chair. Then, Raškić composed himself and wiped his tears on the sleeve without making a sound. He said:

"I don't think my confession will impress the court and the judges. You see, I have done what I have done, and for the sake of the victims, they have to punish me. I must say I didn't think this conversation with my own lost and found daughter would be so difficult."

Paula turned her head and pierced him with her questioning look.

"Jovan Raškić, you're still avoiding my question. When did you become a criminal? When did you turn from a doctor into a murderer?"

Raškić walked around to the sofa and sat down. He shook his head. The guard sat back at the computer relieved that the moment of crisis went by. The old man resumed his narration:

"Have you heard of a little village Baljvine in Bosnia, where Muslims and Serbians have continued to live in peace for centuries and refused to fight each other in the WW2 as well as in the last Balkan war? No, probably you haven't, and you never will. Nobody speaks of Baljvine, for it is a symbol of peace and friendship among nations. You see, politicians can't make money or acquire more power in peace. They need war. The answer to your question, Paula, is in that village. I will tell you why. First, I must tell you that during four years of the war, I saw almost no action. I have never killed a man in person. Only once, during the *Oluja*, I held a rifle in my hands. I was not the muscle. I was the brain of *Republika Srpska* Krajina. I have never raped either a woman or a man. I have never molested a child or tortured the enemy. Often, I tried to help and cure the pain that our soldiers imposed on those people..."

"Are you kidding? Men got raped in the war?"

"Oh, yes, my girl. Men get raped and molested in every war. It is a silent truth, for the victims never speak up. They are afraid they would cease to be men if they prosecute their molesters. Well, I spoke to the tribunal about it and told them about the practices in the prisoners' camps. Men were hurt with gun muzzles, bottlenecks, knives... You know, sexual abuse is the highest show of absolute power over the enemy. There's a lot of logic in the fact that the winners want to show their dominance not only to women, but above all to men."

"Horrible... Can you continue with the Bosnian village story?"

"Yes, Baljvine. I had to stand in for a Bosnia Serbian commander who had gone to Belgrade. My unit was close by. That was nearly the only time I should have seen action and use my gun, and I didn't. I will tell you why. We marched into the village, which was half Muslim, half Serbian. It was scattered around a hill, and the upper part, perched on the slope, was Serbian, the valley was Muslim. In late evening, I gathered the elders and the representatives of the Muslim community and told them that the Muslims had to leave the place within twenty-four hours. The Muslim leader said that it was impossible, that they would never leave their village. I pleaded with him, explaining that the Serbians of the upper part of the village could get violent, hurt them, and make them leave by force. It would be so much easier if they left their homes without a fight. He stood up with the words: 'I can walk among my Serbian neighbors anytime without any fear at all. Watch me!' He left the room and walked to the upper part of the village. It was pitch dark, the middle of the night. We followed him. I was deeply concerned that shots would fall and the fighting would take lives. He came to the first house and walked into the yard of the Serbian elder. 'Miroslave, možemo Bošnjaki ostati u selu? Miroslav, can we, the Bosnians stay in the village?' The Serbian was obviously asleep. After a few calls, he turned on the light in the room on the second floor, and opened the window hastily. 'Šefko, my friend, what is it? Is something wrong? Do you need help? I'll be down in a second...' I stared in the darkness and realized I was a war criminal. I pushed people to fight. I made them hate each other. I inflamed them to cut each other's throats. I was responsible for the atrocities. In the eyes of those good men, who instead of killing decided to love each other, no matter which God they prayed to, I saw the greatness of my crimes. There was no Great Serbia. It was the same joke as the independent Croatia stretching into Herzegovina. The only thing which was great was the greatness of our crimes in the face of humanity. You see, Paula, when you're among the likes of you and everybody around is crying out 'Kill the Croatian! Kill the Turk!' You don't see it. Day by day, you accept bad things happening. Rape, torture, tears – they become a part of your life. You abstract the initial doubts fast, you stop weighing the right and the wrong. Your brain focuses on the efficiency of the task without asking what the task is. Atrocities are the path to a better future. You cut off your conscience. You cut off what you had been before all those evils became part of you, before the Evil is you. Only when you confront the other side of the story, like at Baljvine, you see the magnitude of your wrongdoing. Thus in my mind, the moment my conscience woke up and died, or better to say, when I buried it forever, was in Baljvine. When the good villagers resisted our lunacy, precisely then... that was the moment when I became a war criminal. After Baljvine, there was no way back..."

"But knowing it, why did you continue doing it? Why didn't you abandon everything?"

"I couldn't. Like the villagers of Baljvine were tied by mutual love and understanding, we, the Serbians, and the other two sides accordingly, were tied up by hate and revenge. All I could do afterwards was to avoid the front, to see to the logistics and to plan instead of execute the operations. I saw to it that I did not dirty my hands, but they were smeared with blood all the same. I could not face the other people, the non-Serbians. I could not face the flows of civilians on the roads with their poor belongings piled on trucks and mule carts. They were like ghosts from another story, like characters from old partisan movies. They were ugly and sad. They were angry and humiliated. I didn't want to see them. I didn't want to think who sent them on their sad pilgrimage. I stayed in at the headquarters. There was much work there, too. Some said I was a coward. Now they say, I was not responsible for the crimes, as I was not there, on the territory, where ethnic cleansing was physically taking place. My lawyer says I should plead innocent. I didn't give myself over to lie, though. I know that I am no less responsible than anybody who fired a gun in Srebrenica or molested the prisoners at Omarska. I must take the burden and live with it. I must be a man."

"And what happened to Baljvine? Did you raid it?"

"How could I? Nonplussed, my soldiers and I, we simply left."

"It's a pity you didn't follow their example and stop the war."

"I tried to negotiate ceasefires all the time. But in the mess, nobody actually knew who was shooting who..."

"Yeah, Serbians against Croatians, Croatians against Muslims, Muslims against Serbians and Serbians against Muslims..."

"That is what I am saying. It was a vicious circle... We were everybody at everybody's throat... Tudjman and Milošević got the wheel rolling, they started the war, and we followed like stupid sheep. We jumped off the cliff bleating their sick ideas. That was what your mother was trying to tell me. She was trying to make me go to Belgrade and stop fighting. But I didn't listen to her."

"And you continued to plan murder."

Raškić's face trembled and tears welled up again. He did not hide them from Paula any longer. Why should he? She was the only frail link to life, the only proof that he had once been something else than an ICTY file. What was her judgment of him? Would she ever accept him as a father?

"Paula, please believe me. I loved your mother. Maybe the first time we were together, there was a bit of fear on her part and I might have liked the fact I would subdue her a bit too much. You know, men... You can say I abused the situation. But she received me with passion and devotion. She didn't fake her love. We were together for months. I would have noticed if anything had been so wrong. So, don't think you're a little *Chetnik*... It hurts me to think..."

Paula could not speak. A lump in her throat was pushing tears in her eyes, too. The story of Baljvine, moved her more than she would admit. She heard what she wanted to hear. There was normality, peace, love, and life – and there was war, violence, hate, and death. In between, there was a thin thread of communication and international politics, so vulnerable, yet so important for sustaining the balance, keeping the peace. She swallowed the lump in her throat and held back the tears.

"Why did she leave you then?"

Raškić shook his head.

"I understood her. She wanted to get home to her family. She felt she was betraying her country by sleeping with me. She would cry bitter tears almost every time we made love. Our relationship was precarious, burdened with the bloody baggage. She was a sensitive soul, which made it all the more surprising..."

"What do you mean?"

"I wrote you in the letter that two things happened within the same week – Marica fled and Petar, my aide, stole a bag of money, war provisions for many months, and disappeared. The guard who was supposed to be on duty that night and might have noticed something, was transferred to the front line the following morning and fell during the fights of the day. It was my order, what could I do? I couldn't interrogate him. But I put one and one together. Your mother had prepared the coup meticulously. She must have lured Petar outside the headmaster's house with something, cut his throat in the bush, and taken the money. We weren't very far from Šibenik, only some eighty kilometers. She was sure to have found that out. She could have walked home. She left the original money bag with Petar, so that we would assume that somebody killed and robbed him. I say, I figured it out. On the one hand, I was surprised, she seemed such a gentle person, but on the other, I... Though, in the course of events, I often thought she should have stabbed me instead of Petar..."

For a moment, Paula felt pride, too. Her brave, courageous mother... Then she realized the trap. Was she not approving of violence and murder? What good can it bring when you cut a throat of a man? Was she not celebrating death? She shuddered. Her father, Raškić, said that war changed everybody. He claimed that war turned good people into criminals. Since the dawn of time, society judged and punished the criminals. Would there be then more courts like ICTY in the future? One for Iraq, one for Afghanistan, another for Somalia... How were the political leaders of the future going to justify war and military activities around the world? She said in a weak voice.

"If she had stabbed you, you wouldn't be here to help me now."

Raškić nodded absent-mindedly. Then, he took out of his breast pocket of the gray prisoner's shirt two neatly folded sheets.

"Here, Paula, take this. I have put down all the information about your mother's relatives and my relatives I could remember. Everything, you see... Her surname was Čekić. She came from Šibenik... I know her birthday was in September..."

"It was in spring, the 12th of April, actually..."

He shook his head.

"I don't think so, for we had a small celebration and it was in September. Anyway, if you feel the need to find your relatives, you will be able to. Please, be careful. You never know, how people react..."

"I don't think I will seek them out. They have their life and I hope to have mine..."

With a trembling hand, Raškić presented another sheet of paper, with a neatly arranged family tree.

"For my side, you have more accurate information. Here are my grandparents, my parents, my wife, and my daughters. Their names, birth dates, addresses..."

"Didn't you say your wife and daughters have changed their names and moved to America?"

"Yes, but you can seek them out through our Belgrade relatives. They would not turn you down... Still, they might feel awkward... which reminds me of another matter we must discuss today, Paula."

"Which is?"

Raškić took her hand in his. She jerked to pull it away. Her eyes opened widely in shock, then she sighed, calmed down, and let him hold it. Her feelings were boiling inside her brain. She could not form her thoughts. She came to the ICTY detention unit to meet the butcher of Krajina, and now she found a man... a father... She looked up.

"Paula, it will be entirely your choice, I promise."

"We all have our choices..."

"Would you like me to acknowledge you officially as my daughter?"

She shuddered in shock and pulled her hand away in disgust. She almost yelled at him:

"You mean to bear your name? Raškić?"

He replied in a soothing voice:

"No, Paula, you don't have to take my name. You can be Perić or Čekić or whatever you want to be. It's just that my family owns vast lands around Knin. There is also the house on the hill, below the fortress. You're a Croatian citizen. You could do something with it. I checked with the officials of the court here, and they said there was a fair chance that they would not take my property away from me after the sentence. It has been in the family for generations, long before the war and plundering. Since my daughters and my wife are in America, I can make you my sole heir. If you agree, I will do it. Otherwise, I will not compromise you with my acknowledgement."

Suddenly, Paula felt very tired. She did not need to be this man's daughter. She did not need to suffer from leukemia. She did not need to share his flesh. Why was life so cruel to her? She cannot...

"Mr. Raškić, I will give you my answer before I leave Holland. It's been a lot for one day. I am sorry."

"I understand. I really do. Please, come again, Paula. I am happy to have such a wonderful daughter. Thank you for coming."

He stood up and nodded to the guard. Paula remained seated with her head bent down, looking at the linoleum floor as though she would find the answers there. Finally, she looked up and met Raškić's teary eyes. She sighed and smiled politely.

"I should thank you. I hope the second life you give me will be a better one."

His eyes lit up in hope. He smiled back. The guard took him by the sleeve, and Raškić walked around the pale green leather sofa, offering the man his wrists. Walking towards the exit, he seemed content, almost happy.

Paula asked the guards to ring for a taxi, which drove her to the Scheveningen beach. She phoned the hospital to say she would come in later and skip lunchtime. She desperately needed time alone. She had to run the conversation through in her head and think about what to do next. It was far too soon, to make any decision Raškić had asked for. She wondered if she would ever be able to accept him as a father or as a human being.

The sky was deep blue, all fogs washed away by the early morning rain. The taxi left her above the De Pier shopping gallery, promising to pick her up in two hours' time. The driver left her a card to call him, in case she would like to return earlier. Paula was grateful for the fresh air, the salty breeze bringing the smells of the sea so familiar to her. Yet, the Atlantic was no Adriatic. It was grey and muddy compared to the clear waters of her home island.

She turned towards the open area, skipping the several little tourist shops and stands with souvenir junk claiming to be original Dutch though manufactured in the Far East, probably in China. Paula passed by the racks full of clogs and tulip bulbs like a moonwalker. Her head was heavy with emotions. Was her father, the commander Jovan Raškić, really such a bad person? Was a truly evil man capable of repentance and sincere regret? Poet Shelley wrote "As repentance follows crime, As changes follow time."

Following the boardwalk, she soon reached the less populated and more natural part of the Scheveningen beach. On her right, there were the famous dunes with tiny shrubs exploding in colorful flowers of creamy pink, yellow, and blue. It was a pretty sight, although she could not approach the flowers and pick them. She inhaled the smells of the Atlantic spring in her lungs. The dunes were protected by a low fence with pictograms showing what was allowed and what forbidden. Everywhere there were rules. Everywhere there were signs instructing people how they should live according to the laws of the society, how they should obey the norms of the civilization. It was the essence of our social behavior. Paula read somewhere that laws were the glue of society. What became of men when those laws were broken, when they failed to control themselves? What would she become, should she find herself in such a situation? Her father and her mother became somebody else. It was most ironic that her mother might have murdered with her own hands, while her father was on trial at the Hague tribunal for war crimes. Who was she, then, with two such violent sets of genes? Could she live to put their crimes behind her and lead a decent life? Or, would she flip out at the first conflict and become a criminal like her parents? Would she trespass over that fence to pick those pink flowers on the dunes? Shelley said later in the same poem: "But if Freedom should awake in her omnipotence, and shake. . ." Yeah, she had to fight. She had to use her brain to find her own way. Like the villagers of Baljvine, she had a choice. On her left, her look embraced the open sea, the mighty ocean, where high waves were trying to break the shore, yet billions of tiny grains of sand would not give way and protected the land, kept it whole. The horizon was like a bright open line; it invited her to see the limitless possibilities. She left the boardwalk and stepped onto the vast strip of wet sand, where last night's tide washed empty shells ashore; black mussels, white scallops and colorful sea snails, shells of all sizes and forms. She bent down and started to pick them. She chose them carefully, and when there were so many that her hands could not hold them, she put them into a bag she had improvised from her kerchief. Like those shells from the wet sand, she could pick up her chances in life. She would make her own decisions. She would learn to make the good ones. She would be able to find the balance between the fences and the far away horizon. She would be like that sandy shore; whole by the force of little grains holding it together. First, she had to stay alive.

She turned back towards the Scheveningen beach stands. She could smell deep fried snacks and she realized she was hungry. She stopped by the first stand, where a sporty middle-aged woman with curly blond hair, sky blue eyes, and a wonderful smile was selling *maatjes*, soused herring that the clients were gulping down with raw onions in a bun. Paula preferred deep fried herring and chips. With a can of Amstel beer in one hand, balancing the food and the kerchief with shells in the other, she occupied a little table at the end, facing the sea.

"Careful, Miss!" the joyful vendor cried after her.

"The seagulls will want to have some, too! They are a greedy lot!"

Paula looked back at her, already stuffing her face with the fatty batter dipped in mayonnaise.

"Who is not these days, Madame?"

A bird stole a chip from her platter and she shooed it away. She would not let him eat her last juicy meal before the hospital regime of steamed vegetables and poached chicken would infiltrate her system again.

Riding on the wave

"Dad, what is so urgent that I had to leave my work at the peak of the season and come to see you?"

Olivia was visibly annoyed. She had been working very hard, and with every little success, her life made more sense. In spring, she had bought a small house in Ilirska Bistrica, a town on the Croatian-Slovenian border, but she had no time to renovate it or furnish it, lest to enjoy its lush green garden. Still, it was handy for her, since Andrej had become her boyfriend. They could meet half way. It was almost against their wills that they were a couple. As though an irresistible force of solitude would make their feelings merge and their bodies lie in an embrace. They made no big plans though, for it had been more or less a weekend love so far; Andrej Bak worked in Ljubljana, while Olivia Kadura worked a few weeks in the Croatian Opatija and a few in the Slovenian Portorož.

Mira, still pale as a ghost and thin as a stick, cut in:

"Are you ill, dad?"

Dario shook his white head pensively and stroked grey beard, which he had grown back since Maria's death.

"I am fine, don't worry, baby. Olivia, sorry, but we need to talk."

Olivia, putting up the cafetiera to brew coffee, was still nagging.

"I don't have time to live, dad. I am not seeing my friends, I can't find time to furnish my house, I don't spend time with A... Well, it's a complete nuisance, this compulsory weekend at Mulobedanj at the beginning of July."

"I appreciate your work, Olivia, and I am glad you're taking on the responsibility for the hotels. When we finally sit down and I tell you my intentions, you will see why I summoned both of you..."

Dario took out of the cupboard a bottle of herb brandy and sat at the old oak table, polished with years and thousands of meals. Despite his sister's inheritance, he had not changed his lifestyle. He was a simple man, a former captain and a fisherman. He liked to go to sea and to farm olives. He looked at his younger daughter, who stood by the window, staring at the closed shutters absentmindedly. Mira was still sick with pain. Could he pull her out of her depression?

"Mira, why don't you put some biscuits on the table? Come on, move, do something! Must I and dad do everything?"

Olivia was in her active frenzy. Like always, she took control of the situation and started to order them around. Dario flinched.

"Olivia and Mira, both sit down and listen! Now!"

He did not mean to sound so harsh, but it was necessary. He could see it coming. The girls would start picking at each other,

then quarrelling over who did what. Olivia would reproach Mira
her laziness, at the same time as she was enjoying being the only
one to control the hotels and increasingly making decisions about
how they should run them. Mira did not care for anything, and
had not taken up her studies. She would need another exam year
and a few months to write her thesis, but with every day, her
goal to finish university and to work in their hotel business was
further away. Olivia felt she was doing the job for both of them,
and her sharp tongue never missed the opportunity to scream it
to the world. In a milder tone, Dario pleaded:

"Please, girls. I need to talk to you about my part of the
inheritance."

Now, Mira spoke up:

"Don't we all have enough money and worries as it is? Just
spend it, dad! Buy yourself a new house, a new boat, or
travel... go around the world. Or, whatever..."

"Actually, Mira, I am spending it. I have ordered a new boat
for my fishing trips. It's bigger, yet she will still anchor at Mulobedanj. I will name it Marina..."

Olivia hugged him and kissed him noisily on the cheek.

"That's excellent, dad. Finally, you came back to the living..."

Mira sighed and looked at her older sister as though she was
the weirdest creature on earth. They used to be so close. They
travelled together, took courses, went on holidays, even dated
a few of the same boys... they did everything together. They
were fighting, but it was more a show. After Auntie's death, they
became strangers. No matter how much dad had tried to organize
family gatherings, how much he had tried to bring them together,
talking, eating, planning, Olivia would attack Mira for her grey
moods, for her dress, for her life.

"The boat is one thing, but I have something more important
to tell you..."

"You should also sell Aunt's apartment in Rijeka and buy
yourself a new house, dad! It's been empty since last year..."

Olivia would not give in. She was full of good advice.

"What the hell! Did they not teach you in all your business
courses that there are moments when you should shut up and
listen, Olivia!"

Olivia paled. Mira's face lit a hush of a tiny smile. It served
her big sister right to be put in her place. Olivia made a long
face and just stared at her father.

"Now, I would like to set up a foundation. I will invest my
share of the inheritance. I will sell everything, including the chartering company in Zadar, and it will amount to a serious sum.
The foundation will finance research of marine wildlife and the
influence of pollution on our sea. It will publish the results, in
order to influence the public opinion, which should put pressure

on the politicians to pass the laws to protect the Adriatic better. You know well that the sea is almost devoid of fish compared to the old days. One thing which has not been well known is the influence of aquaculture on the sea."

He paused. He inspected their faces, which were alert with interest. He had their full attention. The sisters exchanged looks. For a change, it was Mira who spoke first.

"Dad, I think this is a great idea. We're not used to living with this heap of money. In this way, you could really make a difference, you could change things..."

Olivia shook her head.

"But dad, how will you go about it? What is the legal status of such a foundation? Have you spoken to Govač? Then, who will work in your foundation... You're retired... you are qualified as a sea captain..."

"My darlings, I have it all figured out. Since spring, I have been in contact with various people, but first I must have your approval. For my foundation will seriously cut into your inheritance when I die."

The sisters nodded at each other. Mira said:

"We all have more than enough, dad. Tell us more about your foundation. Do you have a name for it?"

"It will be called 'Save the Adriatic'. The head office will be in Zagreb, to be closer to the media. Its main task will be to publish research reports and create public interest. We will need a director of the foundation..."

Subconsciously, Dario and Olivia both looked at Mira. Then, the man continued:

"The other office would be positioned in the Rijeka port and it would be floating – on a ship. I have made some enquiries and the foundation could purchase the sister ship of Tito's Galeb, at a very good price. Lasta, the Swallow, has been at the Čiovo shipbuilding dock for some five years. It belonged to the Yugoslav National Army's Navy, but our boys confiscated it in the battle for the bridge to Pag during the last Balkan war. The interior is very modest, no trace of the luxury of the Galeb, but the main engine works like a Swiss clock, and with a little investment, it would be very suitable for navigating the Adriatic and doing research..."

"You mean like Jacques Cousteau, the famous oceanographer..."

"Indeed, Mira. Although instead of Calypso, we will name it Marina's song, like the mermaid's song. I will dedicate my work to Auntie. Thus, she will still be with us not only through her music, but also through our mission. Cousteau set an example. So many years ago, he understood some of the dangers to maritime wildlife which we are seeing today. In Croatia, we have to be careful. The war and the transition have created a climate in which people can do anything, no matter whether it is good for the environment or even legal. Rules and limitations are lenient, and people would do anything for a quick buck. The foundation will provide research and documentary material to point out the dangers. One is, for sure, overfishing."

Olivia smiled at the stream of words; dad could be so energetic when he was after his goals.

"Well, you seem to have thought of many things. Why are you asking us?"

"Olivia, don't you see? I need not only your approval, but also help and support..."

Now Mira spoke up in a clear, matter-of-fact voice:

"First, you need to install internet in your house and start gathering more information as well as communicating with the world. Will you employ scientists? Biologists? Cousteau was also scuba diving, and he even had a little submarine on board of his Calypso."

"I know. There is internet in the house, it is just..."

Olivia looked at Mira, who was virtually resurrecting to life at dad's news. Her cheeks flushed and in the heat of the moment, she asked her big sister:

"What do you say, Olivia, shall we put all our money together?"

"No, no, there's enough only in my share of the inheritance. We must set up the foundation in such a way that it would draw monies from different sources, also from the European Union. We need famous sponsors, famous individuals and companies. There has to be a marketing campaign, in order to mobilize forces. Olivia should continue at the hotels, and in good years, she could donate to our foundation. In bad times, she might be able to borrow from us to bridge a crisis at the Sea Shell."

Somehow, Olivia seemed relieved. She had started to enjoy her work at the Bella Vista and slowly managed to run parts of the business on her own. Mira said in a firm voice:

"Fine, it will be the two of us then, dad. I agree, we should leave the hotels as they are. They're running smoothly and, despite the crisis, Olivia tells me they have more than 70% occupancy around the year, which is great..."

Dario gave his younger daughter a strict look.

"You don't seem to have listened to me, girls. You both keep what you have. I am investing into Save the Adriatic, not you. But since I am getting old and I don't have the knowledge, I would really appreciate it, if you, Mira could help me to start up. It would take you some time from your studies and diploma... If you can..."

"Dad, I didn't know how to tell you, but I am not taking my degree. You see, I was not born for business. I must do something else. I didn't know how to break it to you, but Olivia and I, we have spoken about this a few times. As a co-owner of the hotels, there is no need for me to work there as well, actually. But I didn't know how you would take it... After all the years of education..."

Dario stared at his daughter with his eyes wide open. Nobody ever told him anything. He was shocked and angry. How could she fail in the last year? Had she no shame?

"I think you must finish your studies, Mira. I am serious. Or I will not let you help me. I think it is your duty towards Auntie Marina, who cared so much for your education. It's a shame..."

"But, Dad, I am not interested in Accounting for Hotel Managers or Economy of the Restaurants. Those subjects are boring..."

Dario's face was like stone. He was furious. However, he knew he should not lose his patience.

"How much time do you need if you study very hard, Mira?"

"She needs two months, dad, two months. There are two oral exams and the diploma thesis, which she could do easily with the help of our hotel staff. She could pick the topic of family hotels versus business hotels and compare anything from location to the food and prices. Or, she can pick the future of ecological hotels in Dalmatia and write about the developments so far. She can start with Perovica, and continue with one of our villas in the Opatija hinterland, which Sea Shell might turn into an exclusive ecological place."

"You bitch!"

Mira jolted up so quickly that she turned over the chair behind her back. Her eyes filled with tears. She left the house and slammed the door so wildly that it almost fell out of the jamb. The older girl and her dad sat silently at the table, studying their hands. Finally, Dario stood up and filled his glass with water. Olivia stretched her hand, asking for some for herself.

"I am sorry, dad. I blew it. I should have kept silent."

"Olivia, you're right. You should shut up sometimes. On the other hand, it's good to talk openly. Like you, I don't want Mira to fail now."

He put down the glass and came behind Olivia's back, putting both hands on her shoulders as though he was leaning on his daughter. She was the tough one in the family. She felt his hand and stroked it gently. What could they do now?

"Well, Mira will have to grow up. I cannot tolerate her whims and moods. She should take responsibility for her life, or I will not entrust her with leading the foundation. There are limits to my patience. It is not about money, but about dignity and respect towards her aunt."

Olivia was silent. She knew her little sister, who was like a whirlwind. In a couple of minutes, Mira would come back with a

smile, changing the topic of their conversation as though nothing
had happened. She lifted her face towards her dad.

"Maybe you should take us fishing tomorrow, daddy. Since
we sacrificed our weekend..."

Mira's voice cut in.

"Yes, dad, take us fishing. We have to see what we are going
to save, don't we?"

"And the diploma..."

"Let's talk about it tomorrow, shall we? Today I need a good
dinner and a nice bottle of wine. Let's go to Slavko's and have
some fun!"

Dario took her hand and drew her closer. They joined in a big
family hug. They were a broken family with some broken hearts,
but they were together. Nobody cared that the old man's back
was trembling with sobs. He was so happy. His beloved girls were
home at last!

The miracle of Paula

The bridge from the mainland to the island of Pag was one of the most important traffic points in the whole of Croatia. Built in 1968, the simple construction was a key land connection from the south to the north of Dalmatia during the last Balkan war in the 1990s. The aviation of the Yugoslav National Army rarely missed an opportunity to bomb the long convoys of fugitives, food, and medical supplies which were crossing it day and night. When the Croatian liberators feared that the Serbians could take the bridge and use it for their military purposes to enter northern Dalmatia, they blew it up themselves. An elegant new arch, proudly spanning above the water, replaced the ruins soon after the war. Still, the passage is rather narrow, hardly enough for two vehicles to meet. On the left side, looking towards the island, there is a sidewalk, which the rare pedestrians and more frequent cyclists use to cross the three hundred meters of sea passage below, poetically called *Ljubačka vrata* or Lovers' strait. It is one of the most romantic places in the Adriatic, separating the wild Velebit channel, beaten by the strong *bura*, from the peaceful bay, *Ljubački zaljev*, Lovers' Bay, which shelters the cradle of Croatian culture, the tiny, ancient city of Nin.

Paula slowed down her mother's SUV, opened the window, and put the rap music louder. She was happy, bursting with new energy and life. Her medical in Zadar showed great results. The operation in The Hague was a full success, and the doctors told her she had very good chances of healing completely. After some years, she could even bear children, for should her leukemia not return in the following year, she could consider herself a healthy young woman. After two years of the hospital nightmare, she could not entirely believe them, but on the other hand, she felt great and was grateful for every day of her new life. She celebrated the good news in a local pub, with a fine serving of truffle spaghetti and a glass of white wine. In late afternoon, she was approaching her home island, one of the longest in the Adriatic with its sixty kilometers. On the windy road, it meant another two hours of driving. She looked to the left for a moment, seeing past the old Roman fortress *Fortica* into the bay and smiling at the memory of her mother who took her to Nin, when she was a little girl. It was a real treat, for Maria Perić was a busy woman and rarely left her hotel without supervision.

"My little princess is swimming at the Queen's Beach!"

Paula was happily splashing the clear water behind her tiny body. She could have been seven or eight.

"I am a princess, I am a queen. I have a trail! Look at me, *nona*, I have a trail!"

The white foams behind her back indeed looked like a wedding trail of a noble lady. Her mother was laughing with her, lifting her in her lap and throwing her back in the waves, where she would gulp down salty water, for while giggling she could not keep her mouth shut. When they were driving home, her mother told her the beautiful legend of the Queen's Beach. Paula grew up in the belief that Lovers' Bay got its name after the infinite affection that the first Croatian king, Tomislav, felt for his young wife, the beautiful queen to whom he dedicated the beach at Nin. Paula nourished the romantic legend until one day, she saw in the newspapers the debate regarding the early borders of the first Croatian kingdom under Tomislav. It inflamed nationalist sentiments and quarrels among the historians about whether the river Drina was the eastern border of Croatia or not. Since the last Balkan wars, it was a sensitive point, for the criminal pact between Franjo Tudjman and Slobodan Milošević rested precisely on that assumption, cleansing all foreign elements from the territories west of the river Drina.

The sun was still high, although the warm late June afternoon was fading into the evening. Any day now, Dalmatians, in awe of their old pagan traditions, would be celebrating the longest day of the year, *Ivanje*, the midsummer night, when Velebit mountains would light up with merry bonfires, and parties of young and old would celebrate the new season with wine and song. The bravest among them would risk a jump over the fire, to bring them happiness for the year to come. On the other side of the bridge, Paula stopped the car and stretched her limbs. She took a coke out of the cooler and drank thirstily. She would stop in Novalja to do some shopping. In summer, it was comfortable to enter the air-conditioned shops on hot evenings. Then she would go home and enjoy a good night's sleep. Tomorrow, she would drive to Zrče, one of the biggest beach discos in the Adriatic, famous with young people all around Europe. She should call some friends and tell them the good news. She would party and dance the night away, ecstatic with the most potent drugs of all – life. Oh, no more restraints and no more worries! She would enjoy every moment like it was the last one!

Later in the evening, she drove through the city of Novalja, along the *korso*, the promenade, where the huge *Jadrolinija* speedboat from Rijeka anchored. The crowds who had arrived on it, were dispersing in various directions. The drivers were all trying to spot their friends, so the traffic came to a snail's pace. All of a sudden, Paula could see a young woman, almost a girl, sitting on a big bollard, dialing and redialing on her mobile. Her annoyed gestures showed she could not get through to whomever she was dialing. There was a bright red baby trolley by her side. Paula recognized her friend Emilia, Slavko's niece, and stopped the car in the narrow space of the bus station. She quickly crossed the street and approached her.

"Hello, Emilia. Do you need a ride?"

The young woman's face lit up with a wonderful smile. Emilia jolted up, and, without a word jumped into Paula's embrace. Paula could smell milk on her plump body. She squeezed her old friend, not even two years younger than her and already a mother, in her arms. The little creature in the red trolley did not like that, and a shrill voice pierced the air. Emilia immediately let Paula go.

"Thank you. Let's go quickly, before the police arrests me for disturbing the peace with this screamer. She's a girl, only four months old, but when she's hungry, she's louder than Dario's engine."

"Oh, yeah, your baby girl! I am sorry. It slipped my mind altogether. I received your message while I was away in Holland. What's her name then?"

"Marinka, little Marina. But, let's move, Paula. We can talk in the car. Where did you park?"

As soon as the trolley moved, Marinka stopped crying and observed curiously the woman helping her mother. Her wide baby eyes intelligently appraised the thin, tall figure with hair as short as her father's. When Paula finally threw a look into the red trolley, Marinka welcomed her with a charming, toothless smile and sunrays in her eyes. Paula smiled back. A friendship was born.

"Here, at the bus station. Come!"

They loaded the car with numerous bags and backpacks.

"Have you come on the speedboat with all this junk, Emilia?"

"Oh, it's nothing. People are so friendly. And when Marinka starts her aria...they would do anything to shut her up, you know."

Among laughs and jokes, they took apart the trolley; they folded the frame with the wheels in the trunk, while the carrycot with the precious content landed on the backseat. They drove off in the cacophony of honks and beeps, for a bus had to stop in the middle of the road, blocking the traffic all together. Marinka's eyes were wide open in astonishment. As soon as they left the town centre, Emilia spoke up:

"Oh, I finished my last exam at the high school a week ago. Tomaž still has two exams until the summer term is over. He's studying medicine and it is going really well. He has passed every one of his tests and exams so far. These days, Zagreb is boiling with heat and Slavko has been ringing us every day to ask when we were coming to help him. The old man doesn't need our help, he has employees over the summer. I guess he needs our company. He's alone and bored. After the wedding feast, we promised to help him during the summer. On his calendar, summer started a month ago."

Paula remained silent. She understood the old man's loneliness. After she came back from Holland, unsure whether she would live or die, they sat together many evenings – Dario, Slavko and herself. They talked about Dario's new foundation and Slavko's plans to lure the young couple with the baby to spend summers with him. Although Slavko rarely mentioned it, she knew how eagerly he was waiting for Emilia and the baby.

"Why didn't Slavko come to pick you up then?"

"He rang me in the middle of the afternoon. I think we were passing by the island of Krk then. He said the restaurant was full to the last seat. Apparently the local fire brigade decided that after their monthly training, they would eat dinner at his place. His cook had come down with a cold or something, so there are only two of them there. He asked me to call a taxi, but you know the local taxi service. It's like calling the prime minister... You know they are there, but you cannot reach them. Luckily, you came by. I am so glad to see you, Paula. How are you? You look very well."

"Well, as of today, I am officially healthy for another year. It seems the operation in Holland worked out."

"When was your operation? Wasn't it in April?"

"It was on the fourth of April at noon."

"No, no, it can't be!"

"Yes. Precisely! It was the fourth of April. I will be celebrating the day as my second birthday... There are never enough reasons for good parties..."

Emilia leaned over to Paula and smacked her soundly on her cheek.

"Congratulations, my dear! You were reborn one hour later than my Marinka. I can't believe it, my friend and my daughter born on the same day! This calls for champagne!"

"I agree. I looked into Marinka's eyes, she smiled, and I knew immediately we were connected. We were thrown to the Earth from the same star! We're two space fairies! Two time travelers..."

"You'll hear a witch when you kill the engine. She's asleep now, but she's hungry. She'll scream the hell out of me before I feed her."

"We can stop in the shade by the road and you can feed her. When you come to the village, Slavko will want to hug you and cuddle her."

"Thank you. You're a miracle, Paula."

"Well, the miracle of Paula, love, here it is, in front of your very eyes."

They laughed heartily, remembering their childhood play when they used the huge dresses of Paula's *nona* to stage the Bible. Of course, Paula would always be Saint Paul, so the funny part was her blindness, during which she would bump into a piece of furniture or miss a sweet or, on the pier, clad in a huge beach towel, fall in the water. Before Emilia started to help out in

Slavko's restaurant and before Paula's illness, they used to spend a lot of time together.

"So, tell me, Emilia, how did it go? I mean the birth. Was it painful?"

"Not really. It was over in a couple of hours. Tomaž said my body is perfect for bearing babies. Well, maybe fat helps sometimes..."

"You're not fat, Emilia. Don't wish to be thin like me, for it is for all the wrong reasons. My elegance could be deadly..."

Emilia stroked her friend's hair tenderly. With teary eyes, she replied:

"Sorry, Paula. You really are as thin as a stick. Maybe you should come to Slavko's every day and we can have meals together. I can feed you both, my space fairies..."

The shrill cry from behind reminded them there was a hungry little girl in the cot. Paula pulled up and parked the car in the shade of a huge fig tree. Emilia pressed the baby to her breast. Immediately, smacking sounds replaced the whining. Paula felt blessed to witness the scene. She waited until Emilia started to speak.

"I must confess, Paula, the joy of feeding the baby, the milk which flows, releasing the tension in my breasts... It's almost like sex. It is such a powerful emotion, such a strong bond... I am glad Tomaž understands it and is not jealous, like many other men. As a future doctor, he knows how important it is for both of us."

"Yeah, you're a sight. Next time you will be the Holy Mother!"

They burst out in a laugh and Emilia's nipple jolted out of Marinka's mouth. Marinka cried in protest.

"Here, here, my darling... The dinner is served..."

Paula was still curious.

"Did it hurt a lot? I mean the contractions..."

"It hurt all right. Yet, you wouldn't believe how you cannot feel the pain. You're in another state, full of substances which your body releases into your blood to make you deliver. It wasn't too bad, and it went quickly. Never mind... tell me, rather, Paula, how are you? You said the doctors confirmed you were all right? So the Hague transplant worked?"

"Yes, it did. Obviously, it was the right bone marrow."

"Who was the donor?"

"Oh, they found a match in Holland. I mean my Dutch doctors."

"Amazing... Tomaž said it was very important the genes match, so they usually find a relative..."

"I have practically... you know, no relatives... Nona was, you know..."

"I know. I am very sorry about your *nona*. We all liked and respected Maria. It was so sad. You know, Dario received your message during our wedding party."

"I am sorry, if I spoilt it for you. . . I lost track of events in the hospital in Ljubljana. . . "

"Well, they only told us the following morning, my uncle and Dario. You didn't spoil anything. What could you do, anyway?"

Paula's look turned away, and her face reflected her grief. After her mother, who everybody still held for her grandmother, passed away, Paula was alone in the world. Her father was far away, although she went to see him again before she left Holland. She evaded the question of whether she would accept him as a father, for she was not sure about her feelings. She was not ready to deal with the matter and negotiated some more time to think about everything. Raškić showed understanding to her dilemma and he even joked that he was not going anywhere anyway. They separated with a hug, though, which was a huge step forward. Paula promised to come to visit him again, sometime in late summer.

"Here we go. . . let the air out of your tummy, my little gorger!"

The baby breathed heavily, sliding into a deep sleep after the strains of the voyage. Emilia put Marinka in the cot and took a drink of water out of her bag. Paula's look caught the cover page of the folded daily newspaper *Jutarnji list*. She saw a picture of the man who had become so familiar to her in the past few months. Her father, Raškić. . .

"Emilia, can I see the paper, please?"

Emilia looked at her friend surprised.

"Oh, yeah! I bought it in Rijeka, when Marinka was asleep and I was bored. There's nothing in it. . . "

The paleness of her friend's face stopped Emilia's words. There was something so painful in her protruding cheekbones, something so sad in her huge brown eyes. Paula staggered, and Emilia caught her frail body in her arms.

"What is it, Paula? Are you feeling sick?"

"No, no. . . let me sit down for a minute."

Paula slipped to the rocky ground. She was unable to drag herself to the bench where Emilia was feeding Marinka. Emilia squatted by her side.

"Paula, shall I call the ambulance?"

Paula looked up into her friend's scared eyes. Tears began to slide down her ashen cheeks. She shook her head.

"No, no, Emilia. . . I don't need a doctor. Just give me a minute. . . "

Emilia took a cotton tissue out of her bag and damped it with water. She pressed it on Paula's chin and wiped her cheeks tenderly. Paula was sobbing, first softly, almost inaudibly, then, her cries began to shake her body with pangs of distress. She gripped her friend's hand.

"My Emilia, you don't know...you don't know who I am...you don't know who my mother was...and my father. He's dead, you see..."

Emilia was going through the facts she knew about Paula's parents: they died during the war, and her grandmother brought her up. Why was Paula so upset so many years after the war? Then she remembered the paper and took it in her hands. "Jovan Raškić – a fair judge in his own trial?" Under the headline, a subtitle printed in bold read: "The butcher of Krajina hung himself in the Hague Hilton yesterday."

"Was this man responsible for your parents' death, Paula?"

Unable to speak, Paula was just shaking her head. She continued to sob for a long time before Emilia could hear her say softly:

"Emilia, this man was my father. He donated the bone marrow."

Emilia could not understand what Paula was trying to tell her.

"Who was your father, Paula?"

Paula wiped her eyes and blew her nose. Then, she looked at Emilia, holding her hand.

"Jovan Raškić was my father. My *nona* was not my grandmother. She was my mother. I am their unlucky lucky daughter. A daughter of the war...I must tell you..."

Emilia sat down by her friend. She put her arm around Paula's shoulder and kissed her salty cheeks.

"Tell me, Paula, tell me everything. We have another three hours before Marinka demands her late supper. We have time to talk."

Paula's gaze embraced the horizon on the east, where the dark shades of Velebit were threatening the waves below. She breathed in deeply and stood up.

"Let's sit on the bench. We don't want ants and insects in our clothes, do we?"

Emilia followed her friend to the bench. They sat down. In a low, clear voice, Paula started to tell the story of her mother, the war, the voluntary or involuntary love affair of her mother, and her birth. So many questions welled up during their conversation. It was time to sweep away the dust and ban the shadows of the past. It was time to make space for the sun. Sun meant life. Sun brought warmth and love...

* * *

"War is merely a general term, a collective noun for so many individual stories," wrote Slavenka Drakulić in her beautiful and

horrific novel S.. A week ago, Paula had finished reading the
account of a young teacher, S., a daughter of a Muslim father
and a Serbian mother, who was imprisoned, raped and tortured,
left with an unwanted child. The images of the women's camp,
their suffering and terrible fate somewhere in Bosnia were so vivid
and so compellingly accurate that they could not leave her mind.
She kept digging in her mother's notes, cracking the passwords of
her computer files and searching for a testimony of whether her
mother had undergone the same fate as S. from the novel, had
been subjected to the same horrible ordeals as so many others.
Paula wanted to know whether her mother had told the truth
or she had been raped. The fact of fatherhood was one hundred percent sure, but other questions were opening in front of
Paula's eyes, like tiny ice cracks on a frozen lake, which get wider
and wider, exposing the cold, dark water beneath. Despite all
the sweet words said and written by her late father and despite
her mother's account of the story, Paula knew she would live in
doubts about her conception for the rest of her life. Was she a
fruit of love or a by-product of a crime?

"They loved each other. This is what I am going to believe
and this is what I am going to tell the world."

With terror, Paula realized she spoke her thought aloud. It
did not matter, for she was alone in the house which once had
been her home, the sanctuary, where she could always run into
the warm embrace of her mother. Since last autumn, the house
was empty and its cold walls cried with silence. She should put
on some music...

Paula looked up from her desk into the sunshine outside. The
heavy wooden shutters were closed. It was a lovely autumn day.
The sun shone from the sky weakly, like a tired lover, who had
spent his passionate kisses, his hot energy and warm embraces,
and lay afterwards stretched over the bed of the world, exhausted,
gently caressing the back of his mistress Earth. The rocks and
pebbles at the shore seemed more grey and yellow than white, the
bushes rather blue than green. The silvery leafed olive trees, their
naked branches devoid of fruits after a meager harvest, shook
gently in the soft breeze. After the fluorescence of spring and
summer, the colors were subdued in the diffused afternoon light,
as though autumn wanted to bury all year's secrets deeper under
the velvet surface of the sea.

Paula was finishing marking up a text, which she held printed
in front of her. It was a long personal statement, a confession of
a young Dalmatian woman. The language was accurate and rational, yet the facts, even though stated laconically, desperately
dramatic. The pathos in the structure of the sentences was inten-
tional, her outcry targeted precisely. She was inviting journalists
to Perovica at her own cost. They would spend two days in one
of the loveliest hotels of the Adriatic for free, just for the fact that

they had received an invitation in early August and responded to
it. She included the journalists of the most important mass media
from the territory of the former Yugoslavia. Over two hundred
people wanted to come, so she had to make a thorough selection.
The chosen ones had checked in during the day, and she saw many
of them strolling happily to the beach, as the weather was sunny
and the sea still warm in that last week of October.

However attractive her offer was, Paula knew that most of
them would regret having come. What is more, they would feel
betrayed and angry. For it would not be a free lunch. She would
shake and shock them. She would cause them pain greater than
torture. Studying their work in the papers and on-line media, on
the television, or listening to their radio reports, she took into
account that many of her visiting journalists were cynics. They
liked to address their public as people who knew better, who got
paid to criticize everything and everybody. A good journalist is
always skeptical and aloof, no matter what the content matter.
She expected that the dry professional cynicism would disappear
from their faces as soon as she would play some films. The first
scene involved a baby... She vomited when she had found it on
the internet. With patience, Paula collected the atrocities of the
last Balkan war and pasted them into her horror show, integrating
the narrative, the music and the pictures... In the end, she hired
a movie editor to patch her speech and images together.

She wanted to witness hot tears in their eyes and heavy lumps
in their throats. Her multi-media show was switching from her
personal story to the chronology of events including the lukewarm
reaction of the international peace keepers, cowards, hypocrites,
who should have worked hard day and night to prevent the killing.
Oh, yes, they did work hard, yet only later, when there were more
opportunities for them to fill their pockets with bloody profits.

While she was designing her presentation, Paula had felt like
a pervert. It was crazy to compose a collection of horrible video
clips and shocking photographs. However, it was necessary. She
needed to reach the media's readership, their viewers and listen-
ers. It was a cry to the world. Paula was convinced that, like her
father had done before his death, the people in the three states of
Croatia, Bosnia, and Serbia needed to start the process of repentance; they should take apart their collective guilt layer by layer,
like an ugly old house, and after having atomized their suffering,
they should start to build a new, better life together. They should
condemn their manipulative leaders and stop clinging to their sick
fundamentalist ideas. The endless stupidity of conflicts and the
centuries old hatred with roots in different religions and cultures
should disappear in the reality of the new European stars. What
else could they do? The lands were not moving anywhere. The
churches with their imams and priests would continue to dominate their hills. Better be friends, like the villagers of Baljvine,

than enemies like the citizens of Mostar, where the famous bridge, connecting two cultures for centuries, collapsed in one short day. Paula understood that her existence, the story of her parents and the fact that she had overcome her fatal sickness could symbolize this new cohabitation, this new hope of peace. Moreover, she was physical proof of it.

She stood up and went to the mirror in the bathroom. She combed her hair and put some make up on her face. Since spring, her dark curly hair grew back, and day by day, her body filled with flesh. She was almost satisfied with her image and wanted to ban from her memory her bony grey face gasping for air like a wounded soldier on a stretcher. Still, she had moments of deep doubt and utter confusion. Her mind was like an abandoned minefield, where she could walk peacefully among green grass and colorful flowers for weeks until she chanced upon a memory so painful that it almost blew her brain out. She missed her mother, her loving hand, her soft voice and tender kisses. All she had was her endless stories. . . stories which she doubted more and more were based on true facts and research. For one of them, her own, namely, she found firm proof – her father. Would she ever be capable of forgiving her parents? Who was she anyway? Did she have a right to judge two old people in the whirlwind of war?

Not nearly a month ago, Paula accepted her father's heritage. She decided to revive his estates in Krajina. However, after having read her father's will, she took some more decisions. He had set no conditions under which she was to accept his belated gift, whatsoever. It was her love for life and her deep gratitude for it that made her act.

After Paula discovered that her father had committed suicide on the same day that for the first time in two years her medical tests were positive, she was crushed by remorse and sorrow. Her strengths were gone, and for days in row, she did nothing but shed tears. No matter how much Emilia tried to console her and how many times she came to her house to invite her to a lunch, a dinner or simply to a walk with little Marinka in the cot, Paula closed her pain in her four walls and dwelt in the land of shadows. She sank in ifs. . . What would have happened if her mother had told her who they were earlier. . . if she had found her half-brothers. . . If she had planned to visit her father earlier. . . If she had simply accepted him not only as her donor, but also as her father. . . One grey morning, while the sky was low and dark and the clouds were about to burst with rain, Emilia put a stop to Paula's depression. She came to her door with baby bags and Marinka in a trolley and simply said:

"I must help out Slavko the whole day. The kitchen needs a thorough cleaning or the inspection will close him down. Please, Paula, look after Marinka!"

Paula stared at the show on her doorstep, her eyes red and

swollen with tears, her face grey and pale like during her hospital stays. She faintly objected:

"But how can I feed her? Do you have diapers? I have never changed one in my life..."

Emilia smiled kindly and said in a firm voice.

"That is the only thing I will come to do. When she's hungry, ring me on my mobile. I'll come within minutes and give her the breast. The rest is your responsibility."

"Still, I don't..."

"Sorry, Paula, I need your help. Life calls. Marinka might be a bit peevish this morning. You know, babies hate rain and hate to stay indoors..."

"Emilia, wait!"

But her friend turned her back on Paula, running down the road, leaving her alone with the baby girl, who curiously opened her sleepy eyes. When Marinka saw Paula's sad face, she frowned and her tiny, toothless mouth squinted in an ugly grimace. She let out a piercing cry, at the sound of which Paula could see Emilia shiver. Still, the young mother went on and Paula had to do something. She took the baby in her arms and cradled her softly. When she next looked into her eyes, Marinka's face was forming into a hesitating smile, her rosy cheeks wet with tears. Without another thought, Paula smiled back.

Her days of despair were over. The little sunshine banished her dark depression better than any therapist could. All her love, deceived ideals and subdued warmth, held back during the numerous hospital ordeals, lit up with little Marinka's smile and laughter. They were playing during long walks along the beach while Emilia served the tourists streaming into the little village in masses typical of July. Until August, Paula almost forgot she had had a mother and a father who left her an orphan twice – once with their death, twice with her origins, which she was still hiding from the world. Only her friend Emilia knew about her mother's secret war affair.

Then, a formal blue letter from the local court of the municipality of Knin invited her to a hearing. She dutifully came and received her father's will. There was nobody else present at the hearing. The atmosphere was laden with doubts and suspicions. It was not every day that the court in Knin dealt with their most notorious citizen. In secret, Paula had hoped that Raškić's daughters or his wife might come to claim their share and maybe meet her. Maybe, they would not hate her and she could find a relative at last and stop being so alone. But they did not. The Croatian judge read for the protocol that the wife and the daughters, living under the family name Krajić, Tina, Andrea, Martha and Marijana, in the state of New York, America, had been located and informed according to the regular procedure. In a written reply, they had formally given up the inheri-

tance. They also wrote that they would never set their foot on the
Croatian soil again, and that they reject anything from anybody
within Croatian borders. In their letter, which was stamped by
an American notary, they added that the heritage can go to any
other descendant, which was next in line. They skillfully avoided
writing down Jovan Raškić's name. As though the evil should
not be named, for it could take form again. Paula held their reaction for too radical. What were they thinking? He would not
rise from the dead, would he? Thus the judge confirmed that the
inheritance procedure was legally approved in Croatia, so that
her father's estate could be passed on to her according to his
last will and the medical testimony of their relation in due time,
unless any other relative appealed to the court within the legal
deadline. She accepted and signed her name on the line daughter.
She could feel all the eyes boring in her back while she slid the
pen over the paper. What were they thinking? For them she was
an outcast, a little *Chetnik*. Her cheeks filled with red shame, it
took her a while to scribble her name. Yet, when she looked up
from the document, her mind was firm. She would show all those
hypocrites, war criminals and phonies! She would stop hiding in
her shell, she would tell them all... She took the folder with the
papers including a sealed envelope addressed to her and written
in her father's hand. Another message from beyond...

Back on Pag, in the loneliness of her mother's office, among
walls filled with never-ending volumes of books, she was reading
her father's letter. It was short and to the point, not asking for
anything from her except to find a way to keep for the future
generations the memory of Marica and Jovan, the two enemies
who loved and feared each other, the parents who failed to give
her, Paula, a happy, untroubled life. He wrote in his letter that
he was dying a happy man, knowing that she would find a way
to use the estates at Knin for a good cause, for she is a good
person. The fact that she was reading his letter meant she had
made peace with him in a way, and he thanked her for it.

A while ago, Paula had stopped shedding tears and feeling
sorry for herself. Like both her parents, she was a person of action. She contacted the Knin Tourist Office and tried to hire a
local guide to visit her father's lands and find out more about
the old medical family Raškić. Yet, nobody was available for
weeks. Their excuses went from the high season to the work in
the fields despite a fat euro sum she was offering. Then, she ordered a printout from the Land Registry and took the head of
the food purchases at Perovica Hotel, Silke Wahring, to Knin.
Using the prints from the register and a sophisticated GPS navigator, they inspected the fields together. They were bare and
obviously had not brought crops of wheat, corn or potatoes for
more than a decade. To their dismay, some of the nicest patches
were actually minefields from the war, which nobody cared to

clear. It was the field of an enemy, of a Serbian. Why should the community of Knin be spending good money on clearing the fields of a war criminal? Paula wondered what would happen if a child accidentally stepped on a mine: would it be Serbian or Croatian? She made a mental note to hire professionals to clear all of the Knin's minefields, regardless of whose lands they were or who had planted the sneaky killers in the ground. She should have enough money on her mother's private accounts to pull it off. Silke also noted that on some patches, herds of goats or sheep were grazing nonchalantly, as though they would pace a no man's land. That was compliments of friendly neighbors. Paula realized that she would never be able to live or even spend time in Knin. The memory of her father and the Krajina soldiers would not die in her lifetime. She wondered how her neighbors on Pag would react if they found out whose daughter she was.

Silke took various samples of the soil in glass tubes. Diligently, she also took photographs of every strip of land and the country-side. They picked flowers and cut plants for analyses, and above all, Silke made meticulous notes of everything. Paula trusted her agricultural knowledge and experience. She was sure that this time next year they would be sowing.

The house of the family Raškić in the centre of Knin was deserted and literally falling apart. They did not need the key to enter the hall, as the door was open. There was no furniture inside. Dirty old blinds, which used to be dark green, now all shades of grey and brown, shut out the summer sun. Still, they could smell human excrements and piss in every corner, where piles of plastic bags mixed with used needles. Evidently, local junkies made use of the house for their trips into oblivion. What would Paula do with that ruin?

* * *

The tables in the restaurant of the hotel Perovica formed a circle, with a podium in the middle. Everything was ready for the late afternoon press conference. From several hundred applicants to a free weekend, she chose some seventy journalists from all over Croatia, Bosnia, two from Belgrade and a few from Slovenia. She had read their articles and looked at their footages. On every table, there was a PR package with a huge monograph edition on the island of Pag, a wonderful coffee table book on her home island. She bought several hundreds of the expensive book, some copies also to thank the most faithful guests of the hotel, so the publisher was grateful and helped her print a tiny brochure with The story of Angela Bekić during the last Balkan war. Although names under which Paula had known her mother were confusing, nona Maria Perić, Angela Bekić and Marica Čekić, that was the true story of her mother's life. Names were irrelevant. As an appendix, Paula added what she had found out about her mother

since their arrival on Pag and everything she had found out about
her father, including a summary of their conversation in the ICTY
detention unit in the Hague and his last letter. She hesitated as
to whether she should include some of her mother's historical stories and genealogical notes. However, she abandoned the idea as
it might put her message out of perspective. There would be another time to open her mother's research to the world. She added
a CD-ROM with a richly designed multi-lingual presentation of
the hotel Perovica, which included video shootings of the famous
season parties on the beach. All texts and the rare family photos
were loaded on the disc to ease the work of the journalists later.
While she would be reading and speaking, she wanted all eyes
and all ears open to her message.

The microphones were tested and the cacophony of words,
mostly in *Serbo-Croatian*, the language all three nations had
learnt at school, and which died out not so many years ago. In
a slow, melodic voice, as though it was a fairy tale time, Paula
started her speech and presentation. By the time the screen burnt
with the bloody images of war, the silence in the room was complete, the attention perfect. For days Paula rehearsed in front of
the mirror so as not to cry during her speech. Her voice cracked
when she put up the picture of her mother and, with the next
click, of her father. Be it not for her own photograph from her
most sick days, with her head bald from chemotherapy, explaining
her diagnosis and chances to survive, she would not have made it.
Still, her voice was firm when during the silent movie presenting
unspeakable horrors from the Bosnian and Croatian fronts, the
mass graves at Srebrenica, prisoners at Manjača and wounded
children in Vukovar, she read from her father's last letter:

*While you are reading this letter, I am at peace at last. My soul
is free from all pain and evil. It is free from my sinful, cruel body.
For, my lovely Paula, I realized I must die to kill the evil. My
judges were too mild and the twenty some years in prison in The
Hague, where I might live in comfort, better than many a victim
at home in Croatia, could not kill the evil. It would not be just. I
had to do it myself. I am sure your mother would understand me,
and my only regret is that we cannot be buried together. Yet, I
could not burden your days with such a request. We were apart
before. . .*
*I am dead, but the evil continues to thrive. I killed one man, yet
there are so many others who, under the pretext of political or
religious demands, start the vicious circle of wars. They say they
follow God, yet they pray to Him with blood on their hands.
They say they want Heaven for their fellow men, yet they are
sending them to Hell, to the battle fields, where they are but the
tools of radical ideas, soldiers, tortured captives, raped beings,
devoid of all humanity. They say they want a better world for*

our children, yet they bury mines in the green pastures, where children lose arms, legs, their young, precious lives. What is the future of evil? How can we stop it?

My dear child, I do not know how, for I am the evil. The Devil has lived in my body and fed on my flesh, every day, for more than twenty years. I cannot change and become a human being, no matter how I keep trying. I will be a war criminal, an ICTY case forever. It is better I should not be... But you, you will know how to fight the evil, you with your youth and innocence. By overcoming your hatred for me and by accepting my gift and my lands, you were strong enough to face the evil. Oh, you are a brave girl, a brave girl indeed, just like your mother, who I love deeply and think of her in these last moments of my life.

The last image, an ancient olive tree, taken on the hill behind the hotel at dawn, filled the screen, and the audience took the moment to breathe up.

"So, ladies and gentlemen, one woman, Paula Perić Raškić, is saved. I live. What about the others?"

A man in a velvet jacket in the first row looked at Paula:

"What do you mean?"

"I mean all those silent and abandoned victims of aggression and war who are dying as we speak. I mean the fields, where instead of wheat, mines thrive, to be harvested by women and children. I mean those silent men who instead of providing for their families maintain their weapons, instead of caressing their wives are still handling the guns. I mean all those silent, invisible victims of war who get their moments of fame during the evening news when the infotainment industry distributes their suffering worldwide. Who knows or cares about them? What can we do to help them?"

The silence in the room was so thick it could be cut with a knife. All eyes evaded Paula's questioning look, finding interest in irrelevant details like chair legs or lamp holders. What could they really do? Why is the young woman haunting them? Paula knew her questions would remain unanswered, and her appeal impossible to account for. She sighed:

"I know I have tricked you into witnessing something terrible. You have been trying to forget, as victims in Croatia and Bosnia are trying to forgive. Please help them. Please help me to spread my message across our world, across the Balkans. It cannot be done in one single day, but we have to start somewhere."

The crowd was silent. In spite of the fact that their professional distance was broken and their cynical views crushed, they were just a bunch of journalists in the face of gigantic tasks. They felt sorry for the tormented young woman in front of them. They were not without feelings. They were without impact. They were as helpless as little children in the face of all the dark forces prop-

agating wars around the world. Those forces, the four riders of
the Apocalypse – pestilence, war, famine and death, were moving the world along with love, peace, abundance and birth. Paula
watched her guests. She said:

"You can hold this world together like grains of sand hold
the shore together against the wicked waves. Your grains are
words. You're writers, journalists, use them! Thank you for your
attention. The buffet will open in a minute. Enjoy your stay at
Perovica!"

Nobody moved. They sat still pondering. Maybe new projects
were being thought of and new articles planned. A woman in the
middle slowly stood up.

"One question, please, Miss Perić. I am Stana Treško from
Večernji list. Do you intend to publish a book about your
mother's life?"

The woman's voice was shaky, her dark brown eyes blurred
by tears. It was obvious she was deeply taken by Paula's story.
Paula looked her in the eyes and took her time with the answer.
Stana was one of the most famous and sharp women journalists
in Croatia.

"Well, my mother was a great historical researcher and writer.
She left behind meters of folders with notes and books on the specific periods in Dalmatian history. She was particularly interested
in the women's question across the ages – she has notes going back
to the Greek settlements on Hvar, Korčula and Mljet. I am sorry
to say I have not inherited her gift for the written word."

There was a huge, bear like Slovenian man from Dnevnik in
the first row, his name on the press card read – Janez Fric Sone-
man. He rose slowly to speak up:

"Miss Perić, what you have told us cannot be just life, it
is more. It is literature. You have accepted your father and
you have projects to help the victims of the war in Krajina. I
honestly think you should publish your mother's heritage, too.
I know there will be readers in Slovenia. I cannot imagine that
Croatians would not be interested in what you have to say."

Miss Stana Treško dried her teary eyes with a tissue. Her
head lifted high, she spoke in a clear voice:

"With your cooperation, Miss Perić, this can be the first book
I am going to write."

Paula looked up, her gaze travelled through the window, over
the blue sea, over the bright line of the horizon.

"Anything, my friend, anything... We should do everything
to prevent war. No war no more!"

Appendix

Afterword

Dalmatia, the first book of the Balkan Trilogy (which in the second book will travel north to Istria and Slovenia, and in the third east to Serbia, Kosovo and Macedonia), is dedicated to all those who for years have followed the headlines from the Bosnian war without completely acknowledging what terrible individual suffering each film or photography meant in the lives of its protagonists. It was just a moment in the infotainment industry. I was one of them: the silent and the indifferent. After Slovenia declared independence and the Yugoslav Federal Army left our lands in autumn 1991, my only concern was my young family – a toddler son and an unborn daughter. Yet, the images stayed in my memory, haunting me like an unpaid debt. Questions challenged my conscience: Why did I not help? Where was my humanity as people suffered in Croatia and in Bosnia? Where was I, a compassionate woman? Later, when my publishing house published important books on the world conflicts, I somehow found comfort in the fact that I was doing more than the rest.

However, when I embarked on my new career as a novelist, I had to write my first book about the terrible conflicts, which have been residing in my soul for a decade. I know my writing is not enough. I can only hope that such books as mine can shed light on the terrible consequences of wars. For, weapons have not shut up; as I write, thousands of Syrians are fleeing from violence and living through a hell just like Sarajevo or Dubrovnik in the nineties.

Apart from sources in the bibliography, I have been to the museums along the coast and on the islands, I have sailed the stormy waves of the channels and experienced the warmth and sophisticated nature of the Dalmatian people. Although I have kept to the historical facts, I sometimes had to change things to suit better the story, things like the orphanage in Dubrovnik, established some fifty years later than in the book. Otherwise, the reader can rely on finding the places as they once were still today.

My thanks go to many friends from all around the world who have encouraged me and helped me with advice. I thank also my family, my husband Tadej and my editor Urška Sešek, who were my first critical readers.

Tanja Tuma, May 2013

Historical background

The history of Croatia and Dalmatia is too vast to deal with in such a work of fiction. Hence, I took the liberty to chose only a few places and times, which could enrapture the reader in the atmosphere of wonderful nature and rich civilization.

The Ancient Greeks in Dalmatia, 6th century B.C.

In spring 2011, the City Museum of Ljubljana hosted an exhibition, where exhibits proved that ancient Greeks conquered the island of Korčula and formed their first colony in the Eastern Adriatic in the 6th century B.C. The existence of the Ancient Greek settlements on Hvar, Vis and the findings of the pottery used in male initiation rituals on Palagruža culminated with the discovery of the famous Apoxyomenos near the island of Mali Lošinj. The Croatian Conservation Institute in Zagreb revived the athlete to the present glory and put it on show in the Zagreb Mimara Museum. Having read Erica Jong's wonderful book Sappho's Leap gave me the idea for Agape, a midwife and healer, who fights for her position in the new colony. I have read historical accounts and consulted sources as to Agape's professional knowledge as well as the society structures in the Greek colonies.

Dalmatia within the Roman Empire, 4th century A.D.

Until the present day, Diocletianus (A.D. 244 – 311) remains the most famous politician born on Dalmatian shores. His military skills, his administrative power and cunning rule prevented the decline of the Roman Empire for several decades, if not centuries. As much as I could read about him as a man gave me the frame for his fragile state in the year when he died. It is unsure even today whether he died of natural causes or had been poisoned. In any case, the fish aquaculture on the island of Šolta is a sure fact. Despite his monstrous image as the persecutor of Christians, Diocletian's main character traits were his reason and his sharp intelligence. His main aim was the preservation of the Roman Empire at all cost. Thus, his measures were radical. The rest of the characters are fictitious, although they display the colorful traits of the declining Roman society.

The Republic of Ragusa (today Dubrovnik), 1312 A.D.

In A.D. 1312, Dubrovnik was formally under the Venetian rule in spite of the fact that the only Venetian official was the Rector (Doge) himself. The social structure of the Dubrovnik society was complex and advanced. A handful of old noble families controlled the politics and business, and consequently maintained the power throughout the Venetian rule. Harris writes in his book, Dubrovnik, of a conflict in 1226, when Venice demanded Dubrovnik to pay more taxes. As a form of insurance, the Venetians asked the *Ragusans* to send twenty hostages from noble families to Venice. Silence was all they got and the Ragusa-based Venetian count Griovanni Dandolo, (probably expelled from the city) returned to Venice in 1231. In 1358, the Venetian suzerainty over Dubrovnik was over, and the republic shone in its independent glory once again. The main success of the Ragusan merchants lay in their trading equally with East and West, in their advanced development of business and finance, and last but not least, in their innovative shipbuilding techniques. Their carracks (replicas now sail the Dubrovnik bay every summer) were some of the most successful sea vessels of the time, venturing not only around the Mediterranean, but also on long voyages in the Atlantic Ocean. In addition to sailing the seas, they pursued wide spread consular activities around Europe and authored business innovations such as cargo insurance. Yet, nothing could save them from one of the most successful pirate communities, positioned between Venice and Ragusa, where stormy winds in the channels brought richly loaded ships in danger. At Omiš, a famous pirate leader, Knez Kačić, founded his state-like community. The story revolves around two worlds completely apart; the Ragusan world, founded on old rights and traditions, and, the new, violent (criminal) world of the pirates. Old Dubrovnik chronicles, which are well preserved and subject to on-going study, give us insight in this money driven society of the noble families dominating the life within the thick walls. The names in the book have existed, not all at the same time, but all characters as well as their actions are again product of author's imagination.

Bosnia and the Neretva Delta, A.D. 1501

Looking at the hinterland of Dubrovnik during the Middle Ages, we soon find major changes in Bosnia, which in 1501 had been under the Ottoman rule for more than a century. After the violent Battle of Kosovo in 1389, in which Serbia lost most of its territory to the Ottoman Empire, and many years of plundering the new lands, the Turks settled down around the river Neretva. They started to exploit the lands they had conquered, bringing with them an entirely new religion and culture – the Islam. New crops, modern irrigation systems and many other innovations in administration, architecture and society mark the era of prosperity. Although, today Islam and its radicals have come under suspicion as to their tolerance, the old chronicles report that the early Ottoman governors of Bosnia were broad-minded men and persecuted neither the old Bosnian Christian beliefs nor the Orthodox people. One of the best reads in this aspect is The Bridge on the Drina by so far the only Nobel Literature Prize Winner of the Balkans, Ivo Andrić. The conflict in my book evolves between the three religions and four ethnicities, yet wise women and strong men cunningly deal with it within the walls of the harem. The Neretva delta story also contains also one of the most poetic characters in the book, the Eunuch Ibrahim.

Island of Brač, Monastery Blaca, A.D. 1916 – 1917

During the Great War (1914 – 1918), the island of Brač was under Austro-Hungarian rule. In an aggressive pro-war campaign, Italians claimed back all the lands, which had been under either Roman or Venetian rule in past centuries, including Dalmatia with its islands. When Italy attacked the Austro-Hungarian Monarchy at Isonzo, today the river of Soča, in Slovenia, one of the bloodiest war fields in Europe devoured more than one million lives and devastated the country. During the communist rule (1945 – 1991), there were few accounts of the atrocities during the WW1. Yet, the people around the former front line on the Isonzo, have lived with the mines and craters, remains of the shells and bones for decades. It was an imperialistic war and socialist Yugoslavia had nothing to do with it. In the last decades, many books were published on this topic. The War Museum in Kobarid (Caporetto) is one of the most visited tourist attraction in the country. It offers an impartial account of human suffering on both sides of the line: the Italian and the Austro-Hungarian. The action of our story is set on the Dalmatian island of Brač, the front and its draft haunting the population from a distance. At the Blaca monastery, its last prior set up one of the best well known observatories in this part of Europe. Although the Miličević uncle and nephew play a role of impartial witnesses in the family drama of their cook, they are the very heart of Blaca. Even today, the monastery is on the mailing lists of the most important astrological magazines around the world, all thanks to Nikola Miličević, a famous Dalmatian scientist and astrologist.

The fall of Yugoslavia, 1991

After Josip Broz Tito's death in 1984, the socialist federal state with its motto of brotherhood and unity among three religions (Catholic, Orthodox and Muslim) and seven nations, maintained under Tito's iron fist, started slowly but surely to disintegrate. Tito's successors were weak political leaders and could not cope with Yugoslavia's new drive for national independence and economic liberalism. Slovenia, Croatia and Macedonia declared independence in 1991. Serbians panicked seeing the new constitution of the independent Republic Croatia, and the Plitvice Lakes Incident was one of the first armed conflicts between Serbia and Croatia. In 1991, the Serbians historically living in Croatia's region of Krajina formed an unrecognized state of Republika Srpska Krajina, declaring its loyalty to Yugoslavia, which at that point meant today's states of Serbia, Montenegro and Kosovo. In between, there were vast Croatian Catholic territories and the whole of Bosnia. As soon as the Milošević's destructive ideas of Great Serbia found ground in the new entity of Croatian Serbians, they started ethnic cleansing of the Catholic areas with the aid of the former federal army. For four years, the heart of the Balkans saw continuing military actions, also against the Muslims in Bosnia. Only some hundreds of kilometers away from the western European capitals a cruel war was burning. Slovenia got away with little damage, yet, Slovenians are ashamed to admit that we have profited from our neighbors' and former brothers' hardships; according to some sources our politicians had been selling weapons to Bosnian Muslims and made a fortune on it. That and many other sins prevent Slovenians from forming a just and balanced society, of which you will be able to read in the sequel to this book. The main protagonist, Maria, is at the same time a victim and a profiteer of the war. Despite probable similarities to real persons, all personalities are fictitious.

Until the present day, all states emerging from former Yugoslavia have been suffering under the destructive politics and poor economies, which had already lagged behind in the five decades of communism. Corruption, wild privatization, destruction of industry, poor observance of human rights and freedom of media as well as terrible greed and thirst after the commercial goods from the West have moved our societies into a hostile rat race. Maybe Paula, Tomaž, and Emilia, three young people with honest hearts will be able to cast aside the burdens of their parents and start a new, better world without wars.

Slovenia joined the NATO and the European Union in 2004. Euro as a currency was introduced in 2007 (by the way, the third currency after the Yugoslav dinar and the Slovenian tolar in my lifetime so far), and it became member of the OECD in 2010. Like the rest of the world, it now finds itself in an economic crisis, which is shaking the pillars of democracy. Croatia is to enter the European Union in July 2013, yet, it has big debts and economic problems, too. With its beautiful coast of Istria and Dalmatia, the country should prosper quickly; hopefully not at the expense of its population.

Bibliography

1. John M. Riddle, Eve's Herbs: A history of contraception and abortion in the West, Harvard University Press, 1999.
2. Stephen Williams, Diocletian and the Roman Recovery, Routledge, reprint 1996.
3. Robin Harris, Dubrovnik, a history, SAQI, London, 2003.
4. Noel Malcolm, Bosnia, a Short History, Pan Books, 1994.
5. Mark Thomson, The White War, Basic Books, 2010.
6. Srečko Kosovel, Man in a Magic Square, Mobitel d.d., Ljubljana 2004.
7. Hans Pölzer, Trije dnevi pekla na Soči, Založba Karantanija, 2011.
8. Henrik Tuma, Izza velike vojne, Branko Nova Gorica, 1994.
9. Juraj Batelja, Svećenička pustinja Blaca, Biskupija hvarsko-bračko-viška, Zagreb 1992.
10. Chantal Louis: Monika Hauser, Začenjam vedno znova, Založba Tuma, 2009.
11. Slavenka Drakulić, S. a Novel about the Balkans, Penguin Books, 1999.

* * *

Above is a list of books which can lead one further in the exploration of specific historical periods in Dalmatia and Bosnia. During my research, I have consulted many media, printed and on-line, and was grateful to have found many high quality documentaries on You tube. My special thanks go to Ljubljana City Museum, which inspired the first historical chapter with its wonderful exhibition The Ancient Greeks in Croatia in 2011, and to the Dubrovnik Maritime Museum, Mr. Djivo Bašić, who kindly helped me find out more about shipbuilding in Dubrovnik. The last sad, yet indispensible source worth mentioning is the home page of the International Criminal Tribunal for the Former Yugoslavia (www.icty.org), where I was able to read and follow the trials and the legal epilogue of the war on-line.

Glossary

academia in Ancient Greece, a group of students, mostly men, gathered around a teacher, e.g. Plato. The notion that the famous Greek poet Sappho held such an academy at Lesbos is still widely believed.

Agricola governor of Cappadocia, Lesser Armenia, who in A.D. 316 persecuted St. Blaise and Christians under the orders of the Roman Emperor Licinius.

amphora Latin; plural amphorae; a typical antique container used to transport liquids or wheat on ships.

ankhon old Greek; angina, inflammation of the throat.

Anne Turkish; mother, mom.

apotheca old Greek; repository of medicine; pharmacy.

apoxyomenos old Greek; athlete or scraper; the motive was particularly popular with ancient sculptors and represents an athlete who, after the race, scrapes oil, sand and sweat from his body with a strigil, a small, curved piece of metal. The Croatian Apoxyomenos is one of the most complete specimen in the world, and represents the classic ideal of male beauty.

arnica Latin; famous healing plant used all over Europe since ancient times for ointments and pomades.

As-Salamu 'alayka! Arabic; "Peace be upon you".

auctoritas Latin; authority. It meant more than just certain judicial, administrative and military power in the Ancient Rome; "auctoritas principiis" was the moral authority of the Emperor, which included not only political and ruling power, but also his personal dignity and wisdom.

aureus Latin; plural aurei; gold coins in the Roman Empire; at nowadays prices, one aureus would be worth approximately 100$.

avia Latin; grandmother.

baba Croatian; grandmother.

barba Croatian; an old, respected man, e.g. former sea captain.

barbarophonos old Greek; barbaric, person who does not speak proper Greek, who babbles.

basta Italian; enough, that will do.

Battle of Neretva a famous partisan movie shot in 1969 in the socialist Yugoslavia. The production was heavily sponsored by the state and personally endorsed by the president, Josip Broz Tito. Thus, many international stars like Orson Welles, Sergei Bondarchuk, Yul Brynner and Anthony Dawson acted in it. In 1970 it was nominated for the 42nd Academy Awards.

Battle of Sutjeska a famous partisan movie from 1973, in which the role of the president of Yugoslavia, Josip Broz Tito, was staged by Richard Burton. Tito loved movies and his latest biographers reveal his numerous friendships with famous film stars including Richard Burton and Elisabeth Taylor, who had visited him in his residence on the isles of Brioni a couple of times.

bellum iustum Latin; a just war; Catholicism defines a just war when force is used against an agressor when all other means fail to defend the lives and property of the people under attack, when the prospect of success ending the suffering is realistic and the force used would not cause bigger damage as the initial conflict. Read more under The Just War Theory.

Bene Italian; very well.

bey Turkish; lord, in the Ottoman Empire governor of a province; today; mister.

bimaristan Persian; hospital in the medieval Islamic world.

bonaca Croatian; the absence of all winds and waves at sea.

Bračani plural, Croatian; the inhabitants of the island of Brač, which is the biggest island in the Adriatic Sea.

bratstvo i jedinstvo Croatian; slogan of brotherhood and unity in the Socialist Federative Republic of Yugoslavia.

brodet Croatian; fish stew or soup, which is prepared along the coast from lesser fish, onion, garlic, tomatoes and spices. It is usually served with corn porridge *polenta*.

Bura Croatian; a strong, dry and cold northeast wind, coming in wild shocks from the mountains, particularly dangerous in the channels between the mainland and the islands. The bura is very strong in the Velebit Channel, around the cities of Senj and Makarska. A Dalmatian saying goes that the bura is born in Senj and gets married in Makarska. The speed of the blows have been known to reach 118km/h, so it is very dangerous for sailors and boats. Croatia has a reliable on-line weather service called popularly Aladin. It is also in English and very useful for mariners.

Campus Martius Latin; it was a publicly owned field dedicated to the god of war, Mars, outside the city walls of Rome, where soldiers were trained.

Canus Latin; dog, also used as a curse.

carabinieri Italian; civilian and military police.

Caro nome che il mio cor Italian; Sweet name, you who made my heart...; famous aria from Verdi's opera Rigoletto.

castrato Italian; a boy who was castrated before the puberty to keep his singing voice high. Such boys could sing soprano, mezzo-soprano or contralto. The practice, which was very widely spread in Italy, became illegal in the late 19th century.

Chetnik English spelling; a member of Serbian paramilitary guerilla defending nationalist and monarchist ideals and the

Orthodox faith. The army was established in the first half of the last century to fight against the Ottoman Empire. The Chetniks took part in both Balkan wars, in WW1 and WW2, when their role changed from defending Serbia against the German occupation to cooperating with the Germans in the fight against Tito's partisans. Already during WW2 their aim was the Great Serbia and their strategy ethnic cleansing of Muslims and Croatians. They were cruel to the civilians in the ethnically mixed territories, butchering and raping women and children. In the last Balkan war in the 1990s, the notion kept its initial connotation. Their biggest opponents were the Croatian Catholic Ustashas and the Islamic groups in Bosnia.

crnika Croatian; Quercus Ilex, dwarf evergreen Mediterranean oak.

deli Turkish; a cavalry in the Ottoman Army, formed of recently converted Slaves, who were fanatically fighting against Infidels, mainly by raid and terror. They set whole villages on fire and took young boys for jannisaries.

denarius Latin; plural denarii; a silver coin, approximate worth 25$ today.

Dicentrarchus labrax Latin; kind of fish: European seabass.

dignitas Latin; The notion of dignitas, i.e. dignity, was much more than the English translation. It included a good name, the reputation, achievement, standing and honor of a Roman noble. He would defend his dignitas to the last bit of his person, in extreme cases by a suicide or voluntary exile.

dinar Croatian; silver coin in Ragusa in the middle ages. It was the currency in the Kingdom of Yugoslavia as well as in the socialist Yugoslavia.

divan Arabic; sofa without back, usually set with pillows.

Divide et impera Latin; Divide and rule was a principle which Roman rulers applied since Ceasar, mainly in the provinces. Diocletianus, though, reformed the Empire by dividing it in three parts - Tetrarchy. He appointed two co-emperors, Constantius and Galerius, as Ceasars. The main goals were administrative efficiency and improved tax collection.

dominus Latin; master of the house.

Domobranci Slovenian; defenders of homes, military units during WW2. Their initial role was to protect homes and property against plundering carried out either by German or partisan troops during WW2. When the resistance movement of Tito's partisans was taken over by communists, the Domobranci sided with Germans and fought against the partisans. After the war they were stamped as collaborators. Many immigrated to Argentina and America. Those who could not escape were killed by the partisan units without a legal process. It is still one of the darkest sides of WW2 in Slovenia, dividing the country even today.

dukat Italian; Venetian coin in the middle ages, approximate worth today 44$.

Edictum De Pretiis Rerum Venalium Latin; The Edict on Maximum Prices was issued by Diocletianus in 301 A.D. It should stabilize the Roman economy and bring back prosperity into the Empire. In analogy to his military and administrative success, Diocletianus was eager to reform the monetary and trade system of Rome by introducing first the Edict on Coinage, then, the Edict on Maximum Prices. Namely, various provinces minted their own coins, declaring their value more according to their needs as to the real value of the metal used. So, the trade and business suffered from a flow of money of no worth. The coinage reform defined exact mixtures for certain coins. The administrators surveyed the coins meticulously. The reform was successful and brought stability to the economy. The next reform, with which Diocletianus wanted to eliminate the high profits of the so called men-in-the-middle (transporters, traders, bankers, speculators and profiteers) by prescribing a list of maximum prices for each good (a list of over a thousand articles is preserved), which should be applied in every province of the Roman Empire, no matter where and how the goods were produced. The latter measure was a flop, and Diocletianus could not maintain the maximum prices no matter how much force he used. The Edict is still a famous historical case in business textbooks around the world.

Effendi Arabic; sir, lord.

fez Turkish; plural fezzes; a flat, round red hat, probably of the Ottoman origin. During WW1 the Bosnian troops fighting for the Central Powers wore red fezzes and were dreaded by their enemies, Italians. Not rarely, other Austro Hungarian troops would put on fezzes in order to scare the Itailians on the Isonzo front.

Foibe Italian, singular foiba; deep karstic sinkholes where victims of rapes or mass killings were thrown during WW2; region of Karst in Italy, Slovenia and Croatia.

Fortica Latin; fortress.

Forum Latin; a public square in ancient Greek and Roman times, used for public meetings, discussions, state and judicial affairs.

Fruškogorski biser a famous Croatian sparkling wine.

Garum Latin; a fish sauce produced from salt and fish intestines fermenting in the sun for three months. It was very nutritious and widely used instead of salt in the Ancient Roman cuisine.

gladius Latin; a short sword, famously used in gladiatorial games.

grammaticus Latin; a teacher who taught children to read and write, Greek, Roman history and calculation in the secondary school; usually, only boys were taught.

groši Croatian; singular groš; silver coins of lesser worth in circulation during the Austro-Hungarian rule.

grossi Italian; singular grossum; a Ragusan silver coin, also called dinar.

Gulasch German; typical peasant food popular all over the former Austro-Hungarian territories still today, a beef stew with spices and paprika.

gusle Serbian; a single string musical instrument played all over the Balkans to accompany folk songs.

gymnasium ancient Greek; school where learning, philosophy and bodily training are equally important. Only boys were admitted.

habib Arabic; darling, sweetheart.

Hal beemkanek mosa'adati Arabic; Can you help me?

Hal tatakallamu alloghah alarabiah Arabic; Do you speak Arabic?

hamam Turkish; a steam bath during which the body is cleaned with aromatic soaps and scraped with vulcanic stones.

harem Turkish; a strictly women's household subordinated to one man who is husband to all the wives and father to all the children; typical of the Ottoman society and a custom in Islamic states still today. In a harem, women were attended to by female servants and guarded by eunuchs. Usually, either the mother of the lord of the harem would lead the household or his first, oldest wife.

hass Turkish; a huge estate and a tax unit controlled by one administrator in the Ottoman Empire.

hyperperus Byzanthian, plural hyperperi; a coin of greater value used in the Ragusan trade.

ICTYS abbr. Latin; [Iesos Christos Theou Yios Soter]; Jesus Christ God's Son and Savior.

Imam a Muslim leader of the prayers in the mosque, for Shiites a descendant of Muhammad appointed to lead a community.

Imperium Latin; the supreme power, held by consuls and emperors, to command and administer a territory in military, judicial, and civil affairs.

in medias res Latin; in the middle of the matter.

Ivanje Croatian; Midsummer Night; the 23rd of June.

Jadra Nova the Adriatic town of Biograd, called in the Middle Ages the new Zadar.

Jadranska magistrala Croatian; a windy road along the Adriatic coast, built after WW2 by Yugoslavian volunteers, starting at Istria and ending east of Ulcinj. Nowadays, a modern motorway reaches Split much faster and is to be extended along the Adriatic coast to the border of Albania, including Monte Negro.

Jadrolinija the most popular Croatian state-owned ferry line `www.jadrolinija.hr`.

jinn Turkish; an evil spirit in Islamic beliefs; mean ghost, apparition.

Jugo Croatian; a southeast wind. The jugo usually occurs with rainy and cloudy weather, but it can also blow when the sky is clear. A cyclonic jugo is a warm and very moist wind blowing from the NE and SW direction. It can be severe and can reach a hurricane force with high sea waves. The sky is covered with dense and very low clouds that often bring abundant rain. Croatia has a reliable on-line weather service called popularly Aladin. It is also in English and very useful for mariners.

Jutarnji list the most popular Croatian daily newspaper.

karaka Croatian; carrack – a three to four masted sailing ship built in the late Middle Ages. According to historical sources, Dubrovnik's carracks were as famous as Portuguese ones. The Ragusan shipbuilding was supervised by the state, although the businesses were in private hands. Ragusan merchants rivalled Venetians in every aspect, trading with the Holy Land as well as with the Ottoman Empire. The Ragusan carracks dominated the Mediterranean and sailed into the Atlantic Ocean, harbouring even in London. So one of them found place in Shakespeare's Merchant of Venice: "Your mind is tossing on the ocean; //There, where your argosies with portly sail, //Like signiors and rich burghers on the flood," (William Shakespeare, The Merchant of Venice, 1595) Argosy meant a Ragusan ship. The Santa Maria of Christopher Columbus was a carrack as well, though she was built in Pontevedra in Spain. Today, tourists can revive the naval adventures on numerous replicas which sail around Ragusan waters. Dubrovnik's Maritime Museum is really worth a visit.

karat Croatian; a unit of measurement for gold, yet in the text, it means a business share. "Although some ships were owned by a single man, it was more usual for ownership, profit and risk to be spread. The traditional division of shared ownership in Dubrovnik was by means of karats (karati), each of which represented a share of 1/24. Ownership of the cargo might also be divided, with rich merchants advancing loans to cover a part share of whatever was to be purchased and resold." Dubrovnik, by Robin Harris, SAQI, London, 2003.

kilim Persian; a flat, woven rug, usually in light colors.

klobuk Serbian; typical headgear of the Orthodox Church officials.

Knez Croatian; prince, higher knight. Knez Kačič was a historical personality who lived a century earlier than in the novel. He was one of the most notorious pirates in the 13th century at Omiš. His family received the status of noblemen in 1258 from the King of Hungary, Bela IV.

košava Serbian or Bulgarian; a cold southeastern wind blowing from the Carpathian Mountains along the Danube to Serbia. In winter it causes freezing temperatures.

kolo Serbian; a folk dance, in which dancers dance in a circle, holding hands, sometimes around a solo dancer in the middle. In Tito's Yugoslavia, 1945 – 1991, the kolo symbolized the unity and brotherhood of different nations: Slovenes, Croatians, Bosnians, Serbians, Macedonians, Albanians and Montenegrians. Almost every public dance party ended with a kolo dance entitled Jugoslavija, Jugoslavija.

konoba Croatian; a small pub where simple foods and wine from the region are served.

Korčulani Croatian; the inhabitants of the island of Korčula. The biggest town on the island is also called Korčula. The legend has it that the famous Venetian traveller from the 13th century, Marco Polo, was born in the town of Korčula, which then was a part of the Venetian Republic. Today it is part of Dalmatia, Croatia.

korso Croatian; a promenade by the sea, usually in the city centres of coastal towns.

kruna Croatian; the currency of the Austro-Hungarian Monarchy, which disappeared with the fall of the Empire in 1919.

kuna The Croatian currency. One kuna is worth 0.18$. The word means weasel, and its origin clearly points at the use of weasel pelts as currency in the old times.

lada Croatian; a low, wide boat steered by rowers, very stable and flexible in the blows of the winds. It was popular with the pirates at Omiš, who plundered merchant ships on their way to the Holy Land or Levant.

Lex Diocletiana Feminina Latin; Diocletian's law on women; it did not exist and is only a joke thought of by his Greek slave Filio.

Ljubačka vrata Croatian; Lover's Gate - name of a sea passage between the island of Pag and the Velebit mainland near Zadar.

Ljubački zaljev Croatian; Lovers' Bay, a very shallow sandy bay, very dangerous for sailors even today for the numerous reefs at its western entrance. It hides one of the oldest Croatian capitals, Nin, which has many historical churches and monuments, and a wonderful sandy beach, the Queen's Beach.

loden German; water-resistant cloth made from sheep's wool.

logor Croatian; concentration camp. During the last Balkan war, Serbian women's camps mainly in Bosnia were notorious for the mass rapes, torture and humiliation of the Muslim women. When the detainees were released, they usually found themselves pregnant with unwanted children. The newborns were given up for adoption. Infanticides were frequent. During the war, Monica Hauser (laureate of the Right Livelihood Award), a gynecologist from Switzerland established a safe house for women in Zenica and forced into motion legal steps to declare rape as one of the war crimes. She succeeded, so today the International Court in the Hague recognizes rape as a crime against humanity. A famous Croatian journalist and writer, Slavenka Drakulić, wrote a novel about this issue entitled S. (As if I am not there), translated into English by Marko Ivić and published by Penguin Books.

logos Greek; word. The word meant more than that; rational reasoning, with various connotations in different philosophical doctrines, or word of God.

Lovrijenac St. Lawrence Fort, protecting Dubrovnik, in the old days the Republic of Ragusa; according to a legend (see Robin Harris), a fort was built on this strategically important cape as early as in the 11th century. The main construction was carried out under the supervision of the famous Dalmatian architect and sculptor Juraj Dalmatinac in the 15th century. Today, the fort is not only a tourist attraction, but also a spectacular venue for theatrical and musical performances during the Dubrovnik Summer Festival, in which the most famous play staged is Hamlet by William Shakespeare.

ludus litterarius Latin; Roman primary school for children who could not afford a private tutor; the lessons were focused on reading, writing and basic calculations; both sexes could attend.

lyra a Byzantian bowed string musical instrument used from the Antiquity to the modern times to accompany Balkan folk songs.

maatjes Dutch; raw herring soused in salt.

madrasah Arabic; Islamic higher schools, universities existing still today.

maestral Croatian; a north or north west wind, usually heralding good weather.

mama Croatian, Slovenian, Serbian; mother.

matrona Latin; a strong woman commanding the household.

medicus Latin; medical man, physician.

mentula Latin; obscene word for penis.

mila Croatian; tender and kind.

mincas Croatian; change, small coins used during the Ragusan

Republic - Dubrovnik.

minestrone Italian; mixed vegetable soup with pulses and pasta.

Mrtvo more Croatian; Dead Sea, a very calm bay, sheltered from all winds, on the island of Lopud in front of Dubrovnik.

Mullus barbatus Latin; a species of fish, kind red mullets.

Nezavisna država Hrvatska The Independent State of Croatia was a Nazi puppet state of Croatians during WW2 existing from 1941 to 1945. Until 1943 it was under the Italian protectorate and its official ruler was the Duke of Aosta. Actually, the state was led by Ante Pavelić and Nikola Mandić. The state encompassed today's Croatia, Bosnia and Herzegovina and parts of Serbia. The soldiers, the Ustashas, were very cruel to other nationalities and races - Serbians, Gypsies, Muslims and Jews. They operated several concentration camps, the most notorious of which were Jasenovac and Sisak, a concentration camp for children. After the fall of Yugoslavia, the Serbians living in Croatia, saw a sort of rebirth of the NDH in the new, sovereign Croatia due to some symbols from the past like the coat of arms, the flag and the anthem of the former NDH.

Nihi humanum mihi alienum est Latin; Nothing human is strange or repulsive to me.

no lo so Italian; I don't know.

nomina sunt odiosa Latin; Names are better not said aloud.

Non Bene Pro Toto Libertas Venditur Auro Latin; Freedom is not to be sold for all the treasures in the world; an inscription over the entrance of Lovrijenac, St. Lawrence Fort in Dubrovnik. It conveys the pride and free spirit of the Republic of Ragusa during its most flourishing period.

nona Italian; grandmother; the word is used all over coastal Slovenia and Istria, but not in Dalmatia. It points to Maria's origins from the north.

obitelj Croatian; family.

Oluja Croatian; storm. The decisive military operation and victory of the Croatian War of Independence, which took place between the 4 and 7 August 1995 in the vast area of the Republic of Serbian Krajina on the Croatian and partly Bosnian territory. The fighting parties were the Croatian Army, the Croatian Special Police Force and the Army of the Republic of Bosnia and Herzegovina on one side, and the Army of the Republic of Serbian Krajina and the Yugoslav People's Army on the other side. It was the largest European land battle since WW2 in Europe. After four years, the Croatians regained the territories around Knin. Several towns and villages in Krajina are still uninhabited today, as in the aftermath of the battle, the majority of the Serbian population left.

orada lat. Sparus aurata; Croatian; a tasty Mediaterranean fish, a gilt head bream.

padrona Italian; mistress, lady.

Pagania was a land of Pagans, Slavic tribes living on the Adriatic coast around the fortified town of Omiš, in the delta of the river Cetinja, and the Ragusan border in the delta of the river Neretva. They believed in their own Pagan gods and only very late, in the 9th and 10th century, after some battles and fierce opposition, they accepted Christianity. Apart from growing crops on the narrow strip of land along the coast and in the delta of Neretva, they soon specialized in piracy. Their most profitable business was plundering not only Venetian, but also Ragusan and Ottoman ships carrying precious cargos. The loot and income from collected ransoms as well as profitable slave trade were shared among the members of the community following old Slavic tribal rules. So, their social structure has been idolized as fair. The Venetians tried to crush them, yet, the pirates could easily escape into the Cetinja and Neretva deltas in their quick boats, ladas, built for shallow waters. The galleons and carracks could not sail after them. The Pagans were the most terrible of all the pirates ever operating in the Adriatic sea, and inflicted huge losses on the trade over centuries.

paiderastia old Greek; in direct translation, love of boys, a love among male partners. It was a wide spread custom not only in Ancient Greece, but also in Rome. Still, Roman moralists started to criticize the practice as unnatural. It was the choice of the author to make Diocletian condemn it.

palazzo Italian; palace.

Panem et circenses Latin; bread and games; providing food and entertainment to keep the masses calm.

pater familias Latin; father of the family. Roman society, moulded on the Greek model, was very patriarchic and women had very few civil rights.

patrician Latin; a member of one of the aristocratic families of the Ancient Roman Republic, which before the third century B.C. had exclusive rights to the Senate. The Ragusan notion of the term had the same meaning; only the members of the noble families could take part in the Great Council of the Republic and be appointed Rectors.

pax romana from Latin; Roman peace, a relatively peaceful period of 200 years without civil wars in the 1st and 2nd century A.D. of the Roman Empire.

per partes Latin; one piece at the time, today integration by parts is a well known mathematical method.

phallus plural phalli; Latin; penis.

pharmaca plural, Greek; means medicine and poison, depending on the dosage.

philetor Greek; adult male who has a sexual relationship with a boy; swear word.

pillum Latin; javelin, one of the basic weapons of a Roman soldier.

piscinae plural, from Latin; basin, pool, shallow water.

plebs Latin; plebeans were free citizens in Ancient Rome as opposed to aristocrats, i.e. patricians, slaves and ordinary citizens. The plebs worked for their livelihoods. They were farmers, artisans, traders, and in principle, they owned their businesses and lands. Many of them achieved high positions in the Republic (like Marcus and Cicero) or extreme riches like Crassus.

polenta Croatian, Slovenian, Italian; famous corn porridge cooked with water, salt and fat.

polis Greek; plural poleis; ancient city state.

prošek Croatian; sweet brandy wine, similar to porto.

Qaleelan Arabic; a little bit.

Qanun's materia medica Latin; The Canon of Medicine, a famous encyclopedia of medicine completed by Avicenna in 1025 and translated in all important languages in the Middle Ages.

Quercus Ilex from Latin; evergreen Mediterranean oak, the Croatian name is Crnika.

raša Bosnian; roughly spun wool or garments made of it.

Ragusa today, city of Dubrovnik, has nothing to do with the Italian city on Sicily with the same name. The city was booming as an independent republic for most of the time since the early Middle Ages until the Napoleonic conquest. The Ragusan Chronicles are among the best preserved documents of their times.

Ragusan plural Ragusans; inhabitant of Ragusa, i.e. of the medieval Dubrovnik.

Ragusan Council the ruling body of the Ragusan Republic composed of the members of the Ragusan Aristocracy; between 100 and 200 members, similar function as the Senate in Ancient Rome.

Ragusan Rector a duke in the city state of Dubrovnik. He was elected to office by the Great (Ragusan) Council, which consisted of the male members of the patrician families who were full of age (21). His office lasted only for two months and his power was limited. Ragusa, i.e. Dubrovnik, had one of the most advanced aristocratic republican constitutions in its time, so all the important decisions remained with the Great Council and the aristocratic families. The number of the councillors was between 100 and 200. According to a legend, upon the arrival of Napoleon, who took away their liberty for the first time after centuries in 1806, the Ragusan nobles swore an oath not to bear any more descendants. Several sources claim that Napoleon held the Ragusan constitution and law in such high esteem that even his penal code, the famous Code Civil, one of the foundations for today's legislature, is based on it.

rakija Croatian, Serbian word of Turkish origin for brandy; usually distilled from fruits.

Republika Srpska from Serbian; Republic of Serbian Krajina was established after the referendum of the Croatian Serbians in 1991 and existed as unrecognized client state of Yugoslavia (or better what was left of it - Serbia and Montenegro) until 1995. Its territory was within the boarders of Croatia. Etymologically, Krajina means frontier. The area was populated by the Serbians, Vlachs and other ethnicities fleeing from the territories occupied by the Ottoman Empire after the Battle of Kosovo in 1389 as a sort of defense line to protect the North from the Turks. The Austrian monarchy supported them strongly through the centuries to maintain the fragile border with the Turks. In 1991 Croatians changed their constitution and Serbians did not feel safe under their new right wing government, so they voted to remain a part of Yugoslavia in the form of their own republic, Krajina. The conflict between Krajina and Croatia escalated into a cruel war.

S. Slavenka Drakulić, S. a Novel about the Balkans, Penguin Books, 1999.

sacro egoismo Italian; holy egoism, Antonio Salandra's fascist philosophy, which during WW1 expressed Italian demands to regain the territories of Trentino and Trieste, including all former Venetian territories of Istria, Dalmatia and its islands, from the Austro-Hungarian Empire. With the battle cry, Savoy!, the Italian drafted soldiers stormed the valley of Isonzo trying to establish a corridor from Gorizia to Trieste. Their hopeless war command and poor organization as well as low fighting morale led to one of the biggest defeats at Caporetto, the atmosphere of which Hemingway's novel A Farewell to Arms renders vivid still today.

Salam from Arabic; peace; often used as a greeting.

Salona an Ancient Roman town on the Dalmatian coast, an administrative center close to the port of Split (then called Spalatum). It is the place of birth of Emperor Diocletianus. Today the ruins can be visited.

salve Latin; hello, a usual greeting in Ancient Rome.

scampi al bianco Italian; shrimps in white wine sauce.

Schnaps German; brandy.

Serbo-Croatian The official languages of the Socialist Federative State of Yugoslavia were: Serbo-Croatian (also language of the official documents and the Yugoslav People's

Army), Slovenian and Macedonian, the latter two being really different from Serbo-Croatian. Note that within Yugoslavia, there were also Albanians (Kosovo) and other ethnicities. As to Serbo-Croatian, after the Bosnian war in 1990s, an intellectual fight emerged between the linguists, some claiming Croatian to be a variant of Serbian, the others vice versa. Today politics distinguish Croatian, Serbian, Bosnian (includes lots of Turkish words) and Montenegrin as separate languages, although according to the sources, they all derive from one language: Serbo-Croatian. (see Kordič Snježana, Bernhard Groeschel, Serbo-Croatian Between Linguistics and Politics) Paula in the novel points this cleft out, the separation, which is getting more pronounced as each new state emerging from Yugoslavia is trying to reinvent separate roots of its language.

sipahi Turkish; nobles, Ottoman vassals who belonged to the cavalry units.

Spalato the Middle Age name for Split.

Spalatum the Ancient Roman name for Split.

Sparus aurata Latin; a tasty Mediaterranean fish, a gilt head bream.

stadium plural stadia, Ancient Greek measure for distance. 1 stadium is 185 meters or 607 feet.

starium Latin; plural staria; measure for grain in the Venetian times. One starium was between 64.5kg to 71.5kg.

stećci Bosnian; medieval tombstones along the borders of the medieval Bosnian state prior to the Ottoman occupation in the 15th century. The epitaphs on them are written in the Bosnian Cyrillic alphabet (Bosančica). Since 2009 they have been nominated as UNESCO World Heritage. The largest collection is to be seen near Radimlja in Herzegovina.

stipend fixed regular payment in Ancient Rome; salary.

Stradun the main street of Dubrovnik, where celebrations and the St. Blaise procession take place still today.

strigil Greek; a small curved metal tool used to scrape dirt and sand from the body of athletes and other people in the bath.

Summa Theologica The best known work written by Catholic philosopher and thinker Thomas Aquinas (c.1225-1274).

symposium plural symposia, Greek; in Ancient Greece a gathering of men (Sappho on Lesbos was an exception) debating politics, business or chatting while eating and drinking. Also literary works were read or recited aloud in literary symposia. Sappho's verses quoted in the novel were translated by H.T.Wharton.

šajkača Serbian military headgear originating from the 19th century, particularly popular with the partisans during WW2.

talent plural talents; Ancient Greek measure for mass, 26 kg, i.e. 57 lb.

tata Croatian; father, daddy.

tetka Croatian; aunt, auntie.

Bloody Fairy Tale poem by Desanka Maksimović. The poet expresses the horror of the Kragujevac massacre, where almost 3,000 boys and men were executed by Nazi German occupation forces in October 1941. In Yugoslavia, all students in all federative republics had to learn the poem by heart.

Tica Croatian; bird.

travarica Croatian; a herb brandy distilled from the pressed grapes left over from winemaking. Recipes vary from place to place, yet they usually include dried figs, raisins, rosemary, fennel, sage, lemon zest, etc.

trlja lat. Mullus Sumuletus; Croatian; a kind of fish similar to red mullet.

Tuum nosce hostem Latin; know thy enemy. Diocletianus utters this old Latin saying in the context of his studies of the Christian movement. He understood that by persecuting them, the Romans would only lose in the moral field. The enemies of the Empire became martyrs. Still, Diocletianus supported his co-ruler Galerius in the last Roman persecution of Christians. The next Roman Emperor Constantine formally allowed Christianity by the Edict of Milan in A.D. 313.

tyrant in Ancient Greece, an absolute sovereign, a ruler. The word gained its negative connotation after Plato and Aristotle defined a tyrant as "one who rules without law, looks to his own advantage rather than that of his subjects, and uses extreme and cruel tactics against his own people as well as others". In the 6th century B.C., it was a normal form of government, more so in the new Greek colonies. It had no pejorative or negative meaning.

Uhibbok Arabic; I love you (woman to man)

Uhibboki Arabic; I love you (man to woman)

Una voce poco fa Italian; a famous aria sung by Rosina from Rossini's opera The Barber of Seville.

Untermenschen German; the racist Nazi doctrine, which stamped Jews, Gypsies, and several Slavic nations, among which Serbians, as less than human, lower than the pure Germanic race.

Upravnik Croatian; headmaster of school.

Ustasha Croatian soldiers belonging to the troops of Nezavisna država Hrvatska during WW2; in the last Balkan war pejorative name for a Croatian soldier, i.e. from the point of view of Serbians.

Uzdravlje Croatian; cheers.

Večernji list a popular Croatian newspaper still in print today.

Vespa Italian; the name means wasp, a scooter first manufactured by Piaggio in 1946; still popular today.

villa rustica in Ancient Rome a residence built in the countryside where the household of a family spent summers to escape the cities. There are several ruins of such villas in the littoral of Croatia.

vranac Serbian; horse, steed, mount; also a name of a famous black wine from the area.

Wa 'alayki s-salām! Arabic; an answer to the greeting Peace be with you, meaning And upon you be peace; formal.

Zeus faber Latin; fish, John Dory or St. Peter's fish.

zlato Croatian; gold, also a term of endearment used for children, like my little darling.

žena Croatian; woman.

Živeli Croatian; cheers.

About the author

Tanja Tuma was born in ex-Yugoslavia, behind the Iron Curtain. When the curtain fell, she found herself a citizen of the European Union, based in Slovenia. In college, she studied French, English, and German literature, which propelled her writing and editing career forward. Knowing the ex-Yugoslavian languages, Tanja understands the lands and the peoples she is writing about. After all, she has lived in and travelled around ex-Yugoslavia for half of her life. Tuma has worked in the publishing and bookselling world, which eventually lead to the founding of her own successful company. Once active as a publisher, she reconciled with the motto "live now, write later". In her career Tanja has worked in various areas of publishing, and had the privilege to learn a lot about the international publishing world. When their kids became independent, Tanja and her husband escaped to the solitude of Slovenian woods, where she writes about wild Mediterranean adventures.

For pictures and more news about her books, plans and research, visit her homepage `www.tanjatuma.com` and read her blog.

Made in the USA
Charleston, SC
05 November 2014